The Silent Blade

R. A. Salvatore

D0956861

THE SILENT BLADE

©1998 TSR, Inc.
©2001 Wizards of the Coast, Inc.

Distributed in the United States by Holtzbrinck Publishing. Distributed in Canada by Fenn Ltd.

Distributed to the hobby, toy, and comic trade in the United States and Canada by regional distributors.

Distributed worldwide by Wizards of the Coast, Inc. and regional distributors.

Printed in the U.S.A.

Cover art by Todd Lockwood
First Printing: October 1998
First paperback edition: June 1999
Library of Congress Catalog Card Number: 97-062378

9 8 7 6 5 4

ISBN: 0-7869-1388-6
620-21388-001-EN

U.S., CANADA,
ASIA, PACIFIC, & LATIN AMERICA
Wizards of the Coast, Inc.
P.O. Box 707
Renton, WA 98057-0707
+1-800-324-6496

EUROPEAN HEADQUARTERS
Wizards of the Coast, Belgium
T Hofsveld 6d
1702 Groot-Bijgaarden
Belgium
+322-467-3360

Visit our web site at **www.wizards.com**

By R.A. Salvatore

The Icewind Dale Trilogy
The Crystal Shard
Streams of Silver
The Halfling's Gem
The Icewind Dale Trilogy Collector's Edition

The Dark Elf Trilogy
Homeland
Exile
Sojourn
The Dark Elf Trilogy Collector's Edition

The Cleric Quintet
Canticle
In Sylvan Shadows
Night Masks
The Fallen Fortress
The Chaos Curse
The Cleric Quintet Collector's Edition

Legacy of the Drow
The Legacy
Starless Night
Siege of Darkness
Passage to Dawn
Legacy of the Drow Collector's Edition

Paths of Darkness
The Silent Blade
The Spine of the World
Servant of the Shard
Sea of Swords
Paths of Darkness Collector's Edition
(February 2004)

The Hunter's Blades Trilogy
The Thousand Orcs
The Lone Drow
(October 2003)
The Two Swords
(October 2004)

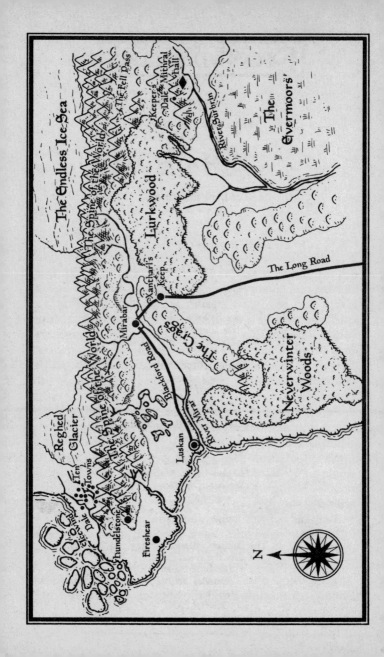

PROLOGUE

Wulfgar lay back in his bed, pondering, trying to come to terms with the abrupt changes that had come over his life. Rescued from the demon Errtu and his hellish prison in the Abyss, the proud barbarian found himself once again among friends and allies. Bruenor, his adopted dwarven father, was here, and so was Drizzt, his dark elven mentor and dearest friend. Wulfgar could tell from the snoring that Regis, the chubby halfling, was sleeping contentedly in the next room.

And Catti-brie, dear Catti-brie, the woman Wulfgar had come to love those years before, the woman whom he had planned to marry seven years previously in Mithral Hall. They were all here at their home in Icewind Dale, reunited and presumably at peace, through the heroic efforts of these wonderful friends.

Wulfgar did not know what that meant.

Wulfgar, who had been through such a terrible ordeal over six years of torture at the clawed hands of the demon Errtu, did not understand.

The huge man crossed his arms over his chest. Sheer exhaustion put him here in bed, forced him down, for he would not willingly choose sleep. Errtu found him in his dreams.

And so it was this night. Wulfgar, though deep in thought and deep in turmoil, succumbed to his exhaustion and fell into a peaceful blackness that soon turned again into the images of the swirling gray mists that were the Abyss. There sat the gigantic, bat-winged Errtu, perched upon his carved mushroom throne, laughing. Always laughing that hideous croaking chuckle. That laugh was borne not out of joy, but was rather a mocking thing, an insult to those the demon chose to torture. Now the beast aimed that unending wickedness at Wulfgar, as was aimed the huge pincer of Bizmatec, another demon, minion of Errtu. With strength beyond the bounds of almost any other human, Wulfgar ferociously wrestled Bizmatec. The barbarian batted aside the huge humanlike arms and the two other upper-body appendages, the pincer arms, for a long while, slapping and punching desperately.

But too many flailing limbs came at him. Bizmatec was too large and too strong, and the mighty barbarian eventually began to tire.

It ended—always it ended—with one of Bizmatec's pincers around Wulfgar's throat, the demon's other pincer arm and its two humanlike arms holding the defeated human steady. Expert in this, his favorite torturing technique, Bizmatec pressed oh so subtly on Wulfgar's throat, took away the air, then gave it back, over and over, leaving the man weak in the legs, gasping and gasping as minutes, then hours, slipped past.

Wulfgar sat up straight in his bed, clutching at his throat, clawing a scratch down one side of it before he realized that the demon was not there, that he was safe in his bed in the land he called home, surrounded by his friends.

Friends . . .

What did that word mean? What could they know of his torment? How could they help him chase away the enduring nightmare that was Errtu?

The haunted man did not sleep the rest of the night, and when Drizzt came to rouse him, well before the dawn, the dark elf found Wulfgar already dressed for the road. They were to leave this day, all five, bearing the artifact Crenshinibon far, far to the south and west. They were bound for Caradoon on the banks of Impresk Lake, and then into the Snowflake Mountains to a great monastery called Spirit Soaring where a priest named Cadderly would destroy the wicked relic.

Crenshinibon. Drizzt had it with him when he came to get Wulfgar that morning. The drow didn't wear it openly, but Wulfgar knew it was there. He could sense it, could feel its vile presence. For Crenshinibon remained linked to its last master, the demon Errtu. It tingled with the energy of the demon, and because Drizzt had it on him and was standing so close, Errtu, too, remained close to Wulfgar.

"A fine day for the road," the drow remarked light-heartedly, but his tone was strained, condescending, Wulfgar noted. With more than a little difficulty, Wulfgar resisted the urge to punch Drizzt in the face.

Instead, he grunted in reply and strode past the deceptively small dark elf. Drizzt was but a few inches over five feet, while Wulfgar towered closer to seven feet than to six, and carried fully twice the weight of the drow. The barbarian's thigh was thicker than Drizzt's waist, and yet, if it came to blows between them, wise bettors would favor the drow.

"I have not yet wakened Catti-brie," Drizzt explained.

Wulfgar turned fast at the mention of the name. He stared hard into the drow's lavender eyes, his own blue orbs matching the intensity that always seemed to be there.

"But Regis is already awake and at his morning meal—he is hoping to get two or three breakfasts in before we leave, no doubt," Drizzt added with a chuckle, one that Wulfgar did not share. "And Bruenor will meet us on the field beyond Bryn Shander's eastern gate. He is with his own folk, preparing the priestess Stumpet to lead the clan in his absence."

Wulfgar only half heard the words. They meant nothing to him. All the world meant nothing to him.

"Shall we rouse Catti-brie?" the drow asked.

"I will," Wulfgar answered gruffly. "You see to Regis. If he gets a belly full of food, he will surely slow us down, and I mean to be quick to your friend Cadderly, that we might be rid of Crenshinibon."

Drizzt started to answer, but Wulfgar turned away, moving down the hall to Catti-brie's door. He gave a single, thunderous knock, then pushed right through. Drizzt moved a step in that direction to scold the barbarian for his rude behavior—the woman had not even acknowledged his knock, after all—but he let it go. Of all the humans the drow had ever met, Catti-brie ranked as the most capable at defending herself from insult or violence.

Besides, Drizzt knew that his desire to go and scold Wulfgar was wrought more than a bit by his jealousy of the man who once was, and perhaps was soon again, to be Catti-brie's husband.

The drow stroked a hand over his handsome face and turned to find Regis.

* * * * *

Wearing only a slight undergarment and with her pants half pulled up, the startled Catti-brie turned a surprised look on Wulfgar as he strode into her room. "Ye might've waited for an answer," she said dryly, brushing away her embarrassment and pulling her pants up, then going to retrieve her tunic.

Wulfgar nodded and held up his hands—only half an apology, perhaps, but a half more than Catti-brie had expected. She saw the pain in the man's sky blue eyes and the emptiness of his occasional strained smiles. She had talked with Drizzt about it at length, and with Bruenor and Regis, and they had all decided to be patient. Time alone could heal Wulfgar's wounds.

"The drow has prepared a morning meal for us all," Wulfgar explained. "We should eat well before we start on the long road."

" 'The drow'? " Catti-brie echoed. She hadn't meant to speak it aloud, but so dumbfounded was she by Wulfgar's distant reference to Drizzt that the words just slipped out. Would Wulfgar call Bruenor "the dwarf"? And how long would it be before she became simply "the girl"? Catti-brie blew a deep sigh and pulled her tunic over her shoulders, reminding herself pointedly that Wulfgar had been through hell—literally. She looked at him now, studying those eyes, and saw a hint of embarrassment there, as though her echo of his callous reference to Drizzt had indeed struck him in the heart. That was a good sign.

He turned to leave her room, but she moved to him, reaching up to gently stroke the side of his face, her hand running down his smooth cheek to the scratchy beard that he had either decided to grow or simply hadn't been motivated enough to shave.

Wulfgar looked down at her, at the tenderness in her eyes, and for the first time since the fight on the ice floe when he and his friends had dispatched wicked Errtu, there came a measure of honesty in his slight smile.

* * * * *

Regis did get his three meals, and he grumbled about it all that morning as the five friends started out from Bryn Shander, the largest of the villages in the region called Ten Towns in forlorn Icewind Dale. Their course was north at first, moving to easier ground, and then turning due west. To the north, far in the distance, they saw the high structures of Targos, second city of the region, and beyond the city's roofs could be seen shining waters of Maer Dualdon.

By mid-afternoon, with more than a dozen miles behind them, they came to the banks of the Shaengarne, the great river swollen and running fast with the spring melt. They followed it north, back to Maer Dualdon, to the town of Bremen and a waiting boat Regis had arranged.

Gently refusing the many offers from townsfolk to remain in the village for supper and a warm bed, and over the many protests of Regis, who claimed that he was famished and ready to lay down and die, the friends were soon west of the river, running on again, leaving the towns, their home, behind.

Drizzt could hardly believe that they had set out so soon. Wulfgar had only recently been returned to them. All of them were together once more in the land they called their home, at peace, and yet, here they were, heeding again the call of duty and running down the road to adventure. The drow had the cowl of his traveling cloak pulled low about his face, shielding his sensitive eyes from the stinging sun.

Thus his friends could not see his wide smile.

Part 1

APATHY

Often I sit and ponder the turmoil I feel when my blades are at rest, when all the world around me seems at peace. This is the supposed ideal for which I strive, the calm that we all hope will eventually return to us when we are at war, and yet, in these peaceful times—and they have been rare occurrences indeed in the more than seven decades of my life—I do not feel as if I have found perfection, but, rather, as if something is missing from my life.

It seems such an incongruous notion, and yet I have come to know that I am a warrior, a creature of action. In those times when there is no pressing need for action, I am not at ease. Not at all.

When the road is not filled with adventure, when there are no monsters to battle and no mountains to climb, boredom finds me. I have come to accept this truth of my life, this truth about who I am, and so, on those rare, empty occasions I can find a way to defeat the boredom. I can find a mountain peak higher than the last I climbed.

I see many of the same symptoms now in Wulfgar, returned to us from the grave, from the swirling darkness that was Errtu's corner of the Abyss. But I fear that Wulfgar's state has transcended simple boredom, spilling into the realm of apathy. Wulfgar, too, was a creature of action, but that doesn't seem to be the cure for his lethargy or his apathy. His own people now call out to him, begging action. They have asked him to assume leadership of the *tribes. Even stubborn Berkthgar, who would have to give up that coveted position of rulership, supports Wulfgar. He and all the rest of them know, at this tenuous time, that above all others Wulfgar, son of Beornegar, could bring great gains to the nomadic barbarians of Icewind Dale.*

Wulfgar will not heed that call. It is neither humility nor weariness stopping him, I recognize, nor any fears that he cannot handle the position or live up to the expectations of those begging him. Any of those problems could be overcome, could be reasoned through or supported by Wulfgar's friends, myself included. But, no, it is none of those rectifiable things.

It is simply that he does not care.

Could it be that his own agonies at the clawed hands of Errtu were so great and so enduring that he has lost his ability to empathize with the pain of others? Has he seen too much horror, too much agony, to hear their cries?

I fear this above all else, for it is a loss that knows no precise cure. And yet, to be honest, I see it clearly etched in Wulfgar's features, a state of self-absorption where too many memories of his own recent horrors cloud his vision. Perhaps he does not even recognize someone else's pain. Or perhaps, if he does see it, he dismisses it as trivial next to the monumental trials he suffered for those six years as Errtu's prisoner. Loss of empathy might well be the most enduring and deep-cutting scar of all, the silent blade of an unseen enemy, tearing at our hearts and stealing more than our strength. Stealing our will, for what are we without empathy? What manner of joy might we find in our lives if we cannot understand the joys and pains of those around us, if we cannot share in a greater community? I remember my years in the Underdark after I ran out of Menzoberranzan. Alone, save the occasional visits from Guenhwyvar, I survived those long years through my own imagination.

I am not certain that Wulfgar even has that capacity left to him, for imagination requires introspection, a reaching within one's thoughts, and I fear that every time my friend so looks inward, all he sees are the minions of Errtu, the sludge and horrors of the Abyss.

He is surrounded by friends, who love him and will try with all their hearts to support him and help him climb out of Errtu's emotional dungeon. Perhaps Catti-brie, the woman he once loved (and perhaps still does love) so deeply, will prove pivotal to his recovery. It pains me to watch them together, I admit. She treats Wulfgar with such tenderness and compassion, but I know that he feels not her gentle touch. Better that she slap his face, eye him sternly, and show him the truth of his lethargy. I know this and yet I cannot tell her to do so, for their relationship is much more complicated than that. I have nothing but Wulfgar's best interests in my mind and my heart now, and yet, if I showed Catti-brie a way that seemed less than compassionate, it could be, and would be—by Wulfgar at least, in his present state of mind—construed as the interference of a jealous suitor.

Not true. For though I do not know Catti-brie's honest feelings toward this man who once was to be her husband—for she has become quite guarded with her feelings of late—I do recognize that Wulfgar is not capable of love at this time.

Not capable of love . . . are there any sadder words to describe a man? I think not, and wish that I could now assess Wulfgar's state of mind differently. But love, honest love, requires empathy. It is a sharing—of joy, of pain, of laughter, of tears. Honest love makes one's soul a reflection of the partner's moods. And as a room seems larger when it is lined with mirrors, so do the joys become amplified. And as the individual items within the mirrored room seem less acute, so does pain diminish and fade, stretched thin by the sharing.

That is the beauty of love, whether in passion or friendship. A sharing that multiplies the joys and thins the pains. Wulfgar is surrounded now by friends, all willing to engage in such sharing, as it once was between us. Yet he cannot so engage us, cannot let loose those guards that he necessarily put in place when surrounded by the likes of Errtu.

He has lost his empathy. I can only pray that he will find it again, that time will allow him to open his heart and soul to those deserving, for without empathy he will find no purpose. Without purpose, he will find no satisfaction. Without satisfaction, he will find no contentment, and without contentment, he will find no joy.

And we, all of us, will have no way to help him.

—Drizzt Do'Urden

Chapter 1
A STRANGER AT HOME

rtemis Entreri stood on a rocky hill overlooking the vast, dusty city, trying to sort through the myriad feelings that swirled within him. He reached up to wipe the blowing dust and sand from his lips and from the hairs of his newly grown goatee. Only as he wiped it did he realize that he hadn't shaved the rest of his face in several days, for now the small beard, instead of standing distinct upon his face, fell to ragged edges across his cheeks.

Entreri didn't care.

The wind pulled many strands of his long hair from the tie at the back of his head, the wayward lengths slapping across his face, stinging his dark eyes.

Entreri didn't care.

He just stared down at Calimport and tried hard to stare inside himself. The man had lived nearly two-thirds of his life in the sprawling city on the southern coast, had come to prominence as a warrior and a killer there. It was the only place that he could ever really call home. Looking down on it now, brown and dusty, the relentless desert sun flashed brilliantly off the white marble of the greater homes. It also illuminated the many hovels, shacks, and torn tents set along roads—muddy roads only because they had no proper sewers for drainage. Looking down on Calimport now, the returning assassin didn't know how to feel. Once, he had known his place in the world. He had reached the pinnacle of his nefarious profession, and any who spoke his name did so with reverence and fear. When a pasha hired Artemis Entreri to kill a man, that man was soon dead. Without exception. And despite the many enemies he had obviously made, the assassin had been able to walk the streets of Calimport openly, not from shadow to shadow, in all confidence that none would be bold enough to act against him.

No one would dare shoot an arrow at Artemis Entreri, for they would know that the single shot must be perfect, must finish this man who seemed above the antics of mere mortals, else he would then come looking for them. And he would find them, and he would kill them.

A movement to the side, the slight shift of a shadow, caught Entreri's attention. He shook his head and sighed, not really surprised, when a cloaked figure leaped out from the rocks, some twenty feet ahead of him and stood blocking the path, arms crossed over his burly chest.

"Going to Calimport?" the man asked, his voice thick with a southern accent.

Entreri didn't answer, just kept his head straight ahead, though his eyes darted to the many rocks lining both sides of the trail.

"You must pay for the passage," the burly man went on. "I am your guide." With that he bowed and came up showing a toothless grin.

Entreri had heard many tales of this common game of money through intimidation, though never before had one been bold enough to block his way. Yes, indeed, he realized, he had been gone a long time. Still he didn't answer, and the burly man shifted, throwing wide his cloak to reveal a sword under his belt.

"How many coins do you offer?" the man asked.

Entreri started to tell him to move aside but changed his mind and only sighed again.

"Deaf?" said the man, and he drew out his sword and advanced yet another step. "You pay me, or me and my friends will take the coins from your torn body."

Entreri didn't reply, didn't move, didn't draw his jeweled dagger, his only weapon. He just stood there, and his ambivalence seemed to anger the burly man all the more.

The man glanced to the side—to Entreri's left—just slightly, but the assassin caught the look clearly. He followed it to one of the robber's companions, holding a bow in the shadows between two huge rocks.

"Now," said the burly man. "Last chance for you."

Entreri quietly hooked his toe under a rock, but made no movement other than that. He stood waiting, staring at the burly man, but with the archer on the edge of his vision. So well could the assassin read the movements of men, the slightest muscle twitch, the blink of an eye, that it was he who moved first. Entreri leaped out diagonally, ahead and to the left, rolling over and kicking out with his right foot. He launched the stone the archer's way, not to hit the man—that would have been above the skill even of Artemis Entreri—but in the hopes of distracting him. As he came over into the somersault, the assassin let his cloak fly wildly, hoping it might catch and slow the arrow.

He needn't have worried, for the archer missed badly and would have even if Entreri hadn't moved at all.

Coming up from the roll, Entreri set his feet and squared himself to the charging swordsmen, aware also that two other men were coming over the rocks at either side of the trail.

Still showing no weapon, Entreri unexpectedly charged ahead, ducking the swipe of the sword at the last possible instant, then came up hard behind the swishing blade, one hand catching the attacker's chin, the other snapping behind the man's head, grabbing his hair. A twist and turn flipped the swordsman on the ground. Entreri let go, running his hand up the man's weapon arm to fend off any attempted attacks. The man went down on his back hard. At that moment Entreri stomped down on his throat. The man's grasp on the sword weakened, almost as if he were handing the weapon to Entreri.

The assassin leaped away, not wanting to get his feet tangled as the other two came in, one straight ahead, the other from behind. Out flashed Entreri's sword, a straight left-handed thrust, followed by a dazzling, rolling stab. The man easily stepped back out of Entreri's reach, but the attack hadn't been designed to score a hit anyway. Entreri flipped the sword to his right hand, an overhand grip, then stepped back suddenly, so suddenly, turning his hand and the blade. He brought it across his body, then stabbed it out behind him. The assassin felt the tip enter the man's chest and heard the gasp of air as he sliced a lung.

Instinct alone had Entreri spinning, turning to the right and keeping the attacker impaled. He brought the man about as a shield against the archer, who did indeed fire again. But again, the man missed badly, and this time the arrow burrowed into the ground several feet in front of Entreri.

"Idiot," the assassin muttered, and with a sudden jerk, he dropped his latest victim to the dirt, bringing the sword about in the same fluid movement. So brilliantly had he executed the maneuver that the remaining swordsman finally understood his folly, turned about, and fled.

Entreri spun again, threw the sword in the general direction of the archer, and bolted for cover.

A long moment slipped past.

Where is he?" the archer called out, obvious fear and frustration in his voice. "Merk, do you see him?"

Another long moment passed.

"Where is he?" the archer cried again, growing frantic. "Merk, where is he?"

"Right behind you," came a whisper. A jeweled dagger flashed, slicing the bowstring and then, before the stunned man could begin to react, resting against the front of his throat.

"Please," the man stammered, trembling so badly that his movements, not Entreri's, caused the first nick from that fine blade. "I have children, yes. Many, many children. Seventeen . . ."

He ended in a gurgle as Entreri cut him from ear to ear, bringing his foot up against the man's back even as he did, then kicking him facedown to the ground.

"Then you should have chosen a safer career," Entreri answered, though the man could not hear.

Peering out from the rocks, the assassin soon spotted the fourth of the group, moving from shadow to shadow across the way. The man was obviously heading for Calimport but was simply too scared to jump out and run in the open. Entreri knew that he could catch the man, or perhaps re-string the bow and take him down from this spot. But he didn't, for he hardly cared. Not even bothering to search the bodies for loot, Entreri wiped and sheathed his magical dagger and moved back onto the road. Yes, he had been gone a long, long time.

Before he had left this city, Artemis Entreri had known his place in the world and in Calimport. He thought of that now, staring at the city after an absence of several years. He understood the shadowy world he had inhabited and realized that many changes had likely taken place in those alleys. Old associates would be gone, and his reputation would not likely carry him through the initial meetings with the new, often self-proclaimed leaders of the various guilds and sects.

"What have you done to me, Drizzt Do'Urden?" he asked with a chuckle, for this great change in the life of Artemis Entreri had begun when a certain Pasha Pook had sent him on a mission to retrieve a magical ruby pendant from a runaway halfling. An easy enough task, Entreri had believed. The halfling, Regis, was known to the assassin and should not have proven a difficult adversary.

Little did Entreri know at that time that Regis had done a marvelously cunning job of surrounding himself with powerful allies, particularly the dark elf. How many years had it been, Entreri pondered, since he had first encountered Drizzt Do'Urden? Since he had first met his warrior equal, who could rightly hold a mirror up to Entreri and show the lie that was his existence? Nearly a decade, he realized, and while he had grown older and perhaps a bit slower, the drow elf, who might live six centuries, had aged not at all.

Yes, Drizzt had started Entreri on a path of dangerous introspection. The blackness had only been amplified when Entreri had gone after Drizzt again, along with the remnants of the drow's family. Drizzt had beaten Entreri on a high ledge outside Mithral Hall, and the assassin would have died, except that an opportunistic dark elf by the name of Jarlaxle had rescued him. Jarlaxle had then taken him to Menzoberranzan, the vast city of the drow, the stronghold of Lolth, Demon Queen of Chaos. The human assassin had found a different standing down there in a city of intrigue and brutality. There, everyone was an

19

assassin, and Entreri, despite his tremendous talents at the murderous art, was only human, a fact that relegated him to the bottom of the social ladder.

But it was more than simple perceptual standing that had struck the assassin profoundly during his stay in the city of drow. It was the realization of the emptiness of his existence. There, in a city full of Entreris, he had come to recognize the folly of his confidence, of his ridiculous notion that his passionless dedication to pure fighting skill had somehow elevated him above the rabble. He knew that now, looking down at Calimport, at the city he had known as a home, at his last refuge, it seemed, in all the world.

In dark and mysterious Menzoberranzan, Artemis Entreri had been humbled.

As he made his way to the distant city, Entreri wondered many times if he truly desired this return. His first days would be perilous, he knew, but it was not fear for the end of his life that brought a hesitance to his normally cocky stride. It was fear of continuing his life.

Outwardly, little had changed in Calimport—the town of a million beggars, Entreri liked to call it. True to form, he passed by dozens of pitiful wretches, lying in rags, or naked, along the sides of the road, most of them likely in the same spot the city guards had thrown them that morning, clearing the way for the golden-gilded carriages of the important merchants. They reached toward Entreri with trembling, bony fingers, arms so weak and emaciated that they could not hold them up for even the few seconds it took the heartless man to stride past them.

Where to go? he wondered. His old employer, Pasha Pook, was long dead, the victim of Drizzt's powerful panther companion after Entreri had done as the man had bade him and returned Regis and the ruby pendant. Entreri had not remained in the city for long after that unfortunate incident, for he had brought Regis in and that had led to the demise of a powerful figure, ultimately a black stain on Entreri's record among his less-than-merciful associates. He could have mended the situation, probably quite easily, by simply offering his normally invaluable services to another powerful guildmaster or pasha, but he had chosen the road. Entreri had been bent on revenge against Drizzt, not for the killing of Pook—the assassin cared little about that—but because he and Drizzt had battled fiercely without conclusion in the city's sewers, a fight that Entreri still believed he should have won.

Walking along the dirty streets of Calimport now, he had to wonder what reputation he had left behind. Certainly many other assassins would have spoken ill of him in his absence, would have exaggerated Entreri's failure in the Regis incident in order to strengthen their own positions within the gutter pecking order.

Entreri smiled as he considered the fact, and he knew it to be fact, that those ill words against him would have been spoken in whispers only. Even in his absence, those other killers would fear retribution. Perhaps he didn't know his place in the world any longer. Perhaps Menzoberranzan had held a dark . . . no, not dark, but merely empty mirror before his eyes, but he could not deny that he still enjoyed the respect.

Respect he might have to earn yet again, he pointedly reminded himself.

As he moved along the familiar streets, more and more memories came back to him. He knew where most of the guild houses had been located, and suspected that, unless there had been some ambitious purge by the lawful leaders of the city, many still stood intact, and probably brimming with the associates he had once known. Pook's house had been shaken to the core by the killing of the wretched pasha and, subsequently, by the appointment of the lazy halfling Regis as Pook's successor. Entreri had taken care of that minor problem by taking care of Regis, and yet, despite the chaos imposed upon that house, when Entreri had gone north with the halfling in tow, the house of Pook had survived. Perhaps it still stood, though the assassin could only guess as to who might be ruling it now.

That would have been a logical place for Entreri to go and rebuild his base of power within the city, but he simply shrugged and walked past the side avenue that would lead to it. He thought he was merely wandering aimlessly, but soon enough he came to another familiar region and realized that he had subconsciously aimed for this area, perhaps in an effort to regain his heart.

These were the streets where a young Artemis Entreri had first made his mark in Calimport, where he, barely a teenager, had defeated all challengers to his supremacy, where he had battled the man sent by Theebles Royuset, the lieutenant in powerful Pasha Basadoni's guild. Entreri had killed that thug and had later killed ugly Theebles, the clever murder moving him into Basadoni's generous favor. He had become a lieutenant in one of the most powerful guilds of Calimport, of all of Calimshan, at the tender age of fourteen.

But now he hardly cared, and recalling the story did not even bring the slightest hint of a smile to his face.

He thought back further, to the torment that had landed him here in the first place, trials too great for a boy to overcome, deception and betrayal by everyone he had known and trusted, most pointedly his own father. Still, he didn't care, couldn't even feel the pain any longer. It was meaningless, emptiness, without merit or point.

He saw a woman in the shadows of one hovel, hanging washed clothes to dry. She shifted deeper into the shadows, obviously wary. He understood her concern, for he was a stranger here, dressed too richly with his thick, well-stitched traveling cloak to belong in the shanty town. Strangers in these brutal places usually brought danger.

"From there to there," came a call, the voice of a young man, full of pride and edged with fear. Entreri turned slowly to see the youth, a tall and gangly lad, holding a club laced with spikes, swinging it nervously.

Entreri stared at him hard, seeing himself in the boy's face. No, not himself, he realized, for this one was too obviously nervous. This one would likely not survive for long.

"From there to there!" the boy said more loudly, pointing with his free hand to the end of the street where Entreri had entered, to the far end, where the assassin had been going.

"Your pardon, young master," Entreri said, dipping a slight bow, and feeling, as he did, his jeweled dagger, set on his belt under the folds of his cloak. A flick of his wrist could easily propel that dagger the fifteen feet, past the awkward youth's defenses and deep into his throat.

"Master," the lad echoed, his tone as much that of an incredulous question as an assertion. "Yes, master," he decided, apparently liking the title. "Master of this street, of all these streets, and none walk them without the permission of Taddio." As he finished, he prodded his thumb repeatedly into his chest.

Entreri straightened, and for just an instant, death flashed across his black eyes and the words "dead master" echoed through his thoughts. The lad had just challenged him, and the Artemis Entreri of a few years previous, a man who accepted and conquered all challenges, would have simply destroyed the youth where he stood.

But now that flash of pride whisked by, leaving Entreri unfazed and uninsulted. He gave a resigned sigh, wondering if he would find yet another stupid fight this day. And for what? he wondered, facing this pitiful, confused little boy on an empty street over which no rational person would even deign to claim ownership. "I begged you pardon, young master," he said calmly. "I did not know, for I am new to the region and ignorant of your customs."

"Then you should learn!" the lad replied angrily, gaining courage in Entreri's submissive response and coming forward a couple of strong strides.

Entreri shook his head, his hand starting for the dagger, but going, instead to his belt purse. He pulled out a gold coin and tossed it to the feet of the strutting youth.

The boy, who drank from sewers and ate the scraps he could rummage from the alleys behind the merchant houses, could not hide his surprise and awe at such a treasure. He regained his composure a moment later, though, and looked back at Entreri with a superior posture. "It is not enough," he said.

Entreri threw out another gold coin, and a silver. "That is all that I have, young master," he said, holding his hands out wide.

"If I search you and learn differently . . ." the lad threatened.

Entreri sighed again, and decided that if the youth approached he would kill him quickly and mercifully.

The boy bent and scooped up the three coins. "If you come back to the domain of Taddio, have with you more coins," he declared. "I warn you. Now begone! Out the same end of the street you entered!"

Entreri looked back the way he had come. In truth, one direction seemed as good as any other to him at that time, so he gave a slight bow and walked back, out of the domain of Taddio, who had no idea how lucky he had been this day.

* * * * *

The building stood three full stories and, decorated with elaborate sculptures and shining marble, was truly the most impressive abode of all the thieving guilds. Normally such shadowy figures tried to keep a low profile, living in houses that seemed unremarkable from the outside, though they were, in truth, palatial within. Not so with the house of Pasha Basadoni. The old man—and he was ancient now, closer to ninety than to eighty—enjoyed his luxuries, and enjoyed showing the power and splendor of his guild to all who would look.

In a large chamber in the middle of the second floor, the gathering room for Basadoni's principle commanders, the two men and one woman who truly operated the day-to-day activities of the extensive guild entertained a young street thug. He was more a boy than a man, an unimpressive figure held in power by the backing of Pasha Basadoni and surely not by his own wiles.

"At least he is loyal," remarked Hand, a quiet and subtle thief, the master of shadows, when Taddio left them. "Two gold pieces and one silver—no small take for one working that gutter section."

"If that is all he received from his visitor," Sharlotta Vespers answered with a dismissive chuckle. Sharlotta stood tallest of the three captains, an inch above six feet, her body slender, her movements graceful—so graceful that Pasha Basadoni had nicknamed her his "Willow Tree." It was no secret that Basadoni had taken Sharlotta as his lover and still used her in that manner on those rare occasions when his old body was up to the task. It was common knowledge that Sharlotta had used those liaisons to her benefit and had climbed the ranks through Basadoni's bed. She willingly admitted as much, usually just before she killed the man or woman who had complained about it. A shake of her head sent waist-length black hair flipping back over one shoulder, so that Hand could see her wry expression clearly.

"If Taddio had received more, then he would have delivered more," Hand assured her, his tone, despite his anger, revealing that hint of frustration he and their other companion, Kadran Gordeon, always felt when dealing with the condescending Sharlotta. Hand ruled the quiet services of Basadoni's operation, the pickpockets and the prostitutes who worked the market, while Kadran Gordeon dealt with the soldiers of the street army. But Sharlotta, the Willow Tree, had Basadoni's ear above them all. She served as the principal attendant of the Pasha and as the voice of the now little seen old man.

When Basadoni finally died, these three would fight for control, no doubt, and while those who understood only the peripheral truths of the guild would likely favor the brash and loud Kadran Gordeon, those, such as Hand, who had a better feeling for the true inner workings, understood that Sharlotta Vespers had already taken many, many steps to secure and strengthen her position with or without the specter of Basadoni looming over them.

"How many words will we waste on the workings of a boy?" Kadran Gordeon complained. "Three new merchants have set up kiosks in the market a stone's throw from our house without our permission. That is the more important matter, the one requiring our full attention."

"We have already talked it through," Sharlotta replied. "You want us to give you permission to send out your soldiers, perhaps even a battle-mage, to teach the merchants better. You will not get that from us at this time."

"If we wait for Pasha Basadoni to finally speak on this matter, other merchants will come to the belief that they, too, need not pay us for the privilege of operating within the boundaries of our protective zone." He turned to Hand, the small man often his ally in arguments with Sharlotta. But the thief was obviously distracted, staring down at one of the coins the boy Taddio had given to him. Sensing that he was being watched, Hand looked up at the other two.

"What is it?" Kadran prompted.

"I've not seen one like this," Hand explained, flipping the coin to the burly man.

Kadran caught it and quickly examined it, then, with a surprised expression, handed it over to Sharlotta. "Nor have I seen one with this stamp," he admitted. "Not of the city, I believe, nor of anywhere in Calimshan."

Sharlotta studied the coin carefully, a flicker of recognition coming to her striking light green eyes. "The crescent moon," she remarked, then flipped it over. "Profile of a unicorn. This is a coin from the region of Silverymoon."

The other two looked to each, surprised, as was Sharlotta, by the revelation. "Silverymoon?" Kadran echoed incredulously.

"A city far to the north, east of Waterdeep," Sharlotta replied.

"I know where Silverymoon lies," Kadran replied dryly. "The domain of Lady Alustriel, I believe. That is not what I find surprising."

"Why would a merchant, if it was a merchant, of Silverymoon find himself walking in Taddio's worthless shanty town?" Hand asked, echoing Kadran's suspicions perfectly.

"Indeed, I thought it curious that anyone carrying such a treasure of more than two gold pieces would be in that region," Kadran agreed, pursing his lips and twisting his mouth in his customary manner that sent one side of his long and curvy mustache up far higher than the other, giving his whole dark face an unbalanced appearance. "Now it seems to have become more curious by far."

"A man who wandered into Calimport probably came in through the docks," Hand reasoned, "and found himself lost in the myriad of streets and smells. So much of the city looks the same, after all. It would not be difficult for a foreigner to wander wayward."

"I do not believe in coincidences," Sharlotta replied. She tossed the coin back to Hand. "Take it to one of our wizard associates—Giunta the Diviner will suffice. Perhaps there remains enough of a trace of the previous owner's identity upon the coins that Giunta can locate him."

"It seems a tremendous effort for one too afraid of the boy to even refuse payment," Hand replied.

"I do not believe in coincidences," Sharlotta repeated. "I do not believe that anyone could be so intimidated by that pitiful Taddio, unless it is someone who knows that he works as a front for Pasha Basadoni. And I do not like the idea that one so knowledgeable of our operation took it upon himself to wander into our territory unannounced. Was he, perhaps, looking for something? Seeking a weakness?"

"You presume much," Kadran put in.

"Only where danger is concerned," Sharlotta retorted. "I consider every person an enemy until he has proven himself differently, and I find that in knowing my enemies, I can prepare against anything they might send against me."

There was little mistaking the irony of her words, aimed as they were at Kadran Gordeon, but even the dangerous soldier had to nod his agreement with Sharlotta's perception and precaution. It wasn't every day that a merchant bearing coins from far away Silverymoon wandered into one of Calimport's desolate shanty towns.

*   *   *   *   *

He knew this house better than any in all the city. Within those brown, unremarkable walls, within the wrapper of a common warehouse, hung golden-stitched tapestries and magnificent weapons. Beyond the always barred side door, where an old beggar now huddled for meager shelter, lay a room of beautiful dancing ladies, all swirling veils and alluring perfumes, warm baths in scented water, and cuisine delicacies from every corner of the Realms.

This house had belonged to Pasha Pook. After his demise, it had been given by Entreri's archenemy to Regis the halfling, who had ruled briefly, until Entreri had decided the little fool had ruled long enough. When Entreri had left Calimport with Regis, the last time he had seen the dusty city, the house was in disarray, with several factions fighting for power. He suspected that Quentin Bodeau, a veteran burglar with more than twenty years' experience in the guild, had won the fight. What he didn't know, given the confusion and outrage within the ranks, was whether the fight had been worth winning. Perhaps another guild had moved into the territory. Perhaps the inside of this brown warehouse was now as unremarkable as the outside.

R. A. Salvatore

Entreri chuckled at the possibilities, but they could not find any lasting hold within his thoughts. Perhaps he would eventually sneak into the place, just to satisfy his mild curiosity. Perhaps not.

He lingered by the side door, moving close enough past the apparently one-legged beggar, to recognize the cunning tie that bound his second leg up tight against the back of his thigh. The man was a sentry, obviously, and most of the few copper coins that Entreri saw within the opened sack before him had been placed there by the man, salting the purse and heightening the disguise.

No matter, the assassin thought. Playing the part of an ignorant visitor to Calimport, he walked up before the man and reached into his own purse, producing a silver coin and dropping it in the sack. He noted the not-really-old man's eyes flicker open a bit wider when he pulled back his cloak to go to his purse, revealing the hilt of his unique jeweled dagger, a weapon well known in the alleys and shadows of Calimport.

Had he been foolish in showing that weapon? Entreri wondered as he walked away. He hadn't any intention of revealing himself when he came to this place, but also, he had no intention of not revealing himself. The question and the worry, like his musing on the fate of Pook's house, found no hold in his wandering thoughts. Perhaps he had erred. Perhaps he had shown the dagger in a desperate bid for some excitement. And perhaps the man had recognized it as the mark of Entreri, or possibly he had noticed it only because it was indeed a truly beautiful weapon.

It didn't matter.

* * * * *

LaValle worked very hard to keep his breathing steady and to ignore the murmurs of those nervous associates beside him as he peered deeply into the crystal ball later that same night. The agitated sentry had reported the incident outside, a gift of a strange coin from a man walking with the quiet and confident gait of a warrior and wearing a dagger befitting the captain of a king's guard.

The description of that dagger had sent the more veteran members of the house, the wizard LaValle included, into a frenzy. Now LaValle, a longtime associate of the deadly Artemis Entreri, who had seen that dagger many times and uncomfortably close far too often had used that prior knowledge and his crystal ball to seek out the stranger. His magical eyes combed the streets of Calimport, sifting from shadow to shadow, and then he felt the growing image and knew indeed that the dagger, Entreri's dagger, was back in the city. Now as the image began to take shape, the wizard and those standing beside him, a very nervous Quentin Bodeau and two younger cocky killers, would learn if it was indeed the deadliest of assassins who carried it.

A small bedroom drifted into focus.

"That is Tomnoddy's Inn," explained Dog Perry, who called himself Dog Perry the Heart because of his practice of cutting out a victim's heart fast enough that the dying man could witness its last beats (though none other than Dog Perry himself had ever actually seen this feat performed).

LaValle held up a hand to silence the man as the image became sharper, focusing on the belt looped over the bottom post of the bed, a belt that included the telltale dagger.

"It is Entreri's," Quentin Bodeau said with a groan.

A man walked past the belt, stripped to the waist, revealing a body honed by years and years of hard practice, muscles twitching with every movement.

Quentin put on a quizzical expression, studying the man, the long hair, the goatee and scratchy, unkempt beard. He had always known Entreri to be meticulous in every detail, a perfectionist to the extreme. He looked to LaValle for an answer.

"It is he," the wizard, who knew Artemis Entreri perhaps better than anyone else in all the city, answered grimly.

"What does that mean?" Quentin asked. "Has he returned as friend or foe?"

"Indifferent, more likely," LaValle replied. "Artemis Entreri has always been a free spirit, never showing allegiance too greatly to any particular guild. He wanders through the treasuries of each, hiring to the highest bidder for his exemplary services." As he spoke, the wizard glanced over at the two younger killers, neither of whom knew Entreri other than by reputation. Chalsee Anguaine, the younger, tittered nervously—and wisely, LaValle knew—but Dog Perry squinted his eyes as he considered the man in the crystal ball. He was jealous, LaValle understood, for Dog Perry wanted, above all else, that which Entreri possessed: the supreme reputation as the deadliest of assassins.

"Perhaps we should find a need for his services quickly," Quentin Bodeau reasoned, obviously trying hard not to sound nervous, for in the dangerous world of Calimport's thieving guilds, nervousness equalled weakness. "In that way we might better learn the man's intentions and purpose in returning to Calimport."

"Or we could just kill him," Dog Perry put in, and LaValle bit back a chuckle at the so-predictable viewpoint and also at his knowledge that Dog Perry simply did not understand the truth of Artemis Entreri. No friend or fan of the brash young thug, LaValle almost hoped that Quentin would give Dog Perry his wish and send him right out after Entreri.

But Quentin, though he had never dealt with Entreri personally, remembered well the many, many stories of the assassin's handiwork, and the expression the guildmaster directed at Dog Perry was purely incredulous.

"Hire him if you need him," said LaValle. "Or if not, then merely watch him without threat."

"He is one man, and we are a guild of a hundred," Dog Perry protested, but no one was listening to him anymore.

Quentin started to reply, but stopped short, though his expression told LaValle exactly what he was thinking. He feared that Entreri had come back to take the guild, obviously, and not without some rationale. Certainly the deadliest of assassins still had many powerful connections within the city, enough for Entreri, with his own amazing skills, to topple the likes of Quentin Bodeau. But LaValle did not think Quentin's fears well-founded, for the wizard understood Entreri enough to realize that the man had never craved such a position of responsibility. Entreri was a loner, not a guildmaster. After he had deposed the halfling Regis from his short rein as guildmaster, the place had been Entreri's for the taking, and yet he had walked away, just walked out of Calimport altogether, leaving all of the others to fight it out.

No, LaValle did not believe that Entreri had come back to take this guild or any other, and he did well to silently convey that to the nervous Quentin. "Whatever our ultimate choices, it seems obvious to me that we should first merely observe our dangerous friend," the wizard said, for the benefit of the two younger lieutenants, "to learn if he is friend, foe, or indifferent. It makes no sense to go against one as strong as Entreri until we have determined that we must, and that, I do not believe to be the case."

Quentin nodded, happy to hear the confirmation, and with a bow LaValle took his leave, the others following suit.

"If Entreri is a threat, then Entreri should be eliminated," Dog Perry said to the wizard, catching up to him in the corridor outside his room. "Master Bodeau would have seen that truth had your advice been different."

LaValle stared long and hard at the upstart, not appreciating being talked to in that manner from one half his age and with so little experience in such matters, for LaValle had been dealing with dangerous killers such as Artemis Entreri before Dog Perry was even born. "I'll not say that I disagree with you," he said to the man.

"Then why your counsel to Bodeau?"

"If Entreri has come into Calimport at the request of another guild, then any move by Master Bodeau could bring dire consequences to our guild," the wizard replied, improvising as he went, for he didn't believe a word of what he was saying. "You know that Artemis Entreri learned his trade under Pasha Basadoni himself, of course."

"Of course," Dog Perry lied.

LaValle struck a pensive pose, tapping one finger across his pursed lips. "It may prove to be no problem at all to us," he explained. "Surely when news of Entreri's return—an older and slower Entreri, you see, and one, perhaps, with few connections left within the city—spreads across the streets, the dangerous man will himself be marked."

"He has made many enemies," Dog Perry reasoned eagerly, seeming quite intrigued by LaValle's words and tone.

LaValle shook his head. "Most enemies of the Artemis Entreri who left Calimport those years ago are dead," the wizard explained. "No, not enemies, but rivals. How many young and cunning assassins crave the power that they might find with a single stroke of the blade?"

Dog Perry narrowed his eyes, just beginning to catch on.

"One who kills Entreri, in essence, claims credit for killing all of those whom Entreri killed," LaValle went on. "With a single stroke of the blade might such a reputation be earned. The killer of Entreri will almost instantly become the highest priced assassin in all the city." He shrugged and held up his hands, then pushed through his door, leaving an obviously intrigued Dog Perry standing in the hallway with the echoes of his words.

In truth, LaValle hardly cared whether the young troublemaker took those words to heart or not, but he was indeed concerned about the return of the assassin. Entreri unnerved the wizard, more so than all the other dangerous characters that LaValle had worked beside over the many years. LaValle had survived by posing a threat to no one, by serving without judgment whomever it was that had come to power in the guild. He had served Pasha Pook admirably, and when Pook had been disposed, he had switched his allegiance easily and completely to Regis, convincing even Regis's protective dark elf and dwarven friends that he was no threat. Similarly, when Entreri had gone against Regis, LaValle had stepped back and let the two decide the issue (though, of course, there had never been any doubt whatsoever in LaValle's mind as to which of those two would triumph), then throwing his loyalty to the victor. And so it had gone, down the line, master after master during the tumult immediately following

Entreri's departure, to the present incarnation of guildmaster, Quentin Bodeau.

Concerning Entreri, though, there remained one subtle difference. Over the decades, LaValle had built a considerable insulating defense about him. He worked very hard to make no enemies in a world where everyone seemed to be in deadly competition, but he also understood that even a benign bystander could get caught and slaughtered in the common battles. Thus he had built a defense of powerful magic and felt that if one such as Dog Perry decided, for whatever reason, that he would be better off without LaValle around, he would find the wizard more than ready and able to defend himself. Not so with Entreri, LaValle knew, and that is why even the sight of the man so unnerved him. In watching the assassin over the years, LaValle had come to know that where Entreri was concerned, there simply weren't enough defenses.

He sat on his bed until very late that night, trying to remember every detail of every dealing he had ever had with the assassin and trying to figure out what, if anything in particular, had brought Entreri back to Calimport.

Chapter 2
RUNNING THE HORSE

Their pace held slow but steady. The springtime tundra, the hardening grasp of ice dissipating, had become like a great sponge, swelling in places to create mounds higher even than Wulfgar . The ground was sucking at their boots with every step, as if it were trying desperately to hold them. Drizzt, the lightest on his feet, had the easiest time of it—of those walking, at least. Regis, sitting comfortably up high on the shoulders of an uncomplaining Wulfgar, felt no muddy wetness in his warm boots. Still, the other three, who had spent so many years in Icewind Dale and were accustomed to the troubles of springtime travel, plodded on without complaint. They knew from the outset that the slowest and most tiresome part of their journey would be the first leg, until they got around the western edges of the Spine of the World and out of Icewind Dale.

Every now and then they found patches of great stones, the remnants of a road built long ago from Ten Towns to the western pass, but these did little more than assure them that they were on the right path, something that seemed of little importance in the vast open stretches of the tundra. All they really had to do was keep the towering mountains to the south, and they would not lose their way.

Drizzt led them and tried to pick a course that followed the thickest regions of sprouting yellow grass, for this, at least, afforded some stability atop the slurpy ground. Of course—and the drow and his friends knew it—tall grass might also serve as camouflage for the dangerous tundra yetis, always hungry beasts that often feasted on unwary travelers.

With Drizzt Do'Urden leading them, though, the friends did not consider themselves unwary.

They put the river far behind them and found yet another stretch of that ancient road when the sun was halfway to the western horizon. There, just beyond one long rock slab, they also came upon some recent tracks.

"Wagon," Catti-brie remarked, seeing the long lines of deep grooves.

"Two," Regis commented, noting the twin lines at each groove.

Catti-brie shook her head. "One," she corrected, following the tracks, noting how they sometimes joined and other times separated, and always with a wider track as they moved apart. "Sliding in the mud as it rolled along, its back end often unaligned with the front."

"Well done," Drizzt congratulated her, for he, too, had come to the same conclusion. "A single wagon traveling east and not more than a day ahead of us."

"A merchant wagon left Bremen three days before we arrived there," Regis, always current on the goings-on of Ten Towns, commented.

"Then it would seem they are having great difficulty navigating the marshy ground," Drizzt replied.

"And might be other troubles they're findin'," came Bruenor's call from a short distance to the side, the dwarf stooping low over a small hump of grass.

The friends moved to join him and saw immediately his cause for concern: several tracks pressed deep into the mud.

"Yetis," the dwarf said distastefully. "And they came right to the wagon tracks and then went back. They're knowin' this for a used trail or I'm a bearded gnome."

"And the yeti tracks are more recent," Catti-brie remarked, noting the water still within them.

Up on Wulfgar's shoulders, Regis glanced around nervously, as if he expected a hundred of the shaggy beasts to leap out at them.

Drizzt, too, bent low to study the depressions and began to shake his head.

"They are recent," Catti-brie insisted.

"I do not disagree with your assessment of the time," the drow explained. "Only with the identification of the creature."

"Not a horse," Bruenor said with a grunt. "Unless that horse's lost two legs. A yeti, and a damned big one."

"Too big," the drow explained. "Not a yeti, but a giant."

"Giant?" the dwarf echoed skeptically. "We're ten miles from the mountains. What's a giant doing out here?"

"What indeed?" the drow answered, his grim tone giving the answer clear enough. Giants rarely came out of the Spine of the World Mountains, and then only to cause mischief. Perhaps this was a single rogue—that would be the best scenario—or perhaps it was an advanced scout for a larger and more dangerous group.

Bruenor cursed and dropped the head of his many-notched axe hard into the soft turf. "If ye're thinkin' o' walking all the way back to the durned towns, then be thinkin' again, elf," he said. "Sooner I'm outta this mud, the better. The towns've been livin' well enough without our help all these years. They're not needin' us to turn back now!"

"But if they are giants—" Catti-brie started to argue, but Drizzt cut her short.

"I've no intention of turning back," he said. "Not yet. Not until we have proof that these tracks foretell a greater disaster than one, or even a handful, of giants could perpetrate. No, our road remains east, and all the quicker because I now hope to catch that lone wagon before the fall of darkness, or soon after if we must continue on. If the giant is part of a rogue hunting group and it knows of the wagon's recent passage, then the Bremen merchants might soon be in dire need of our help."

They set off at a swifter pace, following the wagon tracks, and within a couple of hours they saw the merchants struggling with a loose and wobbly wagon wheel. Two of the five men, obviously the hired guards, pulled hard to try and lift the carriage while a third, a young and strong merchant whom Regis identified as Master Camlaine the scrimshaw trader, worked hard, though hardly successfully, to realign the tilted wheel. Both the guards had sunk past their ankles into the mud, and though they struggled mightily, they could hardly get the carriage up high enough for the fit.

How the faces of all five brightened when they noted the approach of Drizzt and his friends, a well-known company of heroes indeed among the folk of Icewind Dale.

"Well met, I should say, Master Do'Urden!" the merchant Camlaine cried. "Do lend us the strength of your barbarian friend. I will pay you well, I promise. I am to be in Luskan in a fortnight, yet if our luck holds as it has since we left Bremen, I fear that winter will find us still in the dale."

Bruenor handed his axe to Catti-brie and motioned to Wulfgar. "Come on, boy," he said. "Ye'll play come-along and I'll show ye an anvil pose."

With a nonchalant shrug, Wulfgar brought Regis swinging down from his shoulders and set him on the ground. The halfling moaned and rushed to a pile of grass, not wanting to get mud all over his new boots.

"Ye think ye can lift it?" Bruenor asked Wulfgar as the huge man joined him by the wagon. Without a word, without even putting down his magnificent warhammer Aegis-fang, Wulfgar grabbed the wagon and pulled hard. The mud slurped loudly in protest, grabbing and clinging, but in the end it could not resist, and the wheel came free of the soupy ground.

The two guards, after a moment of disbelief, found handholds and similarly pulled, hoisting the wagon even higher. Down to hands and knees went Bruenor, setting his bent back under the axle right beside the wheel. "Go ahead and set the durned thing," he said and then he groaned as the weight came upon him.

Wulfgar took the wheel from the struggling merchant and pulled it into line, then pushed it more securely into place. He took a step back, took up Aegis-fang in both hands, and gave it a good whack, setting it firmly. Bruenor gave a grunt from the suddenly shifting weight, and Wulfgar moved to lift the wagon again, just a few inches, so that Bruenor could slip out from under it. Master Camlaine inspected the work, turning about with a bright smile and nodding his approval.

"You could begin a new career, good dwarf and mighty Wulfgar," he said with a laugh. "Wagon repair."

"There is an aspiration fit for a dwarven king," Drizzt remarked, coming over with Catti-brie and Regis. "Give up your throne, good Bruenor, and fix the carts of wayward merchants."

They all had a laugh at that, except for Wulfgar, who simply seemed detached from it all, and for Regis, still fretting over his muddy boots.

"You are far out from Ten Towns," Camlaine noted, "with nothing to the west. Are you leaving Icewind Dale once more?"

"Briefly," Drizzt replied. "We have business in the south."

"Luskan?"

"Beyond Luskan," the drow explained. "But we will indeed be going through that city, it would seem."

Camlaine brightened, obviously happy to hear that bit of news. He reached to a jingling purse on his belt, but Drizzt held up a hand, thinking it ridiculous that the man should offer to pay.

"Of course," Camlaine remarked, embarrassed, remembering that Bruenor Battlehammer was indeed a dwarven king, wealthy beyond anything a simple merchant could ever hope to achieve. "I wish there was some way I . . . we, could repay you for your help. Or even better, I wish that there was some way I could bribe you into accompanying us to Luskan. I have hired fine and able guards, of course," he added, nodding to the two men. "But Icewind Dale remains a dangerous place, and friendly swords—or warhammers or axes—are always welcomed."

Drizzt looked to his friends and, seeing no objections, nodded. "We will indeed travel with you out of the dale," he said.

"Is your mission urgent?" the scrimshaw merchant asked. "Our wagon has been dragging more than rolling, and our team is weary. We had hoped to repair the wheel and then find a suitable campsite, though there yet remain two or three hours of daylight."

Drizzt looked to his friends and again saw no complaints there. The group, though their mission to go to the Spirit Soaring and destroy Crenshinibon was indeed vital, was in no great hurry. The drow found a campsite, a relatively high bluff not so far away and they all settled down for the night. Camlaine offered his new companions a fine meal of rich venison stew. They passed the meal with idle chatter, with Camlaine and his four companions doing most of the talking, stories about problems in Bremen over the winter, mostly, and about the first catch of the prized knucklehead trout, the fish that provided the bone material for the scrimshaw. Drizzt and the others listened politely, not really interested. Regis, however, who had lived on the banks of Maer Dualdon and had spent years making scrimshaw pieces of his own, begged Camlaine to show him the finished wares he was taking to Luskan. The halfling poured over each piece for a long while, studying every detail.

"Ye think we'll be seeing them giants this night?" Catti-brie asked Drizzt quietly, the two moving off to the side of the main group.

The drow shook his head. "The one who happened upon the tracks turned back for the mountains," he said. "Likely, he was merely checking the route. I had feared that he then went in pursuit of the wagon, but since Camlaine and his crew were not so far away, and since we saw no other sign of any behemoth, I do not expect to see him."

"But he might be bringing trouble to the next wagon along," Catti-brie reasoned.

Drizzt conceded the point with a nod and a smile, a look that grew more intense as he and the beautiful woman locked stares. There had been a notable strain between them since the return of Wulfgar, for in the six years of Wulfgar's absence, Drizzt and Catti-brie had forged a deeper friendship, one bordering on love. But now Wulfgar, who had been engaged to marry Catti-brie at the time of his apparent death, was back, and things between the drow and the woman had become far more complicated.

Not at this moment, though. For some reason that neither of the friends could understand, for this one second, it was as if they were the only two people in all the world, or as if time had stopped all around them, freezing the others in a state of oblivion.

It didn't last, not more than a brief moment, for a commotion at the other side of the encampment drew the two apart. When she looked past Drizzt, Catti-brie found Wulfgar staring at them hard. She locked eyes with the man, but again, it was only for a moment. One of Camlaine's guards standing behind Wulfgar, called to the group, waving his arms excitedly.

"Might be that our giant friend decided to show its ugly face," Catti-brie said to Drizzt. When they joined the others, the guard was pointing out toward another bluff, this one an oozing mud mound pushed up like a miniature volcano by the shifting tundra.

"Behind that," the guard said.

Drizzt studied the mound intently; Catti-brie pulled Taulmaril, the Heartseeker bow, from her shoulder and set an arrow.

"Too small a pimple for a giant to hide behind," Bruenor insisted, but the dwarf clutched his axe tightly as he spoke.

Drizzt nodded his agreement. He looked to Catti-brie and to Wulfgar alternately, motioning that they should cover him. Then he sprinted away, picking a careful and quiet path that brought him right to the base of the mound. With a glance back to ensure that his friends were ready, the drow skipped up the side of the mound, his twin scimitars drawn.

And then he relaxed, and put his deadly blades away, as a man, a huge man wearing a wolf-skin wrap, came out around the base into plain sight.

"Kierstaad, son of Revjak," Catti-brie remarked.

"Following his hero," Bruenor added, looking up at Wulfgar, for it was no secret to any of them, or to any of the barbarians of Icewind Dale, that Kierstaad idolized Wulfgar. The young man had even stolen Aegisfang and followed the companions along when they had gone out onto the Sea of Moving Ice to rescue Wulfgar from the demon, Errtu. To Kierstaad, Wulfgar symbolized the greatness that the tribes of Icewind Dale might achieve and the greatness that he, too, so desired.

Wulfgar frowned at the sight.

Kierstaad and Drizzt exchanged a few words, then both moved back to the main group. "He has come for a word with Wulfgar," the drow explained.

"To beg for the survival of the tribes," Kierstaad admitted, staring at his barbarian kin.

"The tribes fare well under the care of Berkthgar the Bold," Wulfgar insisted.

"They do not!" Kierstaad replied harshly, and the others took that as their cue to give the two men some space. "Berkthgar understands the old ways, that is true," Kierstaad went on. "But the old ways do not offer the hope of anything greater than the lives we have known for centuries. Only Wulfgar, son of Beornegar, can truly unite the tribes and strengthen our bond with the folk of Ten Towns."

"That would be for the better?" Wulfgar asked skeptically.

"Yes!" Kierstaad replied without hesitation. "No longer should any tribesman starve because the winter is difficult. No longer should we be so completely dependent upon the caribou herd. Wulfgar, with his friends, can change our ways . . . can lead us to a better place."

"You speak foolishness," Wulfgar said, waving his hand and turning from the man. But Kierstaad wouldn't let him get away that easily. The young man ran up behind and grabbed Wulfgar roughly by the arm, turning him about.

Kierstaad started to offer yet another argument, started to explain that Berkthgar still considered the folk of Ten Towns, even the dwarven folk of Wulfgar's own adoptive father, more as enemies than as allies. There were so many things that young Kierstaad wanted to say to Wulfgar, so many arguments to make to the big man, to try and convince him that his place was with the tribes. But all those words went flying away as Kierstaad went flying away, for Wulfgar turned about viciously, following the young man's pull, and brought his free arm swinging about, slugging the young man heavily in the chest and launching him into a short flight and then a backward roll down the side of the bluff.

Wulfgar turned away with a low, feral growl, storming back to his supper bowl. Protests came at him from every side, particularly from Catti-brie. "Ye didn't have to hit the boy," she yelled, but Wulfgar only waved his hand at her and snarled again, then went back to his food.

Drizzt was the first one down to Kierstaad's side. The young barbarian was lying facedown in the muck at the bottom of the bluff. Regis came along right behind, offering one of his many handkerchiefs to wipe some of the mud from Kierstaad's face—and also to allow the man to save some measure of pride and quietly wipe the welling tears from his eyes.

"He must understand," Kierstaad remarked, starting back up the hill, but Drizzt had him firmly by the arm, and the young barbarian did not truly fight against the pull.

"This matter was already resolved," the drow said, "between Wulfgar and Berkthgar. Wulfgar made his choice, and that choice was the road."

"Blood before friends—that is the rule of the tribes," Kierstaad argued. "And Wulfgar's blood kin need him now."

Drizzt tilted his head, and a knowing expression came over his fair, ebon-skinned face, a look that settled Kierstaad more than any words ever could. "Is it so?" the drow asked calmly. "Do the tribes need Wulfgar, or does Kierstaad need him?"

"What do you mean?" the young man stammered, obviously embarrassed.

"Berkthgar has been angry with you for a long time," the drow explained. "Perhaps you will not find a position that pleases you while Berkthgar rules the tribes."

Kierstaad pulled roughly away; his face screwed up with anger. "This is not about Kierstaad's position within the tribes," he insisted. "My people need Wulfgar, and so I have come for him."

"He'll not follow you," Regis said. "Nor can you drag him, I would guess."

Frustration evident on his face, Kierstaad began clenching and unclenching his fists at his side. He looked up the bluff, then took a step that way, but agile Drizzt moved quickly in front of him.

"He'll not follow," the drow said. "Even Berkthgar begged Wulfgar to remain and to lead, but that, by Wulfgar's own words, is not his place at this time."

"But it is!"

"No!" Drizzt said forcefully, stopping Kierstaad's further arguments cold. "No, and not only because Wulfgar has determined that it is not his place. Truly I was relieved to learn that he did not accept the leadership from Berkthgar, for I, too, care about the welfare of the tribes of Icewind Dale."

Even Regis looked at the drow with surprise at that seemingly illogical reasoning.

"You do not believe Wulfgar to be the rightful leader?" Kierstaad asked incredulously.

"Not at this time," Drizzt replied. "Can any of us appreciate the agony the man has suffered? Or can we measure the lingering effects of Errtu's torments? No, Wulfgar is not now fit to lead the tribes—he is having a difficult enough time leading himself."

"But we are his kin," Kierstaad tried to argue, but as he spoke them the words sounded lame even to him. "If Wulfgar feels pain, then he should be with us, in our care."

"And how might you tend the wounds that tear at Wulfgar's heart?" Drizzt asked. "No, Kierstaad. I applaud your intentions, but your hopes are false. Wulfgar needs time to remember who he truly is, to remember all that was once important to him. He needs time, and he needs his friends, and though I'll not argue your contention of the importance of blood kin, I tell you now in all honesty that those who love Wulfgar the most are here, not back with the tribes."

Kierstaad started to reply but only huffed and stared emptily back up the bluff, having no practical rebuttal.

"We will return soon enough," the drow explained. "Before the turn of winter, I hope, or in the spring soon after, at the latest. Perhaps Wulfgar will find again his heart and soul on the road with his friends. Perhaps he will return to Icewind Dale ready to assume the leadership that he truly deserves and that the tribes truly deserve."

"And if not?" Kierstaad asked.

Drizzt only shrugged. He was beginning to understand the depth of Wulfgar's pain and could make no guarantees.

"Keep him safe," Kierstaad said.

Drizzt nodded.

"On your word," the young barbarian pressed.

"We care for each other," the drow replied. "It has been that way since before we set out from Icewind Dale to reclaim Bruenor's throne in Mithral Hall nearly a decade ago."

Kierstaad continued to stare up the bluff. "My tribe has camped north of here," he explained, starting slowly away. "It is not far."

"Stay with us through the night," the drow offered.

"Master Camlaine has some fine food," Regis added hopefully. Drizzt knew just from the fact that the halfling was apparently willing to split the portions an extra way that Kierstaad's plight had touched his little friend.

But Kierstaad, obviously too embarrassed to go back up and face Wulfgar, only shook his head and started off to the north, across the empty tundra.

"You should beat him," Regis said, looking back up the hill at Wulfgar.

"How would that help?" the drow asked.

"I think our large friend could use a bit of humility."

Drizzt shook his head. "His reaction to Kierstaad's touch was just that: a reaction," the drow explained. He was beginning to understand Wulfgar's mood a bit more clearly now, for Wulfgar's striking of Kierstaad had been wrought of no conscious thought. Drizzt recalled his days back in Melee-Magthere, the drow school for fighters. In that always dangerous environment, where enemies lurked around every corner, Drizzt had seen such reactions, had reacted similarly on many occasions himself. Wulfgar was back with friends now in a safe enough place, but emotionally he was still the prisoner of Errtu, his constant defenses still in place against the intrusions of the demon and its minions.

"It was instinctual and nothing more."

"He could have apologized," Regis replied.

No, he could not, Drizzt thought, but he kept the notion silent. An idea came over the drow then, one that put a particularly sparkling twinkle in his lavender eyes, a look that Regis had seen many times before.

"What are you thinking?" the halfling prompted.

"About giants," Drizzt replied with a coy smile, "and about the danger to any passing caravans."

"You believe that they will come at us this night?"

"I believe that they are back in the mountains, perhaps planning to bring a raiding party to the trail," Drizzt answered honestly. "And we would be long gone before they ever arrived."

"Would be?" Regis echoed softly, still studying the drow's glowing eyes—no trick of the late-day sun—and the way Drizzt's gaze drifted back toward the snowy peaks shining in the south. "What are you thinking?"

"We cannot wait for the giants' return," the drow said. "Nor do I wish to leave any future caravans in peril. Perhaps Wulfgar and I should go out this night."

Regis's jaw dropped open, his dumbfounded expression bringing a laugh to the drow's lips.

"In my days with Montolio, the ranger who trained me, I learned much about horsemanship," Drizzt began to explain.

"You plan to take one or both of the merchant's horses to go to the mountains?" an incredulous Regis asked.

"No, no," Drizzt replied. "Montolio had been quite a rider in his youth, before he lost his vision, of course. And the horses he chose to ride were the strongest and least broken by saddles. But he had a technique—he called it 'running the horse'—to calm the steeds enough so that they would behave. He would bring them out in an open field on a long lead and snap a whip behind them repeatedly to get them running in wide and hard circles, even to get them bucking."

"Would that not only make them less behaved?" the halfling asked, for he knew little about horses.

Drizzt shook his head. "The strongest of horses possesses too much energy, Montolio explained to me. Thus, he would take them out and let them release that extra layer, and when he would then climb on their backs they would ride strong but in control."

Regis shrugged and nodded, accepting the story. "What has that to do with Wulfgar?" he asked, but his expression changed to one of understanding even as the question came out of his mouth. "You plan to run Wulfgar as Montolio ran the horses," he reasoned.

"Perhaps he needs a good fight," Drizzt replied. "And truly I wish to rid the region of any trouble with giants."

"It will take you hours to get to the mountains," Regis estimated, looking to the south. "Perhaps longer if the giants' trail is not clear to follow."

"But we will move much quicker than you three if you stay, as we promised, with Camlaine," the drow replied. "Wulfgar and I will be back beside you within two or three days, long before you've turned the corner around the Spine of the World."

"Bruenor will not like being left out," Regis remarked.

"Then do not tell him," the drow instructed. Then, before Regis could offer the expected reply, he added, "Nor should you tell Catti-brie. Explain to them only that Wulfgar and I set out in the night, and that I promised to return the day after tomorrow."

Regis gave a frustrated sigh—once before Drizzt had run off, promising Regis to secrecy, and a frantic Catti-brie had nearly beat the information out of the halfling. "Why am I always the one to hold your secrets?" he asked.

"Why are you always sniffing where your nose does not belong?" Drizzt answered with a laugh.

The drow caught up to Wulfgar on the far side of the encampment. The big man was sitting alone, absently tossing stones down to the ground. He did not look up, nor did he offer any apologetic expressions, burying them beneath a wall of anger.

Drizzt sympathized completely and recognized the torment simmering just below the surface. Anger was his friend's only defense against those horrible memories. Drizzt crouched low and looked into Wulfgar's pale blue eyes, even if the huge man did not match the gaze.

"Do you remember our first fight?" the drow asked slyly.

Now Wulfgar did turn his stare up at the drow. "Do you mean to teach me another lesson?" he asked, his tone showing that he was more than ready to accept that challenge.

The words stung Drizzt profoundly. He recalled his last angry encounter with Wulfgar, over the barbarian's treatment of Catti-brie those seven years before in Mithral Hall. They had fought viciously with Drizzt emerging as victor. And he recalled his first fight against Wulfgar, when Bruenor had captured the lad and brought him into the dwarven clan in Icewind Dale after the barbarians had tried to raid Ten Towns. Bruenor had charged Drizzt with training Wulfgar as a fighter, and those first lessons between the two had proven especially painful for the young and overly proud barbarian. But that was not the encounter to which Drizzt was now referring.

"I mean the first time that we fought together side by side against a real enemy," he explained.

Wulfgar's eyes narrowed as he considered the memory, a glimpse at his friendship with Drizzt from many years ago.

"Biggrin and the verbeeg," Drizzt reminded. "You and I and Guenhwyvar charging headlong into a lair full of giants."

The anger melted from Wulfgar's face. He managed a rare smile and nodded.

"A tough one was Biggrin," Drizzt went on. "How many times did we hit the behemoth? It took a final throw from you to drive the dagger—"

"That was a long time ago," Wulfgar interrupted. He couldn't manage to maintain the smile, but at least he did not sink right back into the explosive anger. Wulfgar again found a more even keel, much like his detached, almost ambivalent attitude when they had first started out on this journey.

"But you do remember?" Drizzt pressed, his grin growing across his black face, that telltale twinkle in his lavender eyes.

"Why . . ." Wulfgar started to ask, but stopped short and sat studying his friend. He hadn't seen Drizzt in such a mood in a long, long time, even well before his fateful fight with the handmaiden of the demon queen Lolth back in Mithral Hall. This was a flash of Drizzt from the days before the quest to reclaim the dwarven kingdom, an image of the drow in those times when Wulfgar honestly feared that Drizzt's recklessness would soon put him and the drow in a situation from which they could not escape.

Wulfgar liked the image.

"We have some giants readying to waylay travelers on the road," the drow said. "Our pace will be slower out of the dale, now that we have agreed to accompany

Master Camlaine. It seems to me that a side journey to deal with these dangerous marauders might be in order."

It was the first hint of an eager sparkle in Wulfgar's eye that Drizzt had seen since they had been reunited in the ice cave after the defeat of Errtu.

"Have you spoken with the others?" the barbarian asked.

"Just me and you," Drizzt explained. "And Guenhwyvar, of course. She would not appreciate being left out of this fun."

The pair left camp long after sunset, waiting for Catti-brie, Regis, and Bruenor to fall asleep. With the drow leading, having no difficulty in seeing under the starry tundra sky, they went straight back to the point where the giant and the wagon tracks intersected. There, Drizzt reached into a pouch and produced the onyx panther figurine, placing it reverently on the ground. "Come to me, Guenhwyvar," he called softly.

A mist came up, swirling about the figurine, growing thicker and thicker, flowing and swirling and taking the shape of the great panther. Thicker and thicker, and then it was no mist circling the onyx likeness, but the panther herself. Guenhwyvar looked up at Drizzt with eyes showing an intelligence far beyond that indicated by her feline form.

Drizzt pointed down to the giant track, and Guenhwyvar, understanding, led them away.

* * * * *

She knew as soon as she opened her eyes that something was amiss. The camp was quiet, the two merchant guards sitting on the bench of the wagon, talking softly.

Catti-brie shifted up to her elbows to better survey the scene. The fire had burned low but was still bright enough to cast shadows from the bedrolls. Closest lay Regis, curled in a ball so near to the fire that Catti-brie was amazed the little fellow hadn't gone up in flames. The mound that was Bruenor lay just a bit further back, right where Catti-brie had said good night to her adoptive father. The woman sat up, then got to one knee, craning her neck, but she could not locate two particular forms among the sleeping.

She started for Bruenor, but changed her mind and went to Regis instead. The halfling always seemed to know. . . .

A gentle shake only made him groan and roll tighter into a ball. A rougher shake and a call of his name only had him spitting curses and tightening even more.

Catti-brie kicked him in the rump.

"Hey!" he protested loudly, coming up suddenly.

"Where'd they go to?" the woman asked.

"What're ye about, girl?" came Bruenor's sleepy voice, the dwarf awakened by Regis's call.

"Drizzt and Wulfgar have gone out from camp," she explained, then turned her penetrating gaze back over Regis.

The halfling squirmed under the scrutiny. "Why would I know?" he argued, but Catti-brie didn't blink. Regis looked to Bruenor for support, but found the half-dressed dwarf ambling over, seeming every bit as perturbed as Catti-brie, and apparently ready, like the woman, to direct his ire the halfling's way.

"Drizzt said that they would return to us, and the caravan, tomorrow, or perhaps the day after that," the halfling admitted.

"And where'd they go off to?" Catti-brie demanded.

Regis shrugged, but Catti-brie had him by the collar, hoisting him to his feet before he ever finished the motion. "Are ye meanin' to play this game again?" she asked.

"To find Kierstaad and apologize, I would guess," the halfling said. "He deserves as much."

"Good enough if the boy's got an apology in his heart," Bruenor remarked. Seemingly satisfied with that, the dwarf turned back for his bedroll.

Catti-brie, though, stood holding Regis roughly and shaking her head. "He's not got it in him," she said, drawing the dwarf back into the conversation. "Not now, and that's not where they're off to." She moved closer to Regis as she spoke, but did let go of him. "Ye need to tell me," she said calmly. "Ye can't be playin' this game. If we're to travel half the length o' Faerûn together, then we're needing a bit o' trust, and that ye're not earning."

"They went after the giants," Regis blurted. He couldn't believe that he had said it, but neither could he deny the logic of Catti-brie's argument nor the plaintive look in her beautiful eyes.

"Bah!" Bruenor snorted, stomping his bare foot—and slamming it so hard that it sounded as if he was wearing boots. "By the brains of a pointed-headed orc-cousin! Why didn't ye tell us sooner?"

"Because you would have made me go," Regis argued, but his voice lost its angry edge when Catti-brie moved right in front of his face.

"Ye always seem to be knowing too much and tellin' too little," she growled. "As when Drizzt left Mithral Hall."

"I listen," Regis replied with a helpless shrug.

"Get dressed," Catti-brie instructed Regis, who just looked back at her incredulously.

"Ye heard her!" Bruenor roared.

"You want to go out there?" the halfling asked, pointing to the black emptiness that was the nighttime tundra. "Now?"

"Won't be the first time I pulled that durned elf from the mouth of a tundra yeti," the dwarf snorted, heading for his bedroll.

"Giants," Regis corrected.

"Even worse, then!" Bruenor roared louder, waking the rest of the camp.

"But we cannot leave," Regis protested, motioning to the three merchants and their guardsmen. "We promised to guard them. What if the giants come in behind us?"

That brought a concerned look to the faces of the five members of the merchant team, but Catti-brie didn't blink at the ridiculous thought. She just kept looking hard at Regis, and at his possessions, including the new unicorn-headed mace one of Bruenor's smithies had forged for him, a beautiful mithral and black steel item with blue sapphires set for the eyes.

With a profound sigh the halfling pulled his tunic on over his head.

They were out within the hour, backtracking to the point where wagon track, giant track, and now drow and barbarian track, intersected. They had much more difficulty finding it than had Wulfgar and Drizzt, with the drow's superior night vision. For even though Catti-brie wore an enchanted circlet that allowed her to see in the dark, she was no ranger and could not match Drizzt's keen senses and training. Bruenor bent low, sniffing the ground, then led on through the darkness.

"Probably get swallowed by waiting yetis," Regis grumbled.

"I'll shoot high, then," Catti-brie answered, holding her deadly bow out. "Above the belly, so ye won't have a hole in ye when we cut ye out."

Of course Regis continued to grumble, but he kept his voice lower, not letting Catti-brie hear clearly so that she could not offer any more sarcastic replies.

* * * * *

They spent the dark hours before the dawn feeling their way over the rocky foothills of the Spine of the World. Wulfgar complained many times that they must have lost the trail, but Drizzt held faith in Guenhwyvar, who kept appearing ahead of them, a darker shadow against the night sky, high on rocky outcroppings.

Soon after the break of day, as they moved along a winding mountain path, the drow's faith in the panther was confirmed as the pair came across a distinctive footprint, a huge boot, along a low and muddy depression on the trail.

"An hour ahead, no more," Drizzt explained, examining the print. He looked back at Wulfgar and smiled widely, lavender eyes sparkling.

The barbarian, more than ready for a fight, nodded.

Following Guenhwyvar's lead, they climbed higher and higher until, above them, the land seemed to suddenly disappear, the trail ending at a sheer cliff face. Drizzt moved up first, shadow to shadow, motioning Wulfgar to follow as he determined the way to be clear. They had come to the side of a canyon, a deep and rocky ravine bordered on all four sides by mountain walls, though the barrier to their right, the south, was not complete, leaving one exit from the valley floor. At first, they surmised that the giant encampment must be down there in the ravine, hidden among the boulders, but then Wulfgar spotted a line of smoke drifting up from behind a wall of boulders on the cliff wall almost directly across the way, some fifty yards from their position.

Drizzt scaled a nearby tree, getting a better angle, and soon confirmed that to be the giants' camp. A pair of behemoths were sitting behind the sheltering stones, eating a meal. The drow surveyed the landscape. He could get around, and so could Guenhwyvar, without going down to the valley floor.

"Can you reach them with a hammer throw from here?" he asked Wulfgar.

The barbarian nodded.

"Lead me in, then," the drow said. With a wink, he started off to the left, moving over the lip of the cliff and edging along its facing. Guenhwyvar also started off, picking a higher route than Drizzt along the cliff face.

The dark elf moved like a spider, crawling from ledge to ledge, while Guenhwyvar went along above him in a series of powerful bounds, clearing twenty feet at a leap. Within half an hour, amazingly, the drow had moved beyond the northern wall, around to the eastern facade and within twenty feet or so of the seemingly oblivious giants. He motioned back to Wulfgar, then set his feet firmly and took a deep breath. Not wanting to be spotted, he had come in slightly below the level of the shelf and the boulder wall, and now he measured the short run he would have, and then the distance of the leap to the giants' shelf. He didn't want to have to use his hands to safely land the jump, preferring to come in with both scimitars drawn and ready.

He could make it, he decided, so he looked up at Guenhwyvar. The cat was perched on a shelf some thirty feet above the giants. Drizzt opened his mouth in a mock roar.

The great panther responded, only her roar was far from silent. It rumbled off the mountain walls, drawing the attention of the giants and of any other creatures for miles around.

With a howl, the giants sprang to their feet. The drow ran silently along the ledge and leaped for their position.

Shouting a call to Tempus, the barbarian god of war, Wulfgar hoisted Aegis-fang . . . but hesitated, stung by the sound of that name. The name of a god he had once worshiped but to whom he had not prayed in so many years. A god he felt had abandoned him in the pits of the Abyss. Waves of emotional turmoil rolled over him, dizzying him, sending him careening back to that awful place of Errtu's darkness.

And leaving Drizzt terribly exposed.

* * * * *

They had been guessing as much as trailing, for though Catti-brie could see well in the dark, her night vision still could not match that of the drow, and Bruenor, though skilled at tracking, could not match the hunting prowess of Guenhwyvar. Still, when they heard the panther's roar echoing off the stones about them, they knew their guess had been a good one.

Off they ran, Bruenor's rolling pace matching Catti-brie's long and graceful strides. Regis didn't even try to catch up, didn't even try to follow the same path. While Bruenor and Catti-brie charged off straight in the direction of the roar, Regis veered north, following an easier trail, smooth but angling upward. The halfling wasn't thrilled with the idea of getting into any fights, let alone one against giants, but he did truly want to help out. Perhaps he might find a higher vantage point from which he could call down directions to his friends. Perhaps he might find a place where he could throw stones (and he was a pretty good shot) at safely distant giants. Perhaps he might find—

A tree trunk, the halfling thought, a bit distracted as he rushed around a bend and bumped into a solid trunk.

No, not a trunk, Regis realized. Trees did not wear boots.

* * * * *

Two giants rose up to search out Guenhwyvar; two giants noted the sudden approach of the leaping drow elf. Drizzt timed and aimed his leap perfectly, coming to the lip of the ledge lightly, in full balance. But he hadn't counted on two opponents waiting for him. He had expected Wulfgar's throw to take one down, or at least to distract the behemoth long enough for the dark elf to find steady footing.

Improvising quickly, the drow summoned his innate magical powers—though few remained after all these years on the surface—and brought forth a globe of impenetrable darkness. He centered it on the back wall ten feet from the ground so that it blocked the sight of the behemoths, but, since the globe's radius was about the same length as Drizzt was tall, it left their lower legs visible to Drizzt. He went in hard and fast, skidding down low and slashing wildly with both his scimitars, Twinkle and the newly named Icingdeath.

The giants kicked and stomped, bent low and swung their clubs frantically, and though they were as likely to hit each other as the drow, a giant could take a solid hit from another giant's club.

Drizzt could not.

* * * * *

Damn Errtu! How many evils had he suffered? How many attacks upon body and soul? He felt again Bizmatec's pincers closing about his neck, felt the dull aches of heavy punches as Errtu beat upon him as he lay in the filth, and then the sharp sting of fire as the demon dragged him into the flames that always surrounded its hideous form. And he felt the touch, gentle and alluring, of the succubus, perhaps the worst tormentor of all.

And now his friend needed him. Wulfgar knew that, could hear the battle being joined. He should have led the way with a throw of Aegis-fang, should have put the giants off balance, perhaps even put one down altogether.

He knew that and wanted desperately to help his friend, and yet his eyes were not seeing the fight between Drizzt and the giants. They were looking again into the swirls of Errtu's prison.

"Damn you!" the barbarian cried, and he built a wall of the sheerest red anger, trying to block the visions with pure rage.

* * * * *

It was easily the largest giant Regis had ever seen, towering twenty feet and as wide as buildings Regis had once called home. Regis looked at his new mace, his pitifully small mace, and doubted that he could even raise a bruise on the giant. Then he looked up to see the monster bending lower, a huge hand—a hand big enough to grab the halfling and squeeze the life out of him—reaching down.

"A bit of a meal, then?" the huge creature said in a voice surprisingly sophisticated for one of its kind. "Not much of one, of course, but little's better than nothing."

Regis sucked in his breath and put his hand over his heart, feeling as if he would faint—and then feeling a familiar lump by his collarbone. He reached into his tunic and pulled out a gemstone, a large ruby dangling at the end of a chain. "A pretty thing, don't you think?" he asked sheepishly.

"I think I like my rodents mashed," the giant replied, and up went its huge foot, and off ran Regis with a squeak. A single long stride put the giant's other foot in front of him, though, and he had nowhere to run.

* * * * *

Drizzt rolled over a kicking giant leg, tucking his shoulder as he hit the stone and coming back over to his feet nimbly, reversing direction and stabbing glowing Twinkle into the huge calf. That brought a roar of pain, and then came another yell. It was Wulfgar. The barbarian's curse was followed by an explosion of stone as something—a relieved Drizzt figured it to be Aegis-fang—slammed hard into the cliff.

The missile bounced from the stone wall into the open air beyond, where the drow could see that it was a boulder—thrown by yet another giant, no doubt—and no warhammer.

Even worse for Drizzt, one of the giants moved out far enough on the ledge to see around the globe of darkness. "Argh, ye black-skinned rat!" it said, lifting its club.

Guenhwyvar soared down thirty feet from her perch to slam the bending behemoth on the shoulders, a six-hundred-pound missile of slashing claws and biting teeth. Caught by surprise and off balance, the giant toppled over the stone wall and out into the air, taking Guenhwyvar with it.

Drizzt, dodging yet another stubborn kick, cried out for the cat, but had to turn away, had to focus on the remaining, kicking giant.

As the plummeting giant rolled over Guenhwyvar sprang again, flying out wide and far, back toward the cliff where Wulfgar stood battling his mental demons.

The cat slammed hard against a ledge, far below the barbarian, and there she desperately clung, battered and shaking, while the giant continued its bouncing descent. Down, down the giant fell, a hundred feet and more before it settled, battered and groaning, upon a rocky outcropping.

* * * * *

Another explosion rocked the ledge where Drizzt battled the giant, then a third. The sudden, shocking noise finally broke Wulfgar free of his dark memories. He saw Guenhwyvar struggling to hold her perch on the ledge, nothing but empty air below her all the way to the ravine's floor. He saw Drizzt's globe of darkness, and every now and then a flash of bluish light as the drow sent his scimitar flying fast under the globe but above the blocking boulder wall. He saw the giant's head as it came up straight, and he took aim.

But then another boulder slammed the cliff wall, ricocheting off stone and right into the giant's side, bending it low into the darkness. And then another hit the wall right below Wulfgar's position, nearly shaking him from his feet. The barbarian located the throwers, three more giants on a ledge down and to the right, well concealed behind a barrier of rock, and probably with a cave in the cliff wall behind them. The third threw its rock Wulfgar's way, and the barbarian had to dive aside to avoid being crushed.

He came up and had to scramble again as two more rocks hurtled in.

With a roar—to no god, but just a primal growl—Wulfgar brought Aegis-fang over his head and returned the volley. The mighty warhammer sailed end over end to strike the stone right before the ducking giants. With a thunderous retort it knocked a fair-sized chunk out of the rock wall.

The giants came up staring, obviously impressed with the damage the weapon had inflicted on the stone. When they moved, all three clambered all over each other to retrieve the weapon.

But Aegis-fang disappeared, and when it magically returned to Wulfgar's grasp, the barbarian could see the three giants spread out over the wall in clear view.

* * * * *

Catti-brie and Bruenor came to the lip of the canyon, on the same side as Wulfgar but farther to the south, about halfway between the barbarian and the three giants. They were in time to see the next spinning throw of Aegis-fang. One of the giants managed to get back over the protective wall, and a second was on its way up when the warhammer crashed in, dropping the behemoth onto the back of the third. Solid as the hit was, it didn't kill the giant. Nor did the silver-streaking magical arrow Catti-brie let fly from Taulmaril, scoring a hit on the same giant's back.

"Bah, ye two're to steal all that danged fun!" Bruenor grumbled, skipping off to the south, looking for a way to get at the giants. "Gotta make me a dwarven bow!"

"A bow?" Catti-brie asked skeptically as she set another arrow. "When did you learn to work wood?"

As she finished, Aegis-fang came spinning by once again. Bruenor pointed to it emphatically. "Dwarven bow!" he explained with a wink, then ran off.

Though wounded, the three giants did well to regroup. Up came the first, a huge stone high over its head.

Catti-brie's next arrow drove hard into that stone, cutting right through it, and the two halves slipped down, banging the giant on the head.

The second giant came up fast, throwing hard for Catti-brie, but far wide of the mark. It did get back down in time to dodge her next lightning-streaking arrow, though. The bolt buried itself hard into the cliff wall.

The third giant let fly for Wulfgar even as Aegis-fang returned to the man's hand, and the barbarian had to dive once more to avoid being smashed. Still, the stone rebounded from the back wall at an unexpected angle, clipping Wulfgar painfully on the hip.

Looking up to him, Catti-brie saw that he had an even greater problem, for beyond him, on the north wall and up higher, loomed yet another giant. This one was huge, holding a stone over its head that looked as though it could take down both the barbarian and the ledge he was standing on.

"Wulfgar!" Catti-brie cried in warning, thinking the man doomed.

* * * * *

Drizzt hadn't witnessed any of the missile exchange, though he did get enough of a break from his dodging and slashing to see that Guenhwyvar was all right. The panther had made it onto the lower ledge, and though obviously wounded, seemed more angry at the fact that she could not easily get back into the fight.

The giant's kicks came slower now. As the behemoth tired, its legs stun from many deep cuts. The only trouble the swift drow had now was making sure that he didn't lose his footing in the deepening blood.

Then he heard Catti-brie's cry and was so startled that he slowed too much. The giant's boot caught up to him, hitting him squarely and sending him on a tumbling dive to the far end of the ledge, beyond the edge of the darkness globe. Coming right back to his feet, ignoring the ache, Drizzt ran up the stony wall, climbing a dozen feet before the giant came out in pursuit, bending low, thinking its prey to be on the ground.

Drizzt dropped on the giant's shoulders, wrapping his legs about its neck and double-stabbing his scimitars into the sides of its eyes. The behemoth howled and stood straight. The monster reached for the source of the pain, but the drow was too quick. Rolling over down the giant's back and landing nimbly on his feet, Drizzt cut fast for the lip of the ledge, hopping to the rocky barricade.

The giant batted at its torn eyes, blinded by the cuts and the blood. It waved its hands frantically and turned toward the noise of the drow's movements, lurching to grab him.

But Drizzt was already gone, spinning about the giant and chasing it from behind, prodding hard to keep the behemoth going as it reached for the ledge, overbalancing. Howling with pain, the giant tried to turn around, but that only sent Drizzt in even harder, scimitars biting about the stooping thing's chin.

The giant tried to scramble back but fell into the open air.

* * * * *

Wulfgar turned around at Catti-brie's call but had no time to strike out first or to dodge. Catti-brie got her bow up and level, but the huge giant threw first.

The stone sailed past Wulfgar, past Catti-brie, and Bruenor, down to the ledge in the south. Short-hopping off the stone-blocking wall, it slammed one giant in the chest, throwing it back and to the ground.

Looking down at her drawn arrow, a stunned Catti-brie spotted Regis sitting comfortably on the giant's shoulder. "The little rat," she whispered under her breath, truly impressed.

Now all three—giant, Wulfgar and Catti-brie—turned their attention to the lower ledge. Lightning arrows streaked in one after another, punctuated by a spinning throw of Aegis-fang, or the thunderous report of a huge, giant-hurled boulder. The sheer force of the barrage soon had the three giants dizzy and ducking.

Aegis-fang clipped one on the shoulder as it tried to run out the side down a concealed trail. The force of the hammer blow turned it around in time to see the next streaking arrow, right before the bolt drove through its ugly face. Down it went in a heap. A second giant stepped out, rock high to throw, only to catch a huge boulder in the chest and go flying away.

The third, badly wounded, stayed in a crouch behind the wall, not even daring to creep back the fifteen feet to the cave opening in the wall behind it. Head down, it didn't see the dwarf climb into position on a ledge above it, though it did look up when it heard the roar of a leaping Bruenor.

The dwarf king's axe, buried deep into the giant's brain, sported yet another notch.

Chapter 3
THE UNPLEASANT MIRROR

Well would you do to this one investigate," Giunta the Diviner said to Hand as the man left the wizard's house. "Danger I sense, and we both know who it may be, though to speak the name we fear."

Hand mumbled a reply and continued on his way, glad to be gone from the excitable wizard and Giunta's particularly annoying manner of structuring a sentence, one the wizard claimed came from another plane of existence, but that Hand merely considered Giunta's way of trying to impress those around him. Still, Giunta had his uses, Hand recognized, for of the dozen or so wizards the Basadoni house often utilized, none could unravel mysteries better than Giunta. From simply sensing the emanations of the strange coins Giunta had almost completely reconstructed the conversation between Hand, Kadran, and Sharlotta, as well as the identity of Taddio as the courier of the coins. Looking deeper, Giunta's face had turned into a profound frown, and as he had described the demeanor and general appearance of the one who had given the coins to Taddio, both he and Hand began to put the pieces together.

Hand knew Artemis Entreri. So did Giunta, and it was common knowledge among the street folk that Entreri had left Calimport in pursuit of the dark elf who had brought about the downfall of Pasha Pook, and that the drow was reportedly living in some dwarven city not far from Silverymoon.

Now that his suspicions pointed in a particular direction, Hand knew it was time to turn from magical information gathering to more conventional methods. He went out to the streets, to the many spies, and opened wide the eyes of Pasha Basadoni's powerful guild. Then he started back to the main house to speak with Sharlotta and Kadran but changed his mind. Indeed, Sharlotta had spoken truthfully when she had said that she desired knowledge of her enemies.

Better for Hand that she didn't know.

* * * * *

His room was hardly fitting for a man who had climbed so high among the ranks of the street. This man had been a guildmaster, albeit briefly, and could command huge sums of money from any house in the city simply as a retainer fee for his services. But Artemis Entreri didn't care much about the sparse furnishings of the cheap inn, about the dust piled on the window sills, about the noise of the street ladies and their clients in the adjoining rooms.

He sat on the bed and thought about his options, reconsidering all his movements since returning to Calimport. He had been a bit careless, he realized, particularly in going to the stupid boy who was now claiming rulership of his old shanty town and by showing his dagger to the beggar at Pook's old house. Perhaps, Entreri realized, that journey and encounter had been no coincidence or bad luck, but by subconscious design.

Perhaps he had wanted to reveal himself to any who would look closely enough.

But what would that mean? he had to wonder now. How had the guild structures changed, and where in those new hierarchies would Artemis Entreri fit in? Even more importantly, where did Artemis Entreri want to fit in?

Those questions were beyond Entreri at that time, but he realized that he could not afford to sit and wait for others to find him. He should learn some of the answers, at least, before dealing with the more powerful houses of Calimport. The hour was late, well past midnight, but the assassin donned a dark cloak and went out onto the streets anyway.

The sights and sounds and smells brought him back to his younger days, when he had often allied with the dark of night and shunned the light of day. He noticed before he had even left the street that many gazes had settled upon him, and he sensed that they focused with more than a passing interest, more than the attention a foreign merchant might expect. Entreri recalled his own days on these streets, the methods and speed with which information was passed along. He was already being watched, he knew, and probably by several different guilds. Possibly the tavern keeper where he was staying or one of the patrons, perhaps, had recognized him or had recognized enough about him to raise suspicions. These people of Calimport's foul belly lived on the edge of disaster every minute of every day. Thus they possessed a level of alertness beyond anything so many other cultures might know. Like grassland field rats, rodents living in extensive burrow complexes with thousands and thousands of inhabitants, the people of Calimport's streets had designed complex warning systems: shouts and whistles, nods, and even simple body posture.

Yes, Entreri knew as he walked along the quiet street, his practiced footsteps making not a sound, they were watching him.

The time had come for him to do some looking of his own—and he knew where to start. Several turns brought him to Avenue Paradise, a particularly seedy place where potent herbs and weeds were openly traded, as were weapons, stolen goods, and carnal companionship. A mockery of culture itself, Avenue Paradise stood as the pinnacle of hedonism among the underclass. Here a beggar, if he found a few extra coins that day, could, for a few precious moments, feel like a king, could surround himself with perfumed ladies and imbibe enough mind-altering substances to forget the sores that festered on his filthy skin. Here, one like the boy that Entreri had paid in his old shanty town could live, for a few hours, the life of pasha Basadoni.

Of course it was all fake, fancy facades on rat-ridden buildings, fancy clothes on scared little girls or dead-eyed whores, heavily perfumed with cheap smells to hide the months of sweat and dust without a proper bath. But even fake luxury would suffice for most of the street people, whose constant misery was all too real.

Entreri walked slowly along the street, dismissing his introspection and turning his eyes outward, studying every detail. He thought he recognized more than one of the older, pitiful whores, but in truth, Entreri had never succumbed to such unhealthy and tawdry temptations as could be found on Avenue Paradise. His carnal pleasures, on those very few occasions he took them (for he considered them a weakness to one aspiring to be the perfect fighter), came in the harems of mighty pashas, and he had never held any tolerance whatsoever for anything intoxicating, for anything that dulled his keen mind and left him vulnerable. He had come to Avenue Paradise often, though, to find others too weak to resist. The whores had never liked him, nor had he ever bothered with them, though he knew, as did all the pashas, that they could be a very valuable source of information. Entreri simply could not bring himself to ever trust a woman who made her daily life in that particular line of employ.

So now he spent more time looking at the thugs and pickpockets and was amused to learn that one of the pickpockets was also studying him. Hiding a grin, he even changed his course to bring himself closer to the foolish young man.

Sure enough, Entreri was barely ten strides past when the thief came out behind him, walking past and "slipping" at the last moment to cover his reach for Entreri's dangling purse.

A split second later, the would-be thief was off balance, turned in and down, with Entreri's hand clamped over the ends of his fingers, squeezing the most exquisite pain up the man's arm. Out came the jeweled dagger, quietly but quickly, its tip poking a tiny hole in the man's palm as Entreri turned his shoulder in closer to conceal the movement and lessened his paralyzing grip.

Obviously confused at the relief of pressure on his pained hand, the thief moved his free hand to his own belt, pulling aside his cloak and grabbing at a long knife.

Entreri stared hard and concentrated on the dagger, instructing it to do its darker work, using its magic to begin sucking the very life-force out of the foolish thief.

The man weakened, his dagger fell harmlessly to the street, and both his eyes and his jaw opened wide in a horrified, agonized, and ultimately futile attempt at a scream.

"You feel the emptiness," Entreri whispered to him. "The hopelessness. You know that I hold not only your life, but your very soul in my hands."

The man didn't, couldn't move.

"Do you?" Entreri prompted, bringing a nod from the now gasping man.

"Tell me," the assassin bade, "are there any halflings on the street this night?" As he spoke, he let up a bit on the life-stealing process, and the man's expression shifted again, just a bit, to one of confusion.

"Halflings," the assassin explained, punctuating his point by drawing hard on the man's life-force again, so forcefully that the only thing holding the man up was Entreri's body.

With his free hand, trembling violently through every inch of movement, the thief pointed farther down the avenue in the general direction of a few houses that Entreri knew well. He thought to ask the man a more focused question or two but decided against it, realizing that he might have revealed too much of his identity already by the mere hunger of his particular jeweled dagger.

"If I ever see you again, I shall kill you," the assassin said with such complete calm that all the blood ran from the thief's face. Entreri released him, and he staggered away, falling to his knees and crawling on. Entreri shook his head in disgust, wondering, and not for the first time, why he had ever come back to this wretched city.

Without even bothering to look and ensure that the thief continued away, the assassin strode more quickly down the street. If the particular halfling he sought was still about and still alive, Entreri could guess which of those buildings he might be in. The middle and largest of the three, The Copper Ante, had once been a favorite gambling house for many of the halflings in the Calimport dock section, mostly because of the halfling-staffed brothel upstairs and the Thayan brown pipeweed den in the back room. Indeed, Entreri did see many (considering that this was Calimport, where halflings were scarce) of the little folk scattered about the various tables in the common room when he entered. He scanned each table slowly, trying to guess what his former friend might look like now that several years had passed. The halfling would be wider about the belly, no doubt, for he loved rich food and had set himself up in a position to afford ten meals a day if he so chose.

Entreri slipped into an open seat at one table where six halflings tossed dice, each moving so quickly that it was almost impossible for a novice gambler to even tell which call the one at the head of the table was making and which halfling was grabbing which pot as winnings for which throw. Entreri easily sorted it out, though, and found, to his amusement but hardly his surprise, that all six were cheating. It seemed more a contest of who could grab the most coins the fastest than any type of gambling, and all half dozen appeared to be equally suited to the task, so much so that Entreri figured that each of them would likely leave with almost exactly the amount of coins with which he had begun.

The assassin dropped four gold pieces on the table and grabbed up some dice, giving a half-hearted throw. Almost before the dice stopped rolling, the closest halfling reached for the coins, but Entreri was the quicker, slapping his hand over the halfling's wrist and pinning it to the table.

"But you lost!" the little one squeaked, and the flurry of movement came to an abrupt halt, the other five looking at Entreri and more than one reaching for a weapon. The gaming stopped at several other tables, as well, the whole area of the common room focusing on the coming trouble.

"I was not playing," Entreri said calmly, not letting the halfling go.

"You put down money and threw dice," one of the others protested. "That is playing."

Entreri's glare put the complaining halfling back in his seat. "I am playing when I say, and not before," he explained. "And I only cover bets that are announced openly before I throw."

"You saw how the table was moving," a third dared to argue, but Entreri cut him short with an upraised hand and a nod.

He looked to the gambler at his right, the one who had reached for the coins, and waited a moment to let the rest of the room settle down and go back to their own business. "You want the coins? They, and twice that amount above them, shall be yours," he explained, and the greedy halfling's expression went from one of distress to a gleaming-eyed grin. "I came not to play but to ask a simple question. Provide an answer, and the coins are yours." As he spoke, Entreri reached into his purse and brought out more coins—more than twice the number the halfling had grabbed.

"Well, Master . . ." the halfling began.

"Do'Urden," Entreri replied, with hardly a conscious thought, though he had to bite back a chuckle at the irony after he heard the name come out of his mouth. "Master Do'Urden of Silverymoon."

All the halflings at the table eyed him curiously, for the unusual name sounded familiar to them all. In truth, and they came to realize it one by one, they all knew that name. It was the name of the dark elven protector of Regis, perhaps the highest ranking (albeit for a short while!) and most famous halfling ever to walk the streets of Calimport.

"Your skin has—" the halfling pinned under Entreri's grasp started to remark lightheartedly, but he stopped, swallowed hard and blanched as he put the pieces together. Entreri could see the halfling recall the story of Regis and the dark elf, and the one who had subsequently deposed the halfling guildmaster and then gone out after the drow.

"Yes," the halfling said as calmly as he could muster, "a question."

"I seek one of your kind," Entreri explained. "An old friend by the name of Dondon Tiggerwillies."

The halfling put on a confused look and shook his head, but not before a flicker of recognition has crossed his dark eyes, one the sharp Entreri did not miss.

"Everyone of the streets knows Dondon," Entreri stated. "Or once knew of him. You are not a child, and your gaming skills tell me that you have been a regular to the Copper Ante for years. You know, or knew, Dondon. If he is dead, then I wish to hear the story. If not, then I wish to speak with him."

Grave looks passed from halfling to halfling. "Dead," said one across the table, but Entreri knew from the tone and the quick manner in which the diminutive fellow blurted it out that it was a lie, that Dondon, ever the survivor, was indeed alive.

Halflings in Calimport always seemed to stick together, though.

"Who killed him?" Entreri asked, playing along.

"He got sick," another halfling offered, again in that quick, telltale manner.

"And where is he buried?"

"Who gets buried in Calimport?" the first liar replied.

"Tossed into the sea," said another.

Entreri nodded with every word. He was actually a bit amused at how these halflings played off each other, building an elaborate lie and one the assassin knew he could eventually turn against them.

"Well, you have told me much," he said, releasing the halfling's wrist. The greedy gambler immediately went for the coins, but a jeweled dagger jabbed down between the reaching hand and the desired gems in the blink of a startled eye.

"You promised coins!" the halfling protested.

"For a lie?" Entreri calmly asked. "I inquired about Dondon outside and was told that he was in here. I know he is alive, for I saw him just yesterday."

The halflings all glanced at each other, trying to piece together the inconsistencies here. How had they fallen so easily into the trap?

"Then why speak of him in the past tense?" the halfling directly across the table asked, the first to insist that Dondon was dead. This halfling thought himself sly, thought that he had caught Entreri in a lie . . . as indeed he had.

"Because I know that halflings never reveal the whereabouts of other halflings to one who is not a halfling," Entreri answered, his demeanor changing suddenly to a lighthearted, laughing expression, something that had never come easily to the assassin. "I have no fight with Dondon, I assure you. We are old friends, and it has been far too long since we last spoke. Now, tell me where he is and take your payment."

Again the halflings looked around, and then one, licking his lips and staring hungrily at the small pile of coins, pointed to a door at the back of the large room.

Entreri replaced the dagger in its sheath and gave a gesture that seemed a salute as he moved from the table, walking confidently across the room and pushing through the door without even a knock.

There before him reclined the fattest halfling he had ever seen, a creature wider than it was tall. He and the assassin locked stares, Entreri so intent on the fellow that he hardly noticed the scantily clad female halflings flanking him. It was indeed Dondon Tiggerwillies, Entreri realized to his horror. Despite all the years and all the scores of pounds, he knew the halfling, once the slipperiest and most competent confidence swindler in all of Calimport.

"A knock is often appreciated," the halfling said, his voice raspy, as though he could hardly force the sounds from his thick neck. "Suppose that my friends and I were engaged in a more private action."

Entreri didn't even try to figure out how that might be possible.

"Well, what do you want, then?" Dondon asked, stuffing an enormous bite of pie into his mouth as soon as he finished speaking.

Entreri closed the door and walked into the room, halving the distance between him and the halfling. "I want to speak with an old associate," he explained.

Dondon stopped chewing and stared hard. Obviously stunned by recognition, he began violently choking on the pie and wound up spitting a substantial piece of it back onto his plate. His attendants did well to hide their disgust as they moved the plate aside.

"I did not . . . I mean, Regis was no friend of mine. I mean . . ." Dondon stammered, a fairly common reaction from those faced with the spectre of Artemis Entreri.

"Be at ease, Dondon," Entreri said firmly. "I came to speak with you, nothing more. I care not for Regis, nor for any role Dondon might have played in the demise of Pook those years ago. The streets are for the living, are they not, and not the dead?"

"Yes, of course," Dondon replied, visibly trembling. He rolled forward a bit, trying to at least sit up, and only then did Entreri notice a chain trailing a thick anklet he wore about his left leg. Finally, the fat halfling gave up and just rolled back to his previous position. "An old wound," he said with a shrug.

Entreri let the obviously ridiculous excuse slide past. He moved closer to the halfling and went down in a crouch, brushing aside Dondon's robes that he could better see the shackle. "I have only recently returned," he explained. "I hoped that Dondon might enlighten me concerning the current demeanor of the streets."

"Rough and dangerous, of course," Dondon answered with a chuckle that became a phlegm-filled cough.

"Who rules?" Entreri asked in a dead serious tone. "Which houses hold power, and what soldiers champion them?"

"I wish that I could be of help to you, my friend," Dondon said nervously. "Of course I do. I would never withhold information from you. Never that! But you see," he added, lifting up his shackled ankle, "they do not let me out much anymore."

"How long have you been in here?"

"Three years."

Entreri stared incredulously and distastefully at the little wretch, then looked doubtfully at the relatively simple shackle, a lock that the old Dondon could have opened with a piece of hair.

In response, Dondon held up his enormously thick hands, hands so pudgy that he couldn't even bring the higher parts of his fingers together. "I do not feel much with them anymore," he explained.

A burning outrage welled inside Entreri. He felt as if he would simply explode into a murderous fit that would have him physically shaving the pounds from Dondon's fat hide with his jeweled dagger. Instead, he went at the lock, turning it roughly to scan for any possible traps, then reaching for a small pick.

"Do not," came a high-pitched voice behind him. The assassin sensed the presence before he even heard the words. He spun about, rolling into a crouch, dagger in one hand, arm cocked to throw. Another female halfling, this one dressed in a fine tunic and breeches, with thick, curly brown hair and huge brown eyes, stood at the door, hands up and open, her posture completely unthreatening.

"Oh, but that would be a bad thing for me and for you," the female halfling said with a little grin.

"Do not kill her," Dondon pleaded with Entreri, trying to grab for the assassin's arm, but missing far short of the mark and rolling back, gasping for breath.

Entreri, ever alert, noticed then that both the female halflings attending Dondon had slipped hands into secret places, one to a pocket, the other to her generous waist-length hair, both no doubt reaching for weapons of some sort. He understood then that this newcomer was a leader among the group.

"Dwahvel Tiggerwillies, at your service," she said with a graceful bow. "At your service, but not at your whim," she added with a smile.

"Tiggerwillies?" Entreri echoed softly, glancing back at Dondon.

"A cousin," the fat halfling explained with a shrug. "The most powerful halfling in all of Calimport and the newest proprietor of the Copper Ante."

The assassin looked back to see the female halfling completely at ease, hands in her pockets.

"You understand, of course, that I did not come in here alone, not to face a man of Artemis Entreri's reputation," Dwahvel said.

That brought a grin to Entreri's face as he imagined the many halflings concealed about the room. It struck him as a half-sized mock-up of another similar operation, that of Jarlaxle the dark elf mercenary in Menzoberranzan. On the occasions when he had to face the always well-protected Jarlaxle, though, Entreri had understood without doubt that if he made even the slightest wrong move, or if Jarlaxle or one of the drow guards ever perceived one of Entreri's movements as threatening, his life would have been at an abrupt end. He couldn't imagine now that Dwahvel Tiggerwillies, or any other halfling for that matter, could command such well-earned respect. Still, he hadn't come here for a fight, even if that old warrior part of him perceived Dwahvel's words as a challenge.

"Of course," he replied simply.

"Several with slings eye you right now," she went on. "And the bullets of those slings have been treated with an explosive formula. Quite painful and devastating."

"How resourceful," the assassin said, trying to sound impressed.

"That is how we survive," Dwahvel replied. "By being resourceful. By knowing everything about everything and preparing properly."

In a single swift movement—one that would surely have gotten him killed in Jarlaxle's court—the assassin spun the dagger over and slipped it into its sheath, then stood up straight and dipped a low and respectful bow to Dwahvel.

"Half the children of Calimport answer to Dwahvel," Dondon explained. "And the other half are not children at all," he added with a wink, "and answer to Dwahvel, as well."

"And of course, both halves have watched Artemis Entreri carefully since he walked back into the city," Dwahvel explained.

"So glad that my reputation preceded me," Entreri said, sounding puffy indeed.

"We did not know it was you until recently," Dwahvel replied, just to deflate the man, who of course, was not at all conceited.

"And you discovered this by. . . . ?" Entreri prompted.

That left Dwahvel a bit embarrassed, realizing that she had just been squeezed for a bit of information she had not intended to reveal. "I do not know why you would expect an answer," she said, somewhat perturbed. "Nor do I begin to see any reason I should help the one who dethroned Regis from the guild of the former Pasha Pook. Regis, was in a position to aid all the other halflings of Calimport."

Entreri had no answer to that, so he offered nothing in reply.

"Still, we should talk," Dwahvel went on, turning sidelong and motioning to the door.

Entreri glanced back at Dondon.

"Leave him to his pleasures," Dwahvel explained. "You would have him freed, yet he has little desire to leave, I assure you. Fine food and fine companionship."

Entreri looked with disgust to the assorted pies and sweets, to the hardly moving Dondon, then to the two females. "He is not so demanding," one of them explained with a laugh.

"Just a soft lap to rest his sleepy head," the other added with a titter that set them both to giggling.

"I have all that I could ever desire," Dondon assured him.

Entreri just shook his head and left with Dwahvel, following the little halfling to a more private—and undoubtedly better guarded—room deeper into the Copper Ante complex. Dwahvel took a seat in a low, plush chair and motioned for the assassin to take one opposite. Entreri was hardly comfortable in the half-sized piece, his legs straight out before him.

"I do not entertain many who are not halflings," Dwahvel apologized. "We tend to be a secretive group."

Entreri saw that she was looking for him to tell her how honored he was. But, of course, he wasn't, and so he said nothing, just keeping a tight expression, eyes boring accusingly into the female.

"We hold him for his own good," Dwahvel said plainly.

"Dondon was once among the most respected thieves in Calimport," Entreri countered.

"Once," Dwahvel echoed, "but not so long after your departure, Dondon drew the anger of a particularly powerful pasha. The man was a friend of mine, so I pleaded for him to spare Dondon. Our compromise was that Dondon remain inside. Always inside. If he ever is seen walking the streets of Calimport again, by the pasha or any of the pasha's many contacts, then I am bound to turn him over for execution."

"A better fate, by my estimation, than the slow death you give him chained in that room."

Dwahvel laughed aloud at that proclamation. "Then you do not understand Dondon," she said. "Men more holy than I have long identified the seven sins deadly to the soul, and while Dondon has little of the primary three, for he is neither proud nor envious nor wrathful, he is possessed of an excess of the last four—sloth, avarice, gluttony, and lust. He and I made a deal, a deal to save his life. I promised to give him, without judgment, all that he desired in exchange for his promise to remain within my doors."

"Then why the chains about his ankle?" Entreri asked.

"Because Dondon is drunk more often than sober," Dwahvel explained. "Likely he would cause trouble within my establishment, or perhaps he would stagger onto the street. It is all for his own protection."

Entreri wanted to refute that, for he had never seen a more pitiful sight than Dondon and would personally prefer a tortured death to that grotesque lifestyle. But when he thought about Dondon more carefully, when he remembered the halfling's personal style those years ago, a style that often included sweet foods and many ladies, he recognized that Dondon's failings now were the halfling's own and nothing forced upon him by a caring Dwahvel.

"If he remains inside the Copper Ante, no one will bother him," Dwahvel said after giving Entreri the moment to think it over. "No contract, no assassin. Though, of course, this is only on the five-year-old word of a pasha. So you can understand why my fellows were a bit nervous when the likes of Artemis Entreri walked into the Copper Ante inquiring about Dondon."

Entreri eyed her skeptically.

"They were not sure it was you at first," Dwahvel explained. "Yet we have known that you were back in town for a couple of days now. Word is fairly common on the streets, though, as you can well imagine, it is more rumor than truth. Some say that you have returned to displace Quentin Bodeau and regain control of Pook's house. Others hint that you have come for greater reasons, hired by the Lords of Waterdeep themselves to assassinate several high-ranking leaders of Calimshan."

Entreri's expression summed up his incredulous response to that preposterous notion.

Dwahvel shrugged. "Such are the trappings of reputation," she said. "Many people are paying good money for any whisper, however ridiculous, that might help them solve the riddle of why Artemis Entreri has returned to Calimport. You make them nervous, assassin. Take that as the highest compliment.

"But also as a warning," Dwahvel went on. "When guilds fear someone or something, they often take steps to erase that fear. Several have been asking very pointed questions about your whereabouts and movements, and you understand this business well enough to realize that to be the mark of the hunting assassin."

Entreri put his elbow on the arm of the small chair and plopped his chin in his hand, considering the halfling carefully. Rarely had anyone spoken so bluntly and boldly to Artemis Entreri, and in the few minutes they had been sitting together, Dwahvel Tiggerwillies had earned more respect from Entreri than most would gather in a lifetime of conversations.

"I can find more detailed information for you," Dwahvel said slyly. "I have larger ears than a Sossalan mammoth and more eyes than a room of beholders, so it is said. And so it is true."

Entreri put a hand to his belt and jiggled his purse. "You overestimate the size of my treasury," he said.

"Look around you," Dwahvel retorted. "What need have I for more gold, from Silverymoon or anywhere else?"

Her reference to the Silverymoon coinage came as a subtle hint to Entreri that she knew of what she was speaking.

"Call it a favor between friends," Dwahvel explained, hardly a surprise to the assassin who had made his life exchanging such favors. "One that you might perhaps repay me one day."

Entreri kept his face expressionless as he thought it over. Such a cheap way to garner information. Entreri highly doubted that the halfling would ever require his particular services, for halflings simply didn't solve their problems that way. And if Dwahvel did call upon him, maybe he would comply, or maybe not. Entreri hardly feared that Dwahvel would send her three-foot-tall thugs after him. No, all that Dwahvel wanted, should things sort out in his favor, was the bragging right that Artemis Entreri owed her a favor, a claim that would drain the blood from the faces of the majority of Calimport's street folk.

The question for Entreri now was, did he really care if he ever got the information Dwahvel offered? He thought it over for another minute, then nodded his accord. Dwahvel brightened immediately.

"Come back tomorrow night, then," she said. "I will have something to tell you."

Outside the Copper Ante, Artemis Entreri spent a long while thinking about Dondon, for he found that every time he conjured an image of the fat halfling stuffing pie into his face he was filled with rage. Not disgust, but rage. As he examined those feelings, he came to recognize that Dondon Tiggerwillies had been about as close to a friend as Artemis Entreri had ever known. Pasha Basadoni had been his mentor, Pasha Pook his primary employer, but Dondon and Entreri had related in a different manner. They acted in each other's benefit without set prices, exchanging information without taking count. It had been a mutually beneficial relationship. Seeing Dondon now, purely hedonistic, having given up on any meaning in life, it seemed to the assassin that the halfling had committed a form of living suicide.

Entreri did not possess enough compassion for that to explain the anger he felt, though, and when he admitted that to himself he came to understand that the sight of Dondon repelled him so much because, given his own mental state lately, it could well be him. Not chained by the ankle in the company of women and food, of course, but in effect, Dondon had surrendered, and so had Entreri.

Perhaps it was time to take down the white flag.

Dondon had been his friend in a manner, and there had been one other similarly entwined. Now it was time to go and see LaValle.

Chapter 4
THE SUMMONS

Drizzt couldn't get down to the ledge where Guenhwyvar had landed, so he used the onyx figurine to dismiss the cat. She faded back to the Astral plane, her home, where her wounds would better heal. He saw that Regis and his unexpected giant ally had moved out of sight, and that Wulfgar and Catti-brie were moving to join Bruenor down at the lower ledge to the south, where the last of the enemy giants had fallen. The dark elf began picking his way to join them. At first, he thought he might have to backtrack all the way around to his initial position with Wulfgar, but using his incredible agility and the strength of fingers trained for decades in the maneuvering skills of sword play, he somehow found enough ledges, cracks, and simple angled surfaces to get down beside his friends.

By the time he got there, all three had entered the cave at the back of the shelf.

"Damned things might've kept a bit more treasure if they're meanin' to put up such a fight," he heard Bruenor complaining.

"Perhaps that's why they were scouting out the road," Catti-brie replied. "Might it have been better for ye if we went at them on our way back from Cadderly's place? Perhaps then we'd've found more treasure to yer liking. And maybe a few merchant skulls to go along with it."

"Bah!" the dwarf snorted, drawing a wide smile from Drizzt. Few in all the Realms needed treasure less than Bruenor Battlehammer, Eighth King of Mithral Hall (despite his chosen absence from the place) and also leader of a lucrative mining colony in Icewind Dale. But that wasn't the point of Bruenor's ire, Drizzt understood, and he smiled all the wider as Bruenor confirmed his suspicions.

"What kind o' wicked god'd put ye against such powerful foes and not even reward ye with a bit o' gold?" the dwarf grumbled.

"We did find some gold," Catti-brie reminded him. Drizzt, entering the cave, noted that she held a fairly substantial sack that bulged with coins.

Bruenor flashed the drow a disgusted look. "Copper mostly," he grumbled. "Three gold coins, a pair o' silver, and nothing more but stinkin' copper!"

"But the road is safe," Drizzt said. He looked to Wulfgar as he spoke, but the big man would not match his stare. The drow tried hard not to pass any judgment over his tormented friend. Wulfgar should have led Drizzt's charge to the shelf. Never before had he so failed Drizzt in their tandem combat. But the drow knew that the barbarian's hesitance came not from any desire to see Drizzt injured nor, certainly, any cowardice. Wulfgar spun in emotional turmoil, the depths of which Drizzt Do'Urden had never before seen. He had known of these problems before coaxing the barbarian out for this hunt, so he could not rightly place any blame now.

Nor did he want to. He only hoped that the fight itself, after Wulfgar had become involved, had helped the man to rid himself of some of those inner demons, had run the horse, as Montolio would have called it, just a bit.

"And what about yerself?" Bruenor roared, bouncing over to stand before Drizzt. "What're ye about, going off on yer own without a word to the rest of us? Ye thinking all the fun's for yerself, elf? Ye thinking that me and me girl can't be helpin' ye?"

"I did not want to trouble you with so minor a battle," Drizzt calmly replied, painting a disarming smile on his dark face. "I knew that we would be in the mountains, outside and not under them, in terrain not suited for the likes of a short-limbed dwarf."

Bruenor wanted to hit him. Drizzt could see that in the way the dwarf was trembling. "Bah!" he roared instead, throwing up his hands and walking back for the exit to the small cave. "Ye're always doin' that, ye stinkin' elf. Always going about on yer own and taking all the fun. But we'll find more on the road, don't ye doubt! And ye better be hopin' that ye see it afore me, or I'll cut 'em all down afore ye ever get them sissy blades outta their sheaths or that stinkin' cat outta that statue.

"Unless they're too much for us. . . ." he continued, his voice trailing away as he moved out of the cave. "Then I just might let ye have 'em all to yerself, ye stinkin' elf!"

Wulfgar, without a word and without a look at Drizzt, moved out next, leaving the drow and Catti-brie alone. Drizzt was chuckling now as Bruenor continued to grumble, but when he looked at Catti-brie, he saw that she was truly not amused, her feelings obviously hurt.

"I'm thinking that a poor excuse," she remarked.

"I wanted to bring Wulfgar out alone," Drizzt explained. "To bring him back to a different place and time, before all the trouble."

"And ye're not thinkin' that me dad, or meself, might want to be helping with that?" Catti-brie asked.

"I wanted no one here that Wulfgar might fear needed protecting," Drizzt explained, and Catti-brie slumped back, her jaw dropping open.

"I speak only the truth, and you see it clearly," Drizzt went on. "You remember how Wulfgar acted toward you before the fight with the yochlol. He was protective to the point of becoming a detriment to any battle cause. How could I rightly ask you to join us out here now, when that previous scenario might have repeated, leaving Wulfgar, perhaps, in an even worse emotional place than when we set out? That is why I did not ask Bruenor or Regis, either. Wulfgar, Guenhwyvar, and I would fight the giants, as we did that time so long ago in Icewind Dale. And maybe, just maybe, he would remember things the way they had been before his unwelcome tenure with Errtu."

Catti-brie's expression softened, and she bit her lower lip as she nodded her agreement. "And did it work?" she asked. "Suren the fight went well, and Wulfgar fought well and honestly."

Drizzt's gaze drifted out the exit. "He made a mistake," the drow admitted. "Though surely he compensated as the battle progressed. It is my hope that Wulfgar will forgive himself his initial hesitance and focus on the actual fight where he performed wonderfully."

"Hesitance?" Catti-brie asked skeptically.

"When we first began the battle," Drizzt started to explain, but he waved his hand dismissively as if it did not really matter. "It has been many years since we have fought together. It was an excusable miscue, nothing more." In truth, Drizzt had a hard time dismissing the fact that Wulfgar's hesitance had almost cost him and Guenhwyvar dearly.

"Ye're in a generous mood," the ever-perceptive Catti-brie remarked.

"It is my hope that Wulfgar will remember who he is and who his friends truly are," the drow ranger replied.

"Yer hope," Catti-brie echoed. "But is it your expectation?"

Drizzt continued to stare out the exit. He could only shrug.

* * * * *

The four were out of the ravine and back on the trail shortly after, and Bruenor's grumbling about Drizzt turned into complaining about Regis. "Where in the Nine Hells is Rumblebelly?" the dwarf bellowed. "And how in the Nine Hells did he ever get a giant to throw rocks for him?"

Even as he spoke, they felt the vibrations of heavy, heavy footfalls beneath their feet and heard a silly song sung in unison. There was a happy halfling voice, Regis, and a second voice that rumbled like the thunder of a rockslide. A moment later, Regis came around a bend in the northern trail, riding on the giant's shoulder, the two of them singing and laughing with every step.

"Hello," Regis said happily when he steered the giant to join his friends. He noted that Drizzt had his hands on his scimitars, though they were sheathed (and that meant little for the lightning-fast drow), Bruenor clutched tightly to his axe, Catti-brie to her bow, and Wulfgar, holding Aegis-fang, seemed as if he was about to explode into murderous action.

"This is Junger," Regis explained. "He was not with the other band—he says he doesn't even know them. And he is a smart one."

Junger put a hand up to secure Regis's seat, then bowed low before the stunned group.

"In fact, Junger does not even go down to the road, does not go out of the mountains at all," Regis explained. "Says he has no interest in the affairs of dwarves or men."

"He told ye that, did he?" Bruenor asked doubtfully.

Regis nodded, his smile wide. "And I believe him," he said, waggling the ruby pendant, whose magical hypnotizing properties were well known to the friends.

"That don't change a thing," Bruenor said with a growl, looking to Drizzt as if expecting the ranger to start the fight. A giant was a giant, after all, to the dwarf's way of thinking, and any giant looked much better lying down with an axe firmly embedded in its skull.

"Junger is no killer," Regis said firmly.

"Only goblins," the huge giant said with a smile. "And hill giants. And orcs, of course, for who could abide the ugly things?"

His sophisticated dialect and his choice of enemies had the dwarf staring at him wide-eyed. "And yeti," Bruenor said. "Don't ye be forgettin' yeti."

"Oh, not yeti," Junger replied. "I do not kill yeti."

The scowl returned to Bruenor's face.

"Why, one cannot even eat the smelly things," Junger explained. "I do not kill them, I domesticate them."

"Ye what?" Bruenor demanded.

"Domesticate them," Junger explained. "Like a dog or a horse. Oh, but I've quite a selection of yeti workers at my cave back in the mountains."

Bruenor turned an incredulous expression on Drizzt, but the ranger, as much at a loss as the dwarf, only shrugged.

"We've lost too much time already," Catti-brie remarked. "Camlaine and the others'll be halfway out o' the dale afore we catch them. Be rid o' yer friend, Regis, and let us get to the trail."

Regis was shaking his head before she ever finished. "Junger does not usually leave the mountains," he explained. "But he will for me."

"Then I'll not have to carry you anymore," Wulfgar grumbled, walking away. "Good enough for that."

"Ye're not having to carry him anyway," Bruenor replied, then looked back to Regis. "I'm thinking ye can do yer own walking. Ye don't need a giant to act as a horse."

"More than that," Regis said, beaming. "A bodyguard."

The dwarf and Catti-brie both groaned; Drizzt only chuckled and shook his head.

"In every fight, I spend more time trying to keep out of the way," Regis explained. "Never am I any real help. But with Junger—"

"Ye'll still be trying to keep outta the way," Bruenor interrupted.

"If Junger is to fight for you, then he is no more than any of the rest of us," Drizzt added. "Are we, then, merely bodyguards of Regis?"

"No, of course not," the halfling replied. "But—"

"Be rid of him," Catti-brie said. "Wouldn't we look the fine band of friendly travelers walking into Luskan beside a mountain giant?"

"We'll walk in with a drow," Regis answered before he could think about it, then blushed a deep shade of red.

Again, Drizzt only chuckled and shook his head.

"Put him down," Bruenor said to Junger. "I think he's needin' a talk."

"You mustn't hurt my friend Regis," Junger replied. "That I simply cannot allow."

Bruenor snorted. "Put 'im down."

With a look to Regis, who held a stubborn pose for a few moments longer, Junger complied. He set the halfling gently on the ground before Bruenor, who reached as if to grab Regis by the ear, but then glanced up, up, up at Junger and thought the better of it. "Ye're not thinkin', Rumblebelly," the dwarf said quietly, leading Regis away. "What happens if the big damned thing finds its way outta yer ruby spell? He'll squish ye flat afore any o' us can stop him, and I'm not thinking I'd try to stop him if I could, since ye'd be deserving the flattening!"

Regis started to argue, but he remembered the first moments of his encounter with Junger, when the huge giant had proclaimed that he liked his rodents smashed. The little halfling couldn't deny the fact that a single step from Junger would indeed mash him, and the hold of the ruby pendant was ever tentative. He turned and walked back from Bruenor and bade Junger to go back to his home in the deep mountains.

The giant smiled—and shook his head. "I hear it," he said cryptically. "So I shall stay."

"Hear what?" Regis and Bruenor asked together.

"Just a call," Junger assured them. "It tells me that I should go along with you to serve Regis and protect him."

"Ye hit him good with that thing, didn't ye now?" Bruenor whispered at the halfling.

"I need no protecting," Regis said firmly to the giant. "Though we all thank you for your help in the fight. You can go back to your home."

Again Junger shook his head. "Better that I go with you."

Bruenor glowered at Regis, and the halfling had no explanation. As far as he could tell, Junger was still under the spell of the pendant—the fact that Regis was still alive seemed evidence of that—yet the behemoth was clearly disobeying him.

"Perhaps you can come along," Drizzt said to the surprise of them all. "Yes, but if you mean to join us, then perhaps your pet tundra yetis might prove invaluable. How long will it take you to retrieve them?"

"Three days at the most," Junger replied.

"Well, go then, and be quick about it," Regis said, hopping up and down and wriggling the ruby pendant at the end of its chain.

That seemed to satisfy the giant. It bowed low then bounded away.

"We should've killed the thing here and now," Bruenor said. "Now it'll come back in three days and find us long gone, then it'll likely take its damned smelly yetis and go down hunting on the road!"

"No, he told me he never goes out of the mountains," Regis reasoned.

"Enough of this foolishness," Catti-brie demanded. "The thing's gone, and so should we all be." None offered an argument to that, so they set off at once, Drizzt purposely falling into line beside Regis.

"Was it all the call of the ruby pendant?" the ranger asked.

"Junger told me that he was farther from home than he had been in a long, long time," Regis admitted. "He said he heard a call on the wind and went to answer it. I guess he thought I was the caller."

Drizzt accepted that explanation. If Junger continued to fall for the simple ruse, they would be around the edge of the Spine of the World, rushing fast along a better road, before the behemoth ever returned to this spot.

* * * * *

Indeed Junger was running fast in the direction of his relatively lavish mountain home, and it struck the giant as curious, for just a moment, that he had ever left the place. In his younger days, Junger had been a wanderer, living meal to meal on whatever prey he could find. He snickered now when he considered all that he had told the foolish little halfling, for Junger had indeed once feasted on the meat of humans, and even on a halfling once. The truth was, he shunned such meals now as much because he didn't like the taste as because he thought it better not to make such powerful enemies as humans. Wizards in particular scared him. Of course, to find human or halfling meat, Junger had to leave his mountain home, and that he never liked to do.

He wouldn't have come out at all this time had not a call on the wind, something he still did not quite understand, compelled him.

Yes, Junger had all he wanted at his home: plenty of food, obedient servants, and comfortable furs. He had no desire to ever leave the place.

But he had, and he understood that he would again, and though that seemed an incongruous thought to the not-stupid giant, it was one that he simply couldn't pause to consider. Not now, not with the constant buzzing in his ear.

He would get the yetis, he knew, and then return, following the instructions of the call on the wind.

The call of Crenshinibon.

Chapter 5
STIRRING THE STREETS

LaValle walked to his private suite in the guild house late that morning after meeting with Quentin Bodeau and Chalsee Anguaine. Dog Perry was supposed to attend, and he was the one LaValle truly wanted to see, but Dog had sent word that he would not be coming, that he was out on the streets learning more about the dangerous Entreri.

In truth, the meeting proved nothing more than a gathering to calm the nerves of Quentin Bodeau. The guildmaster wanted reassurances that Entreri wouldn't merely show up and murder him. Chalsee Anguaine, in the manner of a cocky young man, promised to defend Quentin with his life. This LaValle knew to be an obvious lie. LaValle argued that Entreri wouldn't work that way, that he would not come in and kill Quentin without first learning all of Quentin's ties and associates and how powerfully the man held the guild.

"Entreri is never reckless," LaValle had explained. "And the scenario you fear would indeed be reckless."

By the time LaValle had turned to leave, Bodeau felt better and expressed his sentiment that he would feel better still if Dog Perry, or someone else, merely killed the dangerous man. It would never be that easy, LaValle knew, but he had kept the thought silent.

As soon as he entered his rooms, a suite of four with a large greeting room, a private study to the right, bedroom directly behind, and an alchemy lab and library to the left, the wizard felt as if something was amiss. He suspected Dog Perry to be the source of the trouble—the man did not trust him and had even privately, though surely subtly, accused him of the intent to side with Entreri should it come to blows.

Had the man come in here when he knew LaValle to be at the meeting with Quentin? Was he still here, hiding, crouched with weapon in hand?

The wizard looked back at the door and saw no signs that the lock—and the door was always locked—had been tripped, or that his traps had been defeated. There was one other way into the place, an outside window, but LaValle had placed so many glyphs and wards upon it, scattering them in several different places, that anyone crawling through would have been shocked with lightning, burned three different times, and frozen solid on the sill. Even if an intruder managed to survive the magical barrage, the explosions would have been heard throughout this entire level of the guild house, bringing soldiers by the score.

Reassured by simple logic and by a defensive spell he placed upon his body to make his skin resistant to any blows, LaValle started for his private study.

The door opened before he reached it, Artemis Entreri standing calmly within.

LaValle did well to stay on his feet, for his knees nearly buckled with weakness.

"You knew that I had returned," Entreri said easily, stepping forward and leaning against the jamb. "Did you not expect that I would pay a visit to an old friend?"

The wizard composed himself and shook his head, looking back at the door. "Door or window?" he asked.

"Door, of course," Entreri replied. "I know how well you protect your windows."

"The door, as well," LaValle said dryly, for obviously he hadn't protected it well enough.

Entreri shrugged. "You still use that lock and trap combination you had upon your previous quarters," he explained, holding up a key. "I suspected as much, since I heard that you were overjoyed when you discovered that the items had survived when the dwarf knocked the door in on your head."

"How did you get a—" LaValle started to ask.

"I got you the lock, remember?" Entreri answered.

"But the guild house is well defended by no soldiers known by Artemis Entreri," the wizard argued.

"The guild house has its secret leaks," the assassin quietly replied.

"But my door," LaValle went on. "There are . . . were other traps."

Entreri put on a bored expression, and LaValle got the point.

"Very well," the wizard said, moving past Entreri into the study and motioning for the assassin to follow. "I can have a fine meal delivered, if you so desire."

Entreri took a seat opposite LaValle and shook his head. "I came not for food, merely for information," he explained. "They know I am in Calimport."

"Many guilds know," LaValle confirmed with a nod. "And yes, I did know. I saw you through my crystal ball as, I am sure, have many of the wizards of the other pashas. You have not exactly been traveling from shadow to shadow."

"Should I be?" Entreri asked. "I came in with no enemies, as far as I know, and with no intent to make any."

LaValle laughed at the absurd notion. "No enemies?" he asked. "Ever have you made enemies. The creation of enemies is the obvious side product of your dark profession." His chuckle died fast when he looked carefully at the not-amused assassin, the wizard suddenly realizing that he was mocking perhaps the most dangerous man in all the world.

"Why did you scry me?" Entreri asked.

LaValle shrugged and held up his hands as if he didn't understand the question. "That is my job in the guild," he answered.

"So you informed the guildmaster of my return?"

"Pasha Quentin Bodeau was with me when your image came into the crystal ball," LaValle admitted.

Entreri merely nodded, and LaValle shifted uncomfortably.

"I did not know it would be you, of course," the wizard explained. "If I had known, I would have contacted you privately before informing Bodeau to learn your intent and your wishes."

"You are a loyal one," Entreri said dryly, and the irony was not lost on LaValle.

"I make no pretensions or promises," the wizard replied. "Those who know me understand that I do little to upset the balance of power about me and serve whoever has weighted his side of the scale the most."

"A pragmatic survivor," Entreri said. "Yet did you not just tell me that you would have informed me had you known? You do make a promise, wizard, a promise to serve. And yet, would you not be breaking that promise to Quentin Bodeau by warning me? Perhaps I do not know you as well as I had thought. Perhaps your loyalty cannot be trusted."

"I make a willing exception for you," LaValle stammered, trying to find a way out of the logic trap. He knew beyond a doubt that Entreri would try to kill him if the assassin believed that he could not be trusted.

And he knew beyond a doubt that if Entreri tried to kill him, he would be dead.

"Your mere presence means that whichever side you serve has weighted the scale in their favor," he explained. "Thus, I would never willingly go against you."

Entreri didn't respond other than to stare hard at the man, making LaValle shift uncomfortably more than once. Entreri, having little time for such games and with no real intention of harming LaValle, broke the tension, though, and quickly. "Tell me of the guild in its present incarnation," he said. "Tell me of Bodeau and his lieutenants and how extensive his street network has become."

"Quentin Bodeau is a decent man," LaValle readily complied. "He does not kill unless forced into such a position and steals only from those who can afford the loss. But many under him, and many other guilds, perceive this compassion as weakness, and thus the guild has suffered under his reign. We are not as extensive as we were when Pook ruled or when you took the leadership from the halfling Regis." He went on to detail the guild's area of influence, and the assassin was indeed surprised at how much Pook's grand old guild had frayed at the edges. Streets that had once been well within Pook's domain were far out of reach now, for those avenues considered borderlands between various operations were much closer to the guild house.

Entreri hardly cared for the prosperity or weakness of Bodeau's operation. This was a survival call and nothing more. He was only trying to get a feeling for the current layout of Calimport's underbelly so that he might not inadvertently bring the wrath of any particular guild down upon him.

LaValle went on to tell of the lieutenants, speaking highly of the potential of young Chalsee and warning Entreri in a deadly serious tone, but one that hardly seemed to stir the assassin, of Dog Perry.

"Watch him closely," LaValle said again, noting the assassin's almost bored expression. "Dog Perry was beside me when we scried you, and he was far from happy to see Artemis Entreri returned to Calimport. Your mere presence poses a threat to him, for he commands a fairly high price as an assassin, and not just for Quentin Bodeau." Still garnering no obvious response, LaValle pressed even harder. "He wants to be the next Artemis Entreri," the wizard said bluntly.

That brought a chuckle from the assassin, not one of doubt concerning Dog Perry's abilities to fulfill his dream or one of any flattery. Entreri was amused by the fact that this Dog Perry hardly understood that which he sought, for if he did, he would turn his desires elsewhere.

"He may see your return as more than an inconvenience," LaValle warned. "Perhaps as a threat, or even worse . . . as an opportunity."

"You do not like him," Entreri reasoned.

"He is a killer without discipline and thus hardly predictable," the wizard replied. "A blind man's flying arrow. If I knew for certain that he was coming after me, I would hardly fear him. It is the often irrational actions of the man that keep us all a bit worried."

"I hold no aspirations for Bodeau's position," Entreri assured the wizard after a long moment of silence. "Nor do I have any intention of impaling myself on the dagger of Dog Perry. Thus you will show no disloyalty to Bodeau by keeping me informed, wizard, and I expect at least that much from you."

"If Dog Perry comes after you, you will be told," LaValle promised, and Entreri believed him. Dog Perry was an upstart, a young hopeful who desired to strengthen his reputation with a single thrust of his dagger. But LaValle understood the truth of Entreri, the assassin knew, and while the wizard might become nervous indeed if he invoked the wrath of Dog Perry, he would find himself truly terrified if ever he learned that Artemis Entreri wanted him dead.

Entreri sat a moment longer, considering the paradox of his reputation. Because of his years of work, many might seek to kill him, but, for the same reasons, many others would fear to go against him and indeed would work for him.

Of course, if Dog Perry did manage to kill him, then LaValle's loyalty to Entreri would come to an abrupt end, transferred immediately to the new king assassin.

To Artemis Entreri it all seemed so perfectly useless.

* * * * *

"You do not see the possibilities here," Dog Perry scolded, working hard to keep his voice calm, though in truth he wanted to throttle the nervous young man.

"Have you heard the stories?" Chalsee Anguaine retorted. "He has killed everything from guildmasters to battle mages. Everyone he has decided to kill is dead."

Dog Perry spat in disgust. "That was a younger man," he replied. "A man revered by many guilds, including the Basadoni House. A man of connections and protection, who had many powerful allies to assist in his assassinations. Now he is alone and vulnerable, and no longer possessed of the quickness of youth."

"We should bide our time and learn more about him and discover why he has returned," Chalsee reasoned.

"The longer we wait, the more Entreri will rebuild his web," Dog Perry argued without hesitation. "A wizard, a guildmaster, spies on the street. No, if we wait then we cannot go against him without considering the possibility that our actions will begin a guild war. You understand the truth of Bodeau, of course, and recognize that under his leadership we would not survive such a war."

"You remain his principal assassin," Chalsee argued.

Dog Perry chuckled at the thought. "I follow opportunities," he corrected. "And the opportunity I see before me now is one that cannot be ignored. If I—if we—kill Artemis Entreri, we will command his previous position."

"Guildless?"

"Guildless," Dog Perry answered honestly. "Or better described as tied to many guilds. A sword for the highest bidder."

"Quentin Bodeau would not accept such a thing," Chalsee said. "He will lose two lieutenants, thus weakening his guild."

"Quentin Bodeau will understand that because his lieutenants now hire to more powerful guilds, his own position will be better secured," Dog Perry replied.

Chalsee considered the optimistic reasoning for a moment, then shook his head doubtfully. "Bodeau would then be vulnerable, perhaps fearing that his own lieutenants might strike against him at the request of another guildmaster."

"So be it," Dog Perry said coldly. "You should be very careful how tightly you tie your future to the likes of Bodeau. The guild erodes under his command, and eventually another guild will absorb us. Those willing to let the strongest conquer may find a new home. Those tied by foolish loyalty to the loser will have their bodies picked clean by beggars in the gutter."

Chalsee looked away, not enjoying this conversation in the least. Until the previous day, until they had learned that Artemis Entreri had returned, he had thought his life and career fairly secure. He was rising through the ranks of a reasonably strong guild. Now Dog Perry seemed intent on upping the stakes, on reaching for a higher level. While Chalsee could understand the allure, he wasn't certain of the true potential. If they succeeded against Entreri, he did not doubt Dog Perry's prediction, but the mere thought of going after Artemis Entreri . . .

Chalsee had been but a boy when Entreri had last left Calimport, had been connected to no guilds and knew none of the many Entreri had slain. By the time Chalsee had joined the underworld circuit, others had claimed the position of primary assassins in Calimport: Marcus the Knife of Pasha Wroning's Guild; the independent Clarissa and her cohorts who ran the brothels serving the nobility of the region— yes, Clarissa's enemies seemed to simply disappear. Then there was Kadran Gordeon of the Basadoni Guild, and perhaps most deadly of all, Slay Targon, the battle mage. None of them had come near to erasing the reputation of Artemis Entreri, even though the end of Entreri's previous Calimport career had been marred by the downfall of the guildmaster he was supposedly serving and by his reputed inability to defeat a certain nemesis, a drow elf, no less.

And now Dog Perry wanted to catapult himself to the ranks of those four notorious assassins with a single kill, and in truth, the plan sounded plausible to Chalsee.

Except, of course, for the little matter of actually killing Entreri.

"The decision is made," Dog Perry said, seemingly sensing Chalsee's private thoughts. "I am going against him . . . with or without your assistance."

The implicit threat behind those words was not lost on Chalsee. If Dog Perry meant to have any chance against Entreri, there could be no neutral parties. When he proclaimed his intentions to Chalsee, he was bluntly inferring that Chalsee had to either stand with him or against him, to stand in his court or in Entreri's. Considering that Chalsee didn't even know Entreri and feared the man as much as an ally as an enemy, it didn't seem much of a choice.

The two began their planning immediately. Dog Perry insisted that Artemis Entreri would be dead within two days.

* * * * *

"The man is no enemy," LaValle assured Quentin later that same night as the two walked the corridors leading to the guildmaster's private dining hall. "His return to Calimport was not predicated by any desire to reclaim the guild."

"How can you know?" the obviously nervous leader asked. "How can anyone know the mind-set of that one? Ever has he survived through unpredictability."

"There you are wrong," LaValle replied. "Entreri has ever been predictable because he makes no pretense of that which he desires. I have spoken to him."

The admission had Quentin Bodeau spinning about to face the wizard directly. "When?" he stuttered. "Where? You have not left the guild house all this day."

LaValle smiled and tilted his head as he regarded the man—the man who had just foolishly admitted that he was monitoring LaValle's movements. How frightened Quentin must be to go to such lengths. Still, the wizard knew, Quentin realized that LaValle and Entreri were old companions and that if Entreri did desire a return to power in the guild, he would likely enlist LaValle.

"You have no reason not to trust me," LaValle said calmly. "If Entreri wanted the guild back, I would tell you forthwith, that you might surrender leadership and still retain some high-ranking position."

Quentin Bodeau's gray eyes flared dangerously. "Surrender?" he echoed.

"If I led a guild and heard that Artemis Entreri desired my position, I would surely do that!" LaValle said with a laugh that somewhat dispelled the tension. "But have no such fears. Entreri is back in Calimport, 'tis true, but he is no enemy to you."

"Who can tell?" Bodeau replied, starting back down the corridor. LaValle fell into step beside him. "But understand that you are to have no further contacts with the man."

"That hardly seems prudent. Are we not better off understanding his movements?"

"No further contacts," Quentin Bodeau said more forcefully, grabbing LaValle by the shoulder and turning him so he could look directly into the wizard's eyes. "None, and that is not my choice."

"You miss an opportunity, I fear," LaValle started to argue. "Entreri is a friend, a very valuable—"

"None!" Quentin insisted, coming to an abrupt halt to accentuate his point. "Believe me when I say that it would please me greatly to hire the assassin to take care of a few troublemakers among the sewer wererat guild. I have heard that Entreri particularly dislikes the distasteful creatures and that they hold little love for him."

LaValle smiled at the memory. Pasha Pook had been heavily connected with a nasty wererat leader by the name of Rassiter. After Pook's fall, Rassiter had tried to enlist Entreri into a mutually beneficial alliance. Unfortunately for Rassiter, a very angry Entreri hadn't seen things quite that way.

"But we cannot enlist him," Quentin Bodeau went on. "Nor are we . . . are you, to have any further contact with him. These orders have come down to me from the Basadoni Guild, the Rakers' Guild, and Pasha Wroning himself."

LaValle paused, caught off guard by the stunning news. Bodeau had just listed the three most powerful guilds of Calimport's streets.

Quentin paused at the dining room door, knowing that there were attendants inside, wanting to get this settled privately with the wizard. "They have declared Entreri an untouchable," he went on, meaning that no guildmaster, at the risk of street war, was to even speak with the man, let alone have any professional dealings with him.

LaValle nodded, understanding but none too happy about the prospects. It made perfect sense, of course, as would any joint action the three rival guilds could agree upon. They had iced Entreri out of the system for fear that a minor guildmaster might empty his coffers and hire the assassin to kill one of the more prominent leaders. Those in the strongest positions of power preferred the status quo, and they all feared Entreri enough to recognize that he alone might upset that balance. What a testament to the man's reputation! And LaValle, above all others, understood it to be rightly given.

"I understand," he said to Quentin, bowing to show his obedience. "Perhaps when the situation is better clarified we will find our opportunity to exploit my friendship with this very valuable man."

Bodeau managed his first smile in several days, feeling assured by LaValle's seemingly sincere declarations. He was indeed far more at ease as they continued on their way to share an evening meal.

But LaValle was not. He could hardly believe that the other guilds had moved so quickly to isolate Entreri. If that was the case, then he understood that they would be watching the assassin closely—close enough to learn of any attempts against Entreri and to bring about retaliation on any guild so foolish as to try to kill the man.

LaValle ate quickly, then dismissed himself, explaining that he was in the middle of penning a particularly difficult scroll he hoped to finish that night.

He went immediately to his crystal ball, hoping to locate Dog Perry, and was pleased indeed to learn that the fiery man and Chalsee Anguaine were both still within the guild house. He caught up to them on the street level in the main armory. He could guess easily enough why they might be in that particular room.

"You plan to go out this evening?" the wizard calmly asked as he entered.

"We go out every evening," Dog Perry replied. "It is our job, is it not?"

"A few extra weapons?" LaValle asked suspiciously, noting that both men had daggers strapped to every conceivable retrievable position.

"The guild lieutenant who is not careful is usually dead," Dog Perry replied dryly.

"Indeed," LaValle conceded with a bow. "And, by word of the Basadoni, Wroning, and Rakers' guilds, the guild lieutenant who goes after Artemis Entreri is doing no favors for his master."

The blunt declaration gave both men pause. Dog Perry worked through it quickly and calmly, getting back to his preparations with no discernible trace of guilt upon his blank expression. But Chalsee, less experienced by far, showed some clear signs of distress. LaValle knew he had hit the target directly. They were going after Entreri this very night.

"I would have thought you would consult with me first," the wizard remarked, "to learn his whereabouts, of course, and perhaps see some of the defenses he obviously has set in place."

"You babble, wizard," Dog Perry insisted. "I have many duties to attend and have no time for your foolishness." He slammed the door of the weapons locker as he finished, then walked right past LaValle. A nervous Chalsee Anguaine fell into step behind him, glancing back many times.

LaValle considered the cold treatment and recognized that Dog Perry had indeed decided to go after Entreri and had also decided that LaValle could not be trusted as far as the dangerous assassin was concerned. Now the wizard, in considering all the possibilities, found his own dilemma. If Dog Perry succeeded in killing Entreri the dangerous young man who had just pointedly declared himself no friend of LaValle's would gain immensely in stature and power (if the other guilds did not decide to kill him for his rash actions). But if Entreri won, which LaValle deemed most likely, then he might not appreciate the fact that LaValle had not contacted him with any warning, as they had agreed.

And yet LaValle could not dare to use his magics and contact Entreri. If the other guilds were watching the assassin, such forms of contact would be easily detected and traced.

A very distressed LaValle went back to his room and sat for a long while in the darkness. In either scenario, whether Dog Perry or Entreri proved victorious, the guild might be in for more than a little trouble. Should he go to Quentin Bodeau? he wondered, but then he dismissed the thought, realizing that Quentin would do little more than pace the floor and chew his fingernails. Dog Perry was out in the streets now, and Quentin had no means to recall him.

Should he gaze into his crystal ball and try to learn of the battle? Again, LaValle had to consider that any magical contact, even if it was no more than silent scrying, might be detected by the wizards hired by the more powerful guilds and might then implicate LaValle.

So he sat in the darkness, wondering and worrying, as the hours slipped by.

Chapter 6
LEAVING THE DALE BEHIND

Drizzt watched every move the barbarian made—the way Wulfgar sat opposite him across the fire, the way the man went at his dinner—looking for some hint of the barbarian's mindset. Had the battle with the giants helped? Had Drizzt "run the horse" as he had explained his hopes to Regis? Or was Wulfgar in worse shape now than before the battle? Was he more consumed by this latest guilt, though his actions, or inaction, hadn't really cost them anything?

Wulfgar had to recognize that he had not performed well at the beginning of the battle, but had he, in his own mind, made up for that error with his subsequent actions?

Drizzt was as perceptive to such emotions as anyone alive, but, in truth, he could not get the slightest read of the barbarian's inner turmoil. Wulfgar moved methodically, mechanically, as he had since his return from Errtu's clutches, going through the motions of life itself without any outward sign of pain, satisfaction, relief, or anything else. Wulfgar was existing, but hardly living. If there remained a flicker of passion within those sky-blue orbs, Drizzt could not see it.

Thus, the drow ranger was left with the impression that the battle with the giants had been inconsequential, had neither bolstered the barbarian's desire to live nor had placed any further burdens upon Wulfgar. In looking at his friend now, the man tearing a piece of fowl from the bone, his expression unchanging and unrevealing, Drizzt had to admit to himself that he had not only run out of answers but out of places to look for answers.

Catti-brie moved over and sat down beside Wulfgar then, and the barbarian did pause to regard her. He even managed a little smile for her benefit. Perhaps she might succeed where he had failed, the drow thought. He and Wulfgar had been friends, to be sure, but the barbarian and Catti-brie had shared something much deeper than that.

The thought of it brought a tumult of opposing feelings into Drizzt's gut. On the one hand he cared deeply for Wulfgar and wanted nothing more in all the world than for the barbarian to heal his emotional scars. On the other hand, seeing Catti-brie close to the man pained him. He tried to deny it, tried to elevate himself above it, but it was there, and it was a fact, and it would not go away.

He was jealous.

With great effort, the drow sublimated those feelings enough to honestly leave the couple alone. He went to join Bruenor and Regis and couldn't help but contrast the halfling's beaming face as he devoured his third helping with that of Wulfgar, who seemed to be eating only to keep his body alive. Pragmatism against pure pleasure.

"We'll be out o' the dale tomorrow," Bruenor was saying, pointing out the dark silhouettes of the mountains, looming much larger to the south and east. Indeed, the wagon had turned the corner and they were heading south now, no longer west. The wind, which always filled the ears in Icewind Dale, had died to the occasional gust.

"How's me boy?" Bruenor asked when he noticed the dark elf.

Drizzt shrugged.

"Ye could've got him killed, ye durned fool elf," the dwarf huffed. "Ye could've got us all killed. And not for the first time!"

"And not for the last," Drizzt promised with a smile, bowing low. He knew that Bruenor was playing with him here, that the dwarf loved a good fight as much as he did, particularly one against giants. Bruenor had been upset with him, to be sure, but only because Drizzt hadn't included him in the original battle plans. The brief but brutal fight had long since exorcised that grudge from Bruenor, and so now he was just teasing the drow as a means of relieving his honest concerns for Wulfgar.

"Did ye see his face when we battled?" the dwarf asked more earnestly. "Did ye see him when Rumblebelly showed up with his stinkin' giant friend and it appeared as if me boy was about to be squished flat?"

Drizzt admitted that he did not. "I was engaged with my own concerns at the time," he explained. "And with Guenhwyvar's peril."

"Nothing," Bruenor declared. "Nothing at all. No anger as he lifted his hammer to throw it at the giants."

"The warrior sublimates his anger to keep in conscious control," the drow reasoned.

"Bah, not like that," Bruenor retorted. "I saw rage in me boy when we fought Errtu on the ice island, rage beyond anything me old eyes've ever seen. And how I'd like to be seein' it again. Anger, rage, even fear!"

"I saw him when I arrived at the battle," Regis admitted. "He did not know that the new and huge giant would be an ally, and if it was not, if it had joined in on the side of the other giants, then Wulfgar would have easily been killed, for he had no defense against our angle from his open ledge. And yet he was not afraid at all. He looked right up at the giant, and all I saw was . . ."

"Resignation," the drow finished for him. "Acceptance of whatever fate might throw at him."

"I'm not for understanding." Bruenor admitted.

Drizzt had no answers for him. He had his suspicions, of course, that Wulfgar's trauma had been too great and had thus stolen from him his hopes and dreams, his passions and purpose, but he could find no way to put that into words that the ever-pragmatic dwarf might understand. He thought it ironic, in a sense, for the closest example of similar behavior he could recall was Bruenor's own, soon after Wulfgar had fallen to the yochlol. The dwarf had wandered aimlessly through the halls for days on end, grieving.

Yes, Drizzt realized, that was the key word. Wulfgar was grieving.

Bruenor would never understand, and Drizzt wasn't sure that he understood.

"Time to go," Regis remarked, drawing the dark elf from his contemplation. Drizzt looked to the halfling, then to Bruenor.

"Camlaine's invited us to a game o' bones," Bruenor explained. "Come along, elf. Yer eyes see better'n most, and I might be needing ye."

Drizzt glanced back to the fire, to Wulfgar and Catti-brie, sitting very close and talking. He noted that Catti-brie wasn't doing all of the speaking. She had somehow engaged Wulfgar, even had him a bit animated in his discussion. A big part of Drizzt wanted to stay right there and watch their every move, but he wouldn't give in to that weakness, so he went with Bruenor and Regis to watch the game of bones.

* * * * *

"Ye cannot know our pain at seeing the ceiling fall in on ye," Catti-brie said, gently moving the conversation to that fateful day in the bowels of Mithral Hall. Up to now, she and Wulfgar had been sharing happier memories of previous fights, battles in which the companions had overwhelmed monsters and put down threats without so high a price.

Wulfgar had even joined in, telling of his first battle with Bruenor—against Bruenor—when he had broken his standard staff over the dwarf's head, only to have the stubborn little creature swipe his legs out from under him and leave him unconscious on the field. As the conversation wound on, Catti-brie focused on another pivotal event: the crafting of Aegis-fang. What a labor of love that had been, the pinnacle of Bruenor's amazing career as a smith, done purely out of the dwarf's affection for Wulfgar.

"If he hadn't loved ye so, he'd ne'er been able to make so great a weapon," she had explained. When she saw that her words were getting through to the pained man she had shifted the conversation subtly again, to the reverential treatment Bruenor had shown the warhammer after Wulfgar's apparent demise. And that, of course, had brought Catti-brie to the discussion of the day of Wulfgar's fall, to the memory of the evil yochlol.

To her great relief, Wulfgar had not tightened up when she went in this direction, but had stayed with her, hearing her words and adding his own when they seemed relevant.

"All the strength went from me body," Catti-brie went on. "And never have I seen Bruenor closer to breaking. But we went on and started fighting in yer name, and woe to our enemies then."

A distant look came into Wulfgar's light eyes and the woman went silent, giving him time to digest her words. She thought he would respond, but he did not, and the seconds slipped away quietly.

Catti-brie moved closer to him and put her arm about his back, resting her head on his strong shoulder. He didn't push her away, even shifted so they would both be more comfortable. The woman had hoped for more, had hoped to get Wulfgar into an emotional release. But while she hadn't achieved quite that, she recognized that she had gotten more than she could have rightfully expected. The love had not resurfaced, but neither had the rage.

It would take time.

The group did indeed roll out of Icewind Dale the next morning, a distinction made clear by the shifting wind. In the dale, the wind came from the northeast, rolling down off the cold waters of the Sea of Moving Ice. At the juncture to points south, east, and north of the bulk of the mountains, the wind blew constantly no longer, but was more a matter of gusts than the incessant whistle through the dale. And now, moving more to the south, the wind again kicked up, swirling against the towering Spine of the World. Unlike the cold breeze that gave its name to Icewind Dale, this was a gentle blow. The winds wafted up from warmer climes to the south or off the warmer waters of the Sword Coast, hitting against the blocking mountains and swirling back.

Drizzt and Bruenor spent most of the day away from the wagon, both to scout a perimeter about the steady but slow pacing team and to give some privacy to Catti-brie and Wulfgar. The woman was still talking, still trying to bring the man to a better place and time. Regis rode all the day long nestled in the back of the wagon among the generous-smelling foodstuffs.

It proved to be a quiet and uneventful day of travel, except for one point where Drizzt found a particularly disturbing track, that of a huge, booted giant.

"Rumblebelly's friend?" Bruenor asked, bending low beside the ranger as he inspected the footprint.

"So I would guess," Drizzt replied.

"Durned halfling put more of a spell than he should've on the thing," Bruenor grumbled.

Drizzt, who understood the power of the ruby pendant and the nature of enchantments in general, could not agree. He knew that the giant, no stupid creature, had been released from any spell Regis had woven soon after leaving the group. Likely, before they were miles apart, the giant had begun to wonder why in the world he had ever deigned to help the halfling and his strange group of friends. Then, soon after that, he had either forgotten the whole incident or was angry indeed at having been so deceived.

And now the behemoth seemed to be shadowing them, Drizzt realized, noting the general course of the tracks.

Perhaps it was mere coincidence, or perhaps even a different giant—Icewind Dale had no shortage of giants, after all. Drizzt could not be sure, and so, when he and Bruenor returned to the group for their evening meal, they said nothing about the footprints or about increasing the night watch. Drizzt did go off on his own, though, as much to get away from the continuing scene between Catti-brie and Wulfgar as to scout for any rogue giants. There in the dark of night, he could be alone with his thoughts and his fears, could wage his own emotional wars and remind himself over and over that Catti-brie alone could decide the course of her life.

Every time he recalled an incident highlighting how intelligent and honest the woman had always been, he was comforted. When the full moon began its lazy ascent over the distant waters of the Sword Coast, the drow felt strangely warm. Though he could hardly see the glow of the campfire, he understood that he was truly among friends.

* * * * *

Wulfgar looked deeply into her blue eyes and knew that she had purposefully brought him to this point, had smoothed the jagged edges of his battered consciousness slowly and deliberately, had massaged the walls of anger until her gentle touch had rubbed them into transparency. And now she wanted, she demanded, to look behind those walls, wanted to see the demons that so tormented Wulfgar.

Catti-brie sat quietly, calmly, patiently waiting. She had coaxed some specific horror stories out of the man and then had probed deeper, had asked him to lay bare his soul and his terror, something she knew could not be easy for the proud and strong man.

But Wulfgar hadn't rebuffed her. He sat now, his thoughts whirling, his gaze locked firmly by hers, his breath coming in gasps, his heart pounding in his huge chest.

"For so long I held on to you," he said quietly. "Down there, among the smoke and the dirt, I held fast to an image of my Catti-brie. I kept it right before me at all times. I did."

He paused to catch his breath, and Catti-brie placed a gentle hand on his.

"So many sights that a man was not meant to view," Wulfgar said quietly, and Catti-brie saw a hint of moisture in his light eyes. "But I fought them all with an image of you."

Catti-brie offered a smile, but that did little to comfort Wulfgar.

"He used it against me," the man went on, his tone lowering, becoming almost a growl. "Errtu knew my thoughts and turned them against me. He showed me the finish of the yochlol fight, the creature pushing through the rubble, falling over you and tearing you to pieces. Then it went for Bruenor. . . ."

"Was it not the yochlol that brought you to the lower planes?" Catti-brie asked, trying to use logic to break the demonic spell.

"I do not remember," Wulfgar admitted. "I remember the fall of the stones, the pain of the yochlol's bite tearing into my chest, and then only blackness until I awakened in the court of the Spider Queen.

"But even that image . . . you do not understand! The one thing I could hold onto Errtu perverted and turned against me. The one hope left in my heart burned away and left me empty."

Catti-brie moved closer, her face barely an inch from Wulfgar's. "But hope rekindles," she said softly. "Errtu is gone, banished for a hundred years, and the Spider Queen and her hellish drow minions have shown no interest in Drizzt for years. That road has ended, it seems, and so many new ones lie before us. The road to the Spirit Soaring and Cadderly. From there to Mithral Hall perhaps, and then, if we choose, we might go to Waterdeep and Captain Deudermont, take a wild voyage on *Sea Sprite*, cutting the waves and chasing pirates.

"What possibilities lie before us!" she went on, her smile wide, her blue eyes flashing with excitement. "But first we must make peace with our past."

Wulfgar heard her well, but he only shook his head, reminding her that it might not be as easy as she made it sound. "For all those years you thought I was dead," he said. "And so I thought of you for that time. I thought you killed, and Bruenor killed, and Drizzt cut apart on the altar of some vile drow matron. I surrendered hope because there was none."

"But you see the lie," Catti-brie reasoned. "There is always hope, there must always be hope. That is the lie of Errtu's evil kind. The lie about them, and the lie that is them. They steal hope, because without hope there is no strength. Without hope there is no freedom. In slavery of the heart does a demon find its greatest pleasures."

Wulfgar took a deep, deep breath, trying to digest it all, balancing the logical truths of Catti-brie's words—and of the simple fact that he had indeed escaped Errtu's clutches—against the pervasive pain of memory.

Catti-brie, too, spent a long moment digesting all that Wulfgar had shown to her over the past days. She understood now that it was more than pain and horror that bound her friend. Only one emotion could so cripple a man. In replaying his memories within his own mind, Wulfgar had found some wherein he had surrendered, wherein he had given in to the desires of Errtu or the demon's minions, wherein he had lost his courage or his defiance. Yes, it was obvious to Catti-brie, staring hard at the man now that guilt above all else was the enduring demon of Wulfgar's time with Errtu.

Of course to her that seemed absurd. She could readily forgive anything Wulfgar had said or done to survive the decadence of the Abyss. Anything at all. But it was not absurd, she quickly reminded herself, for it was painted clearly on the big man's pained features.

Wulfgar squinted his eyes shut and gritted his teeth. She was right, he told himself repeatedly. The past was past, an experience dismissed, a lesson learned. Now they were all together again, healthy and on the road of adventure. Now he had learned the errors of his previous engagement to Catti-brie and could look at her with fresh hopes and desires.

She recognized a measure of calm come over the man as he opened his eyes again to stare back at her. And then he came forward, kissing her softly, just brushing his lips against hers as if asking permission.

Catti-brie glanced all around and saw that they were indeed alone. Though the others were not so far away, those who were not asleep were too engaged in their gambling to take note of anything.

Wulfgar kissed her again, a bit more urgently, forcing her to consider her feelings for the man. Did she love him? As a friend, surely, but was she ready to take that love to a different level?

Catti-brie honestly did not know. Once she had decided to give her love to Wulfgar, to marry him and bear his children, to make her life with him. But that was so many years ago, a different time, a different place. Now she had feelings for another, perhaps, though in truth, she hadn't really examined those feelings any deeper than she had her current feelings for Wulfgar.

And she hadn't the time to examine them now, for Wulfgar kissed her again passionately. When she didn't respond in kind, he backed off to arms' length, staring at her hard.

Looking at him then, on the brink of disaster, on a precipice between past and future, Catti-brie came to understand that she had to give this to him. She pulled him back and initiated another kiss, and they embraced deeply, Wulfgar guiding her to the ground, rolling about, touching, caressing, fumbling with their clothes.

She let him lose himself in the passion, let him lead with touches and kisses, and she took comfort in the role she had accepted, took hope that their encounter this night would help bring Wulfgar back to the world of the living.

And it was working. Wulfgar knew it, felt it. He bared his heart and soul to her, threw away his defenses, basked in the feel of her, in the sweet smell of her, in the very softness of her.

He was free! For those first few moments he was free, and it was glorious and beautiful, and so real.

He rolled to his back, his strong hug rolling Catti-brie atop him. He bit softly on the nape of her neck, then, nearing a point of ecstasy, leaned his head back so that he could look into her eyes and share the moment of joy.

A leering succubus, vile temptress of the Abyss, stared back at him.

Wulfgar's thoughts careened back across Icewind Dale, back to the Sea of Moving Ice, to the ice cave and the fight with Errtu, then back beyond that, back to the swirling smoke and the horrors. It had all been a lie, he realized. The fight, the escape, the rejoining with his friends. All a lie perpetrated by Errtu to rekindle his hope that the demon could then snuff it out once again. All a lie, and he was still in the Abyss, dreaming of Catti-brie while entwining with a horrid succubus.

His powerful hand clamped under the creature's chin and pushed it away. His second hand came across

R. A. Salvatore

in a vicious punch and then he lifted the beast into the air above his prone form and heaved it away, bouncing across the dirt. With a roar, Wulfgar pulled himself to his feet, fumbling to lift and straighten his pants. He staggered for the fire and, ignoring the pain, reached in to grab a burning branch, then turned back to attack the wicked succubus.

Turned back to attack Catti-brie.

He recognized her then, half-undressed, staggering to her hands and knees, blood dripping freely from her nose. She managed to look up at him. There was no rage, only confusion on her battered face. The weight of guilt nearly buckled the barbarian's strong legs.

"I did not . . ." he stammered. "Never would I . . ." With a gasp and a stifled cry, Wulfgar rushed across the campsite, tossing the burning stick aside, gathering up his pack and warhammer. He ran out into the dark of night, into the ultimate darkness of his tormented mind.

Chapter 7
KELP-ENWALLED

ou cannot come in," the squeaky voice said from behind the barricade. "Please, sir, I beg you. Go away."

Entreri hardly found the halfling's nervous tone amusing, for the implications of the shut-out rang dangerously in his mind. He and Dwahvel had cut a deal— a mutually beneficial deal and one that seemed to favor the halfling, if anyone—and yet, now it seemed as if Dwahvel was going back on her word. Her doorman would not even let the assassin into the Copper Ante. Entreri entertained the thought of kicking in the barricade, but only briefly. He reminded himself that halflings were often adept at setting traps. Then he thought he might slip his dagger through the slit in the boards, into the impertinent doorman's arm, or thumb, or whatever other target presented itself. That was the beauty of Entreri's dagger: he could stick someone anywhere and suck the life-force right out of him.

But again, it was a fleeting thought, more of a fantasy wrought of frustration than any action the ever-careful Entreri would seriously consider.

"So I shall go," he said calmly. "But do inform Dwahvel that my world is divided between friends and enemies." He turned and started away, leaving the doorman in a fluster.

"My, but that sounded like a threat," came another voice before Entreri had moved ten paces down the street.

The assassin stopped and considered a small crack in the wall of the Copper Ante, a peep hole, he realized, and likely an arrow slit.

"Dwahvel," he said with a slight bow.

To his surprise, the crack widened and a panel slid aside. Dwahvel walked out in the open. "So quick to name enemies," she said, shaking her head, her curly brown locks bouncing gaily.

"But I did not," the assassin replied. "Though it did anger me that you apparently decided not to go through with our deal."

Dwahvel's face tightened suddenly, stealing the up-to-then lighthearted tone. "Kelp-enwalled," she explained, an expression more common to the fishing boats than the streets, but one Entreri had heard before. On the fishing boats, "kelp-enwalling" referred to the practice of isolating particularly troublesome pincer crabs, which had to be delivered live to market, by building barricades of kelp strands about them. The term was less literal, but with similar meaning, on the street. A kelp-enwalled person had been declared off-limits, surrounded and isolated by barricades of threats.

Suddenly Entreri's expression also showed the strain.

"The order came from greater guilds than mine, from guilds that could, and would, burn the Copper Ante to the ground and kill all of my fellows with hardly a thought," Dwahvel said with a shrug. "Entreri is kelp-enwalled, so they said. You cannot blame me for refusing your entrance."

Entreri nodded. He above many others could appreciate pragmatism for the sake of survival. "Yet you chose to come out and speak with me," he said.

Another shrug from Dwahvel. "Only to explain why our deal has ended," she said. "And to ensure that I do not fall into the latter category you detailed for my doorman. I will offer to you this much, with no charge for services. Everyone knows now that you have returned, and your mere presence has made them all nervous. Old Basadoni still rules his guild, but he is in the shadows now, more a figurehead than a leader. Those handling the affairs of the Basadoni Guild, and the other guilds, for that matter, do not know you. But they do know your reputation. Thus they fear you as they fear each other. Might not Pasha Wroning fear that the Rakers have hired Entreri to kill him? Or even within the individual guilds, might those vying for position before the coming event of Pasha Basadoni's death not fear that one of the others has coaxed Entreri back to assure personal ascension?"

Entreri nodded again but replied, "Or is it not possible that Artemis Entreri has merely returned to his home?"

"Of course," Dwahvel said. "But until they all learn the truth of you, they will fear you, and the only way to learn the truth—"

"Kelp-enwalled," the assassin finished. He started to thank Dwahvel for showing the courage of coming out to tell him this much, but he stopped short. He recognized that perhaps the halfling was only following orders, that perhaps this meeting was part of the surveying process.

"Watch well your back," Dwahvel added, moving for the secret door. "You understand that there are many who would like to claim the head of Entreri for their trophy wall."

"What do you know?" the assassin asked, for it seemed obvious to him that Dwahvel wasn't speaking merely in generalities here.

"Before the kelp-enwalling order, my spies went out to learn what they may about the perceptions concerning your return," she explained. "They were asked more questions than they offered and often by young, strong assassins. Watch well your back." And then she was gone, back through the secret door into the Copper Ante.

Entreri just blew a sigh and walked along. He didn't question his return to Calimport, for either way it simply didn't seem important to him. Nor did he start looking more deeply into the shadows that lined the dark street. Perhaps one or more held his killer. Perhaps not.

Perhaps it simply did not matter.

* * * * *

"Perry," Giunta the Diviner said to Kadran Gordeon as the two watched the young thug steal along the rooftops, shadowing, from a very safe distance, the movements of Artemis Entreri. "A lieutenant for Bodeau."

"Is he watching?" Kadran asked.

"Hunting," the wizard corrected.

Kadran didn't doubt the man. Giunta's entire life had been spent in observation. This wizard was the watcher, and from the patterns of those he observed he could then predict with an amazing degree of accuracy their next movements.

"Why would Bodeau risk everything to go after Entreri?" the fighter asked. "Surely he knows of the kelp-enwalling order, and Entreri has a long alliance with that particular guild."

"You presume that Bodeau even knows of this," Giunta explained. "I have seen this one before. Dog Perry, he is called, though he fancies himself 'the Heart.'"

That nickname rang a chime of recognition in Kadran. "For his practice of cutting a still-beating heart from the chest of his victims," the man remarked. "A brash young killer," he added, nodding, for now it made sense.

"Not unlike one I know," Giunta said slyly, turning his gaze over Kadran.

Kadran smiled in reply. Indeed, Dog Perry was not so unlike a younger Kadran, brash and skilled. The years had taught Kadran some measure of humility, however, though many of those who knew him well thought he was still a bit deficient in that regard. He looked more closely at Dog Perry now, the man moving silently and carefully along the rim of a rooftop. Yes, there seemed a resemblance to the young thug Kadran used to be. Less polished and less wise, obviously, for even in his cocky youth Kadran doubted that he would have gone after the likes of Artemis Entreri so soon after the man's return to Calimport and obviously without too much preparation.

"He must have allies in the region," Kadran remarked to Giunta. "Seek out the other rooftops. Surely the young thug would not be foolish enough to hunt Entreri alone."

Giunta widened his scan. He found Entreri moving easily along the main boulevard and recognized many other characters in the area, regulars who held no known connection to Bodeau's guild or to Dog Perry.

"Him," the wizard explained, pointing to another figure weaving in and out of the shadows, following the same route as Entreri, but far, far behind. "Another of Bodeau's men, I believe."

131

"He does not seem overly intent on joining the fight," Kadran noted, for the man seemed to hesitate with every step. He was so far behind Entreri and losing ground with each passing second that he could have jumped out and run full speed at the man down the middle of the street without being noticed by the pursued assassin.

"Perhaps he is merely observing," Giunta remarked as he moved the focus of the crystal ball back to the two assassins, their paths beginning to intersect, "following his ally at the request of Bodeau to see how Dog Perry fares. There are many possibilities, but if he does mean to get into the fight beside Dog Perry, then he should run fast. Entreri is not one to drag out a battle, and it seems—"

He stopped abruptly as Dog Perry moved to the edge of a roof and crouched low, muscles tensing. The young assassin had found his spot of ambush, and Entreri turned into the ally, seemingly playing into the man's hand.

"We could warn him," Kadran said, licking his lips nervously.

"Entreri is already on his guard," the wizard explained. "Surely he has sensed my scrying. A man of his talents could not be magically looked at without his knowledge." the wizard gave a little chuckle. "Farewell, Dog Perry," he said.

Even as the words came out of his mouth, the would-be assassin leaped down from the roof, hitting the ground in a rush barely three strides behind Entreri, closing so fast that almost any man would have been skewered before he even registered the noise behind him.

Almost any man.

Entreri spun as Dog Perry rushed in, Perry's slender sword leading. A brush of the spinning assassin's left hand, holding the ample folds of his cloak as further protection, deflected the blow wide. Ahead went Entreri, a sudden step, pushing up with his left hand, lifting Dog Perry's arm as he went. He moved right under the now off-balance would-be killer, stabbing up into the armpit with his jeweled dagger as he passed. Then, so quickly that Dog Perry never had a chance to compensate, so quickly that Kadran and Giunta hardly noticed the subtle turn, he pivoted back, turning to face Dog Perry's back. Entreri tore the dagger free and flipped it to his descending left hand, snapped his right hand around to the chin of the would-be killer, and kicked the man in the back of the knees, buckling his legs and forcing him back and down. The older assassin's left hand stabbed up, driving the dagger under the back of Dog Perry's skull and deep into his brain.

Entreri retracted the dagger immediately and let the dead man fall to the ground, blood pooling under him, so quickly and so efficiently that Entreri didn't even have a drop of blood on him.

Giunta, laughing, pointed to the end of the ally, back on the street, where the stunned companion of Dog Perry took one look at the victorious Entreri, turned on his heel, and ran away.

"Yes, indeed," Giunta remarked. "Let the word go out on the streets that Artemis Entreri has returned."

Kadran Gordeon spent a long while staring at the dead man. He struck his customary pensive pose, pursing his lips so that his long and curvy mustache tilted on his dark face. He had entertained the idea of going after Entreri himself, and now was quite plainly shocked by the sheer skill of the man. It was Gordeon's first true experience with Entreri, and suddenly he understood that the man had come by his reputation honestly.

But Kadran Gordeon was not Dog Perry, was far more skilled than that young bumbler. Perhaps he would indeed pay a visit to this former king of assassins.

"Exquisite," came Sharlotta's voice behind the two. They turned to see the woman staring past them into the image in Giunta's large crystal ball. "Pasha Basadoni told me I would be impressed. How well he moves!"

"Shall I repay the Bodeau guild for breaking the kelp-enwalling order?" Kadran asked.

"Forget them," Sharlotta retorted, moving closer, her eyes twinkling with admiration. "Concentrate our attention upon that one alone. Find him and enlist him. Let us find a job for Artemis Entreri."

* * * * *

Drizzt found Catti-brie sitting on the back lip of the wagon. Regis sat next to her, holding a cloth to her face. Bruenor, axe swinging dangerously at his side, pacing back and forth, grumbled a stream of curses. The drow knew at once what had happened, the simple truth of it anyway, and when he considered it, he was not so surprised that Wulfgar had struck out.

"He did not mean to do it," Catti-brie said to Bruenor, trying to calm the volatile dwarf. She, too, was obviously angry, but she, like Drizzt, understood better the truth of Wulfgar's emotional turmoil. "I'm thinking he wasn't seein' me," the woman went on, speaking more to Drizzt. "Looking back at Errtu's torments, by me guess."

Drizzt nodded. "As it was at the beginning of the fight with the giants," he said.

"And so ye're to let it go?" Bruenor roared in reply. "Ye're thinkin' that ye can't hold the boy responsible?

Bah! I'll give him a beating that'll make his years with Errtu seem easy! Go and get him, elf. Bring him back that he can tell me girl he's sorry. Then he can tell me. Then he can find me fist in his mouth and take a good long sleep to think about it!" With a growl, Bruenor drove his axe deep into the ground. "I heared too much o' this Errtu," he declared. "Ye can't be livin' in what's already done!"

Drizzt had little doubt that if Wulfgar walked back into camp at that moment, it would take him, Catti-brie, Regis, Camlaine, and all his companions just to pull Bruenor off the man. And in looking at Catti-brie, one eye swollen, her bloody nose bright red, the ranger wasn't sure he would be too quick to hold the dwarf back.

Without another word Drizzt turned and walked away, out of the camp and into the darkness. Wulfgar couldn't have gone far, he knew, though the night was not so dark with the big moon shining bright across the tundra. Just outside the campsite he took out his figurine. Guenhwyvar led the way, rushing into the darkness and growling back to guide the running ranger.

To Drizzt's surprise the trail led neither south nor back to the northeast and Ten Towns, but straight east, toward the towering black peaks of the Spine of the World. Soon Guenhwyvar led him into the foothills, dangerous territory indeed, for the high bluffs and rocky outcroppings provided fine ambush points for lurking monsters or highwaymen.

Perhaps, Drizzt mused, that was exactly why Wulfgar had come this way. Perhaps he was looking for trouble, for a fight, or maybe even for some giant to surprise him and end his pain.

Drizzt skidded to a stop and blew a long and profound sigh, for what seemed most unsettling to him was not the thought that Wulfgar was inviting disaster, but his own reaction to it. For at that moment, the image of hurt Catti-brie clear in his mind, the ranger almost—*almost*—thought that such an ending to Wulfgar's tale would not be such a terrible thing.

A call from Guenhwyvar brought him from his thoughts. He sprinted up a steep incline, leaped to another boulder, then skittered back down to another trail. He heard a growl—from Wulfgar and not the panther—then a crash as Aegis-fang slammed against some stone. The crash was near to Guenhwyvar, Drizzt realized, from the sound of the hit and the cat's ensuing protesting roars.

Drizzt leaped over a stone lip, rushed across a short expanse, and jumped down a small drop to land lightly right beside the big man just as the warhammer magically reappeared in his grasp. For a moment, considering the wild look in Wulfgar's eyes, the drow thought he would have to draw his blades and fight the man, but Wulfgar calmed quickly. He seemed merely defeated, his rage thrown out.

"I did not know," he said, slumping back against the stone.

"I understand," Drizzt replied, holding back his own anger and trying to sound compassionate.

"It was not Catti-brie," Wulfgar went on. "In my thoughts, I mean. I was not with her, but back there, in that place of darkness."

"I know," said Drizzt. "And so does Catti-brie, though I fear we shall have some work ahead of us in calming Bruenor." He ended with a wide and warm smile, but his attempt to lighten the situation was lost on Wulfgar.

"He is right to be outraged," the barbarian admitted. "As I am outraged, in a way you cannot begin to understand."

"Do not underestimate the value of friendship," Drizzt answered. "I once made a similar error, nearly to the destruction of all that I hold dear."

Wulfgar shook his head through every word of it, unable to find any footing for agreement. Black waves of despair washed over him, burying him. What he had done was beyond forgiveness, especially since he realized, and admitted to himself, that it would likely happen again. "I am lost," he said softly.

"And we will all help you to find your way," Drizzt answered, putting a comforting hand on the big man's shoulder.

Wulfgar pushed him away. "No," he said firmly, and then he gave a little laugh. "There is no way to find. The darkness of Errtu endures. Under that shadow, I cannot be who you want me to be."

"We only want you to remember who you once were," the drow replied. "In the ice cave, we rejoiced to find Wulfgar, son of Beornegar, returned to us."

"He was not," the big man corrected. "I am not the man who left you in Mithral Hall. I can never be that man again."

"Time will heal—" Drizzt started to say, but Wulfgar silenced him with a roar.

"No!" he cried. "I do not ask for healing. I do not wish to become again the man that I was. Perhaps I have learned the truth of the world, and that truth has shown me the errors of my previous ways."

Drizzt stared hard at the man. "And the better way is to punch an unsuspecting Catti-brie?" he asked, his voice dripping with sarcasm, his patience for the man fast running out.

Wulfgar locked stares with Drizzt, and again the drow's hands went to his scimitar hilts. He could hardly believe the level of anger rising within him, overwhelming his compassion for his sorely tormented friend. He understood that if Wulfgar did try to strike at him, he would fight the man without holding back.

"I look at you now and remember that you are my friend," Wulfgar said, relaxing his tense posture enough to assure Drizzt that he did not mean to strike out. "And yet those reminders come only with strong willpower. Easier it is for me to hate you, and hate everything around me, and on those occasions when I do not immediately summon the willpower to remember the truth, I will strike out."

"As you did with Catti-brie," Drizzt replied, and his tone was not accusatory, but rather showed a sincere attempt to understand and empathize.

Wulfgar nodded. "I did not even recognize that it was her," he said. "It was just another of Errtu's fiends, the worst kind, the kind that tempted me and defeated my willpower, and then left me not with burns or wounds but with the weight of guilt, with the knowledge of failure. I wanted to resist. . . . I . . ."

"Enough, my friend," Drizzt said quietly. "You shoulder blame where you should not. It was no failure of Wulfgar, but the unending cruelty of Errtu."

"It was both," said a defeated Wulfgar. "And that failure compounds with every moment of weakness."

"We will speak with Bruenor," Drizzt assured him. "We will use this incident as a guide and learn from it."

"You may say to Bruenor whatever you choose," the big man said, his tone suddenly turning ice cold once more. "For I will not be there to hear it."

"You will return to your own people?" Drizzt asked, though he knew in his heart that the barbarian wasn't saying any such thing.

"I will find whatever road I choose," Wulfgar replied. "Alone."

"I once played this game."

"Game?" the big man echoed incredulously. "I have never been more serious in all my life. Now go back to them, back where you belong. When you think of me, think of the man I once was, the man who would never strike Catti-brie."

Drizzt started to reply, but stopped himself and stood studying his broken friend. In truth, he had nothing to say that might comfort Wulfgar. While he wanted to believe that he and the others could help coax the man back to rational behavior, he wasn't certain of it. Not at all. Would Wulfgar strike out again, at Catti-brie, or at any of them, perhaps hurting one of them severely? Would the big man's return to the group facilitate a true fight between him and Bruenor, or between him and Drizzt? Or would Catti-brie, in self-defense, drive Khazid'hea, her deadly sword, deep into the man's chest? On the surface, these fears all rang as preposterous in the drow's mind, but after watching Wulfgar carefully these past few days, he could not dismiss the troublesome possibility.

And perhaps worst of all, he had to consider his own feelings when he had seen the battered Catti-brie. He hadn't been the least bit surprised.

Wulfgar started away, and Drizzt instinctively grabbed him by the forearm.

Wulfgar spun and threw the drow's hand aside. "Farewell, Drizzt Do'Urden," he said sincerely, and those words conveyed many of his unspoken thoughts to Drizzt. A longing to go with the drow back to the group, a plea that things could be as they had once been, the friends, the companions of the hall, running down the road to adventure. And most of all, in that lucid tone, words spoken so clearly and deliberately and thoughtfully, they brought to Drizzt a sense of finality. He could not stop Wulfgar, short of hamstringing the man with a scimitar. And in his heart, at that terrible moment, he knew that he should not stop Wulfgar.

"Find yourself," Drizzt said, "and then find us."

"Perhaps," was all that Wulfgar could offer. Without looking back, he walked away.

For Drizzt Do'Urden, the walk back to the wagon to rejoin his friends was the longest journey of his life.

Part 2

WALKING THE ROADS
OF DANGER

We each have our own path to tread. That seems such a simple and obvious thought, but in a world of relationships where so many people sublimate their own true feelings and desires in consideration of others, we take many steps off that true path.

In the end, though, if we are to be truly happy, we must follow our hearts and find our way alone. I learned that truth when I walked out of Menzoberranzan and confirmed my path when I arrived in Icewind Dale and found these wonderful friends. After the last brutal fight in Mithral Hall, when half of Menzoberranzan, it seemed, marched to destroy the dwarves, I knew that my path lay elsewhere, that I needed to journey, to find a new horizon on which to set my gaze. Catti-brie knew it too, and because I understood that her desire to go along was not in sympathy to my desires but true to her own heart, I welcomed the company.

We each have our own path to tread, and so I learned, painfully, that fateful morning in the mountains, that Wulfgar had found one that diverged from my own. How I wanted to stop him! How I wanted to plead with him or, if that failed, to beat him into unconsciousness and drag him back to the camp. When we parted, I felt a hole in my heart nearly as profound as that which I had felt when I first learned of his apparent death in the fight against the yochlol.

And then, after I walked away, pangs of guilt layered above the pain of loss. Had I let Wulfgar go so easily because of his relationship with Catti-brie? Was there some place within me that saw my barbarian friend's return as a hindrance to a relationship that I had been building with the woman since we had ridden from Mithral Hall together?

The guilt could find no true hold and was gone by the time I rejoined my companions. As I had my road to walk, and now Wulfgar his, so too would Catti-brie find hers. With me? With Wulfgar? Who could know? But whatever her road, I would not try to alter it in such a manner. I did not let Wulfgar go easily for any sense of personal gain. Not at all, for indeed my heart weighed heavy. No, I let Wulfgar go without much of an argument because I knew that there was nothing I, or our other friends, could do to heal the wounds within him. Nothing I could say to him could bring him solace, and if Catti-brie had begun to make any progress, then surely it had been destroyed in the flick of Wulfgar's fist slamming into her face.

Partly it was fear that drove Wulfgar from us. He believed that he could not control the demons within him and that, in the grasp of those painful recollections, he might truly hurt one of us. Mostly, though, Wulfgar left us because of shame. How could he face Bruenor again after striking Catti-brie? How could he face Catti-brie? What words might he say in apology when in truth, and he knew it, it very well might happen again? And beyond that one act, Wulfgar perceived himself as weak because the images of Errtu's legacy were so overwhelming him. Logically, they were but memories and nothing tangible to attack the strong man. To Wulfgar's pragmatic view of the world, being defeated by mere memories equated to great weakness. In his culture, being defeated in battle is no cause for shame, but running from battle is the highest dishonor.

Along that same line of reasoning, being unable to defeat a great monster is acceptable, but being defeated by an intangible thing such as a memory equates with cowardice.

He will learn better, I believe. He will come to understand the he should feel no shame for his inability to cope with the persistent horrors and temptations of Errtu and the Abyss. And then, when he relieves himself from the burden of shame, he will find a way to truly overcome those horrors and dismiss his guilt over the temptations. Only then will he return to Icewind Dale, to those who love him and who will welcome him back eagerly.

Only then.

That is my hope, not my expectation. Wulfgar ran off into the wilds, into the Spine of the World, where yetis and giants and goblin tribes make their homes, where wolves will take their food as they find it, whether hunting a deer or a man. I do not honestly know if he means to come out of the mountains back to the tundra he knows well, or to the more civilized southland, or if he will wander the high and dangerous trails, daring death in an attempt to restore some of the courage he believes he has lost. Or perhaps he will tempt death too greatly, so that it will finally win out and put an end to his pain.

That is my fear.

I do not know. We each have our own roads to tread, and Wulfgar has found his, and it is a path, I understand, that is not wide enough for a companion.

—Drizzt Do'Urden

Chapter 8
INADVERTENT SIGNALS

They moved somberly, for the thrill of adventure and the joy of being reunited and on the road again had been stolen by Wulfgar's departure. When he returned to camp and explained the barbarian's absence, Drizzt had been truly surprised by the reactions of his companions. At first, predictably, Catti-brie and Regis had screamed that they must go and find the man, while Bruenor just grumbled about "stupid humans." Both the halfling and the woman had calmed quickly, though, and it turned out to be Catti-brie's voice above all the others proclaiming that Wulfgar needed to choose his own course. She was not bitter about the attack and to her credit showed no anger toward the barbarian at all.

But she knew. Like Drizzt, she understood that the inner demons tormenting Wulfgar could not be excised with comforting words from friends, or even through the fury of battle. She had tried and had thought that she was making some progress, but in the end it had become painfully apparent to her that she could do nothing to help the man, that Wulfgar had to help himself.

And so they went on, the four friends and Guenhwyvar, keeping their word to guide Camlaine's wagon out of the dale and along the south road.

That night, Drizzt found Catti-brie on the eastern edge of the encampment, staring out into the blackness, and it was not hard for the drow to figure out what she was hoping to spot.

"He will not return to us any time soon," Drizzt remarked quietly, moving to the woman's side.

Catti-brie glanced at him only briefly, then turned her eyes back to the dark silhouettes of the mountains.

There was nothing to see.

"He chose wrong," the woman said softly after several long and silent moments had slipped past. "I'm knowin' that he has to help himself, but he could've done that among his friends, not out in the wilds."

"He did not want us to witness his most personal battles," Drizzt explained.

"Ever was pride Wulfgar's greatest failing," Catti-brie quickly replied.

"That is the way of his people, the way of his father, and his father's father before him," the ranger said. "The tundra barbarians do not accept weakness in others or in themselves, and Wulfgar believes that his inability to defeat mere memories is naught more than weakness."

Catti-brie shook her head. She didn't have to speak the words aloud, for both she and Drizzt understood that the man was purely wrong in that belief, that, many times, the most powerful foes are those within.

Drizzt reached up then and brushed a finger gently along the side of Catti-brie's nose, the area that had swelled badly from Wulfgar's punch. Catti-brie winced at first, but it was only because she had not expected the touch, and not from any real pain.

"It's not so bad," she said.

"Bruenor might not agree with you," the drow replied.

That brought a smile to Catti-brie's face, for indeed, if Drizzt had brought Wulfgar back soon after the assault, it would have taken all of them to pull the vicious dwarf off the man. But even that had changed now, they both knew. Wulfgar had been as a son to Bruenor for many years, and the dwarf had been purely devastated, more so than any of the others, after the man's apparent death. Now, in the realization that Wulfgar's troubles had taken him from them again, Bruenor sorely missed the man, and surely would forgive him his strike against Catti-brie . . . as long as the barbarian was properly contrite. They all would have forgiven Wulfgar, completely and without judgment, and would have helped him in any way they could to overcome his emotional obstacles. That was the tragedy of it all, for they had no help to offer that would be of any real value.

Drizzt and Catti-brie sat together long into the night, staring at the empty tundra, the woman resting her head on the strong shoulder of the drow.

The next two days and nights on the road proved peacefully uneventful, except that Drizzt more than once spotted the tracks of Regis's giant friend, apparently shadowing their movements. Still, the behemoth made no approach near the camp, so the drow did not become overly concerned. By the middle of the third day after Wulfgar's departure, they came in sight of the city of Luskan.

"Your destination, Camlaine," the drow noted when the driver called out that he could see the distinctive skyline of Luskan, including the treelike structure that marked the city's wizard guild. "It has been our pleasure to travel with you."

"And eat your fine food!" Regis added happily, drawing a laugh from everyone.

"Perhaps if you are still in the southland when we return, and intent on heading back to the dale, we will accompany you again," Drizzt finished.

"And glad we will all be for the company," the merchant replied, warmly clasping the drow's hand. "Farewell, wherever your road may take you, though I offer the parting as a courtesy only, for I do not doubt that you shall fare well indeed! Let the monsters take note of your passing and hide their heads low."

The wagon rolled away, down the fairly smooth road to Luskan. The four friends watched it for a long time.

"We could go in with him," Regis offered. "You are known well enough down there, I would guess," he added to the drow. "Your heritage should not bring us any problems . . ."

Drizzt shook his head before the halfling even finished the thought. "I can indeed walk freely through Luskan," he said, "but my course, our course, is to the southeast. A long, long road lies ahead of us."

"But in Luskan—" Regis started.

"Rumblebelly's thinkin' that me boy might be in there," Bruenor bluntly cut in. From the dwarf's tone it seemed that he, too, considered following the merchant wagon.

"He might indeed," Drizzt said. "And I hope that he is, for Luskan is not nearly as dangerous as the wilds of the Spine of the World."

Bruenor and Regis looked at him curiously, for if he agreed with their reasoning, why weren't they following the merchant?

"If Wulfgar's in Luskan, then better by far that we're turning away now," Catti-brie answered for Drizzt. "We're not wanting to find him now."

"What're ye sayin'?" the flustered dwarf demanded.

"Wulfgar walked away from us," Drizzt reminded. "Of his own accord. Do you believe that three days' time has changed anything?"

"We're not for knowin' unless we ask," said Bruenor, but his tone was less argumentative, and the brutal truth of the situation began to sink in. Of course Bruenor, and all of them, wanted to find Wulfgar and wanted the man to recant his decision to leave. But of course that would not happen.

"If we find him now, we'll only push him further from us," Catti-brie said.

"He will grow angry at first because he will see us as meddling," Drizzt agreed. "And then, when his anger at last fades, if it ever does, he will be even more ashamed of his actions."

Bruenor snorted and threw his hands up in defeat.

They all took a last look at Luskan, hoping that Wulfgar was there, then they walked past the place. They headed southeast, flanking the city, then down the southern road with a week's travel before them to the city of Waterdeep. There they hoped to ride with a merchant ship to the south, to Baldur's Gate, and then up river to the city of Iriaebor. There they would take to the open road again, across several hundred miles of the Shining Plains to Caradoon and the Spirit Soaring. Regis had planned the journey, using maps and merchant sources back in Bryn Shander. The halfling had chosen Waterdeep as their best departure point over the closer Luskan because ships left Waterdeep's great harbor every day, with many traveling to Baldur's Gate. In truth, he wasn't sure, nor were any of the others, if this was the best course or not. The maps available in Icewind Dale were far from complete, and far from current. Drizzt and Catti-brie, the only two of the group to have traveled to the Spirit Soaring, had done so magically, with no understanding of the lay of the land.

Still, despite the careful planning the halfling had done, each of them began doubting their ambitious travel plans throughout that day as they passed the city. Those plans had been formed out of a love for the road and adventure, a desire to take in the sights of their grand world, and a supreme confidence in their abilities to get through. Now, though, with Wulfgar's departure, that love and confidence had been severely shaken. Perhaps they would be better off going into Luskan to the notable wizards' guild and hiring a mage to magically contact Cadderly so that the powerful cleric might wind walk to them and finish this business quickly. Or perhaps the Lords of Waterdeep, renowned throughout the lands for their dedication to justice and their power to carry it out, would take the crystal artifact off the companions' hands and, as Cadderly had vowed, find the means to destroy it.

If any of the four had spoken aloud their mounting doubts about the journey that morning, the trip might have been abandoned. But because of their confusion over Wulfgar's departure, and because none of them wanted to admit that they could not focus on another mission while their dear friend was in danger, they held their tongues, sharing thoughts but not words. By the time the sun disappeared into the vast waters to the west, the city of Luskan and the hopes of finding Wulfgar were long out of sight.

Regis's giant friend, though, continued to shadow their movements. Even as Bruenor, Catti-brie, and the halfling prepared the camp, Drizzt and Guenhwyvar came upon the huge tracks, leading down to a copse of trees less than three hundred yards from the bluff they had chosen as a sight. Now the giant's movements could no longer be dismissed as coincidence, for they had left the Spine of the World far behind, and few giants ever wandered into this civilized region where townsfolk would form militias and hunt them down whenever they were spotted.

By the time Drizzt got back to camp, the halfling was fast asleep, several empty plates scattered about his bedroll. "It is time we confront our large shadow," the ranger explained to the other two as he moved over and gave Regis a good shake.

"So ye're meanin' to let us in on yer battle plans this time," Bruenor replied sarcastically.

"I hope there will be no battle," the drow answered. "To our knowledge, this particular giant has posed no threat to wagons rolling along the road in Icewind Dale, and so I find no reason to fight the creature. Better that we convince it to go back to its home without drawing sword."

A sleepy-eyed Regis sat up and glanced around, then rolled back down under his covers—almost, for quick-handed Drizzt caught him halfway back to the comfort zone and roughly pulled him to his feet.

"Not my watch!" the halfling complained.

"You brought the giant to us, and so you shall convince him to leave," the drow replied.

"The giant?" Regis asked, still not catching on to the meaning of it all.

"Yer big friend," Bruenor explained. "He's followin' us, and we're thinking it's past time he goes home. Now, ye come along with yer tricky gem and make him leave, or we'll cut him down where he stands."

Regis's expression showed that he didn't much like that prospect. The giant had served him well in the fight, and he had to admit a certain fondness for the big brute. He shook his head vigorously, trying to clear the cobwebs, then patted his full belly and retrieved his shoes. Even though he was moving as fast as he ever moved, the others were already out of the encampment by the time he was ready to follow.

Drizzt was first into the copse, with Guenhwyvar flanking him. The drow stayed along the ground, picking a clear route away from dried leaves and snapping twigs, silent as a shadow, while Guenhwyvar sometimes padded along the ground and sometimes took to the secure low branches of thick trees. The giant was making no real effort to conceal itself and even had a fairly large fire going. The light guided the two companions and then the other three trailing them.

Still a dozen yards away, Drizzt heard the rhythmic snoring, but then, barely two steps later he heard a loud rustle as the giant apparently woke up and jumped to his feet. Drizzt froze in place and scanned the area, seeking any scouts who might have alerted the behemoth, but there was nothing, no evident creatures and no noise at all save the continuous gentle hissing of the wind through the new leaves.

Convinced that the giant was alone, the drow moved on, coming to a clearing. The fire and the behemoth, and it was indeed Junger, were plainly visible across the way. Out stepped Drizzt, and the giant hardly seemed surprised.

"Strange that we should meet again," the drow remarked, resting his forearms comfortably across the hilts of his sheathed weapons and assuming an unthreatening posture. "I had thought you returned to your mountain home."

"It bade me otherwise," Junger said, and again the drow was taken aback by the giant's command of language and sophisticated dialect.

"It?" the drow asked.

"Some calls cannot be unanswered, you understand," the giant replied.

"Regis," Drizzt called back over his shoulder, and he heard the commotion as his three friends, all of them quiet by the standards of their respective races but clamorous indeed by the standards of the dark elf, moved through the forest behind him. Hardly turning his head, for he did not want to further alert the giant, Drizzt did take note of Guenhwyvar, padding quietly along a branch to the behemoth's left flank. She stopped within easy springing distance of the giant's head. "The halfling will bring it," Drizzt explained. "Perhaps then the call will be better understood and abated."

The giant's big face screwed up with confusion. "The halfling?" he echoed skeptically.

Bruenor crashed through the brush to stand beside the drow, then Catti-brie behind him, her deadly bow in hand, and finally, Regis, coming out complaining about a scratch one branch had just inflicted on his cherubic face.

"It bade Junger to follow us," the drow explained, indicating the ruby pendant. "Show him a better course."

Smiling ear to ear, Regis stepped forward and pulled out the chain and ruby pendant, starting the mesmerizing gem on a gentle swing.

"Get back, little rodent," the giant boomed, averting his eyes from the halfling. "I'll tolerate none of your tricks this time!"

"But it's calling to you," Regis protested, holding the gem out even further and flicking it with a finger of his free hand to set it spinning, its many facets catching the firelight in a dazzling display.

"So it is," the giant replied. "Thus my business is not with you."

"But I hold the gem."

"Gem?" the giant echoed. "What do I care for any such meager treasures when measured against the promises of Crenshinibon?"

That proclamation widened the eyes of the companions, except for Regis, who was so entranced by his own gem-twirling that the behemoth's words didn't even register with him. "Oh, but just look at how it spins!" he said happily. "It calls to you, its dearest friend, and bids you—" Regis ended with a squeaky "Hey!" as Bruenor rushed up and yanked him backward so forcefully that it took him right off the ground. He landed beside Drizzt and skittered backward in a futile attempt to hold his balance, but tripped anyway, tumbling hard into the brush.

Junger came forward in a rush, reaching as if to slap the dwarf aside, but a silver-streaking arrow sizzled past his head, and the giant jolted upright, startled.

"The next one takes yer face," Catti-brie promised.

Bruenor eased back to join the woman and the drow.

"You have foolishly followed an errant call," Drizzt said calmly, trying very hard to keep the situation under control. The ranger held no love for giants, to be sure, but he almost felt sympathy for this poor misguided fool. "Crenshinibon? What is Crenshinibon?"

"Oh, you know well," the giant replied. "You above all others, dark elf. You are the possessor, but Crenshinibon rejects you and has selected me as your successor."

"All that I truly know about you is your name, giant," the drow gently replied. "Ever has your kind been at war with the smaller folk of the world, and yet I offer you this one chance to turn back for the Spine of the World, back to your home."

"And so I shall," the giant replied with a chuckle, crossing his ankles calmly and leaning on a tree for support. "As soon as I have Crenshinibon." The cunning behemoth exploded into motion, tearing a thick limb from the tree and launching it at the friends, mostly to force Catti-brie and that nasty bow to dive aside.

Junger strode forward and was stunned to find the drow already in swift motion, scimitars drawn, rushing between his legs and slicing away.

Even as the giant turned to catch Drizzt as he rushed out behind him, Bruenor came in hard. The dwarf's axe chopped for the tendon at the back of the behemoth's ankle, and then, suddenly, six hundred pounds of panther crashed against the turning giant's shoulder and head, knocking him off-balance. He would have held his footing, except that Catti-brie drove an arrow into his lower back. Howling and spinning, Junger went down. Drizzt, Bruenor and Guenhwyvar all skittered out of harm's way.

"Go home!" Drizzt called to the brute as he struggled to his hands and knees.

With a defiant roar, the giant dived out at the drow, arms outstretched. He pulled his arms in fast, both hands suddenly bleeding from deep scimitar gashes, and then he jerked in pain as Catti-brie's next arrow drove into his hip.

Drizzt started to call out again, wanting to reason with the brute, but Bruenor had heard enough. The dwarf rushed up the prone giant's back, quick-stepping to hold his balance as the creature tried to roll him off. The dwarf leaped over the giant's turning shoulder, coming down squarely atop his collarbone. Bruenor's axe came down fast, quicker to the strike than the giant's reaching hands. The axe cut deep into Junger's face.

Huge hands clamped around Bruenor, but they had little strength left. Guenhwyvar leaped in and caught one of the giant's arms, bringing it down under her weight, pinning the hand with claws and teeth. Catti-brie blew the other arm from the dwarf with a perfectly aimed shot.

Bruenor held his ground, leaning down on the embedded axe, and at last, the giant lay still.

Regis came out of the brush and gave a kick at the branch the giant had thrown their way. "Worms in an apple!" he complained. "Why'd you kill him?"

"Ye're seein' a choice?" Bruenor called back incredulously, then he braced himself and tugged his axe from the split head. "I'm not for talking to five thousand pounds of enemy."

"I take no pleasure in that kill," Drizzt admitted. He wiped his blades on the fallen behemoth's tunic, then slid them into their sheaths. "Better for all of us that the giant simply went home."

"And I could have convinced him to do so," Regis argued.

"No," the drow answered. "Your pendant is powerful, I do not doubt, but it has no strength over one entranced by Crenshinibon." As he spoke, he opened his belt pouch and produced the artifact, the famed crystal shard.

"Ye hold it out, and its call'll be all the louder," Bruenor said grimly. "I'm thinkin' we might be finding a long road ahead of us."

"Let it bring the monsters in," Catti-brie said. "It'll make our task in killing them all the easier."

The coldness of her tone caught them all by surprise, but only for the moment it took them to look back at her and see the bruise on her face and remember the cause of her bad mood.

"Ye notice that the damned thing's not working on any of us," the woman reasoned. "So it seems that any falling under its spell are deservin' what they'll find at our hands."

"It does appear that Crenshinibon's power to corrupt extends only to those already of an evil weal," Drizzt agreed.

"And so our road'll be a bit more exciting," Catti-brie said. She didn't bother to add that in this light, she wished Wulfgar was with them. She knew the others were no doubt thinking the exact same thing.

They searched the giant's camp, then turned back to their own fire. Given the new realization that the crystal shard might be working against them, might be reaching out to any nearby monsters in an attempt to get free of the friends, they decided to double their watches from that point forward, two asleep and two awake.

Regis was not pleased.

Chapter 9
GAINING APPROVAL

From the shadows he watched the wizard walk slowly through the door. Other voices followed LaValle in from the corridor, but the wizard hardly acknowledged them, just shut the door and moved to his private stock liquor cabinet at the side of the audience room, lighting only a single candle atop it.

Entreri clenched his hands eagerly, torn as to whether he should confront the wizard verbally or merely kill the man for not informing him of Dog Perry's attack.

Cup in one hand, burning taper in the other, LaValle moved from the cabinet to a larger standing candelabra. The room brightened with each touch as another candle flared to life. Behind the occupied wizard, Entreri stepped into the open.

His warrior senses put him on his guard immediately. Something—but what?—at the very edges of his consciousness alerted him. Perhaps it had to do with LaValle's comfortable demeanor or some barely perceptible extraneous noise.

LaValle turned around then and jumped back just a bit upon seeing Entreri standing in the middle of the room. Again the assassin's perceptions nagged at him. The wizard didn't seem frightened or surprised enough.

"Did you believe that Dog Perry would defeat me?" Entreri asked sarcastically.

"Dog Perry?" LaValle came back. "I have not seen the man—"

"Do not lie to me," Entreri calmly interrupted. "I have known you too long, LaValle, to believe such ignorance of you. You watched Dog Perry, without doubt, as you know all the movements of all the players."

"Not all, obviously," the wizard replied dryly, indicating the uninvited man.

Entreri wasn't so sure of that last claim, but he let it pass. "You agreed to warn me when Dog Perry came after me," he said loudly. If the wizard had guild bodyguards nearby, let them hear of his duplicity. "Yet there he was, dagger in hand, with no prior warning from my friend LaValle."

LaValle gave a great sigh and moved to the side, slumping into a chair. "I did indeed know," he admitted. "But I could not act upon that knowledge," he added quickly, for the assassin's eyes narrowed dangerously. "You must understand. All contact with you is forbidden."

"Kelp-enwalled," Entreri remarked.

LaValle held his hands out helplessly.

"I also know that LaValle rarely adheres to such orders," Entreri went on.

"This one was different," came another voice. A slender man, well dressed and coifed, entered the room from the wizard's study.

Entreri's muscles tensed; he had just checked out that room, along with the other two in the wizard's suite, and no one had been in there. Now he knew beyond doubt that he had been expected.

"My guildmaster," LaValle explained. "Quentin Bodeau."

Entreri didn't blink; he had already guessed that much.

"This kelp-enwalling order came not from any particular guild, but from the three most prominent," Quentin Bodeau clarified. "To go against it would have meant eradication."

"Any magical attempt I might have made would have been detected," LaValle tried to explain. He gave a chuckle, trying to break the tension. "I did not believe it would matter, in any case," he said. "I knew that Dog Perry would prove no real test for you."

"If that is so, then why was he allowed to come after me?" Entreri asked, aiming the question at Bodeau.

The guildmaster only shrugged and said, "Rarely have I been able to control all the movements of that one."

"Let that bother you no more," Entreri replied grimly.

Bodeau managed a weak smile. "You must appreciate our position . . ." he started to say.

"I am to believe the word of the man who ordered me murdered?" Entreri asked incredulously.

"I did not—" Bodeau began to argue before being cut off by yet another voice from the wizard's study, a woman's voice.

"If we believed that Quentin Bodeau, or any other ranking member of his guild knew of and approved of the attack, this guild house would be empty of living people."

A tall, dark-haired woman came through the door, flanked by a muscular warrior with a curving black mustache and a more slender man, if it was a man, for Entreri could hardly make out any features under the cowl of the dark cloak. A pair of armored guards strode in behind the trio, and though the last one through the door shut it behind him, Entreri understood that there was likely another one about, probably another wizard. There was no way such a group could have been concealed in the other room, even from his casual glance, without magical aid. Besides, he knew, this group was too comfortable. Even if they were all skilled with weapons, they could not be confident that they alone could bring Entreri down.

"I am Sharlotta Vespers," the woman said, her icy eyes flashing. "I give you Kadran Gordeon and Hand, my fellow lieutenants in the guild of Pasha Basadoni. Yes, he lives still and is glad to see you well."

Entreri knew that to be a lie. If Basadoni were alive the guild would have contacted him much earlier, and in a less dangerous situation.

"Are you affiliated?" Sharlotta asked.

"I was not when I left Calimport, and I only recently came back to the city," the assassin answered.

"Now you are affiliated," Sharlotta purred, and Entreri understood that he was in no position to deny her claim.

* * * * *

So he would not be killed—not now, at least. He would not have to spend his nights looking over his shoulder for would-be assassins nor deal with the impertinent advances of fools like Dog Perry. The Basadoni Guild had claimed him as their own, and though he would be able to go and take jobs wherever he decided, as long as they did not involve the murder of anyone connected with Pasha Basadoni, his primary contacts would be Kadran Gordeon, whom he did not trust, and Hand.

He should have been pleased at the turn of events, he knew, sitting quietly on the roof of the Copper Ante late that night. He couldn't have expected a better course.

And yet, for some reason that he could hardly fathom, Entreri was not pleased in the least. He had his old life back, if he wanted it. With his skills, he knew he could soon return to the glories he had once known. And yet he now understood the limitations of those glories and knew that while he could easily re-ascend to the highest level of assassin in Calimport, that level would hardly be enough to satisfy the emptiness he felt within.

He simply did not wish to go back to his old ways of murder for money. It was no bout of conscience—nothing like that!—but no thought of that former life sparked any excitement within the man.

Ever the pragmatist, Entreri decided to play it one hour at a time. He went over the side of the roof, silent and sure-footed, picking his way down to the street, then entered through the front door.

All eyes focused on him, but he hardly cared as he made his way across the common room to the door at the back. One halfling approached him there, as if to stop him, but a glare from Entreri backed the little one off, and the assassin pushed through.

Again the sight of the enormously fat Dondon assaulted him profoundly.

"Artemis!" Dondon said happily, though Entreri did note a bit of tension creeping into the halfling's voice, a common reaction whenever the assassin arrived unannounced at anyone's doorstep. "Come in, my friend. Sit and eat. Partake of good company."

Entreri looked at the heaps of half-eaten sweets and at the two painted female halflings flanking the bloated wretch. He did sit down a safe distance away, though he moved none of the many platters in front of him narrowing his eyes as one of the female halflings tried to approach.

"You must learn to relax and enjoy those fruits your work has provided," Dondon said. "You are back with Basadoni, so 'tis said, and so you are free."

Entreri noted that the irony of that statement was apparently lost on the halfling.

"What good is all of your difficult and dangerous work if you cannot learn to relax and enjoy those pleasures your labors might buy for you?" Dondon asked.

"How did it happen?" Entreri asked bluntly.

Dondon stared at him, obvious confusion splayed on his sagging face.

In explanation, Entreri looked all around, motioning to the plates, to the whores, and to Dondon's massive belly.

Dondon's expression soured. "You know why I am in here," he remarked quietly, all the bounce having left his tone.

"I know why you came in here . . . to hide . . . and I agree with that decision," Entreri replied. "But why?" Again he let the halfling follow his gaze to all the excess, plate by plate, whore by whore. "Why this?"

"I choose to enjoy . . ." Dondon started, but Entreri would hear none of that.

"If I could offer you back your old life, would you take it?" the assassin asked.

Dondon stared at him blankly.

"If I could change the word on the street so that Dondon could walk free of the Copper Ante, would Dondon be pleased?" Entreri pressed. "Or is Dondon pleased with the excuse?"

"You speak in riddles."

"I speak the truth," Entreri shot back, trying to look the halfling in the eye, though the sight of those drooping, sleepy lids surely revolted him. He could hardly believe his own level of anger in looking at Dondon. A part of him wanted to draw out his dagger and cut the wretch's heart out.

But Artemis Entreri did not kill for passion, and he held that part in check.

"Would you go back?" he asked slowly, emphasizing every word.

Dondon didn't reply, didn't blink, but in the nonresponse, Entreri had his answer, the one he had feared the most.

The room's door swung open, and Dwahvel entered. "Is there a problem in here, Master Entreri?" she asked sweetly.

Entreri climbed to his feet and moved for the open door. "None for me," he replied, moving past.

Dwahvel caught him by the arm—a dangerous move indeed! Fortunately for her, Entreri was too absorbed in his contemplation of Dondon to take affront.

"About our deal," the female halfling remarked. "I may have need of your services."

Entreri spent a long while considering those words, wondering why, for some reason, they so assaulted him. He had enough to think about already without having Dwahvel pressing her ridiculous needs upon him. "And what did you give to me in exchange for these services you so desire?" he asked.

"Information," the halfling replied. "As we agreed."

"You told me of the kelp-enwalling, hardly something I could not have discerned on my own," Entreri replied. "Other than that, Dwahvel was of little use to me, and that measure I surely can repay."

The halfling's mouth opened as if she meant to protest, but Entreri just turned away and walked across the common room.

"You may find my doors closed to you," Dwahvel called after him.

In truth, Entreri hardly cared, for he didn't expect that he would desire to see wretched Dondon again. Still, more for effect than any practical gain, he did turn back to let his dangerous gaze settle over the halfling. "That would not be wise," was all he offered before sweeping out of the room and back onto the dark street, then back to the solitude of the rooftops.

Up there, after many minutes of concentration, he came to understand why he so hated Dondon. Because he saw himself. No, he would never allow himself to become so bloated, for gluttony had never been one of his weaknesses, but what he saw was a creature beaten by the weight of life itself, a creature that had surrendered to despair. In Dondon's case it had been simple fear that had defeated him, that had locked him in a room and buried him in lust and gluttony.

In Entreri's case, would it be simple apathy?

He stayed on the roof all the night, but he did not find his answers.

* * * * *

The knock came in the correct sequence, two raps, then three, then two again, so he knew even as he dragged himself out of his bed that it was the Basadoni Guild come calling. Normally Entreri would have taken precautions anyway—normally he would not have slept through half the day—but he did nothing now, didn't even retrieve his dagger. He just went to the door and, without even asking, pulled it open.

He didn't recognize the man standing there, a young and nervous fellow with woolly black hair cut tight to his head, and dark, darting eyes.

"From Kadran Gordeon," the man explained, handing Entreri a rolled parchment.

"Hold!" Entreri said as the nervous young man turned and started away. The man's head spun back to regard the assassin, and Entreri noted one hand slipping under the folds of his light-colored robes, reaching for a weapon no doubt.

"Where is Gordeon?" Entreri asked. "And why did he not deliver this to me personally?"

"Please, good sir," the young man said in his thick Calimshite accent, bowing repeatedly. "I was only told to give that to you."

"By Kadran Gordeon?" Entreri asked.

"Yes," the man said, nodding wildly.

Entreri shut his door, then heard the running footsteps of the relieved man outside retreating down the hall and then the stairs at full speed.

He stood there, considering the parchment and the delivery. Gordeon hadn't even come to him personally, and he understood why. To do so would have been too much an open show of respect. The lieutenants of the guild feared him—not that he would kill them, but more that he would ascend to a rank above them. Now, by using this inconsequential messenger, Gordeon was trying to show Entreri the true pecking order, one that had him just above the bottom rung.

With a resigned shake of his head, a helpless acceptance of the stupidity of it all, the assassin pulled the tie from the parchment and unrolled it. The orders were simple enough, giving a man's name and last known address, with instructions that he should be killed as soon as it could be arranged. That very night, if possible, the next day at the latest.

At the bottom was a last notation that the targeted man had no known guild affiliation, nor was he in particularly good standing with city or merchant guardsmen, nor did he have any known powerful friends or relatives.

Entreri considered that bit of news carefully. Either he was being set up against a very dangerous opponent, or, more likely, Gordeon had given him this pitifully easy hit to demean him, to lessen his credentials. In his former days in Calimport, Entreri's talents had been reserved for the killing of guildmasters or wizards, noblemen, and captains of the guard. Of course, if Gordeon and the other two lieutenants gave him any such difficult tasks and he proved successful, his standing would grow among the community and they would fear his quick ascension through the ranks.

No matter, he decided.

He took one last look at the listed address—a region of Calimport that he knew well—and went to retrieve his tools.

* * * * *

He heard the children crying nearby, for the hovel had only two rooms, and those separated by only a thick drapery. A very homely young woman—Entreri noted as he spied on her from around the edge of the drapery—tended to the children. She begged them to settle down and be quiet, threatening that their father would soon be home.

She came out of the back room a moment later, oblivious to the assassin as he crouched behind another curtain under a side window. Entreri cut a small hole in the drape and watched her movements as she went about her work. Everything was brisk and efficient; she was on edge, he knew.

The door, yet another drape, pushed aside and a young, skinny man entered, his face appearing haggard, eyes sunken back in his skull, several days of beard on his chin and cheeks.

"Did you find it?" the woman asked sharply.

The man shook his head, and it seemed to Entreri that his eyes drooped just a bit more.

"I begged you not to work with them!" the woman scolded. "I knew that no good—"

She stopped short as his eyes widened in horror. He saw, looking over her shoulder, the assassin emerging from behind the draperies. He turned as if to flee, but the woman looked back and cried out.

The man froze in place; he would not leave her.

Entreri watched it all calmly. Had the man continued his retreat, the assassin would have cut him down with a dagger throw before he ever got outside.

"Not my family," the man begged, turning back and walking toward Entreri, his hands out wide, palms open. "And not here."

"You know why I have come?" the assassin asked.

The woman began to cry, muttering for mercy, but her husband grabbed her gently but firmly and pulled her back, angling her for the children's room, then pushing her along.

"It was not my fault," the man said quietly when she was gone. "I begged Kadran Gordeon. I told him that I would somehow find the money."

The old Artemis Entreri would not have been intrigued at that point. The old Artemis Entreri would never even have listened to the words. The old Artemis Entreri would have just finished the task and walked out. But now he found that he was interested, mildly, and, as he had no other pressing business, he was in no hurry to finish.

"I will cause no trouble for you if you promise that you will not hurt my family," the man said.

"You believe that you could me cause trouble?" Entreri asked.

The helpless, pitiful man shook his head. "Please," he begged. "I only wished to show them a better life. I agreed to, even welcomed, the job of moving money from Docker's Street to the drop only because in those easy tasks I earned more than a month of labor can bring me in honest work."

Entreri had heard it all before, of course. So many times, fools—camels, they were called—joined into a guild, performing delivery tasks for what seemed to the simple peasants huge amounts of money. The guilds only hired the camels so that rival guilds would not know who was transporting the money. Eventually, though, the other guilds would figure out the routes and the camels, and would steal the shipment. Then the poor camels, if they survived the ambush, would be quickly eliminated by the guild that had hired them.

"You understood the danger of the company you kept," Entreri remarked.

The man nodded. "Only a few deliveries," he replied. "Only a few, and then I would quit."

Entreri laughed and shook his head, considering the fool's absurd plan. One could not "quit" as a camel. Anyone accepting the position would immediately learn too much to ever be allowed out of the guild. There were only two possibilities: first, that the camel would perform well enough and be lucky enough to earn a higher, more permanent position within the guild structure, and second, that the man or woman (for women were often used) would be slain in a raid or subsequently killed by the hiring guild.

"I beg of you, do not do it here," the man said at length. "Not where my wife will hear my last cries, not where my sons will find me dead."

Bitter bile found its way into the back of Entreri's throat. Never had he been so disgusted, never had he seen a more pitiful human being. He looked around again at the hovel, the rags posing as doors, as walls. There was a single plate, probably used for eating by the entire family, sitting on the single old bench in the room.

"How much do you owe?" he asked, and though he could hardly believe the words as he spoke them, he knew that he would not be able to bring himself to kill this wretch.

The man looked at him curiously. "A king's treasure," he said. "Near to thirty gold pieces."

Entreri nodded, then pulled a pouch from his belt, this one hidden around the back under his dark cloak. He felt the weight as he pulled it free and knew that it held at least fifty gold pieces, but he tossed it to the man anyway.

The stunned man caught it and stared at it so intently that Entreri feared his eyeballs would simply fall out of their sockets. Then he looked back to the assassin, his emotions too twisted and turned about for him to have any revealing expression at all on his face.

"On your word that you will not deal with any guilds again once your debt is paid," Entreri said. "Your wife and children deserve better."

The man started to reply, then fell to his knees and started to bow before his savior. Entreri turned about and swept angrily from the hovel, out into the dirty street.

He heard the man's calls following him, cries of thanks and mercy. In truth, and Entreri knew it, there had been no mercy in his actions. He cared nothing for the man or his ugly wife and undoubtedly ugly children. But still he could not kill this pitiful wretch, though he figured he would probably be doing the man a great service if he did put him out of his obvious misery. No, Entreri would not give Kadran Gordeon the satisfaction of putting him through such a dishonorable murder. A camel like this should be work for first year guild members, twelve-year-olds, perhaps, and for Kadran to give such an assignment to one of Entreri's reputation was surely a tremendous insult.

He would not play along.

He stormed down the street to his room at the inn where he collected all his things and set out at once, finally coming to the door of the Copper Ante. He had thought to merely press in, for no better reason than to show Dwahvel how ridiculous her threat to shut him out had been. But then he reconsidered and turned away, in no mood for any dealings with Dwahvel, in no mood for any dealings with anybody.

He found a small, nondescript tavern across town and took a room. Likely he was on the grounds of another guild, and if they found out who he was and who he was affiliated with there might be trouble.

He didn't care.

* * * * *

A day slipped by unremarkably, but that did little to put Entreri at ease. Much was happening, he knew, and all of it in quiet shadows. He had the wherewithal and understanding of those shadows to go out and discern much, but he hadn't the ambition to do so. He was in a mood to simply let things fall as they might.

He went down to the common room of the little inn that second night, taking his meal to an empty corner, eating alone and hearing nothing of the several conversations going on about the place. He did note the entrance of one character, though, a halfling, and the little folk were not common in this region of the city. Soon enough the halfling found him, taking a seat on the long bench opposite the table from the assassin.

"Good evening to you, fine sir," the little one said. "And how do you find your meal?"

Entreri studied the halfling, understanding that this one held no interest at all in his food. He looked for a weapon on the halfling, though he doubted that Dwahvel would ever be so bold as to move against him.

"Might I taste it?" the halfling said rather loudly, coming forward over the table.

Entreri, picking up the cues, held a spoon of the gruel up but did not extend his arm, allowing the halfling to inconspicuously move even closer.

"I've come from Dwahvel," the little one said as he moved in. "The Basadoni Guild seeks you, and they are in a foul mood. They know where you are and have received permission from the Rakers to come and collect you. Expect them this very night." The halfling took the bite as he finished, then moved back across the table, rubbing his belly.

"Tell Dwahvel that now I am in her debt," Entreri remarked. The little one, with a slight nod, moved back across the room and ordered a bowl of gruel. He took up a conversation with the innkeeper while he was waiting for it and ate it right at the bar, leaving Entreri to his thoughts.

He could flee, the assassin realized, but his heart was not in such a course. No, he decided, let them come and let this be done. He didn't think they meant to kill him in any case. He finished his meal and went back to his room to consider his options. First, he pulled a board from the inner wall, and in the cubby space between that and the outer wall, reaching down to a beam well below the floor in his room, he placed his fabulous jeweled dagger and many of his coins. Then he carefully replaced the board and replaced the dagger on his belt with another from his pack, one that somewhat resembled his signature dagger but without the powerful enchantment. Then, more for appearances than as any deterrent, he wired a basic dart trap about his door and moved across the room, settling into the one chair in the place. He took out some dice and began throwing them on the small night table beside the chair, making up games and passing the hours.

It was late indeed when he heard the first footsteps coming up the stairs—a man obviously trying to be stealthy but making more noise than the skilled Entreri would make even if he were walking normally. Entreri listened more carefully as the walking ceased, and he caught the scrape of a thin slice of metal moving about the crack between the door and the jamb. A fairly skilled thief could get through his impromptu trap in a matter of a couple of minutes, he knew, so he put his hands behind his head and leaned back against the wall.

All the noise stopped, a long and uncomfortable silence.

Entreri sniffed the air; something was burning. For a moment, he thought they might be razing the building around him, but then he recognized the smell, that of burning leather, and as he shifted to look down at his own belt he felt a sharp pain on his collarbone. The chain of a necklace he wore—one that held several lock picks cunningly designed as ornaments—had slipped off his shirt and onto his bare skin.

Only then did the assassin understand that all of his metallic items had grown red hot.

Entreri jumped up and tore the necklace from his neck, then deftly, with a twist of his wrist, dropped his belt and the heated dagger to the floor.

The door burst in, a Basadoni soldier rolling to either side and a third man, crossbow leveled, rushing between them.

He didn't fire, though, nor did the others, their swords in hand, charge in.

Kadran Gordeon walked in behind the bowman.

"A simple knock would have proven as effective," Entreri said dryly, looking down at his glowing equipment. The dagger caused the wood of the floor to send up a trail of black smoke.

In response, Gordeon threw a coin at Entreri's feet, a strange golden coin imprinted with the unicorn head emblem on the side showing to the assassin.

Entreri looked up at Gordeon and merely shrugged.

"The camel was to be killed," Gordeon said.

"He was not worth the effort."

"And that is for you to decide?" the Basadoni lieutenant asked incredulously.

"A minor decision, compared to what I once—"

"Ah!" Gordeon interrupted dramatically. "Therein lies the flaw, Master Entreri. What you once knew, or did, or were told to do, is irrelevant, you see. You are no guildmaster, no lieutenant, not even a full soldier as of yet, and I doubt that ever you will be! You lost your nerve—as I thought you would. You are only gaining approval, and if you survive that time, perhaps, just perhaps, you will find your way back into complete acceptance within the guild."

"Gaining approval?" Entreri echoed with a laugh. "Yours?"

"Take him!" Gordeon instructed the two soldiers who had come in first. As they moved cautiously for the assassin Gordeon added, "The man you tried to save was executed, as were his wife and children."

Entreri hardly heard the words and hardly cared anyway, though he knew that Gordeon had ordered the extended execution merely to throw some pain his way. Now he had a bigger dilemma. Should he allow Gordeon to take him back to the guild, where he would no doubt be physically punished and then released?

No, he would not suffer such treatment by this man or any other. The muscles in his legs, so finely honed, tensed as the two approached, though Entreri seemed perfectly at ease, even held his empty arms out in an unthreatening posture.

The men, swords in hand, came in at his sides, reaching for those arms while the third soldier kept his crossbow steady, aimed at the assassin's heart.

Up into the air went Entreri, a great vertical spring, tucking his legs under him and then kicking out to the sides before the startled soldiers could react, connecting squarely on the faces of both the approaching men and sending them flying away. He did catch the one on his right as he landed, and pulled the man in quickly, just in time to serve as a shield for the firing crossbow. Then he tossed the groaning man to the ground.

"First mistake," he said to Gordeon as the lieutenant drew out a splendid-looking sabre. Off to the side the other kicked soldier climbed back to his feet, but the one on the floor in front of Entreri, a crossbow quarrel deep into his back, wasn't moving. The crossbowman worked hard on the crank, loading another bolt, but even more disturbing for Entreri was the fact that there was obviously a wizard nearby.

"Stay back," Gordeon ordered the man to the side. "I will finish this one."

"To make your reputation?" Entreri asked. "But I have no weapon. How will that sound on the streets of Calimport?"

"After you are dead we will place a weapon in your hand," Gordeon said with a wicked grin. "My men will insist that it was a fair fight."

"Second mistake," Entreri said under his breath, for indeed, it was a fairer fight than the skilled Kadran Gordeon could ever understand. The Basadoni lieutenant came in with a measured thrust, straight ahead, and Entreri slapped his forearm out to intercept, purposely missing the parry but skittering backward out of reach at the same time. Gordeon circle, and so did Entreri. Then the assassin came ahead in a short lunge and was forced back with a slice of the sabre, Gordeon taking care to allow no openings.

But Entreri had no intention of following through his movement anyway. He had only begun it so that he could slightly alter the angle of the circling, putting him in line for his next strike.

On came Gordeon, and Entreri leaped back. When Gordeon kept coming, the assassin went ahead in a short burst, forcing him into a cunning and dangerous parrying maneuver. But again, Entreri didn't follow through. He just fell back to the appropriate spot and, to the surprise of all in the room, stamped his foot hard on the floor.

"What?" Gordeon asked, shaking his head and looking about, for he didn't keep his eyes down at that stamping foot, didn't see the shock of the stamp lift the still-glowing necklace from the floor so that Entreri could hook it about his toe.

A moment later Gordeon came on hard, this time looking for the kill. Out snapped Entreri's foot, launching the necklace at the lieutenant's face. To his credit, the swift-handed Gordeon snapped his free hand across and caught the necklace—as Entreri had expected—but then how he howled, the glowing chain enwrapping his bare hand and digging a fiery line across his flesh.

Entreri was there in the blink of an eye. He slapped the lieutenant's sword arm out wide. Balling both fists, middle knuckles extended forward, he drove his knuckles simultaneously into the man's temples. Clearly dazed, his eyes glossed over, Gordeon's hands slipped to his sides and Entreri snapped his forehead right into the man's face. He caught Gordeon as he fell back and spun him about, then reached through his legs and caught him by one wrist. With a subtle turn to put Gordeon in line with the crossbowman, Entreri pulled hard, through and up, flipping Gordeon right into the startled soldier. The flipped man knocked the crossbow hard enough to dislodge the bolt.

The remaining swordsman came in hard from the side, but he was not a skilled fighter, even by Kadran Gordeon's standards. Entreri easily backed and dodged his awkward, too-far-ahead thrust, then stepped in quickly, before the man could retract and ready the blade. Reaching down and around to catch his sword arm by the wrist, Entreri lifted hard and stepped under that wrist, twisting the arm painfully and stealing the strength from it.

The man came ahead, thinking to grab on for dear life with his free hand. Entreri's palm slapped against the back of his twisted sword hand quicker than he could even comprehend, then bent the hand down low back over the wrist, stealing all strength and sending a wave of pain through the man. A simple slide of the hand had the sword free in Entreri's grasp, and a reversal of grip and deft twist brought it in line.

Entreri retracted his hand, stabbing the blade out and up behind him into the belly and up into the lungs of the hapless soldier.

Moving quickly, not even bothering to pull the sword back out, he spun on the man, thinking to throw him, too, at the crossbowman. And indeed that stubborn archer was once more setting the bolt in place. But a far more dangerous foe appeared, the unseen wizard, rushing down the hallway, robes flapping, across the door. Entreri saw the man lift something slender—a wand, he supposed—but then all he saw was a tumble of arms and legs as the skewered swordsman crashed into the wizard and both went flying away.

"Have I yet gained your approval?" Entreri yelled at the still dazed Gordeon, but he was moving even as he spoke, for the crossbowman had him dead and the wizard was fast regaining his footing. He felt the terrible flash of pain as a quarrel dug through his side, but he gritted his teeth and growled away the pain, putting his arms in front of his face and tucking his legs up defensively as he crashed through the wooden-latticed window, soaring down the ten feet to the street. He turned his legs as he hit, throwing himself into a sidelong roll, and then another to absorb the shock of the fall. He was up and running, not surprised at all when another crossbow quarrel, fired from a completely different direction, embedded itself into the wall right beside him.

All the area erupted with movement as Basadoni soldiers came out of every conceivable hiding place.

Entreri sprinted down one alley, leaped right over a huge man bending low in an attempt to tackle him at the waist, then cut fast around a building. Up to the roof he went, quick as a cat, then across, leaping another alley to another roof, and so on.

He went down the main street, for he knew that his pursuers were expecting him to drop into an alley. He went up fast on the side of one wall, expertly setting himself there, arms and legs splayed wide to find tentative holds and to blend with the contours of the building.

Cries of "Find him!" echoed all about, and many soldiers ran right below his perch, but those cries diminished as the night wore on. Fortunately so for Entreri, who, though he was not losing much blood outwardly, understood that his wound was serious, perhaps even mortal. Finally he was able to slide down from his perch, hardly finding the remaining strength to even stand. He put a hand to his side and felt the warm blood, thick in the folds of his cloak, and felt, too, the very back edge of the deeply embedded quarrel.

He could hardly draw breath now. He knew what that meant.

Luck was with him when he got back to the inn, for the sun had not yet come up, and though there were obviously Basadoni soldiers within the place, few were about the immediate area. Entreri found the window of his room easily enough from the broken wood on the ground and calculated the height of his hidden store. He had to be quiet, for he heard voices, Gordeon's among them, from within his room. Up he went, finding a secure perch, trying hard not to groan, though in truth he wanted to scream from the pain.

He worked the old, weather-beaten wood slowly and quietly until he could pull enough away to retrieve his dagger and small pouch.

"He had to have some magic about him!" he heard Gordeon scream. "Cast your detection again!"

"There is no magic, Master Gordeon," came another voice, the wizard's obviously. "If he had any, then likely he sold it or gave it away before he ever came to this place."

Despite his agony, Entreri managed a smile as he heard Gordeon's subsequent growl and kick. No magic indeed, because they had searched in his room only and not the wall of the room below.

Dagger in hand, the assassin made his way along the still-quiet streets. He hoped to find a Basadoni soldier about, one deserving his wrath, but in truth he doubted he could even muster the strength to beat a novice fighter. What he found instead was a pair of drunks, laying against the side of a building, one sleeping, the other talking to himself.

Silent as death, the assassin stalked in. His jeweled dagger possessed a particularly useful magic, for it could steal the life of a victim and give that energy to its wielder.

Entreri took the talking drunk first, and when he was finished, feeling so much stronger, he bit down hard on a fold of his cloak and yanked the crossbow bolt from his side, nearly fainting as waves of agony assaulted him.

He steadied himself, though, and fell over the sleeping drunk.

He walked out of the alley soon after, showing no signs that he had been so badly wounded. He felt strong again and almost hoped he would find Kadran Gordeon still in the area.

But the fight had only begun, he knew, and despite his supreme skills, he remembered well the extent of the Basadoni Guild and understood that he was sorely overmatched.

* * * * *

They had watched those intent on killing him enter the inn. They had watched him come crashing through the window in full flight, then run on into the shadows. With eyes superior to those of the Basadoni soldiers, they had spotted him splayed on the wall and silently applauded his stealthy trick. And now, with some measure of relief and many nods that their leader had chosen wisely, they watched him exit the alley. And even he, Artemis Entreri, assassin of assassins, had no idea they were about.

Chapter 10
UNEXPECTED AND
UNSATISFYING VENGEANCE

ulfgar moved along the foothills of the Spine of the World easily and swiftly, sincerely hoping that some monster would find him and attack that he might release the frustrating rage boiling within him. On several occasions he found tracks, and he followed them, but he was no ranger. Though he could survive well enough in the harsh climate, his tracking skills were nowhere near as strong as those of his drow friend.

Nor was his sense of direction. When he came over one ridge the very next day, he was surprised indeed to see that he had cut diagonally right through the corner of the great mountain range, for from this high vantage point all the southland seemed to spread wide before him. Wulfgar looked back to the mountains, thinking that his chances for finding a fight would be much better in there, but inevitably his gaze swung back to the open fields, the dark clusters of forest, and the many long and unknown roads. He felt a pull in his heart, a longing for distance and open expanses, a desire to break the bounds of his boxed-in life in Icewind Dale. Perhaps out there he might find new experiences that would allow him to dismiss all the tumult of images that whirled in his thoughts. Perhaps divorced from the everyday familiar routines he could also find distance from the horrors of his memories of the Abyss.

Nodding to himself, Wulfgar started down the steep southern expanse. He found another set of tracks—orc, most likely—a couple hours later, but this time he passed them by. He was out of the mountains as the sun disappeared below the western horizon. He stood watching the sunset. Great orange and red flames gathered in the bellies of dark clouds, filling the western sky with brilliant striped patterns. The occasional twinkling star became visible against the pale blue wherever the clouds broke apart. He held that pose as all color faded, as darkness crept across the fields and the sky, broken clouds rushing past overhead. Stars seemed to blink on and off. This was the moment of renewal, Wulfgar decided. This was the moment of his rebirth, a clean beginning for a man alone in the world, a man determined to focus on the present and not the past, determined to let the future sort itself out.

He moved away from the mountains and camped under the spreading boughs of a fir tree. Despite his determination, his nightmares found him there.

Still, the next day Wulfgar's stride was long and swift, covering the miles, following the wind or a bird's flight or the bank of a spring creek.

He found plenty of game and plenty of berries. Each passing day he felt as though his stride was less shackled by his past, and each night the terrible dreams seemed to grab a him a bit less.

But then one day he came upon a curious totem, a low pole set in the ground with its top carved to resemble the pegasus, the winged horse, and suddenly Wulfgar found himself vaulted back into a very distinct memory, an incident that had occurred many years before when he was on the road with Drizzt, Bruenor, and Regis seeking the dwarf's ancestral home of Mithral Hall. Part of him wanted to turn away from that totem, to run far from this place, but one particular memory, a vow of vengeance, nagged at him. Hardly registering the movements, Wulfgar found a recent trail and followed it, soon coming to a hillock, and from the top of that bluff he spied the encampment, a cluster of deerskin tents with people, tall and strong and dark-haired, moving all about.

"Sky Ponies," Wulfgar whispered, remembering well the barbarian tribe that had come into a battle he and his friends had fought against an orc group. After the orcs had been cut down, Wulfgar, Bruenor, and Regis had been taken prisoner. They had been treated fairly well, and Wulfgar had been offered a challenge of strength, which he easily won, against the son of the chieftain. And then, in honorable barbarian tradition, Wulfgar had been offered a place among the tribesmen. Unfortunately, for a test of loyalty Wulfgar had been asked to slay Regis, and that he could never do. With Drizzt's help, the friends had escaped, but then the shaman, Valric High Eye, had used evil magic to transform Torlin, the chieftain's son, into a hideous ghost spirit.

They defeated that spirit. When honorable Torlin's deformed, broken body lay at his feet, Wulfgar, son of Beornegar, had vowed vengeance against Valric High Eye.

The barbarian felt the clamminess in his strong hands—hands subconsciously wringing about the handle of his powerful warhammer. He squinted into the distance, staring hard at the encampment, and discerned a skinny, agitated form that might have been Valric skipping past one tent.

Valric might not even still be alive, Wulfgar reminded himself, for the shaman had been very old those years ago. Again a large part of Wulfgar wanted to sprint down the other side of the hillock, to run far away from this encounter and any other that would remind him of his past.

The image of Torlin's broken, mutilated body, half man, half winged horse, stayed clear in his thoughts, though, and he could not turn away.

Within the hour, he stared at the encampment from a much closer perspective, close enough to see the individuals.

Close enough to understand that the Sky Ponies had fallen on hard times. And into difficult battles, he realized, for many wounded sat about the camp, and the overall numbers of tents and folk seemed much reduced from what he remembered. Most of the folk in camp were women or very old or very young. A string of more than two-score poles to the south helped to clear up the mystery, for upon them were set the heads of orcs, the occasional carrion bird fluttering down to find a perch in scraggly hair, poking down to find a feast of an eyeball or the side of a nostril.

The sight of the Sky Ponies so obviously diminished pained Wulfgar greatly, for though he had sworn vengeance on their shaman, he knew them to be an honorable people, much like his own in tradition and practice. He thought then that he should leave them, but even as he turned to go, one tent flap at the corner of his line of vision pushed open and out hopped a skinny man, ancient but full of energy, wearing white robes that feathered out like the wings of a bird whenever he raised his arms, and even more telling, an eye patch set with a huge emerald. Barbarians lowered their gazes wherever he passed; one child even rushed up to him and kissed the back of his hand.

"Valric," Wulfgar muttered, for there could be no mistaking the shaman.

Wulfgar came up from the grass in a steady, determined walk, Aegis-fang swinging at the end of one arm. The mere fact that he broke through the camp's perimeter without being assaulted showed him just how disorganized and decimated this tribe truly was, for no barbarian tribe would ever be caught so off guard.

Yet Wulfgar had passed the first tents, had moved close enough to Valric High Eye for the shaman to see him and stare at him incredulously before the first warrior, a tall, older man, strong but very lean, moved to block him.

The warrior came in swinging, not talking, launching a sidelong sweep with a heavy club, but Wulfgar, quicker than the man could anticipate, stepped ahead and caught the club in his free hand before it could gain too much momentum, and then, with strength beyond anything the man had ever imagined, turned his wrist and pulled the weapon free, tossing it far to the side. The warrior howled and charged right in, but Wulfgar got his arm across between himself and the man. With a mighty sweep of his arm, Wulfgar sent the man stumbling away.

All the camp's warriors, not nearly as many as Wulfgar remembered from the Sky Ponies, were out then, flanking Valric, forming a semicircle from the shaman out to the sides of the huge intruder. Wulfgar did turn his gaze from the hated Valric long enough to scrutinize the group, long enough to take note that these were not strong men of prime warrior age. They were too young or too old. The Sky Ponies, he understood, had recently fought a tremendous battle and had not fared well.

"Who are you who comes uninvited?" asked one man, large and strong but very old.

Wulfgar looked hard at the speaker, at the keen set of his eyes, the peppered gray hair in a tousled mop, thick indeed for one his age, at the firm and proud set of his jaw. He reminded Wulfgar of another Sky Pony he had once met, an honorable and brave warrior, and that, combined with the fact that the man had spoken above all others, and even before Valric, confirmed Wulfgar's suspicions.

"Father of Torlin," he said, and gave a bow.

The man's eyes widened with surprise. He seemed as if he wanted to respond but could find no words.

"Jerek Wolf Slayer!" Valric shrieked. "Chieftain of the Sky Ponies. Who are you who comes uninvited? Who are you who speaks of Jerek's long-lost son?"

"Lost?" Wulfgar echoed skeptically.

"Taken by the gods," Valric replied, waving his feathered arms. "A hunting quest, turned to vision quest."

A wry smile made its way onto Wulfgar's face as he came to comprehend the tremendous, decade-old lie. Torlin, mutated into a ghastly and ghostly creature had been sent out by Valric to hunt Wulfgar and his companions and had died horribly on the field at their hands. But Valric, likely not wanting to face Jerek with the horrid news, had somehow manipulated the truth, had concocted a story that would keep Jerek in check. A hunting quest or a vision quest, both god-inspired, might last years, even decades.

Wulfgar realized that he had to handle this delicately now, for any wrong or too-harsh statements might provoke the wrath of Jerek.

"The hunting quest did not last," he said. "For the gods, our gods, recognized the wrongness of it."

Valric's eyes widened indeed, for the first time showing some measure of recognition. "Who are you?" he asked again, a hint of a tremor edging his voice.

"Do you not remember, Valric High Eye?" Wulfgar asked, striding forward, and his movement caused those flanking the shaman to step forward as well. "Have the Sky Ponies so soon forgotten the face of Wulfgar, son of Beornegar?"

Valric tilted his head, his expression showing that Wulfgar had hit a chord of recognition there, but only vaguely.

"Have the Sky Ponies so soon forgotten the northerner they invited to join their ranks, the northerner who traveled with a dwarf, and a halfling, and," he paused, knowing that his next words would bring complete recognition, "a black-skinned elf?"

Valric's eyes nearly rolled out of their sockets. "You!" he said, poking his trembling finger into the air.

The mention of the drow, probably the only dark elf any of these barbarians had ever seen, sparked the memories of many others. Whispered conversations erupted, and many barbarians grasped their weapons tightly, awaiting only a single word to begin their attack and slaughter of the intruder.

Wulfgar calmly held his ground. "I am Wulfgar, son of Beornegar," he repeated firmly, focusing his gaze on Jerek Wolf Slayer. "No enemy of the Sky Ponies. Distant kin to your people and to your ways. I have returned, as I vowed I would, when I saw dead Torlin on the field."

"Dead Torlin?" many voices from warriors and those huddled behind them echoed.

"My friends and I did not come as enemies of the Sky Ponies," Wulfgar went on, using what he expected to be the last few seconds of dialogue. "Indeed we fought beside you against a common foe and won the day."

"You refused us!" Valric screamed. "You insulted my people!"

"What do you know of my son?" Jerek demanded, pushing the shaman aside and stepping forward.

"I know that Valric quested him with the spirit of the Sky Pony to destroy us," Wulfgar said.

"You admit this, and yet you walk openly into our encampment?" Jerek asked.

"I know that your god was not with Torlin on that hunt, for we defeated the creature he had become."

"Kill him!" Valric screamed. "As we destroyed the orcs that came upon us in the dark of night, so shall we destroy the enemy that walks into our camp this day!"

"Hold!" shouted Jerek, throwing his arms out wide. Not a Sky Pony took a step forward, though they seemed eager now, like a pack of hunting dogs straining against their leashes.

Jerek stepped out, walking to stand before Wulfgar.

Wulfgar locked his gaze with the man, but not before he glanced past Jerek to Valric, the shaman fumbling with a leather pouch—a sacred bundle of mystical and magical components—at his side.

"My son is dead?" Jerek, barely a foot from Wulfgar, asked.

"Your god was not with him," Wulfgar replied. "For his cause, Valric's cause, was not just."

He knew before he ever finished that his roundabout manner of telling Jerek had done little to calm the man, that the overriding information, that his son was indeed dead, was too powerful and painful for any explanation or justification. With a roar, the chieftain came at Wulfgar but the younger barbarian was ready, lifting his arm high to raise the intended punch, then snapping his hand down and over Jerek's extended arm, pulling the man off-balance. Wulfgar dropped

189

Aegis-fang and shoved hard on Jerek's chest, releasing his hold and sending the man stumbling backward into the surprised warriors.

Scooping his warhammer as he went, Wulfgar charged forward, but so did the warriors, and the northern barbarian, to his ultimate frustration, knew that he would get nowhere near to Valric. He hoped for an open throwing path that he might take down the shaman before he, too, was killed, but then Valric surprised him, surprised everybody, by leaping forward through the line, howling a chant and throwing a burst of herbs and powders Wulfgar's way.

Wulfgar felt the magical intrusion. Though the other warriors, Jerek included, backed away a few steps, he felt as if great black walls were closing in on him, stealing his strength, forcing him to hold in place.

Waves and waves of immobilizing magic rolled on, Valric hopping about, throwing more powders, strengthening the spell.

Wulfgar felt himself sinking, felt the ground coming up to swallow him.

He was not unfamiliar with such magics, though. Not at all. In his years in the Abyss, Errtu's minions, particularly the wicked succubi, had used similar spells to render him helpless that they might have their way with him. How many times he had felt such intrusions. He had learned how to defeat them.

He put up a wall of the purest rage, warding every magical suggestion of immobility with ten growls of anger, ten memories of Errtu and the succubi. Outwardly, though, the barbarian took great pains to seem defeated, to hold perfectly still, his warhammer dropping down to his side. He heard the chants of "Valric High Eye" and saw out of the corner of his eye several of the warriors turning in ceremonial dance, giving thanks to their god and to Valric, the human manifestation of that god.

"Of what does he speak?" Jerek said to Valric. "What quest fell upon Torlin?"

"As I told you," the skinny shaman replied, dancing out from the lines to stand before Wulfgar. "A drow elf! This man, seeming so honorable, traveled beside a drow elf! Could any but Torlin have taken the beast magic and defeated this deadly foe?"

"You said that Torlin was on a vision quest," Jerek argued.

"And so I believed," Valric lied. "And perhaps he is. Do not believe the lies of this one! Did you see how easily the power of Uthgar defeated him, holding him helpless before us? More likely he returned because his friends, all three, were slain by powerful Torlin, and because he knew that he could not hope to find vengeance any other way, could not hope to defeat Torlin even with the aid of the drow."

"But Wulfgar, son of Beornegar, did defeat Torlin in the contest of strength," another man remarked.

"That was before he angered Uthgar!" Valric howled. "See him standing now, helpless and defeated—"

The word barely got out of his mouth before Wulfgar exploded into action, stepping forward and clamping one hand over the shaman's skinny face. With frightening power, Wulfgar lifted Valric into the air and slammed him back down to his feet repeatedly, then shook him wildly.

"What god, Valric?" he roared. "What claim have you of Uthgar above my own as a warrior of Tempus?" To illustrate his point, and still with only one hand, Wulfgar tightened the bulging muscles in his arm and lifted Valric high into the air and held him there, perfectly steady, ignoring the man's flailing arms. "Had Torlin killed my friends in honorable battle, then I would not have returned for vengeance," he said honestly to Jerek. "I came not to avenge them, for they are well, all three. I came to avenge Torlin, a man of strength and honor, used so terribly by this wretch."

"Valric is our shaman!" more than one man yelled.

Wulfgar put him down to his feet with a growl, forcing him down to his knees and bent his head far back. Valric grabbed hard onto the man's forearm, crying out, "Kill him!" but Wulfgar only squeezed all the tighter, and Valric's words became a gurgling groan.

Wulfgar looked around at the ring of warriors. Holding Valric so helpless had bought him some time, perhaps, but they would kill him, no doubt, when he was finished with the shaman. Still, it wasn't that thought that gave Wulfgar pause, for he hardly cared about his own life. Rather, it was the expression he saw upon Jerek's face, a look of a man so utterly defeated. Wulfgar had come in with news that could break the proud chieftain, and he knew that if he killed Valric now, and many others in the ensuing battle before he, too, was finally brought down, then Jerek would not likely recover. And neither, he understood, would the Sky Ponies.

He looked down at the pitiful Valric. While he had been contemplating his next move he had inadvertently pushed back and down. The skinny man was practically bent in half and seemed near to breaking. How easy it would have been for Wulfgar to drive his arm down, snapping the man's spine.

How easy and how empty. With a frustrated roar that had nothing to do with compassion, he lifted Valric from the ground again, clapped his free hand against the man's groin, and brought him high overhead. With a roar, he launched the man a dozen feet and more into the side of a tent, sending Valric, skins, and poles tumbling down.

Warriors came at him, but he quickly had Aegis-fang in hand, and a great swipe drove them back, knocking the weapon from one and nearly tearing the man's arm off in the process.

"Hold!" came Jerek's cry. "And you, Valric!" he emphatically added, seeing the shaman pulling himself from the mess, calling for Wulfgar's death.

Jerek walked past his warriors, right up to Wulfgar. The younger man saw the murderous intent in his eyes.

"I will take no pleasure in killing the father of Torlin," Wulfgar said calmly.

That hit a nerve; Wulfgar saw the softening in the older man's face. Without another word, the barbarian turned about and started walking away, and none of the warriors moved to intercept him.

"Kill him!" Valric cried, but before the words had even left his mouth, Wulfgar whirled about and let fly his warhammer, the spinning weapon covering the twenty feet to the kneeling shaman in the blink of an eye, striking him squarely in the chest and laying him out, quite dead, among the jumble of tent poles and skins.

All eyes turned back to Wulfgar, and more than one Sky Pony made a move his way.

But Aegis-fang was back in his hands, suddenly, dramatically, and they fell back.

"His god Tempus is with him!" one man cried.

Wulfgar turned about and started away once more, knowing in his heart that nothing could be further from the truth. He expected Jerek to run him down or to order his warriors to kill him, but the group behind him remained strangely quiet. He heard no commands, no protests, no movement. Nothing at all. He had so overwhelmed the already battered tribe, had stunned Jerek with the truth of his son's fate, and then had stunned them all by his sudden and brutal vengeance on Valric, that they simply didn't know how to react.

No relief came over Wulfgar as he made his way from the encampment. He stormed down the road, angry at damned Valric, at all the damned Sky Ponies, at all the damned world. He kicked a stone from the path, then picked up another sizable rock and hurled it far through the air, shouting a roar of open defiance and pure frustration behind it. He stomped along with no direction in mind, with no sense of where he should go or where he should be. Soon after, he came upon the trail of a party of orcs, likely the same ones who had battled the Sky Ponies the previous night, an easily discernible track of blood, trampled grass, and broken twigs, veering from the main path into a small forest.

Hardly thinking, Wulfgar turned down that path, still roughly pushing aside trees, growling, and muttering curses. Gradually, though, he calmed and quieted, and replaced his lack of general purpose with a short-term, specific goal. He followed the trail more carefully, paying attention to any side paths where flanking orc scouts might have moved. Indeed, he found one such path and a pair of tracks to confirm it. He went that way quietly, looking for shadows and cover.

The day was late by then, the shadows long, but Wulfgar understood that he would have a hard time finding the scouts before they spotted him if they were on the alert—as they likely would be so soon after a terrific battle.

Wulfgar had spent many years fighting humanoids beside Drizzt Do'Urden, learning of their methods and their motivations. His course now was to make sure that the orcs were not able to warn the larger group. He knew how to do that.

Crouched in some brush by the side, the barbarian wrapped pliable twigs about his warhammer, trying to disguise the weapon as much as possible. Then he smeared mud about his face and pulled his cloak back so that it looked as though it was torn. Dirty and appearing battered, he walked out of the brush and started along the path, limping badly and groaning with every step, and every so often calling out for "my girl."

Just a short time later he sensed that he was being watched. Now he exaggerated his limp, even stumbling down to the ground at one point, using his tumble to allow him a better scan of the area.

He spotted a dark silhouette among the branches, an orc with a spear poised for a throw. Just a few steps more, he realized, and the creature would try to skewer him.

And the other was about, he realized, though he hadn't spotted the wretch. Likely it was on the ground, ready to run in and finish him as soon as the spear took him down. These two should have warned their companions, but they wanted the apparently easy kill for themselves, Wulfgar knew, that they might loot the poor man before informing their leader.

Wulfgar had to take them out quickly, but he didn't dare get much closer to the spear wielder. He pulled himself to his feet, took another staggering step along the trail, then paused and lifted his arm and eyes to the sky, wailing for his missing child. Then, nearly falling over again, shoulders slumped in defeat, he turned around and started back the way he had come, sobbing loudly, shoulders bobbing.

He knew that the orc would never be able to resist that target, despite the range. His muscles tensed, he turned his head just a bit, hearing trained on the distant tree.

Then he spun as the long-flying spear soared in. Deftly, with agility far beyond any man of his size, he caught the missile as he turned, pulling it tight against his side and issuing a profound grunt, then tumbling backward into the dirt, squirming, right hand grasping the spear, left tight about Aegis-fang.

He heard the rustle to the side from an angle above his right shoulder as he lay on his back, waiting patiently.

The second orc came out of the brush, scampering his way. Wulfgar timed the move with near perfection, rolling up and over that right shoulder, letting the spear fall as he went. He came up in a spin, Aegis-fang swiping across. But the orc skidded short, and the mighty weapon swished past harmlessly. Hardly concerned, Wulfgar continued the spin, right around, spotting the spear thrower on the tree branch as he came around and letting fly. He had to continue the spin, couldn't pause and watch the throw, though he heard the crunch and grunt, and the orc's broken body falling through the lower branches.

The orc before him yelped and threw its club, then turned and tried to flee.

Wulfgar accepted the hit as the club bounced off his massive chest. In an instant, he held the creature on its knees as he had held Valric, on its knees, head far back, backbone bowed. He pictured that moment then, conjuring an image of the wicked shaman. Then he drove down, with all his strength, growling and slapping away the orc's flailing arms. He heard the crackle of backbone and those arms stopped slapping at him, stabbing straight up into the air, trembling violently.

Wulfgar let go, and the dead creature fell over.

Aegis-fang came back to his grasp, reminding him of the other orc, and he glanced over and nodded, seeing the thing lying dead at the base of the tree.

Hardly satisfied, his bloodlust rising with each kill, Wulfgar ran, back to the main trail and then down along the clear path. He found the orcish encampment as twilight descended. There were more than a score of the monsters, with others likely out and about, scouting or hunting. He should have waited until long after dark, until the camp had settled and many of the orcs were asleep. He should have waited until he could get a better picture of the group, a better understanding of their structure and strength.

He should have waited, but he could not.

Aegis-fang soared in, right between a pair of smaller orcs, startling them, then on to slam one large creature, taking it and the orc it had been talking to down to the ground.

In charged Wulfgar, roaring wildly. He caught the spear of one startled orc, stabbing it across to impale the orc opposite, then tearing free the tip and spinning back, smashing the spear down across the first orc's head, breaking it in half. Holding both ends, Wulfgar jabbed them into either side of the orc's head, and when it reached up to grab the poles, the barbarian merely heaved it right over his head. A heavy punch dropped the next orc in line even as it moved to draw the sword from its belt, and then, roaring all the louder, Wulfgar crashed into two more, bearing them to the ground. He came up slapping and punching, kicking, anything at all to knock the orcs aside—and in truth, they showed more desire to scramble away than to come at the monstrous man.

Wulfgar caught one, spun it about, and slammed his forehead right into its face, then caught it by the hair as it fell away and drove his fist through its ugly face.

The barbarian leaped about, seeking his next victim. His momentum seemed to be fast waning with the passing seconds, but then Aegis-fang returned to his hand, and he wasted no time in whipping the hammer a dozen feet, its spinning head coming in at just the right angle to drive through the skull of one unfortunate creature.

Orcs charged in, stabbing and clubbing. Wulfgar took one hit, then another, but with each minor gash or bruise the orcs inflicted, the huge and powerful man got his hands on one and tore the life from it. Then Aegis-fang returned again, and the orcish press was shattered, driven back by mighty swipes. Covered in blood, howling wildly, thrashing that terrible hammer, the sheer sight of Wulfgar proved too much for the cowardly creatures. Those who could get away fled into the forest, and those who could not died at the barbarian's strong hands.

Mere minutes later, Wulfgar stomped out of the shattered camp, growling and smacking Aegis-fang against the trees. He knew that many orcs were watching him; he knew that none would dare attack.

Soon after, he came into a clearing on a bluff that afforded him a view of the last moments of sunset, the same fiery lines he had seen on that evening on the southern edges of the Spine of the World.

Now the colors did not touch his heart. Now he knew the thoughts of freedom from his past were a false hope, knew that his memories would follow him wherever he went, whatever he did. He felt no satisfaction at exacting revenge against Valric and no joy in slaughtering the orcs.

Nothing.

He walked on through the night, not even bothering to wash the blood from his clothes or to dress his many minor wounds. He walked toward the sunset, then kept the rising moon at his back, chasing its descent to the western horizon.

Three days later, he found Luskan's eastern gate.

Chapter 11
THE BATTLE-MAGE

o not come here," LaValle cried, and then he added softly, "I beg."

Entreri merely continued to stare at the man, his expression unreadable.

"You wounded Kadran Gordeon," LaValle went on. "In pride more than in body, and that, I warn you, is more dangerous by far."

"Gordeon is a fool," Entreri retorted.

"A fool with an army," LaValle quipped. "No guild is more entrenched in the streets than the Basadonis. None have more resources, and all of those resources, I assure you, have been turned upon Artemis Entreri."

"And upon LaValle, perhaps?" Entreri replied with a grin. "For speaking with the hunted man?"

LaValle didn't answer the obvious question other than to continue to stare hard at Artemis Entreri, the man whose mere presence in his room this night might have just condemned him.

"Tell them everything they ask of you," Entreri instructed. "Honestly. Do not try to deceive them for my sake. Tell them that I came here, uninvited, to speak with you and that I show no wounds for all their efforts."

"You would taunt them so?"

Entreri shrugged. "Does it matter?"

LaValle had no answer to that, and so the assassin, with a bow, moved to the window and, defeating one trap with a flick of the wrist and carefully manipulating his body to avoid the others, slipped out to the wall and dropped silently to the street.

He dared to go by the Copper Ante that night, though only quickly and with no effort to actually enter the place. Still, he did make himself known to the door halflings. To his surprise, a short way down the alley at the side of the building, Dwahvel Tiggerwillies came out a secret door to speak with him.

"A battle-mage," she warned. "Merle Pariso. With a reputation unparalleled in Calimport. Fear him, Artemis Entreri. Run from him. Flee the city and all of Calimshan." And with that, she slipped through another barely detectable crack in the wall and was gone.

The gravity of her words and tone were not lost on the assassin. The mere fact that Dwahvel had come out to him, with nothing to gain and everything to lose—how could he repay the favor, after all, if he took her advice and fled the realm?—tipped him off that she had been instructed to so inform him, or at least, that this battle-mage was making no secret of the hunt.

So perhaps the wizard was a bit too cocksure, he told himself, but that, too, proved of little comfort. A battle-mage! A wizard trained specifically in the art of magical warfare. Cocksure, and with a right to be. Entreri had battled, and killed, many wizards, but he understood the desperate truth of his present situation. A wizard was not so difficult an enemy for a seasoned warrior, as long as the warrior was able to prepare the battlefield favorably. That, too, was usually not difficult, since wizards were often, by nature, distracted and unprepared. Typically a wizard had to anticipate battle far in advance, at the beginning of the day, that he might prepare the appropriate spells. Wizards, distracted by their continual research, rarely prepared such spells. But when a wizard was the hunter and not the hunted he would not be caught off his guard. Entreri knew he was in trouble. He seriously considered taking Dwahvel's advice.

For the first time since he had returned to Calimport, the assassin truly appreciated the danger of being without allies. He considered that in light of his experiences in Menzoberranzan, where unallied rogues could not survive for long.

Perhaps Calimport wasn't so different.

He started for his new room, an empty hovel at the back of an alleyway, but stopped and reconsidered. It wasn't likely that the wizard, with such a reputation as a combat spellcaster, would be overly skilled in divination spells as well. That hardly mattered, Entreri knew. It all came down to connections, and Merle Pariso was acting on behalf of the Basadoni guild. If he wanted to magically locate Entreri, the guild would grant him the resources of their diviners.

Where to go? He didn't want to remain on the open street where a wizard could strike from a long distance, could even, perhaps, levitate high above and rain destructive magic upon him. And so he searched the buildings, looking for a place to hide, an encampment, and knowing all the while that magical eyes might be upon him.

With that rather disturbing thought in mind, Entreri wasn't overly surprised when he slipped quietly into the supposedly empty back room of a darkened warehouse and a robed figure appeared right before him with a puff of orange smoke. The door blew closed behind him.

Entreri glanced all around, noting the lack of exits in the room, cursing his foul luck in finding this place. Again, when he considered it, it came down to his lack of allies and lack of knowledge with present-day Calimport. They were waiting for him, wherever he might go. They were ahead of him, watching his every move and obviously taking a prepared battlefield right with them. Entreri felt foolish for even coming back to this inhospitable city without first probing, without learning all that he would need to survive.

Enough of the doubts and second guesses, he pointedly reminded himself, drawing out his dagger and setting himself low in a crouch, concentrating on the situation at hand. He thought of turning back for the door, but knew without doubt that it would be magically sealed.

"Behold the Merle!" the wizard said with a laugh, waving his arms out wide. The voluminous sleeves of his robes floated out behind his lifting limbs and threw a rainbow of multicolored lights. A second wave and his arms came forward, throwing a blast of lightning at the assassin. But Entreri was already moving, rolling to the side and out of harm's way. He glanced back, hoping the bolt might have blown through the door, but it was still closed and seemed solid.

"Oh, well dodged!" Merle Pariso congratulated. "But really, pitiful assassin, do you desire to make this last longer? Why not stand still and be done with it, quickly and mercifully?" He stopped his taunting and launched into another spellcasting as Entreri charged in, jeweled dagger flashing. Merle made no move to defend against the attack, continuing calmly

203

with his casting as Entreri came in hard, stabbing for his face.

The dagger stopped as surely as if it had struck a stone wall. Entreri wasn't really surprised—any wise wizard would have prepared such a defense—but what amazed him, even as he went flying back, hit by a burst of magical missiles, was Pariso's concentration. Entreri had to admire the man's unflinching spellcasting even as the deadly dagger came at his face, unblinking even as the blade flashed right before his eyes.

Entreri staggered to the side, diving and rolling, anticipating another attack. But now Merle Pariso, supremely confident, merely laughed at him. "Where will you run?" the battle-mage taunted. "How many times will you find the energy to dodge?"

Indeed, if he allowed the wizard's taunts to sink in, Entreri would have found it hard to hold his heart; many lesser warriors might have simply taken the wizard's advice and surrendered to the seemingly inevitable.

But not Entreri. His lethargy fell away. With his very life on the line all the doubts of his life and his purpose flew away. Now he lived completely in the moment, adrenaline pumping. One step at a time, and the first of those steps was to defeat the stoneskin, the magical defense that could turn any blade—but only for a certain number of attacks. Spinning and rolling, the assassin took up a chair and broke free a leg, then rolled about and launched it at the wizard, scoring an ineffective hit.

Another burst of magical missiles slammed into him, following him unerringly in his roll and stinging him. He shrugged through it, though, and came up throwing. A second, then a third chair leg scored two more hits.

The fourth followed in rapid succession. Then Entreri threw the base of the chair. It was a meager missile that would hardly have hurt the wizard even without the magical defense, but one that took yet another layer off the stoneskin.

Entreri paid for the offensive flurry, though, as Merle Pariso's next lightning bolt caught him hard and launched him spinning sidelong. His shoulder burned, his hair danced on end, and his heart fluttered.

Desperate and hurt, the assassin went in hard, dagger slashing. "How many more can you defeat?" he roared, stabbing hard again and again.

His answer came in the form of flames, a shroud of dancing fire covering, but hardly consuming, Merle Pariso. Entreri noted the fire too late to stop short his last attack, and the dagger went through, again hitting harmlessly against the stoneskin—harmlessly to Pariso but not to Entreri. The new spell, the flame shield, replicated the intended bite of that dagger back at Entreri, drawing a deep gash along the already battered man's ribs.

With a howl the assassin fell back, purposely turning himself in line with the door, then dodging deftly as the predictable lightning bolt came after him.

The rolling assassin looked back as he came around, pleased to see that this time the wooden door had indeed splintered. He grabbed another chair and threw it at the wizard, turning for the door even as he released it.

Merle Pariso's groan stopped him dead and turned him back around, thinking the stoneskin expired.

But then it was Entreri's turn to groan. "Oh, clever," he congratulated, realizing the wizard's groan to be no more than a ruse, buying the man time to cast his next spell.

The assassin turned back for the door but hadn't gone a step before he was forced back, as a wall of huge flames erupted along that wall, blocking escape.

"Well fought, assassin," Merle Pariso said honestly. "I expected as much from Artemis Entreri. But now, alas, you die." He finished by drawing a wand, pointing it at the floor at his feet, and firing a burning seed.

Entreri fell flat, pulling what remained of his cloak over his head as the seed exploded into a fireball, filling all the room, burning his hair and scorching his lungs, but harming Pariso not at all. The wizard was secure within his fiery shield.

Entreri came up dazed, eyes filled with heat and smoke as all the building around him burned. Merle Pariso stood there, laughing wildly.

The assassin had to get out. He couldn't possibly defeat the mage and wouldn't survive for much longer against Pariso's potent magics. He turned for the door, thinking to dive right through the fire wall, but then a glowing sword appeared in midair before him, slashing hard. He had to dodge aside and get his dagger up against the blade to turn it. The invisible opponent—Entreri knew it to be Merle Pariso's will acting through the magical dweomer—came on hard, forcing him to retreat. The sword always stayed between the assassin and the door.

On his balance now, Entreri was more than a match for the slicing weapon, easily dodging and striking back hard. He knew that no hand guided the blade, that the only way to defeat it was to strike at the sword itself, and that posed no great problem for the warrior assassin. But then another glowing sword appeared. Entreri had never seen this before, had never even heard of a wizard who could control two such magical creations at the same time.

He dived and rolled, and the swords pursued. He tried to dart around them for the doorway but found that they were too quick. He glanced back at Pariso. Barely, through the growing smoke, he could see the wizard still shrouded in defensive flames, tapping his fireball wand against his cheek.

The heat nearly overwhelmed Entreri. The flames were all about, on the walls, the floor, and the ceiling. Wood crackled in protest, and beams collapsed.

"I will not leave," he heard Merle Pariso say. "I will watch until the life is gone from you, Artemis Entreri."

On came the glowing swords, slashing in perfect co-ordination, and Entreri knew that the wizard almost got what he wanted. The assassin barely, barely, avoiding the hits, dived forward under the blades, coming up in a run for the door. Shielding his face with his arms, he leaped into the fire wall, thinking to break through the battered door.

He hit as solid a barrier as he had ever felt, a magical wall, he knew. He scrambled back out of the flames into the burning room, and the two swords waited for him. Merle Pariso stood calmly pointing the dreaded fireball wand.

But then to the side of the wizard a green-gloved disembodied hand appeared, sliding out of nowhere and holding what appeared to be a large egg.

Merle Pariso's eyes widened in horror. "Wh-who?" he stuttered. "Wha—?"

The hand tossed the egg to the floor, where it exploded into a huge ball of powdery dust, rolling into the air, then shimmering into a multicolored cloud. Entreri heard music then, even above the roar of the conflagration, many different notes climbing the scale, then dropping low and ending in a long, monotonal humming sound.

The glowing swords disappeared. So did the fire wall blocking the door, though the normal flames still burned brightly along door and wall. So did Merle Pariso's defensive fire shield.

The wizard cried out and waved his arms frantically, trying to cast another spell—some magical escape, Entreri realized, for now he was obviously feeling the heat as intensely as was Entreri.

The assassin realized that the magical barrier was likely gone as well, and he could have turned and run from the room. But he couldn't tear his eyes from the spectacle of Pariso, backpedaling, so obviously distressed. To the amazement of both, many of the smaller fires near the wizard then changed shape, appearing as little humanoid creatures, circling Pariso in a strange dance.

The wizard skipped backward, tripped over a loose board, and went down on his back. The little fire humanoids, like a pack of hunting wolves, leaped upon him, lighting his robes and burning his skin. Pariso opened wide his mouth to scream, and one of the fiery animations raced right down his throat, stealing his voice and burning him from the inside.

The green-gloved hand beckoned to Entreri.

The wall behind him collapsed, sparks and embers flying everywhere, stealing his easy escape.

Moving cautiously but quickly, the assassin circled wide of the hand, gaining a better angle as he realized that it was not a disembodied hand at all, but merely one poking through a dimensional gate of some sort.

Entreri's knees went weak at the sight. He nearly bolted back for the blazing door, but a sound from above told him that the ceiling was falling in. Purely on survival instinct, for if he had thought about it he likely would have chosen death, Entreri leaped through the dimensional door.

Into the arms of his saviors.

Chapter 12
FINDING A NICHE

He knew this town, though only vaguely. He'd made a single passage through the place long ago, in the days of hope and future dreams, in the search for Mithral Hall. Little seemed familiar to Wulfgar now as he made his plodding way through Luskan, absorbing the sights and sounds of the many open air markets and the general bustle of a northern city awakening after winter's slumber.

Many, many gazes fell over him as he moved along, for Wulfgar—closer to seven feet tall than to six with a massive chest and shoulders, and the glittering warhammer strapped across his back—was no ordinary sight. Barbarians occasionally wandered into Luskan, but even among the hardy folk Wulfgar loomed huge.

He ignored the looks and the whispers and continued merely to wander the many ways. He spotted the Host-tower of the Arcane, the famed wizard's guild of Luskan, and recognized the building easily enough, since it was in the shape of a huge tree with spreading limbs. But again that one note of recognition did little to guide the man along. It had been so long ago, a lifetime ago it seemed, since he had last been here.

Minutes became an hour, then two hours. The barbarian's vision was turned inward now as much as outward. His mind replayed images of the past few days, particularly the moment of his unsatisfying revenge. The image of Valric High Eye flying back into the jumble of broken tenting, Aegis-fang crushing his chest, was vivid in his mind's eye.

Wulfgar ran his hand through his unkempt hair and staggered along. Clearly he was exhausted, for he had slept only a few scattered hours in three days since the encounter with the Sky Ponies. He had wandered the roads to the west aimlessly until he had spotted the outline of the distant city. The guards at the eastern gate of Luskan had threatened to turn him away, but when he had just swung about with a shrug they called after him and told him he could enter but warned him to keep his weapon strapped across his back.

Wulfgar had no intention of fighting and no intention of following the guards' command should a fight find him. He merely nodded and walked through the gates, then down the streets and through the markets.

He discovered another familiar landmark when the shadows were long, the sun low in the western sky. A signpost named one way Half Moon Street, a place Wulfgar had been before. A short way down the street he saw the sign for the Cutlass, a tavern he knew from his first trip through, a place wherein he had been involved, in some ways had started, a tremendous row. Looking at the Cutlass, at the whole decrepit street now, Wulfgar wondered how he could have ever expected otherwise.

This was the place for the lowest orders of society, for thugs and rogues, for men running from lords. The barbarian put his hand in his nearly empty pouch, fumbling with the few coins, and realized then that this was where he belonged.

He went into the Cutlass half fearing he would be recognized, that he would find himself in another brawl before the door closed behind him.

Of course he was not recognized. Nor did he see any faces that seemed the least bit familiar. The layout of the place was pretty much the same as he remembered. As he scanned the room, his gaze inevitably went to the wall to the side of the long bar, the wall where a younger Wulfgar had set a brute in his place by driving the man's head right through the planking.

He was so full of pride back then, so ready to fight. Now, too, he was more than willing to put his fists or weapons to use, but his purpose in doing so had changed. Now he fought out of anger, out of the sheerest rage, whether that rage had anything to do with whatever enemy stood before him or not. Now he fought because that course seemed as good as any other. Perhaps, just perhaps, he fought in the hopes that he would lose, that some enemy would end his internal torment.

He couldn't hold that thought, couldn't hold any thought, as he made his way to the bar, taking no care not to jostle the many patrons who crowded before him. He pulled off his traveling cloak and took a seat, not even bothering to ask either of the men flanking the stool if they had a friend who was using it.

And then he watched and waited, letting the myriad of sights and sounds—whispered conversations, lewd remarks aimed at serving wenches more than ready to snap back with their own stinging retort—become a general blur, a welcomed buzz.

His head drooped, and that movement alone woke him. He shifted in his seat and noted then that the barkeep, an old man who still held the hardness of youth about his strong shoulders, stood before him, wiping a glass.

"Arumn Gardpeck," the barkeep introduced himself, extending a hand.

Wulfgar regarded the offered hand but did not shake it.

Without missing a beat the barkeep went back to his wiping. "A drink?" he asked.

Wulfgar shook his head and looked away, desiring nothing from the man, especially any useless conversation.

Arumn came forward, though, leaning over the bar and drawing Wulfgar's full attention. "I want no trouble in me bar," he said calmly, looking over the barbarian's huge, muscled arms.

Wulfgar waved him away.

Minutes slipped past, and the place grew even more crowded. No one bothered Wulfgar, though, and so he allowed himself to relax his guard, his head inevitably drooping. He fell asleep, his face buried in his arms atop Arumn Gardpeck's clean bar.

"Hey there," he heard, and the voice sounded as if it was far, far away. He felt a shake then, on his shoulder, and he opened his sleepy eyes and lifted his head to see Arumn's smiling face. "Time for leaving."

Wulfgar stared at him blankly.

"Where are ye stayin'?" the barkeep asked. "Might that I could find a couple who'd walk ye there."

For a long while, Wulfgar didn't answer, staring groggily at the man, trying to get his bearings.

"And he weren't even drinking!" one man howled from the side. Wulfgar turned to regard him and noted that several large men, Arumn Gardpeck's security force, no doubt, had formed a semicircle behind him. Wulfgar turned back to eye Arumn.

"Where are ye stayin'?" the man asked again. "And ye shut yer mouth, Josi Puddles," he added to the taunting man.

Wulfgar shrugged. "Nowhere," he answered honestly.

"Well, ye can't be stayin' 'ere!" yet another man growled, moving close enough to poke the barbarian in the shoulder.

Wulfgar calmly swung his head, taking a measure of the man.

"Hush yer mouth!" Arumn was quick to scold, and he shifted about, drawing Wulfgar's gaze. "I could give ye a room for a few silver pieces," he said.

"I have little money," the big man admitted.

"Then sell me yer hammer," said another directly behind Wulfgar. When he turned to regard the speaker he saw that the man was holding Aegis-fang. Now Wulfgar was fully awake and up, hand extended, his expression and posture demanding the hammer's immediate return.

"Might that I will give it back to ye," the man remarked as Wulfgar slid out of the chair and advanced a threatening step. As he spoke, he lifted Aegis-fang, more in an angle to cave in Wulfgar's skull that to hand it over.

Wulfgar stopped short and shifted his dangerous glare over each of the large men, his lips curling up in a confident, wicked, smile. "You wish to buy it?" he asked the man holding the hammer. "Then you should know its name."

Wulfgar spoke the hammer's name, and it vanished from the hands of the threatening man and reappeared in Wulfgar's. The barbarian was moving even before the hammer materialized, closing in on the man with a single long stride and slapping him with a backhand that launched him into the air to land crashing over a table.

The others came at the huge barbarian, but only for an instant, for he was ready now, waving the powerful warhammer so easily that the others understood he was not one to be taken lightly and not one to fight unless they were willing to see their ranks thinned considerably.

"Hold! Hold!" cried Arumn, rushing out from behind the bar and waving his bouncers away. A couple went over to help the man Wulfgar had slapped. So disoriented was he that they had to hoist him and support him.

And still Arumn waved them all away. He stood before Wulfgar, within easy striking distance, but he was not afraid—or if he was, he wasn't showing it.

"I could use one with yer strength," he remarked. "That was Reef ye dropped with an open-handed slap, and Reef's one o' me better fighters."

Wulfgar looked across the room at the man sitting with the other bouncers and scoffed.

Arumn led him back to the bar and sat him down, then went behind and produced a bottle, setting it right before the big man and motioning for him to drink.

Wulfgar did, a great hearty swig that burned all the way down.

"A room and free food," Arumn said. "All ye can eat. And all that I ask in return is that ye help keep me tavern free o' fights or that ye finish 'em quick if they start."

Wulfgar looked back over his shoulder at the men across the way. "What of them?" he asked, taking another huge swig from the bottle, then coughing as he wiped his bare forearm across his lips. The potent liquor seemed to draw all the coating from his throat.

"They help me when I ask, as they help most o' the innkeepers on Half Moon street and all the streets about," Arumn explained. "I been thinking o' hiring me own and keeping him on, and I'm thinking that ye'd fit that role well."

"You hardly know me," Wulfgar argued, and his third gulp half drained the bottle. This time the burning seemed to spread out more quickly, until all his body felt warm and a bit numb. "And you know nothing of my history."

"Nor do I care," said Arumn. "We don't get many of yer type in here—northmen, I mean. Ye've got a reputation for fighting, and the way ye slapped Reef aside tells me that reputation's well earned."

"Room and food?" Wulfgar asked.

"And drink," Arumn added, motioning to the bottle, which Wulfgar promptly lifted to his lips and drained. He went to move it back to Arumn, but it seemed to jump from his hand, and when he tried to retrieve it he merely kept pushing it awkwardly along until Arumn deftly scooped it away from him.

Wulfgar sat up straighter, or tried to, and closed his eyes very tightly, trying to find a center of focus. When he opened his eyes once more, he found another full bottle before him, and he wasted no time in bringing that one, too, up to his lips.

An hour later, Arumn, who had taken a few drinks himself, helped Wulfgar up the stairs and into a tiny room. He tried to guide Wulfgar onto the small bed—a cot too small to comfortably accommodate the huge barbarian—but both wound up falling over, crashing across the cot then onto thefloor.

They shared a laugh, an honest laugh, the first one Wulfgar had known since the rescue in the ice cave.

"They start coming in soon after midday," Arumn explained, spit flying with every word. "But I won't be needing ye until the sun's down. I'll get ye then, and I'm thinking that ye'll be needin' waking!"

They shared another laugh at that, and Arumn staggered out the door, falling against it to close it behind him, leaving Wulfgar alone in the pitch-black room.

Alone. Completely alone.

That notion nearly overwhelmed him. Sitting there drunk the barbarian realized that Errtu hadn't come in here with him, that everything, every memory, good and bad, was but a harmless blur. In those bottles, under the spell of that potent liquor, Wulfgar found a reprieve.

Food and a room and drink Arumn had promised.

To Wulfgar the last condition of his employment rang out as the most important.

* * * * *

Entreri stood in an alley, not far from his near-disaster with Merle Pariso, looking back at the blazing warehouse. Flames leaped high above the rooftops of the nearest buildings. Three others stood beside him. They were about the same height as the assassin, a bit more slender, perhaps, but with muscles obviously honed for battle.

What distinguished them most was their ebony skin. One wore a huge purple hat, set with a gigantic plume.

"Twice I have pulled you from certain death," the one with the hat remarked.

Entreri looked hard at the speaker, wanting nothing more than to drive his dagger deep into the dark elf's chest. He knew better though, knew that this one, Jarlaxle, was far too protected for any such obvious attacks.

"We have much to discuss," the dark elf said, and he motioned to one of his companions. With a thought, it seemed, the drow brought up another dimensional door, this one leading into a room where several other dark elves had gathered.

"Kimmuriel Oblodra," Jarlaxle explained.

Entreri knew the name—the surname, at least. House Oblodra had once been the third most powerful house in Menzoberranzan and one of the most frightening because of their practice of psionics, a curious and little understood magic of the mind. During the Time of Troubles, the Oblodrans, whose powers were not adversely affected, as were the more conventional magics within the city, used the opportunity to press their advantage, even going so far as to threaten Matron Mother Baenre, the ruling Matron of the ruling house of the city. When the waves of instability that marked that strange time turned again in favor of conventional magics and against the powers of the mind, House Oblodra had been obliterated, the great structure and all its inhabitants pulled into the great gorge, the Clawrift, by a physical manifestation of Matron Baenre's rage.

Well, Entreri thought, staring at the psionicist, not all of the inhabitants.

He went through the psionic door with Jarlaxle— what choice did he have?—and after a long moment of dizzying disorientation took a seat in the small room when the drow mercenary motioned for him to do so. All the dark elf group except for Jarlaxle and Kimmuriel, went out then in practiced order, to secure the area about the meeting place.

"We are safe enough," Jarlaxle assured Entreri.

"They were watching me magically," the assassin replied. "That was how Merle Pariso set the ambush."

"We have been watching you magically for many weeks," Jarlaxle said with a grin. "They watch you no more, I assure you."

"You came for me, then?" the assassin asked. "It seems a bit of trouble to retrieve one *rivvil*," he added, using the drow word, and not a complimentary one, for human.

Jarlaxle laughed aloud at Entreri's choice of that word. It was indeed the word for "human," but one also used to describe many inferior races, which meant any race that was not drow.

"To retrieve you?" the assassin asked incredulously. "Do you wish to return to Menzoberranzan?"

"I would kill you or force you to kill me long before we ever stepped into the drow city," Entreri replied in all seriousness.

"Of course," Jarlaxle said calmly, taking no offense and not disagreeing in the least. "That is not your place, nor is Calimport ours."

"Then why have you come?"

"Because Calimport is your place, and Menzoberranzan is mine," the drow replied, smiling all the wider, as though the simple statement explained everything.

And before he questioned Jarlaxle more deeply, Entreri sat back and took a long while to reflect upon the words. Jarlaxle was, above all else, an opportunist. The drow, along with Bregan D'aerthe, his powerful band of rogues, seemed to find a way to gain from practically every situation. Menzoberranzan was a city ruled by females, the priestesses of Lolth, and yet even there Jarlaxle and his band, almost exclusively males, were far from the underclass. So why now had he come to find Entreri, come to a place that he just openly and honestly admitted was not his place at all?

"You want me to front you," the assassin stated.

"I am not familiar with the term," Jarlaxle replied.

Now Entreri, seeing the lie for what it was, was the one wearing the grin. "You want to extend the hand of

Bregan D'aerthe to the surface, to Calimport, but you recognize that you and yours would never be accepted even among the bowel-dwellers of the city."

"We could use magic to disguise our true identity," the drow argued.

"But why bother when you have Artemis Entreri?" the assassin was quick to reply.

"And do I?" asked the drow.

Entreri thought it over for a moment, then merely shrugged.

"I offer you protection from your enemies," Jarlaxle stated. "No, more than that, I offer you power over your enemies. With your knowledge and reputation and the power of Bregan D'aerthe secretly behind you, you will soon rule the streets of Calimport."

"As Jarlaxle's puppet," Entreri said.

"As Jarlaxle's partner," the drow replied. "I have no need of puppets. In fact, I consider them a hindrance. A partner truly profiting from the organization is one working harder to reach higher goals. Besides, Artemis Entreri, are we not friends?"

Entreri laughed aloud at that notion. The words "Jarlaxle" and "friend" seemed incongruous indeed when used in the same sentence, bringing to mind an old street proverb that the most dangerous and threatening words a Calimshite street vendor could ever say to someone were "trust me."

And that is exactly what Jarlaxle had just said to Entreri.

"Your enemies of the Basadoni Guild will soon call you pasha," the drow went on.

Entreri showed no reaction.

"Even the political leaders of the city, of all the realm of Calimshan, will defer to you," said Jarlaxle.

Entreri showed no reaction.

"I will know now, before you leave this room, if my offer is agreeable," Jarlaxle added, his voice sounding a bit more ominous.

Entreri understood well the implications of that tone. He knew about Bregan D'aerthe being within the city now, and that alone meant that he would either play along or be killed outright.

"Partners," the assassin said, poking himself in the chest. "But I direct the sword of Bregan D'aerthe in Calimport. You strike when and where I decide."

Jarlaxle agreed with a nod. Then he snapped his fingers and another dark elf entered the room, moving beside Entreri. This was obviously the assassin's escort.

"Sleep well," Jarlaxle bade the human. "For tomorrow begins your ascent."

Entreri didn't bother to reply but just walked out of the room.

Yet another drow came out from behind a curtain then. "He was not lying," he assured Jarlaxle, speaking in the tongue common to dark elves.

The cunning mercenary leader nodded and smiled, glad to have the services of so powerful an ally as Rai'gy Bondalek of Ched Nasad, formerly the high priest of that other drow city, but ousted in a coup and rescued by the ever-opportunistic Bregan D'aerthe. Jarlaxle had settled his sights on Rai'gy long before, for the drow was not only powerful in the god-given priestly magics, but was well-versed in the ways of wizards as well. How lucky for Bregan D'aerthe that Rai'gy had suddenly found himself an outcast.

Rai'gy had no idea that Jarlaxle had been the one to incite that coup.

"Your Entreri did not seem thrilled with the treasures you dangled before him," Rai'gy dared to remark. "He will do as he promised, perhaps, but with little heart."

Jarlaxle nodded, not the least bit surprised by Entreri's reaction. He had come to understand Artemis Entreri quite well in the months the assassin had lived with Bregan D'aerthe in Menzoberranzan. He knew the man's motivations and desires—better, perhaps, than Entreri knew them.

"There is one other treasure that I did not offer," he explained. "One that Artemis Entreri does not even yet realize that he wants." Jarlaxle reached into the folds of his cloak and produced an amulet dangling at the end of a silver chain. "I took it from Catti-brie," he explained. "Companion of Drizzt Do'Urden. It was given to her adoptive father, the dwarf Bruenor Battlehammer, by the High Lady Alustriel of Silverymoon long ago as a means of tracking the rogue drow."

"You know much," Rai'gy remarked.

"That is how I survive," Jarlaxle replied.

"But Catti-brie knows it is gone," reasoned Kimmuriel Oblodra. "Thus, she and her companion have likely taken steps to defeat any further use of it."

Jarlaxle was shaking his head long before the psionicist ever finished. "Catti-brie's was returned to her cloak before she left the city. This one is a copy in form and in magic, created by a wizard associate. Likely the woman returned the original to Bruenor Battlehammer, and he gave it back to Lady Alustriel. I should think she would want it back or at least want it out of Catti-brie's possession, for it seems the two had somewhat of a rivalry growing concerning the affections of the rogue Drizzt Do'Urden."

Both the others crinkled their faces in disgust at the thought that any drow so beautiful could find passion with a non-drow, a creature, by that simple definition, who was obviously *iblith*, or excrement.

Jarlaxle, himself intrigued by the beautiful Catti-brie, didn't bother to refute their racist feelings.

"But if that is a copy, is the magic strong enough?" Kimmuriel asked, and he emphasized the word "magic" as if to prompt Jarlaxle to explain how it might prove useful.

"Magical dweomers create pathways of power," Rai'gy Bondalek explained. "Pathways that I know how to enhance and to replicate."

"Rai'gy spent many of his earlier years perfecting the technique," Jarlaxle added. "His ability to recover the previous powers of ancient Ched Nasad relics proved pivotal in his ascension to the position as the city's high priest. And he can do it again, even enhancing the previous dweomer to new heights."

"That we might find Drizzt Do'Urden," Kimmuriel said.

Jarlaxle nodded. "What a fine trophy for Artemis Entreri."

Part 3

CLIMBING TO THE TOP
OF THE BOTTOM

I watched the miles roll out behind me, whether walking down a road or sailing fast out of Waterdeep for the southlands, putting distance between us and the friend we four had left behind.

The friend?

Many times during those long and arduous days, each of us in our own little space came to wonder about that word "friend" and the responsibilities such a label might carry. We had left Wulfgar behind in the wilds of the Spine of the World no less and had no idea if he was well, if he was even still alive. Could a true friend so desert another? Would a true friend allow a man to walk alone along troubled and dangerous paths?

Often I ponder the meaning of that word. Friend. It seems such an obvious thing, friendship, and yet often it becomes so very complicated. Should I have stopped Wulfgar, even knowing and admitting that he had his own road to walk? Or should I have gone with him? Or should we all four have shadowed him, watching over him?

I think not, though I admit that I know not for certain. There is a fine line between friendship and parenting, and when that line is crossed, the result is often disastrous. A parent who strives to make a true friend of his or her child may well sacrifice authority, and though that parent may be comfortable with surrendering the dominant position, the unintentional result will be to steal from that child the necessary guidance and, *more importantly, the sense of security the parent is supposed to impart. On the opposite side, a friend who takes a role as parent forgets the most important ingredient of friendship: respect.*

For respect is the guiding principle of friendship, the lighthouse beacon that directs the course of any true friendship. And respect demands trust.

Thus, the four of us pray for Wulfgar and intend that our paths will indeed cross again. Though we'll often look back over our shoulders and wonder, we hold fast to our understanding of friendship, of trust, and of respect. We accept, grudgingly but resolutely, our divergent paths.

Surely Wulfgar's trials have become my trials in many ways, but I see now that the friendship of mine most in flux is not the one with the barbarian—not from my perspective, anyway, since I understand that Wulfgar alone must decide the depth and course of our bond—but my relationship with Catti-brie. Our love for each other is no secret between us, or to anyone else watching us (and I fear that perhaps the bond that has grown between us might have had some influence in Wulfgar's painful decisions), but the nature of that love remains a mystery to me and to Catti-brie. We have in many ways become as brother and sister, and surely I am closer to her than I could ever have been to any of my natural siblings! For several years we had only each other to count on and both learned beyond any doubt that the other would always be there. I would die for her, and she for me. Without hesitation, without doubt. Truly in all the world there is no one, not even Bruenor, Wulfgar, or Regis, or even Zaknafein, with whom I would rather spend my time. There is no one who can view a sunrise beside me and better understand the emotions that sight always stirs within me. There is no one who can fight beside me and better compliment my movements. There is no one who better knows all that is in my heart and thoughts, though I had not yet spoken a word.

But what does that mean?

Surely I feel a physical attraction to Catti-brie as well. She is possessed of a combination of innocence and a playful wickedness. For all her sympathy and empathy and compassion, there is an edge to Catti-brie that makes potential enemies tremble in fear and potential lovers tremble in anticipation. I believe that she feels similarly toward me, and yet we both understand the dangers of this uncharted territory, dangers more frightening than any physical enemy we have ever known. I am drow, and young, and with the dawn and twilight of several centuries ahead of me. She is human and, though young, with merely decades of life ahead of her. Of course, Catti-brie's life is complicated enough merely having a drow elf as a traveling companion and friend. What troubles might she find if she and I were more than that? And what might the world think of our children, if ever that path we walked? Would any society in all the world accept them?

I know how I feel when I look upon her, though, and believe that I understand her feelings as well. On that level, it seems such an obvious thing, and yet, alas, it becomes so very complicated.

—Drizzt Do'Urden

Chapter 13
SECRET WEAPON

You have found the rogue?" Jarlaxle asked Rai'gy Bondalek. Kimmuriel Oblodra stood beside the mercenary leader, the psionicist appearing unarmed and unarmored, seeming perfectly defenseless to one who did not understand the powers of his mind.

"He is with a dwarf, a woman, and a halfling," Rai'gy answered. "And sometimes they are joined by a great black cat."

"Guenhwyvar," Jarlaxle explained. "Once the property of Masoj Hun'ette. A powerful magical item indeed."

"But not the greatest magic that they carry," Rai'gy informed. "There is another, stored in a pouch on the rogue's belt, that radiates magic stronger than all their other magics combined. Even through the distance of my scrying it beckoned to me, almost as if it were asking me to retrieve it from its present unworthy owner."

"What could it be?" the always opportunistic mercenary asked.

Rai'gy shook his head, his shock of white hair flying from side to side. "Like no dweomer I have seen before," he admitted.

"Is that not the way of magic?" Kimmuriel Oblo-dra put in with obvious distaste. "Unknown and uncontrollable."

Rai'gy shot the psionicist an angry glare, but Jar-laxle, more than willing to utilize both magic and psion-ics, merely smiled. "Learn more about it and about them," he instructed the wizard-priest. "If it beckons to us, then perhaps we would be wise to heed its call. How far are they, and how fast can we get to them?"

"Very," Rai'gy answered. "And very. They had begun an overland route but were accosted by giantkind and goblinkin at every bend in the path."

"Perhaps the magical item is not particular about who it calls for a new owner," Kimmuriel remarked with obvious sarcasm.

"They turned about and took ship," Rai'gy went on, ignoring the comment. "Out of the great northern city of Waterdeep, I believe, far, far up the Sword Coast."

"But sailing south?" Jarlaxle asked hopefully.

"I believe," Rai'gy answered. "It does not matter. There are magics, of course, and mind powers," he added, nodding deferentially to Kimmuriel, "that can get us to them as easily as if they were standing in the next room."

"Back to your searching, then," Jarlaxle said.

"But are we not to visit a guild this very night?" Rai'gy asked.

"You will not be needed," Jarlaxle replied. "Minor guilds alone will meet this night."

"Even minor guilds would be wise to employ wiz-ards," the wizard-priest remarked.

"The wizard of this one is a friend of Entreri," Jar-laxle explained with a laugh that made it sound as if it were all too easy. "And the other guild is naught but halflings, hardly versed in the ways of magic. To-morrow night you will be needed, perhaps. This night continue your examination of Drizzt Do'Urden. In the end he will likely prove the most important cog of all."

"Because of the magical item?" Kimmuriel asked.

"Because of Entreri's lack of interest," Jarlaxle replied.

The wizard-priest shook his head. "We offer him power and riches beyond his comprehension," he said. "And yet he leads us onward as if he were going into hopeless battle against the Spider Queen herself."

"He cannot appreciate the power or the riches until he has resolved an inner conflict," explained Jarlaxle, whose greatest gift of all was the ability to get into the minds of enemies and friends alike, and not with prying powers, such as Kimmuriel Oblodra might use, but with simple empathy and understanding. "But fear not his present lack of motivation. I know Artemis Entreri well enough to understand that he will prove more than effective whether his heart is in the fight or not. As humans go I have never met one more dangerous or more devious."

"A pity his skin is so light," Kimmuriel remarked.

Jarlaxle only smiled. He knew well enough that if Artemis Entreri had been born drow in Menzoberranzan the man would have been among the greatest of weapon masters, or perhaps he would have even exceeded that claim. Perhaps he would have been a rival to Jarlaxle for control of Bregan D'aerthe.

"We will speak in the comfortable darkness of the tunnels when the shining hellfire rises into the too-high sky," he said to Rai'gy. "Have more answers for me."

"Fare well with the guilds," Rai'gy answered, and with a bow he turned and left.

Jarlaxle turned to Kimmuriel and nodded. It was time to go hunting.

* * * * *

With their cherubic faces, halflings were regarded by the other races as creatures with large eyes, but how much wider those eyes became for the four in the room with Dwahvel when a magical portal opened right before them (despite the usual precautions against such magical intrusion), and Artemis Entreri stepped into the room. The assassin cut an impressive figure in a layered black coat and a black bolero, banded about the base of its riser in blacker silk.

Entreri assumed a strong, hands-on-hips pose just as Kimmuriel had taught him, holding steady against the waves of disorientation that always accompanied such psionic dimensional travel.

Behind him, in the chamber on the other side of the door, a room lightless save that spilling in through the gate from Dwahvel's chamber, huddled a few dark shapes. When one of the halfling soldiers moved to meet the intruder, one of those dark shapes shifted slightly, and the halfling, with hardly a squeak, toppled to the floor.

"He is sleeping and otherwise unharmed," Entreri quickly explained, not wanting a fight with the others, who were scrambling about for weapons. "I did not come here for a fight, I assure you, but I can leave all of you dead in my wake if you insist upon one."

"You could have used the front door," Dwahvel, the only one appearing unshaken, remarked dryly.

"I did not wish to be seen entering your establishment," the assassin, fully oriented once more, explained. "For your protection."

"And what form of entrance is this?" Dwahvel asked. "Magical and unbidden, yet none of my wards—and I paid well for them, I assure you—offered resistance."

"No magic that will concern you," Entreri replied, "but that will surely concern my enemies. Know that I did not return to Calimport to lurk in shadows at the bidding of others. I have traveled the Realms extensively and have brought back with me that which I have learned."

"So Artemis Entreri returns as the conqueror," Dwahvel remarked. Beside her the soldiers bristled, but Dwahvel did well to hold them in check. Now that Entreri was among them, to fight him would cost her dearly, she realized.

Very dearly.

"Perhaps," Entreri conceded. "We shall see how it goes."

"It will take more than a display of teleportation to convince me to throw the weight of my guild behind you," Dwahvel said calmly. "To choose wrongly in such a war would prove fatal."

"I do not wish you to choose at all," Entreri assured her.

Dwahvel eyed him suspiciously, then turned to each of her trusted guards. They, too, wore doubting expressions.

"Then why bother to come to me?" she asked.

"To inform you that a war is about to begin," Entreri answered. "I owe you that much, at least."

"And perhaps you wish for me to open wide my ears that you may learn how goes the fight," the sly halfling reasoned.

"As you wish," Entreri replied. "When this is finished, and I have found control, I will not forget all that you have already done for me."

"And if you lose?"

Entreri laughed. "Be wary," he said. "And, for your health, Dwahvel Tiggerwillies, be neutral. I owe you and see our friendship as to the benefit of both, but if I learn that you betray me by word or by deed, I will bring your house down around you." With that, he gave a polite bow, a tip of the black bolero and slipped back through the portal.

One globe of darkness after another filled Dwahvel's chamber, forcing her and the three standing soldiers to crawl about helplessly until one found the normal exit and called the others to him.

Finally the darkness abated, and the halflings dared to re-enter, to find their sleeping companion snoring contentedly, and then to find, upon searching the body, a small dart stuck into his shoulder.

"Entreri has friends," one of them remarked.

Dwahvel merely nodded, not surprised and glad indeed at that moment that she had previously chosen to help the outcast assassin. He was not a man Dwahvel Tiggerwillies wished for an enemy.

* * * * *

"Ah, but you make my life so dangerous," LaValle said with an exaggerated sigh when Entreri, unannounced and uninvited, walked from thin air, it seemed, into LaValle's private room.

"Well done—on your escape from Kadran Gordeon, I mean," LaValle went on when Entreri didn't immediately respond. The wizard was trying hard to appear collected. Hadn't Entreri slipped into his guarded room twice before, after all? But this time— and the assassin recognized it splayed on LaValle's face—he had truly surprised the wizard. Bodeau had sharpened up the defenses of his guild house amazingly well against both magical and physical intrusion. As much as he respected Entreri, LaValle had obviously not expected the assassin to get through so easily.

"Not so difficult a task, I assure you," the assassin replied, keeping his voice steady so that his words sounded as simple fact and not a boast. "I have traveled the world, and under the world and have witnessed powers very different from anything experienced in Calimport. Powers that will bring me that which I desire."

LaValle sat on an old and comfortable chair, planting one elbow on the worn arm and dropping his head sidelong against his open palm. What was it about this man, he wondered, that so mocked all the ordinary trappings of power? He looked all around at his room, at the many carved statues, gargoyles, and exotic birds, at the assortment of finely carved staves, some magical, some not, at the three skulls grinning from the cubbies atop his desk, at the crystal ball set upon the small table across the way. These were his items of power, items gained through a lifetime of work, items that he could use to destroy or at least to defend against, any single man he had ever met.

Except for one. What was it about this one? The way he stood? The way he moved? The simple aura of power that surrounded him, as tangible as the gray cloak and black bolero he now wore?

"Go and bring Quentin Bodeau," Entreri instructed.

"He will not appreciate becoming involved."

"He already is," Entreri assured the wizard. "Now he must choose."

"Between you and . . . ?" LaValle asked.

"The rest of them," Entreri replied calmly.

LaValle tilted his head curiously. "You mean to do battle with all of Calimport then?" he asked skeptically.

"With all in Calimport who oppose me," Entreri said, again with the utmost calm.

LaValle shook his head, not knowing what to make of it all. He trusted Entreri's judgment—never had the wizard met a more cunning and controlled man—but the assassin spoke foolishness, it seemed, if he honestly believed he could stand alone against the likes of the Basadonis, let alone the rest of Calimport's street powers.

But still . . .

"Shall I bring Chalsee Anguaine, as well?" the wizard asked, standing and heading for the door.

"Chalsee has already been shown the futility of resistance," Entreri replied.

LaValle stopped abruptly, turning on the assassin as if betrayed.

"I knew you would go along," Entreri explained. "For you have come to know and love me as a brother. The lieutenant's mind-set, however, remained a mystery. He had to be convinced, or removed."

LaValle just stared at him, awaiting the verdict.

"He is convinced," Entreri remarked, moving to fall comfortably into LaValle's comfortable chair. "Very much so.

"And so," he continued as the wizard again started for the door, "will you find Bodeau."

LaValle turned on him again.

"He will make the right choice," Entreri assured the man.

"Will he have a choice?" LaValle dared to ask.

"Of course not."

Indeed, when LaValle found Bodeau in his private quarters and informed him that Artemis Entreri had come again the guildmaster blanched white and trembled so violently that LaValle feared he would simply fall over dead on the floor.

"You have spoken with Chalsee then?" LaValle asked.

"Evil days," Bodeau replied, and moving as if he had to battle mind with muscle through every pained step, he headed for the corridor.

"Evil days?" LaValle echoed incredulously under his breath. What in all the Realms could prompt the master of a murderous guild to make such a statement? Suddenly taking Entreri's claims more seriously, the wizard fell into step behind Bodeau. He noted, his intrigue mounting ever higher, that the guildmaster ordered no soldiers to follow or even to flank.

Bodeau stopped outside the wizard's door, letting LaValle assume the lead into the room. There in the study sat Entreri, exactly as the wizard had left him. The assassin appeared totally unprepared had Bodeau decided to attack instead of parlay, as if he had known without doubt that Bodeau wouldn't dare oppose him.

"What do you demand of me?" Bodeau asked before LaValle could find any opening to the obviously awkward situation.

"I have decided to begin with the Basadonis," Entreri calmly replied. "For they, after all, started this fight. You, then, must locate all of their soldiers, all of their fronts, and a complete layout of their operation, not including the guild house."

"I offer to tell no one that you came here and to promise that my soldiers will not interfere," Bodeau countered.

"Your soldiers could not interfere," Entreri shot back, a flash of anger crossing his black eyes.

LaValle watched in continued amazement as Quentin Bodeau fought so very hard to control his shaking.

"And we will not," the guildmaster offered.

"I have told you the terms of your survival," Entreri said, a coldness creeping into his voice that made LaValle believe that Bodeau and all the guild would be murdered that very night if the guildmaster didn't agree. "What say you?"

"I will consider—"

"Now."

Bodeau glared at LaValle, as if blaming the wizard for ever allowing Artemis Entreri into his life, a sentiment that LaValle, as unnerved as Bodeau, could surely understand.

"You ask me to go against the most powerful pashas of the streets," Bodeau said, trying hard to find some courage.

"Choose," Entreri said.

A long, uncomfortable moment slipped past. "I will see what my soldiers may discern," Bodeau promised.

"Very wise," said Entreri. "Now leave us. I wish a word with LaValle."

More than happy to be away from the man, Bodeau turned on his heel and after another hateful glare at LaValle, swiftly exited the room.

"I do not begin to guess what tricks you have brought with you," LaValle said to Entreri.

"I have been to Menzoberranzan," Entreri admitted. "The city of the drow."

LaValle's eyes widened, his mouth drooping open.

"I returned with more than trinkets."

"You have allied with . . ."

"You are the only one I have told and the only one I shall tell," Entreri announced. "Understand the responsibility that goes with such knowledge. It is one that I shan't take lightly."

"But Chalsee Anguaine?" LaValle asked. "You said he had been convinced."

"A friend found his mind and there put images too horrible for him to resist," Entreri explained. "Chalsee knows not the truth, only that to resist would bring about a fate too terrible to consider. When he reported to Bodeau his terror was sincere."

"And where do I stand in your grand plans?" the wizard asked, trying very hard not to sound sarcastic. "If Bodeau fails you, then what of LaValle?"

"I will show you a way out should that come to pass," Entreri promised, walking over to the desk. "I owe you that much at least." He picked up a small dagger LaValle had set there to cut seals on parchments or to prick a finger when a spell called for a component of blood.

LaValle understood then that Entreri was being pragmatic, not merciful. If the wizard was indeed spared should Bodeau fail the assassin, it would only be because Entreri had some use for him.

"You are surprised that the guildmaster so readily complied," Entreri said evenly. "You must understand his choice: to risk that I will fail and the Basadonis will win out and then exact revenge on my allies . . . or to die now, this very night, and horribly, I assure you."

LaValle forced an expressionless set to his visage, playing the role of complete neutrality, even detachment.

"You have much work ahead of you, I assume," Entreri said, and he flicked his wrist, sending the dagger soaring past the wizard to knock heavily into the outside wall. "I take my leave."

Indeed, as the signal knock against the wall sounded, Kimmuriel Oblodra went into his contemplation again and brought up another dimensional pathway for the assassin to make his exit.

LaValle saw the portal open and thought for a moment out of sheer curiosity to leap through it beside Entreri to unmask this great mystery.

Good sense overruled curiosity.

And then the wizard was alone and very glad of it.

* * * * *

"I do not understand," Rai'gy Bondalek said when Entreri rejoined him, Jarlaxle, and Kimmuriel in the complex of tunnels beneath the city that the drow had made their own. He remembered then to speak more slowly, for Entreri, while fairly proficient in the drow language, was not completely fluent, and the wizard-priest didn't want to bother with the human tongue at all, either by learning it or by wasting the energy necessary to enact a spell that would allow them all to understand each other, whatever language each of them chose to speak. In truth, Bondalek's decision to force the discussion to continue in the drow language, even when Entreri was with them, was more a choice to keep the human assassin somewhat off-balance. "It seems, from all you previously said that the halflings would be better suited and more easily convinced to perform the services you just put upon Quentin Bodeau."

"I doubt not Dwahvel's loyalty," Entreri replied in the human Calimport tongue, and he eyed Rai'gy with every word.

The wizard turned a curious and helpless look over Jarlaxle, and the mercenary, with a laugh at the pettiness of it all, produced an orb from an inside fold of his cloak, held it aloft, and spoke a word of command. Now they would all understand.

"To herself and her well-being, I mean," Entreri said, again in the human tongue, though Rai'gy heard it in drow. "She is no threat."

"And pitiful Quentin Bodeau and his lackey wizard are?" Rai'gy asked incredulously, Jarlaxle's enchantment reversing the effect, so that, while the drow spoke in his native tongue, Entreri heard it in his own.

"Do not underestimate the power of Bodeau's guild," Entreri warned. "They are firmly entrenched, with eyes ever outward."

"So you force his loyalty early," Jarlaxle agreed,

"that he cannot later claim ignorance whatever the outcome."

"And where from here?" Kimmuriel asked.

"We secure the Basadoni Guild," Entreri explained. "That then becomes our base of power, with both Dwahvel and Bodeau watching to make certain that the others aren't aligning against us."

"And from there?" Kimmuriel pressed.

Entreri smiled and looked to Jarlaxle, and the mercenary leader recognized that Entreri understood that Kimmuriel was asking the questions as Jarlaxle had bade him to ask.

"From there we will see what opportunities present themselves," Jarlaxle answered before Entreri could reply. "Perhaps that base will prove solid enough. Perhaps not."

Later on, after Entreri had left them, Jarlaxle, with some pride, turned to his two cohorts. "Did I not choose well?" he asked.

"He thinks like a drow," Rai'gy replied, offering as high a compliment as Jarlaxle had ever heard him give to a human or to anyone else who was not drow. "Though I wish he would better learn our language and our sign language."

Jarlaxle, so pleased with the progress, only laughed.

Chapter 14
REPUTATION

The man felt strange indeed. Alcohol dimmed his senses so that he could not register all the facts about his current situation. He felt light, floating, and felt a burning in his chest.

Wulfgar clenched his fist more tightly, grasping the front of the man's tunic and pulling chest hairs from their roots in the process. With just that one arm the barbarian easily held the two hundred pound man off the ground. Using his other arm to navigate the crowd in the Cutlass, he made his way for the door. He hated taking this roundabout route—previously he had merely tossed unruly drunks through a window or a wall—but Arumn Gardpeck had quickly reigned in that behavior, promising to take the cost of damages out of Wulfgar's pay.

Even a single window could cost the barbarian a few bottles, and if the frame went with it Wulfgar might not find any drink for a week.

The man, smiling stupidly, looked at Wulfgar and finally managed to find some focus. Recognition of the bouncer and of his present predicament at last showed on his face. "Hey!" he complained, but then he was flying, flat out in the air, arms and legs flailing. He landed facedown in the muddy road, and there he stayed. Likely a wagon would have run him over had not a couple of passersby taken pity on the poor slob and dragged him into the gutter . . . taking the rest of his coins from him in the process.

"Fifteen feet," Josi Puddles said to Arumn, estimating the length of the drunk's flight. "And with just one arm."

"I told ye he was a strong one," Arumn replied, wiping the bar and pretending that he was hardly amazed. In the weeks since the barkeep had hired Wulfgar, the barbarian had made many such throws.

"Every man on Half Moon Street's talking about that," Josi added, the tone of his voice somewhat grim. "I been noticing that your crowd's a bit tougher every night this week."

Arumn understood the perceptive man's less than subtle statement. There was a pecking order in Luskan's underbelly that resisted intrusion. As Wulfgar's reputation continued to grow, some of those higher on that pecking order would find their own reputations at stake and would filter in to mend the damage.

"You like the barbarian," Josi stated as much as asked.

Arumn, staring hard at Wulfgar as the huge man filtered through the crowd once more, gave a resigned nod. Hiring Wulfgar had been a matter of business, not friendship, and Arumn usually took great pains to avoid any personal relationships with his bouncers—since many of those men, drifters by nature, either wandered away of their own accord or angered the wrong thug and wound up dead at Arumn's doorstep. With Wulfgar, though, the barkeep had lost some of that perspective. Their late nights together when the Cutlass was quiet, Wulfgar drinking at the bar, Arumn preparing the place for the next day's business, had become a pleasant routine. Arumn truly enjoyed Wulfgar's companionship. He discovered that once the drink was in the man, Wulfgar let down his cold and distant facade. Many nights they stayed together until the dawn, Arumn listening intently as Wulfgar wove tales of the frigid northland, of Icewind Dale, and of friends and enemies alike that made the barkeep's hair stand up on the back of his neck. Arumn had heard the story of Akar Kessel and the crystal shard so many times that he could almost picture the avalanche at Kelvin's Cairn that took down the wizard and buried the ancient and evil relic.

And every time Wulfgar recounted tales of the dark tunnels under the dwarven kingdom of Mithral Hall and the coming of the dark elves, Arumn later found himself shivering under his blankets, as he had when he was a child and his father had told him similarly dark stories by the hearth.

Indeed, Arumn Gardpeck had come to like his newest employee more than he should and less than he would.

"Then calm him," Josi Puddles finished. "He'll be bringing in Morik the Rogue and Tree Block Breaker anytime soon."

Arumn shuddered at the thought and didn't disagree. Particularly concerning Tree Block. Morik the Rogue, he knew, would be a bit more cautious (and thus, would be much more dangerous), would spend weeks, even months, sizing up the new threat before making his move, but brash Tree Block, arguably the toughest human—if he even was human, for many stories said that he had more than a little orc, or even ogre, blood in him—ever to step into Luskan, would not be so patient.

"Wulfgar," the barkeep called.

The big man sifted through the crowd to stand opposite Arumn.

"Did ye have to throw him out?" Arumn asked.

"He put his hand where it did not belong," Wulfgar replied absently. "Delly wanted him gone."

Arumn followed Wulfgar's gaze across the room to Delly . . . Delenia Curtie. Though not yet past her twentieth birthday, she had worked in the Cutlass for several years. She was a wisp of a thing, barely five feet tall and so slender that many thought she had a bit of elven blood in her—though it was more the result of drinking elven spirits, Arumn knew. Her blond hair hung untrimmed and unkempt and often not very clean. Her brown eyes had long ago lost their soft innocence and taken on a harder edge, and her pale skin had not seen enough of the sun in years, nor proper nutrition, and was now dry and rough. Her step had replaced the bounce of youth with the caution of a woman often hunted. But still there remained a charm about Delly, a sensual wickedness that many of the patrons, particularly after a few drinks, found too tempting to resist.

"If ye're to be killing every man who's grabbing Delly's bottom, I'll have no patrons left within the week," Arumn said dryly.

"Just push them out," Arumn continued when Wulfgar offered no response, not even a change of expression. "Ye don't have to be throwing them halfway to Waterdeep." He motioned back to the crowd, indicating that he was done with the barbarian.

Wulfgar walked away, back to his duties sifting through the boisterous bunch.

Within an hour another man, bleeding from his nose and mouth, took the aerial route, this time a two-handed toss that put him almost to the other side of the street.

* * * * *

Wulfgar held up his shirt, revealing the jagged line of deep scars. "Had me up in its mouth," he explained grimly, slurring the words. It had taken more than a little of the potent spirits to bring him to a level of comfort where he could discuss this battle, the fight with the yochlol, the fight that had brought him to Lolth, and she to Errtu for his years of torment. "A mouse in the cat's mouth." He gave a slight chuckle. "But this mouse had a kick."

His gaze drifted to Aegis-fang, lying on the bar a couple of feet away.

"Prettiest hammer I've ever seen," remarked Josi Puddles. He reached for it tentatively, staring at Wulfgar as his hand inched in, for he, like all the others, had no desire to anger the frightfully dangerous man.

But Wulfgar, usually very protective of Aegis-fang, his sole link to his past life, wasn't even watching. His recounting of the yochlol fight had sent his thoughts and his heart careening back across the years, had locked him into a replay of the events that had put him in living hell.

"And how it hurt," he said softly, voice quavering, one hand subconsciously running the length of the scar.

Arumn Gardpeck stood before him staring, but though Wulfgar's eyes aimed at those of the barkeep, their focus was far, far away. Arumn slid another drink before the man, but Wulfgar didn't notice. With a deep and profound sigh the barbarian dropped his head into his huge arms, seeking the comfort of blackness.

He felt a touch on his bare arm, gentle and soft, and turned his head so that he could regard Delly. She nodded to Arumn, then gently pulled Wulfgar, coaxing him to rise and leading him away.

Wulfgar awoke later that night, long and slanted rays of moonlight filtering into the room through the western window. It took him a few moments to orient himself and to realize that this was not his room, for his room had no windows.

He glanced around and then to the blankets beside him, to the lithe form of Delly amidst those blankets, her skin seeming soft and delicate in the flattering light.

Then he remembered. Delly had taken him from the bar to bed—not to his own, but to hers—and he remembered all they had done.

Fearful, recalling his less-than-tender parting with Catti-brie, Wulfgar gently reached over and put his hand about the woman's neck, sighing in profound relief to find that she still had a pulse. Then he turned her over and scanned her bare body, not in any lustful way, but merely to see if she showed any bruises, any signs that he had brutalized her.

Her sleep was quiet and sound.

Wulfgar turned to the side of the bed, rolling his legs off the edge. He started to stand, but his throbbing head nearly knocked him backward. Reeling, he fought to control his balance and then ambled over to the window, staring out at the setting moon.

Catti-brie was likely watching that same moon, he thought, and somehow knew it to be true. After a while he turned to regard Delly again, all soft and snuggled amidst mounds of blankets. He had been able to make love to her without the anger, without the memories of the succubi balling his fists in rage. For a moment he felt as if he might be free, felt as if he should burst out of the house, out of Luskan altogether, running down the road in search of his old friends. He looked back at the moon and thought of Catti-brie and how wonderful it would be to fall into her arms.

But then he realized the truth of it all.

The drink had allowed him to build a wall against those memories, and behind that protective barrier he had been able to live in the present and not the past.

"Come on back to bed," came Delly's voice behind him, a gentle coax with a subtle promise of sensual pleasure. "And don't you be worrying over your hammer," she added, turning so that Wulfgar could follow her gaze to the opposite wall, against which Aegis-fang rested.

Wulfgar spent a long moment regarding the woman, caretaker of his emotions and his possessions. She was sitting up, the covers bundled about her waist, and making no move to cover her nakedness. Indeed she seemed to flaunt it a bit to entice the man back into her bed.

A large part of Wulfgar did want to go to her. But he resisted, realizing the danger, realizing that the drink had worn off. In a fit of passion, a fit of remembered rage, how easy it would be for him to squeeze her bird-like neck.

"Later," he promised, moving to gather his clothes. "Before we go to work this night."

"But you don't have to leave."

"I do," he said briskly, and he saw the flash of pain across her face. He moved to her immediately, very close. "I do," he repeated in a softer tone. "But I will come back to you. Later."

He kissed her gently on the forehead and started for the door.

"You are thinking that I'll want you back," came a harsh call behind him, and he turned to see Delly staring at him, her gaze ice cold, her arms folded defensively across her chest.

At first surprised, Wulfgar only then realized that he wasn't the only one in this room carrying around personal demons.

"Go," Delly said to him. "Maybe I'll take you back, and maybe I'll find another. All the same to me."

Wulfgar sighed and shook his head, then pushed out into the hall, more than happy to be out of that room.

The sun peeked over the eastern rim before the barbarian, an empty bottle at his side, found his way back into the void of sleep. He didn't see the sunrise, though, for his room had no windows.

He preferred it that way.

Chapter 15
THE CALL OF CRENSHINIBON

The prow cut swiftly through the azure blanket of the Sword Coast, shooting great fins of water and launching spray high into the air. At the forward rail, Catti-brie felt the stinging, salty droplets, so cold in contrast to the heat of the brilliant sun on her fair face. The ship, *Quester*, sailed south, and so south the woman looked. Away from Icewind Dale, away from Luskan, away from Waterdeep, from which they had sailed three days previous.

Away from Wulfgar.

Not for the first time, and she knew not for the last, the woman reconsidered their decision to let the beleaguered barbarian go off on his own. In his present state of mind, a state of absolute tumult and confusion, how could Wulfgar not need them?

And yet she had no way to get to him now, sailing south along the Sword Coast. Catti-brie blinked away moisture that was not sea spray and set her gaze firmly on the wide waters before them, taking some heart at the sheer speed of the vessel. They had a mission to complete, a vital mission, for during their days crossing by land they had come to learn beyond doubt that Crenshinibon remained a potent foe, sentient and intelligent. It was able to call in creatures to serve as its minions, monsters of dark heart eager to grasp at the promises of the relic. Thus the friends had gone to Waterdeep and had taken passage on the sturdiest available ship in the harbor, believing that enemies would be fewer at sea and far easier to discern. Both Drizzt and Catti-brie greatly lamented that Captain Deudermont and his wondrous *Sea Sprite* were not in.

Less than two hours out from port one of the crewmen had come after Drizzt, thinking to steal the crystal. Battered by the flat sides of flashing twin scimitars, the man, bound and gagged, had been handed off to another ship passing by, heading to the north to Waterdeep, with instructions to turn him over to the dock authorities in that lawful city for proper punishment.

Since then, though, the voyage had been uneventful, just swift sailing and empty waters, flat horizons dotted rarely by the sails of another distant ship.

Drizzt moved to join Catti-brie at the rail. Though she didn't turn around, she knew by the footsteps that followed the near-silent drow that Bruenor and Regis had come too.

"Only a few more days to Baldur's Gate," the drow said.

Catti-brie glanced over at him, noting that he kept the cowl of his traveling cloak low over his face—not to block any of the stinging spray, she knew, for Drizzt loved that feel as much as she, but to keep him in comfortable shade. Drizzt and Catti-brie had spent years together aboard Deudermont's *Sea Sprite*, and still the high sun of midday glittering off the waters bothered the drow elf, whose heritage had designed him for walking lightless caverns.

"How fares Bruenor?" the woman asked quietly, pretending not to know that the dwarf was standing behind her.

"Grumbling for solid ground and all the enemies in the world to stand against him, if necessary, to get him off this cursed floating coffin," the ranger replied, playing along.

Catti-brie managed a slight grin, not surprised at all. She had journeyed the seas with Bruenor farther to the south. While the dwarf had kept a stoic front on that occasion, his relief had been obvious when they had at last docked and returned again to solid ground. This time Bruenor was having an even worse time of it, spending long stretches at the rail—and not for the view.

"Regis seems unbothered," Drizzt went on. "He makes certain that no food remains on Bruenor's plate soon after Bruenor declares that he cannot eat."

Another smile found its way onto Catti-brie's face. Again it was short-lived. "Do ye think we'll be seeing him again?" she asked.

Drizzt sighed and turned his gaze out to the empty waters. Though they were both looking south, the wrong direction, they were both, in a manner of speaking, looking for Wulfgar. It was as if, against all logic and reason, they expected the man to come swimming toward them.

"I do not know," the drow admitted. "In his mood, it is possible that Wulfgar has found many enemies and has flung himself against them with all his heart. No doubt many of them are dead, but the north is a place of countless foes, some, I fear, too powerful even for Wulfgar."

"Bah!" Bruenor snorted from behind. "We'll find me boy, don't ye doubt. And the worst foe he'll be seeing'll be meself, paying him back for slapping me girl and for bringing me so much worry!"

"We shall find him," Regis declared. "And Lady Alustriel will help, and so will the Harpells."

The mention of the Harpells brought a groan from Bruenor. The Harpells were a family of eccentric wizards known for blowing themselves and their friends up, turning themselves—quite by accident and without repair—into various animals and all other manner of self-inflicted catastrophes.

"Alustriel, then," Regis agreed. "She will help if we cannot find him on our own."

"Bah! And how tough're ye thinking that to be?" Bruenor argued. "Are ye knowin' many rampaging seven-footers then? And them carrying hammers that can knock down a giant or the house it's living in with one throw?"

"There," Drizzt said to Catti-brie. "Our assurances that we will indeed find our friend."

The woman managed another smile, but it, too, was a strained thing and could not last. And what would they find when they at last located their missing friend? Even if he was physically unharmed, would he wish to see them? And even if he did, would he be in a better humor? And most important of all, would they—would she—really wish to see him? Wulfgar had hurt Catti-brie badly, not in body, but in heart, when he had struck her. She could forgive him that, she knew, to some extent at least.

But only once.

She studied her drow friend, saw his shadowed profile under the edge of his cowl as he stared vacantly to the empty waters, his lavender eyes glazed, as if his mind were looking elsewhere. She turned to consider Bruenor and Regis then and found them similarly distracted. All of them wanted to find Wulfgar again—not the Wulfgar who had left them on the road but the one who had left them those years ago in the tunnels beneath Mithral Hall, taken by the yochlol. They all wanted it to be as it had once been, the Companions of the Hall adventuring together without the company of brooding internal demons.

"A sail to the south," Drizzt remarked, drawing the woman from her contemplation. Even as Catti-brie looked out from the rail, squinting in a futile attempt to spot the too-distant ship, she heard the cry from the crow's nest confirming the drow's claim.

"What's her course?" Captain Vaines called from somewhere near the middle of the deck.

"North," Drizzt answered quietly so that only Catti-brie, Bruenor, and Regis could hear.

"North," cried the crewman from the crow's nest a few seconds later.

"Yer eyes've improved in the sunlight," Bruenor remarked.

"Credit Deudermont," Catti-brie explained.

"My eyes," Drizzt added, "and my perceptions of intent."

"What're ye babbling about?" Bruenor asked, but the ranger held up his hand, motioning for silence. He stood staring intently at the distant ship whose sails now appeared to the other three as tiny black dots, barely above the horizon.

"Go and tell Captain Vaines to turn us to the west," Drizzt instructed Regis.

The halfling stood staring for just a moment, then rushed back to find Vaines. Just a minute or so later the friends felt the pull as *Quester* leaned and turned her prow to the left.

"Ye're just making the trip longer," Bruenor started to complain, but again Drizzt held up his hand.

"She is turning with us, keeping her course to intercept," the drow explained.

"Pirates?" Catti-brie asked, a question echoed by Captain Vaines as he moved up to join the others.

"They are not in trouble, for they cut the water as swiftly as we, perhaps even more so," Drizzt reasoned. "Nor are they a ship of a king's fleet, for they fly no standard, and we are too far out for any coastal patrollers."

"Pirates," Captain Vaines spat distastefully.

"How can ye know all that?" an unconvinced Bruenor demanded.

"Comes from hunting 'em," Catti-brie explained. "And we've hunted more than our share."

"So I heard in Waterdeep," said Vaines, which was why he had agreed to take them aboard for a swift run to Baldur's Gate in the first place. Normally a woman, a dwarf, and a halfling would find no easy—and surely no cheap—passage out of Waterdeep Harbor when accompanied by a dark elf, but among the honest sailors of Waterdeep the names Drizzt Do'Urden and Catti-brie rang out as sweet music.

The approaching ship showed bigger on the horizon now, but it was still too small for any detailed images—except to Drizzt, and to Captain Vaines and the man in the crow's nest, both holding rare and expensive spyglasses. The captain put his to his eye now and recognized the telltale triangular sails. "She's a schooner," he said. "And a light one. She cannot hold more than twenty or so and is no match for us."

Catti-brie considered the words carefully. *Quester* was a caravel, and a large one at that. She held three strong banks of sails and had a front end long and tapered to aid in her run, but she carried a pair of ballistae, and had thick and strong sides. A slender schooner did not seem much of a match for *Quester*, to be sure, but how many pirates had said the same about another schooner, Deudermont's *Sea Sprite*, only to wind up fast filling with sea water?

"Back to the south with us!" the captain called, and *Quester* creaked and leaned to the right. Soon enough, the approaching schooner corrected her course to maintain her intercepting route.

"Too far to the north," Vaines remarked, striking a pensive pose, one hand coming up to stroke the gray hairs of his beard. "Pirates should not be this far north and should not deign to approach us."

The others, particularly Drizzt and Catti-brie, understood his trepidation. Concerning brute force at least, the schooner and her crew of twenty, perhaps thirty, would seem no match for the sixty of Vaines's crew. But such odds could often be overcome at sea by use of a single wizard, Catti-brie and Drizzt both knew. They had seen *Sea Sprite*'s wizard, a powerful invoker named Robillard, take down more than one ship single-handedly long before conventional weapons had even been used.

"Shouldn't and aren't ain't the same word," Bruenor remarked dryly. "I'm not knowing if they're pirates or not, but they're coming, to be sure."

Vaines nodded and moved back to the wheel with his navigator.

"I'll get me bow and go up to the nest," Catti-brie offered.

"Pick your shots well," Drizzt replied. "Likely there is one, or maybe a couple, who are guiding this ship. If you can find them and down them, the rest might flee."

"Is that the way of pirates?" Regis asked, seeming more than a little confused. "If they even are pirates?"

"That is the way of a lesser ship coming after us because of the crystal shard," Drizzt replied, and then the other two caught on.

"Ye're thinking the damned thing's calling them?" Bruenor asked.

"Pirates take few chances," Drizzt explained. "A light schooner coming after *Quester* is taking a great chance."

"Unless they got wizards," Bruenor reasoned, for he, too, had understood Captain Vaines's concerns.

Drizzt was shaking his head before the dwarf ever finished. Catti-brie would have been, too, except that she had already run off to retrieve Taulmaril. "A pirate running with enough magical aid to destroy *Quester* would have long ago been marked," the drow explained. "We would have heard of her and been warned of her before we ever left Waterdeep."

"Unless she is new to the trade or new of the power," Regis reasoned.

Drizzt conceded the point with a nod, but he remained unconvinced, believing that Crenshinibon had brought this new enemy in, as it had brought in so many others in a desperate attempt to wrest the relic away from those who would see it destroyed. The drow looked back across the deck, spotting the familiar form of Catti-brie with Taulmaril, the wondrous Heartseeker, strapped across her back as she made her nimble way up the knotted rope.

Then he opened his belt pouch and gazed upon the wicked relic, Crenshinibon. How he wished he could hear its call to better understand the enemies it would bring before them.

Quester shuddered suddenly as one of its great ballistae let fly. The huge spear leaped away, skipping a couple times across the water far short of the out-of-range schooner, but close enough to let the sailors aboard her recognize that *Quester* had no intention of parlay or surrender.

But the schooner flew on without the slightest course change, splitting the water right beside the spent ballista bolt, even clipping the metal-tipped spear as it hung buoy-like in the swelling sea. Smooth and swift was its run, seeming more like an arrow cutting the air than a ship cutting the water. The narrow hull had been built purely for speed. Drizzt had seen pirates such as this; often similar ships had led *Sea Sprite*, also a schooner, but a three-master and much larger, on long pursuits. The drow had enjoyed those chases most of all during his time with Deudermont, sails full of wind, spray rushing past, his white hair flowing out behind him as he stood poised at the forward rail.

He was not enjoying this scenario, though. There were many pirates along the Sword Coast well capable of destroying *Quester*, larger and better armed and armored than the well-structured caravel, truly the hunting lions of the region. But this approaching ship was more a bird of prey, a swift and cunning hunter designed for smaller quarry, for fishing boats wandering too far from protected harbors or the luxury barges of wealthy merchants who let their warship escorts get a bit too far away from them. Or pirate schooners would work in conjunction, several on a target, a fleet hunting pack.

But no other sails were to be seen on any horizon.

From a different pouch, Drizzt took out his onyx figurine. "I will bring in Guenhwyvar soon," he explained to Regis and Bruenor. Captain Vaines came up again, a nervous expression stamped on his face—one that told the drow that, despite his many years at sea, Vaines had not seen much battle. "With a proper run the panther can leap fifty feet or more to gain the deck of our enemies' ship. Once there she will make more than a few call for a retreat."

"I have heard of your panther friend," Vaines said. "She was much the talk of Waterdeep Harbor."

"Ye better bring the damned cat up soon then," Bruenor grumbled, looking out over the rail. Indeed, the schooner already seemed much closer, speeding over the waves.

To Drizzt the image struck him as purely out of control; suicidal, like the giant that had followed them out of the Spine of the World. He put the figurine on the ground and called softly for the panther, watching as the telltale gray mist began to swirl about the statue, gradually taking shape.

* * * * *

Catti-brie wiped her eyes, then lifted the spyglass once again, scanning the deck, hardly believing what she saw. But again she saw the truth of it all: that this was no pirate, at least none of the kind she had ever before seen. There were women aboard, and not warrior women, not even sailors, and surely not prisoners. And children! Several she had seen, and none of them dressed as cabin boys.

She winced as a ballista spear grazed the schooner's deck, skipping off a turnstile and cracking through the side rail, only missing a young boy by a hands' breadth.

"Get ye down, and be quick," she instructed the lookout sharing the crow's nest. "Tell yer captain to load chain and take her in her high sails."

The man, obviously impressed with the tales he had heard of Drizzt and Catti-brie, turned without hesitation and started down the rope, but the woman knew that the task for stopping this coming travesty had fallen squarely upon her shoulders.

Quester had dropped to battle sail, but the schooner kept at full, kept its run straight and swift, and seemed as if it meant to smash right through the larger caravel.

Catti-brie put up the spyglass again, scanning slowly, searching, searching. She knew now that Drizzt's guess about the schooner's course and intent had been correct, knew that this was Crenshinibon's doing, and that truth made her blood boil with rage. One, or two, perhaps, would be the key, but where . . .

She spotted the man at the forward rail of the flying bridge, his form mostly obscured by the mainmast. She held her sights on him for a long while, resisting the urge to shift and observe damage as *Quester*'s ballistae let fly again, this time in accord with Catti-brie's orders. Spinning chains ripped high through the schooner's top sails. This sight, this man at the rail, one hand gripping the wood so tightly that it was white for lack of blood, was more important.

The schooner flinched, the ship veering slightly, unintentionally, until the crew could work the ballista-altered sails to put her in line again. In that turn, the image of the man at the rail drifted clear of the obstructing mast, and Catti-brie saw him clearly, saw the crazed look upon his face, saw the line of drool running from the corner of his mouth.

And she knew.

She dropped the spyglass and took up Taulmaril, lining her shot with great care, using the mainmast as a guide, for she could hardly even see the target.

* * * * *

"If they've a wizard, he should have acted by now," a frantic Captain Vaines cried. "For what do they wait? To tease us, as a cat to a mouse?"

Bruenor looked at the man and snorted derisively.

"They've no wizard," Drizzt assured the captain.

"Do they mean to simply ram us, then?" the captain asked. "We'll take her down, then!" He turned to yell new instructions to the ballista crews, to instruct his archers to rake the deck. But before he uttered a word a silver streak from the nest above startled him. He spun around to see the streak cut across the schooner's deck, then angle sharply to the right and fly out over the open sea.

Before he could begin to question it another streak shot out, following nearly the same course, except that this one didn't deflect. It soared right past the schooner's mainmast.

Everything seemed to come to a stop, a tangible pause from caravel and schooner alike.

"Hold the cat!" Catti-brie called down to Drizzt.

Vaines looked at the drow doubtfully, but Drizzt didn't doubt, not at all. He put his hand up and called Guenhwyvar—who had moved back on the deck to get a running start—back to his side.

"It is ended," the dark elf announced.

The captain's doubting expression melted as the schooner's mainsail dropped, the ship's prow also dropping instantly, deeper into the sea. Her back beam swung out wide, turning the triangular back sail. She leaned far to the side, turning her prow back toward the east, back toward the far-distant shore.

* * * * *

Through the spyglass, Catti-brie saw a woman kneeling over the dead man while another man cradled his head. An emptiness settled in Catti-brie's breast, for she never enjoyed such an action, never wanted to kill anyone.

But that man had been the antagonist, the driving force behind a battle that would have left many innocents on the schooner dead. Better that he pay for his failings with his own life alone than with the lives of others.

She told herself that repeatedly.
It helped but a little.

* * * * *

Certain that the fight had indeed been avoided, Drizzt looked down at the crystal shard once more with utter contempt. A single call to a single man had nearly brought ruin to so many.

He could not wait to be rid of the thing.

Chapter 16
BROTHERS OF MINDAND MAGIC

he dark elf leaned back in a chair, settling comfortably, as he always seemed to do, and listening with more than a passing amusement. Jarlaxle had planted a device of clairaudience on the magnificent wizard's robe he had given to Rai'gy Bondalek, one of many enchanted gemstones sewn into the black cloth. This one had a clever aura, deceiving any who would detect it into thinking it was a stone the wizard wearing the robe could use to cast the clairaudience spell. And indeed it was, but it possessed another power, one with a matching stone that Jarlaxle kept, allowing the mercenary to listen in at will upon Rai'gy's conversations.

"The replica was well made and holds much of the original's dweomer," Rai'gy was saying, obviously referring to the magical, Drizzt-seeking locket.

"Then you should have no trouble in locating the rogue again and again," came the reply, the voice of Kimmuriel Oblodra.

"They are still aboard the ship," Rai'gy explained. "And from what I have heard they mean to be aboard for many more days."

"Jarlaxle demands more information," the Oblodran psionicist said, "else he will turn the duties over to me."

"Ah, yes, given to my principal adversary," the wizard said in mock seriousness.

In that distant room, Jarlaxle chuckled. The two thought it important to keep him believing that they were rivals and thus no threat to him, though in truth they had forged a tight and trusted friendship. Jarlaxle didn't mind that—in fact, he rather preferred it—because he understood that even together the psionicist and the wizard, dark elves of considerable magical talents and powers but little understanding of the motivations and nature of reasoning beings, would never move against him. They feared not so much that he would defeat them, but rather that they would prove victorious and then be forced to shoulder the responsibility for the entire volatile band.

"The best method to discern more about the rogue would be to go to him in disguise and listen to his words," Rai'gy went on. "Already I have learned much of his present course and previous events."

Jarlaxle came forward in his chair, listening intently as Rai'gy began a chant. He recognized enough of the words to understand that the wizard-priest was enacting a scrying spell, a reflective pool.

"That one there," Rai'gy said a few moments later.

"The young boy?" came Kimmuriel's response. "Yes, he would be an easy target. Humans do not prepare their children well, as do the drow."

"You could take his mind?" Rai'gy asked.

"Easily."

"Through the scrying pool?"

There came a long pause. "I do not know that it has ever been done," Kimmuriel admitted, and his tone told Jarlaxle that he was not afraid of the prospect, but rather intrigued.

"Then our eyes and ears would be right beside the outcast," Rai'gy went on. "In a form Drizzt Do'Urden would not think to distrust. A curious child, one who would love to hear his many tales of adventure."

Jarlaxle took his hand from the gemstone, and the clairaudience spell went away. He settled back into his chair and smiled widely, taking comfort in the ingenuity of his underlings.

That was the truth of his power, he realized, the ability to delegate responsibility and allow others to rightfully take their credit. The strength of Jarlaxle lay not in Jarlaxle, though even alone he could be formidable indeed, but in the competent soldiers with whom the mercenary surrounded himself. To battle Jarlaxle was to battle Bregan D'aerthe, an organization of freethinking, amazingly competent drow warriors.

To battle Jarlaxle was to lose.

The guilds of Calimport would soon recognize that truth, the drow leader knew, and so would Drizzt Do'Urden.

* * * * *

"I have contacted another plane of existence and from the creatures there, beings great and wise, beings who can see into the humble affairs of the drow with hardly a thought, I have learned of the outcast and his friends, of where they have been and where they mean to go," Rai'gy Bondalek proclaimed to Jarlaxle the next day.

Jarlaxle nodded and accepted the lie, seeing Rai'gy's proclamation of some otherworldly and mysterious source as inconsequential.

"Inland, as I earlier told you," Rai'gy explained. "They took to a ship—the *Quester*, it is called—in Waterdeep, and now sail south for a city called Baldur's Gate, which they should reach in a matter of three days."

"Then back to land?"

"Briefly," Rai'gy answered, for indeed, Kimmuriel had learned much in his half day as a cabin boy. "They will take to ship again, a smaller craft, to travel along a river that will bring them far from the great water they call the Sword Coast. Then they will take to land travel again, to a place called the Snowflake Mountains and a structure called the Spirit Soaring, wherein dwells a mighty priest named Cadderly. They go to destroy an artifact of great power," he went on, adding details that he and not Kimmuriel had learned through use of the reflecting pool. "This artifact is Crenshinibon by name, though often referred to as the crystal shard."

Jarlaxle's eyes narrowed at the mention. He had heard of Crenshinibon before in a story concerning a mighty demon and Drizzt Do'Urden. Pieces began to fall into place then, the beginnings of a cunning plan creeping into the corners of his mind. "So that is where they shall go," he said. "As important, where have they been?"

"They came from Icewind Dale, they say," Rai'gy reported. "A land of cold ice and blowing wind. And they left behind one named Wulfgar, a mighty warrior. They believe him to be in the city of Luskan, north of Waterdeep along the same seacoast."

"Why did he not accompany them?"

Rai'gy shook his head. "He is troubled, I believe, though I know not why. Perhaps he has lost something or has found tragedy."

"Speculation," Jarlaxle said. "Mere assumptions. And such things will lead to mistakes that we can ill afford."

"What part plays Wulfgar?" Rai'gy asked with some surprise.

"Perhaps no part, perhaps a vital one," Jarlaxle answered. "I cannot decide until I know more of him. If you cannot learn more, then perhaps it is time I go to Kimmuriel for answers." He noted the way the wizard-priest stiffened at his words, as though Jarlaxle had slapped him.

"Do you wish to learn more of the outcast or of this Wulfgar?" Rai'gy asked, his voice sharp.

"More of Cadderly," Jarlaxle replied, drawing a frustrated sigh from his off-balance companion. Rai'gy didn't even move to answer. He just turned about, threw his hands up in the air and walked away.

Jarlaxle was finished with him anyway. The names of Crenshinibon and Wulfgar had him deep in thought. He had heard of both; of Wulfgar, given by a handmaiden to Lolth and from Lolth to Errtu, the demon who sought the Crystal Shard. Perhaps it was time for the mercenary leader to go and pay a visit to Errtu, though truly he hated dealing with the unpredictable and ultimately dangerous creatures of the Abyss. Jarlaxle survived by understanding the motivations of his enemies, but demons rarely held any definite motivations and could certainly alter their desires moment by moment.

But there were other ways with other allies. The mercenary drew out a slender wand and with a thought teleported his body back to Menzoberranzan.

His newest lieutenant, once a proud member of the ruling house, was waiting for him.

"Go to your brother Gromph," Jarlaxle instructed. "Tell him that I wish to learn of the story of the human named Wulfgar, the demon Errtu, and the artifact known as Crenshinibon."

"Wulfgar was taken in the first raid on Mithral Hall, the realm of Clan Battlehammer," Berg'inyon Baenre answered, for he knew well the tale. "By a handmaiden, and given to Lolth."

"But where from there?" Jarlaxle asked. "He is back on our plane of existence, it would seem, on the surface."

Berg'inyon's expression showed his surprise at that. Few ever escaped the clutches of the Spider Queen. But then, he admitted silently, nothing about Drizzt Do'Urden had ever been predictable. "I will find my brother this day," he assured Jarlaxle.

"Tell him that I wish to know of a mighty priest named Cadderly," Jarlaxle added, and he tossed Berg'inyon a small amulet. "It is imbued with the emanations of my location," he explained, "that your brother might find me or send a messenger."

Again Berg'inyon nodded.

"All is well?" Jarlaxle asked.

"The city remains quiet," the lieutenant reported, and Jarlaxle was not surprised. Ever since the last assault upon Mithral Hall several years before, when Matron Baenre, the figurehead of Menzoberranzan for centuries, had been killed, the city had been outwardly quiet above the tumult of private planning. To her credit, Triel Baenre, Matron Baenre's oldest daughter, had done a credible job of holding the house together. But despite her efforts it seemed likely that the city would soon know interhouse wars beyond the scope of anything previously experienced. Jarlaxle had decided to strike out for the surface, to extend his grasp, thus making his mercenary band invaluable to any house with aspirations for greater power.

The key to it all now, Jarlaxle understood, was to keep everyone on his side even as they waged war with each other. It was a line he had learned to walk with perfection centuries before.

"Go to Gromph quickly," he instructed. "This is of utmost importance. I must have my answers before Narbondel brightens a hands' pillars," he explained, using a common expression to mean before five days had passed. The expression "hands' pillars" represented the five fingers on one hand.

Berg'inyon departed, and with a silent mental instruction to his wand Jarlaxle was back in Calimport. As quickly as his body moved, so too moved his thoughts to another pressing issue. Berg'inyon would not fail him, nor would Gromph, nor would Rai'gy and Kimmuriel. He knew that with all confidence, and that knowledge allowed him to focus on this very night's work: the takeover of the Basadoni Guild.

* * * * *

"Who is there?" came the old voice, a voice full of calmness despite the apparent danger.

Entreri, having just stepped through one of Kimmuriel Oblodra's dimensional portals, heard it as if from far, far away, as the assassin fought to orient himself to his new surroundings. He was in Pasha Basadoni's private room, behind a lavish dressing screen. Finally finding his center of balance and consciousness, the assassin spent a moment studying his surroundings, his ears pricked for the slightest of sounds: breathing or the steady footfalls of a practiced killer.

But of course he and Kimmuriel had properly scouted the room and the whereabouts of the pasha's lieutenants, and they knew that the old and helpless man was quite alone.

"Who is there?" came another call.

Entreri walked out around the screen and into the candlelight, shifting his bolero back on his head that the old man might see him clearly, and that the assassin might gaze upon Basadoni.

How pitiful the old man looked, a hollow shell of his former self, his former glory. Once Pasha Basadoni had been the most powerful guildmaster in Calimport, but now he was just an old man, a figurehead, a puppet whose strings could be pulled by several different people at once.

Entreri, despite himself, hated those string pullers.

"You should not have come," Basadoni rasped at him. "Flee the city, for you cannot live here. Too many, too many."

"You have spent two decades underestimating me," Entreri replied lightly, taking a seat on the edge of the bed. "When will you learn the truth?"

That brought a phlegm-filled chuckle from Basadoni, and Entreri flashed a rare smile.

"I have known the truth of Artemis Entreri since he was a street urchin killing intruders with sharpened stones," the old man reminded him.

"Intruders you sent," said Entreri.

Basadoni conceded the point with a grin. "I had to test you."

"And have I passed, Pasha?" Entreri considered his own tone as he spoke the words. The two were speaking like old friends, and in a manner they were indeed. But now, because of the actions of Basadoni's lieutenants, they were also mortal enemies. Still the pasha seemed quite at ease here, alone and helpless with Entreri. At first, the assassin had thought that the man might be better prepared than he had assumed, but after carefully inspecting the room and the partially upright bed that held the old man, he was secure in the fact that Basadoni had no tricks to play. Entreri was in control, and that didn't seem to bother Pasha Basadoni as much as it should.

"Always, always," Basadoni replied, but then his smile dissipated into a grimace. "Until now. Now you have failed, and at a task too easy."

Entreri shrugged as if it did not matter. "The targeted man was pitiful," he explained. "Truly. Am I, the assassin who passed all of your tests, who ascended to sit beside you though I was still but a young man, to

murder wretched peasants who owe a debt that a
novice pickpocket could cover in half a day's work?"

"That was not the point," Basadoni insisted. "I let
you back in, but you have been gone a long time, and
thus you had to prove yourself. Not to me," the pasha
quickly added, seeing the assassin's frown.

"No, to your foolish lieutenants," Entreri reasoned.

"They have earned their positions."

"That is my fear."

"Now it is Artemis Entreri who underestimates,"
Pasha Basadoni insisted. "Each of the three have their
place and serve me well."

"Well enough to keep me out of your house?" Entreri
asked.

Pasha Basadoni gave a great sigh. "Have you come
to kill me?" he asked, and then he laughed again. "No,
not that. You would not kill me, because you have no
reason to. You know, of course, that if you somehow succeed against Kadran Gordeon and the others, I will
take you back in."

"Another test?" Entreri asked dryly.

"If so, then one you created."

"By sparing the life of a wretch who likely would
have preferred death?" Entreri said, shaking his head
as if the whole notion was purely ridiculous.

A flicker of understanding sharpened Basadoni's old
gray eyes. "So it was not sympathy," he said, grinning.

"Sympathy?"

"For the wretch," the old man explained. "No, you
care nothing for him, care not that he was subsequently murdered. No, no, and I should have understood. It was not sympathy that stayed the hand of
Artemis Entreri. Never that! It was pride, simple, foolish pride. You would not lower yourself to the level of
street enforcer, and thus you started a war you cannot
win. Oh, fool!"

"Cannot win?" Entreri echoed. "You assume much." He studied the old man for a long moment, locking gazes. "Tell me, Pasha, who do you wish to win?" he asked.

"Pride again," Basadoni replied with a flourish of his skinny arms that stole much of his strength and left him gasping. "But the point," he continued a moment later, "in any case, is moot. What you truly ask is if I still care for you, and of course I do. I remember well your ascent through my guild, as well as any father recalls the growth of his son. I do not wish you ill in this war you have begun, though you understand that there is little I can do to prevent these events that you and Kadran, prideful fools both, have put in order. And of course, as I said before, you cannot win."

"You do not understand everything."

"Enough," the old man said. "I know that you have no allegiance among the other guilds, not even with Dwahvel and her little ones or Quentin Bodeau and his meager band. Oh, they swear neutrality—we would have it no other way—but they will not aid you in your fight, and neither will any of the other truly powerful guilds. And thus are you doomed."

"And you know of every guild?" Entreri asked slyly.

"Even the wretched wererats of the sewers," Pasha Basadoni said with confidence, but Entreri noted a hint at the edges of his tone that showed he was not as smug as he outwardly pretended. There was a sadness here, Entreri knew, a weariness and, obviously, a lack of control. The lieutenants ran the guild.

"I tell you this out of admission for all that you did for me," the assassin said, and he was not surprised to see the wise old pasha's eyes narrow warily. "Call it loyalty, call it a last debt repaid," Entreri went on, and he was sincere—about the forewarning, at least—"you do not know all, and your lieutenants shall not prevail against me."

"Ever the confident one," the pasha said with another phlegm-filled laugh.

"And never wrong," Entreri added, and he tipped his bolero and walked behind the dressing screen, back to the waiting dimensional portal.

* * * * *

"You have made every defense?" Pasha Basadoni asked with true concern, for the old man knew enough about Artemis Entreri to take the assassin's warning seriously. As soon as Entreri had left him, Basadoni had gathered his lieutenants. He didn't tell them of his visitor, but he wanted to ensure that they were ready. The time was near, he knew, very near.

Sharlotta, Hand, and Gordeon all nodded—somewhat condescendingly, Basadoni noted. "They will come this night," he announced. Before any of the three could question where he might have garnered that information, he added, "I can feel their eyes upon us."

"Of course, my Pasha," purred Sharlotta, bending low to kiss the old man's forehead.

Basadoni laughed at her and laughed all the louder when a guard shouted from the hallway that the house had been breached.

"In the sub-cellar!" the man cried. "From the sewers!"

"The wererat guild?" Kadran Gordeon asked incredulously. "Domo Quillilo assured us that he would not—"

"Domo Quillilo stayed out of Entreri's way, then," Basadoni interrupted.

"Entreri has not come alone," Kadran reasoned.

"Then he will not die alone," Sharlotta said, seeming unconcerned. "A pity."

Kadran nodded, drew his sword, and turned to leave. Basadoni, with great effort, grabbed his arm. "Entreri will come in separately from his allies," the old man warned. "For you."

"More to my pleasure, then," Kadran growled in reply. "Go lead our defenses," he told Hand. "And when Entreri is dead, I will bring his head to you that we may show it to those stupid enough to join with him."

Hand had barely exited the room when he was nearly run over by a soldier coming up from the cellars. "Kobolds!" the man cried, his expression showing that he hardly believed the claim as he spoke it. "Entreri's allies are smelly rat kobolds."

"Lead on, then," said Hand, much more confidently. Against the power of the guild house, with two wizards and two hundred soldiers, kobolds—even if they poured in by the thousands—would prove no more than a minor inconvenience.

Back in the room, the other two lieutenants heard the claim and stared at each other in disbelief, then broke into wide smiles.

Pasha Basadoni, lying on the bed and watching them, didn't share that mirth. Entreri was up to something, he knew, something big, and kobolds would hardly be the worst of it.

* * * * *

Kobolds indeed led the way into the Basadoni guild house, up from the sewers where frightened were-rats—as per their agreement with Entreri—stayed hidden in shadows, out of the way. Jarlaxle had brought a considerable number of the smelly little creatures with him from Menzoberranzan. Bregan D'aerthe was housed primarily along the rim of the great Clawrift that rent the drow city, and in there the kobolds bred and bred, thousands and thousands of the things. Three hundred had accompanied the forty drow to Calimport, and they now led the charge, running wildly through all the lower corridors of the guild house, inadvertently setting off the traps, both mechanical and magical, and marking the locations of the Basadoni soldiers.

Behind them came the drow host, silent as death.

Kimmuriel Oblodra, Jarlaxle, and Entreri moved up one slanting corridor, flanked by a foursome of drow warriors holding hand crossbows readied with poison-tipped darts. Up ahead the corridor opened into a wide room, and a group of kobolds scrambled across, chased by a threesome of archers.

"Click, click, click," went the crossbows, and the three archers stumbled, staggered, and slumped to the floor, deep in sleep.

An explosion to the side sent the kobolds, half the previous number, scrambling back the other way.

"Not a magical blast," Kimmuriel remarked.

Jarlaxle sent a pair of his soldiers out wide the other way, flanking the human position. Kimmuriel took a more direct route, opening a dimensional door diagonally across the wide floor to the open edge of the corridor from which the explosion had come. As soon as the door appeared, leading into another long, ascending corridor, he and Entreri spotted the bombers. There was a group of men rushing behind a barricade, flanked by several large kegs.

"Drow elf!" one of the men shouted, pointing to the open door. Kimmuriel stood across the dimensional space behind the other door.

"Light it! Light it!" cried another man. A third brought a torch over to light the long rag hanging off the top of one keg.

Kimmuriel reached into his mind yet again, focusing on the keg, on the latent energy within the wood planking. He touched that energy, exciting it. Before the men could even begin to roll the barrel out from behind the barricade it blew apart, then exploded again as the burning wick hit the oil.

A flaming man tumbled out from the barricade, rolling frantically down the corridor, trying to douse the flames. A second, less injured, staggered into the open, and one of the remaining drow soldiers put a hand crossbow dart into his face.

Kimmuriel dropped the dimensional door—better to run through the room—and the group set off, rushing past the burning corpse and the sleeping and badly injured man, past the third victim of the explosion, curled in death in a fetal position in the corner of the small cubby, then down a side passage. There they found three more men, two asleep and a third lying dead before the feet of the two soldiers Jarlaxle had sent out to flank.

And so it went throughout the lower levels, with the dark elves overrunning all obstacles. Jarlaxle had taken only his finest warriors with him to the surface: renegade, houseless dark elves who had once belonged to noble houses, who had trained for decades, centuries even, for just this kind of close-quartered, room-to-room, tunnel-to-tunnel combat. A brigade of knights in shining mail and with wizard supporters might prove a credible enemy to the dark elves on an open field of battle. These street thugs, though, with their small daggers, short swords, and minor magics, and with no foreknowledge of the enemy that had come against them, fell systematically to Jarlaxle's steadily moving band. Basadoni's men surrendered position after position, retreating higher and higher into the guild house proper.

Jarlaxle found Rai'gy Bondalek and half a dozen warriors moving along the street level of the house.

"They had two wizards," the wizard-priest explained. "I put them in a globe of silence and—"

"Pray tell me you did not destroy them," said the mercenary leader, who knew well the value of wizards.

"We hit them with darts," Rai'gy explained. "But one had a stoneskin enchantment about him and had to be destroyed."

Jarlaxle could accept that. "Finish the business at hand," he said to Rai'gy. "I will take Entreri to claim his place in the higher rooms."

"And him?" Rai'gy asked sourly, motioning toward Kimmuriel.

Knowing their little secret, Jarlaxle did well to hide his smile. "Lead on," he instructed Entreri.

They encountered another group of heavily armed soldiers, but Jarlaxle used one of his many wands to entrap them all within globs of goo. Another one did slip away—or would have, except that Artemis Entreri knew well the tactics of such men. He saw the shadow lengthening against the wall and directed the shot well.

* * * * *

Kadran Gordeon's eyes widened when Hand stumbled into the room, gasping and clutching at his hip. "Dark elves," the man explained, slumping in the arms of his comrade. "Entreri. The bastard brought dark elves!"

Hand slipped to the floor, fast asleep.

Kadran Gordeon let him fall and ran on, out the back door of the room, across the wide ballroom of the second floor, and up the sweeping staircase.

Entreri and his friends noted every movement.

"That is the one?" Jarlaxle asked.

Entreri nodded. "I will kill him," he promised, starting away, but Jarlaxle grabbed his shoulder. Entreri turned to see the mercenary leader looking slyly at Kimmuriel.

"Would you like to fully humiliate the man?" Jarlaxle asked.

Before Entreri could respond, Kimmuriel came up to stand right before him. "Join with me," the drow psionicist said, lifting his fingers for Entreri's forehead.

The ever-wary assassin brushed the reaching hand away.

Kimmuriel tried to explain, but Entreri knew only the basics of drow language, not the subtleties. The psionicist's words sounded more like the joining of lovers than anything Entreri understood. Frustrated, Kimmuriel turned to Jarlaxle and started talking so fast that it seemed to Entreri as if he was saying one long word.

"He has a trick for you to play," Jarlaxle explained in the common surface tongue. "He wishes to get into your mind, but only briefly, to enact a kinetic barrier and show you how to maintain it."

"A kinetic barrier?" the confused assassin asked.

"Trust him this one time," Jarlaxle bade. "Kimmuriel Oblodra is among the greatest practitioners of the rare and powerful psionic magic and is so skilled with it that he can often lend some of his power to another, albeit briefly."

"He will teach me?" Entreri asked skeptically.

Kimmuriel laughed at the absurd notion.

"The mind magic is a gift, a rare gift, and not a lesson to be taught," Jarlaxle explained. "But Kimmuriel can lend you a bit of the power, enough to humiliate Kadran Gordeon."

Entreri's expression showed that he wasn't so sure of any of this.

"We could kill you at any time by more conventional means if we so decided," Jarlaxle reminded him. He nodded to Kimmuriel, and Artemis Entreri did not back away.

And so Entreri got his first personal understanding of psionics and walked up the sweeping staircase unafraid. Across the way a concealed archer let fly, and Entreri took the arrow right in the back—or would have, except that the kinetic barrier stopped the arrow's flight, fully absorbing its energy.

* * * * *

Sharlotta heard the ruckus in the outer rooms of the royal complex and figured that Gordeon had returned. She still had no idea of the rout in the lower halls, though, and so she decided to move quickly, to use this opportunity well. From one of the long sleeves of her alluring gown she drew out a slender knife, moving with purpose for the door that would lead into a larger room, with the door of Pasha Basadoni across the way.

Finally she would be done with the man, and it would look as if Entreri or one of his associates had completed the assassination.

Sharlotta paused at the door, hearing another slam beyond and the sound of running feet. Gordeon was on the move, as was another.

Had Entreri gained this level?

The thought assaulted her but did not dissuade her. There were other ways, more secret ways, though the route would be longer. She went to the back of her room, removed a specific book from her bookshelf, then slipped into the corridor that opened behind the case.

* * * * *

Entreri caught up to Kadran Gordeon soon after in a complex of many small rooms. The man rushed out the side, sword slashing. He hit Entreri a dozen times at least and the assassin, focusing his thoughts with supreme concentration, didn't even try to block. Instead he just took them and stole their energy, feeling the power building, building within him.

Eyes wide, mouth agape, Kadran Gordeon back-pedaled. "What manner of demon are you?" the man gasped, falling back through a door into the room where Sharlotta, small dagger in hand, had just come out of another concealed passage, standing along a wall to the side of Pasha Basadoni's bed.

Entreri, brimming with confidence, strode in.

On came Gordeon again, sword slashing. This time Entreri drew the sword Jarlaxle had given him and countered, parrying each slash perfectly. He felt his mental concentration waning and knew that he had to react soon or be consumed by the pent-up energy, so when Gordeon came with a sidelong slash, Entreri dipped the tip of his blade below the angle of the cut, then brought it up and over quickly, stepping under, turning about, and rolling his sword around. He took Gordeon off balance and crashed into the man, knocking him to the floor and coming down atop him, weapon pinning weapon.

* * * * *

Sharlotta lifted her arm to throw her knife into Basadoni but then shifted, seeing the too-tempting target of Artemis Entreri's back as the man went down atop Kadran Gordeon.

But then she shifted again as another, darker form entered the room. She cocked to throw, but the drow was quicker. A dagger sliced her wrist, pinning her arm to the wall. Another dagger stuck in the wall to the right of her head, then another to the left. Another grazed the side of her chest, and then another as Jarlaxle pumped his arm rapidly, sending a seemingly endless stream of steel her way.

Gordeon punched Entreri in the face.

That, too, was absorbed.

"I do grow tired of your foolishness," said Entreri, putting his hand on Gordeon's chest, ignoring the man's free hand as it pumped punch after punch at his face.

With a thought Entreri released the energy, all of it, the arrow, the many sword hits, the many punches. His hand sank into Gordeon's chest, melting the skin and ribs below it. A rolling fountain of blood erupted, spewing into the air and falling back on Gordeon's surprised expression, filling his mouth as he tried to scream in horror.

And then he was dead.

Entreri got up to see Sharlotta standing against the wall, hands in the air—one pinned to the wall—facing Jarlaxle, who had yet another dagger ready. Several other drow, including Kimmuriel and Rai'gy, had come into the room behind their leader. The assassin quickly moved between her and Basadoni, noting the dagger Sharlotta had obviously dropped on the floor right beside the bed. He turned his sly gaze on the dangerous woman.

"It would seem that I arrived just in time, Pasha," Entreri explained, picking up the weapon. "Sharlotta, thinking the guild house secure, had apparently decided to use the battle to her advantage, finally ridding herself of you."

Both Entreri and Basadoni looked at Sharlotta. She stood impassive, obviously caught, though she finally managed to extract the material of her sleeve from the sticking dagger.

"She did not know the truth of her enemies," Jarlaxle explained.

Entreri looked at him and nodded. The dark elves all stepped back, allowing the assassin his moment.

"Should I kill her?" Entreri asked Basadoni.

"Why ask my permission?" the pasha replied, obviously none too pleased. "Am I then to credit you for this? For bringing dark elves to my house?"

"I acted as I needed to survive," Entreri replied. "Most of the house survives, neutralized but not killed. Kadran Gordeon is dead—never could I have trusted that one—but Hand survives. And so we will go on under the same arrangement as before, with three lieutenants and one guildmaster." He looked to Jarlaxle, then back to Sharlotta. "Of course, my friend Jarlaxle desires a position of lieutenant," he said. "One well-earned, and that I cannot deny."

Sharlotta stiffened, expecting then to die, for she could do simple math.

Indeed Entreri did originally mean to kill her, but when he glanced back to Basadoni, when he looked again upon the feeble old man, such a shadow of his former glory, he reversed the direction of his sword and put it through Pasha Basadoni's heart instead.

"Three lieutenants," he said to the stunned Sharlotta. "Hand, Jarlaxle, and you."

"So Entreri is guildmaster," the woman remarked with a crooked grin. "You said you could not trust Kadran Gordeon, yet you recognize that I am more honorable," she said seductively, coming forward a step.

Entreri's sword came out and about too fast for her to follow, its tip stopping against the tender flesh of her throat. "Trust you?" the assassin balked. "No, but neither do I fear you. Do as you are instructed, and you will live." He shifted the angle of his blade slightly so that it tucked under her chin, and he nicked her there. "Exactly as instructed," he warned, "else I will take your pretty face from you, one cut at a time."

Entreri turned to Jarlaxle.

"The house will be secured within the hour," the dark elf assured him. "Then you and your human lieutenants can decide the fate of those taken and put out on the streets whatever word suits you as guildmaster."

Entreri had thought that this moment would bring some measure of satisfaction. He was glad that Kadran Gordeon was dead and glad that the old wretch Basadoni had been given a well-deserved rest.

"As you wish, my Pasha," Sharlotta purred from the side.

The title turned his stomach.

Chapter 17
EXORCISING DEMONS

There was indeed something appealing about the fighting, about the feeling of superiority and the element of control. Between the fact that the fights were not lethal—though more than a few patrons were badly injured—and the conscience-dulling drinks, no guilt accompanied each thunderous punch.

Just satisfaction and control, an edge that had been too long absent.

Had he stopped to think about it, Wulfgar might have realized that he was substituting each new challenger for one particular nemesis, one he could not defeat alone, one who had tormented him all those years.

He didn't bother with contemplation, though. He simply enjoyed the sensation of his fist colliding with the chest of this latest troublemaker, sending the tall, thin man reeling back in a hopping, staggering, stumbling quickstep, finally to fall backward over a bench some twenty feet from the barbarian.

Wulfgar methodically waded in, grabbing the decked man by the collar (and taking out more than a few chest hairs in the process) and the groin (and similarly extracting hair). With one jerk the barbarian brought the horizontal man level with his waist. Then a rolling motion snapped the man up high over his head.

"I just fixed that window," Arumn Gardpeck said dryly, helplessly, seeing the barbarian's aim.

The man flew through it to bounce across Half Moon Street.

"Then fix it again," Wulfgar replied, casting a glare over Arumn that the barkeep did not dare to question.

Arumn just shook his head and went back to wiping his bar, reminding himself that, by keeping such complete order in the place Wulfgar was attracting customers—many of them. Folk now came looking for a safe haven in which to waste a night, and then there were those interested in the awesome displays of power. These came both as challengers to the mighty barbarian or, more often, merely as spectators. Never had the Cutlass seen so many patrons, and never had Arumn Gardpeck's purse been so full.

But how much more full it would be, he knew, if he didn't have to keep fixing the place.

"Shouldn't've done that," a man near the bar remarked to Arumn. "That's Rossie Doone, he throwed, a soldier."

"Not wearing any uniform," Arumn remarked.

"Came in unofficial," the man explained. "Wanted to see this Wulfgar thug."

"He saw him," Arumn replied in the same resigned and dry tones.

"And he'll be seein' him again," the man promised. "Only next time with friends."

Arumn sighed and shook his head, not out of any fear for Wulfgar, but because of the expenses he anticipated if a whole crew of soldiers came in to fight the barbarian.

Wulfgar spent that night—half the night—in Delly Curtie's room again, taking a bottle with him from the bar, then grabbing another one on his way outside. He went down to the docks and sat on the edge of a long wharf, watching the sparkles grow on the water as the sun rose behind him.

* * * * *

Josi Puddles saw them first, entering the Cutlass the very next night, a half-dozen grim-faced men including the one the patron had identified as Rossie Doone. They moved to the far side of the room, evicting several patrons from tables, then pulling three of the benches together so they could all sit side by side with their backs to the wall.

"Full moon tonight," Josi remarked.

Arumn knew what that meant. Every time the moon was full the crowd was a bit rowdier. And what a crowd had come in this evening, every sort of rogue and thug Arumn could imagine.

"Been the talk of the street all the day," Josi said quietly.

"The moon?" Arumn asked.

"Not the moon," Josi replied. "Wulfgar and that Rossie fellow. All have been talking of a coming brawl."

"Six against one," Arumn remarked.

"Poor soldiers," Josi said with a snicker.

Arumn nodded to the side then, to Wulfgar, who, sitting with a foaming mug in hand, seemed well aware of the group that had come in. The look on the barbarian's face, so calm and yet so cold, sent a shiver along Arumn's spine. It was going to be a long night.

* * * * *

On the other side of the room, in a corner opposite where sat the six soldiers, another man, quiet and unassuming, also noted the tension and the prospective combatants with more than a passing interest. The man's name was well known on the streets of Luskan, though his face was not. He was a shadow stalker by trade, a man cloaked in secrecy, but a man whose reputation brought trembles to the hardiest of thugs.

Morik the Rogue had been hearing quite a bit about Arumn Gardpeck's new strong-arm; too much, in fact. Story after story had come to him about the man's incredible feats of strength. About how he had been hit squarely in the face with a heavy club and had shaken it away seemingly without care. About how he lifted two men high into the air, smashed their heads together, then simultaneously tossed them through opposite walls of the tavern. About how he had thrown one man out into the street, then rushed out and blocked a team of two horses with his bare chest to stop the wagon from running down the prone drunk. . . .

Morik had been living among the street people long enough to understand the exaggerated nonsense in most of these tales. Each storyteller tried to outdo the previous one. But he couldn't deny the impressive stature of this man Wulfgar. Nor could he deny the many wounds showing about the head of Rossie Doone, a soldier Morik knew well and whom he had always respected as a solid fighter.

Of course Morik, his ears so attuned to the streets and alleyways, had heard of Rossie's intention to return with his friends and settle the score. Of course Morik had also heard of another's intention to put this newcomer squarely in his place. And so Morik had come in to watch, and nothing more, to measure this huge northerner, to see if he had the strength, the skills, and the temperament to survive and become a true threat.

Never taking his gaze off Wulfgar, the quiet man sipped his wine and waited.

* * * * *

As soon as he saw Delly moving near to the six men, Wulfgar drained his beer in a single swallow and tightened his grip on the table. He saw it coming, and how predictable it was, as one of Rossie Doone's sidekicks reached out and grabbed Delly's bottom as she moved past.

Wulfgar came up in a rush, storming in right before the offender, and right beside Delly.

"Oh, but 'tis nothing," the woman said, pooh-poohing Wulfgar away. He grabbed her by the shoulders, lifted her, and turned, depositing her behind him. He turned back, glaring at the offender, then at Rossie Doone, the true perpetrator.

Rossie remained seated, laughing still, seeming completely relaxed with three burly fighters on his right, two more on his left.

"A bit of fun," Wulfgar stated. "A cloth to cover your wounds, deepest of all the wound to your pride."

Rossie stopped laughing and stared hard at the man.

"We have not yet fixed the window," Wulfgar said. "Do you prefer to leave by that route once more?"

The man next to Rossie bristled, but Rossie held him back. "In truth, northman, I prefer to stay," he answered. "In my own eyes it's yourself who should be leaving."

Wulfgar didn't blink. "I ask you a second time, and a last time, to leave of your own accord," he said.

The man farthest from Rossie, down to Wulfgar's left, stood up and stretched languidly. "Think I'll get me a bit o' drink," he said calmly to the man seated beside him, and then, as if going to the bar, he took a step Wulfgar's way.

The barbarian, already a seasoned veteran of barroom brawls, saw it coming. He understood that the man would grab at him to hold and slow him so that Rossie and the others could pummel him. He kept his apparent focus directly on Rossie and waited. Then, as the man came within two steps, as his hands started coming up to grab at Wulfgar, the barbarian spun suddenly, stepping inside the other's reach. The barbarian snapped his back muscles, launching his forehead into the man's face, crushing his nose and sending him staggering backward.

Wulfgar turned back fast, fist flying, and caught Rossie across the jaw as he started to rise, slamming the man back against the wall. Hardly slowing, Wulfgar grabbed the stunned Rossie by the shoulders and yanked him hard to the side, flipping him to the left to deflect the coming rush of the two men remaining there. Then around went the barbarian again, growling, fists flying, to swap heavy punches with the two men leaping at him from that direction.

A knee came up for his groin, but Wulfgar recognized the move and reacted fast. He turned his leg in to catch the blow with his thigh, then reached down under the bent leg. The attacker instinctively grabbed at Wulfgar, catching shoulder and hair, trying to use him for balance. But the powerful barbarian, simply too strong, drove on, heaving him up and over his shoulder, turning as he went to again deflect the attack from the two men coming in at his back.

The movement cost Wulfgar several punches from the man who had been standing next to the latest human missile. Wulfgar accepted them stoically, hardly seeming to care. He came back hard, legs pumping, to drive the puncher into the wall, wrestling him around.

The desperate soldier grabbed on with all his strength, and the man's friends fast approached from behind. A roar, a wriggle, and a stunning punch extracted Wulfgar from the man's grasp. He skittered back away from the wall and the pursuers, instinctively ducking a punch as he went and grabbing a table by the leg.

Wulfgar spun back, facing the group, and halted the swinging momentum of the table so fully that the item snapped apart. The bulk of the table flew into the chest of the closest man, leaving Wulfgar standing with a wooden table leg in hand, a club he wasted no time in putting to good use. The barbarian smacked it below the table at the exposed legs of the man he had hit with the missile, cracking the side of the soldier's knee once and then again. The man howled in pain and shoved the table back out at Wulfgar, but he accepted the missile strike with merely a shrug, concentrating instead on turning the club in line and jabbing the man in the eye with its narrow end.

A half turn and full swing caught another across the side of the head, splitting the club apart and dropping the attacker like a sack of ground meal. Wulfgar ran right over him as he fell—the barbarian understood that mobility was his only defense against so many. He barreled into the next man in line, carrying him halfway across the room to slam into a wall, a journey that ended with a wild flurry of fists from both. Wulfgar took a dozen blows and gave a like number, but his were by far the heavier, and the dazed and defeated man crumbled to the floor—or would have, had not Wulfgar grabbed him as he slumped. The barbarian turned about fast and let his latest human missile fly, spinning him in low across the ankles of the closest pursuer, who tripped headlong, both arms reaching out to grab the barbarian. Wulfgar, still in his turn, using the momentum of that spin, dived forward, punch leading, stretching right between those arms. His force combined with the momentum of the stumbling man, and he felt his fist sink deep into the man's face, snapping his head back violently.

That man, too, went down hard.

Wulfgar stood straight, facing Rossie and his one standing ally, who had blood rolling freely from his nose. Another man holding his torn eye tried to stand beside them, but his broken knee wouldn't support his weight. He stumbled away to the side to slam into a wall and sink there into a sitting position.

In the first truly coordinated attack since the chaos had begun, Rossie and his companion came in slow and then leaped together atop Wulfgar, thinking to bear him down. But though the two were both large men, Wulfgar didn't fall, didn't stumble in the least. The barbarian caught them as they soared in and held his footing. His thrashing had them both holding on for dear life. Rossie slipped away, and Wulfgar managed to get both arms on the other, dragging the clutching man horizontally across in front of his face. The man's arms flailed about Wulfgar's head, but the angle of attack was all wrong, and the blows proved ineffectual.

Wulfgar roared again and bit the man's stomach hard, then started a full-out, blind run across the tavern floor. Gauging the distance, Wulfgar dipped his head at the last moment to put his powerful neck muscles in proper alignment, then rammed full force into the wall. He bounced back, holding the man with just one arm hooked under his shoulder, and kept it there long enough to allow the man to come down on his feet.

The man stood, against the wall, watching in confusion as Wulfgar ran back a few steps, and then his eyes widened indeed when the huge barbarian turned about, roared, and charged, dipping his shoulder as he came.

The man put his arms up, but that hardly mattered, for Wulfgar shoulder-drove him against the planking— right into the planking, which cracked apart. Louder than the splitting wood came the sound of a groan and a sigh from resigned Arumn Gardpeck.

Wulfgar bounced back again but leaned in fast, slamming left and right repeatedly, each thunderous blow driving the man deeper into the wall. The poor man, crumbled and bloody, splinters deep in his back, his nose already broken and half his body feeling the same way, held up a feeble arm to show that he had had enough.

Wulfgar smashed him again, a vicious left hook that came in over the upraised arm and shattered his jaw, throwing him into oblivion. He would have fallen except that the broken wall held him fast in place.

Wulfgar didn't even notice, for he had turned around to face Rossie, the lone enemy still showing any ability to fight. One of the others, the man Wulfgar had traded blows with against the wall, crawled about on hands and knees, seeming as if he didn't even know where he was. Another, the side of his head split wide by the vicious club swing, kept trying to stand and kept falling over, while a third still sat against the wall, clutching his torn eye and broken knee. The fourth of Rossie's companions, the one Wulfgar had hit with the single, devastating punch, lay very still with no sign of consciousness.

"Gather your friends and be gone," a tired Wulfgar offered to Rossie. "And do not return."

In answer, the outraged man reached down to his boot and drew out a long knife. "But I want to play," Rossie said wickedly, approaching a step.

"Wulfgar!" came Delly's cry from across the way, from behind the bar, and both Wulfgar and Rossie turned to see the woman throwing Aegis-fang out toward her friend, though she couldn't get the heavy warhammer half the distance.

That hardly mattered, though, for Wulfgar reached for it with his arm and with his mind, telepathically calling to the hammer.

The hammer vanished, then reappeared in the barbarian's waiting grasp. "So do I," Wulfgar said to an astonished and horrified Rossie. To accentuate his point, he swung Aegis-fang, one armed, out behind him. The swing hit and split a beam, which drew another profound groan from Arumn.

Rossie, his eager expression long gone, glanced about and backed away liked a trapped animal. He wanted to back out, to find some way to flee—that much was apparent to everybody in the room.

And then the outside door banged open, turning all heads—those that weren't broken open—Rossie Doone's and Wulfgar's included, and in strode the largest human, if he was indeed a human, that Wulfgar had ever seen. He was a giant man, taller than Wulfgar by a foot at least, and almost as wide, weighing perhaps twice the barbarian's three hundred pounds. Even more impressive was the fact that very little of the giant's bulk jiggled as he stormed in. He was all muscle, and gristle, and bone.

He stopped inside the suddenly hushed tavern, his huge head turning slowly to scan the room. His gaze finally settled on Wulfgar. He brought his arms out slowly from under the front folds of his cloak to reveal that he held a heavy length of chain in one hand and a spiked club in the other.

"Ye too tired for me, Wulfgar the dead?" Tree Block Breaker asked, spittle flying with each word. He finished with a growl, then brought his arm across powerfully, slamming the length of chain across the top of the nearest table and splitting the thing neatly down the middle. The three patrons sitting at that particular table didn't scamper away. They didn't dare to move at all.

A smile widened across Wulfgar's face. He flipped Aegis-fang into the air, a single spin, to catch it again by the handle.

Arumn Gardpeck groaned all the louder; this would be an expensive night.

Rossie Doone and those of his friends who could still move scrambled across the room, out of harm's way, leaving the path between Wulfgar and Tree Block Breaker clear.

In the shadows across the room, Morik the Rogue took another sip of wine. This was the fight he had come to see.

"Well, ye give me no answer," Tree Block Breaker said, whipping his chain across again. This time it did not connect solidly but whipped about one angled leg of the fallen table. Then, after slapping the leg of one sitting man, its tip got a hold on the man's chair. With a great roar, Tree Block yanked the chain back, sending table and chair flying across the room and dropping the unfortunate patron on his bum.

"Tavern etiquette and my employer require that I give you the opportunity to leave quietly," Wulfgar calmly replied, reciting Arumn's creed.

On came Tree Block Breaker, a great, roaring monster, a giant gone wild. His chain flailed back and forth before him, his club raised high to strike.

Wulfgar realized that he could have taken the giant out with a well-aimed throw of Aegis-fang before Tree

Block had gone two steps, but he let the creature come on, relishing the challenge. To everyone's surprise he dropped Aegis-fang to the floor as Tree Block closed. When the chain swished for his head, he dropped into a sudden squat but held his arm vertically above him.

The chain hooked around, and Wulfgar reached over it and grabbed on, giving a great tug that only increased Tree Block's charge. The huge man swung with his club, but he was too close and still coming. Wulfgar went down low, driving his shoulder against the man's legs. Tree Block's momentum carried his bulk across the bent barbarian's back.

Amazingly, stunningly, Wulfgar stood up straight, bringing Tree Block up above him. Then, to the astonished gasps of all watching, he bent at the knees quickly and jerked back up straight. Pushing with all his strength, he lifted Tree Block into the air above his head.

Before the huge man could wriggle about and bring his club to bear, Wulfgar ran back the way Tree Block had charged, and with a great roar of his own, threw the man right through the door, taking it and the jamb out completely and depositing the huge man in a jumble of kindling outside the Cutlass. His arm still enwrapped by the chain, Wulfgar gave a huge tug that sent Tree Block spinning about in the pile of wood before he surrendered the chain altogether.

The stubborn giant thrashed about, finally extricating himself from the wood heap. He stood roaring, his face and neck cut in a dozen places, his club whirling about wildly.

"Turn and leave," Wulfgar warned. The barbarian reached behind him and with a thought brought Aegisfang back to his hand.

If Tree Block even heard the warning, he showed no indication. He smacked his club against the ground and came forward in a rush, snarling.

And then he was dead. Just like that, caught by surprise as the barbarian's arm came forward, as the mighty warhammer twirled out, too fast for his attempted deflection with the club, too powerfully for Tree Block's massive chest to absorb the hit.

He stumbled backward and went down with more a whisper than a bang and lay very still.

Tree Block Breaker was the first man Wulfgar had killed in his tenure at Arumn Gardpeck's bar, the first man killed in the Cutlass in many, many months. All the tavern, Delly and Josi, Rossie Doone and his thugs, seemed to stop in pure amazement. The place went perfectly silent.

Wulfgar, Aegis-fang returned to his grasp, calmly turned about and walked over to the bar, paying no heed to the dangerous Rossie Doone. He placed Aegis-fang on the bar before Arumn, indicating that the barkeep should replace it on the shelves behind the counter, then casually remarked, "You should fix the door, Arumn, and quickly, else someone walks in and steals your stock."

And then, as if nothing had happened, Wulfgar walked back across the room, seemingly oblivious to the silence and the open-mouthed stares that followed his every stride.

Arumn Gardpeck shook his head and lifted the warhammer, then stopped as a shadowy figure came up opposite him.

"A fine warrior you have there, Master Gardpeck," the man said. Arumn recognized the voice, and the hairs on the back of his neck stood up.

"And Half Moon Street is a better place without that bully Tree Block running about," Morik went on. "I'll not lament his demise."

"I have never asked for any quarrel," Arumn said. "Not with Tree Block and not with you."

"Nor will you find one," Morik assured the innkeeper as Wulfgar, noting the conversation, came up beside the man—as did Josi Puddles and Delly, though they kept a more respectful distance from the dangerous rogue.

"Well fought, Wulfgar, son of Beornegar," Morik said. He slid a glass of drink along the bar before Wulfgar, who looked down at it, then back at Morik suspiciously. After all, how could Morik know his full name, one he had not used since his entry into Luskan, one that he had purposely left far, far behind.

Delly slipped in between the two, calling for Arumn to fetch her a couple of drinks for other patrons, and while the two stood staring at each other, she slyly swapped the drink Morik had placed with one from her tray. Then she moved out of the way, rolling back behind Wulfgar, wanting the security of his massive form between her and the dangerous man.

"Nor will you find one," Morik said again to Arumn. He tapped his forehead in salute and walked away, out of the Cutlass.

Wulfgar eyed him curiously, recognizing the balanced gait of a warrior, then moved to follow, pausing only long enough to lift and drain the glass.

"Morik the Rogue," Josi Puddles remarked to Arumn and Delly, moving opposite the barkeep. Both he and Arumn noted that Delly was holding the glass Morik had offered to Wulfgar.

"And likely this'd kill a fair-sized minotaur," she said, reaching over to dump the contents into a basin.

Despite Morik's assurances, Arumn Gardpeck did not disagree. Wulfgar had solidified his reputation a hundred times over this night, first by absolutely humbling Rossie Doone and his crowd—there would be no more trouble from them—and then by downing—and oh, so easily—the toughest fighter Half Moon Street had known in years.

But with such fame came danger, all three knew. To be in the eyes of Morik the Rogue was to be in the sights of his deadly weapons. Perhaps the man would keep his promise and let things lay low for a time, but eventually Wulfgar's reputation would grow to become a distraction, and then, perhaps, a threat.

Wulfgar seemed oblivious to it all. He finished his night's work with hardly another word, not even to Rossie Doone and his companions, who chose to stay—mostly because several of them needed quite a bit of potent drink to dull the pain of their wounds—but quietly so. And then, as was his growing custom, he took two bottles of potent liquor, took Delly by the arm, and retired to her room for half the night.

When that half a night had passed he, the remaining bottle in hand, went to the docks to watch the reflection of the sunrise.

To bask in the present, care nothing about the future, and forget the past.

Chapter 18
OF IMPS AND PRIESTS
AND A GREAT QUEST

Your name and reputation have preceded you," Captain Vaines explained to Drizzt as he led the drow and his companions to the boarding plank. Before them loomed the broken skyline of Baldur's Gate, the great port city halfway between Waterdeep and Calimport. Many structures lined the impressive dock areas, from low warehouses to taller buildings set with armaments and lookout positions, giving the region an uneven, jagged feel.

"My man found little trouble in gaining you passage on a river runner," Vaines went on.

"Discerning folk who'd take a drow," Bruenor said dryly.

"Less so if they'd take a dwarf," Drizzt replied without the slightest hesitation.

"Captained and crewed by dwarves," Vaines explained. That brought a groan from Drizzt and a chuckle from Bruenor. "Captain Bumpo Thunderpuncher and his brother, Donat, and their two cousins thrice removed on their mother's side."

"Ye know them well," Catti-brie remarked.

"All who meet Bumpo meet his crew, and admittedly they are a hard foursome to forget," Vaines said. "My man had little trouble in gaining your passage, as I said, for the dwarves know well the tale of Bruenor Battlehammer and the reclamation of Mithral Hall. And of his companions, including the dark elf."

"Bet ye'd never see the day when ye'd become a hero to a bunch o' dwarves," Bruenor remarked to Drizzt.

"Bet I'd never see the day when I'd want to," the ranger replied.

The group came to the rail then, and Vaines moved aside, holding his arm out toward the plank. "Farewell, and may your journey return you safely to your home," he said. "If I am in port or nearby when you return to Baldur's Gate, perhaps we will sail together again."

"Perhaps," Regis politely replied, but he, like all the others, understood that, if they did get to Cadderly and get rid of the Crystal Shard, they meant to ask for Cadderly's help in bringing them magically to Luskan. They had approximately another two weeks of travel before them if they moved swiftly, but Cadderly could wind walk all the way back to Luskan in a matter of minutes. So said Drizzt and Catti-brie, who had taken such a walk with the powerful priest before. Then they could get on with the pressing business of finding Wulfgar.

They entered Baldur's Gate without incident, and though Drizzt felt many stares following him, they were not ominous glares but looks of curiosity. The drow couldn't help contrast this experience with his other visit to the city, when he'd gone in pursuit of Regis who had been whisked away to Calimport by Artemis Entreri. On that occasion, Drizzt, with Wulfgar beside him, had entered the city under the disguise of a magical mask that had allowed him to appear as a surface elf.

"Not much like the last time ye came through?" Catti-brie, who knew well the tale of the first visit asked, seeing Drizzt's gaze.

"Always I wished to walk freely in the cities of the Sword Coast," Drizzt replied. "It appears that our work with Captain Deudermont has granted me that privilege. Reputation has freed me from some of the pains of my heritage."

"Ye thinking that's a good thing?" the so perceptive woman asked, for she had noted clearly the slight wince at the corner of Drizzt's eye when he made the claim.

"I do not know," Drizzt admitted. "I like that I can walk freely now in most places without persecution."

"But it pains ye to think that ye had to earn the right," Catti-brie finished perfectly. "Ye look at me, a human, and know that I had to earn no such thing. And at Bruenor and Regis, dwarf and halfling, and know that they can walk anywhere without earnin' a thing."

"I do not begrudge any of you that," Drizzt replied. "But see their gazes?" He looked around at the many people walking the streets of Baldur's Gate, almost every one turning to regard the drow curiously, some with admiration in their eyes, some with disbelief.

"So even though ye're walking free, ye're not walking free," the woman observed, and her nod told Drizzt that she understood then. Given the choice between facing the hatred of prejudice or the similarly ignorant looks of those viewing him as a curiosity piece, the latter seemed the better by far. But both were traps, both prisons, jailing Drizzt within the confines of the preceding reputation of a drow elf, of any drow elf, and thus limiting Drizzt to his heritage.

"Bah, they're just a stupid lot," Bruenor interrupted.

"Those who know you, know better," Regis added.

Drizzt took it all in stride, all with a smile. Long ago he had abandoned any futile hopes of truly fitting in among the surface-dwellers—his kinfolk's well-earned reputation for treachery and catastrophe would always prevent that—and had learned instead to focus his energy on those closest to him, on those who had learned to see him beyond his physical trappings. And now here he was with three of his most trusted and beloved friends, walking freely, easily booking passage, and presenting no problems to them other than those created by the relic they had to carry. That was truly what Drizzt Do'Urden had desired from the time he had come to know Catti-brie and Bruenor and Regis, and with them beside him how could the stares, be they of hatred or of ignorant curiosity, bother him?

No, his smile was sincere; if Wulfgar was beside them, then all the world would be right for the drow, the king's treasure at the end of his long and difficult road.

* * * * *

Rai'gy rubbed his black hands together as the smallish creature began to form in the center of the magical circle he had drawn. He didn't know Gromph Baenre by anything more than reputation, but despite Jarlaxle's insistence that the archmage would be trustworthy on this issue, the mere fact that Gromph was drow and of the ruling house of Menzoberranzan worried Rai'gy profoundly. The name Gromph had given him was supposedly of a minor denizen, easily controlled, but Rai'gy couldn't know for certain until the creature appeared before him.

A bit of treachery from Gromph could have had him opening a gate to a major demon, to Demogorgon himself, and the impromptu magical circle Rai'gy had drawn here in the sewers of Calimport would hardly prove sufficient protection.

The wizard-priest relaxed a bit as the creature took shape—the shape, as Gromph had promised, of an imp. Even without the magical circle, a wizard-priest as powerful as Rai'gy would have little trouble in handling a mere imp.

"Who is it that calls my name?" asked the imp in the guttural language of the Abyss, obviously more than a little perturbed and, both Rai'gy and Jarlaxle noted, a bit trepidatious—and even more so when he noted that his summoners were drow elves. "You should not bother Druzil. No, no, for he serves a great master," Druzil went on, speaking fluently in the drow tongue.

"Silence!" Rai'gy commanded, and the little imp was compelled to obey. The wizard-priest looked to Jarlaxle.

"Why do you protest?" Jarlaxle asked Druzil. "Is it not the desire of your kind to find access to this world?"

Druzil tilted his head and narrowed his eyes, a pensive yet still apprehensive pose.

"Ah, yes," the mercenary leader went on. "But of late, you have been summoned not by friends, but by enemies, so I have been told. By Cadderly of Caradoon."

Druzil bared his pointy teeth and hissed at the mention of the priest. That brought a smile to the faces of both dark elves. Gromph Baenre, it seemed, had not steered them wrong.

"We would like to pain Cadderly," Jarlaxle explained with a wicked grin. "Would Druzil like to help?"

"Tell me how," the imp eagerly replied.

"We need to know everything about the human," Jarlaxle explained. "His appearance and demeanor, his history and present place. We were told that Druzil, above all others in the Abyss, knows the man."

"Hates the man," the imp corrected, and he seemed eager indeed. But suddenly he backed off, staring suspiciously at the two. "I tell you, and then you dismiss me," he remarked.

Jarlaxle looked to Rai'gy, for they had anticipated such a reaction. The wizard-priest stood up, walked to the side in the tiny room, and pulled aside a screen, revealing a small kettle, bubbling and boiling.

"I am without a familiar," Rai'gy explained. "An imp would serve me well."

Druzil's coal black eyes flared with red fires. "Then we can pain Cadderly and so many other humans together," the imp reasoned.

"Does Druzil agree?" Jarlaxle asked.

"Does Druzil have a choice?" the imp retorted sarcastically.

"As to serving Rai'gy, yes," the drow replied, and the imp was obviously surprised, as was Rai'gy. "As to revealing all that you know about Cadderly, no. It is too important, and if we must torment you for a hundred years, we shall."

"Then Cadderly would be dead," Druzil said dryly.

"The torment would remain pleasurable to me," Jarlaxle was quick to respond, and Druzil knew enough about dark elves to understand that this was no idle threat.

"Druzil wishes to pain Cadderly," the imp admitted, dark eyes sparkling.

"Then tell us," Jarlaxle said. "Everything."

Later on that day, while Druzil and Rai'gy worked the magic spells that would bind them as master and familiar, Jarlaxle sat alone in the room he had taken in the sub-basement of House Basadoni. He had indeed learned much from the imp, most important of all that he had no desire to bring his band anywhere near the one named Cadderly Bonaduce. This was to Druzil's ultimate dismay. The leader of the Spirit Soaring, armed with magic far beyond even Rai'gy and Kimmuriel, might prove too great a foe. Even worse, Cadderly was apparently rebuilding an order of priests, surrounding himself with young and strong acolytes, enthusiastic idealists.

"The worst kind," Jarlaxle said as Entreri entered the room. "Idealists," he explained to the assassin's perplexed expression. "Above all else, I hate idealists."

"They are blind fools," Entreri agreed.

"They are unpredictable fanatics," Jarlaxle explained. "Blind to danger and blind to fear as long as they think their path is according to the tenets of their particular god-figure."

"And the leader of this other guild is an idealist?" a confused Entreri asked, for he thought he had been summoned to discuss his upcoming meeting with the remaining guilds of Calimport, to stop a war before it ever began.

"No, no, it is another matter," Jarlaxle explained, waving his hand dismissively. "One that concerns my activities in Menzoberranzan and not here in Calimport. Let it not trouble you, for you have business more important by far."

And Jarlaxle, too, put it out of his mind then, focusing on the more immediate problem. He had been surprised by Druzil's accounting of Cadderly, never imagining that this human would present such a problem. Though he held firm to his determination to keep his minions away from Cadderly, he was not dismayed, for he understood that Drizzt and his friends were still a long way from the great library known as the Spirit Soaring.

It was a place Jarlaxle had no intention of ever allowing them to see.

* * * * *

"Yes, a pleasure meetin' ye! Oh, a pleasure, King Bruenor, and to yer kin, me blessin's," Bumpo Thunderpuncher, a rotund and short little dwarf with a fiery orange beard and a huge and flat nose that was pushed over to one side of his ruddy face, said to Bruenor for perhaps the tenth time since *Bottom Feeder* had put out of Baldur's Gate. The dwarven vessel was a square-bottomed, shallow twenty-footer with two banks of oars—though only one was normally in use—and a long aft pole for steering and for pushing off the bottom. Bumpo and his equally rotund and bumbling brother Donat had fallen all over themselves at the sight of the Eighth King of Mithral Hall. Bruenor had seemed honestly surprised that his name had grown to such proportions, even among his own race.

Now, though, that surprise was turning to mere annoyance, as Bumpo and Donat and their two oar-pulling cousins, Yipper and Quipper Fishsquisher, continued to rain compliments, promises of fealty, and general slobber all over him.

Sitting back from the dwarves, Drizzt and Catti-brie smiled. The ranger alternated his looks between Catti-brie—how he loved to gaze upon her when she wasn't looking—and the tumult of the dwarves. Then Regis—who was lying on his belly at the prow, head hanging over the front of the boat, his hands drawing pictures in the water—and back behind them to the diminishing skyline of Baldur's Gate.

Again he thought about his passage through the city, as easy a time of it as the drow had ever known, including those occasions when he had worn the magical mask. He had earned this peace; they all had. Once this mission was completed and the crystal shard was safely in the hands of Cadderly, and once they had recovered Wulfgar and helped him through his darkness, then perhaps they could journey the wide world again, for no better reason than to see what lay over the next horizon and with no troubles beyond the fawning of bumbling dwarves.

Truly Drizzt wore a contented smile, finding hope again, for Wulfgar and for them all. He could never have dreamed that he would ever find such a life on that day decades before when he had walked out of Menzoberranzan.

It occurred to him then that his father, Zaknafein, who had died to give him this chance, was watching him at that moment from another plane, a goodly place for one as deserving as Zak.

Watching him and smiling.

Part 4

KINGDOMS

hether a king's palace, a warrior's bastion, a wizard's tower, an encampment for nomadic barbarians, a farmhouse with stone-lined or hedge-lined fields, or even a tiny and unremarkable room up the back staircase of a ramshackle inn, we each of us spend great energy in carving out our own little kingdoms. From the grandest castle to the smallest nook, from the arrogance of nobility to the unpretentious desires of the lowliest peasant, there is a basic need within the majority of us for ownership, or at least for stewardship. We want to—need to—find our realm, our place in a world often too confusing and too overwhelming, our sense of order in one little corner of a world that oft looms too big and too uncontrollable.

And so we carve and line, fence and lock, then protect our space fiercely with sword or pitchfork.

The hope is that this will be the end of that road we chose to walk, the peaceful and secure rewards for a life of trials. Yet, it never comes to that, for peace is not a place, whether lined by hedges or by high walls. The greatest king with the largest army in the most invulnerable fortress is not necessarily a man at peace. Far from it, for the irony of it all is that the acquisition of such material wealth can work against any hope of true serenity. But beyond any physical securities there lies yet another form of unrest, one that neither the king nor the peasant will escape. Even that great king, even the simplest beggar will, at times, be full of the unspeakable anger we all sometimes feel. And I do not mean a rage so great that it cannot be verbalized but rather a frustration so elusive and permeating that one can find no words for it. It is the quiet source of irrational outbursts against friends and family, the perpetrator of temper. True freedom from it cannot be found in any place outside one's own mind and soul.

Bruenor carved out his kingdom in Mithral Hall, yet found no peace there. He preferred to return to Icewind Dale, a place he had named home not out of desire for wealth, nor out of any inherited kingdom, but because there, in the frozen northland, Bruenor had come to know his greatest measure of inner peace. There he surrounded himself with friends, myself among them, and though he will not admit this—I am not certain he even recognizes it—his return to Icewind Dale was, in fact, precipitated by his desire to return to that emotional place and time when he and I, Regis, Catti-brie, and yes, even Wulfgar, were together. Bruenor went back in search of a memory.

I suspect that Wulfgar now has found a place along or at the end of his chosen road, a niche, be it a tavern in Luskan or Waterdeep, a borrowed barn in a farming village, or even a cave in the Spine of the World. Because what Wulfgar does not now have is a clear picture of where he emotionally wishes to be, a safe haven to which he can escape. If he finds it again, if he can get past the turmoil of his most jarring memories, then likely he, too, will return to Icewind Dale in search of his soul's true home.

In Menzoberranzan I witnessed many of the little kingdoms we foolishly cherish, houses strong and powerful and barricaded from enemies in a futile attempt at security. And when I walked out of Menzoberranzan into the wild Underdark, I, too, sought to carve out my niche. I spent time in a cave talking only to Guenhwyvar and sharing space with mushroomlike creatures that I hardly understood and who hardly understood me. I ventured to Blingdenstone, city of the deep gnomes, and could have made that my home, perhaps, except that staying there, so close to the city of drow, would have surely brought ruin upon those folk.

And so I came to the surface and found a home with Montolio deBrouchee in his wondrous mountain grove, perhaps the first place I ever came to know any real measure of inner peace. And yet I came to learn that the grove was not my home, for when Montolio died I found to my surprise that I could not remain there.

Eventually I found my place and found that the place was within me, not about me. It happened when I came to Icewind Dale, when I met Catti-brie and Regis and Bruenor. Only then did I learn to defeat the unspeakable anger within. Only there did I learn true peace and serenity.

Now I take that calm with me, whether my friends accompany me or not. Mine is a kingdom of the heart and soul, defended by the security of honest love and friendship and the warmth of memories. Better than any land-based kingdom, stronger than any castle wall, and most importantly of all, portable.

I can only hope and pray that Wulfgar will eventually walk out of his darkness and come to this same emotional place.

—Drizzt Do'Urden

Chapter 19
CONCERNING WULFGAR

Delly pulled her coat tighter about her, more trying to hide her gender than to fend off any chill breezes. She moved quickly along the street, skipping fast to try and keep up with the shadowy figure turning corners ahead of her, a man one of the other patrons of the Cutlass had assured her was indeed Morik the Rogue, no doubt come on another spying mission.

She turned into an alleyway, and there he was. He was standing right before her, waiting for her, dagger in hand.

Delly skidded to a stop, hands up in a desperate plea for her life. "Please Mister Morik!" she cried. "I'm just wantin' to talk to ye."

"Morik?" the man echoed, and his hood slipped back revealing a dark-skinned face—too dark for the man Delly sought.

"Oh, but I'm begging yer pardon, good sir," Delly stammered, backing away. "I was thinking ye were someone else." The man started to respond, but Delly hardly heard him, for she turned about and sprinted back toward the Cutlass.

When she got safely away, she calmed and slowed enough to consider the situation. Ever since the fight with Tree Block Breaker, she and many other patrons had seen Morik the Rogue in every shadow, had heard him skulking about every corner. Or had they all, in their fears, just thought they had seen the dangerous man? Frustrated by that thought, knowing that there was indeed more than a little truth to her reasoning, Delly gave a great sigh and let her coat droop open.

"Selling your wares, then, Delly Curtie?" came a question from the side.

Delly's eyes widened as she turned to regard the shadowy figure against the wall, the figure belonging to a voice she recognized. She felt the lump grow in her throat. She had been looking for Morik, but now that he had found her on his terms she felt foolish indeed. She glanced down the street, back toward the Cutlass, wondering if she could make it there before a dagger found her back.

"You have been asking about me and looking for me," Morik casually remarked.

"I've been doing no such—"

"I was one of those whom you asked," Morik interrupted dryly. His voice changed pitch and accent completely as he added, "So be tellin' me, missy, why ye're wantin' to be seein' that nasty little knife-thrower."

That set Delly back on her heels, remembering well her encounter with an old woman who had said those very words in that very voice. And even if she hadn't recognized the phrasing or the voice, she wouldn't for a moment doubt the man who was well-known as Luskan's master of disguise. She had seen Morik on several occasions, intimately, many months before. Every time he had appeared differently to her, not just in physical features but in demeanor and attitude as well, walking differently, talking differently, even making love differently. Rumors circulating through Luskan for years had claimed that Morik was, in fact, several different men, and while Delly thought them exaggerated, she realized just then that if they turned out to be correct, she wouldn't be surprised.

"So you have found me," Morik said firmly.

Delly paused, not sure how to proceed. Only Morik's obvious agitation and impatience prompted her to blurt out, "I'm wanting ye to leave Wulfgar alone. He gave Tree Block what Tree Block asked for and wouldn't've gone after the man if the man didn't go after him."

"Why would I care for Tree Block Breaker?" Morik asked, still using a tone that seemed to say that he had hardly given it a thought. "An irritating thug, if ever I knew one. Half Moon Street seems a better place without him."

"Well, then ye're not for avenging that one," Delly reasoned. "But word's out that ye're none too fond o' Wulfgar and looking to prove—"

"I have nothing to prove," Morik interrupted.

"And what of Wulfgar then?" Delly asked.

Morik shrugged noncommittally. "You speak as if you love the man, Delly Curtie."

Delly blushed fiercely. "I'm speaking for Arumn Gardpeck, as well," she insisted. "Wulfgar's been good for the Cutlass, and as far as we're knowing, he's been not a bit o' trouble outside the place."

"Ah, but it seems as if you do love him, Delly, and more than a bit," Morik said with a laugh. "And here I thought that Delly Curtie loved every man equally."

Delly blushed again, even more fiercely.

"Of course, if you do love him, then I, out of obligation to all other suitors, would have to see him dead," Morik reasoned. "I would consider that a duty to my fellows of Luskan, you see, for a treasure such as Delly Curtie is not to be hoarded by any one man."

"I'm not loving him," Delly said firmly. "But I'm asking ye, for meself and for Arumn, not to kill him."

"Not in love with him?" Morik asked slyly.

Delly shook her head.

"Prove it," Morik said, reaching out to pull the tie string on the neck of Delly's dress.

The woman teetered for just a moment, unsure. And then—for Wulfgar only, for she did not wish to do this—she nodded her agreement.

Later on, Morik the Rogue lay alone in his rented bed, Delly long gone—to Wulfgar's bed, he figured. He took a deep draw on his pipe, savoring the intoxicating aroma of the exotic and potent pipeweed.

He considered his good fortune this night, for he hadn't been with Delly Curtie in more than a year and had forgotten how marvelous she could be.

Especially when it didn't cost him anything, and on this nigh, it most certainly had not. Morik had indeed been watching Wulfgar but had no intention of killing the man. The fate of Tree Block Breaker had shown him well how dangerous a proposition that attempt could prove.

He did plan to have a long talk with Arumn Gardpeck, though, one that Delly would surely make easier now. There was no need to kill the barbarian, as long as Arumn kept the huge man in his place.

* * * * *

Delly fumbled with her dress and cloak, all in a fit after her encounter with Morik, as she stumbled through the upstairs rooms of the inn. She turned a corner in the hallway and was surprised indeed to see the street looming in front of her, right in front of her, and before she could even stop herself, she was outside. And then the world was spinning all about.

When she at last re-oriented herself, she glanced back behind her, seeing the open street under the moonlight, and the inn where she had left Morik many yards away. She didn't understand, for hadn't she been walking inside just a moment ago? And in an upstairs hallway? Delly merely shrugged. For this woman, not understanding something was not so uncommon an occurrence. She shook her head, figured that Morik had really set her thoughts to spinning that night, and headed back for the Cutlass.

On the other side of the dimensional door that had transported the woman out of the inn, Kimmuriel Oblodra almost laughed aloud at the bumbling spectacle. Glad of his camouflaging *piwafwi* cloak, for Jarlaxle had insisted that he leave no traces of his ever being in Luskan, and Jarlaxle considered murdered humans as traces, the drow turned the corner in the hallway and lined up his next spatial leap.

He winced at the notion, reminding himself that he had to handle this one delicately; he and Rai'gy had done some fine spying on Morik the Rogue, and Kimmuriel knew the man to be dangerous, for a human, at least. He brought up his kinetic barrier, focused all his thoughts on it, then enacted the dimensional path down the corridor and beyond Morik's door.

There lay the man on his bed, bathed in the soft glow of his pipe and the embers from the hearth across the room. Morik sat up immediately, obviously sensing the disturbance, and Kimmuriel went through the portal, focusing his thoughts more strongly on the kinetic barrier. If the disorientation of the spatial walk defeated his concentration, he would likely be dead before his thoughts ever unscrambled.

Indeed, the drow felt Morik come into him hard, felt the jab of a dagger against his belly. But the kinetic barrier held, and he absorbed the blow. As he found again his conscious focus and took two more hits, he pushed back against the man and wriggled out to the side, standing facing Morik and laughing at him.

"You can not hurt me," he said haltingly, his command of the common tongue less than perfect, even with the magics Rai'gy had bestowed upon him.

Morik's eyes widened considerably as he recognized the truth of the intruder, as his mind came to grips with the fact that a drow elf had come into his room. He glanced about, apparently seeking an escape route.

"I come to talk, Morik," Kimmuriel explained, not wanting to have to chase this one all across Luskan. "Not to hurt you."

Morik hardly seemed to relax at the assurance of a dark elf.

"I bring gifts," Kimmuriel went on, and he tossed a small box onto the bed, its contents jingling. "Belaern, and pipeweed from the great cavern of Yoganith. Very good. You must answer questions."

"Questions about what?" the still nervous thief asked, remaining in his defensive crouch, one hand turning his dagger over repeatedly. "Who are you?"

"My master is . . ." Kimmuriel paused, searching for the right word. "Generous," he decided. "And my master is merciless. You deal with us." He stopped there and held up his hand to halt any reply before Morik could respond. Kimmuriel felt the energy tingling within him, and holding it had become a drain he could ill afford. He focused on a small chair, sending his thoughts into it, animating it and having it walk right past him.

He touched it as it crossed before him, releasing all the energy of Morik's hits, shattering the wooden chair completely.

Morik eyed him skeptically, without comprehension. "A warning?" he asked.

Kimmuriel only smiled.

"You did not like my chair?"

"My master wishes to hire you," Kimmuriel explained. "He needs eyes in Luskan."

"Eyes and a sword?" Morik asked, his own eyes narrowing.

"Eyes and no more," Kimmuriel came back. "You tell me of the one called Wulfgar now, and then you will watch him closely and tell me about him when occasions have me return to you."

"Wulfgar?" Morik muttered under his breath, fast growing tired of the name.

"Wulfgar," answered Kimmuriel, who shouldn't have been able to hear, but of course, with his keen drow ears, certainly did. "You watch him."

"I would rather kill him," Morik remarked. "If he is trouble—" He stopped abruptly as murderous intent flashed across Kimmuriel's dark eyes.

"Not that," the drow explained. "Kyorlin . . . watch him. Quietly. I return with more belaern for more answers." He motioned to the box on the bed and repeated the drow word, "Belaern," with great emphasis.

Before Morik could ask anything else the room darkened utterly, a blackness so complete that the man couldn't see his hand if he had waved it an inch before his eyes. Fearing an attack, he went lower and skittered forward, dagger slashing.

But the dark elf was long gone, was back through his dimensional door into the hallway, then through that onto the street, then back through Rai'gy's teleportation gate, walking all that way back to Calimport before the globe of darkness even dissipated in Morik's room. Rai'gy and Jarlaxle, both of whom had watched the exchange, nodded their approval.

Jarlaxle's grasp on the surface world widened.

* * * * *

Morik came out from under his bed tentatively when the embers of the hearth at last reappeared. What a strange night it had been! he thought. First with Delly, though that was not so unexpected, since she obviously loved Wulfgar and knew that Morik could easily kill him.

But now . . . a drow elf! Coming to Morik to talk about Wulfgar! Was everything on Luskan's street suddenly about Wulfgar? Who was this man, and why did he attract such amazing attention?

Morik looked at the blasted chair—an impressive feat—then, frustrated, threw his dagger across the room so that it sank deep into the opposite wall. Then he went to the bed.

"Belaern," he said quietly, wondering what that might mean. Hadn't the dark elf said something about pipeweed?

He gingerly inspected the unremarkable box, looking for any traps. Finding none and reasoning that the dark elf could have used a more straightforward method of killing him if that had been the drow's intent, he set the box solidly on a night table and gently pulled its latch back and opened the lid.

Gems and gold stared back at him, and packets of a dark weed.

"Belaern," Morik said again, his smile gleaming as did the treasure before him. So he was to watch Wulfgar, something he had planned to do anyway, and he would be rewarded handsomely for his efforts.

He thought of Delly Curtie; he looked at the contents of the opened box and the rumpled sheets.

Not a bad night.

* * * * *

Life at the Cutlass remained quiet and peaceful for several days, with no one coming in to challenge Wulfgar after the demise of the legendary Tree Block Breaker. But when the peace finally broke, it did so in grand fashion. A new ship put in to Luskan harbor with a crew too long on the water and looking for a good row.

And they found one in the form of Wulfgar, in a tavern they nearly pulled down around them.

Finally, after many minutes of brawling, Wulfgar lifted the last squirming sailor over his head and tossed the man out through the hole in the wall created by the four previous men the barbarian had thrown out. Another stubborn sea dog tried to rush back in through the hole, and Wulfgar hit him in the face with a bottle.

Then the big man wiped a bloody forearm across his bloody face, took up another bottle—this one full—and staggered to the nearest intact table. Falling into a chair and taking a deep swig, Wulfgar grimaced as he drank, as the alcohol washed over his torn lip.

At the bar, Josi and Arumn sat exhausted and also beaten. Wulfgar had taken the brunt of it, though; these two had minor cuts and bruises only.

"He's hurt pretty bad," Josi remarked, motioning to the big man—to his leg in particular, for Wulfgar's pants were soaked in blood. One of the sailors had struck him hard with a plank. The board had split apart and torn fabric and skin, leaving many large slivers deeply embedded in the barbarian's leg.

Even as Arumn and Josi regarded him, Delly moved beside him, falling to her knees and wrapping a clean cloth about the leg. She pushed hard on the deep slivers and made Wulfgar growl in agony. He took another deep drink of the pain-killing liquor.

"Delly will see to him again," Arumn remarked. "That's become her lot in life."

"A busy lot, then," Josi agreed, his tone solemn. "I'm thinking that the last crew Wulfgar dumped, Rossie Doone and his thugs, probably pointed this bunch in our direction. There'll always be another to challenge the boy."

"And one day he will find his better. As did Tree Block Breaker," Arumn said quietly. "He'll not die comfortably in bed, I fear."

"Nor will he outlive either of us," Josi added, watching as Delly, supporting the barbarian, led him out of the room.

Just then another pair of rowdy sailors came rushing through the broken wall, running straight for the staggering Wulfgar's back. Just before they got to him, the huge barbarian found a surge of energy. He pushed Delly safely away, then spun, fist flying between the reaching arms of one man to slam him in the face. He dropped as though his legs had turned to liquid beneath him.

The other sailor barreled into Wulfgar, but the big man didn't move an inch, just grunted and accepted the man's left and right combination.

But then Wulfgar had him, grabbing tight under his arms and squeezing hard, lifting the man right from the floor. When the sailor tried to punch and kick at him, the barbarian shook him so violently that the man bit the tip right off his tongue.

Then he was flying, Wulfgar taking two running steps and launching him for the hole in the wall.

Wulfgar's aim wasn't true, though, and the man crashed against the wall a foot or so to the left.

"I'll push him out for ye," Josi Puddles called from the bar.

Wulfgar nodded, accepted Delly's arm again, and ambled away.

"But he will take his share down with him, now won't he?" Arumn Gardpeck remarked with a chuckle.

Chapter 20
DANGLING A LOCKET

My dear Domo," Sharlotta Vespers purred, moving over seductively to put her long fingers on the wererat leader's shoulders. "Can you not see the mutual gain to our alliance?"

"I see Basadonis moving into my sewers," Domo Quillilo replied with a snarl. He was in human form now, but still carried characteristics—such as the way he twitched his nose—that seemed more fitting to a rat. "Where is the old wretch?"

Artemis Entreri started to respond, but Sharlotta shot him a plaintive look, begging him to follow her lead. The assassin sat back in his chair, more than content to let Sharlotta handle the likes of Domo.

"The old wretch," the woman began, imitating Domo's less-than-complimentary tone, "is even now securing a partnership with an even greater ally, one whom Domo would not wish to cross."

The wererat's eyes narrowed dangerously; he was not accustomed to being threatened. "Who?" he asked. "Those smelly kobolds we found running through our sewers?"

"Kobolds?" Sharlotta echoed with a laugh. "Hardly them. No, they are just fodder, the leading edge of our new ally's forces."

The wererat leader pulled away from the woman, rose out of his chair, and strode across the room. He knew that a fight had occurred in the sewers and sub-basement of the Basadoni House. He knew that it concerned many kobolds and the Basadoni soldiers and also, so his spies had told him, some other creatures. These were unseen but obviously powerful, with cunning magics and tricks. He also knew, simply from the fact that Sharlotta still lived, that the Basadonis, some of them at least, had survived. Domo suspected that a coup had occurred with these two, Sharlotta and Entreri, masterminding it. They claimed that old man Basadoni was still alive, though Domo wasn't sure he believed that, but had admitted that Kadran Gordeon, a friend of Domo's, had been killed. Unfortunately, so said Sharlotta, but Domo understood that luck, good or bad, had nothing to do with it.

"Why does he speak for the old man?" the wererat asked Sharlotta, nodding toward Entreri, and with more than a bit of distaste in his tone. Domo held no love for Entreri. Few wererats did since Entreri had murdered one of the more legendary of their clan in Calimport, a conniving and wicked fellow named Rassiter.

"Because I choose to," Entreri cut in sharply before Sharlotta could intervene. The woman cast a sour look the assassin's way, then mellowed her visage as she turned back to Domo. "Artemis Entreri is well skilled in the ways of Calimport," she explained. "A proper emissary."

"I am to trust him?" Domo asked incredulously.

"You are to trust that the deal we offer you and yours is the best one you shall find in all the city," Sharlotta replied.

"You are to trust that if you do not take the deal," Entreri added, "you are thus declaring war against us. Not a pleasant prospect, I assure you."

Domo's rodent's eyes narrowed again as he considered the assassin, but he was respectful enough, and wise enough, not to push Artemis Entreri any farther.

"We will talk again, Sharlotta," he said. "You, me, and old man Basadoni." With that, the wererat took his leave with two Basadoni guards flanking him as soon as he exited the room and escorting him back to the subbasement where he could then find his way back into his sewer lair.

He was hardly gone before a secret door opened on the wall behind Sharlotta and Entreri, and Jarlaxle strode into the room.

"Leave us," the drow mercenary instructed Sharlotta, his tone showing that he wasn't overly pleased with the results.

Sharlotta gave another sour look Entreri's way and started out of the room.

"You performed quite admirably," Jarlaxle said to her, and she nodded.

"But I failed," Entreri said as soon as the door closed behind the woman. "A pity."

"These meetings mean everything to us," Jarlaxle said to him. "If we can secure our power and assure the other guilds that they are in no danger, I will have completed my first order of business."

"And then trade can begin between Calimport and Menzoberranzan," Entreri said dramatically, sarcastically, sweeping his arms out wide. "All to the gain of Menzoberranzan."

"All to the profit of Bregan D'aerthe," Jarlaxle corrected.

"And for that, I am to care?" Entreri bluntly asked.

Jarlaxle paused for a long moment to consider the man's posture and tone. "There are those among my group who fear that you do not have the will to carry this through," he said, and though the mercenary leader had allowed no hint of a threatening tone into his voice, Entreri understood the practices of the dark elves well enough to recognize the dire implications.

"Have you no heart for this?" the mercenary leader asked. "Why, you are on the verge of becoming the most influential pasha ever to rule the streets of Calimport. Kings will bow before you and pay you homage and treasures."

"And I will yawn in their ugly faces," Entreri replied.

"Yes, it all bores you," Jarlaxle remarked. "Even the fighting. You have lost your goals and desires, thrown them away. Why? Is it fear? Or is it simply that you believe there is nothing left to attain?"

Entreri shifted uncomfortably. Of course, he had known for a long time exactly the thing about which Jarlaxle was now speaking, but to hear another verbalize the emptiness within him struck him profoundly.

"Are you a coward?" Jarlaxle asked.

Entreri laughed at the absurdity of the remark, even considered leaping from his chair in a full attack upon the drow. He understood Jarlaxle's techniques and knew that he would likely be dead before he ever reached the taunting mercenary, but still he seriously considered the move. Then Jarlaxle hit him with a preemptive strike that put him back on his heels.

"Or is it that you have witnessed Menzoberranzan?" he asked.

That was indeed a huge part of it, Entreri knew, and his expression showed Jarlaxle clearly that he had struck a nerve.

"Humbled?" the drow asked. "Did you find the sights of Menzoberranzan humbling?"

"Daunting," Entreri corrected, his voice full of force and venom. "To see such stupidity on so grand a scale."

"Ah, and you know it to be a stupidity that mirrors your own existence," Jarlaxle remarked. "All that Artemis Entreri strove to achieve he found played out before him on a grand scale in the city of drow."

Still sitting, Entreri wrung his hands and bit his lip, edging closer, closer, to an attack.

"Is your life, then, a lie?" an unperturbed Jarlaxle went on, and then he sent a verbal dagger flying for Entreri's heart. "That is what Drizzt Do'Urden claimed to you, is it not?"

For just an instant, a flash of seething rage crossed Entreri's stoic face, and Jarlaxle laughed loudly. "At last, a sign of life from you!" he said. "A sign of desire, even if that desire was to tear out my heart." He gave a great sigh and lowered his voice. "Many of my companions do not think you worth the trouble," he admitted. "But I know better, Artemis Entreri. We are friends, you and I, and more alike than either of us wish to admit. You have greatness before you, if only I can show you the way."

"You speak foolishness," Entreri said evenly.

"That way lies through Drizzt Do'Urden," Jarlaxle continued without hesitation. "That is the hole in your heart. You must fight him again on terms of your choosing, because your pride will not allow you to go on with any other facet of your life until that business is settled."

"I have fought him too many times already," Entreri retorted, his anger rising. "Never do I wish to see that one again."

"So you may profess to believe," Jarlaxle said. "But you lie, to me and to yourself. Twice have you and Drizzt Do'Urden battled fairly, and twice has Entreri been sent running."

"In these very sewers he was mine!" the assassin insisted. "And would have been, had not his friends come to his aid."

"And on the cliff overlooking Mithral Hall it was he who proved the stronger."

"No!" Entreri insisted, losing his calm edge for just a moment. "No. I had him beaten."

"So you honestly believe, and thus you are trapped by the pain of the memories," Jarlaxle reasoned. "You told me of that fight in detail, and I did watch some of it from afar. We both know that either of you could have won that duel. And that is your turmoil. If Drizzt had cleanly beaten you and yet you had managed to survive, you could have gone on with your life. And if you had beaten him, whether he had lived or not, you would think no more about him. It is the not knowing that so gnaws at you, my friend. The pain of recognizing that there is one challenge that has not been decided, one challenge blocking all other aspirations you might find, be they a desire for greater power or merely for hedonistic pleasure, both easily within your reach."

Entreri sat back, seeming more intrigued than angry then.

"And that, too, I can give to you," Jarlaxle explained. "That which you desire most of all, if you'll only admit what is in your heart. I can continue my plans for Calimport without you now; Sharlotta is a fine front, and I am too firmly entrenched to be uprooted. Yet I do not desire such an arrangement. For my ventures to the surface, I want Artemis Entreri leading Bregan D'aerthe, the real Artemis Entreri and not this shell of your former self, too absorbed by this futile and empty challenge with the rogue Drizzt to concentrate on those skills that elevate you above all others."

"Skills," Entreri echoed skeptically and turned away.

But Jarlaxle knew he had gotten to the man, knew that he had dangled a treat before Entreri's eyes that the assassin could not resist. "There is one meeting remaining, the most important of the lot," Jarlaxle explained. "My drow associates and I will watch you closely when you speak with the leaders of the Rakers, Pasha Wroning's emissaries, Quentin Bodeau, and Dwahvel Tiggerwillies. Perform your duties well, and I will deliver Drizzt Do'Urden to you."

"They will demand to see Pasha Basadoni," Entreri reasoned, and the mere fact that he was giving any thought at all to the coming meeting told Jarlaxle that his bait had been taken.

"Have you not the mask of disguise?" Jarlaxle asked.

Entreri halted for a moment, not understanding, but then he realized what Jarlaxle was speaking of: a magical mask he had taken from Catti-brie in Menzoberranzan. The mask he had used to impersonate Gromph Baenre, the archmage of the drow city, to sneak right into Gromph's quarters to secure the valuable Spider Mask that had allowed him to get into House Baenre in search of Drizzt. "I do not have it," he said brusquely, obviously not wanting to elaborate.

"A pity," said Jarlaxle. "It would make things much simpler. But not to worry, for it will all be arranged," the drow promised, and with a sweeping bow he left the room, left Artemis Entreri sitting there, wondering.

"Drizzt Do'Urden," the assassin said, and there was no venom in his voice now, just an emotionless resignation. Indeed, Jarlaxle had tempted him, had shown him a different side of his inner turmoil that he had not considered—not honestly, at least. After the escape from Menzoberranzan, the last time he had set eyes upon Drizzt, Entreri had told himself with more than a little convictio, that he was through with the rogue drow, that he hoped never to see wretched Drizzt Do'Urden again.

But was that the truth?

Jarlaxle had spoken correctly when he had insisted that the issue as to who was the better swordsman had not been decided between the two. They had fought against each other in two razor-close battles and other minor skirmishes, and had fought together on two separate occasions, in Menzoberranzan and in the lower tunnels of Mithral Hall before Bruenor's clan had reclaimed the place. All those encounters had shown them was that with regard to fighting styles and prowess they were practically mirrors of each other.

In the sewers the fight had been even until Entreri spat dirty water in Drizzt's face, gaining the upper hand. But then that wretched Catti-brie with her deadly bow had arrived, chasing the assassin away. The fight on the ledge had been Entreri's, he believed, until the drow used an unfair advantage, using his innate magics to drop a globe of darkness over them both. Even then, Entreri had maintained a winning edge until his own eagerness had caused him to forget his enemy.

What was the truth between them, then? Who would win?

The assassin gave a great sigh and rested his chin in his palm, wondering, wondering. From a pocket inside his cloak he took out a small locket, one that Jarlaxle had taken from Catti-brie and that Entreri had recovered from the mercenary leader's own desk in Menzoberranzan, a locket that could lead him to Drizzt' Do'Urden.

Many times over the past few years Artemis Entreri had stared at this locket, wondering over the whereabouts of the rogue, wondering what Drizzt might be doing, wondering what enemies he had recently battled.

Many times the assassin had stared at the locket and wondered, but never before had he seriously considered using it.

* * * * *

A noticeable spring enhanced Jarlaxle's always fluid step as he went from Entreri. The mercenary leader silently congratulated himself for the foresight of spending so much energy in hunting Drizzt Do'Urden and for his cunning in planting so powerful a seed within Entreri.

"But that is the thing," he said to Rai'gy and Kimmuriel when he found them in Rai'gy's room, Jarlaxle finishing aloud his silent pondering. "Foresight, always."

The two looked at him quizzically.

Jarlaxle dismissed those looks with a laugh. "And where are we with our scouting?" the mercenary leader asked, and he was pleased to see that Druzil was still with the mage; Rai'gy's intentions to make the imp his familiar seemed to be well on course.

The other two dark elves looked to each other, and it was their turn to laugh. Rai'gy began a quiet chant, moving his arms in slow and specified motions. Gradually he increased the speed of his waving, and he began turning about, his flowing robes flying behind him. A gray smoke arose about him, obscuring him and making it seem as if he were moving and twirling faster and faster.

And then it stopped, and Rai'gy was gone. Standing in his place was a human dressed in a tan tunic and trousers, a light blue silken cape, and a curious—curiously like Jarlaxle's own—wide-brimmed hat. The hat was blue and banded in red, plumed on the right side, and with a porcelain and gold pendant depicting a candle burning above an open eye set in its center.

"Greetings, Jarlaxle, I am Cadderly Bonaduce of Caradoon," the impostor said, bowing low.

Jarlaxle didn't miss the fact that this supposed human spoke fluently in the tongue of the drow, a language rarely heard on the surface.

"The imitation is perfect," the imp Druzil rasped. "So much does he look like the wretch Cadderly that I want to stick him with my poisoned tail!" Druzil finished with a flap of his little leathery wings that sent him up into a short flight, clapping his clawed hands and feet as he went.

"I doubt that Cadderly Bonaduce of Caradoon speaks drow," Jarlaxle said dryly.

"A simple spell will correct that," Rai'gy assured his leader, and indeed Jarlaxle knew of such a spell, had often employed it in his travels and meetings with varied races. But that spell had its limitations, Jarlaxle knew.

"I will look as Cadderly looks and speak as Cadderly speaks," Rai'gy went on, smiling at his cleverness.

"Will you?" Jarlaxle asked in all seriousness. "Or will our perceptive adversary hear you transpose a subject and verb, more akin to the manner of our language, and will that clue him that all is not as it seems?"

"I will be careful," Rai'gy promised, his tone showing that he did not appreciate anyone doubting his prowess.

"Careful may not prove to be enough," Jarlaxle replied. "As magnificent as your work has been we can take no chances here."

"If we are to go to Drizzt, as you said, then how?" Rai'gy asked.

"We shall need a professional impersonator," Jarlaxle said, drawing a groan from both his drow companions.

"What does he mean?" Druzil asked nervously.

Jarlaxle looked to Kimmuriel. "Baeltimazifas is with the illithids," he instructed. "You can go to them."

"Baeltimazifas," Rai'gy said with obvious disgust, for he knew the creature and hated it profoundly, as did most. "The illithids control the creature and set his fees exorbitantly high."

"It will be expensive," added Kimmuriel, who had the most experience in dealing with the strange illithids, the mind flayers.

"The gain is worth the price," Jarlaxle assured them both.

"And the possibility of treachery?" Rai'gy asked. "Those kinds, both Baeltimazifas and the illithids, have never been known to follow through with bargains nor to fear the drow or any other race."

"Then we will be the first and best at treachery," Jarlaxle insisted, nodding, smiling, and seeming completely unafraid. "And what of this Wulfgar who was left behind?"

"In Luskan," Kimmuriel replied. "He is of no consequence. A minor player and nothing more, unconnected to the rogue at this time."

Jarlaxle assumed a pensive posture, putting all the pieces together. "Minor in fact but not in tale," he decided. "If you went to Drizzt in the guise of Cadderly would you have enough remaining power—clerical powers and not wizardly—to magically bring them all to Luskan?"

"Not I and not Cadderly," Rai'gy replied. "They are too many for any clerical transport spell. I could take one or two, but not four. Nor could Cadderly, unless he is possessed of powers I do not understand."

Again Jarlaxle paused, thinking, thinking. "Not Luskan, then," he remarked, more thinking aloud than talking to his companions. "Baldur's Gate, or even a village near that city, will suit our needs." It all fell into place for the cunning mercenary leader then, the lure that would help separate Drizzt and friends from the crystal shard. "Yes, this could be rather enjoyable."

"And profitable?" Kimmuriel asked.

Jarlaxle laughed. "I cannot have one without the other."

Chapter 21
TIMELY WOUNDS

e always put in here," Bumpo Thunder-puncher explained as Bottom Feeder bumped hard against a fallen tree overhanging the river. The jarring shock nearly sent Regis and Bruenor tumbling off the side of the boat. "Don't like carrying too many supplies all at once," the rotund dwarf explained. "Me brother and cousins eat 'em to dangnabbit fast!"

Drizzt nodded—they did indeed need some food, mostly because of the gluttonous dwarves—and glanced warily at the trees clustered about the river. Several times over the previous two days the friends had noted movements shadowing their journey, and once Regis had seen the pursuers clearly enough to identify them as a band of goblins. By the dogged pursuit, and any pursuit longer than a few hours would be considered dogged by goblin standards, it seemed as if Crenshinibon was calling out yet again.

"How long to resupply and get back out?" the drow asked.

"Oh, not more'n an hour," Bumpo replied.

"Half that time," Bruenor bade him. "And me and me halfling friend'll help." He nodded to Drizzt and

Catti-brie then, and they took the signal; Bruenor hadn't included them because he knew they had to go out and do a bit of scouting.

It didn't take the seasoned pair of hunters long to find goblin sign, the tracks of at least a score of the wicked little creatures. And not far away. The goblins had apparently veered from the river at this point, and when Drizzt and Catti-brie moved to higher ground, looking east to see more of the silvery snake that was the river bending about up ahead, the two understood the goblins' reasoning. *Bottom Feeder* had been going generally north for the past hour, for the river hooked at this juncture, but the boat would soon turn back east, then south, then back to the east once more. Crossing the fairly open ground moving directly to the east, the goblin band would get to the banks in the east far ahead of the dwarves' boat.

"Ah, they're knowing the river then," Bumpo said when Drizzt and Catti-brie returned to report their findings. "They'll be beatin' us to the spot, and the river's narrower there, not wide enough for us to avoid a fight."

Bruenor turned a serious gaze upon Drizzt. "How many're ye figuring, elf?" he asked.

"A score," Drizzt replied. "Perhaps as many as thirty."

"Let's be picking our place for fighting, then," Bruenor said. "If we're to fight, then let it be on ground of our own choosing."

Everyone around noted the lack of dismay in Bruenor's tone.

"They'll be seein' the boat a long way off," Bumpo explained. "If we're to keep it here, tied up, they might be catching on."

Drizzt was shaking his head before the dwarf ever finished. "*Bottom Feeder* will go along as planned," he explained, "but without we three." He indicated Bruenor and Catti-brie, then moved near to Regis, unstrapping his belt so that he could slide off the pouch that held the Crystal Shard. "This remains on the boat," he explained to the halfling. "Above all else, keep it safe."

"So they will come after the boat, and you three will come after them," Regis reasoned, and Drizzt nodded.

"Be quick, if you please," the halfling added.

"What're ye grumbling over, Rumblebelly?" Bruenor asked with a chuckle. "Ye just loaded a ton o' food on the boat, and knowing ye the way I do I'm figuring there won't be much left for me when we get back aboard!"

Regis looked down doubtfully at the pouch, but his face did brighten as he turned to regard the supply-laden boat.

They parted company then, Bumpo, his crew, and Regis pushed off from the impromptu tree landing back into the swift currents. Before they had gone far Drizzt, on the riverbank, took out his onyx figurine, set it down, and called for his panther companion. Then he and his three companions set off, running straight to the east, following the same course as the goblin troupe.

Guenhwyvar took the point position, blending into the brush, barely seeming to stir the grasses and bushes as she passed. Drizzt came along next, working as liaison between the cat and the other two, who brought up the rear, Bruenor with his axe comfortably across his shoulder and Catti-brie with Taulmaril in hand, arrow notched and ready.

* * * * *

"Well, if we're to be fightin', then this'll be the place," Donat said a short while later as *Bottom Feeder* rounded a bend in the river, crossing into a region of narrower banks and swifter current and with many tree limbs overhanging the water.

Regis took one look at the area and groaned, not liking the prospects at all. Goblins could be anywhere, he realized, taking a good measure of the many bushes and hillocks. He took little comfort in the apparent giddiness of the four dwarves, for he had been around dwarves long enough to know that they were always happy before a fight, no matter the prospects.

And even more disconcerting to the halfling came a voice within his head, a tempting, teasing voice, reminding him that with a word he could construct a crystalline tower—a tower that a thousand goblins couldn't breach—if Regis just took control of the crystal shard. The goblins wouldn't even try to take the tower, Regis knew, for Crenshinibon would work with him to control the little wretches.

They could not resist.

* * * * *

Drizzt, looking back with his back against a tree some distance ahead of Bruenor and Catti-brie, motioned for the woman to hold her shot. He, too, had seen the goblin on the branch above, a goblin intent on the river ahead and taking no note of the approaching friends. No need to tell the whole troupe that danger was about, the ranger decided, and Catti-brie's thunderous bow would certainly raise the general alarm.

So up the tree went the drow ranger, one scimitar in hand. With amazing stealth and equal agility, he made a branch level with the goblin. Then, balancing perfectly without using his free hand, he closed suddenly in five quick steps. The drow clamped his empty hand around the creature's side, through bow and bowstring and over the surprised goblin's mouth, and drove his scimitar into the creature's back, hooking the blade upward as he went to slice smoothly through heart and lung. He held the goblin for a few seconds, letting it descend into the complete blackness of death, then carefully set it down over the branch, laying the crude bow atop it.

Drizzt looked all around for Guenhwyvar, but the panther was nowhere to be seen. He had instructed the cat to hold back until the main fighting started and trusted that Guenhwyvar would do as told.

That fight fast approached, Drizzt knew, for the goblins were all about, huddled in bushes and in trees near to the riverbank. He didn't like the prospects for a quick victory here; the region was too jumbled, with too many physical barriers and too many hiding holes. He would have liked the luxury of spending an hour or more locating all the goblins.

But then *Bottom Feeder* came into sight, rounding a bend not so far away.

Drizzt looked back to his waiting friends, motioning strongly for them to come on fast.

A roar from Bruenor and a sizzling arrow from Taulmaril led the way, Catti-brie's missile cutting by the base of Drizzt's tree, diving through some underbrush and taking a goblin in the hip, dropping it squirming to the ground.

Three other goblins emerged from that same brush, running out and screaming wildly.

Those screams fast diminished as the drow, now holding both his deadly blades, leaped down atop them. He struck hard as he crashed in, stabbing one to the side, and felling the one under him by tucking the hilt of his second blade tight against his torso and using his momentum to drive it halfway through the unfortunate creature.

And he nearly collided in midair with another soaring, dark form. Guenhwyvar, leaping strong, crossed by the descending drow and crashed into yet another bush atop a shadowy goblin form.

The one goblin of the three to escape Drizzt's initial leap staggered to the side against the trunk of the same tree from which Drizzt had jumped and turned about, spear raised to throw.

It heard the cursing howl and tried to turn its angle to the newest foe, but Bruenor came in too quick, moving within the sharpened tip of the long weapon and transferring his momentum into his overhead axe with a skidding stop, every muscle in his body snapping forward.

"Damn!" the dwarf grumbled, realizing that it might take him some time to extricate the embedded weapon from the split skull.

Even as the dwarf tugged and twisted, Catti-brie came running by, dropping to one knee and letting fly another arrow. This one blasted a goblin from a tree. She dropped her bow and in one fluid motion drew out Khazid'hea, her powerfully enchanted sword. The blade glowing fiercely, she ran on.

Still Bruenor tugged.

Drizzt, both the other two goblins quite dead, leaped up and ran on, disappearing through a small cluster of trees.

Up ahead, Guenhwyvar ran up the side of a tree, and the terrified goblins on the lowest branches both threw their spears errantly and tried to leap to the ground. One made it; the other got caught in midair by a swiping panther claw and was pulled, squirming wildly, back up to its death.

"Damn," Bruenor said again, tugging and tugging, missing all the fun. "I gotta hit the stinkin' things softer!"

* * * * *

He couldn't raise the crystal tower on the boat, of course, but right over the side, even in the river. Yes, the bottom levels of the structure might be under the water, but Crenshinibon would still show him a way in.

"They got spears!" Bumpo Thunderpuncher cried. "To the wall! To the wall!" On cue, the dwarf captain and his three kinsfolk dived down to the deck and rolled up against the blocking side wall closest to the goblin-infested shore. Donat, who got there first, quickly broke open a wooden locker, each dwarf taking up a crossbow and huddling tight against the shielding planking while loading.

All of the movement finally caught Regis's eye, and he shook away his visions of a crystal tower, hardly believing that he could have even considered raising the thing, and looked, quite startled, at the dwarves. He looked up as the boat drifted beneath an overhanging limb and saw a goblin there, its arm poised to throw.

The four dwarves rolled in unison to their backs, lining up their crossbows and letting fly. Each bolt hit its mark, driving into the goblin and jerking it up and over so that it tumbled into the river behind the floating craft.

But not before it had thrown the spear and thrown it well.

Regis yelped and tried to dodge, but too late. He felt the spear dive into the back of his shoulder. The halfling heard, with sickening clarity, the tip of it prodding right through him to knock against the deck. He was down, facedown, and he heard himself howling, though his voice came from no conscious act.

Then he felt the uneven edges of the decking planks as the dwarves pulled him to the side, and he heard, as if from a great distance, Donat crying, "They killed him! They killed him to death!"

And then he was alone, and so cold, and he heard the splashing of water as swimming goblins made the edge of the boat.

* * * * *

Down from a high branch came the panther, graceful and beautiful, a soaring black arrow. She went past one goblin, one paw kicking out swiftly enough to rake out the oblivious creature's throat, and then crashed upon another pair, bearing one down under her great weight and ripping the life from it in an instant, then skipping on to the next before it could rise and flee.

The goblin rolled to its back, flailed its arms wildly to try to fend off the great cat. But Guenhwyvar was too strong and too fast and soon got her maw clamped about the creature's throat.

Not far to the side, Drizzt and Catti-brie, independently in pursuit of goblins, discovered each other in a small clearing and found that they had become ringed by goblins, who, seeing a sudden advantage, leaped out of the brush and encircled the pair.

"A bit o' good luck, I'd say," Catti-brie remarked with a wink to her friend, and they fell together defensively, back-to-back.

The goblins tried to coordinate their attacks, calling to each other, opposite ones coming in at the same time, while those beside them waited to see if the first attack might leave the two humans vulnerable.

They simply didn't understand.

Drizzt and Catti-brie rolled about each other's back, thus changing their angles of attack, the drow going after those goblins that had come in at Catti-brie and vice versa. Out Drizzt came, scimitars flashing in circling motions, hooking inside spear shafts and turning them harmlessly aside. A subtle shift in wrist angle, a quick step forward, and both goblins staggered backward, guts torn.

Across the way Catti-brie went down low under the high thrust of one spear and sent Khazid'hea slashing across, the wickedly edged blade taking the goblin's leg off cleanly at the knee. A goblin to the side tried to adjust its spear angle down at the woman, but she caught the weapon shaft with her free hand and turned it aside, using it as leverage to propel her up and out, a single thrust taking the creature in the chest.

"Straight on!" Drizzt yelled, rushing by and hooking Catti-brie under the shoulder, helping her to her feet and pushing her along in his charge, their momentum shattering the line of the frightened creatures.

Those behind didn't dare follow that charge, except for one, and thus Drizzt knew that Crenshinibon had crazed this one.

In the span of three heartbeats it lay dead.

* * * * *

Still behind the main fighting, Bruenor heard the commotion, and that made him madder than ever. Twisting and pulling, tugging with all his strength, the dwarf nearly toppled as his axe came free—almost free, he realized with revulsion, for instead of pulling the heavy blade from the creature's skull he had torn the dead goblin's head right off.

"Well, that's pretty," he said with disgust, and then he had no more time to complain as a pair of goblins crashed out of the brush near to him. He hit the closest hard, a roundabout throw that slammed its kin's head right into its belly and sent it staggering backward.

Weaponless, Bruenor took a hit from the second goblin, a club smash across his shoulders that stung but hardly slowed him. He leaped in close, moving right before the goblin, and snapped his forehead into the creature's face, sending it reeling and taking its club from its weakened grasp as it staggered.

Before the goblin could retrieve its bearings, that club smashed down hard once, twice, thrice, and left the thing twitching helplessly on the ground.

Bruenor spun about and launched the club into the legs of the first goblin as it tried to charge at his back, tripping the creature and sending it headlong to the ground. Bruenor quickstepped over it, back to the brush to retrieve his axe.

"Enough playin'!" the dwarf roared. Finesse aside, he slammed his axe against the nearest tree trunk, shattering away the remnants of the head.

Up and spinning, the goblin took one look at the ferocious dwarf and his axe, took one look at the decapitated remains of Bruenor's first kill, and turned and ran.

"No ye don't!" the dwarf howled, and he let fly an overhead throw that sent his axe spinning hard into the goblin's back, dropping it facedown into the dirt.

Bruenor ran by, thinking to pull the axe free in full stride, heading to rejoin his companions.

It was stuck again, this time hooked on the dying goblin's spine.

"Orc-brained, troll-smellin', bug-eater!" Bruenor cursed.

* * * * *

Donat worked hard over Regis, trying to hold the spear shaft steady so the embedded weapon wouldn't do any more damage, while his three kinfolk rushed about frantically, working furiously themselves to keep *Bottom Feeder* free of goblins. One creature nearly made the deck, but Bumpo smashed his crossbow across its face, shattering the weapon and the goblin's jaw.

The dwarf howled in glee, lifted the stunned creature above his head and threw it into two others that were trying to come over the side, dropping all three back into the water.

His two cousins proved equally effective and equally damaging to expensive crossbows, but the boat stayed clear of goblins, soon outdistancing those giving stubborn pursuit in the swift current.

That allowed Bumpo to take up Donat's crossbow, the only one still working, and pluck a few in the water.

Most of the creatures did make the other bank but had seen enough of the fight—too much, actually—and simply ran off into the underbrush.

* * * * *

Bruenor planted his heavy boots on the back of the still-groaning goblin, spat in both his hands, took up his axe handle, and gave a great tug, ripping the head and half the goblin's backbone free.

The dwarf went over in a backward roll to wind up sitting in the dirt.

"Oh, even prettier," he remarked, noting the torn creature and the length of spine lying across his extended legs. He shook his head and hopped to his feet, running fast to join his friends, but by the time he arrived the battle had ended. Drizzt and Catti-brie stood amidst several dead creatures, and Guenhwyvar circled about, searching for any others.

But those held in Crenshinibon's mental grasp were already dead, and those still of free will were long gone.

"Tell the stupid crystal shard to call in thicker-skinned creatures," Bruenor grumbled. He gave Drizzt a sidelong glance as they headed for the riverbank. "Ye're sure we got to get rid of that thing?"

Drizzt only smiled and ran along. One goblin did come out of the river on this side, but Guenhwyvar buried it before the friends ever got close.

Up ahead, Bumpo maneuvered *Bottom Feeder* into a small side pool out of the main current. The three friends laughed all the way, replaying the battle and talking lightheartedly about how good it was to be back on the road.

Their expressions changed abruptly when they saw Regis lying on the deck, pale and very still.

* * * * *

From a dark room in the subbasement of House Basadoni, Jarlaxle and his wizard-priest assistant watched it all.

"This could not be any easier," the mercenary leader remarked with a laugh. He turned to Rai'gy. "Find yourself a human persona in the guise of a priest much like Cadderly and in the same ceremonial dress. Not his hat, though," the mercenary added after a short pause. "That might constitute rank, I believe, or prove more a matter of Cadderly's personal taste."

"But Kimmuriel has gone for Baeltimazifas," Rai'gy protested.

"And you shall accompany the doppleganger to Drizzt and his companions," Jarlaxle explained, "as a student of Cadderly Bonaduce's Spirit Soaring library. Prepare spells of powerful healing."

Rai'gy's eyes widened with surprise. "I am to pray to Lady Lolth for spells with which to heal a halfling?" he asked incredulously. "And you believe that she will grant me such spells, given that intent?"

Jarlaxle, supremely confident, nodded. "She will, because bestowing such spells shall further the cause of her drow," he explained, and he smiled widely, knowing that the outcome of the battle had just made his life a lot easier and much more interesting.

Chapter 22
SAVING GRACE

Regis gasped and groaned in agony, squirming just a bit, which only made things worse for the poor halfling. Every movement made the spear shaft quiver, sending waves of burning pain through his body.

Bruenor brushed aside any soft emotions and blinked away any tears, realizing that he would be doing his grievously injured friend no favors by showing any sympathy at all. "Do it quick," he said to Drizzt. The dwarf knelt down over Regis, setting himself firmly, pressing the halfling by the shoulders and putting one knee on his back to hold him perfectly still.

Drizzt wasn't sure how to proceed. The spear was barbed, that much he recognized, but to push it all the way through and out the other side seemed too brutal a technique for Regis to possibly survive. Yet, how could Drizzt cut the spear quickly enough and smoothly enough so that Regis did not have to endure such unbearable agony? Even a minor shift in the long shaft had the halfling groaning in pain. What might the jarring of the shaft being hacked by a scimitar do to him?

"Take it in both yer hands," Catti-brie instructed. "One hand on the wound, t'other on the spear, right above where ye want the thing broken."

Drizzt looked at her and saw that she had Taulmaril in hand again, an arrow readied. He looked from the bow to the spear and understood her intent. While he doubted the potential of such a technique, he simply had no other answers. He gripped the spear shaft tightly just above the entry wound, then again two handsbreadths up. He looked to Bruenor, who secured his hold on Regis even more—drawing another whimper from the poor halfling—and nodded grimly.

Drizzt then nodded to Catti-brie who bent low, lining up her shot and the angle of the arrow after it passed through, so that it would not hit one of her friends. If she was not perfect, she realized, or even if she simply was not lucky, the arrow might deflect badly, and then they'd have another seriously wounded companion lying on the deck beside Regis. With that thought in mind Catti-brie relaxed her bowstring a bit, but then Regis whimpered again, and she understood that her poor little friend was fast running out of time.

She drew back, took perfect aim, and left fly, the blinding, lightning-streaking arrow sizzling right through the shaft cleanly, and soaring into, and through the opposite deck wall and off across the river.

Drizzt, stunned by the sudden flash even though he had expected the shot, held in place for just a moment. After allowing his senses to catch up with the scene he handed the broken piece of the shaft to Bumpo.

"Lift him gently," the drow instructed Bruenor, who did so, raising the halfling's injured shoulder slowly from the deck.

Then, with a plaintive and helpless look to all about, the drow grasped the remaining piece of shaft firmly and began to push.

Regis howled and screamed and wriggled too much for sympathetic Drizzt to continue. At a loss, he let go of the shaft and held his hands out helplessly to Bruenor.

"The ruby pendant," Catti-brie remarked suddenly, dropping to her knees beside her friends. "We'll get him thinking of better things." She moved quickly as Bruenor lifted the groaning Regis a bit higher, reaching into the front of the halfling's shirt and pulling forth the dazzling ruby pendant.

"Watch it close," Catti-brie said to Regis several times. She held the gemstone, spinning alluringly at the end of its chain before the halfling's half-closed eyes. Regis's head started to droop, but Catti-brie grabbed him by the chin and forced him steady.

"Ye remember the party after we rescued ye from Pook?" she asked calmly, forcing a wide smile across her face.

Gradually she brought him into her words with more coaxing, more reminding of that enjoyable affair, one in which Regis had become quite intoxicated. And intoxicated was what the halfling seemed to be now. He was groaning no more, his gaze locked on the spinning gemstone.

"Ah, but didn't ye have the fun of it in the pillowed room?" the woman said, speaking of the harem in Pook's house. "We thought ye'd never come forth!" As she spoke, she looked to Drizzt and nodded. The drow took up the remaining piece of embedded shaft once more and, with a look to Bruenor to make certain that the dwarf had Regis properly secured and braced, he slowly began to push.

R. A. Salvatore

Regis winced as the rest of the wide-bladed head tore through the front of his shoulder but offered no real resistance and no screaming. Drizzt soon had the spear fully extracted.

It came out with a gush of blood, and both Drizzt and Bruenor had to work fast and furiously to stem the flow. Even then, as they lay Regis gently on his back, they saw his arm discoloring.

"He's bleeding inside," Bruenor said through gritted teeth. "We'll be taking the arm off if we can't fix it!"

Drizzt didn't respond, just went back to work on his small friend, moving aside the bandages and trying to reach his nimble fingers right into the wound to pinch the blood flow.

Catti-brie kept up her soothing talk, doing a marvelous job of distracting the halfling, concentrating so fully on the task before her that she managed to minimize her nervous glances Drizzt's way.

Had Regis seen the drow's face the spell of the ruby pendant might have shattered. For Drizzt understood the trouble here and understood that his little friend was in real danger. He couldn't stop the flow. Bruenor's drastic measure of amputating the arm might be necessary, and even that, Drizzt understood, would likely kill the halfling.

"Ye got it?" Bruenor asked again and again. "Ye got it?"

Drizzt grimaced, looking pointedly at Bruenor's already bloodstained axe blade, and went at his work more determinedly. Finally, he relaxed his grip on the vein just a bit, easing, easing, breathing a bit easier as he lessened the pressure and felt no more blood spurting from the tear.

"I'm taking the damned arm!" Bruenor declared, misinterpreting Drizzt's resigned look.

The drow held up his hand and shook his head. "It is stemmed," he announced.

"But for how long?" Catti-brie asked, genuinely concerned.

Again Drizzt shook his head helplessly.

"We should be going," Bumpo Thunderpuncher remarked, seeing that the commotion about Regis had subsided. "Them goblins might not be far."

"Not yet," Drizzt insisted. "We cannot move him until we're sure the wound will not reopen."

Bumpo gave a concerned look to his brother. Then both of them glanced nervously at their thrice-removed cousins.

But Drizzt was right, of course, and Regis could not be immediately moved. All three friends stayed close to him; Catti-brie kept the ruby pendant in hand, should its calming hypnosis prove necessary. For the time being, though, Regis knew nothing at all, nothing beyond the relieving blackness of unconsciousness.

* * * * *

"You are nervous," Kimmuriel Oblodra remarked, obviously taking great pleasure in seeing the normally unshakable Jarlaxle pacing the floor.

Jarlaxle stopped and stared at the psionicist incredulously. "Nonsense," he insisted. "Baeltimazifas performed his impersonation of Pasha Basadoni perfectly."

It was true enough. At the important meeting that same morning, the doppleganger had impersonated Pasha Basadoni perfectly, no small feat considering that the man was dead and Baeltimazifas could not probe his mind for the subtle details. Of course, his role in the meeting was minor—hindered, so Sharlotta had explained to the other guildmasters, by the fact that he was very old and not in good health. Pasha Wroning had been convinced by the doppelganger's performance. With the powerful Wroning satisfied, Domo Quillilo of the wererats and the younger and more nervous leaders of the Rakers could hardly protest. Calm had returned to Calimport's streets, and all, as far as the others were concerned, was as it had been.

"He told the other guildmasters that which they desired to hear," Kimmuriel said.

"And so we shall do the same with Drizzt and his friends," Jarlaxle assured the psionicist.

"Ah, but you know that the target this time is more dangerous," said the ever-observant Kimmuriel. "More alert, and more . . . drow."

Jarlaxle stopped and stared hard at the Oblodran, then laughed aloud, admitting his edginess. "Ever has it proven interesting where Drizzt Do'Urden is concerned," he explained. "This one has again and again outrun, outsmarted, or merely out-lucked the most powerful enemies one can imagine. And look at him," he added, motioning to the magical reflective pool Rai'gy had left in place. "Still he survives, nay, thrives. Matron Baenre herself wanted to make a trophy of that one's head, and she, not he, has passed from this world."

"We do not desire his death," Kimmuriel reminded. "Though that, too, might prove quite profitable."

Jarlaxle shook his head fiercely. "Never that," he said determinedly.

Kimmuriel spent a long while studying the mercenary leader. "Could it be that you have come to like this outcast?" he asked. "That is the way of Jarlaxle, is it not?"

Jarlaxle laughed again. " 'Respect' would be a better word."

"He would never join Bregan D'aerthe," the psionicist reminded.

"Not knowingly," the opportunistic mercenary replied. "Not knowingly."

Kimmuriel didn't press the point but rather motioned to the reflective pool excitedly. "Pray that Baeltimazifas lives up to his fees," he said.

Jarlaxle, who had witnessed the catastrophe of many futile attempts against the likes of Drizzt Do'Urden, certainly was praying.

Artemis Entreri entered the room then, as Jarlaxle had bade him. He took one look at the two dark elves, then moved cautiously to the side of the reflecting pool—and his eyes widened when he saw the image displayed within, the image of his greatest adversary.

"Why are you so surprised?" Jarlaxle asked. "I told you I can deliver to you that which you most desire."

Entreri worked hard to keep his breathing steady, not wanting the mercenary to draw too much enjoyment from his obvious excitement. He recognized the truth of it all now, that Jarlaxle—damned Jarlaxle!—had been right. There in the pool stood the source of Entreri's apathy, the symbol that his life had been a lie. There stood the one challenge yet facing the master assassin, the one remaining uneasiness that so prevented him from enjoying his present life.

Right there, Drizzt Do'Urden. Entreri looked back at Jarlaxle and nodded.

The mercenary, hardly surprised, merely smiled.

* * * * *

Regis squirmed and groaned, resisting Catti-brie's attempts with the pendant this time, for as the emergency had dictated, she had not begun the charming process until after Drizzt's fingers were already working furiously inside the halfling's torn shoulder.

Bruenor, his axe right beside him, did well to hold the halfling steady, but Drizzt kept growling and shaking his head in frustration. The wound had reopened, and badly, and this time the nimble-fingered drow could not possibly close it.

"Take the damned arm!" Drizzt finally cried in ultimate frustration, falling back, his own arm soaked in blood. The four dwarves behind him gave a unified groan, but Bruenor, always steady and reliable, understood the truth and moved methodically for his axe.

Catti-brie continued to talk to Regis, but he was no longer listening to her or to anything, his consciousness long flown.

Bruenor leveled the axe, lining up the stroke. Catti-brie, having no logical arguments, understanding that they had to stem the bleeding even if that meant cutting off the arm and cauterizing the wound with fire, hesitantly extended the torn arm.

"Take it," Drizzt instructed, and the four dwarves groaned again.

Bruenor spat in his hands and took up the axe, but doubt crossed his face as he looked down at his poor little friend.

"Take it!" Drizzt demanded.

Bruenor lifted the axe and brought it down again slowly, lining up the hit.

"Take it!" Catti-brie said.

"Do not!" came a voice from the side, and all the friends turned to see two men walking toward them.

"Cadderly!" Catti-brie cried, and so it seemed to be. So surprised and pleased was she, and was Drizzt, that neither noticed that the man seemed older than the last time they had seen him, though they knew the priest was not aging, but was rather growing more youthful as his health returned. The great effort of raising the magical Spirit Soaring library from the rubble had taken its toll on the young man.

Cadderly nodded to his companion, who rushed over to Regis. "Good it is that beside you we arrived," the other priest said, a curious comment and in a dialect that none of the others had heard before.

They didn't question him about it, though, not with their friend Cadderly standing beside him, and certainly not while he bent over and began a quiet chant over the prone halfling.

"My associate, Arrabel, will see to the wound," Cadderly explained. "Truly I am surprised to see you out here so far from home."

"Coming to see yerself," Bruenor explained.

"Well, turn about," Baeltimazifas, in the guise of Cadderly, said dramatically, exactly as Jarlaxle had instructed. "I will welcome you indeed in a grand manner, when you arrive at the Spirit Soaring, but your road now is in the other direction, for you've a friend in dire need."

"Wulfgar," Catti-brie breathed, and the others were surely thinking the same.

Cadderly nodded. "He tried to follow your course, it would seem, and has come into a small hamlet east of Baldur's Gate. The downstream currents will take you there quickly."

"What hamlet?" Bumpo asked.

The doppleganger shrugged, having no name. "Four buildings behind a bluff and trees. I know not its name."

"That'd be Yogerville," Donat insisted, and Bumpo nodded his agreement.

"Get ye there in a day," the dwarf captain told Drizzt.

The drow looked questioningly to Cadderly.

"It would take me a day to pray for such a spell of transport," the phony priest explained. "And even then I could take but one of you along."

Regis groaned then, drawing the attention of all, and to the companions' amazement and absolute joy the halfling sat up, looking much better already, and even managed to flex the fingers at the end of his torn arm.

Beside him, Rai'gy, in the uncomfortable mantle of a human, smiled and silently thanked Lady Lolth for being so very understanding.

"He can travel, and immediately," the doppleganger explained. "Now be off. Your friend is in dire need. It would seem that his temper has angered the farmers, and they have him prisoner and plan to hang him. You have time to save him, for they'll not act until their leader returns, but be off at once."

Drizzt nodded, then reached down and took his pouch from Regis's belt. "Will you join us?" he asked, and even then, eager Catti-brie, Bruenor, Regis, and the dwarves began readying the boat for departure. Drizzt and Cadderly's associate moved out of the craft to join the priest.

"No," the doppleganger replied, perfectly mimicking Cadderly's voice, according to the imp who had supplied the strange, creature with most of the details and insights. "You'll not need me, and I have other urgent matters to attend."

Drizzt nodded and handed the pouch over. "Take care with it," he explained. "It has the ability to call in would-be allies."

"I will be back in the Spirit Soaring in a matter of minutes," the doppleganger replied.

Drizzt paused at that curious comment—hadn't Cadderly just proclaimed that he needed a day to memorize a spell of transport?

"Word of recall," Rai'gy, picking up the uneasiness, put in quickly. "Get us home to the Spirit Soaring will the spell, but not to any other place."

"Come on, elf!" Bruenor cried. "Me boy's waiting."

"Go," Cadderly bade Drizzt, taking the pouch and in the same movement, putting his hand on Drizzt's shoulder and turning him back to the boat, pushing him gently along. "Go at once. You've not a moment to spare."

Silent alarms continued to ring out in Drizzt's head, but he had no time then to stop and consider them. *Bottom Feeder* was already sliding back out into the river, the four crew working to turn her about. With a nimble leap Drizzt joined them, then turned back to see Cadderly waving and smiling, his associate already in the throes of spellcasting. Before the craft had gone very far the friends watched the pair dissipate into the wind.

"Why didn't the durned fool just take one of us to me boy now?" Bruenor asked.

"Why not, indeed?" Drizzt replied, staring back at the empty spot and wondering.

Wondering.

Bright and early the next morning, *Bottom Feeder* put in against the bank a couple hundred yards short of Yogerville and the four friends, including Regis, who was feeling much better, leaped ashore.

They had all agreed that the dwarves would remain with the boat, and also, on the suggestion of Drizzt, had decided that Bruenor, Regis, and Catti-brie would go in to speak with the townsfolk alone while the ranger circumvented the hamlet, getting a full lay of the region.

The three were greeted by friendly farm folk, by wide smiles, and then, when asked about Wulfgar, by expressions of confusion.

"Ye thinking that we'd forget one of that description?" one old woman asked with a cackle.

The three friends looked at each other with confusion.

"Donat picked the wrong town," Bruenor said with a great sigh.

* * * * *

Drizzt harbored troubling thoughts. A magical spell had obviously brought Cadderly to him and his companions, but if Wulfgar was in such dire need, why hadn't the cleric just gone to him first instead? He could explain it, of course, considering that Regis was in more dire peril, but why hadn't Cadderly gone to one, while his associate went to the other? Again, logical explanations were there. Perhaps the priests had only one spell that could bring them to one place and had been forced to choose. Yet there was something else nagging at Drizzt, and he simply could not place it.

But then he understood his inner turmoil. How had Cadderly even known to look for Wulfgar, a man he had never met and had only heard about briefly?

"Just good fortune," he told himself, trying logically to trace Cadderly's process, one that had obviously brought him onto Drizzt's trail, and there he had discovered Wulfgar, not so far behind. Luck alone had informed the priest of whom this great man might be.

Still, there seemed holes in that logic, but ones that Drizzt hoped might be filled in by Wulfgar when at last they managed to rescue him. With all that in mind Drizzt made his way around the back side of the hamlet, moving behind the blocking ridge south of the town, out of sight of his friends and their surprising exchange with the townsfolk, who honestly had no idea who Wulfgar might be.

But Drizzt could have guessed as much anyway when he came around that ridgeline, to see a crystalline tower, an image of Crenshinibon, sparkling in the morning light.

Chapter 23
THE LAST CHALLENGE

Drizzt stood transfixed as a line appeared on the unblemished side of the crystalline tower, widening, widening, until it became an open doorway.

And inside the door, beckoning to Drizzt, stood a drow elf wearing a great plumed hat that Drizzt surely recognized. For some reason he could not immediately discern, Drizzt was not as surprised as he should have been.

"Well met again, Drizzt Do'Urden," Jarlaxle said, using the common surface tongue. "Please do come in and speak with me."

Drizzt put one hand to a scimitar hilt, the other to the pouch holding Guenhwyvar—though he had only recently sent the panther back to her astral home and knew she would be weary if recalled. He tensed his leg muscles and measured the distance to Jarlaxle, recognizing that he, with the enchanted ankle bracers he wore, could cover the ground in the blink of an eye, perhaps even get a solid strike in against the mercenary.

But then he would be dead, he knew, for if Jarlaxle was here, then so was Bregan D'aerthe, all about him, weapons trained upon him.

"Please," Jarlaxle said again. "We have business we must discuss to the benefit of us both and to our friends."

That last reference, coupled with the fact that Drizzt had come back this way on the word of an impostor—who was obviously working for the mercenary leader or was, perhaps the mercenary leader—that Wulfgar was in some danger, made Drizzt relax his grip on his weapon.

"I guarantee that neither I nor my associates shall strike against you," Jarlaxle assured him. "And furthermore the friends who accompanied you to this village will walk away unharmed as long as they take no action against me."

Drizzt held a fair understanding of the mysterious mercenary, enough to trust Jarlaxle's word, at least. Jarlaxle had held all the cards in previous meetings, times when the mercenary could have easily killed Drizzt, and Catti-brie as well. And yet he had not, despite the fact that bringing the head of Drizzt Do'Urden back to Menzoberranzan at that time might have proven quite profitable. With a look back to the direction of the town, blocked from view by the high ridge, Drizzt moved to the door.

Many memories came to Drizzt as he followed Jarlaxle into the structure, the magical door sliding closed behind them. Though this ground level was not as the ranger remembered it, he could not help but recall the first time he entered a manifestation of Crenshinibon, when he had gone after the wizard Akar Kessell back in Icewind Dale. It was not a pleasant memory to be sure, but a somewhat comforting one, for within those recollections came to Drizzt an understanding of how he could defeat this tower, of how he could sever its power and send it crumbling down.

Looking back at Jarlaxle, though, as the mercenary settled comfortably into a lavish chair beside a huge upright mirror, Drizzt understood he wouldn't likely get any such chance.

Jarlaxle motioned to a chair opposite him, and again Drizzt moved to comply. The mercenary was as dangerous as any creature Drizzt had ever know, but he was not reckless and not vicious.

One thing Drizzt did notice, though, as he moved for the seat: his feet seemed just a bit heavier to him, as though the dweomer of his bracers had diminished.

"I have followed your movements for many days," Jarlaxle explained. "A friend of mine requires your services, you see."

"Services?" Drizzt asked suspiciously.

Jarlaxle only smiled and continued. "It became important for me to bring the two of you together again."

"And important for you to steal the crystal shard," Drizzt reasoned.

"Not so," the mercenary honestly answered. "Not so. Crenshinibon was not known to me when this began. Acquiring it was merely a pleasant extra in seeking that which I most needed: you."

"What of Cadderly?" Drizzt asked with some concern. He still was not certain whether it really had been Cadderly who had come to Regis's aid. Had Jarlaxle subsequently garnered Crenshinibon from the priest? Or had the entire episode with Cadderly been merely a clever ruse?

"Cadderly remains quite comfortable in the Spirit Soaring, oblivious to your quest," Jarlaxle explained. "Much to the dismay of my wizard friend's new familiar, who holds a particular hatred for Cadderly."

"Promise me that Cadderly is safe," Drizzt said in all seriousness.

Jarlaxle nodded. "Indeed, and you are quite welcome for our actions to save your halfling friend."

That caught Drizzt off guard, but he had to admit that it was true enough. Had not Jarlaxle's cronies come in the guise of Cadderly and enacted great healing upon Regis, the halfling likely would have died, or at the very least would have lost an arm.

"Of course, for the minor price of a spellcasting you gained much of our confidence," Drizzt did remark, reminding Jarlaxle that he understood the mercenary rarely did anything that did not bring some benefit to him.

"Not so minor a spellcasting," Jarlaxle bantered. "And we could have faked it all, providing only the illusion of healing, a spell that would have temporarily healed the halfling's wounds, only to have them reopen later on to his ultimate demise.

"But I assure you that we did not," he quickly added, seeing Drizzt's eyes narrow dangerously. "No, your friend is nearly fully healed."

"Then I do thank you," Drizzt replied. "Of course, you understand that I must take Crenshinibon back from you?"

"I do not doubt that you are brave enough to try," Jarlaxle admitted. "But I do understand that you are not stupid enough to try."

"Not now, perhaps."

"Then why ever?" the mercenary asked. "What care is it to Drizzt Do'Urden if Crenshinibon works its wicked magic upon the dark elves of Menzoberranzan?"

Again, the mercenary had put Drizzt somewhat off his guard. What care, indeed? "But does Jarlaxle remain in Menzoberranzan?" he asked. "It would seem not."

That brought a laugh from the mercenary. "Jarlaxle goes where Jarlaxle needs to go," he answered. "But think long and hard on your choice before coming for the crystal shard, Drizzt Do'Urden. Are there truly any hands in all the world better suited to wield the artifact than mine?"

Drizzt did not reply but was indeed considering the words carefully.

"Enough of that," Jarlaxle said, coming forward in his chair, suddenly more intent. "I have brought you here that you might meet an old acquaintance, one you have battled beside and battled against. It seems as if he has some unfinished business with Drizzt Do'Urden, and that uncertainty is costing me precious time with him."

Drizzt stared hard at the mercenary, having no idea what Jarlaxle might be talking about—for just a moment. Then he remembered the last time he had seen the mercenary, right before Drizzt and Artemis Entreri had parted ways. His expression showed his disappointment clearly as he came to suspect the truth of it all.

* * * * *

"Ye picked the wrong durned town," Bruenor said to Bumpo and Donat when he and the other two returned to *Bottom Feeder*.

The two dwarven brothers looked curiously at each other, Donat scratching his head.

"Had to be this one," Bumpo insisted. "By yer friend's description, I mean."

"The townsfolk might have been lying to us," Regis put in.

"They're good at it, then," said Catti-brie. "Every one o' them."

"Well, I know a way to find out for certain," the halfling said, a mischievous twinkle in his eye. When Bruenor and Catti-brie, recognizing that tone in his voice, turned to regard him, they found him dangling his hypnotic ruby pendant.

"Back we go," Bruenor said, starting away from the boat once more. He paused and looked back at the four dwarves. "Ye're sure, are ye?" he asked.

All four heads began wagging enthusiastically.

Just before the threesome arrived back among the cluster of houses, a small boy ran out to meet them. "Did you find your friend?" he asked.

"Why no, we haven't," Catti-brie replied, holding back both Bruenor and Regis with a wave of her hand. "Have ye seen him?"

"He might be in the tower," the youngster offered.

"What tower?" Bruenor asked gruffly before Catti-brie could reply.

"Over there," the young boy answered, unruffled by the dwarf's stern tone. "Out back." He pointed to the ridge that rose up behind the small village, and as the friends followed that line they noted several villagers ascending the ridge. About halfway up the villagers began gasping in astonishment, some pointing, others falling to the ground, and still others running back the way they had come.

The three friends began running, too, to the ridge and up. Then they too skidded to abrupt stops, staring incredulously at the tower image of Crenshinibon.

"Cadderly?" Regis asked incredulously.

"I'm not thinkin' so," said Catti-brie. Crouching low, she led them on cautiously.

* * * * *

"Artemis Entreri wishes this contest between you two at last resolved," Jarlaxle confirmed.

Drizzt's uncharacteristic outburst made it quite obvious to Jarlaxle just how much he despised Entreri and just how sincere he was in his claim to never want to go against the man again.

"Never do you disappoint me," Jarlaxle said with a chuckle. "Your lack of hubris is commendable, my friend. I applaud you for it and do wish, in all sincerity, that I could grant you your desire and send you and your friends on your way. But that I cannot do, I fear, and I assure you that you must settle your relationship with Entreri. For your friends, if not for yourself."

Drizzt chewed on that threat for a long moment. While he did, Jarlaxle waved his hand in front of the mirror beside his chair, which clouded over immediately. As Drizzt watched the fog swirled away, leaving a clear image of Catti-brie, Bruenor, and Regis making their way up to the base of the tower. Catti-brie was in the lead, moving in a staggered manner, trying to utilize the little cover available.

"I could kill them with a thought," the mercenary assured Drizzt.

"But why would you?" Drizzt asked. "You gave me your word."

"And so I shall keep it," Jarlaxle replied. "As long as you cooperate."

Drizzt paused, digesting the information. "What of Wulfgar?" he asked suddenly, thinking that Jarlaxle must have some information regarding the man since he'd used Wulfgar's name to lure Drizzt and his friends to this place.

Now it was Jarlaxle's turn to pause and think, but just for a moment. "He is alive and well from what I can discern," the mercenary admitted. "I have not spoken with him, but looked in on him long enough to find out how his present situation might benefit me."

"Where?" Drizzt asked.

Jarlaxle smiled widely. "There will be time for such talk later," he said, looking back over his shoulder to the one staircase ascending from the room.

"You will find that your magics will not work in here," the mercenary went on, and Drizzt understood then why his feet seemed heavier. "None of them, not your scimitars, the bracers you took from Dantrag Baenre when you killed him, nor even your innate drow powers."

"Yet a new and wondrous aspect of the crystal shard," Drizzt remarked sarcastically.

"No," Jarlaxle admitted, smiling. "More the help of a friend. It was necessary to defeat all magic, you see, because this last meeting between you and Artemis Entreri must be on perfectly equal footing, with no possible unfair advantages to be gained by either party."

"Yet your mirror worked," Drizzt reasoned, as much trying to buy himself some time as out of any curiosity. "Is that not magic?"

"It is yet another piece of the tower, nothing I brought in, and all the tower is impervious to my associate's attempts to defeat the magic," Jarlaxle explained. "What a marvelous gift you gave to me—or to my associate—in handing over Crenshinibon. It has told me so much about itself . . . how to raise the towers and how to manipulate them to fit my needs"

"You know that I cannot allow you to keep it," Drizzt said again.

"And you know well that I would never have invited you here if I thought there was anything at all you could do to take Crenshinibon away from me," Jarlaxle said with a laugh. He ended the sentence by looking again at the mirror to his side.

Drizzt followed that gaze to the mirror, to see his friends moving about the base of the tower then, searching for a door—a door that Drizzt knew they would not find unless Jarlaxle willed it to be so. Catti-brie did find something of interest, though: Drizzt's tracks.

"He's in there!" she cried.

"Please be Cadderly," both dark elves heard Regis remark nervously. That brought a chuckle from Jarlaxle.

"Go to Entreri," the mercenary said more seriously, waving his hand so that the mirror clouded over again, the image dissipating. "Go and satisfy his curiosity, and then you and your friends will go your way, and I will go mine."

Drizzt spent a long while staring at the mercenary. Jarlaxle didn't press him for many moments, just locked stares with him. In that moment they came to a silent understanding.

"Whatever the outcome?" Drizzt asked again, just to be sure.

"Your friends walk away unharmed," Jarlaxle assured him. "With you, or with your body."

Drizzt turned his gaze back to the staircase. He could hardly believe that Artemis Entreri, his nemesis for so long, awaited him just up those steps. His words to Jarlaxle had been sincere and heartfelt; he never wanted to see the man again, let alone fight with him. That was Entreri's emotional pain, not Drizzt's. Even now, with the fight so close and obviously so necessary, the drow ranger did not look forward to his climb up those stairs. It wasn't that he was afraid of the assassin. Not at all. While Drizzt respected Entreri's fighting prowess, he didn't fear the challenge.

He rose from his chair and started for the stairs, silently recounting all the good he might accomplish in this fight. In addition to satisfying Jarlaxle, Drizzt might well be ridding the world of a scourge.

Drizzt stopped and turned about. "This counts as one of my friends," he said, producing the onyx figurine from his pouch.

"Ah, yes, Guenhwyvar," Jarlaxle said, his face brightening.

"I will not see Guenhwyvar in Entreri's hands," Drizzt said. "Nor in yours. Whatever the outcome, she is to be returned to me or to Catti-brie."

"A pity," Jarlaxle remarked with a laugh. "I had thought you might forget to include the magnificent panther in your conditions. How much I would love a companion such as Guenhwyvar."

Drizzt stood up straighter, lavender eyes narrowing.

"You would never trust me with such a treasure," Jarlaxle said. "Nor could I blame you. I do indeed have a weakness for things magical!" The mercenary was laughing, but Drizzt was not.

"Give it to them yourself," Jarlaxle offered, motioning for the door. "Just toss the figurine at the wall, above where you entered. Watch the results for yourself," he added, motioning to the mirror, which cleared again of fog and produced an image of Drizzt's friends.

The ranger looked back to the door to see a small opening appear right above it. He rushed over. "Be gone from this place!" he cried, hoping his friends would hear, and tossed the onyx figurine through the portal. Thinking suddenly that the whole episode might be just one of Jarlaxle's tricks, he swung about and scrambled to watch in the mirror.

To his relief he saw the trio, Catti-brie calling for him and Regis picking up the panther from the ground. The halfling wasted no time in setting the thing down and calling to Guenhwyvar, and the cat soon appeared beside Drizzt's friends, growling out to the trapped drow even as the other three called for him.

"You know they'll not leave," Jarlaxle said dryly. "But go on and be done with this. You have my word that your friends, all four, will not be harmed."

Drizzt hesitated just one more time, glancing back at the mercenary who still sat comfortably in his chair as though Drizzt presented no threat to him whatsoever. For a moment Drizzt considered calling that bluff, drawing his weapons enchanted or not, and rushing over to cut the mercenary down. But he could not, of course, not when the safety of his friends hung in the balance.

Jarlaxle, so smug in his chair, knew that implicitly.

Drizzt took a deep breath, trying to throw away all the confusion of this last day, the craziness that had handed the mighty artifact over to Jarlaxle and brought Drizzt to this place, to fight Artemis Entreri, no less.

He took a second deep breath, stretched out his fingers and arms, and started up the stairs.

* * * * *

Artemis Entreri paced the room nervously, studying the many contours, staircases, and elevated planks. No simple circular, empty chamber for Jarlaxle. The mercenary had constructed this, the second floor of the tower, with many ups and downs, places where strategy could play in to the upcoming fight. At the center of the room was a staircase of four steps, rising to a landing large enough for only one man. The back side mirrored the front, another four steps back down to the floor level. More steps completely bordered the room, five up to the wall, where another landing ran all the way around. From these, on Entreri's left, went a plank, perhaps a foot wide, connecting the fourth step to the top landing of the center case.

Yet another obstacle, a two-sided ramp, loomed near the back wall beside where Entreri paced. Two others, low, circular platforms, were set about the room by the door across the way, the door through which Drizzt Do'Urden would enter.

But how to make all of these props work for him? Entreri pondered, and he realized that his thoughts mattered little, for Drizzt was too unpredictable a foe, was too quick and quick thinking for Entreri to lay out a plan of attack. No, he would have to improvise every step and roll of the way, to counter and anticipate, and fight in measured thrusts.

He drew out his weapons then, dagger and sword. At first he had considered coming in with two swords to offset Drizzt's twin scimitars. In the end he decided to go with the style he knew best, and with the weapon, though its magic would not work in here, that he loved best.

Back and forth he paced, stretching his muscles, arms, and neck. He talked quietly to himself, reminding himself of all that he had to do, warning himself to never, not for a single instant, underestimate his enemy. And then he stopped suddenly, and considered his own movements, his own thoughts.

He was indeed nervous, anxious and, for the first time since he had left Menzoberranzan, excited. A slight sound turned him around.

Drizzt Do'Urden stood on the landing.

Without a word the drow ranger entered, then flinched not at all as the door slid closed behind him.

"I have waited for this for many years," Entreri said.

"Then you are a bigger fool than I supposed," Drizzt replied.

Entreri exploded into motion, rushing up the back side of the center stairs, brandishing dagger and sword as he came over the lip, as if he expected Drizzt to meet him there, battling for the high ground.

The ranger hadn't moved, hadn't even drawn his weapons.

"And a bigger fool still if you believe that I will fight you this day," Drizzt said.

Entreri's eyes widened. After a long pause he came down the front stairs slowly, sword leading, dagger ready, moving to within a couple of steps of Drizzt.

Who still did not draw his weapons.

"Ready your scimitars," Entreri instructed.

"Why? That we might play as entertainment for Jarlaxle and his band?" Drizzt replied.

"Draw them!" Entreri growled. "Else I'll run you through."

"Will you?" Drizzt calmly asked, and he slowly drew out his blades. As Entreri came on another measured step, the ranger dropped those scimitars to the ground.

Entreri's jaw dropped nearly as far.

"Have you learned nothing in all the years?" Drizzt asked. "How many times must we play this out? Must all of our lives be dedicated to revenge upon whichever of us won the last battle?"

"Pick them up!" Entreri shouted, rushing in so that his sword tip came in at Drizzt's breastbone.

"And then we shall fight," Drizzt said nonchalantly. "And one of us will win, but perhaps the other will survive. And then, of course, we will have to do this all over again, because you believe that you have something to prove."

"Pick them up," Entreri said through gritted teeth, prodding his sword just a bit. Had that blade still been carrying the weight of its magic, the prod surely would have slid it through Drizzt's ribs. "This is the last challenge, for one of us will die this day. Here it is, laid out for us by Jarlaxle, as fair a fight as we might ever find."

Drizzt didn't move.

"I will run you through," Entreri promised.

Drizzt only smiled. "I think not, Artemis Entreri. I know you better than you believe, and surely better

374

than you are comfortable with. You would take no pleasure in killing me in such a manner and would hate yourself for the rest of your life for doing so, for stealing from yourself the only chance you might ever have to know the truth. Because that is what this is about, is it not? The truth, your truth, the moment when you hope to either validate your miserable existence or put an end to it."

Entreri growled loudly and came forward, but he did not, could not, press his arm forward and impale the drow. "Damn you!" he cried, spinning away, growling and slashing, back around the stairs, cursing with every step. "Damn you!"

Behind him Drizzt nodded, bent, and retrieved his scimitars. "Entreri," he called, and the change in his tone told the assassin that something was suddenly very different.

Entreri, on the other side of the room now, turned about to see Drizzt standing ready, blades in hand, to see the vision he so desperately craved.

"You passed my test," Drizzt explained. "Now I'll take yours."

* * * * *

"Are we to watch or just wait to see who shall walk out victorious?" Rai'gy asked as he and Kimmuriel walked out from a small chamber off to the side of the first floor's main room.

"This show will be worth the watching," Jarlaxle assured the pair. He motioned to the stairs. "We will ascend to the landing, and I will make the door translucent."

"An amazing artifact," Kimmuriel said, shaking his head. In only a day of communing with the crystal shard Jarlaxle had learned so very much. He had learned how to shape and design the tower reflection of the shard, to make doors appear and seemingly vanish, to create walls, transparent or opaque, and to use the tower as one great scrying device, as he was now. Both Kimmuriel and Rai'gy noted this as they came around to see the image of Catti-brie, Regis, Bruenor, and the great cat showing in the mirror.

"We shall watch, and they should as well," Jarlaxle said. He closed his eyes, and all three drow heard a scraping sound along the outside of Crenshinibon. "There," Jarlaxle announced a moment later. "Now we may go."

* * * * *

Catti-brie, Bruenor, and Regis stood dumbfounded as the crystalline tower seemed to snake to life, one edge rolling out wide, releasing a hidden fold. Then, amazingly, a stairway appeared, circling down along the tower from a height of about twenty feet.

The three hesitated, looking to each other for answers, but Guenhwyvar waited not at all, bounding up the stairs, roaring with every mighty leap.

* * * * *

They stared at each other for some time, looks of respect more than hatred, for they had come past hatred, these two, losing a good deal of their enmity by the sheer exertions of their running battle.

So now they stared from opposite sides of the thirty-foot diameter room, across the central stairs, each waiting for the other to make the first move, or rather, for the other to show that he was about to move.

They broke as one, both charging for the center stairs, both seeking the higher ground. Even without the aid of the magical bracers Drizzt gained a step advantage, perhaps because though he was twice the assassin's actual age, he was much younger in terms of a drow lifetime than Entreri was for a human.

Always the improviser, Entreri took one step on the staircase, then dived to the side, headlong in a roll that brought him harmlessly past Drizzt's swishing blades. He went right under the raised plank, using it as a barrier against the scimitars.

Drizzt turned completely around, falling into a ready crouch at the top of the stairs and preventing Entreri from coming back in.

But Entreri knew that the ranger would protect his high-ground position, and so the assassin never slowed, coming out of his roll back to his feet and running to the side of the room, up the five steps, then moving along that higher ground to the end of the raised plank. When Drizzt did not pursue, neither by following Entreri's course nor rushing across the plank, Entreri hopped down to that narrow walkway and moved halfway along it toward the center stair.

Drizzt held his ground on the wider platform of the staircase apex.

"Come along," Entreri bade him, indicating the walkway. "Even footing."

* * * * *

They feared climbing that stair, for how vulnerable they would all be perched on the side of Crenshinibon, but when Guenhwyvar, at the landing and looking into the tower, roared louder and began clawing at the wall they could not resist. Again Catti-brie arrived first to find a translucent wall at the top of the stairs, a window into the room where Drizzt and Entreri faced off.

She banged on the unyielding glass. So did Bruenor when he arrived, with the back of his axe, but to no avail, for they could not even scratch the thing. If Drizzt and Entreri heard them, or even saw them, neither showed it.

* * * * *

"You should have made the room smaller," Rai'gy remarked dryly when he, Jarlaxle, and Kimmuriel arrived at their landing, similarly watching the action—or lack thereof—within.

"Ah, but the play's the thing," Jarlaxle replied. He pointed across the way then, to Catti-brie and the others. "We can see the combatants and Drizzt's friends across the way, and those friends can see us," he explained, and even as he did so the three drow saw Catti-brie pointing their way, screaming something that they could not hear but could well imagine. "But Drizzt and Entreri can see only each other."

"Quite a tower," Rai'gy had to admit.

* * * * *

Drizzt wanted to hold the secure position, but Entreri showed patience now, and the ranger knew that if he did not go out, this fight that he desperately wanted to be done with could take a long, long time. He hopped onto the narrow walkway easily and came out toward Entreri slowly, inch by inch, setting each foot firmly before taking the next small step.

He snapped into sudden motion as he neared, a quick-step thrust of his right blade. Entreri's dagger, his left-hand weapon, wove inside the thrust perfectly and pushed the scimitar out wide. In the same fluid movement the assassin turned his shoulder and moved ahead, sword tip leading.

Drizzt's second scimitar was halfway into the parry before the thrust ever began, turning a complete circle in the air, then ascending inside the angle of the thrust on the second pass, deflecting the rushing sword, rolling right over it and around as his first blade did the same with the dagger. Into the dance fully he went, his curving blades accentuating the spinning circular motions, cutting over and around, reversing the direction of one, then both, then one again. Spinning, seeking opening, thrusting ahead, slashing down.

And Entreri matched every movement, his actions in straighter lines, straight to the side or above or straight ahead, picking off the blades, forcing Drizzt to parry. The metal screamed continuously, hit after hit after hit.

But then Drizzt's left hand came in cleanly and cleanly swished through the air, for the assassin did not try to parry but dived into a forward roll instead, his sword knocking one scimitar at bay, his movement causing the other to miss, and his dagger, leading the ascent out of the roll, aimed for Drizzt's heart with no chance for the ranger to bring his remaining scimitar in to block.

So up went Drizzt, up and out, a great leap to the left side, tucking and turning to avoid the strike, landing on the floor in a roll that brought him back to his feet. He took two running steps away as he spun about, knowing that Entreri, slight advantage gained, would surely pursue. He came around just in time to meet a furious attack from dagger and sword.

Again the metal rang out repeatedly in protest, and Drizzt was forced back by the sheer momentum of Entreri's charge. He accepted that retreat, though, quick-stepping all the way to maintain perfect balance, his hands working in a blur.

* * * * *

At the interior landing the three drow, who had lived all their lives around expert swordsmen and had witnessed many, many battles, watched every subtle movement with mounting amazement.

"Did you arrange this for Entreri's benefit or ours?" Rai'gy remarked, his tone surely different, surely without hint of sarcasm.

"Both," Jarlaxle admitted. As he spoke, Drizzt darted past Entreri up the center stairs and did not stop, but rather leaped off, turning in midair as he went, then landing in a rush back to the side toward the plank. Entreri took a shorter route instead of a direct pursuit, leaping up to the plank ahead of Drizzt, stealing the advantage the dark elf had hoped to achieve.

As much the improviser as his opponent, Drizzt dived down low, skittering under the plank even as Entreri got his footing, and slashing back up and over his head, an amazingly agile move that would have hamstrung the assassin had Entreri not anticipated just that and continued on his way, leaping off the plank back to the floor and turning around.

Still, Drizzt had scored a hit, tearing the back of Entreri's trousers and a line across the back of his calf.

"First blood to Drizzt," Kimmuriel observed. He looked to Jarlaxle, who was smiling and looking across the way. Following the mercenary's gaze Rai'gy saw that Drizzt's friends, including even the panther, were similarly entranced, watching the battle with open-mouthed admiration.

And so it was well-earned, Kimmuriel silently agreed, turning his full attention back to the dance, brutal and beautiful all at once.

*   *   *   *   *

Now they came in at floor level, rushing together in a blur of swords and flying capes, their routines neither attack nor defense, but somewhere in between. Blade scraped along blade, throwing sparks, the metal shrieking in protest.

Drizzt's left blade swished across at neck level. Entreri dropped suddenly below it into a squat from which he seemed to gain momentum, coming back up with a double thrust of sword and dagger. But Drizzt didn't stop his turn with the miss. The dark elf went right around, a complete circuit, coming back with a right-handed, backhand down-and-over parry. The inside hook of his curving blade caught both the assassin's blades and turned them aside. Then Drizzt altered the angle of his left before it swished overhead, the blade screaming down for Entreri's head.

But the assassin, his hands even closer together because of Drizzt's block, switched blades easily, then extracted the dagger by bringing his right arm in suddenly, pumping it back out, dagger tip rising as scimitar descended.

Then they both howled in pain, Drizzt leaping back with a deep puncture in his wrist, Entreri falling back with a gash along the length of his forearm.

But only for a second, only for the time it took each to realize that he could continue, that he would not drop a weapon. Both Drizzt's scimitars started out wide, closing like the jaws of a wolf as he and Entreri came together. The assassin, though his blades had the inside track, found himself a split second behind and had to double block, throwing his own blades, and the scimitars they caught, out wide and coming forward with the momentum. He hesitated just an instant to see if he could possibly bring one of his blades back in.

Drizzt hadn't hesitated at all, though, dipping his forehead just ahead of Entreri's similar movement, so that when they came smacking together, head to head, Entreri got the brunt of it.

But the assassin, dazed, punched out straight with his right hand, knuckles and dagger crosspiece slamming into Drizzt's face.

They fell apart again, one of Entreri's eyes fast swelling, Drizzt's cheek and nose bleeding.

The assassin pressed the attack fiercely then, before his eye closed and gave Drizzt a huge advantage. He went in hard, stabbing his sword down low.

Drizzt's scimitar crossed down over it, and he pivoted perfectly, launching a kick that got Entreri in the face.

The kick hardly slowed him, for the assassin had anticipated that exact move indeed, he had counted on it. He ducked as the foot came in, a grazing blow, but one that nonetheless stung his already injured eye. Skittering forward he launched his dagger in a roundabout manner, the edge coming in at the back of Drizzt's knee.

Drizzt could have struck with his second blade, hoping to get it past the already engaged sword, but if he tried and Entreri somehow managed to parry, he knew that the fight would be all but over, that the dagger would tear the back out of his leg.

He knew all of that, instinctively, without thinking at all, so instead he just kicked his one supporting leg forward, falling backward over the dagger. Drizzt was scraped but not skewered. He meant to go all the way around in the roll and come right back up to his feet, but before he even really started he saw that the growling Entreri was fast pursuing and would catch him defenseless halfway around.

So he stopped and set himself on his back as the assassin came in.

On both sides of the room, dark elves and Drizzt's friends alike gasped, thinking the contest at its end. But Drizzt fought on, scimitars whirling, smacking, and stabbing to somehow, impossibly, hold Entreri at bay. And then the ranger managed to tuck one foot under him and come up in a wild rush, fighting ferociously, hitting each of Entreri's blades and hitting them hard, driving, driving to gain an equal footing.

Now they were in it, face to face, blades working too quickly for the onlookers to even discern individual moves, but rather to watch the general flow of the battle. A gash appeared here on one combatant, a gash appeared there on the other, but neither warrior found the opportunity to bring any cut to completion. They were superficial nicks, torn clothes and skin. It went on and on, up one side of the staircase and down the other, and any misgivings that Drizzt might have had about this fight had long flown, and any doubts Entreri had ever had about desiring to battle Drizzt Do'Urden again had been fully erased. They fought with passion and fury, their blades striking so rapidly that the ring came as constant.

They were out on the plank then, but they didn't know it. They came down together, each knocking the other from his perch, on opposite sides, then went under the plank together, battling in a crouch. They moved past each other, coming up on either side, then leaping back atop the narrow walkway in perfect balance to begin anew.

On and on it went, and the seconds became minutes, and sweat mixed with blood and stung open wounds. One of Drizzt's sleeves got sliced so badly that it interfered with his movements, and he had to launch an explosive flurry to drive Entreri back long enough so he could flip his blade in the air and pull the remnants of the sleeve from his arm, then catch his blade as it descended, just in time to react to the assassin's charge. A moment later Entreri lost his cape as Drizzt's scimitar came in for his throat, cutting the garment's drawstring and tearing a gash under Entreri's chin as it rose.

Both labored for breath; neither would back off.

But for all the nicks and blood, for all the sweat and bruises, one injury alone stood out, for Entreri's vision on his right side was indeed blurring. The assassin switched weapon hands, dagger back in left and the longer, better blocking sword back in his right.

Drizzt understood. He launched a feint, a right, left, right combination that Entreri easily picked off, but the attacks had not been designed to score any definitive hit anyway, just to allow Drizzt to put his feet in line.

To the side of the room cunning Jarlaxle saw it and understood that the fight was about to end.

Now Drizzt came in again with a left, but he stepped into the blow and launched his scimitar from far out to the side, from a place where Entreri's closed eye could hardly make out the movement. The assassin did instinctively parry with the sword and counter with the dagger, but Drizzt rolled his scimitar right over the intended parry, then snapped it back out, slashing Entreri's wrist and launching the sword away. At the same time, the ranger dropped his blade from his right hand and caught Entreri's stabbing dagger arm at the wrist. Stepping in and rolling his wrist and turning his weapon hand, Drizzt twisted Entreri's dagger arm back under itself, holding it out wide while before the assassin's free hand could hold Drizzt's arm back the dark elf's scimitar tip came in at Entreri's throat.

All movement stopped suddenly. The assassin, with one arm twisted out wide and the other behind Drizzt's scimitar arm, was helpless to stop the ranger's momentum if Drizzt decided to plunge the blade through Entreri's throat.

Growling and trembling, as close to the very edge of control as he had ever been, Drizzt held the blade back. "So what have we proven?" he demanded, voice full of venom, his lavender orbs locked in a wicked stare with Entreri's dark eyes. "Because my head connected in a favorable place with yours, limiting your vision, I am the better fighter?"

"Finish it!" Entreri snarled back.

Drizzt growled again and twisted Entreri's dagger arm more, bending the assassin's wrist so that the dagger fell to the floor. "For all those you have killed, and all those you surely will, I should kill you," Drizzt said, but he knew even as he said the words, and Entreri did, too, that he could not press home his blade, not now. In that awful moment Drizzt lamented not going through with the move in the first instant, before he had found the time to consider his actions.

But now he could not, so with a sudden explosion of motion he let go of Entreri's arm and drove his open palm hard into the assassin's face, disengaging them and knocking Entreri staggering backward.

"Damn you, Jarlaxle, have you had your pleasure?" Drizzt cried, turning about to see the mercenary and his companions, for Jarlaxle had opened the door.

Drizzt came forward determinedly, as if he meant to run right over Jarlaxle, but a noise behind him stopped him, for Entreri came on, yelling.

Yelling. The significance of that was lost on Drizzt in that moment as he spun about, right to left, his free right arm brushing out and across, lifting Entreri's leading arm, which held again that awful dagger. And around came Drizzt's left arm, scimitar leading, in a stab as Entreri crashed in, a stab that should have plunged the weapon into the assassin's chest to its hilt.

The two came together and Drizzt's eyes widened indeed, for somehow, somehow, Entreri's very skin had repelled the blow.

But Artemis Entreri, his body tingling with the energy of the absorbed hit, with the psionics Kimmuriel had suddenly given back to him, surely understood, and in a purely reactive move, without any conscious thought—for if the tormented man had considered it he would have loosed the energy back into himself—Entreri reached out and clasped Drizzt's chest and gave him back his blow with equal force.

His hand sank into Drizzt's chest even as Drizzt, blood bubbling from the wound, fell to the ground.

* * * * *

Out on the landing time seemed to freeze, stuck fast in that awful, awful moment. Guenhwyvar roared and leaped into the translucent wall, but merely bounced away. Outraged, roaring wildly, the cat went back at the wall, claws screeching against the unyielding pane.

Bruenor, too, went into a fighting frenzy, hacking futilely with his axe while Regis stood dumbfounded, saying, "No, it cannot be," over and over.

And there stood Catti-brie, wavering back and forth, her jaw drooping open, her eyes locked on that horrible sight. She suffered through every agonizing second as Entreri's empowered hand melted into Drizzt's chest, as the lifeblood of her dearest friend, of the ranger she had come to love so dearly, spurted from him. She watched the strength leave his legs, the buckling knees, and the sinking, sinking as Entreri guided him to the floor, and the sinking, sinking, of her own heart, an emptiness she had felt before, when she had seen Wulfgar fall with the yochlol.

And even worse it seemed for her this time.

* * * * *

"What have I done?" the assassin wailed, falling to his knees beside the drow. He turned an evil glare over Jarlaxle. "What have you done?"

"I gave you your fight and showed you the truth," Jarlaxle calmly replied. "Of yourself and your skills. But I am not finished with you. I came to you for my own purposes, not your own. Having done this for you, I demand that you perform for me."

"No! No!" the assassin cried, reaching down furiously to try to stem the spurting blood. "Not like this!"

Jarlaxle looked to Kimmuriel and nodded. The psionicist gripped Entreri with a mental hold, a telekinetic force that lifted Entreri from Drizzt and dragged him behind Kimmuriel as the psionicist headed out of the room, back down the stairs.

Entreri thrashed and cursed, aiming his outrage at Jarlaxle but eyeing Drizzt, who lay very still on the floor. Indeed he had been granted his fight and, indeed, as he should have foreseen, it had proven nothing. He had lost—or would have, had not Kimmuriel intervened—yet he was the one who had lived.

Why, then, was he so angry? Why did he want at that moment, to put his dagger across Jarlaxle's slender throat?

Kimmuriel hauled him away.

"He fought beautifully," Rai'gy remarked to Jarlaxle, indicating Drizzt, the blood flowing much lighter now, a pool of it all about his prone and very still form. "I understand now why Dantrag Baenre is dead."

Jarlaxle nodded and smiled. "I have never seen Drizzt Do'Urden's equal," he admitted, "unless it is Artemis Entreri. Do you understand now why I chose that one."

"He is drow in everything but skin color," Rai'gy said with a laugh.

An explosion rocked the tower.

"Catti-brie and her marvelous bow," Jarlaxle explained, looking to the landing where only Guenhwyvar remained, roaring and clawing futilely at the unyielding glass. "They saw, of course, every bit of it. I should go and speak with them before they bring the place down around us."

With a thought to the crystal shard, Jarlaxle turned that wall in front of Guenhwyvar opaque once more.

Then he nodded to the still form of Drizzt Do'Urden and walked out of the room.

EPILOGUE

He is sulking," Kimmuriel remarked, joining Jarlaxle sometime later in the main chamber of the lower floor. "But at least he has stopped swearing to cut off your head."

Jarlaxle, who had just witnessed one of the most enjoyable days of his long life, laughed yet again. "He will come to his senses and will at last be free of the shadow of Drizzt Do'Urden. For that Artemis Entreri will thank me openly." He paused and considered his own words. "Or at least," the mercenary corrected, "he will . . . silently thank me."

"He tried to die," Kimmuriel stated flatly. "When he went at Drizzt's back with the dagger he led the way with a shout that alerted the outcast. He tried to die and we, and I, at your bidding, stopped that."

"Artemis Entreri will no doubt find other opportunities for stupidity if he holds that course," the mercenary leader replied with a shrug. "And we will not need him forever."

Drizzt Do'Urden came down the stairs then in tattered clothing, stretching his sore arm, but otherwise seeming not too badly injured.

"Rai'gy will have to pray to Lady Lolth for a hundred years to regain her favor after using one of her bestowed healing spells upon your dying form," Jarlaxle remarked with a laugh. He nodded to Kimmuriel, who bowed and left the room.

"May she take him to her side for those prayers," Drizzt replied dryly. His witty demeanor did not hold, though, could not hold, in the face of all that he had just come through. He eyed Jarlaxle with all seriousness. "Why did you save me?"

"Future favors?" Jarlaxle asked more than stated.

"Forget it."

Yet again Jarlaxle found himself laughing. "I envy you, Drizzt Do'Urden," he replied honestly. "Pride played no part in your fight, did it?"

Drizzt shrugged, not quite understanding.

"No, you were free of that self-defeating emotion," Jarlaxle remarked. "You did not need to prove yourself Artemis Entreri's better. Indeed, I do envy you, to have found such inner peace and confidence."

"You still have not answered my question."

"A measure of respect, I suppose," Jarlaxle answered with a shrug. "Perhaps I did not believe that you deserved death after your worthy performance."

"Would I have deserved death if my performance did not measure up to your standards, then?" Drizzt asked. "Why does Jarlaxle decide?"

Jarlaxle wanted to laugh again but held it to a smile in deference to Drizzt. "Or perhaps I allowed my cleric to save you as a favor to your dead father," he said, and that put Drizzt on his heels, catching him completely by surprise.

"Of course I knew Zaknafein," Jarlaxle explained. "He and I were friends, if I can be said to have any friends. We were not so different, he and I."

Drizzt screwed up his face with obvious doubts.

"We both survived," Jarlaxle explained. "We both found a way to thrive in a hostile land, in a place we despised but could not find the courage to leave."

"But you have left now," Drizzt said.

"Have I?" came the reply. "No, by building my empire in Menzoberranzan I have inextricably tied myself to the place. I will die there, I am sure, and probably by the hands of one of my own soldiers—perhaps even Artemis Entreri."

Somehow Drizzt doubted the claim, suspecting that Jarlaxle would die of old age centuries hence.

"I respected him greatly," the mercenary went on, his tone steady and serious. "Your father, I mean, and I believe it was mutual."

Drizzt considered the words carefully and found that he couldn't disagree with Jarlaxle's claims. For all Jarlaxle's capacity for cruelty, there was indeed a code of honor about the mercenary leader. Jarlaxle had proven that when he had held Catti-brie captive and had not taken advantage of her, though he had even professed to her that he wanted to. He had proven it by allowing Drizzt, Catti-brie, and Entreri to walk out of the Underdark after their escape from House Baenre, though surely he could have captured or killed them and such an act would have brought him great favor of the ruling house.

And now, by not letting Drizzt die in such a manner, he had proven it again.

"He'll not bother you ever again," Jarlaxle remarked, drawing Drizzt from his contemplation.

"So I dared to hope once before."

"But now it is settled," the mercenary leader explained. "Artemis Entreri has his answer, and though it is not what he had hoped it will suffice."

Drizzt considered it for a moment then nodded, hoping Jarlaxle, who seemed to understand so very much about everyone, was right yet again.

"Your friends await you in the village," Jarlaxle explained. "And it was no easy task getting them to go there and wait. I feared that I would taste the axe of Bruenor Battlehammer, and given the fate of Matron Baenre, that I did not wish at all."

"But you persuaded them without injuring any of them," Drizzt said.

"I gave you my word, and that word I honor . . . sometimes."

Now Drizzt, despite himself, couldn't hold back a grin. "Perhaps, then, I owe you yet again."

"Future favors?"

"Forget it."

"Surrender the panther then," Jarlaxle teased. "How I would love to have Guenhwyvar at my side!"

Drizzt understood that the mercenary was just teasing, that his promise concerning the panther, too, would hold. "Already you will have to look over your shoulder as I come for the crystal shard," the ranger replied. "If you take the cat, I will not only have to retrieve her but will have to kill you, as well."

Those words surely raised the eyebrows of Rai'gy as he came onto the top of the stairs, but the two were merely bantering. Drizzt would not come for Crenshinibon, and Jarlaxle would not take the panther.

Their business was completed.

Drizzt left the crystalline tower then to rejoin his friends, all together and waiting for him in the village, unharmed as Jarlaxle had promised.

After many tears and many hugs they left the village. But they did not go straight to the waiting *Bottom Feeder* but rather, back up the ridge.

The crystalline tower was gone. Jarlaxle and the other drow were gone. Entreri was gone.

"Good enough for them, if they bring the foul artifact back to yer old home and it brings all the ceiling down atop 'em!" Bruenor snorted. "Good enough for them!"

"And now we need not go to Cadderly," Catti-brie said. "Where then?"

"Wulfgar?" Regis reminded.

Drizzt paused a moment to consider Jarlaxle's words—trustworthy words—about their missing friend. He shook his head. It wasn't time for that road just yet. "We have the whole world open before us," he said. "And any direction will prove as good as another."

"And now we don't have the damned crystal shard bringing monsters in on us at every turn," Catti-brie noted.

"Won't be as much fun then," said Bruenor.

And off they went to catch the sunset . . . or the sunrise.

* * * * *

Back in Calimport Artemis Entreri, possibly the most powerful man on the streets, mulled over the titanic events of the last days, the amazing twists and turns his life's road had shown him.

Drizzt Do'Urden was dead, he believed, and by his hand, though he had not proven the stronger.

Or hadn't he? For wasn't it Entreri, and not Drizzt, who had befriended the more powerful allies?

Or did it even matter?

For the first time in many months a sincere smile found its way onto Artemis Entreri's face as he walked easily down Avenue Paradise, assured that none would dare move against him. He found the halfling door guards at the Copper Ante more than happy to see and admit him, and he found his way into Dondon's room without the slightest hindrance, without even questioning stares.

He emerged a short while later to find an angry Dwahvel waiting for him.

"You did it, didn't you?" she accused.

"It had to be done," was all Entreri bothered to reply, wiping his bloodstained dagger on the cloak of one of the guards flanking Dwahvel, as if daring them to make a move against him. They did not, of course, and Entreri moved unhindered to the outside door.

"Our arrangement is still in force?" he heard a plaintive Dwahvel call from behind. With a grin that nearly took in his ears, the ruler of House Basadoni left the inn.

* * * * *

Wulfgar left Delly Curtie that night, as he did every night, bottle in hand. He went down to the wharves where his newest drinking buddy, a man of some repute, waited for him.

"Wulfgar, my friend," Morik the Rogue said happily, taking the bottle and a deep, deep swallow of the burning liquid. "Is there anything that we two cannot accomplish together?"

Wulfgar considered the words with a dull smile. Indeed, they were the kings of Half Moon Street, the two men who rated deferential nods from everyone they passed, the two men in all of Luskan's belly who could part a crowd merely by walking through it.

Wulfgar took the bottle from Morik and, though it was more than half full, drained it in one swallow.

He just had to.

Servant of the Shard

R.A. Salvatore

An Excerpt

Available in Hardcover
October 2000

LIFE IN THE
DARK LANE

uicker! Quicker, I say!" Jarlaxle howled. His arm flashed repeatedly, a seemingly endless stream of daggers spewing forth at the dodging and rolling assassin.

Entreri furiously worked his sword—a drow-fashioned blade he was not particularly enamored of—and his jeweled dagger. With in-and-out vertical rolls, he caught the missiles and flipped them to the side. All the while he kept his feet moving, skittering about looking for an opening in Jarlaxle's superb defensive posture—a stance made all the more powerful by the constant stream of spinning daggers.

"An opening!" the drow mercenary cried, letting fly one, two, three more daggers.

Entreri sent his sword back the other way but knew that his opponent's assessment was correct. He dived into a roll instead, tucking his head and his arms in tight to cover any vital areas.

"Oh, well done!" Jarlaxle congratulated as Entreri came to his feet after taking only a single hit, and that but a dagger sticking into the trailing fold of his cloak instead of his skin.

Entreri felt the dagger swing in against the back of his leg as he stood up. Fearing that it might trip him, he tossed his own dagger into the air, then quickly pulled the cloak from his shoulders and, in the same fluid movement, started to toss it aside.

An idea came to him, though, and he didn't discard the cloak but rather caught his deadly dagger and set it between his teeth. Entreri stalked a semicircle around the dark elf, waving his cloak, a drow *piwafwi*, slowly about as a shield against the missiles.

Jarlaxle smiled at him. "Improvisation," he said with obvious admiration. "The mark of a true warrior." Even so, the drow's arm flashed yet again, a quartet of daggers soaring for the assassin.

Entreri bobbed and spun a complete circuit, but tossed his cloak as he did and caught it as he came back around. One dagger skidded across the floor, another passed over Entreri's ducking head, narrowly missing him, and the other two got caught in the fabric along with the previous one.

Entreri continued to wave the cloak, but it wasn't flowing wide anymore, weighted as it was by the three daggers.

"Not so good a shield, perhaps," Jarlaxle commented.

"You talk better than you fight," Entreri countered. "A bad combination."

"I talk because I so enjoy the fight, my little friend," Jarlaxle replied, and his arm went back again.

But Entreri was already moving, holding his arm out wide to keep the cloak from tripping him up, then diving into a roll right toward the mercenary, closing the gap between them in the blink of an eye.

Jarlaxle did let fly one dagger, and it skipped off Entreri's back. The drow mercenary caught the next one sliding out of his magical bracer in his hand and snapped his wrist, speaking a command word. The dagger responded at once, elongating into a sword, and as Entreri came over, his sword predictably angled up to gut Jarlaxle, the drow had the parry in place.

Entreri improvised, staying low and skittering forward, swinging his cloak in a roundabout manner to wrap it behind Jarlaxle's legs.

The mercenary quick-stepped, and almost got out, but one of the daggers hooked his boot, and he fell over backward. Jarlaxle was as agile as any drow, but so, too, was Entreri. The man came up over the drow, sword thrusting.

Jarlaxle parried fast, his blade slapping against Entreri's. To Jarlaxle's surprise, the assassin's sword went flying away.

The drow understood soon enough, though, for Entreri's now-free hand came forward, clasping Jarlaxle's forearm. He held the drow's weapon out wide, and there loomed the assassin's other hand, holding again that deadly jeweled dagger. Entreri had the opening, and Jarlaxle couldn't block it or begin to move away from it.

But a wave of such despair, an overwhelming barrage of complete and utter hopelessness, washed over Entreri. He felt as if someone had just entered his brain and begun scattering his thoughts, starting and stopping his reflexes. In the inevitable pause, Jarlaxle brought his other arm forward, launching a dagger that smacked Entreri in the gut and bounced away.

The barrage of discordant, paralyzing emotions continued to blast away in Entreri's mind, and he stumbled back. He hardly felt the motion and was somewhat confused a moment later, as the fuzziness began to clear, to find that he was on the other side of the small room. He was sitting against the wall, facing a smiling Jarlaxle.

Entreri closed his eyes and, at last, forced the confusing jumble of thoughts completely away. For a moment he figured that Rai-guy had intervened. The drow wizard had imbued both Entreri and Jarlaxle with stoneskin spells that they could spar without fear of injuring each other. When the assassin's vision cleared, he saw no sign of the wizard. Entreri turned back to Jarlaxle, guessing then that the mercenary had used yet another in his seemingly endless bag of tricks. Perhaps Jarlaxle had even made use of his newest magical acquisition, the powerful Crenshinibon (which Entreri did not favor at all) to overwhelm the assassin's concentration.

"Perhaps you are slowing down, my friend," Jarlaxle remarked. "What a pity that would be! It is good that you defeated your avowed enemy when you did, for Drizzt has many centuries of youthful speed left in him."

Entreri scoffed at the words, though in truth the thought gnawed at him. He had lived his entire life on the very edge of perfection. Even now, in the middle years of his life, he was confident that he could defeat almost any foe with pure skill or by outthinking his enemy, by properly preparing any battlefield. But Entreri didn't want to slow down, didn't want to lose that edge of fighting brilliance that had so marked his life.

He wanted to deny Jarlaxle's words, but he could not, for he knew in his heart that he had truly lost that fight with Drizzt. He knew that if Kimmuriel Oblodra had not intervened with his psionic powers, then Drizzt would have been declared the victor.

"You did not outmatch me with speed," Entreri started to argue, shaking his head.

Jarlaxle came forward, his glowing eyes narrowing dangerously. It was a threatening expression, a look of rage, that the assassin rarely saw upon the handsome face of the always in control dark elf mercenary leader.

"I have this," Jarlaxle announced, pulling wide his cloak and showing Entreri the tip of the artifact

4

Crenshinibon, the Crystal Shard, tucked neatly into one pocket. "Never forget that! Without it, I could likely still defeat you, though you are good, my friend, better than any human I have ever known. With this in my possession . . . you are but a mere mortal. Joined with Crenshinibon, I can destroy you with but a thought. Never forget that."

Entreri lowered his gaze, digesting the words and the tone, sharpening that image of the uncharacteristic expression on Jarlaxle's always-smiling face. Joined with Crenshinibon? But a mere mortal? What in the Nine Hells did that mean? Never forget that, Jarlaxle had said and indeed, this was a lesson that Artemis Entreri would not soon dismiss.

When he looked back up again, Entreri saw Jarlaxle wearing his typical expression, that sly, slightly amused look that conveyed to all who saw it that this cunning drow knew more than he did, knew more than any human possibly could.

Seeing Jarlaxle relaxed again also reminded Entreri of the novelty of these sparring events. The mercenary leader would not spar with any others. In truth, Rai-guy was stunned when Jarlaxle had told him that he meant to fight Entreri on a regular basis.

Entreri understood the logic behind that thinking: Jarlaxle survived, in part, by remaining mysterious, even to those around him. No one could ever really get a good look at the mercenary leader. He kept allies and opponents alike off-balance and wondering, always wondering. And yet, here he was, revealing so much to Artemis Entreri.

"Those daggers," Entreri said, coming back at ease and putting on his own sly expression. "They were merely illusions."

"In your mind, perhaps," the dark elf replied in his typically cryptic manner.

"They were," the assassin pressed. "You could not possibly carry so many, nor could any magic create them that quickly."

"As you say," Jarlaxle replied. "Though you heard the clang as your own weapons connected with them and felt the weight as they punctured your cloak."

"I *thought* I heard the clang," Entreri corrected, wondering if he had at last found a chink in the mercenary's never-ending guessing game.

"Is that not the same thing?" Jarlaxle replied with a laugh, but it seemed to Entreri as if there was a darker side to that chuckle.

Entreri lifted his cloak to see several of the solid metal daggers still sticking in the folds of its fabric, and found several more holes in the cloth. "Some were illusions, then," he argued unconvincingly.

Jarlaxle merely shrugged, never willing to give anything away.

With an exasperated sigh, Entreri started out of the room.

"Do keep ever-present in your thoughts, my friend, that an illusion can kill you if you believe in it enough," Jarlaxle called after him.

Entreri paused and glanced back, his expression grim. He wasn't used to being so openly warned, or threatened, but he knew, with this one particular companion, that the threats were never, ever idle.

"The real thing can kill you whether you believe in it or not," Entreri replied, and he turned back for the door.

The assassin departed with a shake of his head, frustrated, and yet intrigued. That was always the way with Jarlaxle, Entreri mused, and what surprised him even more was that he found that aspect of the clever drow mercenary particularly compelling.

* * * * *

That is the one, Kimmuriel Oblodra signaled to his two companions, Rai-guy and Berg'inyon Baenre. Berg'inyon was the most recent addition to the surface army of Bregan D'aerthe. The favored son of the most powerful house in Menzoberranzan, Berg'inyon had grown up with all the drow world open before him—to the level that a drow male in Menzoberranzan could achieve, at least. Then Berg'inyon's mother, the powerful Matron Baenre, led a disastrous assault on a dwarven kingdom. The assault ended in her death and threw the great drow city into utter chaos. In that time of ultimate confusion, Berg'inyon had thrown his hand in with Jarlaxle and the ever elusive mercenary band of Bregan D'aerthe. Among the finest of fighters in all the city, and with familial connections to still-mighty House Baenre, Berg'inyon was welcomed openly and quickly promoted, elevated to the status of high lieutenant.

Thus, he was here now serving Rai-guy and Kimmuriel, but as their peer.

He considered the human that Kimmuriel had targeted, a shapely woman posing in the dress of a common street whore.

You have read her thoughts? Rai-guy signaled back, his fingers weaving an intricate pattern, perfectly complimenting the various expressions and contortions of his handsome and angular drow facial features.

Raker spy, Kimmuriel silently assured his companion. *The coordinator of their group. All pass her by, reporting their finds.*

Berg'inyon shifted nervously from foot to foot, uncomfortable around the revelations of the strange and strangely powerful Kimmuriel. He hoped that Kimmuriel wasn't reading his thoughts at that moment, for he was wondering how Jarlaxle could ever feel safe with this one about. Kimmuriel could walk into someone's mind, it seemed, as easily as Berg'inyon could walk through an open doorway. He chuckled then, but disguised it as a cough, when he considered that clever Jarlaxle likely had that doorway somehow trapped. Berg'inyon decided that he'd have to learn that technique, if there was one, to keep Kimmuriel at bay.

Do we know where the others might be? Berg'inyon's hands silently asked.

Would the show be complete if we did not? came Rai-guy's responding gestures, the wizard smiling widely. Soon, all three of the dark elves wore sly and hungry expressions.

Kimmuriel closed his eyes then and steadied himself into long, slow breaths.

Rai-guy took the cue, pulling a pinch of gum arabic in which was enveloped a single eyelash out of one of his several belt pouches. He turned to Berg'inyon and began waggling his fingers, and the warrior drow flinched reflexively—as most sane people would do when a drow wizard began casting in their direction.

The first spell went off and Berg'inyon, rendered invisible, faded from view. Rai-guy went right back to work, now aiming a spell designed to mentally grab at the target, to hold the spy fast.

The woman flinched and seemed to hold fast for a second, then shook out of it and glanced about nervously, now obviously on her guard.

Rai-guy growled and went at the spell again. Invisible Berg'inyon stared at him with an almost mocking smile—yes, there were advantages to being invisible! Rai-guy continually demeaned humans, called them every drow name for offal and carrion. On the one hand, he was obviously surprised that this one had resisted the hold spell—no easy mental task. On the other hand, Berg'inyon noted, the blustering wizard had prepared more than one of the spells, though one, without any resistance, should have been enough.

This time, the woman took one step, then held fast in her walking pose.

Go! Kimmuriel's fingers waved. Even as he gestured, the powers of his mind opened the doorway between the three drow and the woman. Suddenly she was there, though she was still on the street, but only a couple of strides away. Berg'inyon leaped out and grabbed the woman, tugging her hard into the extra-dimensional space, and Kimmuriel shut the door.

It had happened so fast that to anyone watching on the street, it would have seemed as if the woman had simply disappeared.

The psionicist raised his delicate black hand up to the victim's forehead, joining with her mentally. He could feel the horror in there, for though her physical body had been locked in Rai-guy's stasis, her mind was working and she knew indeed that she now stood paralyzed and helpless before dark elves.

Kimmuriel took just a moment to bask in that terror, thoroughly enjoying the spectacle, then he imparted psionic energies to her. He built an armor of absorbing kinetic energy, using a technique he had perfected in Entreri's battle with Drizzt Do'Urden. When it was done, he nodded.

Berg'inyon came visible again almost immediately, as his fine drow sword slashed across the woman's throat, the offensive strike dispelling the defensive magic of Rai'guy's invisibility spell. The drow warrior went into a fast dance, slashing and slashing with both of his fine swords, stabbing hard, even chopping once with both blades, a heavy drop down onto the woman's head.

But no blood spewed forth, no groans of pain came from the woman, for Kimmuriel's armor accepted each blow, catching and holding the tremendous energy offered by the drow warrior's brutal dance.

This went on for several minutes, until Rai-guy warned that the spell of holding was nearing its end. Berg'inyon backed away, and Kimmuriel closed his eyes again as Rai-guy began yet another casting.

Both onlookers, Kimmuriel and Berg'inyon, smiled wickedly as Rai-guy shoved his finger into the woman's mouth and released his spell. A flash of fiery light appeared in the back of the woman's mouth, disappearing as it slid down her throat.

The sidewalk was there again, very close, as Kimmuriel opened a second dimensional portal, and Rai-guy roughly shoved the woman back out.

Kimmuriel shut the door, then they watched, amused.

The hold spell released first, and the woman staggered. She tried to call out, but coughed roughly at the burn in her throat. A strange expression came over her, one of absolute horror.

She feels the energy contained in the kinetic barrier, Kimmuriel explained. *I hold it no longer—only her own will prevents its release.*

How long? a concerned Rai-guy asked. Kimmuriel only smiled and motioned for them to watch and enjoy.

The woman broke into a run. The three noted other people moving around her, some closing cautiously—other spies, likely—and others seeming merely curious. Still others grew alarmed and tried to stay away from her.

All the while, she tried to scream, but just kept hacking from the continuing burn in her throat. All the while, her eyes were wide, so horrifyingly and satisfyingly wide! She could feel the tremendous energies within her, begging release, but she had no idea of how she might accomplish that.

She couldn't hold the kinetic barrier. Her initial realization of the problem transformed from horror into confusion. All of Berg'inyon's terrible beating came out then, so suddenly. All of the slashes and the stabs, the great chop and the twisting heart thrust, burst over the helpless woman, and to those watching, it seemed almost as if the woman simply fell apart, gallons of blood erupting about her face and head and chest.

She went down almost immediately. Before anyone

could even begin to react, before they could run away or charge to her aid, Rai-guy's last spell, a delayed fireball, went off, immolating the already dead woman and many of those around her.

Outside the blast, wide-eyed stares were directed at the charred corpse from comrade and ignorant onlooker alike, expressions of the sheerest terror that surely pleased the three merciless dark elves.

A fine display. Worthy indeed.

For Berg'inyon, the spectacle served a second purpose. It was a clear reminder to him to take care around his fellow lieutenants. Even taking into consideration the high drow standards for torture and murder, these two were particularly adept, true masters of the craft.

Bregan D'aerthe was more tightly knit and interdependent, the followers of Jarlaxle more trusting of each other and reliant upon each other than any other drow institution, even the great ruling houses of Menzoberranzan. But Berg'inyon stared hard at the spectacle of the chopped and blasted spy and took it as a clear warning and reminder of the need to take precautions against Rai-guy and Kimmuriel for his own safety.

These were dark elves, after all.

The Hunter's Blades Trilogy

New York Times best-selling author
R.A. SALVATORE
takes fans behind enemy lines in this
new trilogy about one of the most popular
fantasy characters ever created.

THE LONE DROW

Book II

Chaos reigns in the Spine of the World. The city of Mirabar
braces for invasion from without and civil war within. An orc king
tests the limits of his power. And *The Lone Drow* fights
for his life as this epic trilogy continues.

October 2003

Now available in paperback!

THE THOUSAND ORCS

Book I

A horde of savage orcs, led by a mysterious cabal of power-hungry
warlords, floods across the North. When Drizzt Do'Urden and
his companions are caught in the bloody tide, the dark elf ranger
finds himself standing alone against *The Thousand Orcs*.

July 2003

FORGOTTEN REALMS

R.A. Salvatore's
War of the Spider Queen

Chaos has come to the Underdark like never before.

New in hardcover!

CONDEMNATION, *Book III*
Richard Baker

The search for answers to Lolth's silence uncovers only more complex questions. Doubt and frustration test the boundaries of already tenuous relationships as members of the drow expedition begin to turn on each other. Sensing the holes in the armor of Menzoberranzan, a new, dangerous threat steps in to test the resolve of the Jewel of the Underdark, and finds it lacking.

May 2003

Now in paperback!

DISSOLUTION, *Book I*
Richard Lee Byers

When the Queen of the Demonweb Pits stops answering the prayers of her faithful, the delicate balance of power that sustains drow civilization crumbles. As the great Houses scramble for answers, Menzoberranzan herself begins to burn.

August 2003

INSURRECTION, *Book II*
Thomas M. Reid

The effects of Lolth's silence ripple through the Underdark and shake the drow city of Ched Nasad to its very foundations. Trapped in a city on the edge of oblivion, a small group of drow finds unlikely allies and a thousand new enemies.

October 2003

Starlight & Shadows

New York Times best-selling author Elaine Cunningham finally completes this stirring trilogy of dark elf Liriel Baenre's travels across Faerûn! All three titles feature stunning art from award-winning fantasy artist Todd Lockwood.

New paperback editions!

DAUGHTER OF THE DROW
Book 1

Liriel Baenre, a free-spirited drow princess, ventures beyond the dark halls of Menzoberranzan into the upper world. There, in the world of light, she finds friendship, magic, and battles that will test her body and soul.

February 2003

TANGLED WEBS
Book 2

Liriel and Fyodor, her barbarian companion, walk the twisting streets of Skullport in search of adventure. But the dark hands of Liriel's past still reach out to clutch her and drag her back to the Underdark.

March 2003

New in hardcover – the long-awaited finale!

WINDWALKER
Book 3

Their quest complete, Liriel and Fyodor set out for the barbarian's homeland to return the magical Windwalker amulet. Amid the witches of Rashemen, Liriel learns of new magic and love and finds danger everywhere.

April 2003

The Avatar Series

New editions of the event that changed all Faerûn…and the gods that ruled it.

SHADOWDALE
Book 1 • Scott Ciencin

The gods have been banished to the surface of Faerûn,
and magic runs mad throughout the land.

May 2003

TANTRAS
Book 2 • Scott Ciencin

Bane and his ally Myrkul, god of Death, set in motion a plot to seize
Midnight and the Tablets of Fate for themselves.

June 2003

The New York Times *best-seller!*
WATERDEEP
Book 3 • Troy Denning

Midnight and her companions must complete their quest by traveling
to Waterdeep. But Cyric and Myrkul are hot on their trail.

July 2003

PRINCE OF LIES
Book 4 • James Lowder

Cyric, now god of Strife, wants revenge on Mystra, goddess of Magic.

September 2003

CRUCIBLE: THE TRIAL OF CYRIC THE MAD
Book 5 • Troy Denning

The other gods have witnessed Cyric's madness
and are determined to overthrow him.

October 2003

The foremost tales of the FORGOTTEN REALMS® series, brought together in these two great collections!

LEGACY OF THE DROW COLLECTOR'S EDITION
R.A. Salvatore

Here are the four books that solidified both the reputation of *New York Times* best-selling author R.A. Salvatore as a master of fantasy, and his greatest creation Drizzt as one of the genre's most beloved characters. Spanning the depths of the Underdark and the sweeping vistas of Icewind Dale, Legacy of the Drow is epic fantasy at its best.

January 2003

THE BEST OF THE REALMS
A FORGOTTEN REALMS *anthology*

Chosen from the pages of nine FORGOTTEN REALMS anthologies by readers like you, *The Best of the Realms* collects your favorite stories from the past decade. *New York Times* best-selling author R.A. Salvatore leads off the collection with an all-new story that will surely be among the best of the Realms!

November 2003

"You think we should kiss [...] like a statement instead [...] pumped.

"As a professional, I take my [...]. I know this is an improvisational gig, but a [...] ain amount of rehearsal seems wise. After all, we've been doing it, getting it on, Sugar and Charles that is, for a month. If you want people to believe we're in lust..." Crap. I meant to say *love*. "Well, you know what I mean."

Way to go, Miss Transparent.

He scraped his teeth over his lower lip. Nice teeth. Nice mouth. "Appreciate your dedication, Sunshine."

I couldn't tell if he was serious or sarcastic, and right now I didn't care. I wanted him to kiss me, dammit. "Let's just get it out of the way," I plowed on. "The awkwardness—misaligned mouths, bumping noses and all that."

Except there was no awkwardness. He swooped in without warning, framed my face, ravished my mouth. He kissed the ever-lovin' daylights out of me.

Also available from

Beth Ciotta

Seduced
Charmed
Jinxed
Lasso the Moon

And look for Evie's next adventure in 2008!

ALL ABOUT EVIE

Beth Ciotta

HQN™

ISBN-13: 978-0-373-77207-0
ISBN-10:   0-373-77207-6

ALL ABOUT EVIE

Copyright © 2007 by Beth Ciotta

This book is dedicated to Heather Graham Pozzessere—
an inspiration and a treasured friend. Thank you for all
you have done and all you continue to do. Your talent
is exceeded only by your generosity and kindness.

ACKNOWLEDGMENTS

To my agent, Amy Moore-Benson—You gave me the
courage to spread my wings and now we're flying high.
Thank you for your constant support and guidance!

To my editor, Abby Zidle—You *got* me. You championed
me. I am eternally grateful for your enthusiasm,
storytelling expertise and advice. Keep smiling!

To Tracy Farrell, Dianne Moggy and *everyone*
at HQN Books who helped to make my dreams come
true—thank you from the bottom of my heart.

To Cynthia Valero—Your spirit soars alongside mine on
this one! To Mary Stella and Julia Templeton—You keep
me sane and inspired! To my sister, Barb—Your honesty
and support are priceless. And to my husband, Steve—
Writing about true love is easy when you're living it.

A special thank-you to John Ciotta (my brother-in-law)
and Nicola Mooney (both professional performers
and cruise ship veterans) for answering my gazillion
questions regarding the ins and outs of cruising.
Heartfelt thanks to Al, Alicia and Jean-Marie for sharing
their "cruise" experiences, and to my friend Brooks
for his "magical" expertise.

Dear Reader,

I've been a professional performer for, well, let's just say a long time. I admit, *some* of Evie's adventures and tribulations are loosely based on my own experiences within the entertainment industry; however, she and all the featured characters are purely fictional. In kind, although I extensively researched con artists and scams, *Chameleon* and *A.I.A.* are figments of my overactive imagination. Welcome to my world.

Anchors aweigh!

Beth Ciotta

ALL ABOUT EVIE

CHAPTER ONE

IT FINALLY HAPPENED.

I, Evie Parish, snapped.

At an audition no less. Me, the ultimate professional. In front of several peers and a table of entertainment and marketing executives.

Bad enough I even *had* to audition.

I'd performed in this casino on a number of occasions throughout the years as a singer, an emcee, a dance motivator *and* a character actress. Not just *this* casino, but every casino in Atlantic City. I was known as the poor man's Tracy Ullman. I had versatility out the wazoo. A stellar reputation. A kick-butt résumé. I had more experience in entertainment than any one of the six stony-faced executives who'd insisted upon this live demonstration.

I also had sequined bras older than any of the people deciding my fate.

It wasn't their youth I resented. Okay. That's a lie. It was their inability to afford the performer their respect and attention. In between memorizing the script that I'd been handed on arrival and checking for the umpteenth time to make sure my blush and lipstick hadn't faded, I peeked out from the wings to gauge the reaction of the powers-that-be to the actress on deck. I watched those suits yawn, mumble and fidget through five seamless auditions. The only time they showed interest was during a giggly, stilted presentation from a big-breasted twentysomething-year-old. Granted, *Britney* was young, stacked and beautiful, but she was as green as the bagel I'd found this morning in the back of my fridge.

I traded a disgusted, knowing look with two friends who were also auditioning for this gig, both in their late thirties. Talented, experienced and equally ignored by the Gen-X execs. Nicole and Jayne were already slipping into day clothes and trading their heels for flats.

I should have cut my losses then and there and followed suit. I should have collected my purple fake fur coat and *I Love Lucy* travel tote and vacated the showroom in a dignified manner. But no. I was stubborn, desperate and, dammit, hopeful. Hopeful that they'd see something in me that they didn't see in my friends. Hopeful that talent and experience would win out.

Talk about idealistic.

When my time came I strode onstage with confidence and grace wearing a turquoise bikini top, flowered sarong, three-inch heels and a dazzling smile. I hit my mark and launched into the poorly written promotion intended to *wow* casino patrons. Me, Evie Parish, a mild-mannered, small-breasted, fortysomething.

Normally I excel when reciting monologues and pitches. I can sell camp like Liza Minelli. Unfortunately, I was distracted by an overly loud conversation from the vicinity of the "judges" panel. I stopped midsentence. Did I mention that instead of reading off of the page like Britney, *I'd* memorized the copy? But I digress. No one instructed me to continue, so I didn't. Instead, I shielded my eyes from the bright wash of the spotlight in order to pinpoint the commotion.

I'd endured a lot of humiliation in my twenty-five year career—including a crotchety patron yelling, *"You suck!"* three inches from my face *while* I was performing—but this took the cake. Instead of watching me, the executives were scanning a menu, arguing over what to order for lunch. Three of them, anyway. Another yapped on his cell phone, while the remaining two studied me with bored expressions.

For crying out loud!

Seething, I tugged at the hem of my midthigh sarong. Michael, my agent, who also happens to be my ex-husband—don't ask—had told me the theme was tropical. *Show some skin,* he'd said. Then again he always says that.

"Should I wait?" I asked. "Start over? Pick up where I left off?" *Go tell it on the mountain?*

"Are you wearing bikini bottoms under that skirt?" This from the bored, clean-shaven man who looked young enough to be my...younger brother.

Certain I knew where this was leading, I shifted on my strappy heels and cocked a recently waxed, perfectly shaped eyebrow. "Yes."

"Would you mind losing the sarong?" This from the bored woman sitting next to him. At least she knew it was a sarong.

My heart pounded with fury. The last several months, months of being rejected solely on my advancing age, weighed on my shoulders like an unlucky slot machine. "Yes, I mind."

I heard a collective gasp from the wings. I knew without looking that Nicole and Jayne stood side by side, shocked by my defiance. I didn't cause scenes. I was the calm one, the logical one, the one who sucked it up and took the high road no matter how low the blow.

Up until now, that is.

Now this final injustice compelled me to raise a verbal sword in defense of belittled entertainers everywhere!

I stepped out of the spotlight, allowed my eyes to adjust to the low-lighted house and gave thanks that this was a closed audition. No casino patrons to witness this humiliating debacle. No bartenders, cocktail waitresses, dealers or slot attendants to instigate gossip. Just the six executives and two stage technicians. Oh, and seven performers, including my two closest friends. I glanced toward the left wing and sure enough, Nicole, the rabble-rouser of our clique, was giving me a thumbs-up while Jayne's horrified expression shouted, *Are you mad?*

"Mad as hell," I thought, my inner voice mimicking the deranged anchorman from *Network,* *"and I'm not going to take it anymore!"*

In that same instant, the woman who'd asked me to remove my sarong said, "Thank you for your time, Mrs. Parish."

Since a gigantic vaudevillian hook didn't emerge from the sidelines to yank me off stage, I stood my ground. Hands trembling, I tucked my processed blond hair behind my ears and faced the enemy. "Look, I'm auditioning for the role of an emcee, not a beach bunny." Amazingly, my tone did not betray my inner frustration. Then again, I am a damn good actress. Too bad I seemed to be the only one aware of that.

The entertainment coordinator—was she even twenty?—crossed her arms over her chest and angled her head. She didn't look happy. "As an emcee you'd be representing this property, Mrs. Parish."

She might as well have called me *ma'am.* I curled my French-manicured nails into my sweaty palms. "It's *Ms.* Parish and I realize that, but—"

"What does specialty performer mean?" This from one of the marketing dudes.

My left eye twitched. I tried to wet my lips, but

anxiety had robbed me of saliva. I clasped my trembling hands and twirled my funky chrysoprase ring—a gift from Jayne—around my middle finger. She claimed that the mint-green stone would ease emotional tension and stress. I'm beginning to think she bought me a clunker. Even though I knew full well that, for the sake of my untainted reputation, I should swallow my anger, sarcasm tripped off of my fat, bone-dry tongue. "Excuse me?"

"On your résumé it says specialty performer. What, like an exotic dancer?"

They snickered, turned to one another and traded unfunny quips like the local news reporters at the end of a broadcast. What's up with that? Laughing heartily over something that wasn't clever or funny to begin with.

As I stood there, white noise roaring in my ears, I flashed back on all of the times I—and a slew of other entertainers—had lost a gig because of an unenlightened directive from a higher-up bean counter. A person with no background whatsoever in entertainment. A person who hired and fired acts based on personal taste.

I know amazing female singers who've been passed over because a casino president deemed their hips too big. One even cited a vocalist's ankles too thick. Can you imagine? Never mind that she sang her butt off. *Did you even notice that the audience, your patrons, were thoroughly enjoying themselves, Mr. President? If the ankles bothered you that badly, what about suggesting she wear pants instead of a dress? Wouldn't that be a simple, creative solution? But wait, you're not creative. You're not a visionary.* And neither, I concluded sadly, were the execs seated in front of me.

Heart pumping, I hopped off the stage and approached the long table, demanding everyone's attention with a shrill whistle. *Career suicide,* my logical self warned. Only I wasn't listening to my logical self. I was listening to the injured woman who'd endured a particularly rough year, personally and professionally. There comes a time when a person needs to speak up, to demand common courtesy, respect, no matter the cost, and for me that time was now. Why I hadn't felt this righteous urge when Michael had dumped me for another woman, I couldn't say. Maybe I'd been too stunned, too hurt to speak up. But now I was angry. Angry and insulted and really, *really* pissed.

I climbed up on my soapbox. If this were a TV sitcom, patriotic music would swell in the background.

"Listen up, kids. On behalf of all the other women who auditioned today, we are professionals and expect to be treated as such. Secondly, although the harem girl and French maid costumes stored in my closet might be considered exotic and although I do dance, I am not, nor have I ever been, an exotic dancer. Those costumes, by the way, hang right alongside my fuzzy bumblebee fat-suit and mad scientist lab coat. It's all part and parcel of being a character actress. Translation—an actress with excellent improvisational skills who can represent any given character on any given day at any given private or corporate themed party. And that's just *one* of my God-given talents. I also sing and dance. Hence the term specialty performer."

"Thank you, Ms. Parish. We'll be in touch."

That was it? That was the payoff to my heartfelt tirade? An expressionless don't-call-us-we'll-call-you?

I nodded. "Got it."

Actually, I hadn't. It was the second time I'd been dismissed and yet there I stood, trembling with fury...and fear. Life as I'd known it was fast swirling down the toilet. Again, I twirled the ring. "Just so you know, I'm perfect for this job."

One of the young turks straightened his tie then coughed into his hand. "Yes. Well, thank you."

I didn't budge.

Twirl. Twirl.

The pubescent woman seated to his left drummed her fingers on a stack of résumés. "As a professional, I'm sure you understand that we're looking to please our demographic. We're looking for someone..."

"Younger?" I'd been getting a lot of that lately. Even my husband had opted for a newer model, literally. Oh, yeah. This gig was going to the giggly twentysomething. Youth over experience. Mammary glands over memory skills. "Someone with a bright smile and perky breasts?" I just wanted to be certain I understood the criteria.

The panel of execs looked at me with a collective "duh."

That's when I snapped. "As it happens, I have both." In a moment of righteous insanity, I flashed a thousand-watt smile in tandem with my perky 32Bs.

CHAPTER TWO

YOU'LL NEVER WORK IN this town again droned in my ears as I parked my used Subaru on Atlantic Avenue. I'd heard those words before, but this time, for the first time, I feared they might actually be true. I didn't regret my tirade, just the actions. I'd bared my breasts in public. And for what? It's not as if the execs were amused or impressed enough to give me the job. Nope. No Hollywood moment for me.

Instead they'd had security escort me off the premises, my girlfriends trotting behind, simultaneously applauding and bemoaning my spontaneous wardrobe malfunction. That's when it occurred to me that my antics had probably been caught on film. Casinos are rampant with strategically placed security cameras. Great. Next, they'd be selling the video on QVC. *Specialty Performers Gone Wild.*

Talk about an opening line for tonight's diary entry. Twenty years from now, I'd relive the moment, recorded in vibrant purple-penned detail, and laugh.

Or not.

Back in the parking garage, I'd begged off lunch—Bloody Marys—with the girls, claiming an appointment. As much as I loved them, and as much as they commiserated, panic and despair had me racing toward Michael. He'd put a positive spin on my moment of insanity. He'd salvage my career. At least that's what I'd told myself, over and over, on the three-minute drive from the boardwalk casino to his midtown office.

I left my car and entered the turn-of-the-century brownstone, oblivious to the sights, sounds and smells of town. Though branded a seaside resort, Atlantic City falls miles short of paradise. In order to compete with Vegas, politicians and investors are revitalizing, but mostly it feels like too little too late. Even the Miss America Pageant skipped town. So much for tradition. The only recent addition worth celebrating was an impressive development of designer outlets that appealed to both tourists and locals. Not that I'll ever shop again. Hard to shop without moolah and, as I stated before, chances are I'll never work in this town again.

I climbed the stairs to the second floor and walked toward the door marked Michael Stone Entertainment, Inc. Before I could second-guess the wisdom of this visit, I let myself in. My stomach churned as I hovered on the threshold of Michael's private office. I wondered if he'd heard about *the incident*.

I knocked lightly on the doorjamb, trying not to

notice how handsome he looked in his dress shirt and power tie. Trying not to admire his new funky reading glasses—sexy—and the fact that he was wearing his sandy-brown hair shorter and his sideburns longer—also sexy. Noticing would only depress me. He was no longer mine to admire.

He glanced up from a file and motioned for me to take a seat. He was on the phone. He was always on the phone...or the Internet. He made the majority of his living wheeling and dealing with clients and buyers via modern technology. I assumed he wasn't talking to the people I'd just flashed, otherwise he would've spared me more than a two-second glance.

He didn't know yet.

I blew out a tense breath and sank down on the brown leather wing chair. I should break the news myself, beat the execs to the punch, make my excuses. I could hear Michael now. *Yeah, right.*

Convincing him that I'd bared my boobies in public was going to take some doing. Although I've worn my share of skimpy costumes in the past, in everyday life, real life, I'm preppy-trendy. Kind of a funky, contemporary Doris Day. Even in the privacy of my bedroom. Michael had never appreciated my preference for cartoon pajamas over lace teddies. Oh, yes. He was going to have a very hard time digesting the flashing incident. I was having a hard time with it myself.

He hung up the phone, keyed up a document on his computer. "How did the audition go, hon?"

Michael's pet name for all of his female artists, including his ex-wife.

My cheeks burned. "I'm pretty sure I didn't get it." I twirled the cosmic green ring, scuffed my bargain sandals back and forth over the carpet in a bid to warm my frozen toes. Forty-five degrees outside and here I sat in a bikini, sarong and open-toed shoes. Thank goodness for my knee-length furry coat.

I hugged my arms around my middle, looked everywhere but at Michael. I wanted to confess my sin. My fears. I wanted to crawl onto his lap, to cry on his shoulder, to lament the fact that I was washed up at forty-one. I wanted to smack him because he'd made it impossible to take comfort in his arms by divorcing me and taking up with a lingerie model half my age. Not that I'm bitter. Okay. That's a lie. I'm bitter. But it's something I'm trying very hard to conquer. After all, it's not as if I still love him. I don't.

I don't.

I blinked back tears.

Michael cleared his throat and tapped a Cross pen on his cluttered desk. "You know, Evelyn, I've been thinking about taking on an associate."

The fact that he called me Evelyn instead of Evie signaled we were entering uncomfortable territory. Evelyn is my given name, but only my mom and childhood friends call me that. And Michael…when he has something unpleasant to discuss.

I picked imaginary lint off my sleeve, fidgeted in my seat. I chose to pretend that he wasn't considering *me* for the associate position. In the past, pre-divorce settlement, on those occasions when I hit an abnormally dry spell and gigs were nonexistent, I did have to work a day job, aka real job. Jobs that require right-brain skills. I did not excel at or enjoy any one of those *normal* jobs.

To this day the term *nine-to-five* makes my eye twitch and my stomach spasm. You can imagine all the twitching and spasming going on just now. I focused on relaxing my clenched jaw. I've been struggling with TMJ—Temporomandibular Joint Syndrome—for months. Stress related, my doctor said. Avoid stress. *Riiiight.* This moment I was wired tighter than a newly tuned piano.

Temples throbbing, I massaged the right side of my jaw and prayed it wouldn't lock open when I spoke. I'd hit my quota of embarrassing moments this day, thank you very much. "That's great, Michael. I guess that means business is jamming." Not that he ever suffered slow periods, but he'd always operated solo with the exception of a secretary.

He pushed his trendy glasses up his nose, nodded. "I'm really swamped. You're diplomatic, organized and friendly. You know the business inside and out. You'd make a damned good agent."

To my credit, I refrained from shrieking in horror. In my mind's eye he morphed into Darth Vader. *Come to the dark side, Evie.*

I shuddered. "I appreciate your praise and the job offer, but you know me and nine-to-fives." Wow. He was right. I *am* diplomatic.

"Office hours are ten to six," he said, as if that one-hour difference mattered. It was still eight regimented hours, five days a week, and entailed— ACK!— computer skills. "The job would be steady, hon, with potential for growth."

He rattled off a few more perks. For all my twitching, I had to admit, he knew how to pitch an idea. Then again, Michael could sell a Speedo to an Eskimo. I frowned. "Don't you think that Sasha would have a problem with us working together?" Sasha's the twentysomething hard-body who took my place in his bed. "I mean on a day-to-day basis? Same office and all?"

"She knows there's nothing between us."

Ouch. Okay. We've been divorced for several months, separated even longer. But, still. Didn't fifteen years of amiable bliss count for anything?

The phone rang.

He mouthed an apology and snatched up the receiver. At this point I didn't care if it was the corporate yahoos calling to report *the incident.* I needed a moment to recover from that zinger and to collect my thoughts.

Logically, I knew that Michael thought he was doing me a favor by offering me a job within my field. A job where I could make good money, steady money, if I learned to play both sides of the fence.

There was definite longevity on the business side of entertainment and I couldn't eke out a living by dipping into the proceeds from the sale of our house forever. But instead of doing me a favor, it felt as if he was putting me out to pasture.

I could feel my arteries hardening and the grey hairs sprouting.

My lungs constricted to the size of lima beans.

He hung up the phone, straightened his tie and glanced at his watch. Since he was wearing a suit I assumed he had an impending meeting with a client. Before he could dismiss me, I sucked air into my bean-size lungs and made a last-ditch effort. "I heard through the grapevine that Tropicana is starting up a costumed greeter program."

He set his open briefcase on his cluttered desk. "Yeah, I got a call a couple of days ago. They're looking for attractive, animated women who can interact easily with guests while providing information on sweepstakes, slot tournaments...you know."

Yeah, I knew. That was the point.

"They're looking for someone exactly like you." He tossed three files and a bottle of Tylenol into his briefcase. "Only younger."

He latched shut his case and glanced up, meeting my steady, albeit hurt, gaze. A slight grimace indicated he'd just realized how that sounded. The phone rang, saving us both from addressing what he'd been skirting.

My age.

"Pam, slow down," he said into the mouthpiece as I massaged a sudden, crushing ache in my chest. "I can't understand you. Calm down, hon. Take a breath."

Was he talking to Pam or me? Sweat beaded on my forehead and my fingers tingled. What, I wondered, did a heart attack feel like? I was certainly old enough to have one. Actor John Candy keeled over at forty-four. Okay, he had weight issues, but still.

"A car accident? What… Dammit, Pam." He whipped off his glasses and squeezed the bridge of his nose. "Of course I understand. I'll handle it. Somehow. I'm just glad it's not worse. Take care of yourself and check in when you can. Bye, hon."

He hung up the phone, shoved his glasses back on and scanned computer files. "Who the hell am I going to get to cover this gig on such short notice?"

What about me? I wanted to ask, but didn't. Pride dictated a more subtle route. Besides, I didn't even know what the gig was. I ignored my own sudden and mysterious ailments and voiced concern for Pam what's-her-name. "What's wrong?" I scooted to the edge of my seat in a not-so-subtle attempt to peek at his flat-screen monitor. "What happened?"

"A disaster by way of a three-car pileup," Michael snapped while scanning his database. "Instead of heading for the airport for a contracted engagement, Pam Jones is on her way to the hospital with a broken leg and bruised ribs."

"That's awful, but like you said, at least it's not worse." I didn't know Pam Jones, but I had a good view of her head shot and physical stats via Michael's computer screen. It was almost like looking into a mirror. We both had an all-American vibe going. Pale skin that freckles in the sun, wide blue-green eyes, golden-blond hair. Only Pam had been blessed with long, fairylike curls. The woman could've posed for a Pre-Raphaelite painting whereas I looked like a trendy poster girl for Ivory soap. My pain-in-the-butt, stick-straight hair was currently shoulder length and razor-cut into funky layers.

I refocused on Pam's stats. Okay, she was four inches taller than me and probably a *natural* blonde, but, that and hairstyle aside, we were pretty interchangeable. Why not dull the shock of a last-minute replacement by offering the client a similar product? Meaning, *moi.*

My anxiety over being put out to pasture dampened my sensitivity to Pam's injuries. "Which airport? A.C. or Philly? Maybe I can help. What is it? A meet and greet for conventioneers?" A few years ago I appeared as a mermaid at the Atlantic City Train Station, part of the hoopla to celebrate the arrival of the Miss America contestants. Nothing fazes me. I'm willing to lend atmospheric hoopla to any visiting organization. Well, except the porno convention I saw featured once on HBO. I draw the line at Darla-the-Dancing-Dildo.

Michael spared me a sidelong glance as he stood and rushed to his file cabinet. "It's a—" he waggled his fingers as if to snatch words from the air "—special interest gig. Out of state. Pam was supposed to meet her contact at Philadelphia International. The ship sails out of Fort Lauderdale."

"A cruise ship, huh?" I chewed my thumbnail, musing as he sorted through select head shots and résumés. I'd never performed on a cruise ship, but I was familiar with the venue via the experiences of friends. "How long is the engagement? What's the pay?" Never mind that I was prone to motion sickness. I was desperate to do what I love, what I was born to do, for as long as I could. Even if it meant existing on Dramamine.

"Eight days for three plus all expenses," he mumbled, distracted.

The timing was sweet, but the money… "Three hundred dollars?" For eight days of my life?

"Three thousand."

Zowie. If I rushed home I could pack and be on my way within thirty-five minutes.

Michael chucked the files back into the drawer with a curse, scraped a hand over his cropped hair. "Either they don't have the right look or they're not qualified. What the hell am I going to tell Arch?"

Arch Productions? Never heard of the company, but if they were clients of Michael's they had to be reputable. I stood, looped my travel tote over my arm. "Tell them I'm on my way."

He met my gaze, bit the inside of his cheek. He wasn't sold.

"I'm a quick study, Michael. If you're worried about me learning my lines—"

"No script. There's a character profile, but mostly this job hinges on improvisation."

"Bonus."

He peeled back his shirt cuff, checked the time. "You'd have to participate in passenger activities."

"What, like bingo and shuffleboard? Is that supposed to scare me? Me, who's led many a conga line not to mention limbo and hula hoop contests?" I rolled my eyes. "I can't believe you're hesitating. This job has me written all over it."

Visibly frustrated, he braced his hands on his hips and raised one brow. "You'd have to room with a man."

That was a problem *because…?* I knew only headliners rated private cabins. So my roommate would be a guy. So what? If he was a dancer, ten to one he was gay. If not gay, he was probably in his twenties, which also nixed hanky-panky. Although I hadn't had sex in a year, good sex in even longer, I couldn't imagine screwing around with someone young enough to be my…well, I just couldn't imagine. That didn't mean I wouldn't appreciate the company and the view. I'm divorced, not dead.

I matched his stance and expression. "Not to repeat myself, but, bonus." I waited a beat. Two beats. Three.

Not a flicker of jealousy.

Irritated, I narrowed my eyes. "I'm perfect for this job and you know it."

My ex-husband, soon to be ex-agent if he didn't buckle, sighed. "This isn't a normal gig, Evie."

But it *was* a gig. I shifted my weight, wishing I'd had time to swap my high-heeled sandals for my high-top sneakers. My feet smarted as badly as my conscience. I still hadn't told him about my botched audition. The words wouldn't come. Instead I said, "I need to get out of town for a while." I pictured Michael and that barely legal model doing the horizontal mambo, let the hurt and anger swell. I nabbed his yellow-and-blue-striped tie and jerked him down to my eye level. A considerable distance since I was a foot shorter than his six foot two. "You owe me."

Hunched over and momentarily frozen in his calfskin oxfords, he stared me down for a full minute. I don't know what won him over—my persistence or my thinly veiled desperation. Maybe he'd read my mind and was feeling the teensiest bit guilty about Sasha. Or maybe he was considering my mental stability. After all, I had a death grip on the silk fabric looped around his neck.

Seemingly considering my sanity, he pried loose my fingers then smoothed his shirt and tie. "You do favor Pam in coloring."

I performed a victory happy dance, giddy with excitement and relief. Eight days far and away from the city that no longer considered me an asset. Eight days to contemplate my future, padding my bank account in the process. Pam's misfortune was my blessing.

Ignoring my comical jig—a routine that *used* to amuse him—Michael glanced at his watch, the phone. "You'll be stepping into the shoes of a free-spirited newlywed."

"A comedic role. My specialty."

"Except we're not talking eccentric kook."

"What are we talking?

"Think Judy Holliday in *Born Yesterday*."

The mental image was crystal clear, the irony priceless. "Ditsy ex-showgirl?"

He smirked. "You'd need to provide your own wardrobe. Miniskirts, microshorts, crop tops and stiletto heels. A Wonderbra wouldn't hurt."

It never did. Since I was dead set against a boob job, I owned several bust-enhancing brassieres. On occasion I've been hired to portray a zaftig, although usually zany, character. As a freelance entertainer I often provide my own costumes, although in this instance it struck me as odd. A low-budget production show? On a cruise ship? Maybe it was an inter-active murder mystery or improvisational theater like *Tony n' Tina's Wedding*.

I started to ask specifics but was sidetracked by Michael's cocky expression. Clearly, he expected me to back down. Clearly, he thought he knew me, which he did. Familiarity used to make me feel special. Just now I felt predictable, boring and somewhat ill.

My self-esteem plummeted by the nanosecond. The need to escape Michael, this town, my life, was excruciating. I shrugged. "So I'll have to flaunt my body. I don't have a problem with that."

"Since when?"

"Since today." This was it. Time to 'fess up. I waited until he turned his back in search of his briefcase. "Just so you know, I flashed the execs at the audition."

He snapped the lid closed. "What do you mean, you flashed them?"

"They were looking for T & A, so I showed them T."

He smiled. "Yeah, right." Shaking his head, he leaned over, signed on to the Internet and speed-typed an e-mail.

I squelched a smug retort. I wasn't the only predictable one in this room.

Case closed, I thought, as he signed off AOL, snagged his briefcase and shooed me toward the door.

"What time am I expected at the airport?" I asked, more than happy not to elaborate on the botched audition.

"In three hours. You'll have to haul ass. I'll call you on your cell with details." He followed me out the door, down the stairs and onto the buckled sidewalk.

I glanced over my shoulder, cursing myself for wanting to impress him even as the words left my mouth. "You won't regret this, Michael."

"It's not you I'm worried about," he said as we moved toward separate cars, separate lives. "It's Arch."

CHAPTER THREE

THIRTY-SEVEN MINUTES later I was packed and on my way to Philadelphia International Airport.

Arch, it turned out, was my contact. Arch Reece. An acquaintance of Michael's, although not once in the fifteen years that we'd lived together had he uttered the man's name. Michael hit the highlights of the gig during a cell phone call as I sped west on the Atlantic City Expressway. Details were minimal and cryptic.

"Arch has your ticket. He'll be waiting for you at American Airlines."

"What's he look like?"

"Today? I'm not sure."

Cryptic statement number one.

"Don't worry about it, Evie. He'll approach you."

"How will he know what *I* look like?"

"I e-mailed your head shot, along with a brief explanation about Pam. Be sure your phone's charged. You always forget and—"

"It's charged," I grumbled. So I forgot once in a while. So what? My world, unlike Michael's, did not revolve around phones and the Internet.

"He's not going to like the last-minute switch," he said, blowing over my snippy tone, "but he's desperate and he trusts me and I trust you. You're anal when it comes to nailing a gig."

"Gee, thanks."

My sarcasm garnered an exasperated sigh. "That was a compliment."

Actually, it was. Michael respected my work ethics. He considered me a rarity. He'd told me so hundreds of times over the years. *I wish every performer was as conscientious as you, Evie.*

Too bad you can't retire on stellar ethics, I thought moodily. Although rebelling hadn't secured my future, either.

My cheeks burned with contrition. Even though my anger was righteous, I regretted my rash behavior. A spotless reputation tarnished in one bonehead moment. *Flash. Poof. Tah-dah!* Optimistic professional turns into cynical hoyden. It felt scary. Like I'd contracted a mysterious disease.

Like the *me* I knew was dying.

If I wasn't me, the girl who brightened people's lives with a skit, song or dance, who was I? All my life, I'd felt as if I'd been put on this earth for one reason. To entertain. Even when my marriage crumbled, I still had purpose.

"Are you all right, hon?"

No. My world was falling apart, and my jaw hurt due to some hearty teeth grinding. I opened my mouth as little as possible for fear my jaw would lock. "I'm peachy."

I squeezed the steering wheel, punched the gas. Must. Escape. Town. "So about Arch."

"He'll prep you for the job before you board the ship. When he relays specifics, just remember I warned you."

Cryptic statement number two.

Suddenly I wondered about the outrageously high but wonderful salary quote. "Meaning?"

"There's a small level of risk."

"Define risk."

"Just follow Arch's directive implicitly, otherwise…"

A pregnant pause raised the hair on my arms. "What?"

"Never mind. Just don't deviate from Arch's script and everything will be fine."

"I thought there was no script."

"You know what I mean."

"Not really." Approaching a toll booth, I eased left and zipped through the EZ-Pass lane, my imagination soaring. "Oh, jeez, Michael. Is this a variety act? You said I'll be playing the free-spirited newlywed. Is Arch the daredevil groom? Is he going to saw me in half or shoot an apple off of my head?" Visions of Folies Bergère sashayed through my head. "Please tell me this doesn't involve a rhinestone G-string and sequined pasties!"

He snorted. "As if you would bare your breasts for art."

I smirked, slowing from seventy to sixty-five. The last thing I needed was a cop on my tail. I couldn't afford the time or the ticket. "You think you know me so well."

"I know I know you."

"Because you lived with me for fifteen years?"

"Yes."

"Meaning I'm predictable. Boring."

"Meaning you're a creature of habit. Jesus, Evie, what's gotten into you? I've never known you to pick a fight."

"I'm not—"

"On second thought maybe this gig is a blessing in disguise. Time away and a change of scenery can do wonders for the soul."

He was worried about my soul? About me? Just as my blood started pumping with old, mushy feelings, his phone blipped with an incoming call.

"I've got to take this, hon. It might be Sasha."

Cold resentment replaced the warm fuzzies. What was left of the professional me bid Michael a pleasant goodbye. The new cynical me, her voice growing ever louder, mentally shouted, *screw you, you traitorous bastard*.

The bastard called back three minutes later. His tone was clipped. "You flashed your tits for half a dozen execs?"

"And I didn't even get any beads." This time it was me who hung up.

ONCE I CROSSED the Walt Whitman Bridge I spent the rest of the drive navigating heavy traffic. Two accidents on I-95 South, a bumper-to-bumper nightmare. Finding an opening in the airport's economy parking lot proved difficult. After driving up and down several long aisles, I spied a space. Finally. *Yes!*

As I pulled into the tight space—why don't people park between the appropriate lines?—it occurred to me that I should contact the client to let him know I was on the way. Yes, it would be close but I'd make it.

Except…I didn't have Arch's number. Michael hadn't given it to me and I hadn't asked. He did say he gave Arch my number, intimating *he* would call *me*…which he hadn't. What if he'd refused to take me on as a substitute for Pam? Although if that were the case, Michael would've called me. My phone hadn't rung, so…

Oh, no.

I rooted through my purse, snagged my cell phone, and… Crap! No juice. Surely, I hadn't…

But of course I had.

I'd forgotten to charge it last night. This was all Michael's fault. He'd jinxed me.

Bastard.

I hurriedly plugged the phone into the cigarette lighter. *Come on, come on.*

Meanwhile, I climbed out of the idling car,

dragged my supersize cherry-red suitcase off the backseat and positioned it by the driver's door. With my luck, check-in would charge extra for being overweight. Not me, the suitcase. It couldn't be helped. The zipper on my second suitcase busted, so I had to cram everything into Big Red. Thank goodness it was one of those expandable jobs. Something I'd spied on QVC. Still, it weighed a ton. Again, not my fault. I'd packed for two. Me and my alter ego—the ditzy, sexpot newlywed.

Cursing the brisk temperature, I plopped back down in the driver's seat and powered on my cell. I punched speed dial to retrieve my messages. There were four. Three from Arch. One from Michael. I ignored Michael, who only ranted that Arch was trying to get in touch with me.

I searched my purse for a pen. Settling on an eyeliner pencil, I relistened to Arch's last message and scribbled his number on a fast-food napkin. Gosh, he had a sexy voice, and that accent—British? Scottish? I couldn't put my finger on it, but, *yum*.

Heart racing, I punched in his cell phone number.

He answered on the first ring. "Where the bloody hell are you?"

As far as greetings went, I'd heard better. "The airport parking lot. Economy. I'm so sorry, Mr. Reece. As you know, I didn't have much notice and there was an accident—"

"You, too? Bollocks. Are you all right?"

I blinked as a transport shuttle breezed by, hoping

another was directly on its tail. The economy lot was a good five minutes from the actual terminal, and that's after you actually got *on* the minibus and hit the highway. "What? Oh, no. Not me. I wasn't involved in an accident. I was delayed by one. Two actually. Traffic was a mess and then parking... I didn't think I'd ever—"

"Ms. Parish."

"Yes?"

"The plane, our plane, boards in twenty minutes. I need you here, yeah? Now."

"Right. Of course. No problem." Great. I was botching this gig before it even began. "I'll be there in—"

"What are you wearing?"

"Excuse me?"

"I know what you look like. I need to know what you're wearing," he said in that Sean Connery-esque accent. "My wife has a distinct style."

"Why does my style need to complement your wife's?"

"You *are* my wife."

It took a minute to sink in. "I'm playing your wife?" A fantasy reared. Bulging biceps. Rippled abs. A delicious accent to boot. Evie and the hunk.

"I thought Stone told you—"

"He did. I mean, he said I'd be playing a ditzy newlywed. He just didn't specify that *you'd* be playing my husband."

"Now you know, Sugar."

Flirty, too. I quirked a brow, grinned. "Gotcha, honey."

"That's your name," he said, and my smile slipped. "Sugar Dupont. My alias is Charles Dupont."

I wasn't sure which was more disconcerting: my name, Sugar, for cryin' out loud, or the fact that he'd called a stage name an alias. Must be a foreign thing. "Charles and Sugar Dupont. Got it." I glanced at my phone, noted it was somewhat charged, pulled the plug and cut the engine.

"I'm an eccentric novelist and you're a Vegas showgirl. Retired."

"Me or you?" I asked, lest he think I wasn't paying attention. More and more this was sounding like an improvisational murder mystery. The kind where you mill about all day with the patrons, only you're in character the entire time. One of the cast members kicks the bucket and it's the patrons' job to determine the identity of the killer. I'd acted in a few of these over the years and they were always a hoot. "Which one of us is retired?"

"You, Sugar. I'm merely in between books."

I knew he wasn't flirting but, between the low timbre of his voice and that accent, he had a devastating effect on my libido. It had been aeons since I'd felt this sexually charged. Please, I thought, as I looped my purse and Lucy tote over my shoulder and abandoned the car, let him be in his midthirties at least. No way could I fool around with a twenty-year-old, but a guy in his thirties? A gorgeous Brit, Scot—whatever—with a hunky body? I'm pretty sure I could get down and dirty with a *slightly* younger man, especially if he had a mature outlook on life. "Are you by chance my roommate?" Buzzing with anticipation, I locked the car door and pocketed the keys.

"As we are married, it would make sense, yeah?"

I pumped my fist in the air. *Yes.* Smiling, I grabbed my bulging suitcase and, juggling tote, purse and phone, dragged Big Red toward the shuttle vestibule.

"Are you on your way yet?"

"Yup. Should be there in—"

"What are you wearing?"

Back to that. I glanced at my shuffling feet. "Lime and pink-flowered sneakers, khaki capris and a lime-green T-shirt. Although, you can't see my T-shirt because of my coat—a pink trench. Oh, and I have an aqua wool scarf wrapped around my neck."

After a long pause he said, "You call that sexy?"

"I call it comfortable." I'd be spending the next couple of hours on a plane and then transferring onto the ship. Who gets sexed-up to travel?

"Sugar Dupont is an ex-showgirl. A fun-loving exhibitionist."

"I know. Michael told me. I packed appropriate costumes for when I'm onstage."

"In this business, the world is our stage, Ms. Parish. You'll be *on* the moment you meet me at check-in. This is a round-the-clock performance. If you have a problem with this, tell me now. I *cannae* afford—"

"No problem." I did a one-eighty and raced—as much as one can race when lugging one hundred pounds of luggage—back to my car. I couldn't afford to lose this job. I would not, *could not* face working a nine-to-five. Then there was the flashing incident. Must. Escape. Town. "I'll call you back in two minutes."

I severed the connection before he could argue, whipped open the bulging suitcase right there between my car and the blue van parked next to me. I rooted out a Sugar Dupont ensemble and hunkered down in my backseat for a quick change. I'm no stranger to quick changes, but usually these occur in a dressing room or a curtained, or at least darkened, space backstage. Wiggling in and out of clothes in the backseat of my compact four-door, in broad daylight, was a new experience.

I traded my baggy khaki capris for tight black capris. My funky, flowered sneakers for stiletto, fruit-garnished sandals. I sank lower in the seat, whipped off my T-shirt and pulled on a formfitting halter top—also featuring a fruit motif. I shifted and glanced in the rearview mirror.

Bra strap alert!

Sugar may be an exhibitionist, but I'd be damned if she was a fashion disaster. I needed to trade the bra I was wearing for a strapless push-up—which was somewhere in my suitcase, which was lying open in the parking lot. I unhooked my bra with one hand, eased open the back door and, just as I reached for my suitcase, the halter top came undone and fell down revealing my breasts, nips to the chilly March wind. Before I could cover myself I heard a little boy say, "Look, Daddy. I see bubbies."

Mortified, I looked up to find a family of four loading into the blue van parked in the adjacent space. I smiled—what else could I do?—yanked up my top and knotted the ties behind my neck.

The father grinned, hefted the little boy into a toddler seat then rounded to the driver's side. The mother scowled while buckling in her daughter.

Thirty seconds later they were gone, and I still fussed over details. I finger-teased my hair—sexy-tousled—doused it with hair spray and shoved on a pair of Jackie O sunglasses. Big, round and black, the Gucci knockoffs concealed a good portion of my face but they were trendy and fun and, in my estimation, screamed showgirl on holiday. No offense, Mrs. O.

Lastly, because I refused to catch pneumonia, I pulled on a red cashmere shrug. Not appropriate outerwear considering the temperature, but at least my arms would be warm. Since the cropped sweater was sexy tight, I didn't figure Arch would object.

Satisfied that I looked the part, I hauled my butt and luggage back toward the vestibule—a precarious task while balancing on four-inch stilettos. Nervous laughter bubbled in my throat as I anticipated falling into a hole to China or getting hit by a clown car. This entire day qualified as a segment on *Saturday Night Live.*

I didn't call Arch back until I'd claimed a seat on the shuttle chugging toward the terminal. "On my—" *gasp, cough* "—way." I used my free hand to dab away the sweat on my upper lip. In between gulps of air—I really need to start exercising—I described my new attire.

"Brilliant," he said with a smile in his voice. "Sugar?"

I squeezed my tingling thighs together and applied red lipstick—Sugar struck me as a Cajun Crimson kind of gal—one-handed and without the aid of a mirror. God, I was good. "Yes?"

"A bit of character profile here." He paused, and I waited with bated breath. "You're crazy *aboot* me. *Cannae* keep your hands off of me."

If he looked anything like what I was imagining—a beefed-up James Bond—that wouldn't be a trial. Getting paid to grope a sexy stranger? Talk about your dream gig. I tried my best to sound nonchalant, bored even. "So what do you look like, *Charles?* I don't want to paw the wrong guy."

He chuckled, a husky rumble that made my stomach flutter. "Ever see the flick *Some Like It Hot?*"

I snorted. "Only a bazillion times."

"Brilliant."

"I'll say. Can Billy Wilder direct, or what?"

"Brilliant is slang for excellent, love."

And *love* was slang for *baby, hon, doll*—some sort of endearment. Where was a Bridget Jones lingo guide when you needed one? "Right," I said with conviction. I'd catch on quick enough, quick study that I am. "So is that the gig? Are we doing a stage reenactment of *Some Like It Hot?*" I chucked the lipstick and powdered my nose. I'd have to tease my hair higher and unload an entire can of hair spray if I had to cop Marilyn Monroe's helmet-head. "Wait. Marilyn played Sugar Kane, not Sugar Dupont."

"I was drawing a comparison of myself to Tony Curtis."

I snickered at the memory of Curtis and Lemmon in fishnets and heels, disguised as Josephine and Daphne, the homeliest members of an all-girl band. "You're in drag?"

"Not today. Visualize the part in the movie where Curtis assumes the role of the oil tycoon."

"Meaning you look like a nearsighted yachting snob?" Even with those goofy pop-bottle glasses, Tony had looked adorable. Okay, so we're talking geeky. More stuffed shirt than superspy. The nerd and the showgirl. Works for me. My overactive imagination had me seducing Arch much as Monroe had seduced Curtis in a steamy scene on a stolen yacht.

Brilliant.

"Bang on," he said in that bone-melting accent. "With a slight variation."

The shuttle neared the American Airlines departure area and my pulse accelerated. I squinted out the window, searching for a young Tony Curtis. Did this mean Arch had full lips and big, moony brown eyes? "The shuttle's curbside," I said, hoping I didn't sound as breathless as I felt. "I need to sign off so I can grab my bags."

"I'll be waiting just inside the doors," he said, skepticism lacing his tone. "You're sure you're up to this? Seriously, Evie, it's important that you play your part convincingly at all times, yeah?"

After I got over the thrill of hearing him say my real name, I remembered what Michael had said about a level of risk, and realized that I still didn't fully understand what I was getting into. Assignment? Alias? I should probably bail.

Three thousand dollars and eight days to reevaluate your life. And, if you're lucky, a hot fling.

What would Michael think if he knew I was contemplating a lusty romp? Would he care?

He wouldn't believe it. I'd never had a meaningless fling in my life. *You're a creature of habit, Evie.*

Resentment and conviction propelled me to my feet. "There won't be any screwups," I said as I gathered my luggage. "Lucky for you, Arch Reece, I'm one hell of an actress."

CHAPTER FOUR

NEVER BE MORE NERVOUS than the person in charge.

Jayne had calmed me with those words of advice seven years ago after I'd struggled to learn a choreographed routine on very short notice. Martha Graham I am not. But I do have excellent rhythm, natural talent and those work ethics that please Michael so. I was determined to nail that dance routine even though it strained my technical knowledge. Jayne, bless her soul, couldn't understand why I was busting my hump. We're talking a Bar Mitzvah, not Broadway. I was doing the choreographer a favor. She didn't expect perfection. Why was I stressing?

"Never be more nervous than the person in charge," Jayne had soothed after I'd broken out in a rash.

Arch didn't seem overly nervous about my trial-by-fire performance, and he was the man in charge. I'd meet the production manager or director after we boarded, but just now, Arch Reece was the man, and, aside from him asking if I was up to the task, he seemed cool as a chilled gel mask.

Despite his calm and Jayne's advice, I had a major case of the butterflies. Fortunately, nervous excitement worked in my favor. Sugar would be anxious about running late and jazzed about her impending trip with her new husband.

I scrambled off of the minibus in full Sugar mode. When portraying stereotypical characters, ninety percent of the illusion hinges on makeup, hair and costume. Look the part, feel the part. Shallow, but there it was. The heels helped with the wiggle I was certain she had. The push-up bra pumped up my sensuality. Tousled hair and red lipstick broadcasted fun and bold.

I stumbled twice—not so fun—on my short trek from shuttle to terminal due to my cumbersome suitcase and stiletto heels. Chin held high, I teetered on—across the sidewalk crowded with people and luggage, navigating the mammoth-wide revolving doors. I had a job to do, people to impress, a life to escape.

Heads turned in my harried wake. It didn't surprise me. A clumsy poster girl for Fredericks of Hollywood, lugging an *I Love Lucy* tote and a huge red suitcase, was bound to attract attention. I wasn't self-conscious because I wasn't me. I was Sugar Dupont. A ditzy newlywed looking for her brainiac husband.

My racing pulse stuttered as I cleared the revolving doors and noted a mature, silver-bearded gentleman, leaning on a fancy walking stick. I wouldn't have given him a second look except he was dressed in foppish yachting attire. White oxford shirt, beige trousers, a navy-blue blazer. He'd accented the conservative ensemble with a striped ascot, Panama straw hat and black-rimmed, round lenses—similar to the thick spectacles Curtis had worn when posing as the mild-mannered millionaire playboy, only sepia-tinted.

It couldn't be, but then he smiled and said, "Sugar, love, time's ticking," in a quasi Cary Grant accent, and I knew that it was. My steamy fantasy evaporated, striking me momentarily breathless with disappointment. If Arch had a six-pack, it was in the fridge. The only kind of iron this round-shouldered, paunch-bellied man pumped was Geritol.

At least he had all of his teeth.

Sugar's sugar daddy abandoned his luggage and limped forward just as an overeager skycap nabbed Big Red with such enthusiasm that he jerked me off balance. If I were me I would have screamed, but I was Sugar, so I squealed as I careened forward and plowed into my bespectacled *husband*.

We landed with a bone-jarring *thwack*. Arch, flat on his back. Me, flat on top of Arch.

My first thought was that he smelled like my dad—Old Spice. My second thought was that I'd just tackled an injured elder—*crap*. The memory of his cane clattering to the marbled tiles flooded me with an ocean of remorse.

Simultaneously, we reached out to adjust each

other's glasses—silly glasses to begin with, down-right comical now that they sat crooked on our tip-to-tip noses. His manicured fingertips brushed my perfectly made-up skin, and my already burning cheeks flushed hotter.

Zing. Zap.

Electrified lust shocked my deprived body. His hat had flown off, revealing a head of thick, silver waves. Distinguished came to mind, followed by sexy. Granted, I'd always had a thing for older men, but not *this* old. Then there was the matter of those Truman Capote shades, his snobby attire and Pills-bury Doughboy gut. This man was so far from my fantasy ideal we may as well have been on opposite poles. Regardless, I couldn't deny a magnetic attraction. It had nothing to do with looks and everything to do with high-octane testosterone. The heat kindling between my legs could peel the paint off of my Subaru.

He quirked a lopsided grin and I realized, with a start, that the attraction was two-sided. Arch Reece might have a soft midsection, but there was nothing soft about the anatomy south of his brown leather belt!

Knowing it would be just my luck today, I glanced down at my cleavage and, yes, indeed, my halter top had shifted. If I breathed too deep, there'd be nipplage.

I adjusted my plunging neckline, ignoring his smirk. Addressing his erection would embarrass us both, I assumed, so instead I prodded his noggin for injuries. His hair felt as dry as his skin looked. Being a cosmetic freak, I could suggest restorative treatments, but my instincts told me to shelve the beauty advice. I knew without looking that we'd acquired an audience. Remembering Arch's lecture regarding being in character 24-7, I settled on a high-pitched voice and a Brooklyn accent. The need to prove myself as a competent actress, especially given this morning's botched audition, was fierce. "Charlie, baby, are you all right?"

The arrogant SOB answered at a volume for my ears only and, I swear, his lips barely moved. "Stone said you take direction well."

It only took a millisecond to realize…I had my hands all over him.

He acknowledged the audience with a coy smile. "My wife," he drawled, shifting into Charles mode as he wrangled us into a sitting position. "She's crazy about me."

Smiling and nodding, the gawkers peeled away. They had places to go, people to see. I had a gig to protect. I resisted an eye roll as I scrambled off Arch's lap, weak-kneed at the memory of his hard-on. I might've bruised his backside, but there was nothing wrong with his ego. From what I'd felt, it was *massive*. "Oh, you," I teased, punctuating my bemused expression with a ridiculous giggle.

I swear the skycap who'd confiscated my suitcase actually sighed. Apparently, he was enchanted with my seemingly low IQ and pumped-up cleavage.

Men.

Speaking of, two security guards swooped in to save the day—albeit belatedly. They hauled Arch to his unsteady feet—good thing his trousers were baggy—dusted him off and displayed, finally, appropriate concern.

I scooped up my purse and travel tote, and retrieved the renegade cane.

My brain wrapped around an idea the same moment I wrapped my fingers around that brass-tipped spindle of polished oak. What if his walking stick, like my sunglasses, was a prop? I'd applied makeup and a hairstyle in keeping with my character. Who's to say Arch hadn't done the same?

A security guard offered my stage husband his hat while the skycap rolled our luggage to the ticket counter. Arch locked hold of his cane with one hand, my elbow with the other. "Our flight boards in eight minutes," he said while finessing me to one of those self-serve, check-in computers. "I hope you can walk fast in those heels."

"I hope you can keep up with that cane."

The corners of his mouth curved as he swiped a credit card and punched the appropriate buttons under the monitor. No verbal response, just that damnable crooked smile. What was going through that mind of his? Was he pleased with my appearance? My performance? *Did I pass the audition?* I wanted to ask, but didn't. If he said something like, *Not particularly, but you'll have to do,* chances were, I'd self-destruct.

Scraping the bottom of my emotional well for an iota of self-confidence, I hung back and checked out the scene. Why were we in character *now?* Were other cast members present and currently blending in? How did this play into our cruise ship performance? I had a dozen questions but didn't want to alienate Arch. I didn't want to blow this gig, whatever it was. I needed the distraction as badly as the money. As if this day hadn't been wacky enough, what was with my bizarre attraction to a stuffed-shirt actor who appeared to be several years my senior?

Older man-younger woman.

Visions of Michael and Sasha rolling around in our old bed flashed in my head.

Ouch.

Old news. Old hurt. Why did it feel so fresh?

"Dinnae get skittish on me now, Sugar," Arch said as he punched more buttons.

Did he sense my turmoil or was he merely pointing out the fact that I wasn't hanging all over him as directed? I couldn't help comparing the two of us to Michael and Sasha. The age difference chafed. Not to mention the thought of snuggling with another woman's man. Did Arch have a significant other? I knew our alliance was a charade. All the same, guilt pumped through me at the thought of groping someone's loved one.

I squeezed in close, my voice a controlled hush. "Are you married?"

"Is that a trick question, love, or did that tumble ball up your memory?" The automated system spit out our boarding passes. He retrieved the e-tickets with his right hand while waggling his ring finger. "You and I were married three weeks ago in Vegas."

"I mean for real," I cringed at my obvious impatience, swallowed hard when Arch turned to face me.

His expression and tone were neutral, but his words stung like salt to an open wound. "So that's what he meant by conservative, yeah?"

He, I assumed, was Michael. I interpreted conservative to mean predictable, boring. Had Michael bitched to this man about my inadequacies? My temper flared in tandem with buried hurt. *Conservative.* I suddenly felt like a Hush Puppies loafer in a closet of Jimmy Choo high heels.

Before I could lash out, Arch moved in. He cradled the back of my head, nuzzled my ear. "No spouse. No one special. This is strictly business, yeah?"

So, he was unattached, available. *Single.* My knees wobbled with relief, or…something. His gentle touch and caring tone worked like balm on my raw nerves. He brushed his lips across my cheek and the heat between my legs raged. Good Lord.

"In or *oot?*" he asked when the ticket agent called, "Dupont!"

Because I suspected Michael expected me to bail, and because going back to what I knew in Atlantic City was scarier just now than sailing the Atlantic with a complete stranger, I croaked, "in," swallowing a sentimental lump when Arch produced a wedding band and slipped it onto my third finger. I'd ditched Michael's ring the day he'd ditched me. Wish I could say the same for my lingering affections.

I wrestled with my issues as Arch wrestled with our luggage. Whether his grunting effort was feigned or real, I didn't know. The ticket agent and I both gave him a hand with Big Red. When she advised him of an additional charge due to the excess weight, he produced a wad of bills and paid cash. He didn't comment, though he did cast me a sidelong glance.

I smiled, trying to look cute and clueless.

The ticket agent looped destination tags around the baggage handles. "I need to see your boarding passes and photo IDs, please."

I reached into my purse, but Arch squeezed my free hand, offering the agent two passports from his inner jacket pocket.

The woman gave the documents a cursory glance before handing them back. "Your flight leaves out of gate A6. If you don't hurry, you'll miss it." She noted Arch's cane. "I'll have transportation waiting on the other side of the security screening checkpoint."

Though curious about those passports, my thoughts centered on Arch as we ascended the escalator. He moved pretty fast for a man with a limp. I started to say, a man of his age, but I didn't know his age. I reminded myself that this was an act. Charles Dupont was a character. Were the deep creases in his forehead genuine or the result of expertly applied makeup? Was that trimmed beard—one of those perpetual five-o-clock shadows—homegrown or store-bought? Were his shoulders truly stooped or was he purposely slouching? What about his awkward gait? Real or affected? His current accent differed slightly from the one I'd heard on the phone, and again I couldn't pinpoint it, except to say it was Cary Grant-like, which was in keeping with Curtis's portrayal of the snobby oil tycoon.

I pushed my sunglasses up on top of my head, trying to see through Arch's disguise, and saw that other people were staring, as well. Not at Arch per se, but at us as a couple. The novelist and the showgirl. Arthur Miller and Marilyn Monroe. Talk about your odd couple.

For a moment, I identified with the young woman who'd professed undying love for Michael Stone. Then I thought about my love for the same man, and quickly threw up barriers. I didn't want to sympathize with Sasha. I didn't even like her. She'd stolen my husband.

Conflicting emotions stormed the wall around my heart like a battering ram. The best I could do was smile Sugar's smile and walk Sugar's walk as Arch maneuvered me through the security checkpoint and onto the golf cart thing that sped us to our gate.

By the time we boarded our plane and took our seats, he'd flashed those passports twice more. As soon as I caught my breath, I intended to ask for a look. Just now I absorbed the captain's announcement regarding rough weather, dug in my tote for a Dramamine and struggled with the rumblings of a full-blown panic attack.

CHAPTER FIVE

I WOKE UP IN A DARK ROOM in a strange bed. Where was I? Where was Arch?

My heart and head pounded with a ferocity that made my stomach roil. I'd been dreaming about going down in flames—my career, not the plane. Standing in front of a car dealership in ninety-degree weather, wearing a gorilla costume and holding a sign that said, You'll go APE for our prices!

That's what you get for flashing those forty-one-year-old tits, Michael had admonished, standing next to a Cadillac, his arms wrapped around pubescent versions of Sasha and Britney.

I massaged my aching chest, waited for the depressing fog of the nightmare to dissipate. But, dammit, it clung. Just as I'd clung to my alcoholic beverage as the plane had dipped and bounced through that electrical storm. Probably hadn't been smart to mix Dramamine with two glasses of vodka and cranberry. In fact, I sort of remembered someone saying so. An older man with nerves of steel and a sexy smile.

Arch.

I also sort of remembered him half carrying me out of the airport and finessing me into a cab. I had a vague memory of peeling off my cashmere shrug because the air was hot and sticky, and noting the palm trees and Monet sunset with a slurred, "Beautiful, beautiful."

Arch had agreed.

Everything else was a blur.

At least my jaw hadn't locked, and I hadn't puked my guts into an airsick bag. Not that I recalled, anyway.

Determined to pull myself together, I flicked on the bedside lamp and padded toward the bathroom, wiping drool from the corner of my mouth—*lovely*. I needed to wash my face, down two glasses of water and pee. Not necessarily in that order.

A scream lodged in my throat when I eased open the door. A dark-haired, broad-shouldered man hovered over the sink, squirting hair product into his hand. Smoke curled from the cigarette anchored between his lips. Black wires dangled from the buds lodged in his ear.

Paralyzed, or maybe I should say *mesmerized* since this stranger's body was freaking *hot*, my gaze trailed down his sculpted back, following the wires that led to a superslim MP3 player clipped to the threadbare hotel-issue towel wrapped around his taut waist. I glanced farther down and caught his bare foot tapping to whatever music he was listening to.

Whoever he was, he'd just showered. The steamy room smelled of Irish Spring, tobacco and shaving cream. It was a sexy scent, smoke and all. Probably because it was so manly. I breathed in the testosterone-charged air and nearly climaxed on the spot.

He shifted and dragged his gelled fingers through his wet hair, the muscles in his shoulders rolling with the effort. I told myself to stop staring at his impressive biceps—was that a Celtic band tattooed on his right arm?—and to back away from the threshold with my dignity intact. Was this another cast member? The producer? Where was Arch and why had he left me alone with a stranger?

My fantasies took a detour and kicked into hyperdrive along with my pulse. What if this was all a bizarre plot to get rid of me? For good. Maybe Sasha had brainwashed Michael. Lord knows she'd done something to get him to the gym every day. Maybe Arch had been hired to deliver me to this guy. Maybe he was going to whack me or sell me to some wife-collecting sheik!

Maybe I should lay off Dramamine and B movies.

The dark stranger snuffed his cigarette, nabbed a hand towel and swiped it over the fogged-up mirror. Our gazes locked.

He turned and pulled out the earbuds.

I yelped and shot backward, tripping over something big and red—Big Red—screaming—I was me, not Sugar—when the stranger rushed out of the bathroom.

I landed flat on my back.

He landed flat on top of me, his big hand covering my mouth. "Stop screaming, for fuck's sake. It's me. Arch."

I recognized the voice, the accent, if not the man. I blinked up at him, amazed. Although, I should've known. All that testosterone. "Wah hahpn oo yor air?"

He removed his hand from my mouth. "What?"

"What happened to your hair?" I repeated. This afternoon it had been stark silver. Now it was jet-black, although it would probably lighten a shade when it dried.

"Temporary dye. Washes *oot* in the shower."

A thigh-tingling image came to mind. Mr. Manly Man buck naked. Hot water sluicing over that hot bod. My insides melted as I stared up at him transfixed. He was handsome, in a bad boy sort of way, early to mid-thirties. That closely trimmed beard, when silver, had made him look significantly older. Just now he looked rebellious. His grey-green gaze sparked with mischief. His face, less creased and more defined than upon first meeting, suggested a hard-knock maturity. His body suggested he worked out religiously. Amen.

Snap out of it, Evie. "Did your wrinkles wash off, too?" I asked, tongue-in-cheek as opposed to tongue-hanging-out-of-mouth. *Pant. Pant. Drool. Drool.*

His sinfully attractive lips quirked. "Peeled off, actually. Prosthetics."

If I'd had the slightest doubt, that crooked grin confirmed his identity. Arch Reece had a killer smile to go with his killer form. A rock-hard body that was presently squished against me. My heart continued to race although it had nothing to do with fear. "Um. So I guess that beer gut was fake, too."

"Strap on, strap off." The grin turned wicked. "What *aboot* you, Sunshine?"

My mind blanked then he raised himself up an inch or so and leered down at my bountiful cleavage.

Oh.

I smirked. "They're real."

"Impressive."

"With the help of major padding, yes." The ogling continued so I cleared my throat. I wanted him to roll aside. The pressure on my bladder reminded me how badly I needed to pee. "Do you mind?"

"Not at all. I value the benefits of push-up brassieres."

"I mean, do you mind getting off?"

"Why, Ms. Parish, we hardly know each other."

Lingering chemicals dulled my wit. By the time light dawned, he'd shifted his weight.

"You may want to close your eyes, love."

"Why?" I asked at the same time I realized something hard pressed against my thigh. Something massive. I rolled my eyes to cover my own arousal. "What are you, on Viagra?"

"What can I say? You're lovely."

If I'd thought he was sincere, I would have blushed with joy. "Yeah, right." I could only imagine what I looked like just now. Tangled hair, bloodshot eyes, wrinkled clothes. I'd probably smeared red lipstick across my chin when I'd wiped away the drool. Lovely. *Snort*. "Bet you say that to all of your costars."

"Only the stunners."

Oh, brother. Now I knew he was playing me. This guy was a textbook charmer. And *I* was way too vulnerable and horny. "I have to pee." There. That should kill the moment.

"Right." He stared down at me, one brow raised. *Those eyes*. My heart pitter-pattered. *Can't. Breathe*. Now I knew why he wore those kooky, tinted glasses in public. They kept the average woman from swooning in his path. If that failed, he could beat them off with his cane.

"Fair warning, love. Lost my towel in the tumble."

Still going for worldly, I said, "Nothing I haven't seen before."

Yeah, boy, *that* was a lie. If this were a Warner Brothers cartoon, *ah-ooo-gah!* would have been the sound effect accompanying the visual of my eyeballs literally springing out of my head as Arch pushed to his feet—full monty. It's not as if he stood there posing. I got a two-second glimpse, tops.

Regardless, the image was burned into my brain. Holy smoke.

Then he turned around to step into a pair of grey sweatpants and I got a good look at his butt. A spectacular butt. Not quite as breathtaking as John Thomas, but impressive all the same.

I scrambled to my feet and into the bathroom before I said something stupid like, *"Nice ass,"* or *"Is that penis for real?"* While I was in there doing my thing, I collected my wits and memories. In one day, I'd been a flasher *and* a flashee. If you asked me, I was fast on my way to forfeiting my conservative crown. Sullying my reputation and rubbing Michael's nose in it was a tempting goal.

At least I had something to work toward. I'd already turned cynical; surely I could handle adventurous. So long as it didn't involve turbulence or rocky seas.

The plane ride came back in mortifying chunks. By the time I'd washed my hands and finger-combed my hair, I'd remembered everything right up until I'd fallen asleep—make that passed out—which was probably one hour into the flight from hell.

I opened the bathroom door and leaned against the doorjamb, feeling foolish and confused.

Arch sat at the desk, his callus-free fingers attacking the keyboard of a laptop. My first thought was that he was writing me out of the script. My second thought was that he looked nearly as sexy wearing sweats and a baggy T-shirt as he did wearing a towel. Nearly.

"You held my hand when we hit that bad patch of turbulence. You engaged me in a game of movie trivia to distract me from getting sick." His knowledge of the classics floored me. Michael used to disappear when I indulged in any film dated pre-Technicolor. I cleared my throat, tucked my hair behind one ear. "Thank you for being so understanding."

"Thank you for not hurling on me."

"So am I, you know, fired?"

"For what?"

"For getting wasted on the job."

"This *job* requires an actress who can convincingly play the role of Sugar Dupont whenever in public," he said, typing and talking at the same time. *How did he do that?* "You followed my cues and stayed in character even though you were pissed. That's bloody impressive, yeah?"

I blushed at the compliment. "Well, thank you. Except, I wasn't angry."

He glanced at me over his shoulder.

"Wait. Don't tell me. Across the pond, *pissed* is slang for trashed. Heard it in a movie." I shifted my weight, angled my head. "So what are you? Scottish? British? Irish?"

"Aye." He pushed out of his chair. "Are you hungry?"

I blinked at the swift change of subject. Plus, I wasn't clear on his answer to my question. Maybe he was a little of all three. *Aye* was Scottish, right?

But *pissed*…wasn't that a Brit thing? Yet at other times I caught a twinge of a "Danny Boy" lilt.

I glanced around the generic hotel room. "Where are we, anyway?" Surely I would've remembered boarding a honking-big cruise ship. Granted, I'd been looped—I'm one of those people who gets fog-brained on cold medicine—but not *that* looped.

"An airport hotel. Tomorrow morning we'll cab over to the cruise port, board the ship. That's when the real work begins." He snatched a room service menu from a side table, gave it a three-second glance, then passed it to me. "It's half-past eight and I haven't eaten since morning."

Come to think of it, neither had I. "I could stand a little something." Like a big, juicy cheeseburger and a plate of fries smothered in brown gravy. I settled on a mixed salad and bottled water with lemon. After seeing Arch's body, I was more than a little self-conscious about my soft spots. Tomorrow I might even do aerobics. *Gag.*

He shifted back to his laptop, closed the file he'd been working in and shut down. "You want a sandwich with that salad?"

Yes. "No."

"Hung over?"

No. "Yes." Sort of. Mostly, I wanted to tone up overnight. Like that was going to happen. But, hey, that's what I do. Dream. Imagine. Pretend. According to my mom, my free spirit was at the root of all my problems. If I'd gone to college like my brother,

I would have had a teaching degree to fall back on. Instead, I was looking at life as a gorilla.

"Why *dinnae* you shower?" Arch said as he moved toward the phone. "Change into something comfortable?"

"As in skimpy?" The notion appalled and intrigued me. Talk about confused.

His lips twitched. "Would you be comfortable eating dinner and going over your character profile in your bra and panties?"

"Are you asking Sugar or me?"

"You."

"Then, no."

"*Didnae* think so."

His cocky grin liquefied my bones. Wow. Instead of melting into a puddle, I dropped to my knees and popped the latches of Big Red.

Arch chuckled and reached for the phone. It chimed, which was weird since he was calling out. He replaced the receiver and snagged a cell phone off the desk. "Yeah?"

He really needed to work on his greetings.

"Are you mental?" He jammed a hand through his damp waves. "Bugger off, mate. It's too late."

I tried not to listen. Okay. That's a lie. My curiosity kept me from discreetly escaping into the bathroom. I dawdled over my suitcase, located my toiletry bag and picked through my loungewear.

"Why *dinnae* we leave it up to Evie?"

I froze at the sound of my name, looked up just as Arch reached down and handed me his phone.

My skin sizzled from his touch, brief though it was. Without a word he settled on the bed, kicked back—ankles crossed, hands behind his head. Like me, I guess he intended to eavesdrop.

Heart pounding, I sat back on my heels, pressed the cell to my ear. "Yeah?" Lame greeting. An Arch greeting. But the best I could manage since I didn't know who was on the other end of the line.

"Do not get on that ship with Arch."

Michael. "Why not?"

"I made a mistake, hon. Come home."

My stomach knotted. I broke into a clammy sweat. *Don't puke. Don't puke.* Was he talking about Sasha? Suddenly, after a year of hootchy-kootchy with Miss January of the Beach Hut Babe calendar, he wanted to reunite with me? Insane hope surged through my blood. "What are you saying?"

"You're not up to this job."

Good thing I was sitting, otherwise, my knees would've buckled. I clenched my jaw, cursed the dreamer in me and willed my heart to keep beating. "Why not?"

"For one you get seasick."

"I have Dramamine." *I wish I had a pill to cure me of you.*

"I don't trust Arch."

"I don't trust you. But we still work together. Sort of."

Dead air.

He was probably trying to formulate an excuse for my lack of bookings without targeting my age. Somehow I resisted the urge to launch Arch's phone against the wall.

"I wasn't thinking straight when I booked you on this," he finally said. "I was in a hurry and you were…"

"Desperate?"

"Yes, dammit." He sighed. "Come home, Evie. I just got a call from Dooley's. They're looking for someone to host karaoke on Tuesday nights."

"Pass."

"Something else will come up."

"Something already did." I scooped up my toiletry bag and a change of clothes, forced myself to my feet. "I'll see you in eight days, Michael."

He lowered his voice, and I had to wonder if Sasha was within earshot. "I don't want you to get hurt, hon."

"Like Arch said…too late." I thumbed off the power, calmly placed the phone on the desk. I headed for the bathroom without looking at the man my ex didn't trust. I didn't want to consider why. My brain was already reeling. "I'll be out in a few minutes."

"I'll order room service."

I waited until I was in the shower, hot water pounding, before I gave in to tears.

CHAPTER SIX

LIFE WAS CRUEL.

I watched Arch inhale a deluxe burger and fries while I picked at my salad. I didn't even like salad. He also swilled beer while I sipped calorie-free, flavor-free water.

The waiter had forgotten my wedge of lemon.

"Do you always eat like that?" I asked.

He aimed a ketchup-drenched fry at my boring rabbit food. "Do you?"

"I'm watching my weight."

"Why?"

"You're kidding. Are you or are you not in entertainment?"

"I'm a man," he said by way of an answer. "Men like curves." He chewed the fry, swilled more beer. "Let's go over it one more time, yeah?"

Considering my generous hips, I think he just complimented me, but I couldn't be sure, and I wasn't going to ask. Bad boy was all business now. Michael's call had dampened his playful mood. I wasn't happy about the call, either, although I felt better since the cry in the shower. I couldn't wash away the hurt, but I did manage to rejuvenate my body. Swapping Sugar's tight clothes for drawstring pants and an oversize Betty Boop T-shirt also helped. Ah, comfort.

I'd taken longer in the bathroom than I'd intended, but no way, no how was I going to face Mr. Manly Man on our first night together sans beauty products.

After drying my hair, I slathered my skin with French Vanilla lotion then applied mascara and sheer pink lip balm. Anything more would have been ridiculous considering we were going to turn in after dinner.

"Would it help if I gave you the written profile?" Arch asked, offering me a sheet of paper from his notebook. "Gave you more time to absorb? I know it's a bit of information."

I ignored the profile, stabbed a tomato wishing it were a meatball. Michael would have ordered me the burger without asking. Even though the salad held the appeal of grass, I decided it was kind of nice being in the company of a man who didn't know me any better than I knew him. I decided now was a good time to dazzle Arch with one of my special skills.

"My name is Sugar Louise Dupont, maiden name Jones. Born and raised in Brooklyn, New York." Something he'd revised since I'd adopted the accent on my own. "I'm a singer. Was a singer. A Vegas lounge lizard to be exact." Another revision since I was too short to be a showgirl. "I bounced from stage to stage, man to man, looking for the perfect fit." I batted my lashes. "Then I met you. It was love at first sight, well, for you, anyway. No wonder. You had a front-row seat at the midnight show as I performed "Fever" in a skintight gown—red—cut down to my navel and slit up to my thigh."

I ignored his knee-melting grin and plowed on. "You sent a bottle of champagne backstage. Attached was a romantic note. An original poem that won my heart. I adored you before we even met. Later that night you took me out to dinner, swept me off my acrylic stilettos. One week later we were married in Gabriel's Chapel of Love. All told we've only known each other for one month, hence we're still learning the details of one another's lives. Convenient," I said, ditching the tomato for a cucumber. "In case you screw up."

Arch leaned forward, picked at the label of his bottle. "I *willnae* screw up."

"Neither will I." I leaned in, as well. "I'm a quick study."

"So I've noticed."

"My improvisational skills rock."

"Witnessed that on the plane, yeah?"

The plane. "About that. I just want you to know, I'm not much of a drinker."

"I gathered."

"I mean, I'm not a lush. I've just had… It's been a rough…day."

"Want to talk *aboot* it?"

"No, thanks." I nibbled on a cucumber.

He took a long pull of his beer, settled back in his chair. "Right then. Tell me *aboot* Charles Dupont."

Every now and then I was ultraconscious of his accent and I found myself smiling because, gosh, it was sexy. *About* sounded like *aboot* and *will not* came out *willnae*. We won't talk about what his tongue did to *R*s. A nimble tongue like that could probably—well, we won't go there.

He quirked a brow as if to say, what's the holdup? I didn't want to explain that I was aroused by his accent. So, I repeated everything he'd told me, down to the year his first wife died and the names of his deceased pets and estranged children. Not that I was trying to impress him.

Well, yeah, I guess I was.

He lived on an estate in Connecticut—Charles, not Arch. Came from old money. I, Sugar, didn't know where it originated exactly, only that he had tons of it. Yup, Charlie was loaded. He was also a writer. Published under a pseudonym. Unlike Sugar, the man shunned the spotlight.

He also shunned women his own age.

He'd sprained his ankle, hence the cane, after tripping while chasing me around the room in the midst of playful sex.

Too bad that was only part of the profile. Sounds like fun.

Arch leaned back in his chair, considered me with those lightning eyes.

Zap.

Yeah, boy, I felt *that*. Interest.

"You're good."

"Thanks." If those casino execs would've paid attention when I'd delivered that copy, they, too, might have been impressed with my memory skills. It felt good to be appreciated. "You're not so bad yourself." It wasn't my style to gloat—even though I was sort of needy in the compliment department just now—so I turned the attention on him. Besides, I truly was impressed with Arch Reece the Actor. "When I first saw you, I thought you were, like, I don't know, sixty."

"Prosthetics."

"I get that, and I'm in awe. I've never explored anything outside of traditional theatrical makeup. But it's more than that. Your body language, the costume. You came off like a foppish tycoon with the hots for a brainless bimbo. Just like in *Some Like It Hot*. Although, Tony Curtis?" I snorted. "Try Truman Capote."

Actually, he'd more closely resembled a bespectacled Sean Connery, post-James Bond. Like Arch, Connery possessed a timeless charisma. No way was I confessing a bad case of thigh-sweats for either man.

One side of his mouth kicked up. "If you recall, I did say Curtis with a twist, yeah?"

"Yeah." That was another thing about his accent. Three-quarters of his statements sounded like questions, even when he didn't finish with his signature, *yeah?* I remember I used to think the same thing about the dude in *The Highlander* TV series. *Why does everything sound like a question, and why do I find that so sexy?* Of course, the whole package was sexy…like Arch.

Zing. Zap.

I squeezed my legs together. Best not to think about Arch's package.

"By the way," I added, while pushing aside my salad, "if this weren't a slapstick murder mystery, I'd be totally offended by Sugar's stereotypical personality. I know lots of casino lounge singers— hello, *I'm* one—and none of them—" I paused "—well, ninety-eight percent of them are not brainless bimbos."

"If you remember, Sugar was originally a showgirl, and who said anything *aboot* a murder mystery?"

I opened my mouth to defend dancers who just happened to be comfortable wearing pasties on their nips and balancing extravagant headpieces on their pretty noggins, but I got sidetracked by that murder mystery part. "I just assumed, I mean, we are acting in an interactive production of some sort, right?"

"Is that what Stone told you?"

"No. He said that I'd be playing a ditzy character and that I needed to participate in passenger activities."

"That's the sum of it."

"There's no show?"

"It's more of an illusion."

"Like magic?"

"Like smoke and mirrors."

"For what purpose?"

"For the greater good."

What did *that* mean? "Is there a production manager, director, someone in charge?"

He spread his hands wide. "You're looking at him, love."

"You're the whole enchilada? Cast, crew, management?"

"Is that a problem?"

I didn't know. I'd heard of a one-man or -woman show, but those generally took place in a theater. I thought back to something he'd said earlier today. *The world is our stage.* I guess he meant that literally. Needing to work off the anxiety sparking along my spine, I pushed away from our makeshift dining table, stood and paced. "Can you be more specific about our purpose? That greater good thing?"

"No."

Huh. Well, okay, this was just weird.

He shifted in his seat, rested his forearms on his thighs. His sleeves rode up and I got another glimpse of those defined biceps. That Celtic tattoo sensitized my body like foreplay. Tribal. Hot. *Yowza.*

"Here's the deal, Evie. I need you to play Sugar,

my attentive wife. I need you to be the life of the party, yeah? A social butterfly. I want you to have a fantastic time on the ship."

"Do I look like I just fell off of a turnip truck?"

"What do you mean?"

I stopped in front of him, hands on hips. "You're paying me a lot of money to have *fun?*"

"I'm paying you to create a unique deception."

My pulse fluttered at the word *deception*. "Is it illegal?"

"No." He looked me dead in the eye, his expression serene as a monk. "We good?"

It took me a second to catch my breath. Those eyes of his were…I don't know. Mesmerizing, I guess. They made you want to say yes, to anything. This guy was flipping dangerous.

So, why wasn't I backing away?

"Just so I have this straight. The goal is to deceive someone. Someone bad, I guess, since we're doing this for the greater good. That would also explain Michael's mention of risk. That bad person, I guess he's dangerous."

So much for serene. The flash of annoyance was brief, but I caught it before he broke eye contact and nabbed the beer bottle. "You're safe with me."

I believed him. It wasn't the fact that he looked as though he could pound the hell out of "The Rock," it was more the sense that he could talk himself out of a pact with the devil.

Oh, yeah, I was curious about this man. I was

curious about a lot of things, but he'd made it clear that we were operating on a need-to-know basis. And, hey now, there was a thought—maybe the less I knew, the better off I'd be.

"Michael doesn't think I'm up for this job," I said more to myself than Arch.

He stood, putting us toe-to-toe and warping my brain cells with a heady dose of machismo. "What do you think?"

I peered up at him, wet my lips. "I think I love a challenge."

He grinned. "My kind of girl."

Blood thundered in my ears like a rocker's bass drum—louder, harder. Oh, crap, my heart was going to pull an *Alien* and burst through my chest. Wouldn't *that* be lovely?

I waited for him to touch me. My hair was in my eyes. Why didn't he reach up and tuck those rebel locks behind my ears like they do in romance novels? Yes, I read them—what's not to like about happily-ever-afters? Someday, I fully expected mine.

Arch was not following the script in my head, so I revised it. I brushed my own hair out of my eyes, held his gaze. Talk about a challenge. "I'm crazy about you. Can't keep my hands off of you."

No expression. No response.

"Sugar," I clarified, trying to get a bead on him and failing. "That's what you said, right?"

"Right."

"So I guess that means hugging and kissing and stuff."

"When in public, aye."

What about behind closed doors? I wanted to ask, but didn't. "As an actor I'm sure you know how uncomfortable it can be doing it with a stranger. Kissing, that is. For the first time, I mean." I willed my voice not to warble. Blushing was another matter. "So I'm thinking our first time shouldn't be in front of an audience."

"You think we should kiss. Now."

For once his response sounded like a statement instead of a question. My blood pumped. The spirit of my friend Nicole cheered in my ear. *You go, girl!*

"As a professional, I take my job seriously. I know this is an improvisational gig, but a certain amount of rehearsal seems wise. After all, we've been doing it, getting it on, Sugar and Charles that is, for a month. If you want people to believe we're in lust—um, love—we should look like we've been around. Each other, that is. Intimately."

He scraped his teeth over his lower lip. Nice teeth. Nice mouth. "Appreciate your dedication, Sunshine."

I couldn't tell if he was serious or sarcastic, and right now I didn't care. I wanted him to kiss me, dammit. I wanted something in this miserable day to go right. Was that so wrong?

"Let's just get it out of the way," I plowed on. "The awkwardness—misaligned mouths, bumping noses and all that."

Except there was no awkwardness. He swooped in without warning, framed my face, ravished my mouth. He kissed the ever-lovin' daylights out of me.

His beard scratched and ignited my skin. Rough. Hot. *Primal*.

His tongue… Oh sweet, Lord, my panties were damp and all he was doing was *kissing* me!

It seemed like forever. It seemed like a blip. Next thing I knew, he was standing six inches back, draining the last of his beer.

I fought a dizzy spell and resisted the urge to glance down to see if JT had roared to life. I was, after all, a professional. Those superior acting skills kept my knees and voice from quaking. "I guess we're good then." We were better than good. We were Bogie and Bacall, sizzling hot!

"Right." Arch tugged on a ball cap and denim jacket, snatched a cigarette from the pack on the desk and announced he needed a smoke. "*Dinnae* open the door for anyone. I have a key, yeah?"

I watched as he left and shut the door behind him.

Yeah. That went well.

Not.

Bewitched, bothered and bewildered, as the song goes, I weaved across the room, drunk on the headiness of that kiss. Hands trembling, I rooted through Big Red for my most current diary, a girlie-pink-and-white journal entitled *Secrets of a Diva*.

Knowing I tended to bottle up my feelings, my dad had bought me my first diary when I was ten, telling me when my brain and heart were all jammed up, I should pour my thoughts onto the pages. My brain and heart were definitely jammed. Today had been a total freak-fest. And that *kiss*…

I unlocked the diary using the key I kept hidden in my wallet then grabbed my purple pen. The familiarity of the process provided me with a small dose of comfort. At this point, I'd take what I could get.

Dear Diary, Why are men such asses?

CHAPTER SEVEN

Atlantic City, New Jersey
The Chameleon Club

MILO BECKETT STOOD at the living room window of his second-floor apartment, hands braced on the scarred sash. Jaw set, he stared out at the Atlantic Ocean. Not that he could see it. He'd invest in a bottle of glass cleaner, but it would ruin the desired effect. His apartment was directly above his place of business—The Chameleon Club.

Seedy was the objective. He didn't want the Inlet Tavern to attract a large clientele. The club was a front. The government operative's goal was to blend in.

Like a chameleon.

Milo was good at fooling the masses. He'd learned from the best. His mentor, his nemesis, his partner in crime. Right now he was pissed as hell at the man.

Ocean gazing usually lowered his blood pressure, but he couldn't see the damned ocean. A grainy film of sand and dirt streaked the outer pane, compliments of a nor'easter. The quarter moon skulked behind ominous clouds. An occasional flash of lightning illuminated choppy seas and the driving rain battering the Inlet's boardwalk. One working streetlamp flickered on and off. Mostly off. The scene was dark and dangerous.

Like Milo's mood.

Downstairs, a cheap audio system dished jazz classics, his music of choice. Jazz soothed his soul and kept the twentysomething customers at bay. John Coltrane's version of "My Favorite Things" floated up through the heating ducts along with patron chatter. A couple of local seniors nursed drinks and swapped stories with Samuel Vine, The Chameleon Club's primary bartender, the man who ran the tavern when Milo was in the field. Pushing seventy, the dark-skinned ex-boxer was still formidable, but also dependable as the rising sun. Honesty in Milo's line of work was as rare as a thirty-year-old virgin. He'd learned long ago not to trust anyone.

Especially Arch Duvall.

He smelled more than heard Woody, the newest member of the unconventional dream team, enter the room through the secret stairwell. Dumped by his girlfriend, the twenty-five-year-old techno-geek had been trying to win her back for weeks. New haircut, new clothes. This week: new cologne.

It reeked. Aside from flies, all he'd attract with that flowery stench were curious looks.

Milo didn't figure it was worth mentioning since

they weren't on a case. Woody, nicknamed The Kid, was a sensitive bastard. He was also brilliant. He'd been holed up in the basement for the past few hours doing what he did best—cracking and tracking.

"Did you find him?" Milo asked without turning.

"How'd you know it was me and not Vine?"

"I'm psychic."

Woody snorted. "You saw my reflection in the window, right?"

Milo couldn't see shit in that window. "You got me." Another thing he'd learned from Arch. The art of lying. He turned, folded his arms over his chest. "So?"

"It wasn't easy, sir."

"Milo," he prompted, although it was wasted breath. Woody had been on the team for three months. He'd yet to drop formalities where his boss was concerned. Respect had been ingrained in the Midwestern boy by the grandparents who'd raised him. He twanged *ma'am* and *sir* without thought. *Sir* made Milo's balls twitch. Aside from making him feel old, it reminded him of the bureaucratic bullshit that had resulted in him overstepping and his wife stepping out.

The only time anyone referred to him as *Sir* or *Agent Beckett* was when he was at HQ, which, to their mutual relief, wasn't often. He'd earned a reputation as a hot dog. If he weren't so tight with the director, he'd be out on his forty-seven-year-old ass. As far as his team was concerned, the A.I.A.—Artful Intelligence Agency—operated on a "the-less-we-know-the-better" policy. He had a directive. Results, within blurred reason, were all that mattered.

Like the ones tucked away in Woody's eccentric mind. Milo angled his head. "Where is he?"

"Fort Lauderdale. Traveled under the name of Charles Dupont."

Arch was a pro at operating under the radar. Woody was good, but he shouldn't have been able to track him this fast. Arch must have slipped.

Something was wrong.

"Tomorrow he's sailing for San Juan on an adults-only cruise. The Fiesta line focuses on romance in the golden years. Caters mostly to second honeymooners, couples celebrating anniversaries. Kind of a geriatric *Love Boat*."

The Benson file.

"Son of a bitch." Milo strode to the hall closet, yanked a suitcase from the shelf.

The flowery stench followed him into his bedroom. "Do you think he's up to his old tricks, sir?"

"I think he's taking an unauthorized vacation." Read: Defying team policy by acting solo. Worse, acting outside of A.I.A. jurisdiction. Chameleon's license-to-shill wasn't valid on foreign soil. They had domestic leeway, not international carte blanche.

And Arch knew it.

Milo crammed the case full of casual and formal wear, processing details. Vine and Woody could handle the bar. He'd have to keep A.I.A in the dark in order to keep Arch's ass, and his own, out of a sling.

Woody scratched at his sparse goatee, also new. "Guess you're going after him." For a smart kid, he often stated the obvious.

"I need you to make travel arrangements." This was the second time in eight months Arch had gone renegade. Milo's patience was spent.

"Done."

He glanced up.

The shaggy-haired boy, who presently resembled a modern-day beatnik, shrugged. "Figured it was the next logical move given your mood when you ordered me to track Ace."

Aka Arch. Grifters referred to their underworld aliases as *monikers*. Thanks to Arch, every team member had one. Even Milo. Woody referred to everyone on the team by their monikers, except for Milo. Nope. Milo was *Sir*.

Ignoring his twitching balls, he clasped shut his case, pulled on a leather jacket and silently cursed Arch "Ace" Duvall. "I don't know why I bother," he muttered.

"Because it's what friends do."

He let that pass. His relationship with Arch was complicated. No one, aside from Milo and Arch, knew the particulars. He intended to keep it that way.

Woody handed him a stuffed envelope. "I made arrangements for two. It's a couples' cruise."

Woody hadn't been on the team for long but he

knew Arch's history. Knew he was up to something and that he'd just reeled in his *friend*. Whether he wanted in or not, Milo was now part of Arch's game. He'd stick out like a sore thumb if he showed up single for a couples' cruise.

"I called Hot Legs. She's packing. You can pick her up on the way to A.C. International."

Gina Valente, aka Hot Legs, was an ex-cop with a gift for grifting. A valuable asset, she often ensnared marks via her feminine wiles. He wasn't keen on dragging her into this mess, but now, thanks to Arch, this was Chameleon business. "You're two steps ahead of me, Kid."

"Three." He gestured to the envelope.

Milo thumbed through the contents. Travel documents. Passports. Character profiles… Aw, hell. "Why this guy?"

"You've played him before. You're already prepped. We've got the wardrobe in stock and we're on a tight schedule. He's middle-aged, but he's rich."

"He's annoying."

"He gets on Ace's nerves, that's for sure."

Milo cracked his first smile of the day. He shrugged out of the leather jacket, opened the suitcase to swap out the wardrobe.

Woody hovered nearby, rubbing the back of his neck—his nervous tell.

"What?"

"There's something else, sir."

"Spit it out."

"Ace enlisted an unsanctioned player."

CHAPTER EIGHT

AFTER AN HOUR of scribbling in my diary, rehashing a day of rash actions, and checking in with Nicole via a brief phone call, I'd fallen into a fitful sleep. Most people have nightmares about showing up at an important event in their underwear. I showed up topless.

I'd have to ask Jayne, a new age enthusiast, to look up the interpretation of breasts in one of her dream books. Or not. Maybe I didn't want to know. Maybe it symbolized a need for my mother—please save me from the big, bad world. Only the last person I'd run to is my I-told-you-so mom who *told* me to go to college. *You could've been a teacher,* I could hear her saying. *Instead you're a gorilla.* Or maybe the topless bit simply meant that I was destined to lose my shirt.

Great.

I blinked up at the ceiling, thought about the days to come and how I'd be spending them with Arch. Surprisingly, the hurricane of loneliness that generally ruined my mornings weakened to a Category One. Last night's kiss lingered and sparked under my skin like a summer lightning storm. The man was not only dangerous, but potent.

I kicked off the sheets, scooted to the edge of the bed and scanned the darkened room.

He was also missing.

My heart raced with familiar pangs of desertion. *He found you lacking. He's gone.* My jaw throbbed. Falling asleep without my splint—the retainerlike appliance provided by my TMJ specialist—hadn't been smart. Stressful dreams on top of a stressful day make Evie a prime candidate for lockjaw.

I massaged my chest with one hand, my jaw with the other. I told myself to chill. *You've survived a year without Michael. You don't need a man. You don't need Arch.*

I marched over to the window and wrenched open the curtains. Florida sunshine flooded the room. Craving a glass of orange juice, I palmed the warm plate glass and squinted at the blue skies, palm trees and hedges bursting with pink and white flowers.

I thought about Disney World. Maybe I could relocate and get a job there. Maybe I could snag a gig as Goofy or Minnie Mouse—full-body costume. Better than a gorilla suit. At least I'd be hawking fairy tales instead of cars.

Sighing, I turned away from the tropical scenery, my spirits lifting when I realized Arch hadn't vamoosed. His suitcase yawned open, propped up on one of those metal luggage stands. His laptop sat on the desk. A cushioned chair overflowed with rumpled blankets and a pillow, the only proof he'd even returned last night. Add scary-quiet to his bag of tricks.

Since the bathroom door was closed, I assumed Houdini was in there peeing or preening. Maybe he was taking a shower. Maybe I should join him. Yeah, boy, wouldn't *that* be fun? Except I was too chicken to risk rejection. He hadn't seemed impressed with my kissing skills, certainly not enough to join me in bed. I couldn't imagine he'd welcome me in his shower. Last night I'd endured several hours of dreamed humiliation. I had no interest in making them come true, thank you very much.

My gaze skipped back to the chair heaped with bed linens.

Okay. So my stage husband had opted to stretch out in a chair or on the floor rather than next to me. Disappointing, but not devastating. At least he hadn't split. At least I wasn't a total failure, losing husband number two after day number one.

Nicole grumbled in my imagination. *I say he slept on the floor because you gave him a hard-on and he couldn't whack off lying next to you. Well, he could but—*

Yeah, Jayne interrupted. *He didn't sleep with you because he wants to get down and dirty, and he can't because he assured you this is business. At least he's honorable.*

It was a confidence-boosting fantasy and I intended to revel in it like a day at the spa.

The bathroom door creaked open. My pulse accelerated, then stalled. I looked like I'd just rolled out of bed. Which I had. Not the point. The point was cartoon loungewear, bed-head and morning breath. *Ugh.*

I fished a mint out of my purse just as Arch stepped into the room, only it wasn't Arch but Charles. Either he'd risen predawn or he was a quick-change artist of extraordinary skill. My knowledge of the application of prosthetics was nil, however, I'd read in some celebrity rag that it was a long and tedious process. Of course, that had involved transforming a mortal man into a beastly alien. Arch had merely accelerated the aging process.

I blinked at his wrinkles and beer gut, those absurd glasses, and marveled at my lustful reaction. Not a sign of Mr. Manly Man and my engine still revved. I even got a sexual charge out of the scent of Old Spice. Did I ever have it this bad for Michael? I mean, I am-was-am physically attracted to my ex, but I don't remember my body buzzing and humming and my mind blanking as it was now. I knew I should say something but couldn't think of anything other than, *Take me. Take me now.*

"Good morning," he said.

Yeah. *That* would have been the icebreaker. "Good morning." I tugged at the hem of my T-shirt, feeling self-conscious about my appearance. Not that he'd actually looked at me yet.

I crossed my arms over my braless chest and watched as he tucked an artfully knotted red scarf into the mouth of his starched white shirt. Amazing that a man these days even knew *how* to tie an ascot knot. The dated image reminded me of old Hollywood, royal races and Thurston Howell the Third.

Suddenly, I didn't feel quite as silly. I even managed a smile. "Sleep well?"

He nodded. "You?"

"Like a baby." Okay. That was a lie. But I wasn't about to admit I'd tossed and turned when he'd copped forty winks. Unless he was lying, too. Call me hopeful.

I smoothed my hand over my tangled hair, took in his crisp white oxford shirt and creased navy trousers. Talk about conservative. But it somehow worked with his silver hair and those kooky glasses. He really looked like the camera-shy author.

I looked like a delusional fan from a cartoon convention.

Turning away, I rooted through Big Red for a change of clothes. I waited for Arch to bring up that atomic kiss, but he didn't. *Guys avoid mushy talk,* said the spirit of Jayne, to which Nicole added, *Like he's going to admit the earth moved.*

Right. Thanks, girls. I looked over my shoulder to ask him a question and caught him staring. At *me.* Even though he wore an enigmatic expression, the air crackled like the Fourth of July.

Jolted, I cleared my throat and almost choked on my breath mint. *Smooth, Parish.* "Are you…" I flitted a hand toward the bathroom, trying not to hack and cough.

"All yours."

"I'll be out in a few minutes."

"I'll order room service."

We'd spoken those same lines last night. It smacked of an unsettling connection that had me racewalking toward the bathroom. Snap, crackle, *sizzle.* How is it possible he didn't feel that sizzle? He seemed so calm, so unaffected.

I shut the door between us, wanting to die. Then I heard a muffled "Bollocks," and decided this day might be worth living after all.

I DRESSED TO KILL because it was my first official day on the job and first impressions are vital.

And, okay, I wanted to make Arch suffer.

After catching him watching me and hearing that curse, I was pretty certain I'd stirred up *something* with my tongue. I'm not exactly inexperienced in the kissing department. Damn him for making me doubt my sensuality, even if only for a few restless hours. As if Michael hadn't done enough damage.

But I digress.

My job, as described by Arch, was to be the life of the party, to dupe some bad sort into believing that I'm a free-spirited, head-over-heels-in-love newly-wed. For the greater good, he'd said. For art, I added on my own, because I wanted to show the world that a convincing performance comes from within. Honed skills over physical perfection. Age is moot.

With each stroke of the makeup brush, I thought more about Sugar and less about Arch. Her background and dreams. Specific character traits—socially outgoing, expressive, a desire to be admired. We had a lot in common—upbeat and imaginative, flying through life by the seat of our pants. Those aspects of Sugar's personality would come to me naturally. The klutz factor would require effort, although I could count on the stilettos to keep me off balance. Flaunting my body wouldn't be too much of a trial since it wasn't my body, but Sugar's. A character's clothes, or lack of, provided superficial motivation.

The true challenge lay in adopting her excessive-talking, heart-on-her-sleeve mentality. I'd have to battle my suppressed Midwestern upbringing in order to gab about anything and everything that came to mind, especially personal fears and desires. Unlike Sugar, I internalize. I'm not one for unleashing my inner demons. Giving those casino execs hell had been totally out of character.

I thought back on yesterday—post-booby-baring, pre-contemplating-the-consequences. For a brief moment, I'd felt empowered and free. Sugar, I decided as I supersized my breasts to 34Cs via the "extreme cleavage" bra, felt empowered and free around the clock.

Must be nice.

Then again, being in character allowed me to act out of character. Bonus. I could do with a little acting out.

I crammed my feet into strappy stilettos and squeezed my curves into a skintight, low-cut, purple-flowered sundress because Sugar felt better dolled up.

And because I wanted to make Arch suffer.

Glamour makeup—check. Sex kitten hair—check. Lots of skin…well, way more than I generally showed—check.

"Brilliant," was all he said when I emerged from the bathroom an hour later in my Doris Day meets Pamela Anderson splendor. A man of few words this morning, but at least the words were positive. Whether he meant them personally or profession-ally, I didn't know and didn't care. A glimmer of his flirty nature returned as we reviewed our profiles over the breakfast he'd ordered in. Arch-Charles in flirty mode was more fortifying than a bowl of Wheaties.

It wasn't until we'd loaded into the cab and were on our way to the cruise port that my *husband* became chatty. "My wife's first cruise," he said to Ramon the cabbie, an apologetic explanation for my enthusiastic rambling.

Though I gabbed with a Brooklyn accent, used exaggerated hand gestures and occasionally giggled, the bubbling nervous energy was every bit mine as it was Sugar's. I'd never been to Florida, never been on a cruise. I'd never performed in a two-person show, an entire ship as my stage. Considering the escalating traffic as we neared the cruise port, my audience—passengers and crew—would number in the thousands.

My neck tingled with the promise of a rash. My jaw throbbed. What if I bombed? What if someone saw through my ruse and pegged me as a fake? *You're not Sugar Dupont, the sexy, vibrant, wife of a wealthy author. You're that over-forty divorcée with the washed-up career!*

I scratched at my prickly skin and wrestled with a monster called stage fright, while Ramon navigated traffic and delivered his tour guide spiel. His description of Lauderdale's Blue Wave Beach—white sand and crystal-clear surf—provided an escape from my imagination's crash-and-burn scenario. "Gee, it sounds beautiful. Think we can take a detour, Charlie?"

"Paradise awaits in the Caribbean," Arch said, heavy on the Cary Grant accent. "Patience, love."

He halted my scratching by clasping my hand and nuzzling my ear. My eyes rolled back in my head. Not that he noticed since I was wearing my mambo-big and dark sunglasses. The orgasmic groan, he noticed.

"Newlyweds," he explained to Ramon.

The dark-eyed Cuban checked me out via the rearview mirror. Men of various ages and ethnicities had been checking me out all morning—the bellhop, the front desk clerk, a group of conventioneers. Jayne would've shot them a disapproving look. Nicole would've twitched her hips or flipped them the bird, depending on her mood. I didn't have a standard reaction. Men didn't leer at women like me.

Except, I wasn't me. I was Sugar.

Every smarmy wink and suggestive smile validated my acting skills and boosted my damaged ego. I'd probably wake up tomorrow or the day after feeling cheap, but just now I felt desirable. *Take that, Sasha.*

I sensed myself sinking deeper into fantasyland, disconnecting with Evie Parish and embracing Sugar Dupont.

"Lucky man," Ramon said with a sexy smile.

"Yes, I am."

I pretended that Arch was sincere, another positive charge to my confidence. I'll take all the zaps I can get. Then I thought about something else he'd said. Not the paradise part, because that only summoned visions of us doing the horizontal rumba, but the part about the Caribbean. I hadn't given thought as to *where* we'd be sailing. I'd been too focused on my performance. My mind fast-reeled with movies filmed in the islands. Tropical images burned bright. I could hear Bob Marley—"*One love, one heart.*" I could taste the rum. I could feel my cares slipping away.

Paradise.

Who needed Calgon when they had the Caribbean? Turquoise waters, sunshine, sunscreen. Arch in a bathing suit. Arch in a bathing suit rubbing sunscreen on my bare back.

My rash ebbed as my imagination soared.

"Here we are," Ramon announced, cutting my fantasy short. "Port Everglades."

The cab rolled to a stop at a security checkpoint and Arch handed the guards the requisite passports and travel documents through the window. Pleasantries were exchanged and, when they handed back the passports, I nipped them out of Arch's hands for a look-see. Mostly I was interested in mine.

Amazing how official it looked. It boasted Sugar's name and my professional head shot. I remembered then that Michael had e-mailed a JPEG, but how had Arch transferred it onto a government document?

I quirked a suspicious brow and handed the falsified booklet back to my not-entirely-truthful husband. I resisted the urge to punch him in the arm for lying to me. Socking my cane-wielding, AARP-card-carrying husband might not look so good to Ramon, shattering the illusion of newly wedded bliss. Not that I should give a flying fig about Arch's illusion. The deception might not be illegal, but that passport was. If I landed in a foreign prison because of him, I'd…I'd…well, at the very least, he'd never work with this actress again.

Either he was a mind reader or he could hear me grinding my teeth. He derailed my runaway thoughts by pressing his mouth to mine. His tongue teased open my mouth and a fierce hunger caused me to feast. The ache in my jaw instantly eased. Kissing—the new treatment for TMJ. I melted in his arms, my senses fully and wonderfully compromised. For a few blissful seconds I was sweet sixteen and making out in the backseat with the high school hunk. My insides bubbled with girlie excitement. *Don't giggle, Parish.* Jeesh.

When he eased away and lowered my sunglasses, it took me a minute to focus on his intent gaze. The man had kissed me blind.

He smiled. "No worries, love."

I would have believed him if he told me the sky was green. I contemplated his top-notch bullshitting skills as I fought to recapture my breath and he angled away to look out the side window.

"Third-busiest cruise port in the world," Ramon said while maneuvering heavy traffic. "*Mucho* ships set sail on Sunday. Between all of the cruise lines, day like today, you're looking at 35,000 embarking passengers."

Arch mumbled something like, "35,000 marks." Or maybe it was *max.* Mumbling plus accent equals Greek to me. Plus my heart still thudded in my ears, an aftereffect of that supernova kiss. He'd messed with my hearing as well as my vision and if that wasn't bad enough, I felt as if I was hurtling through space. Had I really thought Arch merely potent? Try lethal.

I surveyed our surroundings seeking to ground

myself. No businesses or shops, just massive lots of land teeming with trailer containers, like the ones on the back of a semitruck.

Then the ships came into view! About a dozen of them, docked side by side. A fleet of floating hotels and entertainment resorts. I flashed back to my favourite episodes of *The Love Boat*. As a teen, I'd loved that sitcom. Although deep down I'd always believed I would become a professional performer, I sometimes toyed with the idea of pursuing a career as "cruise director." Maybe I should have taken those interests more seriously. I'm beginning to think the concept of destiny is a load of hooey.

A fervent believer in mystical hooey, Jayne would argue differently. According to Nicole, yesterday our friend had visited her psychic. Madame Helene had seen a tragic event in Jayne's future. A loved one will suffer.

My gaze zeroed in on the lifeboats. Scenes from *Titanic,* which I saw, like, ten times, assaulted my brain accompanied by Celine Dion's "My Heart Will Go On."

Great. Better to focus on *The Love Boat* and its schmaltzy theme.

Ramon delivered us to the appropriate gate. A porter carted off our luggage and placed it into a large square cage along with a lot of other luggage. Arch tipped the men, bade them farewell.

"I hope they don't deliver Big Red to the wrong

cabin. My feet are killing me." Sugar could look sexy in sneakers, couldn't she?

"Who's Big Red?" Arch asked softly as we hobbled toward the glass doors of the terminal.

"My suitcase." I didn't have a cane to lean on, so I leaned into Arch. Besides, *his* limp was fake.

"You name your suitcases?"

"People name their cars, don't they?"

"Some people." He lowered his voice even more. "You *dinnae* talk to Big Red, do you?"

"Of course not."

"Typically, people who name their cars talk to them, yeah? *Come on, baby. Turn over,*" he lulled in a husky voice. "*Purr for me, and I'll fill you up with the good stuff.*"

It's impossible to squeeze your thighs together while walking at a brisk clip, so I had to endure the erotic tingle. Heavenly hell. "I don't talk to Big Red."

He grinned, and the tingling intensified.

He'd probably charmed his way through life, wielding his sexual charisma like a suggestive spell. Harry the Hypnotist had nothing on Arch. During the aftershock of one of his kisses, if he directed me to squawk like a chicken, I'd probably flap my arms for good measure. Part of me reveled in the magic. Part of me felt manipulated. Mostly I felt challenged. I knew that in order to hold my own with this Bad Boy, I needed to connect with my inner Bad Girl. The same girl who'd flashed the execs. This was war.

As soon as we breezed through the doors, I threw my arms around his neck. "Oh, Charlie, baby, I'm so excited!" Yeah, boy, *that* was the truth. "My first cruise!" I kissed him. Openmouthed with lots of tongue. No mercy. I slid my hands to his spectacular butt. I wiggled against JT—not easy given that strap-on belly—and...*hello!*

Someone cleared their throat. Couldn't have been Arch. We had a tonsil-teasing kiss going on.

He pushed me to arm's length and the throat-clearer came to light. A uniformed greeter. A round-eyed young chick with a Crest Whitestrips smile. Her freckled cheeks burned bright.

"Newlyweds," Arch and I said in our pseudo accents, our smiles nearly as broad and fake as hers.

"I, um, I was just noticing—" she glanced toward Arch's cane and ended up staring at his crotch "—your limp."

I—Sugar, rather—laughed. "I beg to differ, honey."

Arch, rather, Charles, coughed.

The girl blushed brighter and focused on something in the distance. "If we can ease your discomfort, I mean, assist, I mean...would you like a wheelchair, sir?"

"Gee, we've never done it in a wheelchair, Charlie." I winked at the poor girl. She looked as though she wanted to be anywhere but here. Arch, the one I meant to ruffle, looked amused.

"I say, dear girl, that's most kind of you. Sprained ankle," he said. "Dreadful pain."

"I'll summon a wheelchair, sir." She couldn't get to the phone fast enough.

Arch smiled at me—slow, evil.

Then I got it.

Ramon had warned it could take as long as two hours to check in. Arch would be in a wheelchair.

I'd be on my feet.

Oh, yeah. This was war.

CHAPTER NINE

CHECK-IN WAS HECTIC and tedious. Don't get me wrong. The cruise ship representatives were helpful and friendly, but, given the mob of embarking passengers, the process took forever.

My feet and good humor took a serious hit.

Just after crossing over the gangway, Arch and I encountered the ship's photographer and two young women dressed in fun, flirty sailor suits. I know fellow entertainers when I see them. The hairpieces, theatrical makeup and outgoing personalities were dead giveaways. They engaged us in a classic meet and greet and invited us to join them for a souvenir photo. Part of their job was to distract boarding customers from yet another line forming in the ship's atrium. Even though they made me smile, I endured a stab of envy as they worked their magic.

I used to make people happy.

I'm not a competitive person, but my adrenaline spiked. I could still make people happy. To prove it, I ratcheted up the schmaltz—Sugar, full blast. I used ditzy banter to amuse the security guards who inspected our Fiesta Cards—a plastic card thingy that worked as a boarding pass, room key and on-board charge card. I cracked up the assistant cruise director, Gavin King, by nabbing a hairbrush out of my purse to demonstrate my microphone technique when he mentioned a karaoke night. "Although I don't know that it would be fair of me to participate," I said in my cutesy voice. "I'm a lounge singer, you know."

"Retired lounge singer." Arch grasped my left hand, thumbed my fake wedding band. He smiled up at me all lovey-dovey, and I froze, my next line forgotten! "We recently married," he continued. "I fear life on my remote estate can be quite boring. I trust my wife will be well entertained upon this cruise."

"Absolutely." Gavin enthusiastically listed several other activities. A consummate people person, this man was responsible, along with his boss, for coordinating passenger activities and creating excitement and fun.

I could create excitement and fun.

Again, it occurred to me that maybe I'd missed the boat—no pun intended. Maybe I should've pursued my fleeting childhood dream to fill Julie McCoy's canvas shoes. Was there an age limit on newbies in the cruise director field? Except experience had taught me that you don't pull special events out of your butt. A lot of preplanning and day-of details go into coordinating one measly function. I prefer performing to paperwork. Rehearsals over red tape.

My mom's voice barked in my ears. *When are you going to grow up? You're over forty now, you know.*

Yeah, I know.

Rebelling, I regressed another few years, singing "Conga" and weaving Arch's wheelchair on a serpentine route through the Atrium—a spacious public area that resembled the lobby of a high-class hotel. Stepping onto a Fiesta cruise ship was like stepping into Oz. An overwhelming glitz factor and multitudes of happy, peppy characters. Umm, staff. One would think that, since I work in casinos, I'd be used to glitz and pep. Except I work in Atlantic City, not Vegas. With the exception of one or two of the East Coast resorts, there's not a lot of emphasis on glitz. And though most casinos preach customer service to their employees, consistent downsizing made hotel and gaming staff cranky rather than peppy. Costumed performers used to spread cheer, but the strolling entertainment programs in A.C. were obsolete.

Making *me* obsolete.

I buried the sobering thought. I was Sugar, not me. *"Come on shake your body, baby, do the conga!"*

Hubby craned around, peered up at me through his tinted lenses. "Nice voice."

I'm not sure if it was the compliment or the sexy tilt of his mouth, but my insides went all gooey. Again. I reflected on his atomic kisses. Again. I wanted to ask if he was as hot for me as I was for him or just a total horndog who could get it up for any woman—but I didn't. It had to be the latter. Men like Arch Reece, enigmatic, dark and dangerous charmers, didn't chase women like me. Sexpots like Sugar, maybe. But not Ivory-soap Evie.

My jaw throbbed and again I cursed the fact that I'd fallen asleep without my splint. Sugar didn't have TMJ. Sugar wasn't stressed. Then Cher materialized in my mind as she'd appeared in *Moonstruck* and slapped me twice. *Snap out of it!*

Right.

You are Sugar.

Right.

I rounded the wheelchair and, hands on Arch's thigh, bent over to give him a prime view of my pumped-up cleavage. "Ah, Charlie, you were a sucker for my voice from the start." Mimicking Peggy Lee's sultry voice, I crooned a line of "Fever." Then I leaned in closer, winked. "Or was it that split-up-to-there red dress?"

He stroked his silver whiskers, started to say something, but was distracted.

I glanced in the direction he was looking. Speaking of red dresses… A dark-haired woman wearing a chiffon halter dress glided toward the elevators. The hem kissed the back of her superlong legs midthigh. Since we couldn't see her face or breasts, I took it Arch was a leg man.

I pressed my mouth close to his ear. "Hey, you're

a newlywed, remember? You shouldn't be checking out other women." I eased back, forced a smile and twirled my ring. "Not that I care."

He studied me, grinned. "You care."

Of all the…

"I only have eyes for you, Sugar." He hauled me onto his lap and sealed that vow with a kiss. The crowd noise faded and the schmaltzy *The Love Boat* theme blared in my head. "Set a course for adventure, your mind on a new romance." Arch's tongue danced circles around mine and lulled me into a stupor. *Again.* Holy guacamole, this man could kiss.

Just as it was getting good, meaning the tingling between my thighs had intensified to a moan-inducing ache, he broke contact. The schmaltzy crooner in my head choked. No, wait. That was a cough. And it wasn't the crooner in my head, but another happy, peppy crew member at our side.

Arch, or rather, Charles, winked up at the kid. "Newlyweds."

"Congratulations!" he chirped, then manned the wheelchair. "Might I be of service?"

"Good of you to offer, son. I'm looking for the shore excursion director."

I scrambled to my feet, scrambled for a thought that didn't involve getting naked with Arch. I teetered alongside as the crewman steered the wheelchair across the Atrium. Sporting a dazzling white grin, he rattled off vital information. Most notably: the mandatory lifeboat drill. Yeah, boy, *that* worked like a cold shower. Aware that this cruise would be attended by a good thousand or more, I massaged my jaw while trying not to obsess on the lifeboat-to-passenger ratio.

The crewman circumvented the crush of passengers and ushered us to a vacant section of the front desk. Arch thanked him, abandoned the wheelchair and introduced himself to the shore excursion director.

"Welcome aboard, Mr. and Mrs. Dupont. My name is Lucas." If he was shocked by our age difference, he didn't show it. All of the crew members thus far had seemed unfazed. Like me, they'd probably seen it all. "Our official Shore Excursion Talk takes place in the Fiesta Theater tomorrow at 10:30 a.m. At that time I'll provide you with an extensive overview of visits to San Juan, St. Thomas, La Romana and Nassau. You can book your excursions directly after. However, if you'd like to preview a brochure…"

I drifted as he launched into a sales pitch, noting that most of the other guests were seniors. I felt oddly at home. Although the Atlantic City casinos were currently angling to hook the younger generation, the meat of their revenue, minus high rollers, came from the over-sixty crowd. The blue hairs that bus in and drop their disposable income into the slots and buffet food into their purses. I've been entertaining and mingling with seniors for years.

Maybe this Sugar gig wouldn't be so hard after all. At least the demographics were familiar.

The bad-guy element, now that was another matter.

While Arch discussed ports of call with Lucas, I surreptitiously scanned the bustling area, looking for whomever it was we were supposed to deceive. *Smoke and mirrors.* All I saw were pleasant, smiling faces. Couples on vacation. Harmless, not dangerous. Certainly no one who looked suspicious.

On the other hand, there were a scattered few who looked plain silly. Like the cat-eye-spectacled grandma who walked away from the balloon artist wearing a latex palm tree on her head. On second thought, the fact that she was brave enough to wear the sculptured balloon hat was kind of cute. I couldn't say the same for the fashion disaster, sitting in a club chair, chomping on an unlit cigar while reading the newspaper. Seriously, what kind of man combines a Texan Stetson, Hawaiian shirt, Bermuda shorts and combat boots, thinking he looks good?

Then again, I was wearing a skintight flowery sundress and carrying an *I Love Lucy* travel tote. Nothing criminal about quirky taste. Okay, Tex Aloha. Whatever rings your bell.

My mind zipped back to the element of risk. I twisted my ring, wishing I knew specifics. *For the greater good,* I told myself.

Arch wrapped a strong arm around me as if sensing my unease, all the while chatting amiably with Lucas. He really was a top-notch actor. Quietly friendly to the crew members and overtly adoring of me—uh, Sugar.

"Feel free to contact me if I can be of further assistance," Lucas said. He then gestured toward the bustling area decorated with an abundance of plants and festive balloon sculptures. Whatever they were paying that balloon artist, he was worth every penny. "The Atrium bar is to our left. Danny, our most popular pianist, is performing there now. He knows at least four bars of any song ever written. There's also a Welcome Aboard party in progress, poolside, Deck Nine. Live music. Dancing. Drink of the day, Fiesta Fandango." He nodded toward a bank of elevators. "A cabin steward will direct you to the party or to the proper deck for your cabin, should you choose. You have plenty of time to explore the ship before the lifeboat drill."

Again with the lifeboat drill. Dread shivered down my body, zapping life into my numb toes. I imagined Arch and I dangling from the stern, à la Jack and Rose, as the ship nosedived to the bottom of the deep blue sea. "At least they don't have icebergs in the Caribbean," I mumbled as we hobbled away from the desk.

"No," Arch said with a smile in his voice. "Just hurricanes."

Smart-ass.

I wrapped an arm around his augmented waist

and leaned into him to ease the weight off of my cramped feet. Since I was pressed against him anyway, I took advantage and playfully nipped his earlobe. "You're looking a little tuckered, baby. Whaddaya say we hit the cabin?"

Nudge. Nudge. Wink. Wink.

Not that I really wanted to fool around. Okay. That's a lie. But not this minute. I *really* wanted to get off of my flippin' feet.

He smiled down at me and my heart thumped. "Sweet of you to be concerned, love, but I wouldn't dream of cheating you of a moment's adventure." He eyed the bar. "Let's have a drink, shall we? Test Danny's repertoire?"

So in other words it wasn't time to break. "Sure."

I sucked it up because I'm a trooper, and because Sugar wouldn't turn down a drink. Why did I have this sinking feeling the fun-loving newlywed was going to be the death of me?

Don't think the words sink, sinking or sunk while on a ship, Parish.

Right.

And don't forget about the mandatory lifeboat drill.

Crap.

Dangerous men? Sinking ships? A drink suddenly sounded like a very good idea.

CHAPTER TEN

"GLAD I'M NOT claustrophobic."

Milo shut the door with a quiet click and moved into the cabin behind Gina. Two steps in and he'd navigated half of the room. It wasn't the square footage that surprised him as much as the monochrome decor. The carpet. The bedspreads. The cushion of the lone chair. Pink. The flower arrangement. The nightstand jimmied in between the twin beds. Pink.

Christ. "Cozy."

Gina flipped her long brown ponytail over her shoulder, clipping Milo in the chin. He was standing *that* close. Back to him, she snorted her disgust. "Couldn't The Kid book anything less…"

Cramped? he expected her to say.

"Pink?"

He smiled at that. He should've known. Although the five-foot-eight beauty was all woman, there wasn't a delicate bone in her amazing body. Trained in self-defense and skilled in the art of love, she could seduce and throat-punch a man with equal proficiency. He liked that she could take care of herself. Unlike his ex-wife, Gina didn't need a man to complete her. She didn't hold men up to fairy-tale expectations. She understood Milo's obsession with con artists, a like obsession that had driven her off the force. Gina Valente looked at the world with eyes wide open instead of through rose-tinted glasses. Next time he mated for life, he wanted a lioness, not a lamb.

Gina was a lioness.

She gestured to the beds. "Which one do you want?"

"Take your pick." Both promised to cramp his six-foot-two frame. Hands on hips, he surveyed the accommodations, noted the limited storage space, the lack of windows. The thirteen-inch television had been shelved in a decorative corner box and suspended from the ceiling. Basic amenities. Given the last-minute booking, cabin selections were slim. Since suites and rooms-with-a-view were completely sold out, they'd had to settle on this interior stateroom.

Gina tossed her handbag on the bed nearest the postage-stamp-size bathroom. "What do you want to bet Ace has a suite?"

"Sucker bet." Arch always traveled in style and rarely at his own expense.

Gina sank down on the bed, crossed those mile-long legs. "You snore?"

Although they'd worked together before, they'd never shared a room. "No. You?"

"No. But I sometimes talk in my sleep."

To his knowledge, she'd slept with the enemy on at least two occasions in the line of duty. "Sounds dangerous."

She smiled coyly as if reading his mind. "In those instances, I usually don't sleep."

He waited for the boner that never came. Annoyed, he stuffed his hands in the pockets of his cargo shorts, rocked back on his rubber heels. "Thanks for doing this, Gina."

"Please. Like this is work. Well, technically it is, but it's a lot better than enduring subzero temperatures to bust a Ponzi scheme up in Juno."

Last month's reverse sting. Milo didn't argue. February in Alaska was brutal.

Her keen brown gaze shifted around the room. "The cabin's nauseating, but the ship's a dream. A hop to the Caribbean? I plan on having fun, Jazzman. You could do with some yourself." She looked him in the eye, blasted him with a sultry smile. "Fun, that is."

He recognized flirting. What he couldn't determine was her sincerity. He refrained from comment as she slipped into the bathroom and shut the door. Even if she was interested in a casual slam, it wouldn't happen. Unlike Arch, he didn't mix business with pleasure. Also, although he considered Gina hot, she didn't light his fuse.

Not like the little firecracker he'd spotted down in the Atrium. The first woman to raise his flag in months and he was undercover. He'd looked away almost as soon as he'd noticed her. Who needed the torture? His divorce had been final a year ago. He was a free man. No ties. No obligations. Yet his sex life was freaking pathetic.

Meanwhile, he'd yet to corner his partner. He wanted answers, and they'd better be good. Although this was Arch, so of course he'd plead a convincing defense. Milo would need thigh-high boots to wade through the bullshit. Nothing new. The twist that threw Milo was Arch taking on a case Chameleon had determined dead in the water. This was uncharted territory.

Two weeks ago, HQ had alerted Milo to a beef filed by a Ms. Celia Benson, the granddaughter of Herman Stokes, a senior who'd claimed he'd been bilked in an investment scam. He'd died a month later, but not before filing complaints with a local bunco squad. Unfortunately, the police investigation tanked. Meanwhile, the crook who'd bilked him in the first place sent henchmen to dissuade him from making further complaints. They ended up scaring him to death. Or so Ms. Benson claimed. After a preliminary investigation, Chameleon had rejected the case. No proof. The complaint was based on hearsay and complicated by territorial laws. Bottom line, this scam was out of their jurisdiction. What the hell had possessed Arch to act?

With an unsanctioned player, no less.

The bathroom door opened and Gina reentered, freshly primped.

"I need to locate Arch's cabin."

She smoothed her hands over her sundress. "I'll corner a steward." She slinked toward the door. "How *hard* can it be?"

Definite flirting. Shit.

CHAPTER ELEVEN

MENTAL NOTE: Fiesta Fandangos are toxic. A mild, fruity drink, the menu had said, with rum the only alcoholic ingredient. One word: *False advertising.* Okay, that's two words, but those suckers are powerful. Pardon my muddled brain. I'd sipped the Fandango at the Atrium bar. It was the second drink, the one Arch had bought me poolside, that went down like water. I refused to let on that I was light-headed. My pride was at stake. No way, no how would I have Arch assuming I was a wimp…or a lush.

No way.

I'm a gifted actress. I can do sober. So act I did when, an hour later, a cabin steward showed us to our room. Hanging on Arch to keep my balance wasn't a problem. I was only following directions, conscientious worker that I am. Michael would be so proud.

Yesterday's cynicism welled up, but I pushed it down again. Besides, I was Sugar, not me. And Arch was Charles, an eccentric, potbellied, nearsighted

author who'd sipped scotch and conversed spar-
ingly with the bartender while I'd boogied with
three energetic senior ladies at the poolside wel-
coming party. Calypso music and Gavin's promise
of a prize for the best mambo dancers had lured us
away from our drinks. Since our menfolk didn't
want to participate, we'd latched on to each other.
I'd partnered with Martha, the same woman I'd seen
wearing the balloon hat, who had no sense of
rhythm. We didn't win, but we had fun.

Arch had watched the festivities with a crooked
smile. *"I need you to be the life of the party, yeah?
A social butterfly."* I guess he was pleased with my
efforts. All I could think was, this was just the first
day in a week full of contests and activities. My feet
hurt. My back hurt. The thought, *I'm too old for this,*
crossed my mind and I shuddered.

I'd been *on* since we'd left the hotel this morning.
I'd performed five hours straight. I was burned. I ask
you—how am I supposed to maintain a vibrant,
over-the-top personality for several days, hours at a
time? As a lounge singer I'm used to forty minutes
on, twenty off. Sure, I've worked harder. High-roller
parties and high-stakes slot tournaments are murder.
When booked as a dancer or an actress, I've gone
as long as two hours without a break.

But this…*this* was a challenge. Challenge is
good for the soul—the soul of body, not the feet.
As soon as the steward vamoosed and the cabin
door shut, I flopped facedown on the bed and

groaned. "Whoever invented high heels should be shot. And as soon as I can figure out how to get even, *you* are dead meat."

"Look forward to your efforts, Sunshine."

I sat up to make a wisecrack and instead said, "Zowie." The cabin was nothing like I'd imagined. I'd expected confined. Instead, I got spacious. A queen-size bed. Two, no, *three* rooms. Plus a balcony! TV-VCR, minibar, a love seat and cushy chairs. The entire setup was decorated in muted gold and shades of beige. Classy. I unbuckled the ankle straps, toed off the pain-in-the-foot stilettos and mentally happy-danced around the suite. That's right, *suite!*

"I, um, wow. This is nice."

"Charles is accustomed to comfort."

"And you?"

"I'm a lot like Charles."

"Filthy rich? Reclusive?"

He smiled then studied his reflection in a vanity mirror, re-knotted his ascot. "I need to go *oot*. You settle in. Relax. I'll be back before we set sail, yeah?"

Hard to believe we hadn't even left the dock and I'd already put in a week's work. Ugh. Maybe he was right. Maybe I should rest. Recharge. "Yeah. I mean, okay." I massaged the ball of my foot. "Where are you going?" It wasn't my business, but curiosity preempted good manners.

"*Oot*."

Out. Right. I frowned as the door hit him in his admirable ass. In his absence followed silence, and a flutter of anxiety. That desertion thing, I guess.

I twirled my chrysoprase ring, willing tranquility. None came. *Get a grip, Parish.* So I was alone. I could do alone. I'd been alone for months. More than a year, in fact.

Even though I was fuzzy headed, I didn't feel like napping. I'd unpack, but our luggage had yet to arrive. I assured myself Big Red had not been mistakenly delivered to a stranger's room, Big Red was in transit.

I stood and paced. I needed to walk off the Fandango and work out the charley horse cramping my left foot. I could also use a breath mint. I limped to the marble table where I'd ditched my Lucy tote, rooted for my Breath Savers. My cell phone chirped, announcing a new message. I popped a mint in my mouth, plucked the cell from the tote's side pocket. As I connected to voice mail it occurred to me that I'd never listened to Jayne's messages. According to Nicole, she'd left five. Was this the sixth?

Or maybe it was Michael.

Wince.

The first four were Jayne in frantic *where-are-you* mode. The fifth was Jayne again, only the morning after she knew I'd arrived safely in Florida. After a brief scolding, she turned upbeat.

"I just got a call from my agent and guess who got the spokesperson gig? Uh-huh. Britney. What

was she, like, twelve? Whatever. So listen, Evie. I had a mass e-mail from Zippo-the-Clown. Fannie's Flowers is looking for outgoing delivery people who can sing and dance. I know, I know. But it's better than flipping burgers or typing status reports. Think of it as temporary, you know, until something legit comes along. At least you'd still be performing. Think about it, and be sure to e-mail me when you get settled on the ship. Love ya. Bye."

My knees buckled. Thank goodness a chair was directly beneath my butt. Singing telegrams? That was only a notch above the gorilla gig!

I deleted Jayne's absurdly chipper voice and moved on to message number six.

"Evelyn. It's Mom."

Great.

"I feel your pain. Now I know what it feels like to be betrayed," she said with a sniff. *"Don't bother calling home hoping to speak to Daddy. He doesn't live here anymore."*

End of message.

Panic buzzed in my ears. I signed off, stared at the phone. Dad cheated on Mom? I couldn't imagine. Nor could I imagine him bailing on a forty-three-year marriage. She must've kicked him out. *That* I could imagine.

I punched speed dial.

A horn blasted.

"Jesus!" I nearly jumped out of my skin, nearly dropped the phone. I pressed it back to my ear, heard a ring and...another blast. More rings. Another blast. That made three—blasts, not rings.

Mom wasn't answering and I was running out of time. Blast four. Five. Six. Seven. Then a long blast that had me chucking the phone and Mom's crisis. That's assuming the crisis was legit. Probably they'd just had a humdinger fight. Yeah, that was it. Call me the Queen of Denial.

Heart pounding, I zipped around the cabin looking for the life preserver. Our cabin steward had reiterated there'd be a lifeboat drill before we sailed. Mandatory, he'd repeated. Well, duh! As if I didn't want to know what to do, if we sank like the *Titanic*. Celine Dion trilled in my ear. "Shut. *Up!*"

I scrambled for the life jacket which was...there! Suspended on a hook in the closet. Got it. Where was Arch? I inspected the bulky, freakishly orange jacket, thinking it looked somewhat like a toilet seat with a box attached. Did the fat black straps latch around your shoulders or waist? I'd drown before figuring out how this thing worked. I'd ask Arch to help me except he wasn't here! Meanwhile, his life jacket hung in the closet. I grabbed it, too. Maybe I'd run into him in the hall.

I buckled on my stilettos, seeing as I had no other available shoes, and rushed across the room—*ouch, ouch*—to read the sign on the back of the door. At least the toxic Fandangos hadn't obliterated my memory. *"Look for the location of your muster station on the back of your door,"* the steward had said. Squinting at the fine print, I located my assigned meeting place and, with a life jacket looped over each arm, dashed out into the hall.

The door slammed behind me. Celine crooned in my ear…"My heart will go on and on…" What a pain—my stilettos, not Celine.

I hobbled to the elevator, punched the button and waited, obsessing on the boat going down and my parents breaking up. Several other passengers streamed past me and into a stairwell.

"Not supposed to use the elevator, miss," one kindly old man reminded me as he pulled a toilet seat flotation device over his graying head.

Right. I limped after the gang then remembered I'd left my purse in the room. What if someone stole it? Not that I suspected anyone on the housekeeping staff would stoop so low, but I've seen those scenarios in movies. *All* of the passengers would be at a *mandatory* lifeboat drill. A crafty, dishonest person could easily scarf up a few valuable items.

My ID was in the purse. My *real* ID. What if my forgetfulness somehow compromised Arch's…well, whatever it was he was doing for the greater good? I hurried back to my cabin only to realize I'd left something else inside.

The key. The Fiesta Card. The thing I was supposed to have with me at all times!

Screw it. Fear of not knowing what to do in case of an emergency overrode fear of exposing Arch and propelled me toward the stairwell. The Fandangos and stilettos compromised my judgment and speed. Jayne's and Mom's messages buzzed in my ears, heightening my anxiety as I navigated the stairs, two unwieldy life preservers slung over my arms.

I could feel my jaw tightening, and as I breached the last step and burst through a door, my heel caught on something. I opened my mouth to scream, *"Watch out!"* but my jaw locked.

"Wah ow!" was all I managed as I sailed forward and tackled Tex Aloha.

CHAPTER TWELVE

I'M USED TO MAKING A spectacle of myself. Believe you me, I have a colorful history. Like the time I showed up in a stretch limo as Officer Buzzby the Safety Bee at a government function on the Boardwalk. I raised eyebrows and doubts about my sanity when I emerged from the limo in a furry bumblebee fat suit complete with bopping head antennae and state trooper sunglasses. The casino I worked for at the time donated the limo and my services. The character and costume were mine. The absurdity of it all lasted an hour tops.

Sugar's latest antic promised to haunt me for life.

I'm guessing about three hundred passengers plus assorted crew witnessed me plowing into Tex Aloha—him landing face-first on deck, me landing face-first on Tex. No doubt the shocked onlookers got a peek at my lace panties. Could have been worse, I told myself. I could've been wearing a thong. Tex suffered the greatest injury, a nasty gash on his forehead. Since he cushioned my fall, all I really suffered was embarrassment. Okay, huge embarrassment.

I couldn't close my mouth. Locked wide open, I couldn't even voice a proper apology. Thinking I'd hurt myself in the fall, a crewman escorted both Tex and me to the ship's medical center. The nurse ushered us in and we sat on opposing beds. After I scribbled TMJ on a notepad, the doctor advised the nurse and turned his attention to Tex.

All I needed was anti-inflammatory medication and an ice-pack. Oh, and to relax.

Tex needed stitches. The handkerchief he'd pressed to his forehead was soaked red. Blood streamed down his face, dripping on his tropical shirt.

"Hell's Bells. It's a friggin' scratch, Doc." He glanced at me then the nurse. "Pardon my French."

The doctor shook his head. "That cut is more than a quarter inch deep. If you want it to heal properly—"

"Then get on with it, goddammit. There's a pitcher of beer waitin' with my name on it."

He didn't sound angry, just loud and abrasive. Definitely Texan. His gaze fastened on my breasts— typical man—before settling on my face. My cheeks flooded with heat. *Yes, I know,* I mentally screamed, I look like a wide-mouth bass! Did he have to deepen my mortification by staring? For the umpteenth time I tried to close my mouth. The inability to do so flooded me with irrational panic. What if my jaw stuck open like this forever?

Annoyance flashed in Tex's ochre-brown eyes. He hadn't blasted me yet for knocking him over and busting up his head and cigar. I sort of wished he'd let it out and get it over with.

He swiped off his Stetson and clamped his teeth around the shredded stogie. His salt-and-pepper hair and the crinkles framing his eyes hinted he was closing in on fifty. His facial features were too angular for my taste. His hair was cropped close, military style. The muscles in his arms and legs well-defined. I glanced down at his combat boots. My imagination zoomed. Had I injured a vet? A soldier on leave?

Specialty performer attacks war hero! News at eleven.

Doctor Drake rolled over a tray of shiny instruments. He stood between us, so it's not like I could really see him going to work on Tex's gash, but still. Feeling woozy, I turned my face away, focused on the door. I pressed the ice pack against my jaw, thumbed my ring.

"Don't worry, Twinkie. Head wounds bleed like a mother. Ain't nothin' but a scratch."

I assume he was talking to me, not Doctor Drake. The pastry reference irritated me, but I guess Sugar did look like a cream puff. Instinct told me this guy was a womanizer. Sure, Arch probably was, too, but at least Arch was charming. Tex was obnoxious.

A heartbeat later, the charming womanizer limped in à la Charles, looking sick with worry. In character even in crisis. Impressive.

"Sugar, love, they told me…" He glanced at Tex. "Bloody hell."

Wasn't that the truth.

"She's fine," the nurse assured him. "Her TMJ flared up, causing her jaw to lock. As you know, these episodes are often brought on by extreme stress. I understand that she was upset when she fell into the muster station. Perhaps you can help to calm her, Mr. Dupont."

To his credit, he didn't betray, in words or expression, that he was in fact unaware that I had TMJ. I wondered if he even knew what TMJ was. He thanked the nurse and gestured to a partition. "I say, would you mind pulling that drape?"

She complied, and thankfully, mercifully, now there was no chance whatsoever that I'd see the doctor stitching up Tex. My shoulders sagged with relief. I blushed head to toe when Arch smoothed back my hair and studied my face. Jaw locked, mouth wide open, I had to look as stupid as I felt.

He took the ice pack from my hand, set it on the bed. Then he pressed his fingertips to each side of my jaw and gently massaged. "I say, I've been racking my brain, love, and for the life of me can't recall Joe and Jerry's feminine names."

It took me a second to realize that he was talking about Curtis and Lemmon in *Some Like It Hot*. I couldn't *say* their drag names, so I wrote them. Josephine and Daphne. Jeesh. How could he forget? And why was that important now?

He glanced at the notepad. "Ah, yes." He smiled and continued to massage my jaw. His touch was gentle and warm, just like his gaze. He glanced down at my stilettos. "I was thinking about the part in the movie where Joe and Jerry are hurrying toward the train in drag."

Wigs, tight skirts, nylons and high heels. I smiled, nodded. It was one of several hilarious scenes.

Quoting from the movie, he affected Daphne's high-pitched, feminine voice, "How *do* they walk in these things, huh? How do they keep their balance?" Then in Josephine's voice, "It must be the way the weight is distributed."

I laughed. I couldn't help it. Sure, the lines were funny, but it was Arch's expression and his girlie delivery that tickled my funny bone and unlocked my jaw. My palms flew to my cheeks *Home Alone* style. "Oh, my, God. Thank you!" I threw my arms around his neck and hugged tight. He'd distracted me completely, putting me at ease by talking about something I loved—movies. "You're a genius."

I heard a grunt from the other side of the curtain. I imagined the doctor puncturing Tex's skin with a needle and grimaced. "That poor man."

"He'll live." Arch maneuvered me off the bed and out of the medical station. "Let's get you back to the cabin and into flat shoes, yeah?"

"Wait, I need… I want to say…" I thought about the blood, the stitches. "Would you go back, tell him I'm sorry? Please?"

Arch pushed his Panama hat to the back of his head, dragged a hand over his silver whiskers. "Right then. Stay here."

He was back a minute later, ushering me toward an elevator.

"Is he angry?" I asked.

"No."

"Is he suing?" Sweat beaded on my forehead thinking about all the people who sued casinos because of one or another mishap. Considering my pathetic bank account, if he sued, I was sunk. *Don't think the word* sunk. *You can't sink. You missed the drill.*

"He's not suing."

A relief, but I'd still apologize later in person. "Did you get his name?"

"Vic Parker."

I DIDN'T SEE VIC PARKER for the rest of the day. Nor did I reconnect with Jayne or my mom. My cell phone was useless out at sea and a call from our cabin's phone would cost a small fortune. I did manage to steal away to the Internet Lounge to zip off a couple of e-mails.

Hey, Jayne,

Sorry for the scare. I'm on board. All's well. Re: Britney. Figures. Re: The singing telegram. I'd rather flip burgers.

Will e-mail again tomorrow. Kiss Nic for me. Miss you much!

Love, Evie

Then I typed a quick note to my brother.

Christopher,
   Mom called. Said Daddy split. Should I be
worried? Best to Sandy and the kids.
Love, Evie

Even though Christopher and I weren't close, surely he wouldn't leave me hanging—unlike Mom. Until then, I chose not to think about the possibility that my parents had separated.

There were a lot of things that I chose not to think about just now. The last thing I needed or wanted was another lockjaw episode. I can only liken the feeling to being trapped in a coffin. The frustration. The panic. The fear of never unlocking the hinges.

If I hadn't been distracted by Tex's bloody injury, I probably would've hyperventilated. It's happened before. Tonight, no matter what, I'd wear that blasted splint.

I kept waiting for Arch to grill me about TMJ. He had to wonder what set it off and if it would happen again. It had to bug him. It didn't fit Sugar's profile. But he didn't bring it up. Instead, he lavished attention on me, treating me to a spa visit. A full-body massage by a highly skilled masseuse. Yeah, boy, talk about relaxed.

I returned to our cabin to find Big Red waiting for me. Hallelujah, *something* was going right with this day. After a quick shower, I changed into bright red capris, a red-and-white-flowered halter top and white tennis shoes. Sugar accessories included huge silver hoop earrings, Cajun Crimson lipstick and two perky ponytails. When I came out of the bathroom, Arch was hanging up the phone. "Dinner reservations," he explained.

Not that I'd asked. I was too busy staring. He'd stripped off his jacket, his oxford shirt and that fake padded belly. The man was naked from the waist up. I devoured his buff torso and that Celtic armband tattoo in a ravenous starefest. The hair and face belonged to Charles, but the body was all Arch.

Then he said, "Sexy," and I realized the staring was mutual.

My cheeks heated. "Even with the sneakers?"

"Especially with the sneakers."

Oh, man.

He strapped on the gut, pulled on a clean under-shirt and slipped back into his oxford. "Are you up for a stroll? Fresh air might help, yeah?"

If we didn't leave this cabin, I'd faint from a toxic dose of raw lust. Sure, he had a great body, but it was his thoughtfulness that seduced me. The memory burned bright of how he'd eased my misery in the medical station, how he'd gifted me with an expensive massage. "Sure."

The moment we exited the cabin we were *on*. The world is our stage and all that. Again, I was impressed with his acting skills, and hoped the feeling was mutual. We strolled Deck Ten arm in arm. I encountered a few curious glances, but I was pretty sure that was because of tackling Tex, not snuggling with my older husband.

On a whim, I swung around, wrapped my arms around his neck and pressed a lingering kiss to his mouth. His thumbs brushed beneath my breasts. Now *that* was a new twist. I shivered with orgasmic delight, easing back before I got carried away.

He studied me through his sepia-tinted, Truman Capote glasses. "What was that for?"

"For being you."

"You *dinnae* know me."

"I know enough." Well, not really. But I knew he was innately kind, and for now, that was enough. Energized, I bounded out of his arms and looked out over the railing. Fort Lauderdale was a shrinking spec on the horizon. The farther we drifted from land, away from my unstable life, the lighter my heart felt. I gazed up at the cloudless sky and thanked my lucky stars for this opportunity and for the fact that I wasn't seasick.

I'd heard that, because of a cruise ship's immense size, one barely senses any movement except in extreme rough seas. The water glittered before me like a vast, magical pond. No waves. No rocking. Things were looking up.

I breathed in the salt air, and with it, the scent of Old Spice. I knew it came from Arch, but it made me think of my dad. Distraction was vital. "I need a drink."

"I know just the place."

ARCH AND I ENDED UP on Deck Nine, the poolside bar. This time instead of calypso, a sequined duo cranked out seventies hits. The keyboard player belted "Staying Alive" in his falsetto. The female singer harmonized along with recorded vocal tracks. If I closed my eyes, I'd think I was listening to the Bee Gees. They were that good, and the audience visibly enjoyed their efforts.

Although it was a party atmosphere, many passengers reclined in lounge chairs, sipping beverages and chatting with loved ones or friends. A few brave souls had joined a dance instructor to learn the line dance from *Saturday Night Fever*. I knew that dance. I wondered if I should jump in—at least I was wearing comfortable shoes—but Arch ushered me onto a stool at the bar.

I felt as if I'd been given a reprieve from being the life of the party. Did he worry he'd worked me too hard this morning? Did he think I was stressed out because of the job, hence my bout with TMJ? Well, darn. That was my fault. I'd planted the seed in his head with my big mouth. *Michael doesn't think I'm up for this.*

I wanted to set him straight, but I couldn't. Not here. Not in public.

The bartender came over, the same guy we'd had earlier today—Beau, his name tag read. "Scotch, Mr. Dupont?"

"Good of you to remember, old boy."

Except Beau wasn't really old. He was middle-aged. Average height. Average build. Not handsome, not ugly. Average. He smiled at me. "Fiesta Fandango for the lady?"

"Virgin piña colada, please." Between the Motrin I'd taken earlier and the pills the nurse had given me, it didn't seem wise to mix medication and alcohol. I'd done that yesterday. Oh, and earlier today. Jeesh. For someone who didn't want to be the stereotypical artist numbing her emotions with drugs or booze, I was doing a pretty good job of it.

I'd barely taken two sips of the frozen concoction when Martha-of-the-two-left-feet appeared. She pushed her cat-eye glasses up her nose, squinted at me and smiled. "It *is* you. We were taking bets."

For a moment my insides chilled like my drink. What did she mean by that? I glanced over at a group of huddled seniors. They stood near an outdoor shuffleboard court, cues in hand. Four of them. Two men, two women. When they saw me looking, they waved. Forcing a smile, I waved back. Had one of them taken a bus trip to Atlantic City? Had someone recognized me from one of the casinos?

I turned back to Martha. Five foot, *maybe*, with yellow—yes, yellow—tightly permed hair. The corners of her black cat-eye glasses sparked with rhinestones. She wore purple Bermuda shorts, black-and-white basketball sneakers and a Mickey Mouse T-shirt. She looked like one of my zany characters. The thought occurred: *This is me in thirty years.* I cleared my throat, locked in the Brooklyn accent. "Um, where did we meet exactly?"

"Don't you remember? The mambo contest. I didn't recognize you with your pigtails and Keds. You look like a little girl." Her gray gaze fell to my chest. My cups still runneth over thanks to the extreme cleavage bra. "Well, from a distance, anyway."

I was relieved that my cover hadn't been blown, ecstatic that she'd thought me so young. Although I guess even forty-one was young in the opinion of a seventy-two-year-old. "You remember my husband, Charlie."

"Certainly, dear." She squinted at him through her sparkly bifocals.

For a moment I thought that she was going to be the first person to comment on our age difference, but then Charles kissed her age-spotted hand and said, "Pleasure to see you again, madam."

"The pleasure's mine," Martha murmured, transfixed.

Seems I'm not the only one affected by Arch's crooked grin. Yeah, boy, he knew what he was doing.

"Would you like to join us for a drink, Martha?"

She fluffed her Harpo-hairdo, smiled at Charles then looked my way. "Actually, Sugar, we were hoping you'd join us in a game of shuffleboard. I need a partner."

Martha was a widower. While we'd mamboed, .

she'd explained that she had no one special in her life. Even though this cruise had been advertised as a "couples cruise," she'd tagged along with a group of her married friends intending to let loose and have fun. Life's too short, she'd said, especially when you're seventy-two.

"I'd be happy to team up with you, Martha." I hopped off my stool before Arch could stop me. Sure, there was a part of me that wanted to prove to him that I was up to this job, that I have boundless energy, that I'm the life of the party. But more, I wanted to make someone happy. I wanted to make a difference in Martha's life because someday…that could be me.

CHAPTER THIRTEEN

TALK ABOUT A GRUELING, traumatic day. If I weren't so professional—okay, obsessed—I would've faked a headache and begged off dinner. The need to prove myself as an entertainer kept me charged like the Energizer bunny. Besides, it was hard to say no to Arch, who continued to play the thoughtful, loving husband, treating me to displays of public affection and a gourmet meal.

Dinner conversation focused on movie trivia and an improvised discussion about an inside tip on procuring an unearthed masterpiece for Charles's private art collection. The feigned intrigue caused my pulse to race with excitement. I'd never advocate anything illegal, but Sugar would.

We left The Cha-Cha Club sometime around nine. I could barely keep my eyes open. As much as I wanted to do the nasty with Arch, sleep was uppermost in my mind as we stepped into an elevator. I bit my lip to keep from complaining when he ushered me out onto Deck Nine. What now? A moonlit walk? A nightcap poolside?

Worse.

He guided me into the ship's casino.

I AMAZE MYSELF sometimes. I have no formal training, yet I delivered an Oscar-winning performance. I stood behind Charles, my French-manicured hand gripping his shoulder, bouncing and squealing like a brainless twit every time he won a hand of blackjack. In reality, I wanted to bash him on his silver head for dragging me into a place that reminded me of Atlantic City. I didn't care that he was winning. The longer we stayed, the more I felt like a loser. I performed in the casinos. I, unlike Sugar, had not happily retired. *I* was being forced out. I, unlike Sugar, did not have a wealthy, attentive husband. *I* was divorced. Divorced, unemployed, and over forty. It was all I could do not to scream my frustration to the gilded rafters.

Oh, yeah. I was good.

I retained my composure, my Brooklyn accent and Sugar's vibrant personality for another forty-five minutes until Arch cashed in his chips. I zoned out as we crossed the festive red-and-gold carpet, as we passed the craps and roulette tables and rows and rows of slots.

Hold it in, Evelyn. Good girls don't cause scenes. Even though I left home when I was seventeen, my mom *still* influenced my behavior. I could almost see her standing in front of me, wagging her finger.

I know, I know, I thought to myself. *If I'd gone to college, learned a noble profession, I wouldn't be in this mess.* I fisted my hands, longing to punch something. Not that I would. *Violence is wrong.*

By the time we reached our cabin I was shaking.

"You're angry," Arch said in his own accent after closing and latching the door.

"No, I'm not."

"You're trembling."

"I'm cold."

"It's eighty degrees out there, yeah?"

"Are you asking me or telling me?" I snapped.

"Pardon?"

"Never mind." I turned my back. "Would you unzip this, please?" Heat should have pooled down below as he performed the intimate task, but now the only thing burning was my buns. "Thank you." I snatched up a change of clothes, stomped into the bathroom and slammed the door.

I ditched the evening gown in favor of blue-and-green-striped pajama bottoms and a green ribbed tank top. I removed all traces of makeup, scrubbed my face and teeth. I told myself to get over it, to suck it up, but the more I suppressed my feelings, the more they intensified. Thoughts whirled and raced and collapsed in on each other.

I blew out of the bathroom and rooted through Big Red in search of my diary. *When your heart and mind jam up,* I could hear Daddy saying, *pour your feelings onto the page.*

Without a word, Arch, who'd stripped to his trousers, escaped into the bathroom.

I plopped my butt in a chair and wrote.

Dear Diary, Why are men such asses?

Okay. So last night's entry had started the same way. So sue me for being unoriginal. I'd shot my creative load by being in character for twelve flippin' hours.

I deserve an Oscar, dammit. I deserved that emcee job, not Britney. I deserved a happily-ever-after with the man I gave my best years to, not Sasha!

I ranted and whined, spewed everything I couldn't say out loud because good girls don't complain. I scrambled to finish my last thought just as Arch ventured out of the bathroom.

"What are you doing?"

"Writing in my diary."

"What are you writing?"

"Private stuff."

"Like what?"

"If I told you it wouldn't be private." I closed and locked the diary just as he stepped in behind me.

He hovered over my shoulder, reading the cover. *"Secrets of a Diva."*

I didn't need to turn to know that he'd shed the prosthetics, showered off the hair dye and snuck a smoke. All I had to do was breathe. Irish Spring, tobacco and shaving cream. The return of Mr. Manly Man. Criminy.

"You *dinnae* strike me as a diva," he said. "Divas let everyone know their feelings."

Avoid eye contact. Maintain your composure. I sidled out of my seat and crossed the room without looking at him. "I voice my feelings."

"Not at the risk of confrontation."

"Are you saying I'm a wuss?"

"I'm saying you're nice."

Why did that feel like a strike against me? I buried my diary in my suitcase, hid the key. "You were going to say something else."

"Repressed."

As in distant? Cold? Michael told him I was conservative. As in *frigid?* The frustration I'd committed to paper resurfaced, simmering under my skin. I turned, fists balled at my side, ready to knock Arch on his butt. There'd been a lot of "firsts" in the past two days. It could happen. But he was already on the floor, on his hands and toes...doing *push-ups*.

My thoughts stalled as I reacquainted myself with Arch Reece, the dark and dangerous rebel. I hadn't seen him without his aging makeup since last night. How had I forgotten how insanely handsome he was? I watched his muscles flex as he continued to work his upper body, dressed in loose-fitting sweatpants and a tight black T-shirt. Jeesh. I couldn't bring myself to rise for an early jog, and here he was exercising after a long day. He'd performed twelve flipping hours, too. Then again, he was probably ten years younger than me.

Since he wasn't looking at me, I continued to admire his arms and shoulders. It also made it easier for me to speak freely. I couldn't bring myself to ask if Michael had spoken to him about our sex life, but I could address that confrontation thing. "If you had seen me in action yesterday morning, you'd take back that repressed crack."

"It was an observation, not an insult." He continued the push-ups. Nine. Ten. "What did you do?"

"Told off a group of executives." I didn't mention the flashing biz. It was too embarrassing. Too childish.

"Why?"

"Because they talked through my audition. It was rude."

"What were you auditioning for?"

"A casino spokesperson." Anxious, I fingered my ring. It made me think of Jayne. She would have been perfect for the job, as well. Another victim of ageism. "You know. A costumed greeter who answers patrons' questions and fills them in on the latest tournaments and sweepstakes."

"Sounds like a waste of your talent, yeah? You're an actress. A singer."

"I'm also over forty." Oh, great. Reveal your age. Burst his bubble. Kiss the horizontal mambo goodbye. What vibrant thirtysomething guy wants to get it on with an over-forty has-been?

He paused in the middle of his twenty-fifth push-up—yes, I'd been counting—and studied me.

My cheeks burned under his bold appraisal. Why hadn't I at least put on some lip gloss? "I know. I don't look my age. But I don't look twenty, either, and that's what everyone wants."

"Not everyone."

I blinked. Was that a come-on? Was he admitting he appreciated older women? Me?

He focused back on the carpet, resumed his push-ups. "Fuck 'em."

Who? The casinos or Michael? They'd all abandoned me for younger women.

"There are other places to perform."

I snorted. "What, like New York? Hollywood? Nashville?" I clenched my jaw against a surge of anger. I paced the spacious suite, patriotic music swelling in my head. "The recording and movie industries are youth oriented. Opportunities for female performers over the age of forty are slim. And that's for the ones who have already established themselves."

"There are other options."

"Sure. Singing telegrams and hawking cars in a gorilla suit."

He chuckled as he rose to his feet. "Not exactly what I had in mind."

"Oh, right. I could host karaoke night at Dooley's." I shot him a look of disgust as I paced by. "I'd rather be shot and put out of my misery than put out to pasture."

He ran a hand over his mouth, probably to disguise another smile, stroked those sexy black whiskers. "That's a wee bit dramatic, yeah?"

How dare he trivialize my career crisis! "Easy for you to be blasé. You're a man."

"You noticed."

I blew over his playful sarcasm. "Men have greater longevity in entertainment. Look at Sean Connery, Harrison Ford, Robert Redford, Clint Eastwood. They're over sixty and they still land lead roles, some of them romantic. Pierce Brosnan stayed on as James Bond even after fifty. Do you think they'd let an over-fifty woman play a Bond Girl? No! Why? Because Hollywood and fashion magazines have brainwashed people into thinking that the older a woman gets the less beautiful she becomes."

"That's *bullshite*."

"That's entertainment."

"So get out."

I threw my arms wide. "And do what? I've spent the last twenty years performing in casinos, Arch. It's what I do. It's who I am. They don't want me anymore. Do you have any idea of what it's like to not be able to do what you do best?"

"Aye."

I stopped in front of him, heart hammering. He'd just done fifty push-ups and wasn't even breathing hard. "You do?"

He dragged a hand through his dark, wet hair. "Sometimes life throws you a curve, Sunshine. Sometimes you're forced to move on."

"What were *you* forced to move on from?"

He quirked a lopsided smile. "Doing what I do best."

"You talk in circles, you know that?" No doubt about it. He rivaled Michael in the art of saying something without saying anything at all. I spun away and fell back on the bed with a weary sigh.

"Change is never easy, Evie."

"It sucks."

"Usually."

He stretched out next to me on the bed and my pulse skyrocketed. We lay side by side, staring at the ceiling. My body tensed with excitement and dread. Was he going to make a move? Did I want him to make a move?

Yes.

No.

Not this minute. This minute I longed to be held and comforted. Would he sense that? Should I ask? Take the initiative and roll into his arms? "I wanted to get away from it all," I said, my voice sounding as fragile as I felt. *Crap.* "To forget. Then you dragged me into that stupid casino."

"Ah."

"Did we have to go in there?"

"Afraid so."

"Smoke and mirrors?"

"Aye."

I felt the back of his hand knock against mine. I opened my palm, casually, heart in throat, and, yes… *yes,* he interlaced his fingers with mine. I waited for him to roll on top of me, to turn this into something sexual. Michael would. Well, at least he used to. He never understood the concept of cuddling. When Arch made no move other than to hold my hand, I wondered if it was because he wasn't interested or because he was being sensitive. Instead of forty-one, I felt fourteen. I plucked at an imaginary daisy. *He wants me, he wants me not.* "I'd feel better if you'd tell me who we were duping and why."

"Maybe."

"But you're not going to tell me."

"No."

I finally looked away from the ceiling and at the man lying beside me. "Because you think I can't handle it? That I'll freak out and my jaw will lock? Because that's not why it happened. I'm not stressed about this job."

He shifted, met my gaze and I swear, he looked straight into my soul. "What, then?"

I realized suddenly that I was doing something with Arch that I rarely did with Michael. Discussing my feelings. He stroked his thumb over the back of my hand, and again I felt a spark, a connection that I couldn't name. My heart thudded as I felt the world shift. Or maybe it was the ship. Yes, we were definitely rocking. Subtly, but still… Since he'd asked, and since I was feeling uncharacteristically chatty, I started with my most recent and nagging source of anxiety. "Did you ever see *Titanic?*"

CHAPTER FOURTEEN

A SOFT KNOCK WOKE Milo out of a sound sleep.

"Room service," a muffled voice called.

They'd had room service hours ago. He squinted at his travel alarm. Two-fifteen in the morning.

Arch.

Gina had established contact earlier this evening. Their renegade teammate had agreed to a meeting, though he hadn't specified a time. Just like the irritating bastard to show up in the middle of the night.

Milo sat up and switched on a bedside lamp. Gina was already in motion. She slept in boxer shorts and a tank top. Palming his aching head, he took in her toned legs and arms, her sexy, rumpled hair. He glanced down at his limp dick. *What the hell's wrong with you?*

She shoved her arms into a bathrobe, opened the door. Enter a mustached steward of seemingly Mediterranean descent, carrying a tray boasting two long-stemmed crystal flutes and a bottle of Perrier-Jouet.

He didn't ask where or how Arch had gotten the uniform or the champagne. He didn't care. "If the Agency finds out about this trip, my ass is grass."

"Your arse shouldn't be here. I flew out of Philly incognito to avoid this. Figured The Kid would track me, but not until after we'd sailed."

"You underestimated Woody."

"Either that or I'm slipping."

You said it, Milo thought, *not me.*

Arch placed the tray on the nightstand, turned and surveyed the room. "Flamingo. Fuchsia. What the bloody hell would you call this?"

"Fuck you."

"Uh-uh." Arch snapped his fingers. "Pink." He grinned. "Sweet."

Gina grabbed the bottle and popped the cork.

Milo waved off the glass she offered. He'd taken a painkiller just before midnight. "Dammit, Arch, Chameleon passed on this case."

"No, *you* passed." The career confidence man sat in the room's only chair, stretched out his legs and thumbed open the top two buttons of his white jacket.

"One complaint doesn't carry much weight, especially one lodged on hearsay. I did a preliminary check and Celia Benson's story—or rather her grandfather's deathbed ramblings—didn't wash."

"I paid a call on Ms. Benson."

"Son of a—"

"Relax. I *didnae* go as myself."

"Of course not."

"Or on behalf of Chameleon. I introduced myself as a private investigator. Said I'd been tipped off by an anonymous do-gooder from her local bunco squad. Since it was the first stop in her grandfather's chain of complaints regarding the fraud, she bought my story."

"Why the hell did you make contact at all?" Milo tempered his aggravation by reminding himself of all the times *he'd* sidestepped policy. "Even if Ms. Benson's complaint is valid, we can't touch this team of grifters. Not legally. Be it one or fifty victims."

"They're fleecing the elderly."

"Lots of con artists target the elderly. We've got no evidence. And one—" he held up a finger "—*one* official beef."

Arch laughed. "For fuck's sake, Jazzman. You know as well as I do that most marks never report falling prey to a scam. Especially the old folk. They know they were fools, but if they press charges friends and neighbors will know, too. Who wants to risk a family member charging them incompetent and committing them to a nursing home? It's a valid fear, yeah?"

"Let's not forget the psychological manipulation," Milo gritted out. "Once you're done with a mark, you've not only robbed him of his money, but also his dignity. Goodbye, self-esteem. Hello, guilt and shame."

Arch deflected Milo's sarcasm with an arrogant

grin. "We're not talking *aboot* me, but since you're pointing the finger, I've never stolen a bloody penny. I *dinnae* have to."

"You fleece them with your charm. Got it. Spare me the lecture in Scams 101." He knew the drill. He'd committed himself to learning the confidence game inside and out. Rule number one: Professional swindlers don't employ violence. The mark willingly hands over his or her money, making con artists, if they are indeed caught, difficult to convict. Where's the crime? Local law enforcement's inefficiency in investigating and prosecuting fraud is what prompted Milo's midthirties career crisis. The result: Men in Black over Men in Blue.

Arch leaned forward, braced his forearms on his thighs. "You're pissed because I blew you off. Sorry, mate, but you wouldn't budge and I couldn't leave go. These bastards broke the code."

"What *code?*"

Arch dragged his hands down his face, looking as though he regretted his words.

Gina piped in. "I assume he's referring to the violent aspect of the case. Professional grifters don't employ thugs to work over marks."

Milo popped another painkiller, hoping to ease a headache that had worsened with Arch's arrival. "There's no forensic evidence to support Ms. Benson's claim that *thugs* are responsible for her grandfather's death. According to the autopsy report, Stokes died of natural causes. A heart attack. Period.

Not inconceivable considering his advanced age and depressed state of mind. His wife died not two weeks before."

"Had you dug deeper—"

"Ms. Benson's report indicated that, according to her grandfather, the come-on and sting took place in La Romana. The Dominican Republic, Arch. That falls under territorial law. Out of our jurisdiction." Milo glanced at Gina, who knew the law as well as he did. She sat cross-legged on her bed, glass in one hand, the bottle in the other. Apparently, she wasn't inclined to share with their guest. The fact that they hadn't exchanged pleasantries also piqued Milo's curiosity.

"If that's not enough to deter you, and it should be," Milo continued, "the alleged mark and alleged roper were of two different nationalities, the ship from a third country. The alleged crime, for Christ's sake, took place in a *fourth* country."

Arch studied him with an enigmatic expression. "The difference between you and me is that you play by the rules."

"Not always." If he played by the rules, Arch would be serving time. "You're determined to make my life hell, aren't you?"

Arch smiled. "Just returning the favor."

Again, Milo was aware of Gina's silence. She sat drinking, taking it all in, her keen brown eyes ping-ponging between the two men. "Bad enough you acted without the team," he said to Arch. "You had to pull in an unsanctioned player?"

"Evie wasn't my first choice. A last-minute glitch. Lemonade out of lemons, yeah?"

"You could've used me." Gina's first words since Arch had entered the room. She smirked. "Oh, wait. You did." She drained her champagne, poured more.

Milo assessed the situation. *Son of a bitch.* His partner had bedded and dumped Gina. He glared at the bastard who had the balls to shrug. Tension between team members. Great. Just great. "Do you even know this Evie?"

"I knew *of* her."

"Can she be trusted?" What was he saying? Only a fool trusts a grifter. He listened as Arch explained the personalities and background of Charles and Sugar Dupont. Sugar was a party girl, a free spender who had her wealthy husband wrapped around her finger. Charles, it would seem to anyone who observed, would do anything to keep his young wife happy, including investing in a good-time time share.

"So the brainless-bimbo thing is an act," Gina said. "She's pretending to be the kind of twit that will fall for anything. That's always attractive to a roper." She smirked. "Good call, Ace. The outside man won't be able to resist her."

Actually, it was. Milo shot her a look, while asking his partner, "What do you know about this woman?"

"She's a professional actress. She's good."

"An actress? Not a player? You're joking, right?"

"She can handle it."

"How much did you tell her?"

"Not much." He smiled, shook his head. "Christ, she's easy."

Gina leveled Arch with a deadly glare. "I almost feel sorry for her."

Milo frowned. "I'm inclined to agree."

Arch unleashed a rare show of temper. "Listen, you weren't supposed to know *aboot* this. Not until I'd lured these bastards back onto American soil. I mean, that was your bloody problem, right? That you can't touch them *legally?* As long as they're within your jurisdiction, as long as there's proof or a confession, then you can arrest the buggers, take them out of commission, yeah?"

"Yeah."

"Right, then. Now that you're here, you're in." He leaned forward, rested his forearms on his knees and lowered his voice. "We'll divide and conquer. We know the roper's a crew member."

Milo held up a hand. "Hold on. How do we know they're still working *this* ship?"

"I know," Arch said without further explanation. "What I don't know is the roper's identity. And unfortunately, Mr. Stokes *didnae* provide his granddaughter with the name or description."

"Just an overview of the sequence of events," Gina said, "that led to the poor sucker forking over seventy thousand dollars for a 'once-in-a-lifetime' investment."

"The roper directed Mr. Stokes to a Mr. Simon Lamont of Dragonfly Cruises," Milo said, recalling the granddaughter's written statement.

"The inside man," Gina said.

The big guy. The boss. The smooth-talking hustler who pitched the irresistible deal—the come-on. Milo wrung his hands together as frustration with Arch gave way to anticipation of the hunt. "We dock in La Romana on Thursday. That gives us three days."

Gina whistled low. "Do you know how many employees are on this ship?"

"Stokes said he considered the man who introduced him to Lamont a *good egg*. We're talking someone he and his wife had a lot of contact with. Someone in a highly visible position. Hospitality or entertainment." Arch rubbed the back of his neck. "The key is to be as visible as possible. Between the four of us we can spread a lot of *bullshite*, yeah? We have the advantage. We're savvy to the psychological aspects. I've already targeted three likely suspects. The assistant cruise director, the shore excursion director and Beau, the poolside bartender."

"I'll feel them out," Milo said.

"I ran into a dance instructor who also conducts various activities and games," Gina said. "Fred. A real silver-tongued Romeo."

"Fred?" Milo asked.

"You know. Like Astaire." She rolled her eyes.

"Get with it, Jazzman. Like that's his real name. He's a hot-blooded Spaniard with more lines than Disney World. Trust me, he's suspect. Although if he got to Stokes, it was probably through *Mrs*. Stokes. This one works the ladies."

"So we keep an eye on these few while scoping other possibilities," Arch said. "Once we determine our mark—"

"—we con the hustler into believing we're *his* perfect marks," Gina finished.

"Between the two couples, one of us will win an introduction to Lamont and that team will hook and lure him back to the States."

A bastardized version of a Turnaround Confidence. At times like this Milo wondered who was in charge of Chameleon, him or Arch? He usually soothed his ego with the A.I.A's mantra: *Results are all that matter*. But something felt off-kilter with this one. Mainly the unsanctioned player. "What's the bait?"

Arch checked his watch, stood. "I'll explain when we meet up again. Tomorrow morning in the Fiesta Theater. Ten-thirty."

Milo raised a guarded brow. "What's wrong with now?"

He secured his buttons, smoothed the uniform and picked up the empty tray. "I need to get back. I *dinnae* want Evie to wake up alone."

Gina poured more bubbly. "God forbid."

The door closed behind Arch and Milo dropped

his throbbing head into his hands. In the space of ten minutes, he'd seen a flash of his partner's temper and a peek at his tender side. Genuine emotions. Arch was definitely off his game.

Gina abandoned her glass and robe, wiggled under the sheets. "Notice he didn't explain why he contacted Ms. Benson in the first place?"

Fending off a feeling of doom, Milo switched off the lamp. "I noticed."

CHAPTER FIFTEEN

THE SEX WAS GREAT.

In my dreams, anyway. I fell asleep talking. Stretched out on the cushy, queen-size bed, I'd spewed my fears about drowning. Although, maybe that was preferable to enduring the demise of my career—*Did I mention three casinos are requesting lounge bands with twentysomething members only?*

Arch mostly listened to my self-pitying rant. Unlike Nicole and Jayne, he didn't add fuel to the fire. His calm demeanor eventually cooled my jets. I fell asleep reminiscing, telling him about the time I fell off a trapeze in a casino showroom. I guess that's why I dreamed about having creative monkey sex in a Bungee Sex Swing. No, I didn't have practical experience. I saw it featured on *The Tonight Show*. But there could be a first time. Call me adventurous—my new motto.

I woke up disoriented and frisky, a man's arm wrapped around my waist. At first I basked in the fact that I wasn't alone. I felt safe and cherished and, if this was a lucid dream, I never wanted to wake.

Spooning was heaven, except…Michael didn't like to spoon. Reality poked at my hazy brain. Something else poked at my backside. Something massive and granitelike. Not Michael, I realized, now fully awake. Arch.

Oh, boy, oh, boy.

I blinked at the sunshine pouring through the parted drapes like a spotlight. My heart pounded. My body froze. *Showtime.* Only I was unsure of my lines, the blocking. What should I say? Do? This was totally awkward. He was either sleeping or pretending to be asleep. He was *not* taking the lead. JT, however, was ready to rumble.

I hadn't partied with the one-eyed monster in over a year. I'd never partied with a John Thomas as daunting as Arch's. Not that size mattered. At least, I don't think it does.

One way to find out, Nicole taunted from afar.

My hoo-ha tingled in anticipation. Have mercy, I begged. Instead, time dragged. Maybe he was waiting for me to make the first move. Waiting for a sign. I could wiggle my fanny against him or turn into him and run my fingers through his devilish dark hair. I could flash a playful smile, sing a line from an old disco fave. *"Do you wanna get funky with me?"* But not with morning breath and bedhead. And, crap, no makeup. Could I ease out of his arms, sneak into the bathroom, brush my teeth and hair, apply minimal cosmetics and crawl back into bed without waking him?

Not the way my luck had been running.

If he woke up while I was in the bathroom, he might rise and start his morning rituals—my chance for sex blown. Or maybe he'd instigate conversation and I'd say something stupid and wilt his erection—my chance for sex blown.

My mind continued to spin the possible scenarios. I'd fallen asleep without that stupid splint. What if I opened my mouth to respond and it locked open again? What if he deemed me unfit for this job? Left me behind at the first island stop? No money, nowhere to go but home where there was no work, no husband, no *life*.

Maybe we could have sex without kissing.

Not.

Arch was an Olympic kisser—gold medal. No way did I want to miss out on that. My mouth watered just thinking about his naked body. Exploring all that sinew would be a sensual thrill. Nipping and licking that six-pack was at the top of the list, followed closely by running my tongue along that tribal tattoo.

I thought about him nipping and licking me and the tingling intensified. Except wait. That meant him seeing *me* naked. No sinew. No sexy piercings. And sans the extreme-cleavage bra, no boobs. Well, I have boobs, of course, perky boobs—that's a plus—but they're small. Although, wait. Arch was a leg man, right? I had decent legs. Maybe he'd focus on those.

"I can hear your wheels turning."

Did he mean my teeth grinding?

"Morning, Sunshine." He kissed the back of my neck and rolled away and out of bed before I could act. Hadn't considered *that* scenario.

"Well, darn," I mumbled as he shut himself in the bathroom and day two of this gig began—*without* a bang.

MENTAL NOTE: Cruises are fattening. My waist expanded two inches just reading the culinary choices featured on the daily itinerary sheet. Aside from regular meals, the ship offered round-the-clock pizza and hot dogs and a midnight buffet. And what was up with the ice-cream-sundae-making contest? Let's not even talk about the twenty-four-hour room service—Arch's choice for breakfast.

As was our routine, he ordered while I showered. The fact that we *had* a routine fascinated me. We'd known each other less than three days and yet we joked and bickered like old friends. Old friends with the hots for each other. I'd never experienced anything like it.

Sitting across from each other at the suite's balcony table, tropical skies as our backdrop, I was superaware of the sexual tension we'd yet to address. No way would I bring it up first. What if I'd misread the situation? What if the attraction was, in reality, one-sided? Maybe that morning wood had been the result of a sexy dream.

What did a man like Arch fantasize about, anyway? Probably something really risqué. Probably something I shouldn't ponder over breakfast, especially since he was way more appetizing than my veggie omelet.

I nibbled on a piece of rye toast and refocused on the itinerary. Arts and crafts, bingo, a fashion show and cha-cha lessons. Plenty of contests and activities to keep Sugar-the-social-butterfly fluttering.

"Something wrong with your food?"

I glanced from the itinerary to my traveling companion, my boss, my stage husband, the man I'd slept with, only literally. He'd yet to apply the prosthetics, so I was forced to endure his staggering good looks. I swallowed a groupie sigh. "No. There's just a lot of it."

He lit a cigarette, shrugged. "Not so much. You *didnae* finish your meal last night, either. You must be starving."

"Not so much." Not for food, anyway. I watched him take a long drag, blow out a lazy stream of smoke and marveled that I actually found it sexy. Why did he have to be so flipping bad-boy gorgeous? And so *young?*

Yeah, boy, when he wasn't sporting Charles's wrinkles and silver hair our age difference remained a tough pill to swallow. "How old are you, anyway?"

He scraped white teeth over his sexy bottom lip, poured more coffee.

Cheeks burning, I set the itinerary aside and

sipped my green tea. "That was rude. I'm sorry. Forget I asked."

He stirred sugar, *real* sugar, into his java. Sure, *he* had a youthful metabolism. Never mind that earlier, while I was in the bathroom transforming into Sugar, he'd tackled sit-ups and push-ups and jogged in place for thirty minutes listening to whatever music pumped out of his MP3 player. Yeah, never mind that, I thought as I gripped and twirled my ring.

"Age is a real issue with you, yeah?"

"No."

His mouth quirked.

Was my nose growing? "I mean, yes, obviously. Hence my rant last night." *Twirl, twirl.* "Not that you'd understand. You're a man. A young one at that. Not that it matters."

He glanced at my ring, at me. "It matters."

I fidgeted in my seat. "I know you're my employer and all, but I have to tell you…that's kind of irritating. That *I-know-your-mind* thing that you do. You don't know me."

"I *dinnae* have to know you, Evie. You're easy to read."

"Meaning I'm predictable?"

"Meaning your body language betrays your feelings."

I stiffened.

He snuffed the cigarette then shoved out of his chair. "You're a gifted actress, but a wretched liar."

Was that a compliment? An insult? I sat there, contemplating an appropriate comeback as he snatched up stuffy cruise wear and a black makeup case.

"Thirty-nine," he said and disappeared into the bathroom.

Thirty-nine years old? No way! I would've sworn early thirties, not late, although his personality smacked of a mature, confident man. *Thirty-nine?* One year from forty. Only two years younger than me. Not that I felt like the elder. I felt like a besotted teen. Two years' age difference. In the older woman–younger man scheme of things, that didn't even count. Did it?

I imagined Nicole and Jayne rolling their eyes, speaking in unison. *Jump him.*

Right. The age issue melted away. Two years. Heh. Nothing. Certainly nothing like the quarter-century Michael-Sasha age difference. Still, having a hot and sweaty fling with a hot and hunky guy, an associate of Stone Entertainment no less, would absolutely tarnish my conservative crown. I'm not one to boink and tell, but, I gotta confess, I was pretty jazzed about rubbing Michael's nose in my sex-capades.

All I had to do was have one.

Come on, creative monkey sex! The only thing holding me back was, well, *me.* I'd never been the aggressor. Never had casual sex. Before Michael, there'd been three other men—all serious relationships. I wasn't the type to seduce a mysterious, vibrant stranger.

But Sugar was....

I scrambled toward the vanity mirror, rolled up my rib-hugging T-shirt and studied my lily-white stomach. Skimping on dinner and breakfast had paid off. I didn't look buff, but I didn't look fat. Just soft. Most of the women on this ship were over fifty. I thought about Martha, over seventy and battling elephant skin and varicose veins. That didn't stop her from wearing shorts. I wouldn't be surprised if I caught her in a two-piece bathing suit.

I pointed at my reflection and spoke some nonsense at myself. "You're not Evie. You're Sugar. Age is a state of mind and Sugar's a kid at heart. You're fun-loving and proud of your body. You're sexy. Arch said so yesterday. Wear the Keds."

I sashayed across the room, peeling off my tee and singing Sugar's new signature song. "I'm too sexy for my shirt, too sexy for my shirt. So sexy it hurts."

I dipped into Big Red and pulled out a bright green bikini. I dressed quickly, doubled up the padding in the cups, pulled white denim shorts over the French-cut bottoms and slipped on my flowery Keds. I was bent over, tying the laces when Arch exited the bathroom and uttered my new favorite word.

"Bollocks."

INSTEAD OF ATTENDING the shore excursions talk in the Fiesta Theater, Arch asked me to visit the shops in the Atrium. "I need you to make some purchases, yeah?" He pulled on the Panama straw hat, completing his transformation into Charles. "Perfume, clothes, trinkets. Whatever catches Sugar's eye. Charge it to our Fiesta Card."

The card that doubles as room key and passenger ID. At the end of the cruise those charges would be transferred to whatever credit card Arch had provided at check-in. I had to ask. "Who's paying for this?"

"The company."

"What company?"

"TCC."

"TCC Productions? Never heard of them." Truth was I no longer believed that Arch was affiliated with a legitimate production company. I suspected he wasn't a professional actor as much as a master of disguise. So what exactly was TCC and what exactly was Arch's profession? All I'd been told was that we were duping some creep for the greater good. It was no longer enough. "You and I need to chat."

"Not now."

"But—"

He tweaked my nose. "Later, Sunshine."

I could do without the nose tweaking, but at least he kept eyeballing my body. Two points for skimpy attire! I'm pretty sure I'd hooked him. All I had to do was reel him in. I was banking on Sugar's help in that department.

Before she/I could act, Arch/Charles snatched up his cane and strode toward the cabin door. Once in the hall, I was sure he'd incorporate that fake limp. Why did he have to have a limp, anyway? How did that play in? More questions to be answered *later.* "Where should I meet you? When?"

"You mentioned a dance class."

"Cha-cha Fever with Fred and Ginger." I already knew the traditional steps, *plus* the Cha-cha Slide and the Cowboy Cha-cha. But it was dance class or a basketball tournament, and the only balls I wanted to handle were Arch's. "Eleven-thirty. Deck Nine. Poolside."

"I'll find you."

"You stay alive, no matter what occurs!" I mimicked in an overdramatic voice. "I will find you!"

"Hawkeye to Cora. *Last of the Mohicans.* Nineteen ninety-two film adaptation."

"You're amazing."

"That's what they all say." He winked and then he was gone.

ONE HOUR TO SHOP. One hour to buy perfume, clothes or some sort of trinket. Nicole, Jayne and I have been known to spend entire days shopping. But they weren't here and I wasn't me. Sugar, I decided as I slipped into the Internet Lounge, was an impulse buyer. She could do serious damage in half an hour.

I located an open computer terminal, sat in a high-backed leather chair and signed on. Connecting to my server took longer than I was used to, and the rates were costly, so I vowed to read fast and respond briefly.

I clicked on an e-mail from Jayne.

So glad you wrote, Evie. I wasn't up to another conversation with Michael. He's such a jerk. Sure you don't want to sign on with my agent?

Re: The singing telegram position. I need the extra money so I'm going for it. Please don't think less of me.

Re: Lisa LeFarre's breasts. Gossip is a certain VP of Table Games is groping them.

Speaking of groping... Have you done any? Nic said you're rooming with a Gerard Butler look-alike. Lucky you! I loved him in *Phantom of the Opera*. Can your Scot sing?

Having dinner at Nic's tonight. Will give her your love. Miss you much!

Love, Jayne

P.S. Please be extra careful. Madame Helene said that one of my loved ones is in danger and she's never wrong. Well, hardly ever.

I whipped off a quick response.

How can you leave me hanging like that, Jayne? Which VP? Which casino? Dying of curiosity. Watch. She'll marry the guy and be set for life. What's up with men's obsession with youth and breasts?

Speaking of...what does your dream book say about gorillas and breasts? Two separate subjects.

Re: The singing telegram position. Of course I don't think less of you. Go for it!

Groping. Um, yes, a little. Several atomic kisses. I don't know if he sings, but he likes music. Oh, and he insisted I go shopping, his treat. He's too good to be true, right? Right.

I have to run. Wish you were here.

Love, Evie

P.S. You know what I think about Madame Helene.

Skimming past junk mail, I spied a note from my brother. Yes! Whether it was good news or bad, at least I wouldn't be in purgatory. Once I knew the situation, at least I'd know whether to laugh or cry.

Evelyn,

Dad bought the Corner Tavern. Can you blame Mom for blowing a gasket? Don't worry. I'll handle it.

Mom says you're on a cruise ship. Work or pleasure?

Christopher

My heart hammered as my fingers flew over the keys in ticked response.

What do you mean Dad bought the Corner

Tavern? When? Why? If you don't want me to worry, please be more forthcoming with details.

Yes, I'm on a cruise ship. Work. Did you give Sandy and the kids my best?

Love, Evie

I sat staring at the computer screen, my body vibrating with a half-dozen emotions. I felt bad about the potshot I'd taken at the singing telegram position in my initial e-mail to Jayne. I didn't realize she was considering the job, although I know she's nearly as desperate as me for work. Ten years ago, I would have taken that gig. A temporary fix. Certainly better for my artistic soul than working a cash register or serving up today's special. *Now* the thought of showing up on a stranger's doorstep and singing "Happy Birthday" filled me with… I don't know. Contempt? Humiliation? Hardly a job for a forty-one-year-old woman. Whether that was my or my mom's thought, I don't know. But the notion nagged my brain. As did the thought, *I'm meant for something more.*

The question was what?

Speaking of…*what* was my brother's problem? Great. Torture me with minimal information then flaunt your influence. *I'll handle it.* Of course he'd *handle it.* He was, after all, a male version of Mom. Logical and controlling. I resisted a second response. Resisted lashing out. I told myself to sign off and back away from the computer.

But then a new e-mail came in. An e-mail from Nicole.

Did you boink his brains out yet?
Nic

I laughed. Thank God for my friends.

CHAPTER SIXTEEN

HE SPIED ARCH SITTING on the right side of the theater, beneath the balcony overhang. Most of the audience sat closer to the stage, listening to the shore excursion director, Lucas, flag fun-filled day trips to exotic ports of call. Arch had positioned himself away from the bulk of the crowd.

Milo took advantage of the semiprivacy and slouched into the seat next to him.

Arch peered over the rims of his tinted glasses, noted his palm tree bowler shirt and jungle boots with a raised brow. "The disguise is almost as obnoxious as your alias's personality, yeah?"

"I live to offend." Milo grinned around the cigar clamped between his teeth. "You."

The man's lips twitched.

Milo itched to test his good humor by addressing Arch's fling with Gina. She wouldn't talk about it, but he knew she was pissed and that didn't bode well for the team. Unfortunately, time was limited and they needed to discuss the mission.

He veered his thoughts from Gina and tuned in

to Lucas's sales pitch. Informative. Enticing. He noted the body language of the crowd. Hooked. By the time the charismatic man wrapped, the majority of the audience would line up to book guided tours of multiple ports of call. The adventurous sort would taxi ashore and explore on their own. Very few would stay on board. Even a good portion of the crew would enjoy free time at port.

"The roper could be making his play on land as easily as at sea," Milo ventured softly. "A chance meeting in a local bar or shopping bazaar."

"True."

"Safer than being overheard by undercover security while on the job. I guarantee there are plainclothes officers circulating. Security surveillance on this ship is top-notch. Have you noticed all the cameras?"

"Aye. Public access areas are well protected."

"Watch your ass," Milo said. "They are."

"You doubt my abilities? I'm wounded."

"Like hell. So what's the plan?"

"You mean aside from giving the impression that we're wealthy opportunists?" His gaze slid to Milo. "Some of us morons?"

"Yeah, asshole. Aside from that."

Arch tapped his forefinger on the decorative tip of his cane. "We should book excursions."

"Genuine cruise enthusiasts would take advantage of ports of call." He nodded. "Got it. So tomorrow we trek into San Juan."

"Tomorrow, I'm going to have a setback with my ankle."

"That right?"

"You and Hot Legs go ashore. Evie and I will stay aboard."

"Divide and conquer."

"You're not in Stokes's age group, so you'll have to work the arrogant big-spender angle."

"I know my role, Arch."

"If our man's ashore and watching, we want him to peg you and your *wife* as perfect marks."

"If he stays on board and goes pigeon hunting he'll find the Duponts." Milo tamped down his annoyance. "Figured that out on my own. Imagine."

Arch grinned. "I'd cite the likeness of great minds, but your head's big enough, yeah?"

"Nothing compared to yours."

He scratched his silver whiskers. "Might help if the two couples bond publicly. Establishing a relationship would make meeting more convenient."

Milo considered. "Let's bump into each other at the poolside bar."

"Sunset. Beau's shift."

The bartender Arch had nominated as a possible roper. If he was their man and if Milo played his cards right, Beau would try to gain *his* confidence. Fine by him. Since he'd come this far, he wanted to be the mark. Safer because he'd be on the inside, not Arch. Even now he could feel a suppressed edginess to the man that he'd felt only once before.

Lamont broke the code. What frickin' code? No honor among thieves...or grifters. So what had prompted Arch to circumvent Chameleon and investigate Ms. Benson's beef on his own? The man didn't act without purpose. "Why are we here, Arch? What's in it for you?"

"Peace of mind."

He knew when he was being stonewalled. He let it slide. Pushing would get him nowhere and might end up garnering unwanted attention. He'd press later. In private. He wanted to know why he was risking A.I.A's wrath before this reverse sting went down.

He tongued his cigar to the other side of his mouth. "Most hustlers would have hit and run, transferred their game to another cruise line. The longer Lamont plucks pigeons from this ship, the greater his chances of being caught."

"He'll move on. Eventually. He's cocky and he's got a good thing going. I *dinnae* think his roper's a career grifter. More like a disgruntled employee who took the position when presented with a get-rich-quick scheme."

There had to be more to it. "What do you know that you're not telling me?"

Arch rolled back his shoulders, visibly weighed his words, the cagey bastard. "I'm familiar with Lamont."

"Why didn't you say something before?"

"I wasn't sure at the time. I needed to be sure. I

made some quiet inquiries within the circle and…this is something I need to do."

"So this is personal."

"Yeah."

"Christ."

Arch shrugged. "Pull *oot*. Turn a blind eye. You and Gina can catch a flight out of San Juan and be home by tomorrow night."

"And leave you alone? Risk you landing your ass in a foreign prison?" Milo dragged a hand down his face. "No offense, but your emotions are showing."

"Bugger."

"Yeah." In this game, genuine emotions made a man vulnerable. Compromised his judgment. He knew it and Arch knew it. *Mistake #1*: He'd dragged an inexperienced player into this. What if things went wrong and Evie paid the price? Arch didn't have much of a conscience, but Milo did.

They sat in silence for a moment, listening to Lucas's accented patter. Milo sighed. "So what's the bait? Say the roper introduces you to Lamont. How are you going to tempt him back to the States?"

"Art."

"Art?"

Arch nodded. "Lamont's fingers are in a lot of pots, yeah? He occasionally appropriates masterpieces for a private art collector."

"He's an art thief?"

"He's a criminal with varied interests and contacts. A scum-artist. This collector shells out astronomical money for priceless paintings. Lamont's orchestrated a few scams, substituted forgeries for genuine articles."

"So the galleries, museums, whatever, are unaware that they've been robbed," Milo surmised.

"Aye."

"Art theft *and* investment fraud."

"Like I said, varied interests. Thing is, the last scam Lamont pulled for this collector curdled. As a result, they're on shaky terms just now. Given the buyer's obsession and deep pockets, Lamont would like nothing better than to get back in his good graces."

Milo mulled over the information. "Okay. So I'm guessing Charles Dupont possesses something that would be of particular interest to this collector. Something valuable enough, rare enough to lure Lamont back to the States for a lucrative switch." He glanced sideways at Arch. "Am I close?"

"Bang on."

"You seem awfully sure of yourself."

"I'm sure of Lamont's greed."

Milo blew out a breath. "Fine. So art is your bait. What if the roper passes you over, introduces me to Lamont instead? That angle won't work for my alias, unless that collector's interested in an Elvis on black velvet."

Arch cracked a smile. "We'll figure something out before and if that time comes."

"Why didn't Woody turn up this art forgery information when he ran a background check on Lamont?"

"Simon Lamont's an alias. One of many. The Kid's good, but Lamont's slippery, hence his moniker, Simon the Fish."

Again Milo sensed an edginess in Arch that set off warning bells. "You know, whatever your beef is with Lamont, you can be up-front with me. We're partners." That comment earned him a raised brow. "More or less."

The Scot bit back a smile. "This dance of ours, it's a bit mystifying, yeah? Why the hell do we put up with each other?"

"Good question."

ARMED WITH MY FIESTA CARD, I perused the shelves of an exclusive gift shop in the ship's Atrium. I'd spent more time online than I'd anticipated, so I really needed to buy and run. I wish Arch had stipulated a price range. Normally a frugal person, my eyes bulged at most of the ticketed merchandise. I didn't need a new bathing suit; I'd packed three. The jewelry was pricy and not really to Sugar's taste. Perfume, I decided, was the way to go.

I picked up a small decanter of Chanel, sniffed. Nice. Chloé had a light, fruity scent. Also nice.

"If you really want to drive your man insane, try this."

I looked up to find a tall, striking brunette standing beside me at the cosmetic counter. The same brunette that I'd seen floating through the Atrium yesterday in a red chiffon dress. The one who'd caught Arch's eye. Today she was wearing another halter sundress—canary yellow—and carrying a Gucci purse that matched her gold strappy sandals. Her arms were toned, her skin flawless, and her supergorgeous legs stretched from here to the moon. She exuded confidence and expensive taste. Her face was you-gotta-hate-her gorgeous—a cross between Angelina Jolie and Catherine Zeta-Jones. Arch had admired her from the rear. I could only imagine his reaction to her exotic beauty full on.

I stiffened with jealousy, which was crazy because Arch and I weren't an item. Well, not in real life, anyway. Tall, Dark and Beautiful passed me a sample bottle of the perfume she'd just spritzed into the air. The scent, floral. The label, French. "I'm not familiar with this brand." Or the language, I thought, squinting at the foreign script.

"It's the scent that matters," she drawled in a lazy Southern accent. "Jasmine. Alleviates stress, promotes self-confidence and, best of all, works as an aphrodisiac. Sweet yet exotic." She raised a dark brow. "Appeals to a man's Madonna-whore fantasy."

I blinked at her bluntness. I reserved this kind of talk for close friends. This woman was less inhibited and so, I reminded myself, was Sugar. I sucked it up and played the role, relying on a portion of the profile Arch had drilled me on. "I know what you mean about the good girl–bad girl thing. My Charlie chased me around the bed after I surprised him with a Catholic schoolgirl getup." I cocked my head in deep bubble-brain thought. "I'm not sure what riled him most, the short plaid skirt or the bobby socks. Anyway, he sprained his ankle in the process, poor baby."

The woman's plump red lips curved into a coy smile, and for the first time in my life I wondered if I should brave collagen injections. Even *I* wondered how it would feel to kiss a mouth like that. No, I'm not bi, just imaginative and, okay, envious.

"Last night I surprised my husband wearing this fragrance and nothing else," she went on as I stood there mesmerized by her blatant sexuality. She leaned closer, spoke in a conspiratorial tone. "The man ate me up—head to toe." She straightened and summoned one of the salesclerks. "I'll take two bottles of Les Fleurs de Provence Jasmine, please."

So that was how you pronounced it.

"Forty percent off. Duty-free. Can't beat that," she said with a man-eating smile then slunk to the front cash register.

I'm sure she was just trying to be helpful, and I did want to seduce Arch, but instead of grateful I felt competitive. Call me crazy. Or insecure. I needed all the help I could get. I motioned to the second clerk. "I'll have what she's having."

I stood my ground as the brunette exited the shop without a "see ya" or a second look. I bristled, deciding without any real basis that I didn't like her very much. And, mostly, I like everybody. Mostly. But that woman struck me as a manipulator.

I flashed on yesterday's conversation with Nicole. *Michael blabbered something about the guy you're working for being a manipulator.*

My overactive imagination ran amok. Arch had watched the brunette glide through the atrium. Maybe he knew her. Was it possible? Could it be? Was Tall, Dark and Beautiful the bad sort we were striving to deceive? Was she a modern-day Mata Hari? A double agent? A sexy spy who used her feminine wiles to seduce top-secret information out of political and military lovers? Was Arch the undercover agent sent to bring her down? A real-life James Bond?

My heart pounded as the fantasy mushroomed in my mind like hype on Paris Hilton.

Get a grip, Evie.

It was only after she left that I realized Mata Hari stuck out on this ship more than I did. Far younger than most of the passengers, younger than me. Her beauty and confidence demanded attention as did her conditioned body. If we attended the same function, all eyes would swerve to her, and *I* was supposed to be the life of the party.

I snorted as I passed the clerk my Fiesta card. Well, duh, no wonder I didn't like her.

CHAPTER SEVENTEEN

IT'S EASY TO FORGET one is on a boat, excuse me, *ship,* when the vessel is several stories high and approximately as long as three football fields. We're talking huge! A fifty-thousand-ton floating resort hotel and, although I'd spent the day shopping, dining and participating in various games and classes, I'd only ventured onto three decks. I hoped to explore more of the ship before returning to Fort Lauderdale. Selfishly, I almost wished that we'd fall victim to the Bermuda Triangle so I wouldn't *have* to return home.

Just now I was on Deck Nine, the center of my social activities, in the middle of a late-afternoon dance party, a spin-off from this morning's cha-cha class. A few passengers splashed around in the Olympic-size pool, while others lounged and sipped margaritas. The poolside servers—smiley guys wearing Bermuda shorts and tropical shirts—certainly kept the frozen concoctions coming. Arch sat at the bar, sipping scotch, chatting intermittently with Beau-the-bartender and Dirk and Nan Iverson, an obnoxiously friendly couple from California. Every now and then he'd glance over at me.

Although I still wore a bikini, I'd swapped my short shorts for a floral ankle-length sarong and my Keds for platform sandals. The sandals weren't as comfy as my sneaks, but they looked adorable with the sarong—call me shallow. Besides, I reveled in the way Arch checked out my legs every time I twirled and the sarong parted. Since I was dancing with a pro and my insecurities do not extend to my ballroom techniques, I'll admit to showing off.

This morning, Fred and Ginger had noted right away I wasn't a novice. Since I was the only one in class without a partner—even Martha-of-the-Two-Left-Feet had shown up with a man—they'd matched me with Fred. Spicy hot, Brazilian-born Fred—definitely *not* his real name. The man was built and the man could dance, an ultrasexy combination. Like a latino Patrick Swayze in *Dirty Dancing*. This evening, Fred swept me into his arms the moment he realized Charles was out of the dancing picture, what with his, *ahem*, bum ankle. Fred looked at this as a chance to perform with an accomplished partner. I looked at this as an opportunity to make Arch squirm.

I'd been dancing with Fred for about ten minutes when Martha bopped up to the bar and engaged Arch in conversation. I continued to dance, but my mind wandered, rehashing the day thus far. I'd flitted from one activity to another—cha-cha lessons, bingo,

ceramic painting, merengue lessons—sitting only
long enough to have lunch with my husband. The
only activity he'd participated in was bingo. Otherwise, he'd loitered at the closest bar, sipping scotch
while chatting amiably with passengers and crew
members. How he could drink so much without
getting even a little drunk was a mystery.

Another mystery, I should say.

Although I mingled and frolicked as Sugar, part
of me remained sharp and in tune with my surroundings. Who specifically was I performing for?
Michael had cited a level of risk. Arch had confirmed that we were dealing with a dangerous sort.
You're safe with me, he'd promised. Obviously, I
believed him, because I wasn't scared, just curious.

The *unique deception* was us posing as the
wealthy Duponts. I got that. In public, Charles
lavished his new wife with affection, gourmet meals,
spa visits and shopping sprees. I rolled my eyes, remembering how I'd pegged the bombshell brunette
as a double agent. Jealousy, envy, insecurity,
whatever, makes you crazy. Me, anyway. Jeez. Earth
to Evie.

Arch wanted someone to believe that he was
enamored with his young wife and would do
anything to make her happy—that much I'd puzzled
through. What I couldn't figure was why I had to be
a sexy social butterfly. I guess it meant I usually
ended up the center of attention. I'd certainly made
a spectacle of myself at bingo when I'd instructed

Gavin to shake his balls. What? He kept calling *B*s and I needed a *G!* And, it's not like the majority of the geriatric crowd hadn't heard that one before. They proved their knowledge of clichéd bingo retorts when Gavin called B11 and they chorused *chicken legs!*

But I digress.

Everywhere I turned, everywhere I played I was surrounded by jovial vacationers. Mostly seniors. Mostly couples. Honeymooners, second honeymooners, couples celebrating aeons of togetherness. Couples like my parents—only my parents were no longer a couple. Another mystery. One I blocked out in consideration of my TMJ. Besides, my brother was handling the crisis and Christopher was enterprising and competent—so Mom had told me a billion times.

Truth be told, he was in a better position to engineer the reconciliation seeing that he lives in their—and my—hometown. I'm presently sailing through turquoise waters past a bunch of islands— the Caicos Archipelago, according to the daily itinerary sheet. Fat lot of good I could do from paradise.

I turned my face toward the sky, soaked in the sunshine, breathed in the salt air. I willed myself to steep in the fantasy of Sugar Dupont. A gift, really. A respite from real life.

If only I could seduce Arch, the fantasy would be complete. Later tonight, I'd spray on that Jasmine perfume, channel Sugar's confident sexuality and make my move. Tomorrow I aimed on knocking Nic's socks off when I e-mailed that, yes, indeed, *I'd boinked his brains out*. The mere notion made me dizzy—or maybe that was the four-revolution spin I'd just come out of. The more I kept up with Fred, the more complex his moves got. I wondered if I'd be able to keep up with Arch—in bed, not on the dance floor. Although if he wanted to do it on the floor, or in the shower, or against the wall...call me willing.

Martha stepped away and I refocused on getting a rise out of JT, er, Arch.

The setting was perfect. Sunset. Skies of pink, orange and red. The moon newly visible on the horizon. Music—dirty, sexy—more salsa than cha-cha. Fred gripped my scantily clad body and we undulated in joint expression. Hot. Sensual. Our gazes locked—Arch's and mine, not Fred's. Heat pooled in my southern hemisphere. I danced seductively with my instructor, but I was seducing my roommate. I felt naughty, empowered. I could feel the conservative crown slipping. I sensed Arch's interest, could feel the sparks zapping between us, even though we were yards apart.

Just then Tex Aloha sauntered up to the bar wearing patriotic swimming trunks and his cowboy hat. Flip-flops, no shirt. He edged in between Dirk and Nan, motioned Beau for a drink. His timing, once again, sucked. He claimed Arch's attention and ruined my seduction!

Fred ground his lower region against me and nuzzled my ear. *Uh-oh.*

Cheeks flaming, I stammered that I should get back to my husband, only Fred held tight.

"Rarely do I get to dance with someone as beautiful and talented as you, Mrs. Dupont. Surely your husband wouldn't mind if we finished this song."

I might have been flattered if his hand hadn't shifted from the small of my back to the swell of my rear. Since I'd unwittingly stirred him up to begin with, I figured he deserved a diplomatic set-down as opposed to a slap in the face. "Listen, *Fred*. I think you misunderstood my…enthusiasm."

"I understand that you are full of energy and passion."

"I'm a married woman—"

"And I have been indiscreet." He returned his hand to a respectable body part, spoke close to my ear. "Later tonight. After he falls asleep. Meet me—"

I misstepped, accidentally on purpose, and crushed his instep.

He cursed and faltered. I spun around and smacked into, of all people, Tex. Thankfully, he didn't teeter. In fact, he was rock solid. Not bulked up, just well toned—not that I noticed.

"We keep meetin' like this, Sugar, one of us is gonna break somethin'. Probably me."

I tore my gaze from his admirable torso and focused on those nasty stitches. "I owe you an apology."

"I'll take a dance instead." He smiled over my shoulder at Fred. "You don't mind, do ya, boy?"

I'm not sure if it was the "boy" that irked him or if I'd seriously injured his foot, but Fred excused himself and limped toward Ginger.

Tex, um, Vic, took me in his arms as the music changed and the tempo slowed. A ballad. Apparently, the Latin segment was over. Crap. I looked around his body at Arch, who toasted me with his scotch and smiled. Great. Apparently, being the life of the party included dancing with every Tom, Dick and Tex who got the itch.

"You ain't gonna stomp on my foot, are ya?"

"I didn't stomp. I…" His expression said he'd seen enough to know that I'd wanted to escape Fred. I shrugged. "He was getting a little fresh."

"I noticed."

"I'm married."

"Met your husband in the infirmary, remember?"

"Actually, I'm trying to forget that entire mishap."

"Jaw get stuck like that often?"

I blushed. "No."

"What you need is to relax."

"I am relaxed."

"Feels like I'm dancing with a two-by-four."

How rude of you to say so. But he was right. I'd stiffened up. Subconsciously, I suppose I didn't want to give him the wrong idea. After all, he'd seen me grinding with Fred. Although Sugar was supposed to be a free spirit and I *was* trying to seduce my husband, not Salsa-Fred, so it's not as if I'd done anything wrong.

Then why did I feel so uncomfortable?

I decided it was because Tex, Vic, whoever, was half-naked and I was half-naked and even though he wasn't my type, he wasn't half-bad. As a dancer that is. Like Fred, I appreciate a partner with skill. Someone who moves in time and doesn't step on my toes. What I didn't appreciate was the way my skin tingled under his competent hands. Was I *that* desperate for physical intimacy? Tex's unwavering stare bothered me, too. I'm not sure if he was sizing me up or checking me out. Either way, I felt exposed and scrutinized and it chafed. To make matters worse, the man wore a wedding band! How would his wife feel if she saw him holding me close and ogling my cleavage? I know how I felt when I'd once caught Michael ogling a model's portfolio. Said portfolio belonging to *Sasha*.

This dance was over.

Before I could misstep, he spun me out of his arms. "Your husband bought me a drink. I'm thinkin' I should get to it before the ice melts."

An innocent enough statement, yet there was nothing innocent about Tex. He was arrogant and slick, putting me in mind of a used-car salesman. Which made me think of the gorilla suit. Which made my skin itch. Scratching my neck, I dodged three bar servers carrying loaded trays and rushed into Arch's open arms.

"Did you see my moves, baby?" I asked a little too brightly.

"I could watch you all night, love." He nixed my scratching by pulling me into a kiss.

By now I was used to him scrambling my thoughts, but this kiss obliterated brain cells. Aggressive. Possessive. Was it the scotch? My sexy dancing? My body trembled in answer to his unexpected and extremely public lust.

Someone cleared their throat. What was up with that? Every time we made out, someone intruded. I'm not an exhibitionist, but, hello? What did they expect? We're newlyweds. Arch eased away and I willed my wobbly legs steady. Buster Poindexter blasted in the background. "*Feeling hot, hot, hot!*"

Yeah, Buster. That's an understatement.

My bespectacled husband motioned Beau for another scotch and ordered me a Fandango. If I drank the ship's potent special, things would get a whole lot hotter. I told myself to show some restraint, for God's sake. Sip, don't gulp.

Arch grinned at me, while directing his question to the bartender. "What did you think of my wife's dancing, old boy?"

Beau smiled. "Impressive."

"You should hear her sing."

I knew it was part of our ruse, but Arch sounded sincerely impressed. I must've gotten to him with that verse of "Fever." I filed away the knowledge, nipped his bottom lip then smiled at the bartender. "Charlie's my biggest fan."

Beau presented me with the tall, deadly drink. "There's a karaoke dance party tomorrow night," he said. "You should sign up, Mrs. Dupont."

"Gavin said the same thing, but it wouldn't be fair. You see, I'm a professional."

"That right?"

I frowned at the sound of Tex's voice. Unlike the overly friendly Iversons, he hadn't moseyed off to mingle with the entertainment staff. Nope. Just my luck. He was still here and invading my personal space. Could the officious redneck stand any closer? I glanced from his smirking mug to his mug of beer. *Thinkin' I should get to it before the ice melts.*

"A professional *singer,*" I clarified, with a calculated friendly smile. "By the by, Mr. Parker, there's no ice in your beer."

"Call me Vic, and, by the by, I wasn't talking about my beer."

So he was talking about *me?* He'd compared me to a two-by-four. A piece of wood. As in rigid. Frigid. *Cold.* Only his bold appraisal had ignited my temper and triggered a meltdown. I'd planned to accidentally stomp on his toes, but he'd spun me away in the nick of time. He'd read me like a book, seen through Sugar's carefree persona. That worried me. And bugged me. I decided I didn't like *Vic* any more than Ms. Tall, Dark and Beautiful.

"I say, Beau, I think you're right," Charles piped in. "Sugar should perform a number at that party."

"I should?"

Something clicked. Yes, we'd been *on* all day, whenever in public. But this moment I felt like Arch and I had taken center stage. This was it. This was real. A premium performance was crucial. Just like that, Evie and Arch were no more.

"She misses the spotlight," Charles said to the other men. "Won't admit it, but, at times, I do believe she's bored to tears on the estate."

"I'm *not!* You take that back," I said, fussing with his ascot. "I can't think of anything more thrilling than being Mrs. Charles Dupont!"

"Chucked your career for marriage, did ya?" Vic asked while gnawing on a swizzle stick. At least it was better than those nasty cigars.

"I didn't chuck anything, Mr. Parker. I happily walked away. Showbiz is fickle and unstable. Contracts aren't worth the paper you sign on and most of the casinos stopped investing in new sound equipment in 1981. Trust me, there is no joy in singing over an inferior audio system."

"Where did you perform, Mrs. Dupont?" Beau asked. "Vegas? Reno? Atlan—"

"Vegas," Charles said.

"It's where we met," I said. "Love at first sight."

"Married a week later."

"This is our one-month anniversary."

"Ain't that something?" Vic said. "The little

woman and I are celebrating our anniversary, too. Fifteen years."

"Spectacular," Charles said. "Pour this man another ale, Beau. On me."

"Decent of you, Dupont. Figure I can down one more while I'm waiting on Carol. We aim on making use of that pool while everyone else dines." He grinned, winked. "The wife's fond of underwater sports, if you catch my drift."

Oh, brother. "So where are you and Mrs. Parker from?" I asked, craving a hot shower and disinfecting soap.

"We've got a spread outside of Dallas. You?"

"Born in Brooklyn. Transplanted to Vegas. Now I'm in Connecticut with Charlie."

Vic sipped out of his replenished mug. "On an estate, you said."

"A lovely place with loads of privacy and a view of Long Island Sound." My voice vibrated with excitement as I embraced the fantasy. "Katharine Hepburn owned a home nearby. Sometimes I step outside and breathe deep, hoping to absorb some of her creative energy."

"*The* Katharine Hepburn?" Beau glanced over while loading up a server's tray with various drinks. "The movie star?"

I nodded. "Rest her soul."

"Impressive," Vic said, toasting Charlie. "What do you do for a living, Dupont?"

I beamed with pride and answered for him. He

was, after all, painfully private about his literary pursuits. "He's a writer."

"Must be a bestseller, one of them Tom Clancy types, if you're livin' next to a celebrity."

I bristled. Vic was crass, although Charles didn't seem to notice. Or maybe he noticed, but didn't care.

"Alas, I am not a bestseller. I inherited my father's fortune and invested wisely."

"Got an eye for investments myself," Vic said.

When he didn't elaborate, I asked, "What business are you in…Vic?"

"Oil."

"Oil?"

"Oil."

TV junkie that I am, I flashed back to the soap of all nighttime soaps: *Dallas*. Was Vic Parker a living, breathing J. R. Ewing? A vain, conniving oil baron? A man who engineered intricate business deals using cloak-and-dagger methods, employing that same sneaky mentality to cheat on his wife?

More likely, he was a grease monkey at Jiffy Lube. Still…I sipped my Fandango, deciding, either way, the man was a slippery jerk.

"Carol and I are set for life," he bragged. "Speakin' of, here comes the little lady now."

I turned and choked on my drink when I locked eyes on a lean, mean brunette in an itty-bitty bikini. *The* brunette. Ms. Tall, Dark and Beautiful. What were the chances? Tex Aloha and Mata Hari were a couple!

Charles thumped lightly between my shoulder blades as I scrambled to recover from my coughing fit. "Wrong pipe," I hacked out. Desperate, I nabbed a glass of water off the passing bar server's tray and gulped deeply.

Beau gasped. "Mrs. Dupont, that's not water, that's—"

Schnapps. Peppermint schnapps. It burned and overwhelmed, spraying out of my mouth and soaking Tex as I hooked my toe on the leg of a stool and lost my footing. Teary-eyed, I thrust out my hands to cushion my fall…and glommed on to Mata Hari's breasts.

CHAPTER EIGHTEEN

"DO YOU THINK THE Parkers think I'm a pervert?"

"I think they think you're accident prone."

"What do you think?"

"I think you're accident prone."

Hard to take issue considering my calamities over the last few days. I laid my beaded purse on the night-stand and watched as my partner took off his glasses and set them on the vanity. Next he chucked his dinner jacket and dress shirt, then unstrapped the fake gut.

Thank goodness the charade, at least for tonight, was over. The Iversons had invited themselves to join us for dinner. Making conversation with Dirk and Nan was impossible as they didn't allow a person to get in a word edgewise. Enduring their company had been exhausting and irritating. Even so, not half as irritating as my obsession with the offensive Parkers. They'd consumed my thoughts all through dinner. Tex's ogling. Carol's risqué talk. The groping incident, followed by a lesbian innuendo, and then the two of them traipsing off to indulge in underwater sports. *Pah-leeze.*

"Well, I think they're perverts," I blurted. "Or something."

Arch chuckled as he pulled his T-shirt over his head. "Yeah?"

"Yeah." Rather than admiring his upper body when he sat on a chair and unlaced his shoes, I turned away and took my time shedding Sugar's plentiful rhinestone jewelry.

"What struck you as twisted, Sunshine?"

"For one, she licked schnapps off his chest."

"I've seen racier behavior."

"Me, too." When Michael and I had vacationed in New Orleans. The things women *and* men did for beads. "That's not the point. It's the way she took her time, like she was putting on a show."

I heard a shoe drop.

"For you," I added as his second shoe thudded to the floor.

No comment. But he *must* have noticed. Ms. Tall, Dark and Beautiful had been less than discreet in her appraisal of *Charles*. Gold digger immediately sprang to mind, followed by the recurring notion that she was a seducing evil agent. Neither one of us had given up that we'd met earlier in the gift shop. I'm not sure why, although I'd again sensed a competitive edge.

"I think she was putting on a show for everyone," Arch finally said. "She likes attention."

"Ya think?" Carol Parker wasn't loud like her husband, but she certainly made her presence known.

"That scrap of material masquerading as a bathing suit screamed, *Hey everyone, check out my hot bod!*"

Arch mimicked a cat yowl.

"Yeah, yeah. I'm envious. Whatever. I understand the 'if you've got it, flaunt it' mentality. She probably worked very hard for that lithe body and her breasts were magnificent. Trust me, I know."

He laughed.

"They're real, if you're wondering."

"I'm not wondering."

I glanced over my shoulder. He sat at the desk attacking the keys of his laptop computer. Again I marveled that he could type and talk at the same time. And, I confess, I itched to know *what* he typed. Did he journal his thoughts and feelings like me? Naw. Guys with beefy muscles and tribal tattoos probably aren't in touch with their inner selves. More likely he was documenting the day for business purposes, making a laundry list of things to do, entering data into an expense report.

He was certainly an enigma. He'd shed all of *Charles* but his trousers, silver hair, wrinkles and jowls. His face looked twice as old as his body. An odd combination and yet it worked because, although Arch had confessed to being thirty-nine, he had a weathered soul. I had a sudden image of a small boy who'd grown up much too fast.

I cocked a brow. "Are you telling me you didn't notice Carol Parker's breasts?"

"I noticed."

"You didn't wonder if they were real? They're *perfect*."

"Yours are perfect and they're real."

"Yes, but you wondered. You asked me outright, remember?"

"Aye."

His smile was hot and lethal. Before my bones liquefied, I pivoted and palmed the cool wall. I gazed out of the porthole at the moonlit sea seeking clarity. I didn't think my chrysoprase stone covered that, not that it was working, anyway.

My mind jumped tracks and chugged toward TV land. Tex and Mata. *Boris and Natasha. Bonnie and Clyde.* Partners in life and maybe, just maybe, in crime. My imagination whipped up a steamy political scenario involving a crooked American oilman and his femme fatale sidekick en route to meet a shifty Arab sheik on a secluded tropical isle. Or maybe their identities were fake—*like ours.* They *could* be international jewel thieves…or weapons couriers. What if they're in cahoots with terrorists or Cuban militants?

The muscles in my shoulders bunched. *For the greater good.*

Was *company* code for *agency?* As in government agency? Was TCC like the CIA or FBI? I'd never heard of it. But how many people outside of the casino industry knew what the CCC was? Was Arch a real-life, Bond-type superspy? He was fit enough, cagey enough, smart enough. It would explain his subtle allusions to risk, his superior acting chops and ability to alter his appearance. Not to mention the false travel documents and his constant calm in the face of chaos. The man was unshakable.

I sneaked a peek just as he shut down his computer. Maybe he'd sent a coded message to TCC. Did this room provide Internet access?

"We were really pouring it on for the Parkers," I ventured.

"No more than for Beau or the Iversons and everyone else within visual and audio range."

No straight answers. Like Michael, he knew how to skirt issues. A troubling trait in a lifetime partner, but something I could forgive in a one- or five-night stand. Knowing that this was a short-run gig and that my unstable life waited for me back in Atlantic City, I wanted to milk this adventure for all it was worth. "One question. Have I met whomever it is we're trying to dupe for reasons I don't understand?"

"I'm not sure." He opened the closet and locked the computer in the security safe.

I clenched my teeth and refocused on the meditative scenery beyond the porthole. Registering the tightness in my jaw and shoulders, I told myself to loosen up, to play it cool. As cool as Arch. "Are you sure you're not sure? Are you sure it isn't the Parkers? Because I sensed something. I can't explain it exactly. At all, really." I furrowed my brow, pondered aloud. "Are they part of the unique deception or are they the targets? Are you friends? Rivals?" *Lovers? Ex-lovers?* "The way Carol looked at you…"

"One question, eh?" He moved in behind me and caressed my upper arms. "You worry too much, Sunshine."

I'd heard that before. Was I blowing things out of proportion? Overreacting? The feel of Arch's hands on my bare arms and shoulders obscured my focus. Resisting the urge to lean against him, I watched moonlight dance on ripples of endless water. It would be cake to lose myself in the illusion of the moment. Floating on the Caribbean Sea, locked away in a beautiful cabin with a beautiful man. The gaga stuff that makes up the best parts of romance novels.

Except for the third-wheel feeling.

I likened Carol to Sasha, the other woman, Arch to Michael, the wandering husband, and me to me. The odd one out. "I'm not worried. I'm curious and annoyed. I know what I saw. She's interested in you. She wasn't even all that subtle. What's worse, Vic has wandering eyes, too."

"Yeah?"

"Yeah. I caught him checking me out a couple of times. Don't tell me you didn't notice."

"I noticed."

Was that why he'd kissed me so possessively in front of Tex? A silent warning to the guy to back off? My stomach fluttered with the possibility that he'd actually been jealous. I cleared my throat, focused. "The point is, when you're married, you're supposed to only have eyes for each other."

"It's human nature to admire what one deems beautiful," Arch said as he massaged my knotted shoulders. "Just as one admires a work of art."

I worked my tight jaw. "That's all well and good if one can keep one's eyes in one's pants." I knocked my forehead against the pane. "You know what I mean."

"Aye." He kneaded the strained muscles in my neck. "You were magnificent this evening, Evie. You stayed in character, rolled with the punches. Bloody brilliant."

Heat flooded from my hair follicles to my pinched toes. Damn these narrow pumps. I was more flattered than turned-on. I shifted to thank him and found myself staring at his bare chest, that Celtic tattoo, his piercing, hypnotic eyes. Okay, maybe I was more turned-on.

He moistened his bottom lip and I thought about making love with a superspy, a man who risked torture and death for leader and country. As fantasies went, it was a knee-buckler. I tilted my face upward, closed my eyes and waited.

And waited.

"I'm going to wash *oot* this dye, yeah?"

Noooo! I opened my eyes, sagged against the wall as he zipped into the bathroom.

He mumbled something and shut the door.

Unbelievable.

Disappointment whacked my system like a base-ball bat. After years in the fickle entertainment business, you'd think I'd be numb to rejection. No such luck. Just as with failed auditions, I obsessed on where I'd gone wrong. Was it my breath? My timing? Was my obvious infatuation a turnoff? James Bond never ran from a ready and willing lady. What the hell?

Then I thought about what he'd said. He wanted to wash away the remnants of Charles. Maybe he was in a hurry to clean up so we could get down and dirty. Yeah, that was it. I'd showered before dinner, slipped into this sequined cocktail dress. Now I needed to get out of said dress and into something sexy.

Sexier. Except, I didn't own any risqué lingerie.

Last night I surprised my husband wearing this fragrance and nothing else.

Not that I wanted advice from Ms. Tall, Dark and Beautiful, but if she could do it, so could freaking I!

I stepped out of my heels, peeled off the dress and panty hose and tossed the whole kit and caboodle into Big Red. Naked as a blue jay, as Mom would say—don't think about Mom!—I rooted through my beaded purse for face powder and red lipstick. *Pat, pat. Swish, swish…*done. I fussed with my hair while examining my reflection in the vanity mirror. If I wanted to get picky I could bemoan a few crow's feet

and soft spots. Then again, bemoaning would under-
mine my confidence. I closed my eyes and imagined
Sugar, ten years younger with ten times the confidence.

Steeled, I sidestepped the mirror and searched the
dresser drawer for this afternoon's purchase. I bit
my lower lip and liberally doused my body with Les
Fleurs de Provence Jasmine.

*It promotes self-confidence and, best of all, works
as an aphrodisiac.*

Yeah, baby, yeah. Work your magic. Giddy with
anticipation, I shut off all but one light and dived
into bed, pulling the covers up to my chin. Gripping
the edge of the cream-colored spread, I waited, listening for the sound of the shower shutting off, cal-
culating the time it took him to finger gel through
his hair and to step into sweatpants. The door
squeaked open and I pasted on what I hoped was a
come-hither smile.

He stepped into the room wearing boxers and a
baggy gray T-shirt. He looked dark and roguish and
utterly edible. My heart raced like a rabbit as he moved
at a snail's pace across the room. He finally made it
to the edge of the bed. "You're tuckered out, yeah?"

"No."

He sneezed. "No?"

"Bless you. No."

He sneezed again. Twice more. "Bloody hell." He
backed away, sniffed the flowers in the vase.

I turned on my side, careful not to expose

anything, and propped myself up on one elbow. "What's wrong?"

"Not these. These are silk." He backed up, neared the bed and sneezed again…and again.

"What is it, Arch?"

"Something's triggering my allergies."

I swallowed a lump of dread. It couldn't be. "What are you allergic to?"

He sneezed four times in rapid succession. "Certain flowers and nuts. Almonds. Lilacs. Jasmine." He sneezed twice more. "Fuck me!"

I wish. "Here's an idea," I said, scrambling to the opposite side of the bed as he neared and sniffed. "Why don't you go out for a breath of fresh air and I'll—"

He sneezed three times fast. "It's you."

Curse you, Mata Hari! "You said to buy something. Trinkets, clothes, perfume. I bought perfume. I didn't know."

He snatched a tissue from a nearby box. "Jasmine, yeah?"

"Yeah."

Blowing his nose—not so roguish—he stalked toward the balcony, flung open the sliding door. A warm breeze circulated but I didn't imagine it would air out the room while I continued to stink it up. I wanted to flee to the bathroom, to shower off the offending scent, but…I clutched the bedspread to my chest. "I'm so sorry."

"Not your fault." *Aw-choo!*

"Maybe if you took a walk—"

"I'm *oot* of disguise." *Sniffle*.

"Right. Okay. Well, then, step out on the balcony and don't come back until you hear the door shut."

"What door?" He turned and nailed me with a watery gaze. "Where are you going?"

"Nowhere. Just…the bathroom. I need to shower off this—"

Aw-choo!

"Bless you. Now go back out—"

"Why do I have to hang *oot* there until…" He sneezed, three big, wet sneezes.

"Bless—"

"Bugger!"

"Would you—"

"Why?"

"BECAUSE I'M NAKED!"

He blinked, blew his nose without taking his eyes off of me, and then cocked a brow. "As in nude? In the buff? In the raw? Bare-assed—"

"Naked." My embarrassment fast morphed into anger.

He grinned, slow, sinful. "Nothing I haven't seen before."

I was in no mood to be teased. My seduction was ruined. What would be the point in accepting what was so obviously a challenge and baring all? He was allergic to me! He couldn't touch me, couldn't come within six inches of me without sneezing his head off and now, now… Oh, God. Was he *wheezing?*

Just like a man to be more concerned about copping a look than dealing with the fact that his throat was closing up!

With a Herculean tug, I yanked the queen-size spread, taking it with me as I wormed off the bed. "Maybe you should get back into costume, visit Doctor Drake. You don't look so good."

"You could look better yourself," he teased, gesturing to the yards of fabric wrapped around my bare form. "Why *dinnae* you drop—"

"No."

"If you *dinnae* want me to see you naked, then why—"

"Oh, shut up." I had no right to be surly. He was the one with the swollen eyes and running nose. But I was pissed. Really pissed. Not at him. At Carol Parker. I could almost hear her laughing at me. If I didn't know better, and I didn't, I'd think she'd tricked me into buying that perfume. The more I thought about it, the madder I got. I shut the door, wrenched on the shower and mentally scribbled in my journal.

Dear Diary, Today I met a witch.

CHAPTER NINETEEN

INSTEAD OF TEARING UP the sheets with Arch as planned, I lay in the center of the bed alone. Arch had bedded down on the couch. I no longer smelled of jasmine, he'd explained, but the sheets did.

Damn you, Carol Parker.

That long shower had washed away everything except for a welling resentment. She was young, beautiful and confident. Everything Michael had seen in his new squeeze. My mind replayed Carol's every word and action, summing her up with one word: *devious*.

Two o'clock in the morning and my mind still churned. No sleep for an overimaginative movie fanatic and reformed TV addict. I nurtured my hypothesis about the Parkers, the criminal angle, because I didn't like them, especially her, and I wanted a good reason other than petty envy. Also, as long as I spun political-thriller scenarios, I couldn't mourn my botched seduction. Except for the bit of teasing before I'd escaped into the bathroom, Arch hadn't mentioned the naked thing.

Honestly, I'm grateful he didn't address my intentions head-on. I mean, he had to know that I'd had sex on the brain, right? What was there to say that wouldn't A, embarrass me *or* B, turn me on? As long as we didn't discuss it, he couldn't express disinterest. My fantasy could thrive, and, believing what I thought I saw in his eyes—desire—I could make another play, another day. Like tomorrow. Maybe.

"You should put in your splint."

I jumped at the sound of his voice. "What?"

"The mouth guard."

"I know what a splint is. *Why?*"

"You're grinding your teeth."

"I am?" For crying out loud. Could this night get any *more* unromantic? I fidgeted beneath the sheets, my body now fully clothed in pink cotton pajamas. The bed felt big and lonely, and I had to resist wallowing in the notion that this is how I spent my nights at home. These past two days, I'd felt happy, mostly, and vital. I clung to Sugar, to the fantasy, like a lifeline.

"What's on your mind, Sunshine?"

Work. Companionship. Sex. "Stuff."

"If you're worried—"

"I'm not."

"It's not that I'm not tempted. It's just—"

"Please don't say it."

"—I don't mix business and pleasure."

"Ever?"

"Messy."

I thought about my relationship with Michael. Definitely messy. The good news was Arch and I wouldn't be working together after this cruise. I could cool my jets for now and pursue a relationship later, except I didn't want a relationship with Arch. I just wanted to dance with JT. Since man and beast could live in Scotland or England or Timbuktu for all I knew, I wanted to mix it up while I had the chance. How messy could it get?

Arch broke the silence. "What did you think I was going to say?"

"What do you mean?"

"You said, 'please don't say it.' Say what?"

I didn't bother lying. According to him, I stank at it. "Nice girl. I thought you were going to call me a nice girl, and that would be—"

"What?"

"Awful."

"Why?"

"Because nice girls finish last."

Silence greeted that statement. Even I was stunned by the bitterness in my voice. I wanted to show Michael that I could be unpredictable and wild, except things weren't going my way. I sucked at lying. Sucked at promiscuity. Maybe I needed to hang around someone like Mata Hari—watch and learn.

"Stone really fucked with your head, yeah?"

It was the first time he'd mentioned my ex since

their tense phone conversation two days before. I rolled to my side and squinted at his silhouette. Lying supine on the love seat, his feet hung over the end. He couldn't be comfortable. Yet he hadn't complained or blamed me for the perfume episode even once. Unshakable. "How well do you know Michael?"

"Well enough."

"Are you friends?"

"Business associates."

"That's it?"

"That's all."

I rolled my eyes. Trying to get any information out of this man was like trying to interview a reclusive celebrity. Not only was he unshakable but also a master of evasion. Did they teach those skills in spy school? Unlike him, I decided to be direct. "Are you an agent?"

"Like Stone?"

"Like Bond. James Bond."

He laughed. "You have a vivid imagination, Sunshine."

"I'm famous for it." I also possessed a lesser-known stubborn streak. "So are you?"

"No."

"Why don't I believe you?"

"Have I ever lied to you?"

"How would I know?"

"Exactly."

"You didn't answer my question."

"Didn't I?"

I fell back with an *oomph*. "My brain hurts."

"Then give it a rest."

I imagined him smiling and it chafed. "I can't," I snapped. "There's a lot going on in my life right now."

"Like?"

"You mean aside from my husband dumping me?"

"Ex-husband. Yeah. Aside from that."

"My career is on the fast road to Deadsville."

"Anything else?"

"Isn't that enough?"

He didn't answer and I suddenly felt like an immature, self-absorbed whiner. He no doubt had problems of his own, like saving the ship from a terrorist attack or something. "My parents split up." There. That was news to him and I even managed not to sound like a churlish kid.

"When?"

"Recently."

"For good?"

"For a while." I refused to think that their separation would end in divorce. Sure, they bickered, but they loved one another. They belonged together. This was just a temporary glitch. "My brother said he'd patch things up."

"You're worried he'll fail?"

I snorted. "Christopher accomplishes everything he sets his mind to. He's smart and successful, always makes the right choices."

"You sound resentful."

"Envious." I squinted up into the darkness, conjured an image of my brother chained to a regimented job and bossy wife. "Wait. That's not true. I don't want his life. He works a high-pressure nine-to-five and married a stuck-up conniver who came with two bratty kids, compliments of her first marriage. Unfortunately, Sandy and her demon offspring are now part of my family so I have to be civil. Family is family, even if they're not blood, right?"

"Tricky stuff, that."

"What?"

"Family."

"I'll say. Anyway, at least I don't live in Indiana anymore."

"That's where you're from, yeah?"

"Born and raised."

"Ah, a nice Midwestern girl."

I flipped over and punched my pillow. "I'm not nice."

"If you say so."

"Enough about me. What about your family?"

"Not as interesting as yours."

That statement roused me like a bucket of cold water. "I doubt that." I sat up and hugged my knees to my chest. It was that or sail across the room and pummel him with my pillow. "Give it up, Arch." I was so over his aloofness.

"What?"

"Something. Anything." I focused on his relaxed silhouette, bristled at his blasé tone. Good grief, was he falling asleep? "You're right. I don't know you. I don't know anything about you. Including whether or not you're trustworthy. How do I even know you're going to pay me at the end of this gig?" Okay. That wasn't my biggest concern, but it's what came out in the moment's heat.

"Don't insult me, Evie."

"For the greater good. Whose good? Your good? The country's good? What country? You won't even own up to your birth nation."

"Scotland."

"What?"

"I'm a Scot."

I noted the strained revelation, wondered why it had cost him so much to share so little. "But you sort of sound…the words you use…sometimes you sound British."

"I've spent a lot of time in England."

"Oh." I didn't know where to steer the conversation. There was so much I wanted to know and yet I instinctively knew deeper questioning at this point would prove fruitless. Even though Arch was easy to talk to, even though we had entered swiftly and easily into what suspiciously felt like a friendship, the man himself was a closed book. A mystery. An enigma. Which, truth told, was probably a huge part of his appeal. Well, aside from the obvious physical aspect.

"So what's on tomorrow's agenda?" I asked.

His head lolled sideways and, because of an exceptionally well-directed moonbeam, I made out his perplexed expression. He blinked. "Sorry?"

I grinned, pleased that I'd tipped his infuriating balance. "The ship's docking in San Juan. Are we going ashore? Or staying aboard? Where do you think our...what would you call the person we're trying to dupe? Our victim?"

"Mark."

The term was familiar. I'd once worked a two-week stint as a magician's assistant. My friend, known as Marko the Magnificent in theatrical circles, had referred to an audience member we were about to play a trick on as a mark. Not that I thought Arch was a conventional magician. More like a charming trickster—smoke and mirrors. "Where do you think our mark will be?" I swung my legs over the side of the bed, gripped the mattress to keep myself rooted. It was that or pace off my nervous energy. Since I'd been rolling in the sheets I probably smelled like jasmine again. The last thing I wanted to do was to stir up scents and set off another allergy attack.

Sit tight and *talk* it off, I told myself when he failed to answer my question. "How can you not know whether or not I've met the mark? Don't you know who we're after? Who we're trying to fool? Is that why you said the world is our stage? Because this guy could be anywhere, so we're, like, what? Trying to smoke him out?"

"Go to sleep, Evie."

"Is he even a he? Or are we dealing with a she?" Mata Hari sprang to mind.

"He's a he. A crew member. Hospitality or entertainment."

"One of *my* people? Is that why I'm here? Like attracts like?"

He sighed, an unusual show of exasperation. "You're here because you were in the right place at the wrong time."

"You mean right place at the right time."

"No, I don't."

I skated over that, circled around the mysterious crew member. The faster my mind churned the tighter my hold on the mattress. "What did he do? Why is he dangerous? You know, I could be more effective if I were better informed."

"Need-to-know basis, Sunshine."

"And that's all I need to know?" My heart raced, my voice jumped an octave. "That we're trying to fool some man, some member of this crew, someone like, well, like me, into, what? Into believing we're happily married and…rich. The money thing. That must be key because we've spent a boatload. No pun intended. And…" I chewed my bottom lip, processed conversations we'd had throughout the two days in front of various crew members. "And we want him to think that I'm bored in Connecticut and happy as a pig in mud on this floating party. And there's the expendable income thing." I snapped my fingers. *"To Catch a Thief."*

"What?"

"Hitchcock classic. 1955. Cary Grant and Grace Kelly."

"Evie—"

"Grant pretends to be someone he's not, utilizing rich eye candy Kelly, to catch a thief. So, what? Does this guy sneak into passenger's rooms when they go ashore? Steal their jewels? Their money?" I slapped a hand to my pounding chest. "Or worse. Personal information so that he can rob them later. Identity theft. That's, like, a huge thing now, right? I—"

I gasped as he hauled me to my feet and into his arms. When had he crossed the room? Why was he holding me? "What are you doing?"

"Giving you something else to think *aboot*." He crushed his lips against mine.

Who could think? *Oh, my God. Oh, my God.* Heaven. No, hell. This was hell. Hot. Sinful. *Wicked.* I wrapped my arms around his neck and held on for dear life as he kissed me dizzy. My knees quaked as he claimed and conquered. Tongue. Lips. Teeth. One hand cradled the back of my head. The other, holy…down my pants. Fingers. Touching me…there. Holy…Cripes. Friction. Intense. Erotic. Can't think. Can't breathe.

My sexually deprived body exploded with decadent sensations as he kissed and stroked me to a mind-blowing, limb-melting climax.

My knees buckled. I moaned into his mouth and sagged against his body. He laid me on the bed, stifled a sneeze and I knew it would go no further. I couldn't dredge up the energy to be upset. I knew, deep down in my fibrillating heart, this was only a teaser.

So much for not mixing business with pleasure.

He disappeared into the bathroom and my warped brain cells fired up a medley of Bond theme songs—"Goldfinger"—Ha!—followed by "Nobody Does It Better," and "All Time High."

Exhausted and deliciously sated, I closed my eyes and gave over to thoughts of Pussy Galore, Operation Grand Slam and a spy with a license to thrill.

Dear Diary, My life doesn't suck.

CHAPTER TWENTY

DAY THREE OF THE CRUISE. Four days after meeting Arch. Life was looking up.

Viva la orgasm.

I woke up feeling refreshed. Energized. *Optimistic*. I'd slept better than I had in months. If I dreamed, I don't remember. I think Arch melted my brain with that white-hot sex.

We didn't speak of it. The orgasm, that is. Arch, I assumed, was being a gentleman. Or maybe he was kicking himself. He'd broken his policy, mixed business with pleasure. As for me, even though I was ecstatic, my old-fashioned upbringing kept me from verbalizing my reawakened appreciation for foreplay.

But I thought about it.

A lot.

I tried not to obsess. But, hey. Come on. Arch was hot. Getting pawed by Arch, a wham, bam, third-base slam in the middle of the night, was hot. I'm pretty sure the sexy episode was on his mind, too, because I caught him looking at me five or ten times while we readied for the day.

One of us, I decided while tying the laces of my Keds, was going to have to break the tension. I voted for me. It had been a long time since I'd felt this vibrant and motivated. Taking charge would only enhance the rush. I steeled myself when he stepped out of the bathroom in full Charles regalia sans the tinted glasses. I could do this, especially dressed as Sugar. This morning our united energy and optimism bubbled through my system like expensive champagne.

Giddy with bravado, I locked gazes with Arch. "About last night," we said at the same time. We laughed, the ice broken, then proceeded to step on each other's lines.

"It was—"

"—a mistake," he said.

"—amazing," I said.

Pregnant pause.

We took stock of each other and our conflicting attitudes. The mood shifted from awkward to jovial to tense in ten seconds flat.

"This is complicated enough without making it personal, Sunshine."

"It would be less complicated if you cleared some things up for me." Suddenly I was thinking less about the mind-blowing orgasm and more about this mind-boggling gig. Arch's tight-lipped expression prompted me to fight fire with fire. I folded my arms under my pumped-up cleavage. "Okay. You want to keep things strictly business? Then I want some professional courtesy."

"Meaning?"

"I'm not leaving this room unless you shed some light on this gig. I hate being uninformed. Not knowing what's expected of me."

If Michael had been more communicative, maybe I could have changed my ways, my appearance, sought marriage counseling. Some honesty, some direction would've been nice. I never suspected he was falling out of love with me. Never saw the signs of an affair. God, I was naive. Or dense. Maybe both.

"I *cannae—*"

"Basics. That's all I'm asking for. I don't need names. You don't have to divulge any secrets of national importance."

He pressed his lips together to suppress a smile or a curse. I didn't know which nor did I care.

I palmed my forehead, closed my eyes and groaned. "I feel an excruciating headache coming on. You'll have to make merry yourself today." I peered at him through thick, lowered lashes, my lips curled in a taunting grin. "Except Charles wouldn't leave Sugar suffering alone in the cabin, now would he?"

"You're bluffing."

I plopped my butt on the bed, toed off my Keds. "It's not like we have a contract. I didn't sign anything. We're operating on faith and it's been pretty one-sided. Time for you to even out the percentage, Arch. Trust me when I say, the more I know about a part, a client, the better my performance."

He braced his hands on his hips. "The more you know about *this* job, the higher your stress level, the greater the chances you'll crack out of turn."

"What?"

"Miss a cue."

My back went up. "I've never missed a cue in my life."

"Never?"

I pursed my lips, scanned my memory. "Well, maybe once. During a performance in regional theater. But I had a high fever and the heat from the par cans only heightened my delirium."

He grinned and suddenly the air crackled with another kind of tension. Sexy, sizzling tension that fried my brain cells and melted my bones.

"You're cute when you're cocky, Sunshine."

I raised a brow. "If you think you're going to charm me into leaving this room without some specifics, you're in for a big disappointment, buster."

The grin widened and his gorgeous eyes danced with amusement.

I applauded myself for not sliding off the bed in a pool of wanton lust.

"The person I need to hook just now is a small fish," he said, knocking me off balance with the unexpected revelation. "He'll lead me to my primary mark, a vicious shark who preys on the gullible, especially the elderly."

People like Martha and her cronies. "Bastard."

"Aye."

"And you're going to blow him out of the water."

"Something like that."

"The greater good." I hopped to my bare feet and paced, my senses vibrating with curiosity and excitement. "Okay. So how are we going to hook this small fish?"

"By making him believe that we're rich and gullible." He pushed up the brim of his Panama hat and calmly watched as I wore a path in the carpet. "You were bang on last night, Sunshine. I want him to think that you're bored in Connecticut and happy as a pig in mud on this floating party."

I pumped my fist in the air. "Yes!" Okay. That was smug. But I couldn't help it. I was proud of myself for making at least one correct deduction. Besides, there was that whole cute-when-cocky thing. Maybe I was turning him on a little. He'd certainly revved my engine by confiding in me. Every revelation stimulated my brain and body and ratcheted up my confidence.

"I want him to believe," Arch went on, "that I'm so smitten, I'd do anything, spend a fortune if need be, to keep you content."

Hence the public affection. I absorbed that information, nodded, trying my best to keep my mind on business, not pleasure. It's the first time he'd been forthcoming with details and I wanted to milk his generous mood. "About this small fish. You mentioned he's in hospitality or entertainment. Have you narrowed it down at all?"

He worked his jaw and I knew I'd gotten just about all of the specifics I was going to get. For now. "The shore excursion director is a likely suspect," he said. "And Beau."

"The bartender? But he seems so nice."

"Being nice is a brilliant way to win someone's confidence, yeah?"

My cheeks flushed and I cursed my naiveté. "Anyone else?"

"The assistant cruise director."

"Gavin?" I swallowed my disbelief. Neither Beau nor Gavin struck me as disreputable. I hadn't had much contact with the shore excursion guy. Easier to believe he was the stinky small fish. "Anyone else?"

"Sure. The dance instructor who couldn't keep his hands off of you. The pianist who knows four bars of any song ever written. The chatty steward who replenishes the fruit basket in our room every day or any one of the several bartenders or waiters or…" He angled his head. "You get the picture, yeah?"

"Yeah." I rolled my eyes. "So much for narrowing it down."

Arch readjusted his hat and slid on his glasses, effectively ending the discussion.

I stepped into my Keds, wanting him to know that his faith in me had paid off. Jazzed, I pushed for one more bit of information. "How will we know when he's hooked?"

"When he offers us the chance of a lifetime."

THE PLAN FOR THE MORNING was basic and I felt inspired simply because Arch, who I now knew was absolutely not in entertainment but most probably in espionage, had trusted me with a few details of our mission.

We divided our morning efforts for maximum coverage. Pad and pen in hand, *Charles* visited various lounges under the guise of outlining a new book. Mostly he sat at the bar, drank scotch, conversed with bartenders, servers and featured musicians, while intermittently jotting notes in a leather journal. I participated in midmorning fun and games, bouncing in from time to time to report my adventures and to torture him with playful kisses. Perfectly legit. I was Sugar, not me.

As Sugar, I socialized and frolicked on a grand scale. A Ping-Pong tournament, a five-minute makeover. I even braved a Bachata dance lesson with Fred and Ginger. Our mark was in hospitality or entertainment, Fred's area, and Fred was definitely slimy.

Knowing what I knew now, which wasn't much, I regretted cutting him off last night when he suggested a rendezvous. What if he was our man? What if he was going to seduce me and pitch the deal of a lifetime?

Unfortunately, Fred regarded me with wary eyes, pairing me with bowlegged Mr. Pachinko, whose wife had opted for a game of canasta. Still, I blessed the smarmy dance instructor with a few flirty smiles and by lesson's end he'd promised me a dance at the karaoke party. I wasn't sure if we'd be back in time for the party, as we were going ashore to do some sightseeing in San Juan. But maybe I'd run into him after.

Martha-of-the-two-left-feet, who'd somehow hooked up with a much younger man—and I mean like thirty years younger—informed me that she'd be at the party. She'd been practicing her disco steps. *Burn, blue-hair, burn.*

Speaking of infernos, an inextinguishable fire raged inside of me all day, fueling boundless energy and enthusiasm. It wasn't because I'd finally gotten some, well, a little, after a year in the no-man zone—although I'm sure that put *some* spring in my step. No, this was different. Purpose, I guess. My country, or let's just say, "the good guys" since this was for the greater good, needed me. My acting and singing talents were in demand. I was a valuable asset. No one cared that I was over forty. No one treated me like an over-the-hill has-been.

Then again, I wasn't acting or thinking like an over-the-hill has-been. Sugar wasn't insecure or cynical. She lived life to the fullest, and damn anyone who found fault with her quirky exuberance—not that anyone did.

Throughout the day, my mind bounced from one concern to another, processing, assessing. Midday, just after changing into suitable clothes for the shore excursion, I slipped away from Arch and into the Internet Lounge. No update from my brother, though that didn't come as a shock. I could almost hear him. *Chill, Evie. I'm handling it.*

Okay. Sure. Whatever.

With my family it was always one thing or another. My parents' separation, I decided for the sake of my sanity and TMJ, was just *another*, and Christopher would handle it because Christopher was a problem solver. I massaged my jaw and clicked on an e-mail from Jayne.

Atomic kisses with muscled, tattooed dude? OMG! So, like, tongue and everything, right?

Moving on to your gorilla and breast question…this is just one school of thought, but if you're dreaming about apes then beware of a mischief maker in your business or social circle. Unless the gorilla was docile. Then the dream is forecasting a new and unusual friend.

Really, Evie. I need more details.

Anyhoo, let's talk breasts. Did the dream involve someone laying their head on your breast? If so, this means you're primed to meet a new, valuable friend. I'm seeing a theme here. Otherwise, dreaming about boobs in general is a good omen.

I reread Jayne's analysis, my already awesome mood brightening. Anyone looking at me surely needed sunglasses. Obviously, Arch was the new and unusual friend. The good omen thing was a surprise.

If one put stock in dream interpretation, which I sort of did, then I had every reason to believe good things were in my future. I very badly needed to believe that. So I memorized Jayne's e-mail and stroked her ring for good measure. *Trust in the chrysoprase. It attracts abundance and promotes successful new ventures.*

An abundance of orgasms would be nice, especially with Arch. As for the new venture, maybe I had a shot at this spy thing. What? Kate Jackson made an incredible transition in *Scarecrow and Mrs. King*. A secret agent accidentally involved the divorced housewife in one of his covert missions. She proved herself valuable and by the end of the series she was a full-fledged agent. Yes, I know that was television. But who says life can't imitate art?

The loudspeaker jerked me out of my daydream, alerting those going ashore to report to their designated meeting place. Not wanting to be harried and late—been there, done that with the lifeboat drill— I whipped off a quick response to Jayne. Then I clicked on an e-mail from Nicole.

So did you boink him yet?

God, I love my friends.

CHAPTER TWENTY-ONE

MILO WATCHED ARCH limp toward the theater. He knew what was coming. Did Evie? Did she know Arch was going to fake a fall? Beg off the tour due to aggravating his wrenched ankle? Did he rehearse her reaction or was he trusting her instincts? What did they talk about when they were alone? How much had Arch revealed? What had he asked of her? What had been his *come-on*? More importantly, what had he promised in return?

For a man who normally played by the book, his partner was playing loose. A source of curiosity and frustration for Milo. Once ashore, he'd contact Woody and enlist his computer skills. He wanted answers.

Top of the list: Who exactly was Evie?

He ignored a hitch in his breath when she laughed in response to something Arch said. Bottling and selling that kind of infectious cheer could fund his retirement. He ignored the way her skintight, knee-length pants and red-and-pink T-shirt accentuated her kick-ass curves. And were those…?

Hell, yeah, they were. Flowered sneakers. He ignored them, too, because they were surprisingly cute.

Even though Arch had claimed Evie was a last-minute snarl, Milo was still pissed that he'd involved an unsanctioned player. But as always, the man had lucked out. In spite of her inexperience, she made a great shill. Like Gina, she could easily distract a mark while another team member worked his magic. Only Evie was Gina's flipside. Adorable versus siren. A valuable asset. Not that Chameleon needed another full-time team member. But maybe as an extra…

Stop thinking with your dick, Beckett.

At least Mr. Happy wasn't broken.

He adjusted his cargo shorts, backed deeper into the Fiesta Theater. He had a clear view of the oncoming mismatched couple through the propped-open doors. Evie had yet to notice him because she was staring up adoringly at *Charles*. If she was acting, then she was as good as Arch claimed. If she had genuine feelings for the cagey Scot then she was screwed, and not in a good way. Arch didn't do long term.

Never attach yourself to anyone that you can't walk away from in a split second.

Gina knew Arch's creed. So why was her nose out of joint? Did she think she was different? Did she think she could change him? No. She was smarter than that. She knew the psychological makeup of a grifter. Even though Arch now worked the right side of the law, the man was not reformed. To reform one must admit to behaving badly in the first place. Career con artists were basically amoral. They felt no remorse. They could sleep at night because they believed the weak and gullible deserved what they got.

Ten to one, Arch slept like a rock last night.

Milo slept like hell.

After a premeditated R-rated swim with his *wife,* he'd retired to his cabin, his own bed, silently cursing the Scot for complicating his already knotty life. He'd mentally reviewed the Benson case and his conversations with Arch, trying to connect the dots.

Somewhere, somehow Lamont had crossed Arch or someone he cared about. Since the man kept the more intimate aspects of his life under wraps, the personal angle eluded Milo. Rolling a kink out of his neck, he tamped down his musing and focused on the unfolding drama.

With Sugar in tow, Charles Dupont cleared the threshold of the theater, the meeting place of those going ashore to tour San Juan, Puerto Rico. Gina stood a few feet away amongst the throng, obtaining the numbered sticker that corresponded with the number of their tour bus. At some point today, the roper might approach them with the same bull he'd shoveled Stokes. The bait: *"How would you like to 'live' on a six-star cruise ship and travel the world? I know this guy, this deal. Very hush-hush…"* And so on.

Or maybe he'd make his move tomorrow. The most he and Gina could do was perpetuate the ruse. Patience was vital.

Milo made eye contact with Arch, touched the brim of his Stetson in greeting.

The conservatively dressed man raised his cane in response and—BAM!—there it was. He faltered and went down hard.

Evie yelped and fell to her knees beside him. "Charlie, baby, honey. Are you okay?"

Her shock and concern seemed genuine. If she was acting, Milo thought as he joined in the ruse, she was damned good. "Hell's fire, Twinkie," he joked, while helping Arch to his feet. "Wherever you go, men fall at your feet."

"Only not in the way a girl hopes," some woman added.

Curious onlookers chuckled.

Evie's face turned as crimson as her sexy lipstick.

Arch winced for show when he tried to stand on his own. "Wretched ankle," he complained in his concocted blue-blood accent, leaning against Milo for support.

Lucas, the golden-tongued shore excursion director, elbowed his way through the gawkers. "Should I call Doctor Drake, Mr. Dupont?"

"No need, old boy. However, I'm afraid I won't be able to go ashore. Damned disappointing, but the less I walk today, the better."

"I'll call for a wheelchair," Lucas said. "Please

don't try to make it back to the cabin on your own. I insist," he added, when Arch looked as though he might argue. He scrambled for the house phone as fellow passengers voiced their concern and Sugar fussed over Charles.

Milo squelched an eye roll as Arch lapped up the attention.

Gina joined them and he prayed she wouldn't crack out of turn while battling the green-eyed monster.

"I heard what you said about not going ashore, Charles. Don't worry," she said, her voice a husky contralto, "we'll look after Sugar."

Shit. "Hell, yeah," Milo said—as if he had a choice. "No reason the little lady should have to miss out on the fun while you're icing that ankle."

"We can shop till we drop," Gina added.

"Good of you to offer," Arch said with an easy smile. "I'll leave it up to Sugar."

Twinkie blinked a couple of times then chirped, "Don't be silly, baby. I'm not going anywhere without you." She quirked a coy grin. "We'll make our own fun."

Good girl, Milo thought.

"Isn't that sweet," Gina said.

"All ashore that's going ashore," someone announced.

The crowd clamored toward the door just as Lucas greeted a steward pushing a wheelchair.

"Where's your cane, Charles?" Gina asked in her husky *Carol* voice.

"I believe it rolled down that aisle," he said, gesturing behind him.

"I'll get it," she said, just as Evie announced she'd grab the wheelchair.

The level of noise and activity among passengers accelerated and for a moment chaos reigned.

Arch turned to retrieve his cane from Gina, and Milo watched, amazed, as Evie tripped over someone or something and plowed into the shore excursion director.

What a frickin' klutz, he thought, as she faltered and flung her arms around Lucas, grabbing hold of the man's ass. The pair babbled apologies while catching their balance and righting themselves.

Her execution was almost flawless. If Milo didn't have a trained eye, he, like everyone else in the theater, would've missed it. He clamped down on his cigar so his mouth wouldn't fall open.

I'll be damned.

CHAPTER TWENTY-TWO

"YOU'RE A NATURAL."

"You're a bastard." Heart pounding, I double-checked that we hadn't been followed, then locked the cabin door behind us. My adrenaline pumped for all kinds of reasons and it spiked when Arch sprang out of the wheelchair. I tossed my Lucy tote on the bed and slugged him in the arm. Hard.

With the exception of thirty years ago when I lost it and pummeled my know-it-all brother—much like Ralphie whaled on the bully in *A Christmas Story*—I've never retaliated physically. *Violence is wrong.* Thing was, lately my inner bad girl refused to play nice.

Annoyingly amused, Arch rolled back his offended shoulder. "And that was for…"

"Throwing me to the wolves."

"I *didnae*—"

"You could have told me that we weren't going ashore, that you planned to fake an injury. Do you have any idea how I felt when you crumpled to the floor? I thought you were hurt for *real*."

"Evie—"

"And then Tex—"

"Who?"

"—Vic implied I'm a dangerous klutz and called me *Twinkie!* I hate it when he calls me that. It makes me sound fluffy. Sweet."

Arch placed his glasses and Panama hat on the vanity. "In his defense—"

"I'm not sweet."

"If you say so."

"I used to be sweet, before people, including my own husband, started rejecting me based on age. Now I'm bitter. Cynical, shifty and *violent*."

I stopped in my heated tracks, slumped back against the wall. "I just hit you. I can't believe I *slugged* you. Maybe it's hormones. Maybe I'm premenopausal. Mood swings. Anxiety." I slapped a hand to my clammy brow, wondering if I was having a hot flash. "Great. What's next? Wild chin hairs?"

Arch unbuttoned his shirt, unstrapped the fake gut. "What is it *aboot* you and your age? So you're forty-one. Big fuckin' deal. Stone didn't know a good thing when he had it and the casinos are missing *oot* on a brilliant talent."

That prodded a tiny smile out of me. He scored points for validating my worth on both the personal and professional front. Still… "If you think I'm a brilliant talent, why didn't you prep me for your pratfall and plans to bail on San Juan? And don't you dare give me that crack-out-of-turn excuse."

"I wanted a real moment, yeah?"

I willed the top of my head not to blow off. "What?"

"This morning you asked for a show of faith. I *dinnae* trust easily, but I do believe in your caring nature. I knew you'd react strongly and with genuine concern when I fell. I wanted a real moment and I got it." He toed off his loafers and padded into the bathroom.

I followed him, my heart thudding in my ears. "Yes, but after the initial fall, I knew that you were faking. I ended up acting my butt off, *improvising* my butt off because you didn't clue me in. I didn't know if you wanted me to go ashore, you know, split our efforts, or stay on board, status quo." I twirled my ring, focused on the cheery sneakers. "I didn't want to make the wrong decision. But then I thought about Sugar's profile. She wouldn't abandon Charlie, leaving him to nurse his injury alone. She'd stay on board and fuss over him, keep him entertained. Sugar can have fun anywhere."

"Like I said. You're a natural." He looked over his shoulder. "That's a good thing, yeah?"

In other words, he'd just paid me a compliment. I mumbled a begrudging, "Thank you." I was angry, not rude.

I leaned against the doorjamb, watched as he began to remove the foam latex appliances from his face. I tried not to ogle his half-naked body. No easy feat. His sculpted shoulders and tapered back were droolworthy. His arms were to-die-for ripped and that Celtic band around his bicep killed me. Amazing that I could be ticked off and turned-on at the same time. Swear to heaven, if he got in the shower, I'd join him. Best-case scenario, we'd have sex. Worst case, we'd almost have sex.

I blew out a tense breath. "I'm sorry I hit you."

"Hate to break it to you, but your punch lacks power, Sunshine."

"That's not the point. I lost my temper."

"But not in public, yeah? Not where it counted. I couldn't have scripted it better."

"Let's not go there, huh?" I watched him dip a brush in a tiny jar, transfixed and transported back to the days when I shared a dressing room with a dozen other strolling entertainers. Stilt walkers, mimes, clowns, magicians and character actors like me. Swapping makeup tips was a daily ritual. "So what do you use to make the latex adhere? Spirit gum?"

"Aye." He loosened one edge of his faux jowls, swabbed underneath.

"So, the gook on the brush. Spirit gum remover?"

"Uh-huh."

I watched, fascinated as he repeated the brush and peel process, gently loosening the latex appliance bit by bit. "I read somewhere that it takes hours to apply prosthetics. I know you get up early to get a head start, but you're never in the bathroom for more than ninety minutes tops."

"I wear the tinted glasses so I *dinnae* have to screw with crow's feet or under-eye bags. Jowls and a wrinkled forehead? Pretty basic. Plus, I've had a lot of practice."

"Where'd you learn how to do this?"

"Someone in the biz."

"Someone in TCC? What does that stand for, anyway? The Covert Connection? The Counterintelligence Council?"

He caught my gaze in the mirror and winked. "Nice try."

I smirked. "So, what? If you told me, you'd have to shoot me?"

"Between the eyes."

I blinked.

He shook his head, sighed. "Christ, you're easy."

"I prefer the term *trusting* or *naive*." Was he *trying* to rile me? "Don't look so disgusted. There are worse things in this world."

"Not if it costs you your pride or your savings, or worse, your life."

"Are you talking about the vicious shark, the man who preys on gullible seniors?"

"He doesn't stop there, Sunshine."

My pulse skipped. "What do you mean? What did he do?"

"Never mind." He powdered the underside of each appliance, to absorb or reduce moisture I assumed, and returned them to a special case. Then he scrubbed his face with soap and water. The longer his silence, the shorter my patience. I wanted him to trust me, to enlist my help in making the world a better place.

"What's it going to take to convince you that I'm not a…a Twinkie?" I snapped my fingers. *The wallet!* I whirled and raced into the bedroom. Plucked the brown leather billfold from my Lucy tote, swiveled back around and knocked into the shirtless bad boy.

He grasped my shoulders and steadied me.

"This," I said, waving the evidence of my deceptive behavior beneath his nose, "proves that I am not a crème puff."

Grinning, he nabbed the goods. "And this would be?"

"Lucas's wallet."

The grin slipped. "Where'd you get it?"

"Out of his back pocket."

"You pinched his wallet?"

"*No*. That would be stealing. I have every intention of returning it with its contents intact. I just… borrowed it."

His brow furrowed. "Why?"

I rolled my eyes. "Because maybe there's something in there to confirm or negate his little fish status. Because he probably keeps his Fiesta card in there, which means we can search his room while he's ashore."

"Where did you learn how to pick pockets?"

I frowned. "You make it sound criminal."

"It is."

"No, it's not. It's hoodwinking. You know. Calculated deception. The Misdirection—distraction. The Dip—dipping into the pocket, taking the wallet. A little sleight of hand to hide it, in this case, in my Lucy tote." I shrugged. "All it takes is practice."

"Plus steady nerves and bang-on timing." He stared at me as if I had two heads. "Who taught you?"

"Someone in the biz," I said, tossing his own words back at him. "A magician friend," I added when a muscle jumped under his left eye. Jeez, had I finally managed to piss him off? "His regular assistant had to take a maternity break and I filled in for a few weeks. Lifting an item from an audience member was part of the act. Took me a while to get the technique down. Since I haven't done it in a while I assumed I'd lost my touch. Guess not."

I grinned for a millisecond before losing my patience and huffing a breath. "Why are you looking at me that way? It's not like you're Mr. Clean. You forged my passport. So I borrowed a wallet! I thought you'd be happy or impressed, not annoyed. It's for the greater good, for goodness' sake. Say something, dammit!"

"Bollocks."

He tossed the wallet on the table and yanked me into his arms. Suddenly, I was crushed against a wall of half-naked bad boy. He smothered my gasp with his mouth, blew my mind with his tongue.

I didn't protest, hell, no. That would require coherent thought and speech. He'd robbed me of both. I flung my arms around his neck, pressed closer, kissed deeper. I wanted this. I wanted more. I ground my pelvis against him to let him know I was game. Given our height difference, it was my lower stomach that endured the sweet, torturous pressure of his hard-on. Apparently criminal behavior was a turn-on for this man. I filed away the knowledge while smoothing my hands down his muscular back. I grabbed his stellar butt and bemoaned the fact he was still wearing pants.

Whatever Midwestern inhibitions I harbored vanished when his hands slipped beneath my T-shirt and splayed across my bare skin. His fingers skimmed and unhooked my bra strap and—*tingle, zing, zap*—I was his for the taking. Lest he miss the *take me, take me now* vibes I radiated, I gave him a more concrete *go*. I unbuckled his belt and fumbled with his fly, trembling with an exhilarating dose of anticipation.

I whimpered when he broke our hot, wet kiss. Mentally cheered when he tugged my shirt over my head, simultaneously ridding me of my bra. I stood before him topless and aroused, and loving the hungry look in his eyes as his gaze swept over my small, but perky breasts.

"I *dinnae* do relationships, Sunshine."

I took that as a *If you want me to stop, speak now*. "How convenient," I croaked, his heavy accent raging through me like an injected aphrodisiac. "I don't want one." *Not with you,* I thought as I boldly dipped my hands into his white briefs. *You're a heartbreaker*. He was also hard and huge and I couldn't believe I was actually caressing JT.

He groaned—Arch, not John Thomas—when I stroked his impressive length.

"Payback," I said, reflecting on last night. Since he'd taken liberties, I figured I was entitled to a little groping myself. Only he had something different in mind. In a flash, I was flat on my back—the bed beneath me, Arch above, kicking off his pants while peeling away my capris.

"I've wanted you naked from the moment you tripped though the airport's revolving doors."

His blunt admission struck me dizzy. I felt desired, and emotional. A warning bell gonged in my head causing me to go rigid when he pressed his magnificent body against mine and kissed my neck.

"I haven't done this in a while," I whispered, my nipples pebbling when he nipped and sucked my earlobe. "In fact, it's been aeons since I've done it with anyone but—"

"I'll take it slow, yeah?"

"No." The tenderness in his voice undid me. "I don't want slow. I don't want intimate." That would summon affection and compromise my fragile heart. "I just want—"

"Sex."

He flipped me onto my stomach and straddled me. I felt the weight of his erection on the small of my back as he skimmed his fingers over my shoul-

ders and back, featherlight. I shivered and moaned.
Delicious sensations rolled through me as he shifted
his weight and swept his hands over the swell of my
backside, his fingers probing and stroking the
wetness between my thighs. *Yes.*

My feverish brain flashed on the image of us, of
me in bed with a seriously hunky bad boy. Having
sex. With a spy…or something. With a man I barely
knew. I felt naughty and sensual and desperate to
feel him inside of me, filling me. "Do it," I whispered as want and need assaulted my sexually
deprived body.

His arm slipped beneath my stomach and lifted
me onto my knees. I knew what was coming. I
think I might have begged for it. I couldn't be sure.
My mind was mush. I choked out my last coherent
word. "Condom."

"Done."

When? I wondered, then he slid into me and my
mind exploded with vibrant fireworks and a string
of dirty words. A couple may have slipped out. That
or Arch was a mind reader. He rode me hard, one
hand on my hip, one on my shoulder, holding me
captive as he made love—no—*boinked* me blind.

Oh. My. Gaaaawd.

Decadent shock waves pounded my writhing
body, pulled me under into dark erotic waters as his
granite-hard shaft filled me to the hilt. As his hands
stroked and kneaded, as his fingers skimmed and

pinched. He slammed into me deep and hard, and yet I cried, "More!"

I glanced back, caught a glimpse of that rugged face and tribal tattoo. Every muscle in my body quivered. My stomach coiled into a tight knot and my lungs seized.

"Easy," he soothed in a tight voice and I realized I was moving against him, frantic. Frantic for release. The climax started from deep within and fanned its way through my body, zapping nerves I'd thought long severed.

"Coming," I managed in a strained whisper. Overpowered by a glorious wave of ecstasy, I cried out, my body trembling beneath Arch.

I felt his heated torso against my slick back, his warm breath against my neck. "I'm with you, lass."

Together we crested, shuddered. He bit and kissed my shoulder and, after an erotic, mumbled curse, fell to his side and pulled me into a spooning position. My pliant body curved into him as I struggled for an even breath and a clear thought. I didn't know what to say, what to do. I certainly wasn't going to admit I was a stranger to sweaty casual sex. I tried to relax against him, to enjoy the delicious satiation. *You can do worldly,* I told myself. *If all else fails, channel Sugar.*

Arch smoothed his palm over my shoulder and down my arm. My already thumping heart thumped harder when he interlaced his fingers with mine. "Evie?"

"Hmm?" I didn't turn. Somehow I'd managed not to make eye contact throughout the entire scene. It made the coupling less personal. Since a relationship was out of the question, I needed the emotional distance. Part of me wished he wasn't so touchy-feely in the aftermath. That he'd roll away and go out on the balcony for a smoke.

Instead, he cuddled and held my hand.

"Was I too rough?"

"You were perfect." Sex, just, sex. That's all I want. Okay. That's a lie, but it's how it had to be.

"That was—"

"If you say a mistake, I'll have to hurt you."

He smiled against my neck. "I was going to say bloody amazing, yeah?"

"Oh." Since I was facing away, I grinned like an idiot. I'd satisfied a bad boy. *Woo-hoo!* "Yes, it was very nice."

"Nice?" He chuckled. "You're full of surprises today, Sunshine."

I wasn't sure if he was referring to the hot sex or hot wallet, but the observation caused me to stir.

"Where are you going?" He tightened his grip, anchored me to the bed.

I shifted and made eye contact, willed my heart and mind steady. "We need to act before Lucas returns. Surely it won't take long for him to discover that his wallet is missing." My eyes widened with a fresh thought. "I was hoping he'd think he left it in his room, but what if he assumes it was stolen?

What if he goes to the island police or ship's security?"

He smoothed my hair from my face. "*Dinnae* worry. I'll take care of it." He kissed my forehead. "You stay here."

"But I want to help."

"You already did." He flipped through the wallet. "No key card. So much for a quick and easy entrance. I'll have to track down his room number and charm my way into his cabin."

Via a pretty, impressionable housekeeper? I raised a brow. "*Or* you could just break in. I'm betting you know how."

"But it wouldn't be as much fun."

"Fun, huh?"

He squeezed my hand then rolled away and out of bed.

Chilled and self-conscious, I pulled the quilted spread over my exposed body while openly admiring his naked form. The man was built. "Don't you think it'll look a little suspicious if Charles Dupont is seen roaming the halls of the crew's quarters?"

"I'm not going as Charles Dupont." He pulled a white outfit from a garment bag in the closet and disappeared into the bathroom.

I glanced at the digital clock, amazed that so little time had passed since we'd hit the sheets. Then again, I had asked for a fast and furious coupling. I didn't regret it. It had been exhilarating. Purely physical. Exactly what I hungered for, though I knew satisfaction would be fleeting. Dallying with Arch was like dining on Chinese food. In an hour, I'd want more.

He exited the bathroom dressed in a white uniform and my stomach fluttered with a familiar craving. An hour? Try five minutes.

I realized that he was dressed as a crew member, but with a little bit of imagination—and I had a boatload—he looked like a naval officer. An Italian naval officer, if there was such a thing. The fake moustache looked like the real deal. Sexy. He'd slicked his hair back with a colored gel, darkening his natural brown hair to black. His eyes were no longer green, but a dark chocolate brown. Dreamy.

"Contact lenses?" I asked, impressed and turned-on by his new swarthy look.

He winked and pocketed the wallet. "I *willnae* be longer than necessary."

I clutched the blanket to my chest and sat upright. "What should I do while you're gone?"

"Rest up."

My body hummed with anticipation. My lip quirked. "What for?"

"Karaoke."

I blinked.

"Since we *didnae* go ashore, we can attend the karaoke party. Gavin will be there along with several other possibilities. We need to continue with our ruse, Sunshine. Lucas may or may not be the little fish. We *willnae* know for sure until whoever it is offers us—"

"A chance of a lifetime."

"Aye." He paused at the door. "Are you going to be all right with what just happened?"

Ooh, boy. Bad boy was back to business. Now was the time to dredge up my worldly facade. "Are you referring to the meaningless sex and the understanding that it won't lead anywhere?" I shrugged. "Why wouldn't I be?"

He angled his head and studied me with those new dark eyes. "Because, aside from Stone, I'm the only man you've shagged in, how many years?"

"We were married for fifteen years. Hooked up two years before that."

He whistled low.

"Don't get a swelled head," I said, needing to trivialize the relevance of…*shagging* a man I barely knew. "You just happened to be in the right place at the wrong time."

"You mean the right time."

"No, I don't."

He smoothed his fingers over that moustache, a grin tugging at his mouth. "Your ability to recall my exact words is a bit disturbing, yeah?"

"It's a gift. Unlike lifting wallets, no practice necessary. I was born with a scary-good memory."

"Possess any other skills I should know *aboot?*"

I grinned, stretched. "Does being unbelievably flexible count?"

"And here I thought you were a nice girl."

"That would be the old me."

"Huh. Should I be nervous?" he asked while exiting the cabin.

Sensing I'd unbalanced the unflappable man, my grin turned evil. "Absolutely."

CHAPTER TWENTY-THREE

SEVERAL HOURS LATER, dressed as Mr. and Mrs. Charles Dupont, Arch and I made our way toward the Don Juan Lounge. "You're absolutely positive that there wasn't anything in his wallet or room to suggest he might be...fishy?"

Even though I'd asked in a whisper-soft voice, Arch still hushed me. "For the fiftieth time, I'm sure. Let it go, yeah?"

I'd been trying. I just hated to think that I'd *borrowed* a man's wallet and put us at risk for nothing. Arch hadn't complained, but somehow I felt as though I'd botched my first attempt at duping the bad guys. I huffed an exasperated sigh as we passed the Fiesta Theater. "Well, even though I missed San Juan, at least I didn't have to experience it with Carol Parker."

"Friendly gesture, yeah?"

No. "Our last shopping endeavor proved disastrous."

He blinked. "What shopping endeavor?"

"Yesterday. In the gift shop. I ran into her at the

counter. If it wasn't for her, I never would have bought that jasmine perfume. I mean, it had to be coincidence, bad timing, rotten luck, but..." I glanced up and caught him frowning. "What?"

"Nothing."

"It was a coincidence, right?"

"What else?"

"You tell me."

"Nothing to tell."

Hard to believe we'd gotten naked and sweaty only a few hours before. We were back to square one. Me, clueless. Him, secretive. Ugh. "She's shifty if you ask me. Not that you did. I'm just saying."

"Do me a favor, love," he said, affecting Charles's accent as he escorted me into the lively lounge. "Don't ruffle Carol's feathers."

I started to ask why but was distracted by the loud music and party atmosphere. My gaze swept across the room, taking it all in. A swarm of crazed butterflies attacked my stomach.

"You all right, love?"

"Peachy keen," I answered in Sugar's high-pitched voice.

It wasn't a lie, precisely. I'm a professional. A veteran. I've performed in countless capacities on countless stages in countless venues. I know the joy of thunderous applause and the agony of chirping crickets. I've survived auditions, rejections, accolades, insults, catty women, grabby men, competitive artists, loud drunks, affectionate drunks, lewd drunks and drunks who puked on the dance floor. Due to booze, not my performance.

I've seen it all, experienced it all. Yet eyeing the room, my stomach knotted, my mouth dried, my pulse skipped. It wasn't the posh setting that intimidated me. Don Juan's was an upscale lounge, but no more so than any of the casino lounges I've played. Nor was I put off by the stage. A DJ had set up his gear stage right. A lone mike stand stood center stage cradling a wireless Shure 58. Audio monitors and a TV monitor were positioned down front. Standard equipment. Familiar ground.

Since bean counters long ago scaled back on budget and the use of live drummers—don't ask— I'm used to singing with smaller groups, which almost always means using sequenced tracks. So, it wasn't the thought of singing along to inflexible karaoke CDs that had me shaking in my four-inch, metallic, pointy-toed pumps.

It was the thought of performing in front of Arch.

Sure, he'd heard me noodle around with a verse of "Conga" and "Fever." But this was different. The pressure to impress was enormous. I seriously wanted to turn tail, find a secluded corner and a bag of oatmeal raisin cookies.

Good thing I was Sugar, not me. Sugar bopped into the lounge ready to boogie.

Arch, who'd transformed back into Charles, and who'd declared his ankle now strong enough to forgo the wheelchair, limped toward a vacant table with the use of his cane. I bobbled alongside him, my spiky heels sliding over the marbled foyer then sinking into plush carpet.

"Boogie Oogie Oogie" pulsed through the speakers suspended from the ceiling. Several dancers had already taken to the floor, including Martha and her young friend. "I'm surprised at how crowded it is considering what Gavin said about slow nights in port." It didn't look slow to me, although maybe he'd been speaking specifically about participation in karaoke.

"Can't hear you well, love. What do you say we sit away from the speakers?"

I recognized more than a few people as he led me to a table at the rear of the lounge. Several waved. I smiled and waved back, feeling a tad overdressed. Then again Sugar's taste in fashion was faithfully over the top.

Dress code for the evening was casual, but I'd glitzed up. A sparkly, clingy pink cocktail dress with a modest neckline and a plunging back. I'd applied dramatic makeup—smoky eye shadow, kohl liner, ebony mascara, shimmering blush and Sugar's signature Cajun Crimson lipstick. Between my teased hair, high heels and short hemline, I *almost* looked leggy and tall. Overall, the look was va-va-voom sexy.

Arch had taken one look and said, "Bollocks."

Yeah, baby, yeah.

I'd had three things in the back of my mind when I glammed up. One: To bolster my confidence on the off chance Carol-the-witch Parker joined the festivities, equally spiffed up, trying to steal my thunder and my husband. Two: To wow Arch. I was seriously hoping to extend our one-night stand by a day or five. Three: I wanted to impress Gavin. If he was the little fish, I'd hook him and reel him in. If he was a straight-up cruise director, I'd put a bug in his ear—at some point—about hiring me on as an entertainer. A performer's age was less of a factor on cruise ships. No sense in ignoring an alternative for the future.

I wasn't sure how I felt about a six-month tour away from my friends, but I couldn't ignore my unemployed status at home and my bolstered spirits here on the ship. It wasn't merely the attraction to Arch, but the change of scenery, the positive atmosphere. Here everyone, passengers and crew, seemed happy.

I could hear Nicole impersonating Madame Helene. *Go to the happy place.*

I'd rather tag along with Arch.

Evie Parish: Sidekick to an international spy.

The dreamer in me wanted to pursue a future in espionage. I mean, they must utilize people like me from time to time, otherwise why was I here?

The realist in me, which was really the ever-present voice of my mom, said, *You'd better have something to fall back on.* That's why I wanted to impress Gavin, second-in-command regarding entertainment. At forty-one, I could no longer afford to ignore my mom's sound—gag—advice.

So basically, I was looking at this karaoke thing as an audition.

Considering my last audition, you can see where I'd be a tad apprehensive.

Arch and I settled at a four-seat table. He ordered a scotch, what else? I ordered a glass of vodka and cranberry. If I had to sing "Crazy" or "I Will Survive" for the eight-billionth time in my life, I needed inspiration. With any luck the alcohol would melt the knot in my stomach and provide a little false courage.

Charles and I held hands and ad-libbed about remodeling his estate or possibly purchasing an apartment in Manhattan. He could work anywhere, he said. He emphasized the fact that he wanted me to be happy. *The ruse*.

I thought about all the places, all the people we'd touched over the last couple of days with our fabricated tale. We'd been visible, friendly and open about our well-off status. Employees talk. No matter the department, gossip gets around. I know that from my years in the casino industry. Even if we hadn't had optimum exposure to whomever Arch was after, surely the mark knew what we were about. Surely he'd pitch his deal in the next day or so. Maybe even tonight.

The more I thought about it, the more my pulse

raced. Or maybe that was because of the way Arch brushed his thumb back and forth across my hand. My breath caught when he wrapped one arm around me and leaned close. My eyes rolled back as he kissed my neck, nipped my lobe.

"Listen close, love."

I had to listen hard because something was pounding in my ears. Oh. My heart.

"If anyone approaches you with an exclusive opportunity, play along. But make it clear, I handle the finances, yeah?"

Before I could respond, he kissed me. Slow, deep. So not fair, the way he could muddle my mind. I wanted the kiss to go on forever. I wanted to drag him off to a coat closet and rip off his prosthetics and clothes. No particular order.

He eased away and my fantasies fizzled. I opened my eyes to find him leaning back in his seat, sipping scotch and watching me through those sepia-tinted glasses. He knew the effect he had on me. Damn him. I smiled as if to say, you'll get yours. The roaring in my ears reduced enough to hear the DJ, Elliot, relaying the objective of the evening.

"It's easy," he said. "Pick a song from the extensive list being passed about and I'll call you up in the order that I receive the requests. Don't worry if you don't know the words. The lyrics will scroll across this television monitor. No fuss, all fun. It's your night to shine!"

I saw Gavin mingling with various passengers,

handing out song lists and encouraging guests to sign up for a turn. I saw him coming my way, knew what was expected. Knew what I had to do. For Arch. For the greater good.

For myself.

Mental note: No matter what happens, don't flash your boobs.

CHAPTER TWENTY-FOUR

WHEN MILO ENTERED the Don Juan Lounge, Twinkie was leading a conga line, weaving through tables and encouraging patrons to join in. He guesstimated a good twenty had already grabbed on. The second in line was a stoop-shouldered geezer with a wide denture smile. He had plenty to smile about. He was gripping the hips of a devilishly cute woman with a knockout figure. Lucky bastard. The fact that she'd pickpocketed a man earlier today only increased Milo's fascination. In spite of her deft technique, he was relatively certain she wasn't a pro. What she was, was an enigma.

A sparkly bloused grandma with curly yellow hair and cat-eye glasses stood onstage squinting at a monitor and belting out some Latin-Disco song—badly. Something about the rhythm getting you. It had certainly gotten Evie.

He hadn't realized he was staring until Gina elbowed him in the ribs. "There's Charles," she said, with a nod toward Arch.

They made their way through a lounge that was

growing more crowded by the minute. People who'd returned from their shore excursions, dropping in for a nightcap or a late night of dancing. The party, he'd read, went until 2:00 a.m.

"Well, if it ain't our friend, Dupont," Milo drawled over the loud music. "Mind if me and the Mrs. join ya?"

Arch-Charles straightened his ascot, motioned them into a seat. "How was San Juan?"

"Festive. How's your ankle?"

"Better."

Milo sat across from Arch. Gina sat in between them.

Arch smiled at her. "How was the shopping?"

She shrugged. "No irresistible bargains."

"Unlike the gift shop's duty-free perfume."

She matched Arch's smile, a fake smile, and Milo felt like a voyeur at a bizarre chess game. *Check. Checkmate.* "How about you and Sugar?" he asked, breaking the tension. "Trip upon any deals here on the ship?"

"Nothing special, no."

So they'd all struck out. Milo snagged a waitress. "Darlin', couple of beers here. And another round for the Duponts." Although they hadn't been ap-proached by the roper, he had touched base with Woody. The Kid, being the overenthusiastic whiz he was, had colored in a few grey areas. Wanting to drag Arch away for a private word, he glanced at his watch. Midnight. "How long you been here?"

"Couple of hours."

He glanced at the conga queen. "She perform yet?"

"Multiple times. The crowd loves her."

"I can see that." Milo marveled at her energy, admired the deep cut of the back of her dress as she shimmied past, a train of people in tow. She blew a kiss at Arch, and Milo felt a tug of resentment. "Nice dress," he commented dryly.

Gina pushed out of her chair with a disgusted snort. "I'm going to the bar to see if they have any pretzels."

Milo sharpened his wits, turned back to his partner intending to persuade him to step outside. But then the song ended and the DJ made an announcement. "Let's have a round of applause for Martha!" The crowd responded kindly. But then he announced Sugar and the applause tripled. She took center stage, caressed the microphone and, in a breathless voice said, "This one's for you, Charlie, baby."

Given her sex-kitten appearance, Milo half expected her to break into a Marilyn Monroe rendition of "Happy Birthday." He sure as hell wasn't prepared for Peggy Lee's "Fever."

As soon as the bass line kicked in and Evie started singing, he scraped a hand over his jaw thinking, *I'm toast*. He wondered what Arch was thinking. After all, the sultry performance was directed at him.

She was good. A little off-key in her upper range,

but oddly it didn't bother him. Her voice had character. A husky alto, far and away from her high-pitched speaking voice, her rich tone rivaled that of Diana Krall, one of Milo's contemporary favorites. But it was something else, something beyond her singing. Charisma? He couldn't pinpoint it exactly but she stirred him.

Instead of making love to the camera, as they say, she made love to Arch. But it was Milo and Mr. Happy who felt the effects. *Damn.*

The song ended and he sat there, stunned. Everyone else applauded. Sugar stepped off the stage, her eyes on Arch, but the old woman, Martha, hugged her and pulled her onto the crowded dance floor. The DJ had launched into "Y.M.C.A." and Sugar, party girl extraordinaire, was now spelling letters out with her arms.

He couldn't believe it. He was almost willing to endure The Village People to watch Twinkie dance. He downed his beer, stood. "I need some fresh air."

"I'll join you."

He and Arch were nearly to the front entrance when they ran into Gina. She was carrying a bowl of party mix and smirking at the dance floor. "Quite the performance."

"Keep an eye on her," Milo said.

"Gee, I thought you'd never ask."

OKAY. THIS SUCKED. I'd planned to return to our table, to snuggle down on Arch's lap to see if his beast had responded to my call of the wild. I knew *I* was hot to trot. The fact that Elliot had had "Fever" in his collection, the song Sugar supposedly sang in Vegas the night Charles first spotted her, seemed serendipitous to my seduction. Instead of snuggling with Arch, I was dancing with Martha, participating in a choreographed song that I disliked as much as "The Chicken Dance." But I couldn't say no to Martha, and Gavin was watching. He'd been watching all night.

I'm not bragging—okay, that's a lie—but I'm pretty sure I'd snagged his interest. The Motown hit "My Guy" had been a calculated pick, a guaranteed crowd pleaser, and something I could ham up for *my husband*. Couples flocked to the dance floor, and the enthusiastic applause that came after jolted my system like a drug. The familiar rush propelled me through the next two hours, although I'd had to kick off my skyscraper heels a few times.

It had seemed only natural to start the conga line when Martha launched into "Rhythm is Gonna Get You." It's what I get paid to do at home—initiate and perpetuate fun. Arch had hired me to be the life of the party and since I'm anal about my work… If Gavin didn't hire me as a singer or a party motivator, maybe he'd hire me as an assistant because I'd darn well proven I could create excitement and fun! Maybe I could fill Julie McCoy's canvas shoes after all. At least the thought of being a cruise director didn't make my eye twitch and my stomach spasm.

I'd still rather be a sidekick to a spy, but at least I had backup. Maybe. If Gavin did offer me a job, I'd have to explain my "Sugar" ruse. I'd cross that bridge if I came to it.

Elliot segued into Donna Summer's "Bad Girls" and I explained to Martha that I really needed to get back to Charlie. She boogied over to her friends, but before I could boogie off anywhere, Fred nabbed my hand and reeled me in.

"You promised me a dance, yes?"

Crap. "You bet, Freddie, baby. You know how to hustle?"

"It is," he said with a dazzling smile, "my specialty."

Even though the balls of my feet were cramping, I allowed him to lead me into the seventies dance. It's not that I wanted to dance, although I do love to hustle, but there loomed the chance that he was the man Arch was after. My pulse raced as he glided and spun me around the floor, and it had little to do with physical exertion. Although three minutes into it, I was sweating big-time. Keeping up with his moves was a challenge. The man was a champion hustler.

"We make a good team," he said.

"Uh-huh," I managed, because at this point I was breathless—from dancing, not because he was looking at me all, well, Don Juan-like.

"I have a proposition for you."

Uh-oh. "I'm all ears."

"Not here. It's too loud."

Before I knew it, he was *hustling* me toward the door. I glanced anxiously in Arch's direction, only he wasn't there. Ms. Tall, Dark and Beautiful, of all people, was sitting at our table, conversing with Martha's young and handsome dance partner. Tex was nowhere in sight.

I told myself to focus as Fred guided me through an alternate exit. *Stay in character. Play along and remember, Charlie makes all the financial decisions.* Check.

If the guy got fresh, well, Sugar would slug him. Double check.

MILO WAITED UNTIL he and Arch were outside, alone on deck, before he slipped out of Vic's accent. "I talked to Woody," he said at a volume considerably lower than that of his Texan alter ego.

They stood side by side, leaning against the rail and staring out at the twinkling lights of San Juan. In less than an hour the ship would set sail for St. Thomas. Arch shoved his tinted glasses to the top of his silver head, pinched the bridge of his nose. "Did he win Kara back yet?"

"The only thing he's won lately is an award for most obnoxious cologne."

"As long as it doesn't smell like jasmine."

"Aren't you allergic—"

"Yeah. So what did The Kid have to say?"

"He did a background check on Evie Parish."

"I *didnae* tell you her last name."

"I snapped a digital shot of her this morning. You take it from there."

Arch glanced up at the stars, seemingly unruffled. "So, let me guess. No criminal record. Not even a speeding ticket, yeah?"

"A real Shirley Temple." Milo pulled a cigar out of his shirt pocket—a handmade Cuban he'd purchased on the sly in Old San Juan—and lit up. He hadn't smoked in years, but tonight he succumbed to the guilty pleasure, thinking there were worse things. Like lusting after his partner's unexpected glitch. "So where did she learn how to pick pockets?"

He glanced sideways. "You saw?"

"Don't worry. I'm the only one. Everyone else in the theater was distracted, including you. Lucas didn't feel a thing. She's good. So good that she's never been caught."

"She's not a pro."

"So what gives?"

"Learned it from a magician. She worked as his temporary assistant for a while. The Dip was part of the act."

"No shit." He processed. "So you knew this and asked her to lift Lucas's wallet?"

He shook his head. "Didn't know until after. She thought it might help in establishing whether or not the man's our roper."

"You told her—"

"Very little. But what I do say sticks." He blew

out a breath. "She memorized Sugar's profile after one hearing. And other things… Possible she has an eidetic memory."

"Total recall?"

"Or close to it." Arch angled his head. "She's more of a glitch than I first anticipated."

"How so?" When he didn't answer, Milo took another route. "Why didn't you tell me she's married to Michael Stone?"

"Was married. They're divorced."

Per Arch's referral, they'd used the entertainment agent to book two dozen shills for a sting up in Newark several months back. Operating on a standard need-to-know, the actors had been shielded from the true nature of the "gig" as well as the true identity of their employer. Milo had only dealt with Stone on the phone, but had formed an immediate opinion of his character. "Stone's an ass."

"Agreed."

"So why are you dealing with him?"

"That's my business, yeah?" He replaced his glasses, looked over his shoulder. "I want to get back to Evie. Let's wrap."

"I want to know about Simon Lamont. Who is he to you?" When he remained tight-lipped, Milo pushed. "Gina and I are putting our asses on the line for you. If A.I.A—"

"Screw the Agency. If you really want to go after the scum-artists, go freelance."

"Career advice from a man who should be

serving time. Huh." Used to Arch tap-dancing
around a subject until you'd forgotten your original
question, Milo pressed. "What's your beef with
Lamont?"

"You're not going to leave go, are you, mate?"

"No."

Arch worked his jaw, blew out a breath. "He
lured a respected associate *oot* of retirement to work
a forgery scam. When the artist delivered the goods,
Lamont reneged on the price. This artist, my...friend,
was old school, stood up to Lamont on principle.
Don't cheat a cheater, yeah? Someone silenced his
protests. Permanently."

Fuck. "Lamont?"

"Or hired muscle. I'm not clear on specifics,
only the circumstances. Because of Lamont, a
good man is dead."

Milo rubbed the back of his neck. "A man you
cared about."

"Aye."

He sighed. "So because of that personal debacle
you believe Ms. Benson's claim that Lamont and
his muscle were responsible for her grandfather's
heart attack."

"Do I think they could have scared a frail, frustrated man to death through intimidation? You bet."

"Earlier you said Simon Lamont is an alias."

"Also known as Simon LaCrosse. Simon the
Fish. David Krebs. David Kinere..."

"David Krebs. I know that name." Milo took a

heady drag off of the Cuban, racked his brain. Ah, shit. "Fell under investigation last year. Suspected of being involved in heavy rackets on the West Coast."

"Bit of a violent streak, yeah."

"Skipped the country to avoid arrest."

"You should've dug deeper, Beckett."

"You shouldn't have involved an unsanctioned player." He tempered the rising volume of his voice. "Jesus Christ, Arch. Krebs, Lamont, whatever the hell name he's going by, is dangerous."

Arch dragged a hand over his face. "Like you said, my emotions are showing. I fucked up but it's too late now."

The ragged edge to the man's tone sawed through Milo's anger. He didn't trust Arch, but he liked him. Even when they'd been on opposite sides of the law, when the grifter had slipped through his fingers time and again, making him look like a dumb-ass with the boys at A.I.A., he'd liked him. And because Arch was willing to stick his neck out for this associate, someone he actually cared about, he liked him even more.

Shit.

"It's not too late," he said. "We'll fly Evie out of St. Thomas tomorrow, concoct a story, salvage our covers. Chameleon will take down Lamont."

"Even though it's *oot* of the Agency's jurisdiction?"

"Even though."

"Why?"

"Because it just became personal."

Presently, Gina stepped in and upped the stakes. "We've got trouble."

CHAPTER TWENTY-FIVE

"I CAN'T BELIEVE I broke his foot, Gavin. I am *so* sorry."

"Please stop apologizing, Sugar. The man accosted you. Are you sure you don't want to press charges?"

"I'm sure. I mean, I feel sort of at fault. I did walk out on deck with him in the middle of the night and…" I groaned, pressed the ice pack Doctor Drake had given me against the knot on my forehead as Gavin escorted me to my cabin. How stupid could I be? Fred was slick. A smooth-talking, sultry-eyed flirt. He'd made a play for me the night before. I should have known his proposition would be of a lewd nature.

Problem was, he wouldn't take no for an answer. When he maneuvered me into a dark corner and pawed me, I'd panicked. Not being able to push out of his arms, I stomped on his foot with my spiky heels. Hard. "How will he teach your dance classes with a cast up to his knee?"

"After my boss and the head of security get

through with him, he'll be lucky if he doesn't spend the night in the brig. Believe me, fulfilling his obligations as dance instructor is the last thing on our minds. Are you sure you don't want to press charges?"

"I'm sure." Filing a complaint, involving authorities... What if I somehow compromised Arch's mission? What if they looked up Sugar Dupont in the computer only to discover she didn't exist?

"Here we are." Gavin tugged me to a stop at my cabin door.

I felt a bit fuzzy. The struggle. Fred shoving me aside, causing me to bonk my head on the railing after I mashed his foot. The shock of knowing I'd sent yet another man to the infirmary. Staying in character throughout the entire episode had been exhausting. The rolling of my stomach rivaled the throbbing of my head.

"Do you have your Fiesta Card?"

"No, I... No. It's in my purse and I think I left that in the lounge." At least I'd had the forethought to tuck my wallet, holding my real ID, into Big Red.

"Maybe a waitress picked it up or someone turned it in. I'll check." He cleared his throat. "Is your husband inside?"

"I don't know. I don't think so." I had no idea where Arch had gone. Maybe he'd returned to the lounge by now. Maybe *he* had my purse.

"No problem," Gavin said. "I have a passkey."

He opened the door and I ventured inside,

stalling just over the threshold. "He's not here," I said, a big, fat knot forming in my throat. *Don't cry. Don't cry.*

"I can have him paged."

"No. Thanks, but no." I just stood there, feeling disoriented and wishing he'd go away. What would Sugar do?

"Again. I can't apologize enough for this unfortunate incident," Gavin said. "I wish there was something I could do. Make this up to you somehow." He sighed. "Wait. I know. Although…" He shook his head. "Never mind."

Whoa. I was fuzzy headed, not unconscious. A few brain cells still sparked. I turned, careful not to sound too eager. "What?"

"I'm not really supposed to talk about it." He glanced over both shoulders, up and down the hall.

I glanced at the crystal vase, thinking I could bean him if he got frisky like Fred. I was getting pretty good at hurting people. Because of me Tex needed stitches. Fred, a cast. I wondered if Arch had a bruise where I'd punched him. "How rude of me to leave you standing in the hall. I'm sorry. Please, come in."

"The ship frowns upon staff visiting passengers' cabins."

"Nonsense. You saw me safely to my room. I can at least offer you a drink." *Come on, come in.*

"I'll pass on the drink, but I will come inside for a moment. Let's leave the door ajar."

Okay. So maybe he was a straight-up guy as I'd first thought. The surge of energy I'd experienced fizzled. I sank down on the love seat, kicked off my sparkly bone-crushers. "You were saying?"

He hovered near the doorway, lowered his voice. "I'm not really supposed to talk about this. Dragonfly hasn't gone public yet. It's all very hush-hush. Only a select few will receive an invitation to get in on the ground floor. But it's perfect for you and I owe you. You really made me look good in front of my boss tonight. Don Juan's was jumping. The only downer was Fred." He frowned. "I definitely owe you for that buffoon's behavior. I am, after all, one of his superiors. However, this would have to remain between you and me. This thing."

"I'm not following you, Gavin." Really. I wasn't.

Again he looked over his shoulder then back at me. "How would you like to live on a cruise ship full-time? Own your own cabin. Travel the world."

"Sounds expensive."

He smiled. "Actually, it's quite affordable. A once-in-a-lifetime opportunity for a limited few."

This was it! The offer Arch had tipped me off to. I felt a bit dizzy and I was pretty sure it wasn't solely due to the bonk on my head. Gavin was the mark! The bad guy. Only he didn't seem threatening and I wasn't nervous so much as excited. "I want in."

He blinked at me and I realized I'd practically

squealed the words. *Simmer down, Parish.* Stay in character. "What I mean is, Charlie and I, we were just talking about purchasing a second home. And, like, well, a cabin could be a second home, right? Kind of a floatin' condominium?"

His shoulders relaxed and the smile returned. "Right."

"Only, well, I don't handle our money. That's Charlie's department."

"I understand." He shifted his weight, considered.

I pressed the ice pack more firmly to my head to keep it from exploding. *Play it cool.* "Here's the thing. I don't know if you've noticed, but I've had a blast these past couple of days."

"I noticed."

"Between you and me, Connecticut is a little boring. Livin' like this more often? That would make me very happy." I smiled. "Charlie wants me to be happy."

He nodded. "All right then. I'll have a talk with your husband. But not here. I really can't stay any longer. I'm expected."

"We're going into St. Thomas tomorrow," I blurted.

"So am I. Tell him to meet me at the Coconut Shack, say, one in the afternoon? It's near Magens Bay. And, Sugar," he said as he backed toward the door, "make sure Mr. Dupont realizes this is an inside tip. Very hush-hush."

I gave him a thumbs-up. "Mum's the word."

He shut the door and I pumped my fist in the air. "Yes!" Then promptly fell back on the love seat and pressed the ice pack to my aching head.

"I TOLD YOU TO KEEP an eye on her."

"I'm a player, not a babysitter." Gina threw her handbag on her bed.

Milo tossed his Stetson on the vanity. "She could have been seriously hurt."

"She did all right. She broke the slimeball's foot."

"The nurse said she had a contusion."

"Self-inflicted. She bobbled and bashed her head. You said it yourself, she's a klutz." Gina sat on the bed, pried off her heels. "Calm down, Jazzman. Jesus, they can probably hear you in the next cabin."

Milo breathed deep, rolled his neck to ease a kink. "What the hell happened back there?" He still sounded surly, but at least he wasn't yelling.

She shifted, sat cross-legged and massaged the balls of her feet. "I *was* watching her. She was smack in the middle of a crowd of old farts, dancing and having a high old time. Then this pretty-boy approached me, introduced himself as Horatio and started laying it on thick. Turns out he works for the ship. A dance escort. Strictly kosher, so he said. But I'm thinking, okay, so he could be a candidate."

She glanced up and nailed Milo with a calm, sincere gaze. "I was doing *business*. The moment I noticed she was missing, I blew off Horatio and tracked her down. Fred's anguished cry worked like a beacon."

Milo ran his tongue over his teeth, scraped both hands over his buzz cut. "I need a drink."

"Beer in the minibar. Grab me one, too, will you?"

He snagged two longnecks, tossed her one, then sank down on his bed. "Sorry about—"

"Forget it." She took a long pull of her beer then angled her head. "Why don't you fill me in on your discussion with Ace. Given your shitty mood, I'm guessing things are going to get rocky."

I'M NOT SURE HOW LONG Gavin had been gone before the door swung open and Arch blew in. A minute? Five? I'd been lying on the sofa, nursing my noggin and committing my discussion with Gavin to memory. Time sort of blurred.

I heard the door shut, heard my name. I pushed myself up, adjusted the hem of my dress and leaned back against the sofa. "You're not going to believe what happened."

"Fred attacked you. I heard." He flashed my clutch purse then tossed it on the table.

"Oh, good. Thank you."

"Sure."

I narrowed my eyes. "You sound funny."

"I *dinnae* feel funny."

I realized then that he was slipping out of costume, slowly, meticulously. Jeez. Didn't he see the goose-egg on my forehead? Wasn't he concerned? "What *are* you feeling?"

"Angry."

"Really? Your angry is like most people's bored." He didn't respond. He didn't even look at me. Stripped down to his trousers and a T-shirt, he moved into the bathroom. The elation that I felt regarding Gavin's proposition wilted. Dread blossomed in its place. Was Arch going to go postal? Pull a Beretta or Glock—or whatever spies used these days—and go gunning for Fred? "If it's any consolation, he didn't attack me exactly. He just sort of groped."

Silence.

"I broke his foot. I didn't mean to. I'm not a violent person…usually. Must have been the adrenaline…or something."

Silence.

Crap. I pushed off of the love seat and approached the bathroom. He'd left the door open, so I dawdled on the threshold. Tonight, he removed the prosthetics with greater speed and far less care. Uh-oh.

"I think they're going to throw him in the brig," I said. "Which is a fancy nautical term for jail. I saw this movie once and—"

"This is real life, Evie. Not a movie."

It was then that I realized he wasn't angry with Fred so much as *me*. My pulse accelerated, my breathing quickened. I stood there frozen, catapulted back in time to when I'd disappointed my mom. Too many times to count. But it didn't matter. Each time I felt like a loser. A failure.

"Why did you put yourself in a compromising position?"

"You told me if anyone propositioned me…" I swallowed hard, summoned a backbone. "You said your guy, your *mark,* was in entertainment or hospitality. That's Fred. You said if anyone offered me a *chance of a lifetime*…well, he said he had a proposition. What was I supposed to do? You said play along. So I did. But his proposition involved sex. I'm pretty sure that's not what you meant. And even if it was, I declined. He refused my refusal. I broke his foot. And that was that."

Arch scrubbed his face with soap and water. I stood there, vibrating as he completed the transformation from Charles to Arch. I stood there thinking, *I don't know you at all. Not an iota.* I didn't know his background or values. Why did I care what he thought of me?

But I did. I cared.

Big-time.

"I hate that you're not honest with me. I hate that you're not direct. Hello? I can't fix what I don't know is broken." I tapped my temples. "Not a mind reader."

My anguished words echoed in my head. I shivered and rubbed my goose pimply arms. Who was I blasting? Arch or Michael? Again, I was reminded of how alike they were when it came to manipulating emotions. Sleeping with Arch, even for the pure thrill, had been one big-ass mistake.

My stomach cramped as I waited for him to explain his bonehead behavior. Still he said nothing, just peeled his T-shirt over his head. I watched his back muscles roll with the effort and again bemoaned the attraction.

He turned and faced me, his eyes riveted on the floor tiles.

Why won't you look at me? My breath caught in my throat, along with my words. He looked so guarded, so unapproachable. I grappled for a coherent thought, spewed my good news. "Gavin is your mark. He walked me to our cabin, pitched a once-in-a-lifetime opportunity. He said he'll meet you at the Coconut Shack tomorrow, one o'clock."

Yeah, boy, *that* got his attention. His gaze locked with mine and my desert-dry tongue knotted. The intensity of that gray-green stare was staggering. He braced his hands on his hips. "What else did he say?"

Thinking I'd finally broken through, I blew out a breath, shook off my anger and focused on the job. I repeated our conversation verbatim, or close to it, because I have a kick-ass memory. I expected him to comment. To question. To acknowledge that I'd supplied him with valuable information. Something. Anything. I would've settled for "well done."

Silence. Stony-faced silence.

He stripped off his pants and shorts. He bypassed me and the whirlpool tub, stepped into the shower stall and severed our conversation by shutting the door and blasting the water.

I stared at the frosted shower pane, blood burning, skin sizzling. Great. Now in addition to being fired up I was turned-on. Mr. Manly Man in all his naked splendor was branded on my corneas for life. All those glorious muscles, that tribal tattoo, his rebel good looks, not to mention JT.

Fascinated with a one-eyed beast. Obsessed with sex. So unlike me. Thing was, I hadn't been "me" in days. It was as if a mad scientist had attached a mind-bending contraption to my head in an effort to alter my behavior patterns. The old me avoided confrontation. *Good girls don't cause scenes*. Since that humiliating spokesmodel audition, I'd been anything but *good*. I'd been acting out, speaking my mind, for several days running. Yup. Just as I'd first thought, after forty-one years of internalizing, I'd finally snapped.

"I know I'm not trained in this spy stuff, but I'm a good actress, and I have good instincts. I'm a natural. You said so yourself. If I did something wrong, didn't get enough information from Gavin, then that's *your* fault, not mine. That need-to-know policy of yours is a little restricting. Insulting, too. It's like you don't trust me."

I jabbed a finger at the fogged-over pane. "Let me tell you, *buster*, I am completely, utterly trustworthy! It's one of my better qualities, along with being a trouper. If you'd had the courtesy to look at me, you might have noticed the knot on my forehead.

Groped and wounded in the line of duty, yet I haven't whined. You could have at least asked if I'm okay!"

Winded from my rant, I jerked open the door, reestablishing face-to face confrontation. "What *is* your problem?"

"You."

His arm snaked out, wrapped around my waist. He hauled me into the shower fully clothed. Pressed against the tiled wall, my heart thudded as he plastered his soaked naked body against me, and kissed me blind.

Did I mention he was naked?

This was better than a sexy scene out of a romance novel, because *this* was real. I wrapped my arms around his neck and held tight as my bones melted. Steamy, hot, wet. Me. Arch. The shower. I intensified the kiss, opening my mouth wider, hungrily seeking his tongue, his affection. I wanted more, needed more.

Fill the emptiness.

I moaned in frustration when he framed my face in his hands and eased away. But then he studied my forehead and gently kissed my bump. "You scared the *shite oot* of me, Sunshine."

In that instant, I understood his bonehead behavior. He cared about me, even if only a little. Cared that I'd been hurt, and that it had, on some level, been his fault. If not for him, I wouldn't be here at all. He felt responsible, guilty. But for whatever reason, personal or professional, he fought hard to suppress his feelings.

I knew all about suppression.

Water sprayed out of the shower nozzle, steam swirled, and I felt myself slipping in more ways than one. Arch annihilated any vestiges of self-restraint with a sincere and caring gaze. *Snap.* "I know you don't do relationships. I know we're not a good idea, but—"

He silenced me with a ravenous kiss. His hands moved swiftly, peeling my soaked dress off my trembling form, exploring every inch of me. Every curve, every crevice.

My eyes rolled back as he stroked me much as he had the night before, only slower this time. I squirmed against his hand, moaned into his mouth, as he coaxed me toward a mind-bending climax. Fireworks burst behind my eyelids when he rounded the bases, suckling my breasts and then sliding his tongue home. Three flicks and…BAM!

The Big *Ooooh!*

I sagged against him, exhausted, cross-eyed, thinking this was it, the end of the erotic scene and that was okay, because the sheer electricity of the moment would power me through another year of celibacy.

Only he killed the shower spray, hauled me out of the stall and into the dimly lit bedroom.

Next thing I knew I was spread-eagle in the center of the bed, Arch sprawled on top of me—naked, wet—and… "No! Not like this," I cried. "Too intimate."

"You're killing me." Yet he hauled me out of bed and bent me over the bureau.

I scattered cosmetics and magazines, clearing the surface and holding on for dear life. *"Ooooh!"* He gripped my hips and filled me from behind with one deep thrust. Huge. Hard. "Condom!" I cried in a fraction of rational thought.

"Done."

I didn't question his lightning-speed abilities. I'd lost the capacity to form sentences. My mind shut down as every nerve ending sparked to life. So many sensations. He shagged me fierce and fast. I came and came, a series of earth-rocking orgasms. Sex, for me, had never been like this. So carnal and all-consuming.

Arch urged me to slow down, but I didn't want slow. I wanted frenzied and mind-blowing. I might have even said it out loud, because he flipped me around and suddenly we were wrestling on the carpeted floor. He rolled beneath me so that I straddled him, JT buried deep within me.

"Have at it," was all he said and I took control, riding him, catching wave after wave of delicious ecstasy. I explored his amazing body with my hands. Licked his tattoo. Plundered his sensuous mouth. Inhibitions blew apart and away as I indulged in a purely physical connection with a man I felt safe with.

Oh. My. *"Yeeeees!"*

He gripped my hips, rammed deep and held firm, reaching his own peak as I shuddered and collapsed on top of him.

I could scarcely breathe, let alone think. I couldn't

move, but I could hear…our pounding hearts, our ragged breath…

And Arch. "Bollocks."

CHAPTER TWENTY-SIX

I WOKE UP to the smell of coffee. Fuzzy headed, I squinted against the natural light streaming in through the windows. Sunrise. I glanced at the digital alarm clock—7:00 a.m. I'd conked out after sex, fallen asleep damp and naked in Arch's arms. I don't remember him carrying me to bed. Don't remember dreaming, just floating in deep, dark space.

I stretched, feeling delicious despite my achy muscles. Besides, if not for the small discomforts, I might have chalked up the white-hot sex to a wicked dream. I was still in awe. I, Evie Parish, a small-breasted, over-forty divorcée was having wild monkey sex with a slightly younger, ultrasexy spy.

Wait until I got hold of my diary. This was definitely a tale for posterity. Or at least a tale *I* wanted to read again and again. And I had to share the news with Nic and Jayne. Once I got home. Once…

No, I couldn't think about home. There were still four days left on this journey. Still time to convince Arch that I could be an asset to TCC, whatever that was. I could be a superspy assistant. I could. I already was. Wasn't I?

This new life did not have to end. *That's the fighting spirit,* Jayne whispered in my thoughts. I smiled.

My eyes finally adjusted to the sun and found Arch sitting across the room watching me—his expression somber.

Uh-oh.

I pushed myself up to my elbows, heart pounding. I felt something swirl in my gut, like the bottom might drop out of my fragile, repairing confidence if he spoke that look. My mind scrambled. I had to save myself. *Now.* "Are you thinking about my tussle with Fred, my conversation with Gavin or my tumble with you?" I rasped, voice gravelly from too much karaoke and too little sleep.

"A bit of each." He pointed to the cup of tea sitting on the nightstand.

I took a sip, startled by his thoughtfulness. It was still warm. The heat sliding down my throat helped to bolster me. I decided to attack his possible guilt issues straight on. "I'm releasing you from your promise."

His brow quirked. "What promise?"

"Well, it wasn't a promise exactly. More like a vow, I guess. That first day, you said I was safe with you, intimating I'd come to no harm. You don't need that kind of pressure. You should be concentrating on netting that shark. You're my employer, Arch. Not my bodyguard. I can take care of myself."

The other brow rose.

I lifted a hand to my goose egg, compliments of the smarmy dance instructor. "It's just a bump for goodness' sake. Fred has a broken foot. I'd say I came out on top."

"A position you favor," he said with a twinkle in his eye.

I flashed on an image of me tackling Arch to the floor and having my way with his body. "Was I too rough?" I asked, cheeks flushing.

He smiled a little. "I was *aboot* to ask you the same thing."

I shook my head and fought a head-to-toe raging blush. "I thought it was exciting."

"No argument there."

"I'm not normally so…aggressive." I nearly choked on the honesty. My previous sex life suddenly seemed so bland. "You bring out the devil in me."

"You bring *oot* something in me, as well, Sunshine. Not so wicked as the devil, yeah? But equally dangerous."

I pursed my lips. "Are you trying to scare me off?"

"Aye."

"It's not working."

He stroked his beard, gaze intense. I realized belatedly that he'd already transformed into Charles. Interesting how my brain only registered the man beneath the disguise. I tumbled on. "If you're worried about me getting all clingy, don't. I'm not interested in a serious relationship. I just got out of one of those and I, well, as Ann-Margret sang, I've gotta lot of livin' to do."

"*Bye, Bye, Birdie*. 1963."

I shook my head. "I can't believe you got that reference." "Lot of Livin' To Do" was a schmaltzy song from a schmaltzy movie musical. One of my favorites. "Kind of weird, our common obsession with movies."

He shrugged. "Not really. Just happens we both have above-average memories."

"We also write daily—you in your laptop, me in my diary—private stuff. And we internalize, you know, mask our feelings."

He angled his head.

"Okay. I've been pretty expressive lately. Unusual for me. I seem to be going though a change. *A* change, not *the* change," I clarified.

He rolled his eyes.

"I just think it's interesting that we have so much in common." I tucked the sheets firmly beneath my armpits, scooted into a sitting position and hugged my knees to my chest. "I think we make a good team."

He leaned back in his seat, sipped his coffee. "I thought you weren't interested."

"I'm not." The man had heartbreaker written all over him. I'd already gone that route. "Not personally. I'm speaking professionally. Professionally we make a good team, yeah?" Oh, Lord. I was even beginning to sound like him.

"What are you driving at, Sunshine?"

"The company you work for, TCC. Do you think they'd hire me?"

"No."

"Why not?"

"You're not qualified."

I twisted my ring around my finger in a bid to retain my calm. At some point over the past couple of days I'd come to the realization that over forty did not equal over the hill. Call me hopeful once more. It was the feeling of outlasting my usefulness that terrified me. "Have I failed you somehow on this gig?"

"No."

"Then—"

"You're not qualified."

"So you said. I could learn, take classes, attend—"

"You're too soft."

I blinked, swallowed hard. "I can fix that. Start working out, lifting weights."

"Not physically. Emotionally." He shook his head, lit a cigarette. "Stone's right. You're not up to this job." He blew out a stream of smoke. "I'm sending you home, yeah?"

"No." A dull roar filled my ears—fury. Why did he have to bring up Michael? Rouse my insecurities? I twirled the ring faster. "I won't go."

"What?"

"To steal your words, are you mental? My leaving would compromise your mission. Blow everything we've worked for. Gavin is going to offer you an irresistible deal and—"

"No. He's going to *steer* me toward the inside man who's going to offer me an irresistible deal. A criminal, Evie. Investment fraud is nothing compared to his usual rackets. He's scum."

"Your assignment is to take him out, or whatever. For the greater good. I want to be a part of that. I want to do something worthwhile. Make a difference."

"Coordinate a charity fund-raiser."

"I'm serious."

"So am I. You're going home."

"But—"

"After the meeting with Gavin we'll head back to Charlotte Amalie, take advantage of the duty-free shopping. Before reboarding the ship, you're going to catch me embracing Carol Parker."

My stomach dropped. "Why Carol Parker?"

"Because she's convenient. Three-quarters of the ship have seen the Parkers and Duponts socializing, yeah? As you said, she's been flirtatious. I'm sure you're not the only one who noticed. You're going to make the most of that, misinterpret the embrace, and *we* are going to have a bloody great row."

How did he know Carol would be around? How did he know she'd play along?

I narrowed my eyes. "I suppose Sugar's going to go ballistic, have a petty, tearful tantrum, storm off to the airport and leave Charles behind." I snorted. "Then of course, more than ever, Charles will want to invest in that cruise ship deal. A peace offering to his beloved bride."

He grinned. "Great minds, eh, love?"

I smirked. "Forget it."

"Evie—"

"Shove it!" I batted my long bangs out of my eyes, wincing when I clipped my tender bump. "I have never walked out on a job. I won't start now."

He crushed his cigarette in the ashtray. "You're not walking *oot*. I'm firing you."

My mouth dropped open. I quickly closed it for fear it would lock. Tension vibrated in my jaw and shoulders. "If you fire me, then I have no reason to keep up the pretense of being Sugar Dupont. I'll walk out that door as Evie Parish."

I was bluffing, of course. I wouldn't sabotage the greater good for my selfish pride. But he didn't have to know that.

I shimmied off the bed, yanking a sheet with me. Draped in yards of one hundred percent cotton, I shuffled toward the bathroom. "The Skyline Drive and Magen's Bay tour group meets in the theater in forty-five minutes. I'll be ready in thirty. That leaves you fifteen minutes to explain whatever it is I *need-to-know*. Unless you want to rely on my instincts. Up to you." I shut myself in the bathroom before he could cut me off at the knees.

Body trembling with fury, I leaned back against the door and breathed deep. I resented his lack of faith. *I'm not soft. I can handle this job. I'm capable. I'm creative.* If he didn't provide me with direction, I'd proceed on instinct.

I'm a natural.

Willing calm, rational thoughts, I embraced my future with the heart of a lion. "I won't give up my new life without a fight."

ARCH'S DIRECTION boiled down to, *"Whatever happens, stay in character."* He'd claimed there was no plan other than to listen to Gavin's pitch and to cement a meeting with the shark. *I can't set the trap until I know the terrain,* he'd said. Whatever that meant. I'm guessing he held back because he still planned on sending me home before he swam into shark-infested waters. That wasn't going to happen but I didn't belabor the point. I didn't want to risk him locking me in the cabin for safekeeping. I had a job to do, islands to see. I'd already missed San Juan. No way was I skipping St. Thomas.

Even if it meant putting up with the Parkers.

The tropical isle with its mountainous terrain, white sandy beaches and turquoise waters was like nothing I'd ever seen. Yet for all of the tour guide's charisma and expertise, the Parkers, or more to the point *Carol* Parker, voiced boredom during the scenic drive overlooking the north side of the island and Charlotte Amalie harbor. Apparently she was more into sunbathing than sightseeing.

I wondered if Arch had known we'd be on the same tour bus. How convenient considering he'd threatened to use Carol to hasten my exit. Not that I was going anywhere.

By the time our bus reached Mountain Top, the island's highest peak, I wanted to stuff a sock in Carol's mouth. Her incessant snarky comments irritated the hell out of me. *Negative energy,* I could hear Jayne saying. *Steer clear.* I tried, but then Dirk and Nan Iverson, the chatty couple from California, glommed on to me. They weren't snarky, just boring. They talked my ear off for fifteen minutes as I tried to admire the assorted exotic birds and kick-butt scenery. I didn't retain a thing they said. Me, with the scary-good memory.

Next stop on the tour was Estate St. Peter Great House, a former governor's retreat. Citing his ankle, Arch lingered on a balcony, sipping complimentary rum and enjoying a spectacular view of the surrounding islands while I explored the botanical gardens with the tour group. Since his ankle was presumably *healing,* his limp less pronounced, I figured he'd really opted out because of his allergies. Unfortunately, Carol stayed behind with Arch, preferring alcohol to flowers. Tex, er, Vic, tagged along with me, claiming an interest in horticulture.

"Exotic orchids are beautiful," he drawled, "but not near as interestin' as a field of wild bluebonnets."

I wouldn't have given that statement a second thought except he was looking at me when he said it. It wasn't the first time I'd caught him staring. The first time was earlier this morning when he noted the purplish-yellow bump on my noggin. I'd tried to cover it with makeup and strategically combed bangs, but he'd noticed.

I'd gestured to his stitches, then my own badge of ill luck. "Thinking this is poetic justice?"

"Thinkin' you've got guts, Twinkie."

Guess he'd heard about my tangle with Fred. Mostly everyone had. I'd endured sympathetic looks from other passengers throughout the day. But no one looked at me quite like Vic. Granted, I was dressed a little on the skimpy side—short denim shorts and a sheer blouse knotted at my waist—but it was balmy and everyone else had dressed light. After this, we were going to the beach.

No, there was something other than sexual interest in Vic's disturbing gaze, something I couldn't pinpoint, and *that's* what made me squirm. Even though Gavin was our mark, I still had a niggling feeling that the Parkers were somehow involved. That was the only thing that kept me from telling the cowboy oilman to stick his bluebonnets where the sun don't shine.

Since Arch had revealed so little, my imagination saw fit to explore every possible scenario ingrained in my brain from umpteen years of movie watching. I came up with some doozies, most of them featuring underworld plots, maniacal villains and a surprise ending involving lots of stuff blowing up. My nerves were pretty shot by the time we reached Magens Bay. But I smiled, laughed and cavorted because I was Sugar, not me. Because I had assured Arch I could keep up the ruse of the free-spirited, fun-loving newlywed, no matter what. I wanted to prove I was qualified as a spy's sidekick. Not that today posed a real challenge, except for enduring the Parkers. My mission, as described by Arch in his succinct need-to-know lecture, was to play the enthusiastic sightseer and enjoy St. Thomas. Oh, and to follow his lead. Once again, he'd opted to rely on my instincts. I took that as a compliment, even though I was dying for details.

Take it slow, Evie. Earn his confidence and trust.

I stroked my ring and summoned patience. There was nothing to be done, he'd said, until his meeting with Gavin. Which, according to my watch, was about thirty minutes from now. *Tick. Tick.* We were standing on what had to be one of the most beautiful beaches in the world, yet I was eager to escape to a dark, smoky bar to fight crime.

The tour guide left us to our own devices, allowing us ninety minutes for beachcombing and swimming. I knew we wouldn't need that long because of the scheduled meeting at the Coconut Shack, so I didn't much care.

Carol, on the other hand, cared plenty. "An hour and a half? He's joking, right?" She swept an arm wide, indicating the picturesque surroundings. "*This* is why I came to the Caribbean. To soak up the sun. This is damned gorgeous."

I couldn't argue. Powdery white sand. Intense, clear blue waters. Palm trees. Coconut groves. The pristine beach offered a unique blend of sun and shade and was surrounded by lush green mountains. Yup. Damned gorgeous. It was also a popular spot. Leave it to Carol to point that out. "It's too crowded here," she said, continuing along the east side of the bay and heading down a trail marked Little Magens Bay. "Let's see where this leads."

It *led* to a secluded stretch of beach, and yeah, boy, I wished I'd followed my instincts and plopped in the sand back with the other tourists. The *clothed* tourists.

"Hell's fire, darlin'," Vic said to Carol with a muffled choke. "Looks like you stumbled onto a topless beach."

I started to point out that quite a few bottoms were showing, as well, but I was momentarily speechless. I hadn't seen this much male flesh since the time Nicole leafed through a *Playgirl* magazine while we waited at a cattle call audition.

Charles tugged at the brim of his Panama hat. "I say, not to sound priggish, but I'm not one for dropping my drawers in public."

Carol tugged a rolled-up towel out of her tote and

snapped it open. "I say, when in Rome." She peeled her sundress over her head, whipped off her bikini top, plopped down on the towel and slathered lotion over her toned, flawless form. At least she hadn't opted to go full monty. That was something, I guess.

The men showed no signs of shock, although they did drink their fill. What man wouldn't? Carol Parker's lithe body was to die for. But then they focused on the other nudes—mostly male—and I felt a shift in attitude. Not disapproval so much as discomfort. From the way the sun-worshippers were paired, I'm pretty sure the majority were gay.

Carol broke the silence. "You're making spectacles of yourselves. I'm sure these liberal-minded sunbathers don't appreciate three fully clothed snowbirds gawking at their privates. Vic, honey, I know you're not shy. Charles, you may be a prig, but Sugar's a kindred free spirit." She nailed me with a challenging gaze. "Right?"

"Right," I heard myself saying. Because Sugar *was* a free spirit. Her habit of dressing provocatively proved she wasn't inhibited. She wouldn't think twice about sunbathing topless on a clothing-optional beach. Also, I'd told Arch I could keep up the ruse, no matter what. Here was a chance to prove my determination. Talk about a test. I didn't even walk around my own house naked.

Just then, something clicked. The way Charles-Arch's attention kept floating back to Carol. Yeah, boy, this was a perfect setup for Sugar's-my tantrum later on when-if I caught him in a "compromising embrace" with the pretentious slut. Unbelievable.

No doubt he expected me to buckle now. To follow through with his planned "bloody row" and to fly home. *You're too soft*. Meaning too sensitive. Too nice.

Had he forgotten? That was the old me.

I kicked off my shoes and shorts and unbuttoned my blouse. It's not as if I hadn't bared my boobies before. First the audition, then the airport parking lot. Maybe the third time would be the charm. If Jayne was right and breasts were a good omen then all the more reason to go for it, what with underworld plots and maniacal villains in my future.

At the very least, I'd prove that, although ten to fifteen years older, my boobs were just as perky as Carol's. I wanted to impress Arch in more ways than one. I didn't want to think about the man standing next to him. I blocked Tex from my mind as I casually slipped off my bikini top and flopped facedown on my beach towel. "Charlie, baby, could you rub some sunscreen on my back?"

At least it was one way to get Arch's hands on me. Although his portrayal of Charles continued to be flawless, I knew he was ticked at me for blackmailing him. I knew he wanted me gone. Partly because he was worried about my safety. Partly because he thought I was going to screw up. And partly, the part that intrigued me most, because he had a thing for me. I was sure of it. Those thoughts caused me to dig in my heels. I liked being here. In the soup with a spy, that is. Yesterday I'd rediscovered passion. Today I'd found purpose.

For the greater good.

Charlie's Angels had nothing on me. Well, except for great hair and martial arts training.

I was feeling pretty cocky until I felt the pressure of a large, strong hand on my bare skin. Then the warm lotion. Then two hands, moving in a steady circular motion over my shoulders, middle and lower back. I closed my eyes, shivering as my body endured sensual aftershocks from our previous encounters. I reveled in the gentle massage, the sound of the water lapping at the shore, the lulling heat of the afternoon sun. The smell of coconut oil and Old Spice.

Arch.

I envisioned wild monkey sex and sighed.

Carol called someone a bastard.

"It's hot as the devil's kitchen," Vic said, snapping me out of my daze. "I ain't risking a sunburned ass. I'm headin' back to that beach bar we passed and grabbin' a beer."

The Coconut Shack. The meeting. It had to be close to time. I would have jerked straight up, if Arch hadn't pinned me down. "Stay, love," he said. "Enjoy the sun and surf. I believe I'll join Vic for a cool drink. Why don't you ladies join us in an hour?"

"Don't worry about us," Carol drawled with a

sickeningly sweet smile. "We'll get along just fine. Right, Sugar?"

"You bet." I pushed my vintage black sunglasses up my sweaty nose, grateful that no one could see the daggers shooting out of my eyes and aimed at the topless she-devil. *Follow my lead,* Arch had said. Obviously, he didn't want me in on the meeting with Gavin. If I didn't know better, I'd suspect him of conspiring with Carol back at the governor's mansion while Vic and I toured the gardens. Which led me back to my original thought that they had a previous relationship—Arch and Carol. Which made me think of Mata Hari and double-crossing spies, which made my imagination soar.

So, I wondered as I heard the men walk off, how did Tex Aloha figure into this?

"BLOODY HELL."

"Yeah." They were far enough away from the women to speak freely. Still, Milo kept his voice low and an eye trained for anyone within earshot. "Did you know Little Magens was for nudists?"

"Hell, no. You?"

"No." Milo tipped back his Stetson, dragged his forearm across his moist brow. "I'm thinking Gina knew."

Arch glared at him over the rim of his glasses.

"She's royally pissed at you, Arch."

"And using Evie to exact revenge."

"Is it working? Are you sorry you screwed a

teammate—literally and figuratively? Because I am. Gina's a vital member of Chameleon. If she resigns or forces me to fire her ass because she can't get past this *woman scorned* shit, then *I* will be the one who's royally pissed."

"You've been pissed since I've known you," Arch said.

"How about that?"

"I never thought she'd go that far. Baring her breasts. *Bugger.*"

"Gina or Evie?"

"Evie." Arch dabbed at the sweat trickling over his prosthetics with a folded handkerchief. "So did you look?"

"What do you think?" He wished to hell he hadn't. Bad enough he'd gotten a full frontal of Gina. Made it harder to think of her as "one of the boys." Now he'd worry about her more in the field. That sucked. But it was Evie who promised to haunt his dreams. That compact body in those green bikini bottoms and nothing else. She was curvier than Gina, softer. Feminine over buff, his personal preference. He'd only gotten a glimpse of her breasts before she'd belly-flopped on her towel, but he'd seen enough to know that they were firm, high and perfectly shaped. Oh, yeah, he'd be dreaming about those breasts. To pile misery upon misery, he couldn't get her husky singing voice out of his head.

"Every time I think I have her pegged, she surprises me," Arch complained.

"Gina or Evie?"

"Evie. For fucksake, mate, pay attention. I had no idea she was that comfortable with her body."

"Evie? The blond bunny who skips around in tight, skimpy outfits?"

"That's Sugar, not Evie."

"Hell."

Arch stuffed the handkerchief in his pocket, expression grim as they continued along the rocky shoreline. "She stripped off her top to prove she's got balls. To prove she's qualified."

"For what? To compete in the Ms. Tropic Babe contest?"

Arch shot him a look. "To join the team."

Milo waited for two young sunbathers to pass them, and then nudged his partner off the trail and into a thicket of trees. "You told her about Chameleon?"

"Not exactly."

"What exactly?"

Arch thumbed up the brim of his hat. "I mentioned I work for a company, TCC. She assumed the initials stood for a covert intelligence agency."

He crossed his arms to keep from punching the man. "Like the CIA. FBI. Something like that?"

"More like SIS. MI6."

"British Intelligence?"

Arch grinned. "She has a bit of a James Bond fixation, yeah?"

"You're telling me Twinkie—"

"Evie."

"—thinks you're a frickin' secret agent? An international spy? Well, that's just…" He laughed, shook his head. "Let her have her fantasy. It's not like she can look you up after this."

Arch rubbed the back of his neck.

Milo's gut kicked. "Tell me you didn't give her your real name and number?"

"Gave her a fake last name and real cell number to an alternate phone, yeah?"

"Lose the phone."

"Done."

"What about Stone? Can she get to you through him?"

"That would mean him having to explain our connection."

"Something I'd like to know about myself."

"Wouldn't endear him to you, mate."

"Not looking for a friend." Milo swatted away a bug, checked his watch. "All right. Ten minutes until you're supposed to meet our man. Only natural that we enter the Coconut Shack together. The Parkers and the Duponts have established themselves as cruise buddies. When you see Gavin, make your excuses and I'll hang back. We'll better know what we're dealing with after the *come-on*. Once back in Charlotte Amalie, we'll put Evie on a charter jet, brainstorm the sting and—"

"She's not going."

"What?"

Arch shrugged. "I told her the plan. She told me to shove it."

"Shove it?" Milo looked over his shoulder, then back at Arch. "Over the years you've snowed thousands of people, from salesmen to sheiks, corporate presidents to seasoned cops. You're telling me you couldn't persuade one unstable lounge entertainer to get on a plane?"

"Piss off."

"Fuck you."

Arch checked the time. "Ready to dance?"

Summoning Vic's laid-back persona, he swept a hand toward the trail. "You lead."

Arch, the arrogant bastard, smiled. "Always do."

CHAPTER TWENTY-SEVEN

I WAS DYING OF CURIOSITY. Dying, I tell you. By the time Carol and I reunited with Vic and *Charles* the meeting was over. No sign of Gavin. No update from Arch. No telling hints from his expression or body language. I couldn't grill him because I couldn't get him alone.

We rejoined our tour group and returned to Charlotte Amalie via the crammed shuttle bus. Everyone was in a grand mood. Everyone but me. Well, and Carol, who bitched the whole way back about the limited beach time. If you ask me the hour had been fifty-nine minutes too long. An hour alone with Ms. Tall, Dark and Obnoxious was eternity. Not that we'd exchanged three words. Luckily, sunbathing was the ultimate silent sport.

Still, retaining Sugar's clueless, perpetually cheery attitude proved a major feat as the bus zipped back into the bustling port town. I had to know if the meeting went all right. Did Gavin pitch the ultimate deal or did Tex butt in and muck things up? Gavin had specified Dragonfly was hush-hush. Did he clam up when Arch didn't show up alone?

Arrrrgh!

It's not as though I could glean a clue from Arch's mood, because he was Charles. Not that it was easy to get a bead on Arch anyway. The man flatlined on emotions.

Imagine my frustration when he performed a song and dance, ditching me in downtown Charlotte Amalie in favor of shopping with *Vic*. To make matters worse, he told me to stick with *Carol*. My only solace was in knowing he wasn't going to send me packing, not today, anyway, because he'd told me to meet him back on the ship. But that didn't guarantee he wouldn't try to trick me into leaving tomorrow. Understanding his motivations was harder than working the *New York Times* crossword puzzle.

Amid the verbal shuffle, he'd told me he wanted to buy me something special. A *surprise*. I didn't argue. I couldn't argue. I was Sugar and Sugar would be over-the-moon ecstatic that her beloved *Charlie-baby* wanted to buy something special.

Man. I was really beginning to despise the free-spirited twit.

I needed an immediate distraction before I blew my top or horrors, cracked out of turn. Maybe shopping *was* the ticket. Main Street boasted designer shops like Ralph Lauren, Benetton and Gucci. Century-old warehouses converted into restored retail stores lined the waterfront. Leather, jewelry, perfume, cameras and exotic trinkets. You name it, Charlotte Amalie had it, and most of it was duty-free.

Just my luck. Stuck in the flipping "Shopping Mecca of the Caribbean" with Carol Parker.

Sugar, I decided, had limits. I turned to the leggy brunette and smiled. "I know our husbands told us to stick together, but, and please don't take this the wrong way, I could use some time alone."

She surveyed the crowded street and narrow alleyways while clutching her tote and Gucci handbag close. "Safety in numbers."

"I can take care of myself." If only I had a glove, I'd challenge her with a haughty slap. Alas, I simply quirked one brow. "You?"

Her glossy lips curled into an amused smirk. "See you back on the ship...*Sugar.*"

I scooted off with a halfhearted wave. As much as I disliked her I found it impossible to be totally rude. My parents had drilled common courtesy and respect into my head. Along with suppressing dramatic emotions—bad and good—and the concept that violence is wrong and good girls don't complain. If I was *too soft,* then my parents were to blame. Except I know they had my best interests at heart and I truly did believe in most of their teachings. Maybe I just needed to find a healthy medium.

Maybe that was part of this perplexing change. Maybe the "snap" was me growing up into my own

balance of beliefs. I didn't know whether to celebrate or to cry. I decided to spend some money.
Who knows what tomorrow would bring and I really
wanted to buy gifts for Nicole and Jayne. Maybe
something for Mom and Dad. Something romantic.
Something to remind them that they belong
together. At least, I think they belong together. I'm
not exactly an authority on happy marriages.

On a whim, I ducked into the foyer of an Italian
bistro, out of the crush and cacophony of the main
drag, and dug through my Lucy tote. I hadn't
received an e-mail update from Christopher, so I
decided to try Dad. *Why did you buy the Corner
Tavern? Why can't you move back home? And, oh,
by the way, remember when I was young and wanted
to be a kick-butt crime fighter?*

No signal. Darn. I hadn't been able to get a
signal while at port in San Juan, either. If I did
end up working for TCC—The Counterintelligence
Corps?—I'd have to upgrade my long-distance plan.
Maybe they had some kind of company phone, one
with video, a tracking system and secret-gadget
functions. Wouldn't that be cool?

"Sugar?"

Ack! Startled out of my daydream, I spun to find
Martha and her cronies exiting the dining area and
heading toward me, their arms loaded with bags of
duty-free booty. I mentally reviewed their names
and relationships. Joyce and Earl—married fifty-
two years. Ethel and Sid—second marriage, twenty-

five years. All longtime friends of Martha and her husband, Bert, who'd long since passed. I thought about the inside man, the shark who gobbled up sweet, trusting seniors, and saw red.

"We thought it was you, honey," Martha said. She gestured to one of her friends, the white-haired fellow with the big nose, the one who reminded me of Grandpa Munster sans the vampire cape. "Actually, Earl spied you. He keeps swearing he knows you from somewhere."

"I just have one of those faces," I said nonchalantly, slipping my phone back into my tote. Surely Earl hadn't seen my work in Atlantic City. Weren't they from the Carolinas? Of course, he could've been part of a junket.

Martha shoved her cat-eye glasses up her sunburned nose and peeked around my shoulder. "Where's Charles?"

"He's off shopping with Mr. Parker." I smiled and conjured a blush. "He wanted to buy me something special."

"Jewelry, I'll bet," Joyce said. "Diamond International is around here somewhere. What was that other place we passed?"

"Diamond Palace," Earl said. "If I was him I'd go for a bottle of one of those exotic fragrances we smelled in the Perfume Shoppe."

"That's because you're cheap," Joyce said.

"Well, you can't walk around on your own, dear," Martha said. "Frankly, I'm surprised Charles allowed you to do so, especially after that dreadful incident last night."

"I knew Fred was a lecher," Joyce said with a righteous sniff. "Good for you for breaking his leg."

"Oh, I didn't break his leg. It was just his—"

"I would have kneed him in the privates," Ethel said.

Earl and Sid winced.

I suppressed a smile. "At any rate, it was sort of my fault for being so trusting."

Martha patted my arm. "Another reason why you shouldn't stroll these streets without a chaperone. Safety in numbers."

"So I've heard."

Martha looped her arm through mine and steered me back out onto Main Street. "We can shop as we head toward the docks. We need to board the ship by four-thirty."

"But—"

"Where did Charles say he'd meet up with you?"

"Back on the ship, but—"

"It's settled then," Joyce said. "You're coming with us. Anything special you want to buy?"

They huddled around me, all smiley and protective. I craned my head around for sight of Arch. Despite his leaving me behind to do God-knows-what with Vic—I was convinced more than ever something was going on there—I was hesitant to leave the area. As if he might need me. Or I might miss something I was needed to do.

Oh, well. If nothing else maybe I could find out how these couples managed to stay happily married for so long and glean some insight on my parents' issues. Also, they were doing a pretty good job of keeping my mind off Arch and his mission. Resigned to a shopping spree with the golden girls and boys, I smiled. "I'd like to purchase a designer purse for one friend and a watch for another."

"I know the perfect spot," Ethel said.

"Maybe a camera for myself. Nothing too expensive or complicated. I left mine at home and, well, pictures would be nice." Who knew if I'd ever get to the Caribbean again? Maybe I could even snap a picture of Arch to show Nicole and Jayne.

Martha squeezed my arm and smiled. "Let's go get your camera, dear."

AFTER DISAPPEARING into a maze of shops, Milo phoned Woody, asking him to e-mail specific information to his secured account. Meanwhile Arch purchased a few items for show, and soon after they made their way back to the ship.

They maintained casual banter, two friendly acquaintances retiring to Dupont's suite for drinks and smokes while awaiting the return of their spendthrift wives. Once inside, they dropped the ruse and got down to business.

Arch retrieved his laptop out of the safe, placed it on the desk and fired it up.

Milo grabbed two beers out of the minifridge,

tossing one to Arch after he typed in his password. "Fucking hot out there."

"Better than freezing your balls off in Alaska, yeah?"

"Not so sure." He noted Arch's fat suit and prosthetics with a raised brow. "You gotta be dying in that getup."

"Suffer for my art, yeah?" The Scot slugged back a quarter of his beer then started shedding layers. He angled his head toward the computer. "Go ahead. I want to peel off a few years, wash my face. I'll be right *oot*."

He disappeared into the bathroom and Milo settled in a chair to access his secured account. He pressed the cool green bottle against his flushed cheek as he waited for files to download. He still couldn't believe his good fortune. He'd planned to hang back when they'd entered the Coconut Shack. After spying Gavin King, Charles had begged off cocktails with Vic, claiming he owed Gavin a drink for escorting Sugar safely to their cabin after the Fred fiasco. But King had insisted Vic join them. Said he'd heard the Texan was keen on investments and since the Duponts and Parkers were friends…

"Figured he'd double his score," Milo said to himself. The man's pitch had been scripted and sparse in detail. If they were interested, and they were, he'd introduce them to the man with his finger on the pulse of Dragonfly Cruises. The man with the inside scoop on this exclusive business opportunity—Mr. Simon Lamont. King had cleared his throat throughout, a nervous tell. Not the smoothest roper Milo had ever encountered.

Nursing his beer, he opened the first file and read. "You're right," he said as Arch exited the bathroom, drying his face with a towel. "King's not a pro." He angled the screen when the man pulled a chair in alongside him. "Been with Fiesta Cruises for ten years. Passed over twice for promotion. The last time, this past year. Looks like you had him pegged, Arch. Disgruntled employee."

"Sticking it to the company by bilking its customers, yeah?"

"Word will eventually get around," Milo said. "Fiesta's reputation will take a hit. By that time King will be long gone, his bank account well padded."

"*Dinnae* know *aboot* the padded account," Arch said. "Look at these financial statements. Our boy's in serious debt."

"Gambling problem. Special fondness for cards," Milo said, reading on. He glanced at Arch. "Explains the location of tomorrow's meet." The Coco Casino. King would meet them there and make the introductions to Lamont—a man he'd described as a wealthy entrepreneur who routinely spearheaded hospitality resorts, including but not limited to the Coco Casino. *Imagine if you will,* he'd said, *an international Donald Trump.*

"I *dinnae* like going into the Coco blind. We need a floor plan."

"Woody's working on it."

"Step ahead of me, yeah?"

Milo smiled. "Whenever possible."

Arch lit a cigarette. "Plenty of casinos in the Dominican Republic, legit and otherwise. Odds are the Coco Casino is a sucker gambling house. Lamont either owns a piece of it or he rented a meeting room to use as the big store."

Milo nodded, his thoughts traveling a similar path. "If Lamont frequents the casino, he could've run into King at the tables, learned his story and reeled him in as a roper. Our friendly cruise director could be using his cut to feed his habit."

"Or maybe he lost a wad to Lamont and/or his casino cohorts," Arch said. "Maybe he's working off debts. Doesn't matter. Gavin King's vengeful, greedy, and in deep."

"He's also the least of our problems."

Arch blew out a stream of smoke, chugged more beer. "I *cannae* send her away now. Not after King mentioned he'd bragged *aboot* Sugar and how Lamont's looking forward to meeting her. *She's* the reason Dupont wants to purchase this dream residential cabin. Like it or not, Evie has become vital to the sting."

"You want this guy so bad that you're willing to put a civilian at risk?"

Arch flashed a brief smile. "You *willnae* let anything happen to her."

Milo didn't buy his flippant manner. He sensed concern, but more bothersome, a restrained rage.

Arch ground out his half-finished smoke. "Let's just do this, yeah? I'll protect Evie."

"I suppose you have a plan."

"*Dinnae* I always?"

Milo was all ears. He was also tired of being jerked around. He nailed Arch with a look that telegraphed his mind-set. "The artist, the man Lamont betrayed and silenced. Who was he to you?"

The grifter looked away, took a lazy pull off the longneck. After a long moment, he spoke a single word. "Family."

Milo raised a brow. "You mean like Chameleon?" Arch and Gina's rift aside, the team considered themselves a family. They shared the same vision, watched each other's backs, provided emotional support though no one ever asked for it.

"Blood."

No shit? As far as he knew, Arch had no siblings. His father had run off before he was born. His mother had died years ago. This was a surprising twist to a man he thought he knew well. As well as anyone could know Arch Duvall. He waited for the man to look at him. "Okay."

Arch blew out a breath, nodded. "I'd appreciate it if—"

"Between you and me." The admission, he knew, had cost Arch. Under normal circumstances, he wouldn't have given up the personal information.

Still, Milo found it hard to accept the man's angst at face value. He'd been sidestepping grifter bullshit for too long. On the surface, he'd shared the insight to cinch Milo's determination in felling Lamont. Played the compassion card. Milo got that. Question was, did he have an ulterior motive? *Smoke and mirrors.* The cagey Scot always had an ace up his sleeve, hence his moniker.

"One thing, Arch. This better be about justice and not revenge."

"Meaning?"

"Meaning I'll be damned unforgiving if your intention all along was to finesse a meeting with Lamont in order to end his grifting for good—eye for an eye."

"I'm not a killer."

"Doesn't mean you're not capable of killing under extreme circumstances."

Arch flashed an easy smile. "Good thing I have you along to keep me in line."

Milo snorted. "Yeah. Good thing." Acknowledging a pang of dread, he clicked on an incoming file from Woody.

The Coco Casino's floor plan.

CHAPTER TWENTY-EIGHT

"OH, GOOD. YOU'RE HERE." I closed the door behind me, dropped my shopping bags near the bed. I was flushed and winded from rushing to board on time. Or maybe it was the sight of Arch, freshly showered and wearing nothing but a towel and an MP3 player, that left me breathless. Throughout the afternoon my imagination had concocted several scenarios. Most of them ended with the ship setting sail and leaving my superspy behind on St. Thomas where he shot it out with Vic while stuff blew up all around them.

Finding him in our cabin sans blood and gore was a major relief. I didn't want to consider the possibility that my feelings ran beyond concern for an associate. Thoughts that we'd bonded as friends were just as troubling since we might say goodbye in four days. Since there was a very real possibility—since he'd made it clear I wasn't TCC material—that I would never see him again. So I focused on the physical.

He stood at the bathroom mirror, just as he had

that first night in the hotel, his back to me, a cigarette dangling from the corner of his mouth. I breathed in the scent of Irish Spring and Marlboro cigarettes. I fixated on that tribal tattoo and thought naughty, primal thoughts.

He raked gel through his short dark hair and caught sight of me in the mirror. This time I didn't scream and back away. This time I stayed and stared as he snuffed his cigarette, pulled out the earbuds and turned to face me.

Breathe, Evie, breathe. "Oh, good," I squeaked. "You're here," I repeated, figuring he didn't hear me the first time. "What are you listening to?" I'd been wondering for days.

He unclipped the player from the towel. "*Dinnae* laugh."

"Okay."

"Boy George."

I smiled.

"You're laughing."

"No, I'm not. I'm just, well, surprised."

"You expected heavy metal?"

"Or Celtic rock." My smile widened. Movies and music. What else did we have in common? "I love Culture Club."

"How do you feel about Madonna?"

"Brilliant."

"As in a marketing genius?"

"As in excellent."

He smiled and my heart slammed against my

ribs. I locked my knees as he moved toward me. *Don't melt, you ninny.*

He pushed my big black sunglasses on top of my head, examined my face. "You look like you got too much sun, yeah?"

"I'm just flushed from running. I was shopping, lost track of time." Yeah. That sounded good.

"I was a bit worried. If you weren't with Carol—"

"I wasn't with Carol."

"What?"

I shrugged, eased away and moved into the bedroom. "I'm sorry, but I don't like her. First there was the perfume thing and then today, the beach. I'm telling you, she took off her top and challenged me to do the same just to embarrass me. She's mean."

He dropped his chin, scratched his dark whiskers. "She's not mean."

"Did you tell her to dare me with that topless bit? You know, when you two were together at the governor's mansion. Did you conspire against me? Did you expect me to run screaming for the airport?"

"I *didnae* know *aboot* the nude beach. I did ask her to watch over you when I wasn't around. As a favor. *Dinnae* take this wrong, but she's not as gullible as you."

I blushed from head to toe. "I'm not gullible."

"Fred."

"Trusting."

"Same thing."

Talk about cynical. I didn't know how to respond without looking more foolish, so I stayed with something I knew. Or thought I knew. "Are you and Carol Parker having an affair?"

"No."

"Is she a double agent?"

He laughed. "Carol Parker is a spoiled rich girl who's married to a spoiled rich boy."

"There's something weird about that couple. I don't care what you say, she's mean. And Vic, he's…"

"What?"

"He's always watching me."

"Everybody watches you, Sunshine. You're adorable."

Blushing, I sat on the bed, unlaced my sneakers, and peered up at him through lowered lashes. "You mean Sugar's adorable."

"Meant what I said."

Okay. That was sweet. That was…hot. I blew my bangs out of my eyes, toed off my shoes. "About the topless thing. Since I was Sugar, and since I don't know how the Parkers fit into this, and I'm convinced they do, somehow…I did what I had to do. I was quick about it, hoping Vic wouldn't notice." I caught my bottom lip between my teeth, replayed the moment and cringed. "Do you think he noticed?"

Arch crossed his arms over his impressive pecs.

"You think he noticed."

He raised a brow.

"Oh, crap. He noticed."

"When are you going to get it through that thick head of yours, Evie? You're worth noticing."

That perked me up. "You are incredible for my ego."

He just smiled that secret smile of his then turned his back, dropped the towel. The sight of his bare ass perked me up even more. Must be a European thing, I thought. The man had no qualms about walking around naked. Viva la Europe.

"Let's get back on track," he said, while stepping into a pair of grey sweatpants.

"I didn't know we were off track."

"Are you telling me you walked around town alone?" He sounded sort of bored.

Uh-oh. One thing I'd learned about Arch. There was a calm before his storm. "Actually, I ran into Martha and her friends. So there were six of us. Trust me, I wasn't alone. Speaking of shopping—"

"Were we?"

"Yes. When did you replace my driver's license and credit cards with Sugar's?"

"That first night in the hotel. You just noticed?"

"It's the first time I needed anything other than my Fiesta Card. How did you do that? Get my picture on a license with Sugar's info? And the credit cards…"

"Trade secret."

"They were all I had. I only had so much cash and I wanted to buy some gifts so I used them."

"That's what they're for."

"But who's going to pay?"

"*Dinnae* worry about it." He shook his head. "I *cannae* believe Carol ditched you."

"To be fair, I ditched her. Tell me about *your* day." I wanted to avoid a lecture on personal safety, but mostly I was curious. Horribly curious. I stretched out on my stomach, my chin cupped in my hands. "Everything. Don't leave anything out. Starting with your meeting with Gavin. Did he mention Dragonfly?"

"He did."

"Did he tell you when and where to meet the guy in charge?"

"Uh-huh." He swung open the minibar. "Would you like something to drink?"

"Water would be great, thanks."

He handed me a bottle then nabbed a beer for himself and sat in a seat near the balcony door.

I sipped and shifted to keep him in full view. "So?"

"Tomorrow evening. There's a casino on the outskirts of La Romana. King will meet us there, introduce us to Simon Lamont."

He was filling me in, giving me details. *Trusting* me. Maybe he had come to consider me a sidekick after all, even if only for this job. It was a start, and made me feel more hopeful about my life than I had in a long time. Even more wonderful than any compliment about how cute I might be—though those didn't hurt. Arch Reese and his metro-macho mystery had brought the shine back into my life.

"He's the shark? This Lamont?"

"He is."

My stomach fluttered at the thought of facing an honest-to-gosh criminal.

"I know how you feel *aboot* casinos, Sunshine. If you want to pull *oot*—"

"No way."

"He's dangerous."

"Okay."

"Why aren't you scared?"

"Because, whether or not I released you from that promise, you won't let anything happen to me."

"Your faith in me is…unsettling."

Something in his voice, something indefinable but potent, caused my heart to swell. He hadn't trusted very often. Probably never had the kind of support my dad had given me. He struck me as someone who'd grown up too fast. Someone who had it rough. Someone afraid to feel.

He looked away, over his bare shoulder, out the balcony door. "We're pulling *oot* of St. Thomas."

It took a second for his words to sink in. Then I registered the gentle movement of the ship and the sight of the colorful red roofs and vibrant green hills growing more distant. "Crap!" I catapulted off of the bed and rooted through three shopping bags. "I wanted to take a picture!"

I found the shrink-wrapped package and tore at the plastic. I opened the box and… "What the hell?"

"What's wrong?'

I stared. Blinked. Blinked again. "There are rocks in this box."

"What?"

"Rocks. In. *Box.*" I dumped the contents on the table. No camera. Just rocks. Stones. Pebbles. "I don't get it."

"Fuck." Arch walked over, examined the manufacturer's box, the plastic wrapping…the rocks. He palmed his forehead and let out a sigh that sounded half-frustrated, half-amused. "I *cannae* believe you fell for this."

"For what?"

"Rocks in box."

"I know! I see!"

He shook his head. "That's the name of the con."

"What con?"

"The short con. The grift. The scam. Where did you buy this?"

My head reeled as I continued to sift through the pile of rubble in search of my newly purchased digital camera. "From a man."

"On the street?"

"In an alley."

"Christ. I suppose he had a whole table of these boxes. All sealed. One actual camera on display. One that he showed you and allowed you to try *oot.*"

I swallowed hard. "Yes."

"He told you that he worked for a trucking firm or a retailer. Said something *aboot* overinventory. He offered you a bargain. An irresistible deal."

Uh-oh.

"Rocks in the box. It's one of the oldest short cons *oot* there along with the Pigeon Drop, Three Card Monte, Shell Game…"

"Are you saying I was scammed?"

"Royally."

I sank down on the edge of the bed, palmed my own forehead. "He seemed so honest."

Arch sat next to me. "He won your confidence, appealed to your good nature and your desire for a bargain, yeah? Good deal syndrome. No offense, Sunshine, but you're an easy mark. A female Walter Mitty."

I knew the story, of course. A mild man with a vivid fantasy life. A regular Joe who imagined himself experiencing wondrous adventures. For instance, kicking criminal butt alongside an international spy. Tears pricked at my eyes. So much for superspy sidekick. "You think I'm a Walter Mitty?"

"I think you're…trusting."

"Same thing."

"We're going to have to do something about that."

"Like what?"

"Like educating you to how it works in the real world."

"You mean your world."

"Aye. The *real* world. The world where a sucker is born every minute."

"That's awfully pessimistic."

"Realistic."

I felt my head drifting out of the clouds, my feet nearing solid ground. It was a sickening sensation. "You're not an international spy, are you?"

"No."

"Then why did you tell me—"

"You assumed. I played along. It's what I do. I tell people what they want to hear. Perpetuate fantasies. Smoke and mirrors, love."

My perpetuated fantasies started to crack, along with my heart. "Who are you?"

"A man who's trying to do the right thing."

"You talk in circles."

"Aye."

"You're just like Michael."

"Worse."

"Do you *want* me to despise you?"

"It would be best."

For whom? What was he saying? "I don't understand."

"I'm a con artist, Evie."

I pressed my hands to my aching chest, gasped for air. "Oh, God."

He clasped the back of my neck, forced my head between my legs. "Breathe."

I squeezed my eyes shut, squeezed off the tears. I told myself to breathe, to live, if only to take

Ethel's advice and knee a lech in the groin. My brain scrambled as I sucked air. I knocked away Arch's hand and lunged to my feet. I didn't want to cry. Instead I let myself get angry, the very same emotion that landed me in this mess.

"The Parkers aren't the bad guys here," I said, starting to pace, needing to move. "You are. You and this Simon Lamont, and Gavin and whomever else is in your gang. You're using me to set up the Parkers. You took Vic to that meeting to suck him into the Dragonfly ruse. You're going to try to sell him a cabin on a cruise ship that doesn't exist. What did you call it? Investment fraud. You're going to steal—"

"I never steal. I persuade."

I looked at him aghast. "You think there's a difference?"

"Aye."

"I can't believe I'm having this conversation." I studied the posh suite as I continued my frantic pacing. If I kept moving, maybe I wouldn't pass out from shock. "I can't believe I'm here. With you. A *thief.*"

"Grifter."

"Same thing."

"Someday I'll explain why that's insulting, yeah?"

"How could Michael do this to me? He said there was an element of risk. Called you a manipulator. He had to know." I whirled to face Arch. "Does he? Does he know what you do?"

"Aye."

I palmed my forehead to keep my brain inside. "How can you be so calm?"

"Someone has to be."

"Are you making fun of me?"

"No."

I hugged my arms around my middle, forced myself to maintain eye contact, even though angry tears blurred my vision. "I'm not sure when I ever felt such a fool. Except for when Michael told me he'd fallen in love with someone else. Sasha. Oh wait, maybe you've met her. Then of course, you understand why he chose her over me. Pretty. Young. Built. Is that why you took pity on me? Was I so pathetic that you created a fantasy for me? Was it just fantasy? Smoke and mirrors? A con to keep me in character?"

"Now you're pissing me off."

I swiped away a renegade tear and sneered. "Really? I can't tell. You look more bored than anything. Then again, according to Michael I'm boring. An unadventurous, predictable, goody two-shoes. No wonder he left—"

Arch body-slammed me against the wall, knocking away my words and breath. "I'm not after the Parkers' money. I'm here for Simon Lamont. Period."

Stunned, I stared up into his eyes, speechless, my heart thundering in my ears. His heart pounding against my chest.

"So tell me, Sunshine, do you still believe me when I say I'd never let anything bad happen to you?"

It was the craziest thing. "Yes."

"Stone's a fuckin' idiot." He tangled his fingers in my hair, studied my face with an intensity that singed my soul. "I've never encountered a more dangerous woman in my life."

He smothered my protest with a kiss that spiraled through my trembling body, obliterating my doubts and insecurities. My struggles ceased as he conquered my mouth and curves. The feel of his hands laying claim to my body stirred my blood. He set me on fire, burned off my anger. Rational thought—gone. Good girl—gone.

In a burst of frenzied passion, I managed to flip our position—trapping Arch against the wall as I deepened the kiss. I felt a snap, a connection. *Kindred spirits,* Madame Helene whispered. Holy smoke.

Gripping his shoulders, I tore away my mouth and searched the shielded windows to his soul. "Is Simon Lamont a criminal?"

"Aye."

"More unscrupulous than you?"

"Absolutely."

"Would the world be a better place if he were… taken out?"

"He's fleecing the elderly out of their savings. He terrorizes the weak and naive in order to control them. He betrayed a good man, robbed him of his earnings and his life. He's scum."

So on top of everything else this shark was a killer? "Why should I believe you? How can I trust you?"

"You can't."

Those devastating eyes that said nothing and everything. My heart and mind imploded. "I'm going to take a shower."

"I'll order room service."

That *connection*. I barely made it into the sanctity of the bathroom before bursting into tears.

CHAPTER TWENTY-NINE

MILO KNOTTED HIS TIE. Dress code for tonight was informal, but he'd promised Gina a fancy dinner in the Cha-Cha Club by way of an apology for a hasty reprimand. He'd blasted her for allowing Evie to wander off in a town rife with muggers and pickpockets before allowing her to explain. It was the second time in two days that he'd jumped to the wrong conclusion. He blamed Arch. The man's erratic behavior of late had put them all on edge.

A soft rap sounded at the door. "Your towels, sir."

He shrugged into his suit jacket on the way to the door. Gina stepped out of the bathroom dressed to the nines just as Arch, dressed as a room steward, pushed in and past Milo.

Grim-faced, the Scot dumped a stack of folded bath towels on the bed and unloaded on their female teammate. "I *thought* you were a professional."

She braced her hands on her hips, worked her jaw. "I'd watch my step, Ace."

"First the perfume—"

"You deserved that."

"Then the Fred fiasco."

"I explained at the mansion."

"Magens Bay—"

"That's enough," Milo said. "Gina and I have been through this."

"I can defend myself, Jazzman."

Milo watched as the lethal beauty moved forward, thinking that if Arch had any sense, he'd apologize now or leave. The stupid bastard stood his ground.

"We were *'on'* at that beach, you prick. Surrounded by passengers who'd already witnessed Vic and Carol's racy behavior on board. Not to mention Sugar's. I played my role. I admit I pushed, but you're asking me to work a sting with a civilian. An accident-prone, emotional half pint. I wanted to see what she was made of."

"So you threw a vulnerable woman to the wolves of Charlotte Amalie."

Milo whistled low just as Gina swung out and gut-punched Arch. "Feel better?" he asked her.

"A little."

"Take a walk."

She slid him an annoyed look.

"Now."

He waited until she'd left the room to address his partner. "Evie blew Gina off. She couldn't stick close without risking her cover. So she tailed her. All day. Most of the time your girl was in the company of five seniors. The couple of times she was alone, Gina was close enough to step in if things got rough."

Arch sucked in a breath, rubbed his stomach. "She let her fall prey to a street grifter."

Milo raised a brow. "In your own words—if the mark's stupid or greedy enough to fall for a scam, they got what they deserved."

"Still true."

"What makes Evie different?"

He didn't answer so Milo took another route. "Are you in love with that woman?"

"No."

"Sure?"

"I'm sure."

Milo wasn't.

Arch dragged his hands over his damp hair. "I'm off my game, that's all. You said it yourself, yeah?"

"I'm hoping taking down Lamont is the cure. I, Chameleon, we can't work like this, Arch. *You* can't work like this. Not without getting yourself killed or incarcerated."

Arch smoothed his fingers over his fake moustache, studied the toes of his boat shoes. After a long, agonizing moment thick with tension, he said, "Did you prep Gina on tomorrow night's confidence?"

"She's good to go. What about Evie?"

"Haven't discussed details yet."

"Second thoughts?"

"Deep thoughts. Weighing what I want to reveal."

Milo said nothing. He trusted Arch's judgment, even if he didn't trust the man.

The sober Scot turned to leave. "Tell Gina—"

"Tell her yourself."

He nodded, then he was gone.

ARCH WAS MISSING when I came out of the bathroom. All I felt was numb. I'd had a good cry in the shower. I was all cried out. No more crying. Done. I wasn't upset or angry. I wasn't anything. Just…numb.

Like a zombie rag doll, all loose-limbed and wide-eyed, I dressed in yellow-and-pink striped lounging pants and a SpongeBob T-shirt. My hair was freshly washed and dried, the funky layers sticking out every which way. I'd scrubbed away the day's sweat, sunscreen and fading makeup, and, after careful consideration in the mirror, applied a bit of eye crème and lip balm. Arch was right. I'd gotten too much sun. My face was beet-red, my nose and cheeks dotted with freckles. Lovely.

Barefoot, I padded over to Big Red and fished out my journal and purple pen. I sat at the desk, opened the book to a blank page and wrote.

Dear Diary,

I tapped the pen against my teeth. I doodled a broken heart and lots of question marks. I scribbled stick figures in bed. Stick figures of a con man and an actress. I wrote…

Who am I? Why am I here? What is my purpose?

I doodled a picture of the earth and clouds. I scratched out the earth and wrote…

I like perpetuating fantasies. Violence is wrong. People who terrorize the weak and naive are scum.

I stared at the blank pages a little longer, then closed the journal knowing that I was going to help Arch take down Simon Lamont, and little else. Despite what Arch had said, he wasn't worse than Michael. I'd known him less than a week, and though our relationship, friendship, affair, whatever, had started off dishonestly, he'd come clean. I'd been with Michael for fifteen years and yet the entire marriage felt like a sham. Did I know him at *all*? What was his connection with Arch? He knew he was a con artist. Did he supply him regularly with actresses for scams? Was he involved in other illegal activities?

I felt another snap. A *dis*connection. More numbness.

Arch walked through the door, noted my journal. "Private stuff?"

"Yeah." I closed and locked the diary, returned it to Big Red. I didn't ask him why he was dressed like a room steward. Brain full.

He slipped out of the uniform and into his own sweats and a T-shirt. I watched. Still numb.

"You know your laptop?"

"Yeah?"

"Can you get Internet access in here?"

"Sure."

"Could I—"

"Absolutely."

In less than three minutes it was booted up and waiting for me. "Just let me know what it costs," I said as I signed on to my e-mail account.

His reply was a look that said, *don't insult me*. He was touchy about the weirdest things.

Room service arrived, snagging his attention.

I skimmed my e-mail, looking for news from home. Home, home. Thank goodness, I spied an e-mail from Christopher. But there were ten, no, eleven from Nicole, all with the same subject header: CALL ME.

My heart raced, but I still clicked on my brother's e-mail first.

Evelyn,

Still working on it. Mom and Dad are stubborn.

Blah. Blah. Blah. No new news. I moved on to one of Nicole's messages, then the next, and the next. They all said the same thing. Call Me. Now.

It was then that I noticed there were no e-mails from Jayne. Not even one.

Dread swam through my numbness, threatening to attack. Still, I couldn't ignore Nicole's distress. Had something happened to Jayne? I signed off the Internet, glanced over to Arch, who was setting our food on the table. "I need to use the phone. Call a friend. It's important."

"Go ahead."

"It's really expensive, the ship-to-shore thing."

"Make the call."

It occurred to me that he was being super nice. Gentle. As if he thought I was going to break or something. *You're too soft.* "I'm going to help you," I said while punching numbers. "That is, if you still want my help."

"I do."

"I'm up to the job."

"I know."

I swallowed hard, focused on the call. The process took a few moments. Finally, a connection and Nicole's husky voice. "Hello?"

"I got your e-mails. What's wrong? Is Jayne all right?"

"Jayne's fine. No one's hurt…yet."

Dread took a bite out of the numbness. I gripped the receiver tighter. "What do you mean?"

"Did you get any other e-mails?"

"I got lots of e-mails. Probably mostly junk. Only opened my brother's and yours."

"Good. That's good." I heard her light a cigarette, blow out a pent-up breath. "Word's out. Everyone's talking. E-mails are flying. Jayne and I didn't want you to learn about this in a casual gossipy bit from someone in the biz. We flipped a coin. I lost."

"Must be bad. Have I been barred from the casinos for the flashing incident?" I half joked. "I'll never work Atlantic City again? Is that the buzz?"

At this point, nothing would surprise me. Oddly, the thought of being washed up as a casino performer didn't even faze me. Subconsciously, I guess I'd accepted it as a done deal. I didn't know what I was going to do when I got home, but I knew I'd changed. My world had been turned upside down. There was no going back to the life I knew. I didn't want that life, anyway, I realized, sinking into a notion and a nearby chair. I wanted something else. Something more.

"It's about Michael," she said, softly, tentatively. "And Sasha."

I glanced over my shoulder. Arch was lounging in a chair, sipping beer and watching me. I schooled my expression, lowered my voice. "Let me guess. They're getting married. Didn't take him long to get back on the matrimonial horse, did it?" I felt a zing, but that's all. No crushing pain. No panic. After all, I didn't even know the man. "You can relax, Nic. I'm not upset. I'm over it. Over Michael."

"Truly?"

"Completely."

"Great. That makes this a little easier." I heard her take another drag. "I don't know about the marriage thing, although I assume it's in their future. That is if Michael does the right thing. Not that I have faith in his sense of right and wrong. If he had a decent bone, he would have contacted you and told you himself. The bastard."

"Nic…"

"Sasha's pregnant."

Good thing I was sitting down, because you could have knocked me over with a feather. Huh. Okay. Life did indeed hold more surprises. I placed a hand over my flat belly, acknowledged a hollow feeling in my gut and tucked conflicting feelings deep within my mangled heart.

"Evie?"

"I'm okay." I was. "Good for them."

"You mean that?" She sounded incredulous.

"Yes." Sort of. "I have to go, Nic. I appreciate you breaking the news to me, but this call is costing me a small fortune."

"You sure you're okay?"

"I'm in the Caribbean with a nice man. Complicated, but nice."

She laughed. "Right. How's that going, anyway?"

"I'll let you know." We said our goodbyes. I joined Arch at the table.

He caught my gaze. "Don't you mean a rat bastard thief?"

I uncovered my dish, expecting a salad. Cheeseburger and fries. Comfort food. I smiled a little. "Meant what I said."

CHAPTER THIRTY

I COULDN'T SLEEP. My mind wouldn't shut down. Arch had bunked on the couch, wanting to give me some distance. The truth about who he was had driven a wedge between us. Even though there was a physical attraction, even though I felt an emotional connection, I couldn't wrap my mind around his core beliefs. How was convincing someone to give you their money of their own free will different or better than stealing? The fact that he fleeced only those who could afford the loss did little to ease my discomfort. It still seemed wrong. I mean, he wasn't exactly Robin Hood, seeing that he kept the spoils.

Speaking to my Hollywood sensibilities, he'd assured me that, although there was a dark side to his world, a world depicted in movies like *House of Games* and *The Grifters,* his immediate circle more closely mirrored *Ocean's Eleven.* Of course he'd liken himself and his associates to that sexy, witty crew. The arrogant comparison made me smile. Then he'd added, "Or *Dirty Rotten Scoundrels.*" I'd chuckled, envisioning him in the goofy Steve Martin role. Arch's ability to put me at ease was astonishing. Just one of a confidence man's talents, I'd reminded myself.

"When we go into this tomorrow night," he'd said, "think *The Sting* with a twist. Two con men, one experienced—me—and one green—you—avenging the wronged by conning a ruthless rat bastard and putting him out of commission."

That made me feel better. Sort of.

"There are scam-artists and scum-artists," he'd gone on to say. "Scam-artists prey on greed and vanity. Scum-artists prey on fear and loneliness, the weak and elderly. We all use scare tactics, emotional manipulation to dissuade ~~a mark from~~ contacting the authorities. But some, like Lamont, follow through on threats. Some terrorize and employ violence. Those are scum-artists. *Dinnae* confuse the two, Sunshine."

He'd certainly given me something to think about. Something to toss and turn over—4:00 a.m. and I was still wide-awake. I rolled over for the umpteenth time, fluffed and punched my pillow. I shoved away thoughts of his occupation and mentally reviewed the Lamont sting. If I fell asleep, I'd probably be plagued with anxiety dreams. Either way, tomorrow I was going to need a gallon of coffee and a bucket of antacid.

"You need to sleep, Evie."

He sounded bored. I twirled my ring and stared out the balcony door at the starry sky. "I can't."

"Do you know what a *tell* is?"

"I think so." I glanced toward his silhouette, surprised by the question. "I've heard the term used by poker players. It's an unconscious gesture, expression, like tugging at your ear or rocking in your chair, something that betrays a person's mind-set. Something that screams, *I'm bluffing*."

"Or nervous. Lamont would be sensitive to a tell."

I realized then that I was twisting my ring round and round my finger. A new habit. Every time I needed encouragement or calm, I fingered the ring. "Oh." Embarrassed, I pulled off Jayne's mystical gift and laid it on the nightstand. It was a clunker, anyway. Better to rely on my inner strength and wisdom than a green stone.

"Do you want to talk *aboot* it?"

"What?"

"The phone call."

Although he'd blatantly eavesdropped, he hadn't commented on my conversation with Nicole. Until now. "I wasn't thinking about the phone call." Until now. I blocked feelings and images and focused on the sting. My part in the takedown was minimal. As soon as Lamont finished with his initial pitch, or as Arch called it, the come-on, ditzy, fun-loving Sugar was supposed to remark on Charles's art collection and how the cost of owning a cabin suite on the Dragonfly paled in comparison to what he'd paid for his most recent acquisition. Then, after fawning over her skeptical hubby and begging *pretty please,* Sugar would skip off to hit the slot machines, leaving Charles to handle the financial details. "What if Lamont gets suspicious when I duck out of the meeting early?"

"He won't. Because you're a hell of an actress, yeah?"

"Flattery will get you, well, a thank-you."

"You're welcome."

"Maybe I should stay for the whole thing." Whatever that was. Arch hadn't shared the specifics of how he was going to entrap Lamont. All I knew was that the *rat bastard* was going to end up in prison where he'd *hopefully rot.*

"As I explained, I have people on the inside. Professionals." He cut me off before I could take exception. "This isn't *aboot* ability, but experience. I need you to trust me on this."

"But you said—"

"I'm asking for a leap of faith."

Something in his voice, that nuance that made me envision him as a deprived, hard-knock child, whittled away that wedge. Not completely. Just enough to expose my caring nature. In some ways, I felt that Arch was as lost as me.

"In return," he said, "I'll share a secret."

My heart pounded, sensing this was a rare moment. I held my breath.

"You *cannae* tell—"

"I won't. Not a soul."

He blew out a breath, waited a beat. Two. "The man Lamont betrayed, a man who died because he dared to stand up to the bastard, was my grandfather."

"Oh, Arch." I wasn't sure what I heard in his voice. Anger? Sadness? I only know that it tore at my heart.

"I grew up in Scotland. He lived in England. Although I saw him infrequently during my youth, he was always there for me—financially, emotionally. I never knew my father. He was, as it happens, a con man. Constantly on the move. I was a result of a long-running sporadic affair. Marriage was out of the question, as was settling in one place. Emotional attachments compromise a grifter's judgment. When he learned my ma was pregnant, he cut ties completely."

I shuddered. "How could he be so cold?"

"Not cold. Practical. Merciful, if you asked my ma. His coming and going mangled her heart. She *didnae* wish the same for me."

"She must've been a very strong woman."

He smiled. "Aye. Worldly, too. She knew what she was in for when she fell in love with a grifter. Her own da, my grandfather, was an artist, a painter, who lived his life in the gray."

I scrunched my brow. "Meaning?"

"He had a miraculous gift for re-creating works of the masters."

I still wasn't following.

"He primarily made his living as an art forger."

"Wow." I tried to imagine Arch's childhood, his

influences. So different from my conventional up-bringing. "So the smoke and mirrors thing. That's pretty much in your blood."

"Pretty much."

"Wow."

"You may not approve of how my grandfather utilized his talents, but I guarantee, you would have approved of the man, Evie. He was kind and funny, a true gentleman. He deserved a better fate, yeah?"

I massaged an ache in my chest. "Why does all of this have to be secret?"

"The more people know about me, the more vulnerable I become." He fell silent while I mulled that over. After a moment he said, "We good?"

I blew out a breath, replayed his explanation on the differences between scam-artists and scum-artists. I acknowledged the admiration and genuine grief when he spoke of his grandfather. I didn't know how I felt about Arch as a whole, but Arch the man was an irresistible puzzle that I wanted to work out. "You can't be comfortable on that couch."

He didn't answer.

I figured just now he needed me as badly as I needed him. My performance jitters and the lack of physical contact made me nuts. As crazy as it was, as much as I didn't want to, I considered him a friend. "You're going to make me ask, aren't you?"

Silence.

"You want me to ask."

Nothing.

The gentleman con artist. The man was an infuriating enigma. I rolled my weary eyes. "All right. I'll ask. Would you please sleep with me?"

He rolled off the couch and joined me in bed, naked except for his boxers.

"I don't want sex."

"Too bad for me."

My stomach fluttered and a smile touched my lips. "Could you just, would you—"

"Absolutely." He maneuvered me into his arms, my back nestled against his front, spooning-style.

An uneasy thought kept me from relaxing. "Arch?"

"Hmm?"

"The story you just told me. Was it solely to cement my help in roping Lamont? Or was it also your way of telling me you're a chip off your father's block? Is that why you don't do relationships? Because it would compromise your professional judgment?"

He smoothed his palm down my arm. "When my ma realized I was destined to grift, she offered advice that I adopted as my personal code. Never attach yourself to anyone that you can't walk away from in a split second."

I bit my lip, not wanting to ponder what that said about *us*. He had, after all, been up-front on that score. What chafed more was the thought that he was capable of abandoning a child. "So, if you ever found yourself in your father's shoes, you'd walk away?"

"I'd do what was best for the babe."

"You sort of danced around the question."

"I know." He interlaced his fingers with mine,

rested his brow against the back of my head and mumbled a graphic curse. "Evie?"

"Yes?"

"I am not my father's son."

Not a direct answer, but the sentiment I was hoping for. I swallowed an emotional lump and decided not to press further on the subject. *The more people know about me, the more vulnerable I become.* It had cost him to confide in me. It made me feel special. And though he was probably fighting it tooth and nail, hence the curse, it smacked of *some* sort of relationship. At the very least, we were friends.

Smiling, I relaxed in Arch's embrace, reflected on tomorrow and beyond. I felt safe, yet anxious, as if primed for adventure. I closed my eyes, envisioned a scene from *Titanic*. Not the one where Jack and Rose dangled off the stern of a sinking ship, but the one where they balanced on the prow flying into their future with childlike optimism.

I felt myself drifting, and against my better judgment, falling just a little bit in love. *"Titanic,"* I murmured.

He pulled me closer against him, spoke close to my ear. "We're not going down, Sunshine."

"The scene in steerage. Jack and Rose. Celtic music."

"Ah."

I quoted Rose. *"I don't know this dance."*

"Neither do I," he answered in Jack's American accent. *"Just go with it."*

CHAPTER THIRTY-ONE

THE AFTERNOON SUN set low in the sky. The first shore excursion of the day was complete. Milo stood on the promenade deck, leaning against the railing and admiring Catalina Island as the ship set sail for the Dominican Republic, specifically La Romana. In less than two hours, they'd be at the Coco Casino eating up Simon the Fish's slippery bait. A once-in-a-liftetime opportunity, he'd told Herman Stokes, for which the old man had forked over a lifetime's savings.

In turn, Arch would pitch a come-on of his own. Sugar would spill the beans about Charles's art collection, in particular, a previously undiscovered painting by Vermeer. Something rare enough to lure Lamont back onto American soil for the sting.

Milo had spent the night reminding himself that today was about more than entrapping the man who'd killed a blood relative of his partner. He thought about Herman Stokes and the countless seniors like him. Unsuspecting pigeons.

As a result, he hadn't gotten much sleep. Arch

was right. He should've dug deeper. But Chameleon was inundated with cases. A.I.A. had been pushing high-profile scams. Ponzi schemes. Boiler room scams. Managed earning scams. Scams that targeted the rich or pointed to corporate and political corruption. Meanwhile scum-artists, as Arch called them, preyed on the old, the weak and the needy. People like Mr. Stokes, who, knowing he'd been bilked, had died a humiliated and broken man.

I should've dug deeper.

"You look pissed, mate."

Milo tongued his unlit cigar to the other side of his mouth, glanced sideways at Arch and raised a brow.

Decked out as Charles Dupont, the grifter angled toward the sea, toward Milo, averting his face from any CCTV cameras. "More pissed than usual, that is."

"Thinking about the future."

"Whose?"

"Chameleon's."

Arch adjusted his tinted glasses. "I know I've put the team at risk—"

"Forget it. Where's Evie?"

"In our cabin with her head in the toilet."

Hell. "Nerves?"

Arch shook his head. "Seasick. The tender boat."

Since the ship didn't dock at Catalina Island, anyone wanting to go ashore needed to shuttle back and forth in a small tender boat. In order to keep up the ruse of the happy cruise enthusiasts, the Duponts and Parkers had booked passage, albeit separate excursions. Seas were choppy.

"Will she be able to perform?"

"I asked her the same thing before she ordered me *oot*. Afraid I insulted her. She's never missed a day of work in her life, or so she bellowed, just before she hurled."

"Glad I'm not a superstitious man," Milo said in a low voice. "This sting has clusterfuck written all over it."

"What's the problem?"

"Something smells."

"Fishy?" Arch tugged down the brim of his straw hat, rolled back his shoulders. "Relax. After King reported our names, Lamont would've done a background check, looked into our financial standings. I made sure my bogus records were in place before I left Atlantic City. I was meticulous."

"I'm sure you were."

"The Kid wouldn't screw up on your end."

"No, he wouldn't. Still, we're leaving too much to fate."

"I'm working with what I know, yeah?" Arch said calmly. "I *cannae* anticipate Lamont's actions like most marks. He may offer a trade—the Vermeer for a cabin. He may attempt a Big Con—sucker me *oot* of the painting or replace it with a fake."

"Replacing a fake with a fake." Milo's lip twitched. "Talk about poetic justice."

"It *willnae* get that far. I don't know how he'll respond to today's come-on. But I know he'll make a move. No matter how this goes down, the result will be the same, yeah? Simon the Fish will travel to the U.S. to pinch that painting. You'll arrest him once he's on home soil and earn points with A.I.A. I'll celebrate his incarceration. Countless pigeons will remain unplucked." He smiled though his tone held no humor. "And they all lived happily ever after."

Milo's gut kicked. "Clusterfuck."

"Don't borrow trouble, Jazzman."

He repositioned his Stetson, pushed his aviator sunglasses up his nose. "Try to get some crackers and ginger ale into Evie. Better yet, mix a couple of tablespoons of bitters into a glass of club soda." He pushed off the rail, trying like hell not to borrow trouble. "See you on the dance floor."

I WANTED TO DIE. No amount of ginger ale or antacid had been able to cure my nausea. Too late for Dramamine or any other motion-sickness medication to do any good. I was weak from throwing up. The bump on my noggin throbbed from banging my forehead against the toilet seat in my haste to hug the porcelain princess. I was embarrassed. I know Arch had been trying to help, and I guess it was sweet, but his holding my hair back as I puked up my guts had been mortifying. Okay. I'm exaggerating. I still had my guts, but everything else was true.

Glamming up for a night at the casino had been difficult. A, because I looked like crap. B, because I felt like crap. But I managed to perform miracles. Because C, I wanted to come through for Arch. When I'd told Nicole that he was complicated, I hadn't been lying. Last night he'd confided in me. He'd schooled me. He'd comforted me and held me through the wee morning hours. Even if I never saw him again after this gig, I was convinced we'd been brought together for some cosmic reason. My life would never be the same, and I'm thinking that's a good thing. I figured I owed him big-time.

So I twisted my hair into a funky chignon, swept my long bangs over my forehead to hide the yellowish bump and spackled on foundation and blush to cover my greenish tint. I accented my eyes with smoky shadows and my lips with my signature red lipstick. I squeezed my curves into a little black dress, a sexy number that I'd worn when emceeing a few high-roller craps tournaments, and slid into my bone-crusher stilettos. More showy than classy, but hey, I was Sugar, not me. Even though I felt like hell, I looked like heaven. Or so Arch said. Okay, he'd said *bollocks,* but to me it was the same.

I barely registered the trek from cabin to gangway. My mind raced a million miles a minute, psyching myself up, mentally reviewing the plan.

Luckily, the ship docked at La Romana, so I was spared the nightmare of the small craft bouncing over rough seas—*gag.* A taxi was waiting to take us to the Coco Casino. The Parkers shared the ride. Arch had told me Gavin had included Vic in his come-on. It occurred to me that the Parkers were the insiders, the professionals, Arch had mentioned. Where they were concerned, I could never get a straight answer. So instead of asking again, I gave up and played along.

I fed off my nervous energy to channel Sugar's bubbly personality. I assured everyone that the nausea had passed. Even Carol surprised me by voicing concern. I played my part. I focused. Arch, or, rather, Charles, nuzzled and kissed me on the ride. He was playing a part, too. The besotted husband. But there was genuine respect and affection in his gaze. Maybe that's what energized me most, distracted me from my upset stomach, throbbing head and shaky legs.

By the time we arrived at the Coco Casino, I felt like I was on drugs. Like I'd crossed over to an alternate plane. It had to be a combination of my weakened state and a heady burst of adrenaline. I was completely at ease as Arch ushered me into the casino. Though far smaller and less high-tech than any Atlantic City casino, the atmosphere and objective were the same. To seduce hardworking people out of their hard-earned money. The flashing lights, green-felt tables, spinning wheels. *Ka-ching!* Games of chance.

Listen to the come-on. *Check.* Voice my excitement. *Check.* Mention the painting and then split for the slots, leaving the finances to Charlie-baby. *Check, check.*

I was fine. Perfect. In the zone. Then I saw Gavin coming toward us with…Martha.

"What's she doing here?" I asked in a ragged whisper.

Arch squeezed my hand, and did that thing where he talks without hardly moving his lips. "Easy, love."

She waved excitedly. "Sugar! Charles!"

I smiled so hard my cheeks hurt.

Charles kissed her hand. "Martha, dear. What a pleasant surprise. What brings you here?"

"Same as you." She winked, swooped in on the other side of me and looped her arm through mine. "Isn't this exciting? When Gavin told me about, well, you know, I just had to look into the possibility of living on a—" she looked around, lowered her voice "—you know. This past week I've had the time of my life!"

"You, too?" I said, responding for both Sugar and me.

"I've decided when I go, I'm going on a…" She bopped her curly head in lieu of a *you know*. "I'm so grateful to Gavin for letting me in on this deal." She gave the cruise director's shoulder a playful rap. He looked so at ease, I wanted to slug him. "Such a sweetie, this boy," Martha said.

Yeah, I thought, blood burning. *A real prince of a man who wants to cheat you out of seventy thousand dollars.* "Martha, don't you think—"

"What do you say we get this show on the road, King?" Vic interrupted. "Me and the missus want to get some gamblin' in tonight."

"I understand," Gavin said. "Right this way."

We walked toward the rear of the gaudy casino floor, past blackjack tables and roulette wheels. I swear some of the players barely looked sixteen. Didn't they card anyone in this joint? Joint, I decided on keener inspection, was more appropriate than *casino*. It had a distinctly smarmy feel.

Gavin opened a door, led us down a hall and through another door into an office. Spacious. Clean. Much like any ordinary corporate office. Desk. Chairs. Couch. Bar. Tasteful art on the walls. A model of a cruise ship and what looked like rolled-up blueprints on a conference table.

Two suited men, one a hulking guy with mile-wide shoulders and the other a squirrely-looking dude, stood behind the leather couch. They smiled.

We smiled.

A dark-haired, good-looking gentleman, wearing an expensive tailored suit, rose from behind the cherrywood desk. "Simon Lamont," he said in a deep, pleasant voice. He smiled and offered his hand in greeting to each person in the room, listening intently as Gavin made the introductions. He didn't look like a criminal. He looked like a casino VP. Kind of like Alec Baldwin in that movie where William Macy plagued gamblers with bad luck. *The Cooler*. The same movie where Alec Baldwin's character broke scammers' bones with a baseball bat, come to think of it. My stomach turned at the possibility.

"Mrs. Dupont," he said, taking my hand. "Gavin has raved about you. Seems you're the social hit on the Fiesta."

And you're the man who killed Arch's grandpa, the shark who preys on the trusting and vulnerable. People like Martha. I despised Lamont, but my disgust had to pale in comparison to what Arch was feeling. I glanced sideways, half expecting him to lunge at the creep. He didn't lunge. Not even an eye twitch. He looked amiable and relaxed. My admiration for the man soared. More than ever I wanted to do whatever I could to advance his cause. Lamont was the lowest piece of scum I'd ever had the misfortune of meeting and yet I smiled graciously and shook his hand.

"It's a pleasure to finally meet you," he said with a sincere smile.

I wished I could say the same. "Aren't you a peach?" *You rat bastard scum-artist.*

Lamont chuckled, seemingly charmed.

Gavin left us to business, promising to meet up after for dinner.

Squirrelly-dude moved in. "You look familiar."

I realized with a start that he was talking to me.

"My friend Earl says she's got one of those faces," Martha said, cleaning her glasses with her shirt.

"No," the man said, narrowing his eyes. "We've met."

Oh, no. Oh, God. He *did* look familiar. "Ever been to Vegas?" I asked brightly.

"Lots of times."

I smiled, clueless and casual. "You probably saw me performing in one of the casinos. I'm a lounge singer. Well, was a lounge singer. I'm retired now. Charlie and me, we're married."

"Living in Connecticut now, old boy." Arch shifted his cane to his right hand, slid his left arm around my waist.

Martha shoved on her glasses. "Earl thought he saw you in Atlantic City," she said. "Working a Fourth of July Sweepstakes dressed as the Statue of Liberty." She snorted. "I told him he was cracked. Told him I'd asked you about your career and that you moved straight from Brooklyn to Vegas."

"Look," Vic said. "I ain't got all night. I'm here to do business. Maybe. That's if this deal is as sweet as King says."

"It's a once-in-a-lifetime opportunity," Lamont said, smiling at Vic, then glancing at me.

My neck prickled with a rash. *Don't scratch. Don't tell.*

"Our screening process is quite intensive. We're only allowing a select—"

"Atlantic City." Squirrelly-dude snapped his fingers. "Craps tournament. You presented me with a trophy. We had our picture taken together. In fact, you were wearing that same dress."

Crap!

"Only your name wasn't Sugar. What was it?"

"Speaking of gambling," Carol said in a husky voice, "I'd like to get some in before we have to return to the ship."

"Speaking of ships," Vic said to Lamont, "King said you have floor plans and sketches of this supposed six-star wonder. Seeing's believing, if you know what I'm saying."

"Lucy. You went by the name Lucky Lucy." Squirrelly-dude smiled as though he'd just answered the winning question on *Who Wants to be a Millionaire?* "Am I right?"

"Wrong," Martha said. "Sugar never worked Atlantic City. Although, crazy world, she's an *I Love Lucy* fanatic. Carries the cutest tote with Lucy's picture all over it. Her father gave it to her for her birthday last year. For luck."

The silence was brief but suffocating. I sucked in a breath and launched into a ditzy explanation. I'd forgotten all about the short stint I'd done in Atlantic City last year. *Thunk to the forehead.* "Jeez. Am I a bubble brain, or what?"

Arch backed me up, a brilliant bit of improvising. Vic and Carol lamented the delay. *Was this a business meeting or a social?* Martha argued with Squirrelly-dude.

My stomach lurched.

This smacked of a live performance gone wrong.

That horrible moment when someone drops a line or misses a cue or a piece of scenery topples.

The moment after, where someone or everyone tries to cover, and usually does because usually they're professionals. If you're lucky the audience doesn't notice, or thinks it's part of the act. Martha, for sure, was not a professional and I, for damn sure, did not feel lucky. I felt cursed. My role had been simple, the direction clear. Yet nothing was going to script. *Warning, Will Robinson! Danger! Danger!*

Through my vertigo, I heard Lamont ask Hulking-guy to show Martha and the Parkers to another room for refreshments. "I like to spend quality time with each prospective investor."

I slowly let out my breath when Martha exited, asking if they had piña coladas. However, I felt a little cold fear when Carol and Vic left, too, leaving us alone with Lamont and Squirrelly-dude. So maybe they weren't the insiders. Then who was?

Lamont unbuttoned his suit jacket and settled on the corner of his desk. "As I said, we have an intensive screening process." He looked at me with a quizzical smile. "According to my information, your parents passed on five years ago, Mrs. Dupont."

In that space of a moment I knew I'd committed a cardinal sin in the world according to Arch. I'd cracked out of turn, messed up, deviated from my character profile and mentioned a true life occurrence. *My* dad. *My* birthday. Not Sugar's.

I wanted to scratch my itchy neck, but I kept smiling that clueless smile as Arch segued into a song and dance. Only Lamont wasn't buying it, his face hard as stone. "Forgive me, but my experiences with cutthroat competitors have made me a cautious man. If there's any chance you're not the real Mr. and Mrs. Dupont…"

"I understand, good man," Arch said in his blue-blood accent. "I'm equally cautious when purchasing art for my collection. One needs to be sure they're dealing with the genuine article." He reached into his suit jacket and passed Lamont his wallet. "My identification."

Lamont inspected the contents, though his gaze kept flitting back to Arch. "I'm a bit of an art connoisseur myself."

"Charlie's into paintings," I said, following Arch's cue. Train wreck averted. Get the show back on track. "He just purchased a Vermin."

Lamont's brow rose. "You mean Vermeer?"

"The guy they did that movie about," I said with a chipper smile. "*Girl with a Pearl Earring*. Did you see it?" I rolled my eyes while passing him my own fake identification. "*Boooring*."

"That painting is in a museum," Lamont said.

"I'm in possession of another Vermeer," Arch said. "An earlier work. But that's neither here nor there. About the Dragonfly—"

"Found this on the grandma, boss." Hulking-guy strode back into the room and laid a small handgun on Lamont's desk.

I stared at the firearm, stunned. What the—

"Pat them down," Lamont ordered. "Security

precautions," he said to us with a tight smile. "You understand."

A jolt of panic rushed through my system. Arch's fake gut. The prosthetics. What if he took off Arch's glasses and found the smooth skin around his eyes? My heart pounded against my ribs. Did Arch carry a gun? Did the goons? Martha had been packing. The mystery of the century! "I don't feel so good." It wasn't wholly a lie. On instinct, I went limp, falling into a dead faint, directly in Hulking-guy's path.

I banged my head hard on the floor, suppressed a groan when he tripped and landed partly on top of me. I couldn't see anything, well, because my eyes were closed. But even when I peeked all I saw were the legs of the couch. I could hear, though. Still in character, Charles protested. "Get your hands off of me, old boy. Allow me to help my wife."

"He's wearin' a fat suit," Squirrelly-dude said. "And a fuckin' wire!"

Wire?

I heard cursing, shuffling. Hulking-guy scrambled off me, so I scrambled, too. Only I was disoriented from the head banging. Cross-eyed, I saw Arch clobber Squirrelly-dude with his cane, throw a punch at Hulking-guy. Saw Lamont pull a gun. Aim it at Arch.

"No!" I lunged to knock away the gun. Only Squirrelly-dude pushed me. I whacked my head on the desk. Saw stars. Heard voices. Vic?

Then a bang, a loud, sickening bang that reverberated in my ears as my eyes glazed over and the scene faded to black.

CHAPTER THIRTY-TWO

I DREAMED ABOUT AN APE. A docile ape. *A new and unusual friend,* Jayne said. I flashed my breasts. The ape grinned. *Bollocks.* I heard a bang. Saw blood. Heard Madame Helene. *I see a tragic event in your future. A loved one will suffer.*

"No!" My eyes flew open. Tex Aloha hovered inches above me, watching me with that brown stare. Startled, I slapped his face.

He eased back, rubbed his cheek. "Welcome back, Twinkie."

I blinked. "What are you doing here?"

"Making sure you're okay."

The adrenaline from my dream made me snappish. "Doesn't your wife care that you ogle other women?"

"My *wife* divorced me and married another man. I can ogle all I want."

My throat felt scratchy and raw, my mind muddled. "Carol divorced you?"

"There is no Carol. No Vic, either. Thank God."

"I don't understand." Then I realized I didn't

even know where I was. Sun streamed in through a window, and then I heard beeping and saw machines. Hospital machines. My bed had rails. My adrenaline shot up again. I tried to push myself up on my elbows, felt woozy and plopped back down. "Where's…Charles?"

"You mean Arch?"

"You know Arch?"

"As well as anyone can."

"You're his insider. The professional. You and Carol—"

"Gina."

"You knew each other all along. I was right." Sort of. Instead of spies, they were con artists. My head throbbed. My stomach pitched. I touched my head, felt thick bandages and fought a dizzy spell. "Was I shot?"

"No."

"Arch?"

"He's fine. Martha, too."

"Why in the world did she have a gun?"

"Some street punk sold it to her earlier in the day. Told her the island wasn't a safe place for little old ladies." His eyes twinkled with amusement. "She was pretty pissed when Lamont's muscle took it off of her. Kicked him in the shin."

"He's lucky she didn't kick him somewhere else. Martha may look fragile, but she's got spunk."

"That makes two of you. To hear Arch tell it, you tried to defend him."

"Lamont aimed a gun at him and…" I palmed my bandages. "I thought I heard—"

"You did. There was a struggle. Lamont took a bullet."

"Is he—"

"Yeah."

I closed my eyes. I didn't expect to feel bad for Lamont, and maybe I didn't. But a man had been shot dead. In front of me. We'd come to put him in prison, not six feet under. Right?

"An accident," he said, as if reading my mind. "Self-defense. Luckily, Arch was wired. He intended to record the come-on as security. Instead, he got the altercation. That squared us with local law enforcement. Still, Arch needs to lie low for a while."

I swallowed past the lump in my throat. "Where is he?"

"Someplace safe."

"Can I see him?"

"He's already left the island."

"Oh." My dismal mood worsened. I noted Tex's attire. A tasteful shirt and pants that matched. No cowboy hat. No cigar. Younger than I first thought and good-looking in a quiet way. "Who are you?"

He produced identification. Government ID. Only I didn't recognize the branch. I squinted at his name. "Agent Beckett?"

"Call me Milo." He returned the wallet to his pocket. "We were here unofficially."

"Arch works with you? He told me he was a con artist."

"Reformed." He scratched his clean-shaven jaw. "Supposedly. We head a special team. Chameleon. Our objective, simply put, is to con cons, bust scams."

"Fraud investigators?"

"In a way."

"Smoke and mirrors. For the greater good." My splitting head reeled as I tried to absorb the information. So Arch *was* a good guy. Tears pricked my eyes. I wasn't a total Walter Mitty. Arch wasn't a superspy, but he *did* work for the government. "I've never heard of Chameleon, or the Artful Intelligence Agency."

"We're covert."

I furrowed my brow, studied his face and tried to adjust to his non-Texan, nonabrasive personality. "So, you probably shouldn't have told me about the team."

"Probably not. But I figure you're owed some sort of explanation for being dragged into this. I'm hoping you can keep a secret."

My heart ached, my thoughts centered on Arch. We didn't even get to say goodbye. Was he angry because I botched his sting? Was he glad to put some distance between us? It couldn't end like this. I didn't want it to end at all. Even though I'd unintentionally mucked things up. Even though I'd ended up in the hospital and another man had ended up dead. A *scum-artist,* I reminded myself. A man who preyed on the weak. Something exploded inside of me. Something positive. Something electric.

Purpose.

I pushed myself into a sitting position, ignored the aches and pains. "I can keep a secret, but I want in."

He crossed his arms, poked a tongue in his cheek. "Ms. Parish. Are you blackmailing me?"

I blushed. "No." One of Jayne's affirmations rang in my ears. *Glory awaits those who accept the challenge.* "Yes. Sort of."

He smiled, studied me as he had so many times before. Only this time he didn't give me the willies. This time I recognized the glint in his eyes for what it was. Interest. Curiosity. I intrigued him. Okay. That was good, right? Because it meant he wouldn't mind having me around. Maybe.

"You're not qualified."

The thought of working with Arch, of doing something vital bolstered my confidence. "You're wrong. Arch explained that a con artist is a one-person theater troupe—set designer, writer, director, actor. I've done all of those things. I have more than twenty-five years' experience in entertainment. I create illusions. Perpetuate fantasies. I can blend in anywhere. Just like a Chameleon." My heart thundered in my chest. "Plus I have sleight-of-hand skills and a kick-butt memory. I can think of a dozen scenarios where those talents might come in handy."

He grinned.

Optimism sparked and burned through my blood. Call me hopeful. "I was born for this job."

"You talk a good game."

"I can bullshit with the best of them."

"I've seen you in action." He rocked back on his heels, studied me, hard. I didn't flinch. As auditions went, this was cake. All I had to do was be myself. A woman with dreams and goals. A woman of many talents.

"There might be a position, but—"

"Great. I'll go through the training. Whatever it takes. I'm your girl."

"I'm thinking you're Arch's girl."

My heart fluttered. "Why would you think that?"

He didn't answer directly, just studied me with those disconcerting eyes. "Mixing business with pleasure is dangerous. Especially in our field, Ms. Parish."

"You can call me Evie, Agent Beckett."

"Only if you call me Milo."

"Milo." Now, I decided, was a good time to utilize my acting skills. "No offense, but you've misread the situation. I was just pretending to be enamored with Arch and vice versa. It was part of our ruse. We're just…friends."

"Friends, huh?"

I smiled and lied through my teeth. "The last thing I want is a romantic entanglement with a man who has secrets. Trying to get a straight answer out of Arch is—"

"Frustrating?" He smiled then glanced away and blew out a breath. Unease danced along my spine, but then he turned back and offered his hand. "I'll give you a shot on a trial basis."

I pumped my fist in the air. "Yes!" Remembering myself, I clasped his hand, shook. "I mean, thank you, Agent Beckett, um, sir."

"Milo."

"Milo." So different from Tex. Then again this man was nothing like that obnoxious character. I didn't know this man at all. But he was…interesting.

He nodded to the door. "I'm going to have a conversation with your doctors. You have some serious bumps and bruises, but I figure you're fit enough to fly home. I have a chartered jet on standby. We can discuss Chameleon on the flight." He gave me a hard look. "You're sure this is what you want?"

I don't know this dance.

Neither do I. Just go with it.

"I've never been more sure of anything in my life."

When he was gone, I turned to the table next to the bed, poured water from a pitcher into a glass and drank. My tongue was bone-dry. Performance jitters, I thought with a wry smile. I noticed my Lucy tote on the table and pulled it onto my lap. Agent Beckett—Milo—must have put it there. The sun shone through the window and heated my sheets. I could see palm trees through the glass. We were still in the islands. I probably couldn't get a signal, but I wanted to check my cell. Maybe Arch had left me a message. When I opened my tote my fingers connected with a book wrapped in tissue paper. I yanked it out, tore away the wrapping.

A journal.

With a picture of tropical skies and a beautiful, brilliant ball of fire.

Sunshine.

I opened the bright yellow journal, stared at the inside cover. Teary-eyed, I smiled at his terrible penmanship.

For private stuff.—Arch

Okay, the note wasn't mushy, but he wasn't a mushy kind of guy. It was a start. Of what I didn't know. The gift itself was priceless. A new journal to chronicle my new life. Beaming with passion and purpose, I titled the first page.

The Chameleon Chronicles.

CHAPTER THIRTY-THREE

THE NEXT DAY, I was fit enough to travel. Milo Beckett, who'd insisted on escorting me back to the States, had been cordial and generous, handling the hospital bills and arranging for a charter flight. I think he felt guilty about my head injury, though it really wasn't a big deal.

Gina had flown home the day before. Gavin was in the brig with Fred. Lamont's goons were being detained by local law. And Martha was back on the ship with her cronies. He didn't seem concerned in the least about Arch.

I, on the other hand, couldn't get the complicated Scot off my mind. Mostly, I wondered how he was handling the fact that he'd killed a man. One might assume he was thinking tit for tat, an eye for an eye, but I was fast learning not to assume anything about Arch. Maybe, just maybe, he was wrestling with remorse. According to Milo, there'd been a struggle, the gun had gone off. A bullet meant for Arch had ended up in Simon the Fish. Self-defense. I'm not sure either one of us truly believed that, but we wanted to.

Though I didn't fully understand the dynamics of Chameleon, I did sense a history between Arch and Milo. Another mystery to unravel. Even though I was returning to my old stomping grounds, a new world awaited. I couldn't wait to dig in and explore.

"We've got a few minutes before we board," Milo said, as we navigated the small but crowded La Romana airport.

"I need to use the ladies' room."

"Up ahead on the left," he said. "I'm going to slip into the gift shop. Buy some gum and a magazine. Want anything?"

"I could use some Dramamine. Just in case we hit turbulence."

"Motion sickness. Right." He smiled and pointed. "I'll meet you by that water fountain."

I peeled off, still marveling that this nice guy, dressed in tasteful jeans and a funky T-shirt, was the same guy I'd dubbed Tex Aloha a few days before. *Smoke and mirrors.*

I pushed into the bathroom, another woman close behind. She edged me aside, almost knocking me over. Jeez, not to be catty, but what a clumsy moose. Might help if she wore flats. I never realized they made pumps in a size thirteen! She slammed shut the stall door and proceeded to moan and whine and shuffle around. "For heaven's sake," she said in a nasally American accent. "This is the second time today... If this don't beat all. Anybody out there?" she asked.

I paused, my hand on my own stall door. The

only one *out here* was me. Another woman occupied the toilet down the way. Other than that…just me. Just my luck. "Something wrong?"

"My zipper's stuck and I can't reach around."

Been there. "If you come out, I'll help—"

"The teeth are caught in my panty hose and…I can't come out. And I really need to…go. You'll have to come in. Please. Oh! This is dreadful!"

I sort of believed in Karma, so I couldn't ignore her. A story for my new diary I told myself as I gently knocked. "Hello?" The door swung open and she hauled me inside. Suddenly I was squished between the wall and an Amazonian, heavily made-up brunette. "What the—"

"I *cannae* believe you fell for that."

I blinked. "Arch?"

He, as a big, unattractive *she,* gestured to me to lower my voice. "Lured into a compromising situation by a stranger. What if I was a thief, or worse? I could rob you right now. Or I could have my way with you."

"Do I get a choice?"

"This isn't funny."

"You're right. It's hilarious." I grinned ear to ear. "You're wearing a pencil skirt, a silk blouse and panty hose. Hey, is that a padded bra?"

He slapped my hand away. "*Dinnae* touch. Do you think I'm easy?"

"I'm hoping." The grin faded and I threw my arms around him and clung. "I was worried about you."

"And I you."

"Milo said you have to lie low."

"Aye."

"He told me you'd already left the island."

"He's under that impression. *Dinnae* tell him otherwise. He'll be pissed. He likes to think he's in control."

"Is he?"

"Sometimes. He was right to shelter you after what happened with Lamont. I'm sorry I dragged you into that, Sunshine."

I framed his face between my hands, looked for the man beneath the mascara and rouge. "You changed my life for the better. Please don't apologize."

He dropped his forehead to mine. "I should not be here."

"So why are you?"

"You *didnae* look so good last time I saw you. I wanted to make you smile, yeah?"

I laughed softly. "By dressing as Josephine?"

"I was going for Daphne."

"Wrong hair color, but hey, great legs."

"Flattery will get you…" He pressed papers into my hands.

I eased away and read. "A ticket to London?"

"My grandfather had a flat there. I need to handle some of his affairs. Having you there would be…nice."

My heart hammered against my chest. He didn't want a relationship. No emotional ties. But he was inviting me to share a part of his life he didn't want other people to know about? *Danger, Will Robinson!* "I only have a couple of free weeks. I'm supposed to be starting a new job. Speaking of—"

"You can tell me *aboot* it when I pick you up at Heathrow. You depart from Philly day after tomorrow."

"But—"

He kissed me, a lingering, hot kiss that set my blood ablaze and melted brain matter. Common sense—up in smoke.

Next thing I knew he was gone and I was stumbling out of the stall dazed. A woman who'd been washing her hands regarded me with a raised brow. Guess she thought I'd been making out with another girl in the stall. All I could do was smile.

I exited the bathroom, still a tad dazed, Arch nowhere in sight. Milo, however, was exactly where he said he'd be. I neared the water fountain, telling myself to play it cool. The trip to London would have to be on the Q.T. I'd sworn to Milo that Arch and I were just friends. And I'd sworn to Arch not to reveal any details regarding his grandfather. Ooh, boy. Life was about to get complicated. And exciting.

"Weather's turned iffy. Might get bumpy," Milo said. "Think you can handle it?"

I nabbed the Dramamine out of his hand, chucked it in my Lucy tote alongside my ticket to London and grinned. "Bring it on."

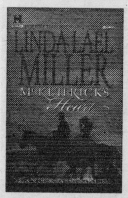

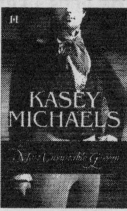

REQUEST YOUR FREE BOOKS!

2 FREE NOVELS FROM THE ROMANCE/SUSPENSE COLLECTION PLUS 2 FREE GIFTS!

YES! Please send me 2 FREE novels from the Romance/Suspense Collection and my 2 FREE gifts. After receiving them, if I don't wish to receive any more books, I can return the shipping statement marked "cancel." If I don't cancel, I will receive 4 brand-new novels every month and be billed just $5.49 per book in the U.S., or $5.99 per book in Canada, plus 25¢ shipping and handling per book plus applicable taxes, if any*. That's a savings of at least 20% off the cover price! I understand that accepting the 2 free books and gifts places me under no obligation to buy anything. I can always return a shipment and cancel at any time. Even if I never buy another book from the Reader Service, the two free books and gifts are mine to keep forever.

185 MDN EF5Y   385 MDN EF6C

Name _____ (PLEASE PRINT) _____

Address _____ Apt. # _____

City _____ State/Prov. _____ Zip/Postal Code _____

Signature (if under 18, a parent or guardian must sign)

Mail to **The Reader Service:**
IN U.S.A.: P.O. Box 1867, Buffalo, NY 14240-1867
IN CANADA: P.O. Box 609, Fort Erie, Ontario L2A 5X3

Not valid to current subscribers to the Romance Collection,
the Suspense Collection or the Romance/Suspense Collection.

Want to try two free books from another line?
Call 1-800-873-8635 or visit www.morefreebooks.com.

* Terms and prices subject to change without notice. NY residents add applicable sales tax. Canadian residents will be charged applicable provincial taxes and GST. This offer is limited to one order per household. All orders subject to approval. Credit or debit balances in a customer's account(s) may be offset by any other outstanding balance owed by or to the customer. Please allow 4 to 6 weeks for delivery.

Your Privacy: Harlequin is committed to protecting your privacy. Our Privacy Policy is available online at www.eHarlequin.com or upon request from the Reader Service. From time to time we make our lists of customers available to reputable firms who may have a product or service of interest to you. If you would prefer we not share your name and address, please check here. ☐

BOB07

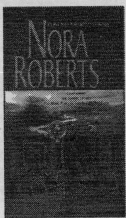